The Sisters

3 in 1

PAPERCUTZ

 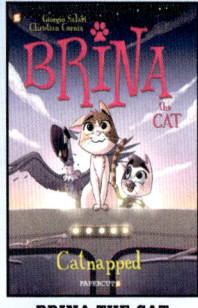 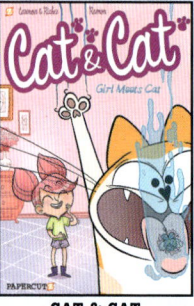 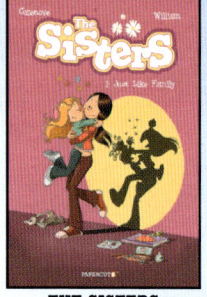 

THE SMURFS TALES | BRINA THE CAT | CAT & CAT | THE SISTERS | ATTACK OF THE STUFF

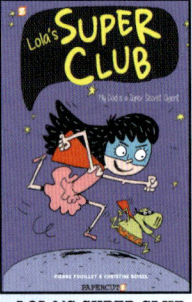 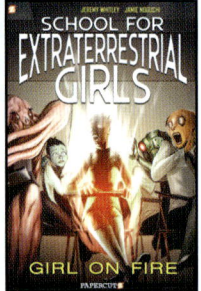   

LOLA'S SUPER CLUB | SCHOOL FOR EXTRATERRESTRIAL GIRLS | GERONIMO STILTON REPORTER | THE MYTHICS | GUMBY

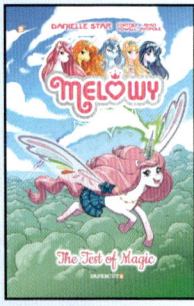 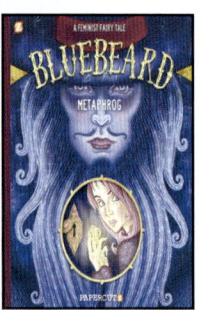 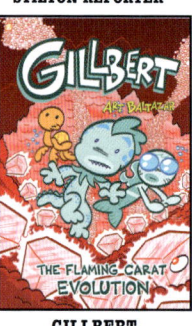 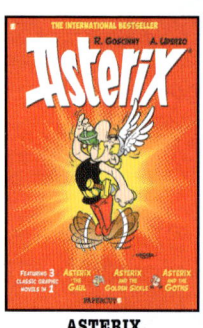 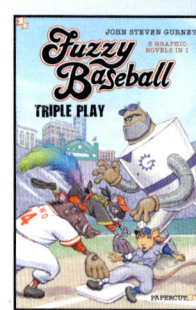

MELOWY | BLUEBEARD | GILLBERT | ASTERIX | FUZZY BASEBALL

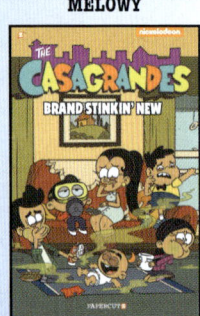 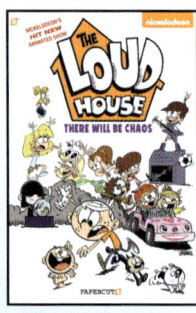 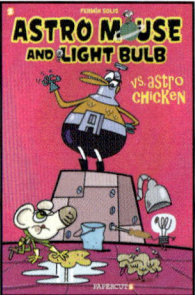 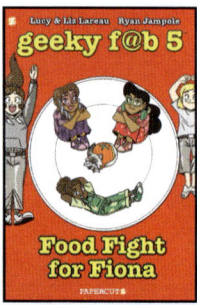 

THE CASAGRANDES | THE LOUD HOUSE | ASTRO MOUSE AND LIGHT BULB | GEEKY F@B 5 | THE ONLY LIVING GIRL

MORE GREAT GRAPHIC NOVEL SERIES AVAILABLE FROM

PAPERCUTZ

WWW.PAPERCUTZ.COM

ALSO AVAILABLE WHERE EBOOKS ARE SOLD.

3 in 1

Story
Cazenove & William
Art and colors
William

PAPERCUT#
New York

THE SISTERS 3 IN 1
Les Sisters [The Sisters] by Cazenove and William
Originally published in French as *Les Sisters* [THE SISTERS] Volume 1, 2, and 3. ©2008-2010, 2009, 2010 BAMBOO ÉDITIONS
Sisters, characters and related indicia are copyright, trademark and exclusive license of *Bamboo Édition*.
English translation and all other editorial material © 2022 by Papercutz.
All rights reserved. www.papercutz.com

Cazenove and William — Writers
William — Artist
William — Colorist
Nanette McGuinness and Anne & Owen Smith — Translation
Wilson Ramos Jr. and Dawn Guzzo — Lettering

Mark McNabb — Production
Carol M. Burrell, Jeff Whitman,
and Robert V. Conte — Original Editors
Zach Harris — Editor
Stephanie Brooks — Assistant Managing Editor
Editor-in-Chief
Jim Salicrup

Special thanks to Catherine Loiselet

No part of this book may be stored, reproduced or transmitted in any form or by any means, electronic or mechanical, including photocopying, recording, or by any information storage and retrieval system, without written permission from the copyright holder.

For information address
Bamboo Édition –
290 route des Allogneraies, 71850 Charnay-Lès-Mâcon, FRANCE
bamboo@bamboo.fr – www.bamboo.fr

ISBN: 978-1-5458-0969-3

Printed in China
October 2022

Papercutz books may be purchased for business or promotional use. For information on bulk purchases please contact Macmillan Corporate and Premium Sales Department at
(800) 221-7945 x5442

Distributed by Macmillan
First Papercutz Printing

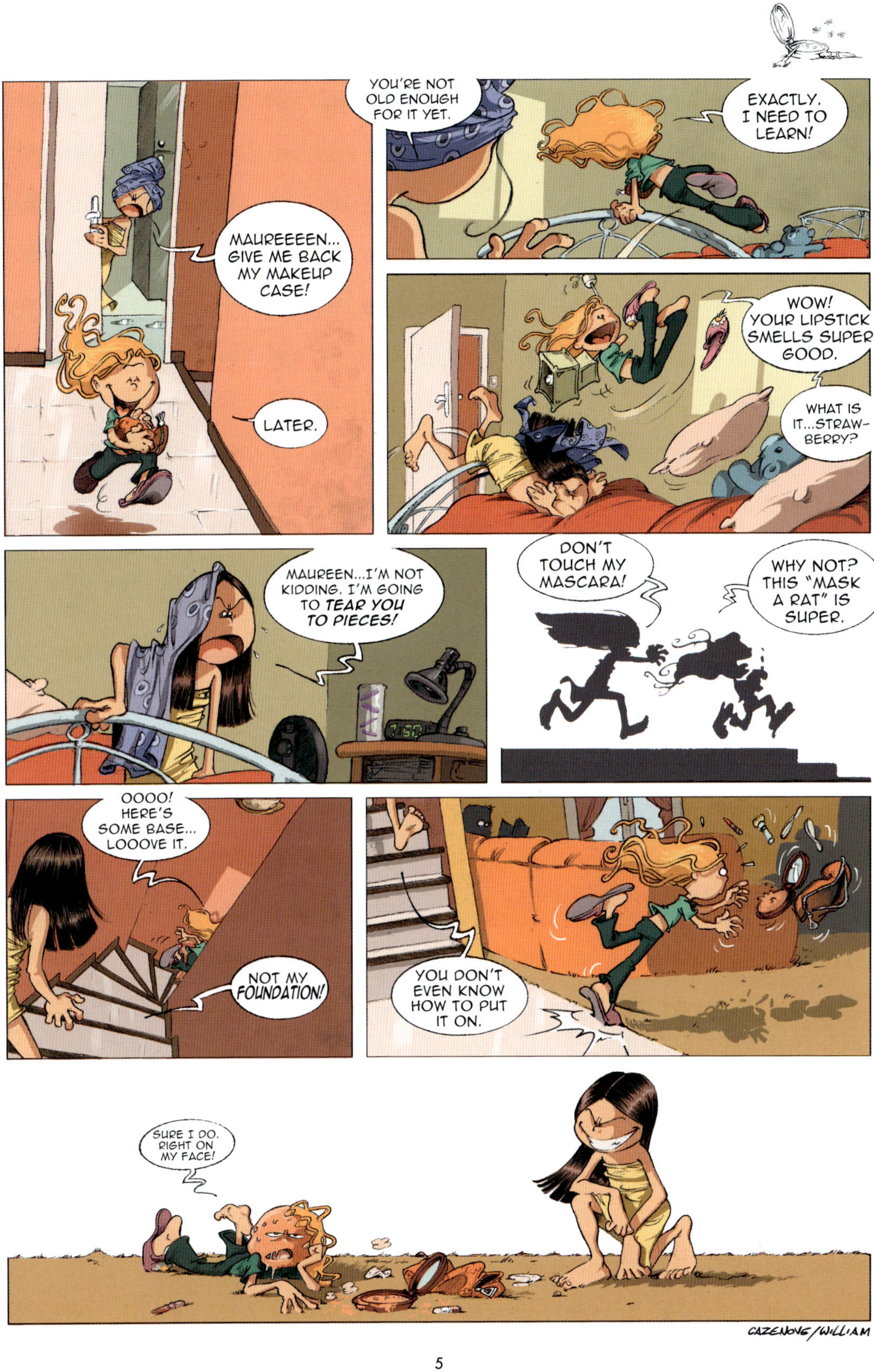
MAUREEEEN... GIVE ME BACK MY MAKEUP CASE!
LATER.
YOU'RE NOT OLD ENOUGH FOR IT YET.
EXACTLY. I NEED TO LEARN!
WOW! YOUR LIPSTICK SMELLS SUPER GOOD.
WHAT IS IT...STRAWBERRY?
MAUREEN...I'M NOT KIDDING. I'M GOING TO TEAR YOU TO PIECES!
DON'T TOUCH MY MASCARA!
WHY NOT? THIS "MASK A RAT" IS SUPER.
OOOO! HERE'S SOME BASE... LOOOVE IT.
NOT MY FOUNDATION!
YOU DON'T EVEN KNOW HOW TO PUT IT ON.
SURE I DO. RIGHT ON MY FACE!
CAZENOVE/WILLIAM

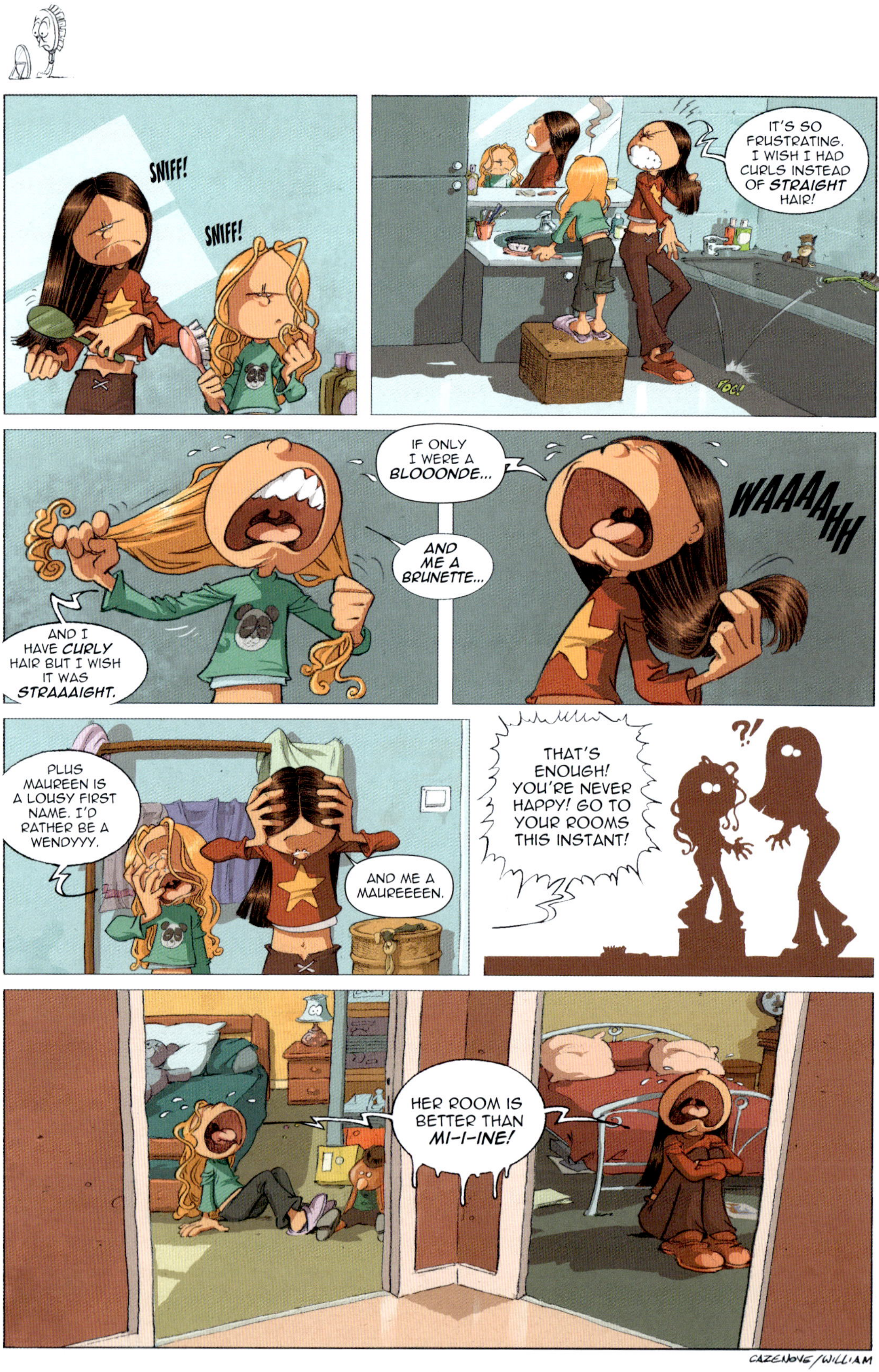
SNIFF!
SNIFF!
IT'S SO FRUSTRATING. I WISH I HAD CURLS INSTEAD OF STRAIGHT HAIR!
IF ONLY I WERE A BLOOONDE...
WAAAAHH
AND ME A BRUNETTE...
AND I HAVE CURLY HAIR BUT I WISH IT WAS STRAAAIGHT.
PLUS MAUREEN IS A LOUSY FIRST NAME. I'D RATHER BE A WENDYYY.
AND ME A MAUREEEEN.
THAT'S ENOUGH! YOU'RE NEVER HAPPY! GO TO YOUR ROOMS THIS INSTANT!
?!
HER ROOM IS BETTER THAN MI-I-INE!
CAZENOVE/WILLIAM

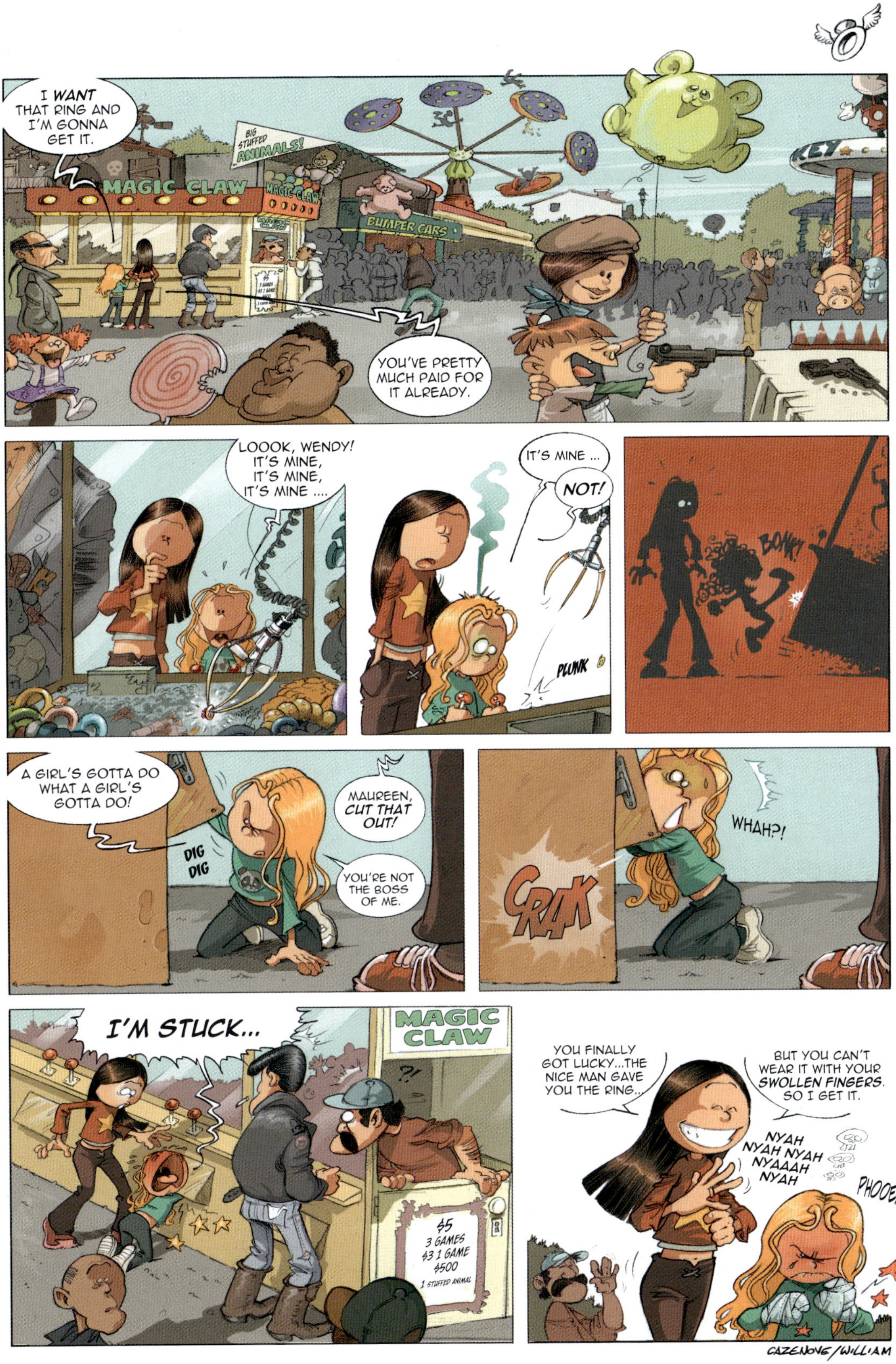

I WANT THAT RING AND I'M GONNA GET IT.
MAGIC CLAW
BIG STUFFED ANIMALS!
BUMPER CARS
YOU'VE PRETTY MUCH PAID FOR IT ALREADY.
LOOOK, WENDY! IT'S MINE, IT'S MINE, IT'S MINE ....
IT'S MINE ...
NOT!
PLUNK
BONK!
A GIRL'S GOTTA DO WHAT A GIRL'S GOTTA DO!
DIG DIG
MAUREEN, CUT THAT OUT!
YOU'RE NOT THE BOSS OF ME.
CRAK
WHAH?!
I'M STUCK...
MAGIC CLAW
?!
$5 3 GAMES $3 1 GAME $500 1 STUFFED ANIMAL
YOU FINALLY GOT LUCKY...THE NICE MAN GAVE YOU THE RING...
BUT YOU CAN'T WEAR IT WITH YOUR SWOLLEN FINGERS. SO I GET IT.
NYAH NYAH NYAH NYAAAH NYAH
PHOOEY!
CAZENOVE/WILLIAM

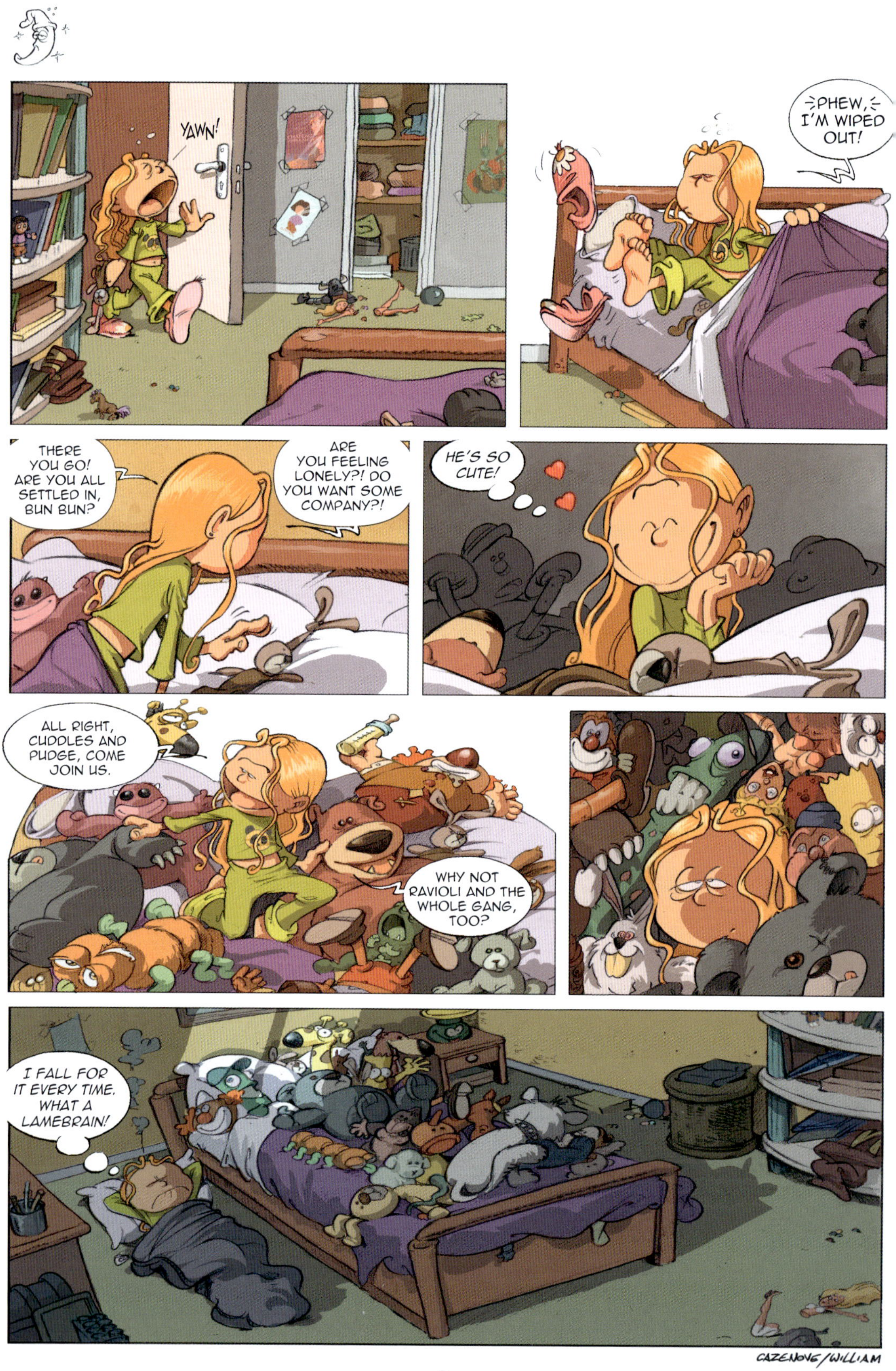
YAWN!
PHEW, I'M WIPED OUT!
THERE YOU GO! ARE YOU ALL SETTLED IN, BUN BUN?
ARE YOU FEELING LONELY?! DO YOU WANT SOME COMPANY?!
HE'S SO CUTE!
ALL RIGHT, CUDDLES AND PUDGE, COME JOIN US.
WHY NOT RAVIOLI AND THE WHOLE GANG, TOO?
I FALL FOR IT EVERY TIME. WHAT A LAMEBRAIN!
CAZENOVE/WILLIAM

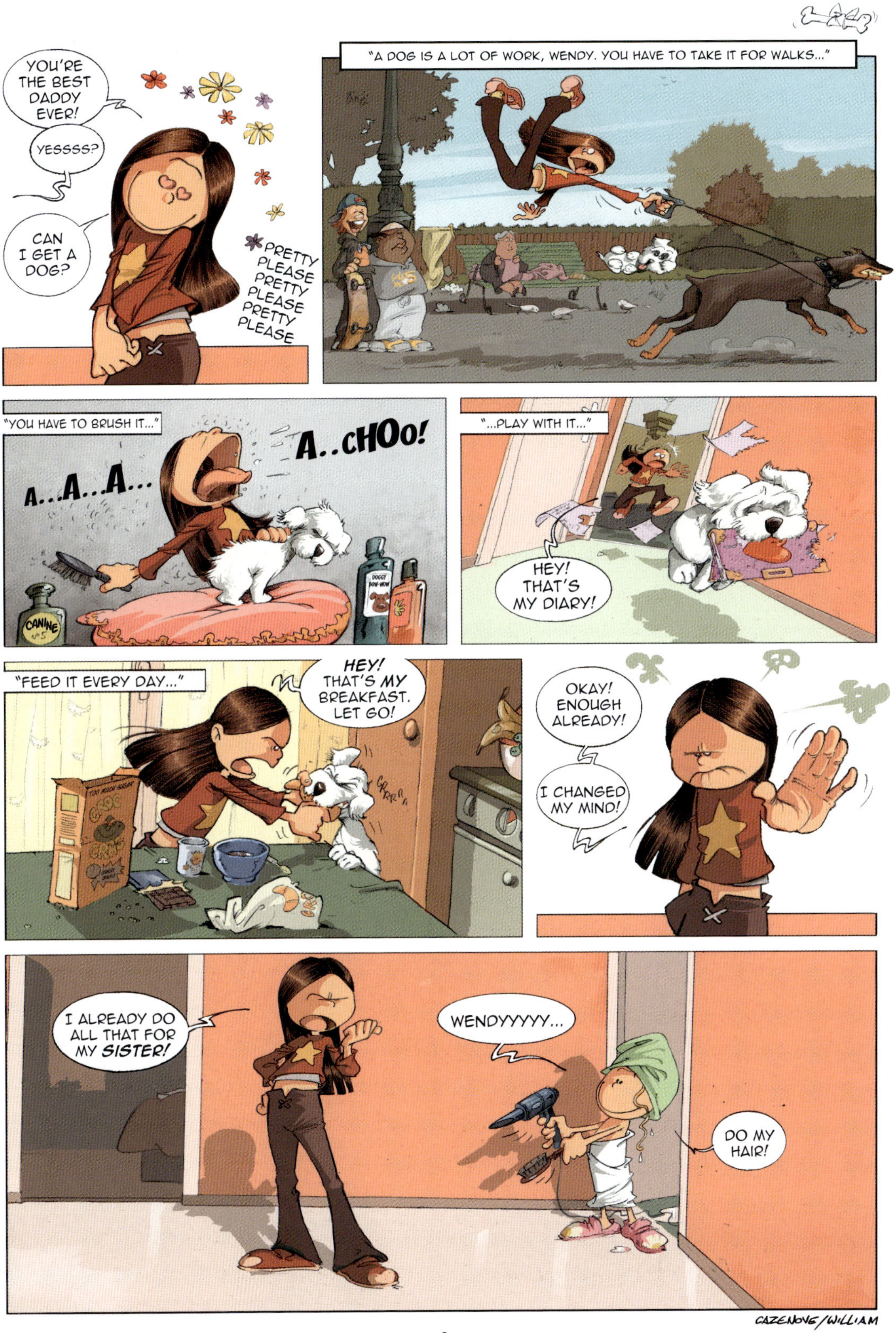
YOU'RE THE BEST DADDY EVER!
YESSSS?
CAN I GET A DOG?
PRETTY PLEASE PRETTY PLEASE PRETTY PLEASE
"A DOG IS A LOT OF WORK, WENDY. YOU HAVE TO TAKE IT FOR WALKS..."
"YOU HAVE TO BRUSH IT..."
A...A...A...
A..CHOO!
CANINE Nº5
DOGGY BOW-WOW
"...PLAY WITH IT..."
HEY! THAT'S MY DIARY!
"FEED IT EVERY DAY..."
HEY! THAT'S MY BREAKFAST. LET GO!
TOO MUCH SUGAR
GRRR...
OKAY! ENOUGH ALREADY!
I CHANGED MY MIND!
I ALREADY DO ALL THAT FOR MY SISTER!
WENDYYYYY...
DO MY HAIR!
CAZENOVE/WILLIAM

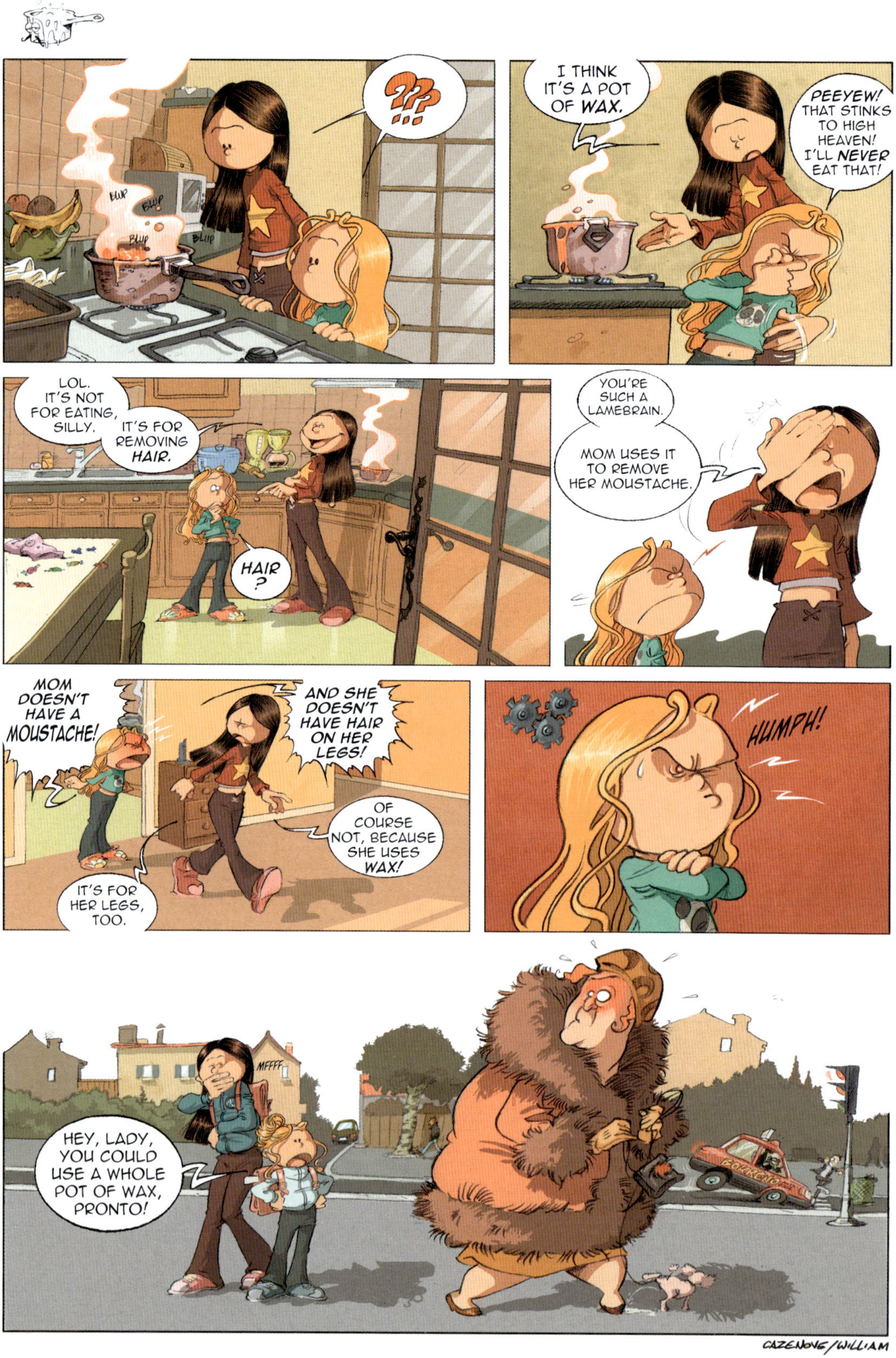
BLUP
BLUP
BLUP
BLUP
???
I THINK IT'S A POT OF WAX.
PEEYEW! THAT STINKS TO HIGH HEAVEN! I'LL NEVER EAT THAT!
LOL. IT'S NOT FOR EATING, SILLY.
IT'S FOR REMOVING HAIR.
HAIR?
YOU'RE SUCH A LAMEBRAIN.
MOM USES IT TO REMOVE HER MOUSTACHE.
MOM DOESN'T HAVE A MOUSTACHE!
AND SHE DOESN'T HAVE HAIR ON HER LEGS!
IT'S FOR HER LEGS, TOO.
OF COURSE NOT, BECAUSE SHE USES WAX!
HUMPH!
MFFFF
HEY, LADY, YOU COULD USE A WHOLE POT OF WAX, PRONTO!
CAZENOVE/WILLIAM

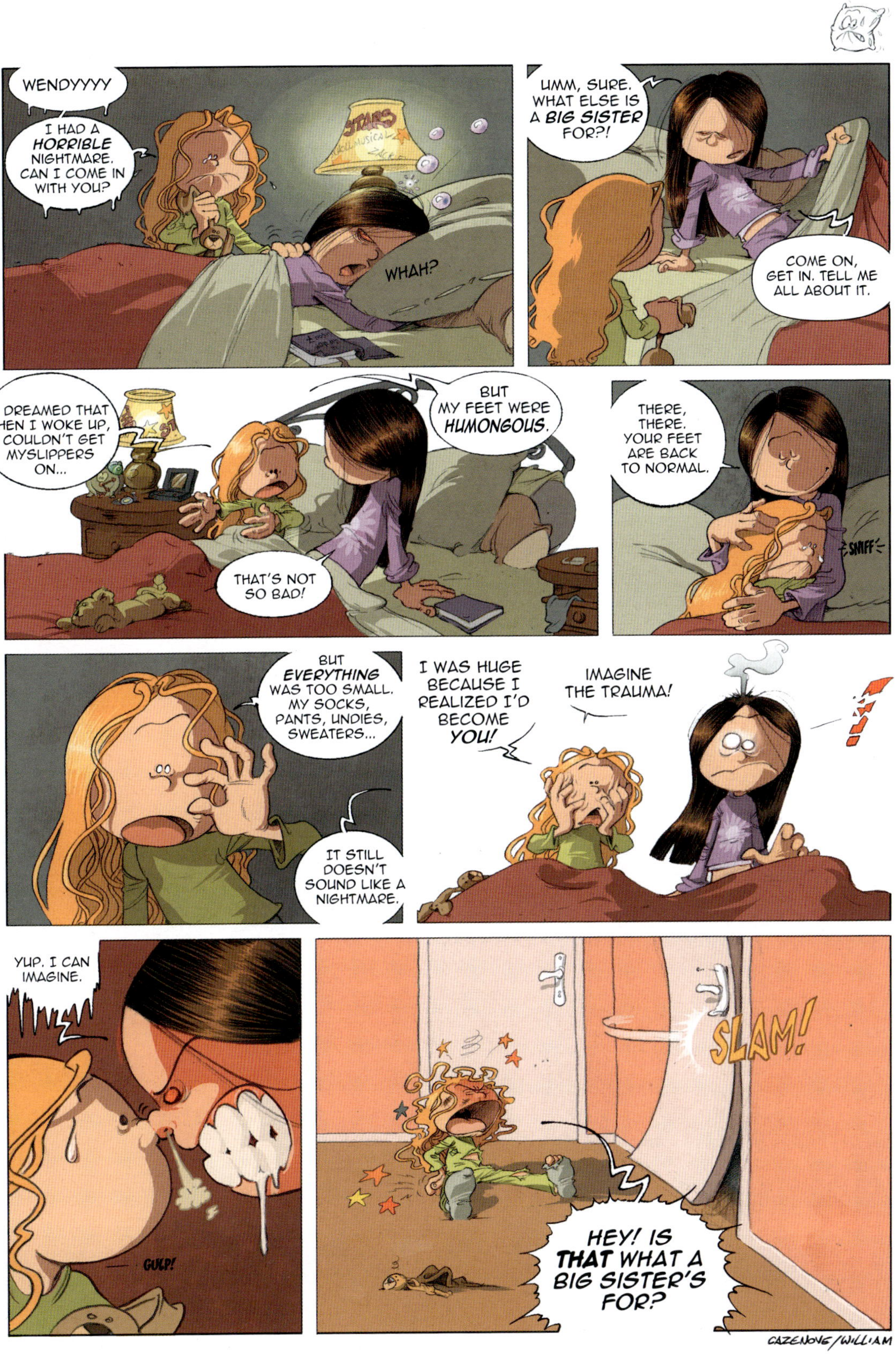

WENDYYYY
I HAD A HORRIBLE NIGHTMARE. CAN I COME IN WITH YOU?
WHAH?
UMM, SURE. WHAT ELSE IS A BIG SISTER FOR?!
COME ON, GET IN. TELL ME ALL ABOUT IT.
I DREAMED THAT WHEN I WOKE UP, I COULDN'T GET MY SLIPPERS ON...
BUT MY FEET WERE HUMONGOUS.
THAT'S NOT SO BAD!
THERE, THERE. YOUR FEET ARE BACK TO NORMAL.
SNIFF
BUT EVERYTHING WAS TOO SMALL. MY SOCKS, PANTS, UNDIES, SWEATERS...
IT STILL DOESN'T SOUND LIKE A NIGHTMARE.
I WAS HUGE BECAUSE I REALIZED I'D BECOME YOU!
IMAGINE THE TRAUMA!
YUP. I CAN IMAGINE.
GULP!
SLAM!
HEY! IS THAT WHAT A BIG SISTER'S FOR?
CAZENOVE/WILLIAM

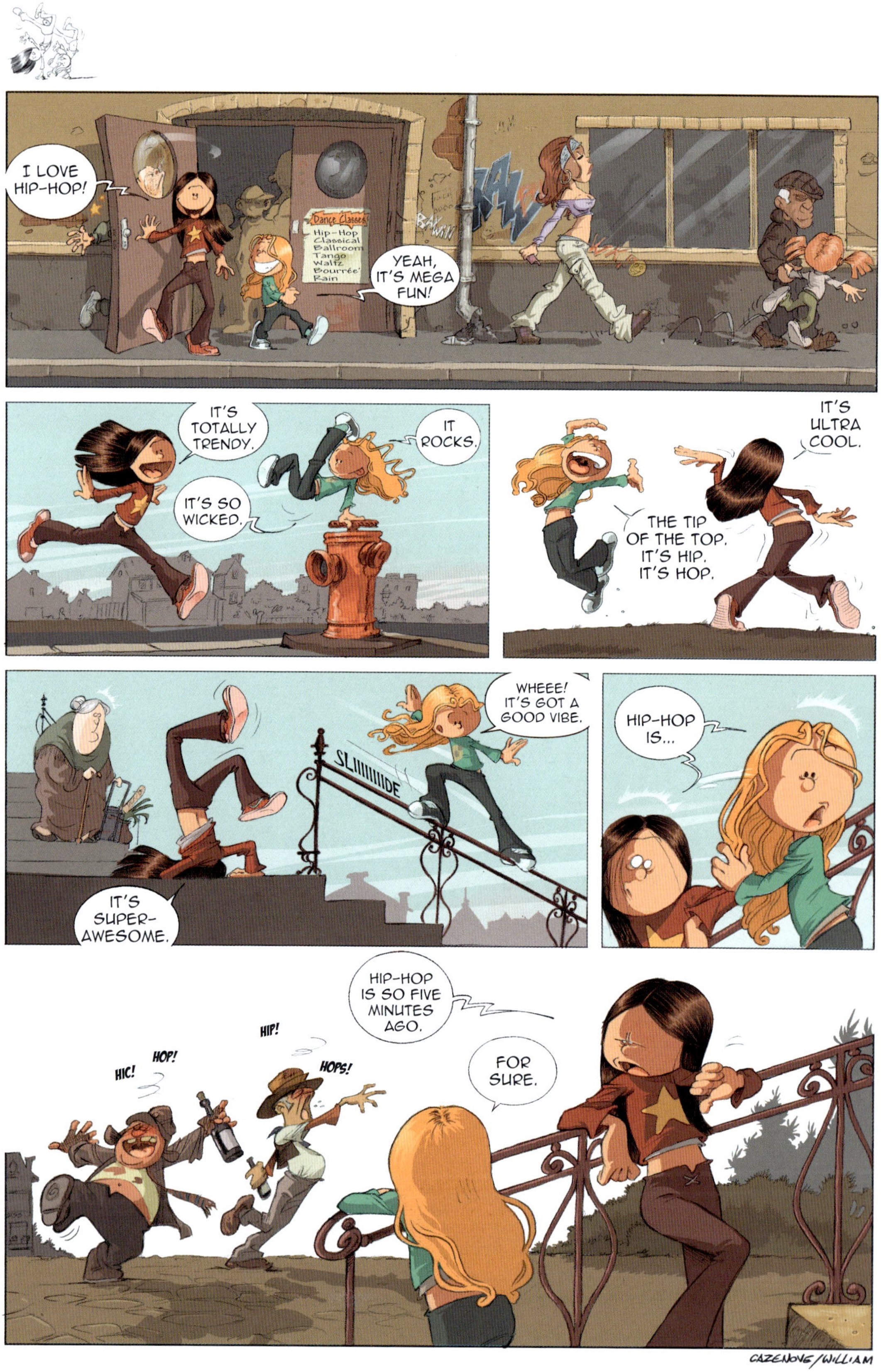
I LOVE HIP-HOP!
Dance Classes
Hip-Hop
Classical
Ballroom
Tango
Waltz
Bourrée
Rain
YEAH, IT'S MEGA FUN!
IT'S TOTALLY TRENDY.
IT ROCKS.
IT'S SO WICKED.
IT'S ULTRA COOL.
THE TIP OF THE TOP. IT'S HIP. IT'S HOP.
WHEEE! IT'S GOT A GOOD VIBE.
SLIIIIIIIIDE
IT'S SUPER-AWESOME.
HIP-HOP IS...
HIP-HOP IS SO FIVE MINUTES AGO.
HIC!
HOP!
HIP!
HOPS!
FOR SURE.
CAZENOVE/WILLIAM

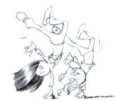

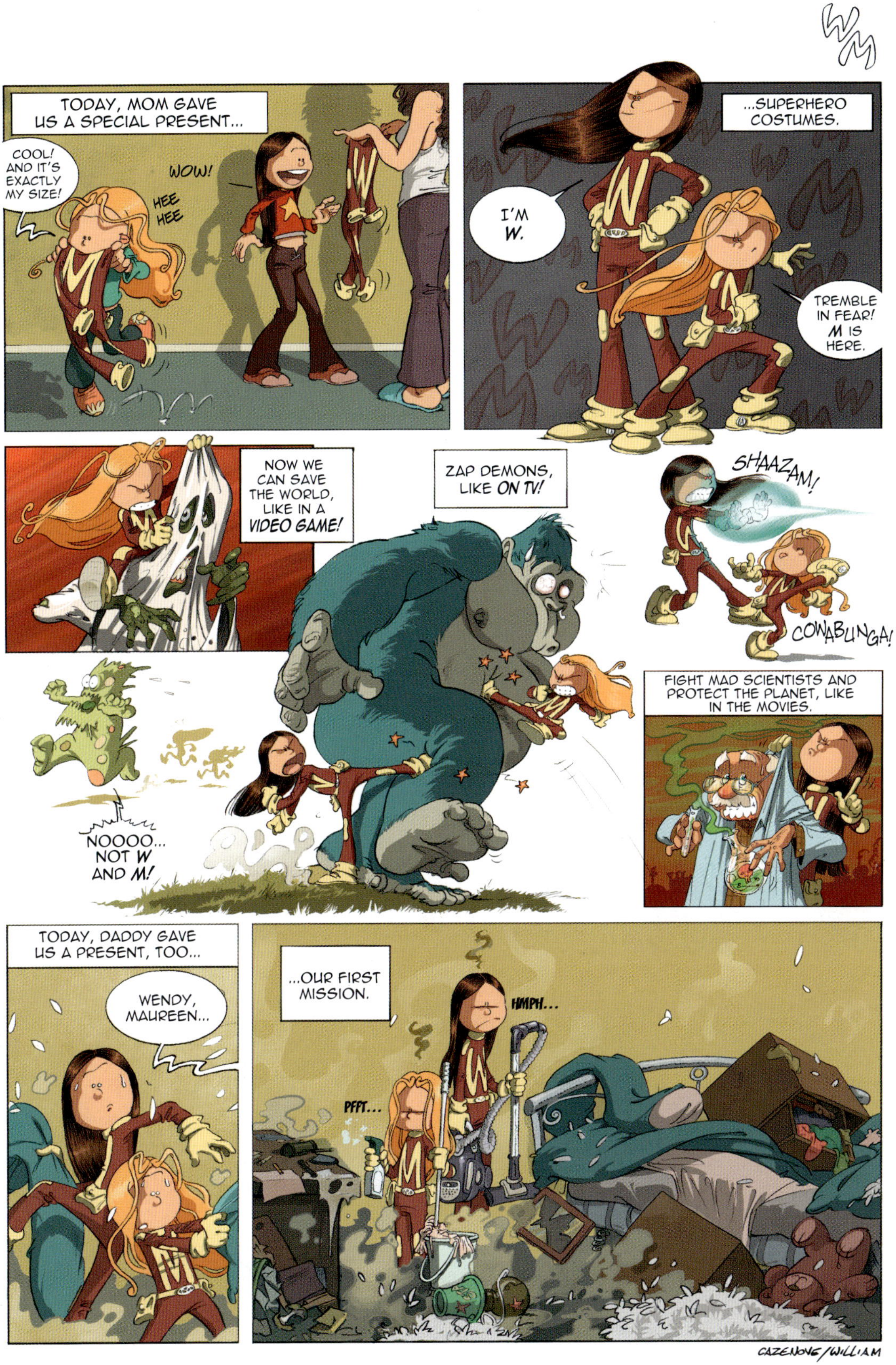
TODAY, MOM GAVE US A SPECIAL PRESENT...
COOL! AND IT'S EXACTLY MY SIZE!
WOW!
HEE HEE
...SUPERHERO COSTUMES.
I'M W.
TREMBLE IN FEAR! M IS HERE.
NOW WE CAN SAVE THE WORLD, LIKE IN A VIDEO GAME!
ZAP DEMONS, LIKE ON TV!
SHAAZAM!
COWABUNGA!
NOOOO... NOT W AND M!
FIGHT MAD SCIENTISTS AND PROTECT THE PLANET, LIKE IN THE MOVIES.
TODAY, DADDY GAVE US A PRESENT, TOO...
WENDY, MAUREEN...
...OUR FIRST MISSION.
HMPH...
PFFT...
CAZENOVE/WILLIAM

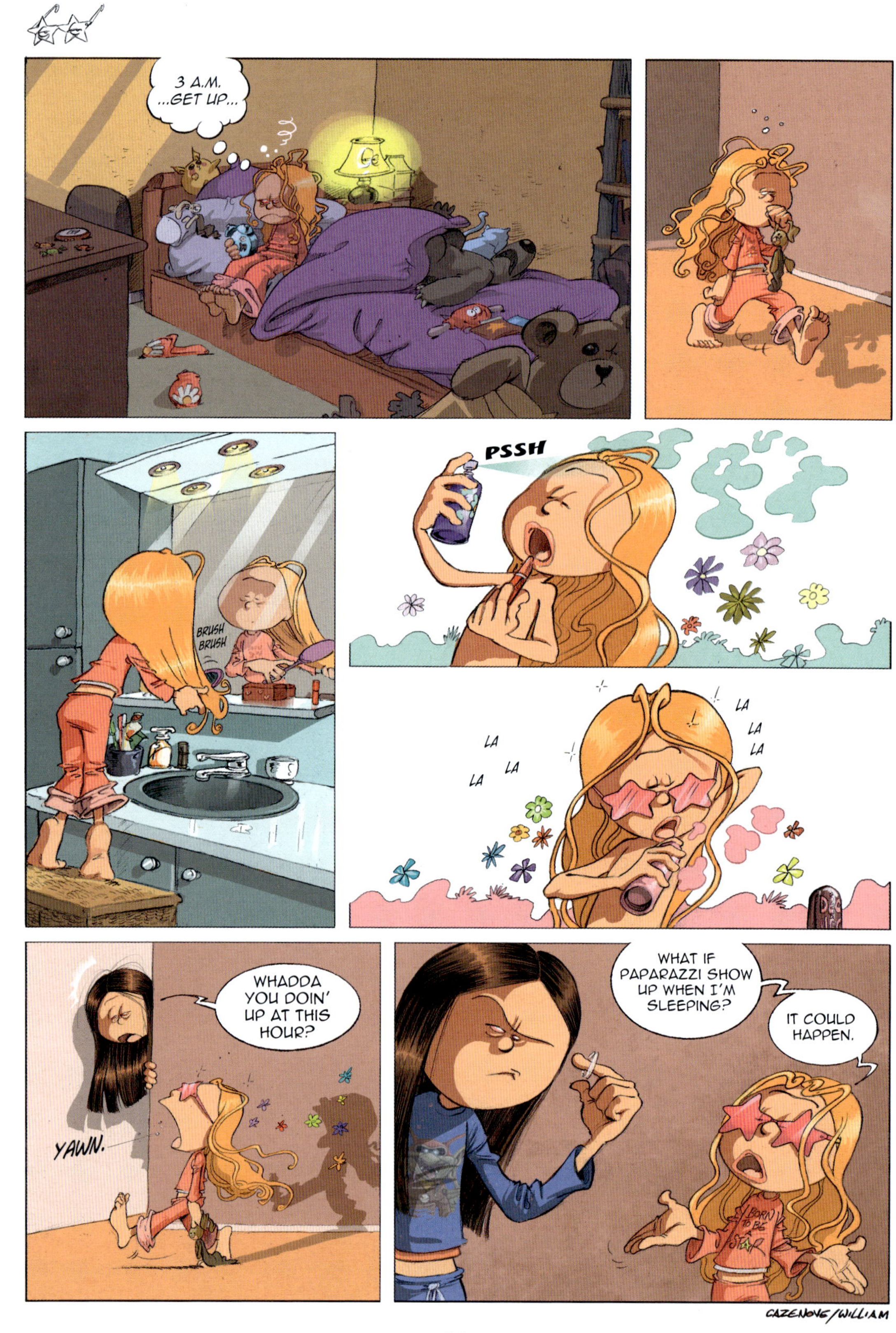
3 A.M. ...GET UP...
PSSH
BRUSH BRUSH
LA LA LA LA LA LA
WHADDA YOU DOIN' UP AT THIS HOUR?
YAWN.
WHAT IF PAPARAZZI SHOW UP WHEN I'M SLEEPING?
IT COULD HAPPEN.
BORN TO BE A STAR

CAZENOVE/WILLIAM

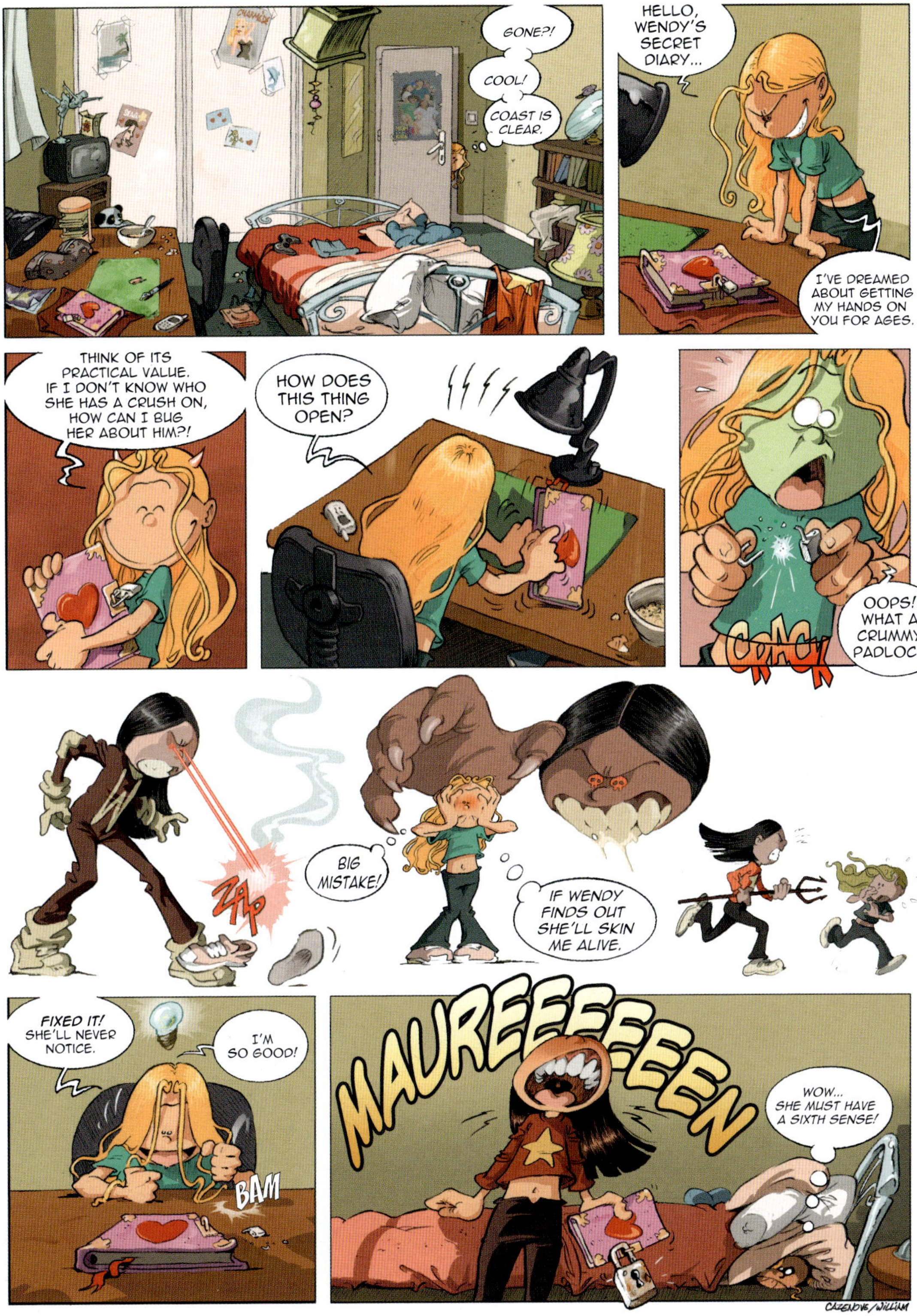
GONE?!
COOL!
COAST IS CLEAR.
HELLO, WENDY'S SECRET DIARY...
I'VE DREAMED ABOUT GETTING MY HANDS ON YOU FOR AGES.
THINK OF ITS PRACTICAL VALUE. IF I DON'T KNOW WHO SHE HAS A CRUSH ON, HOW CAN I BUG HER ABOUT HIM?!
HOW DOES THIS THING OPEN?
CRACK
OOPS! WHAT A CRUMMY PADLOCK!
ZAP
BIG MISTAKE!
IF WENDY FINDS OUT SHE'LL SKIN ME ALIVE.
FIXED IT! SHE'LL NEVER NOTICE.
I'M SO GOOD!
BAM
MAUREEEEEEN
WOW... SHE MUST HAVE A SIXTH SENSE!
CAZENOVE/WILLIAM

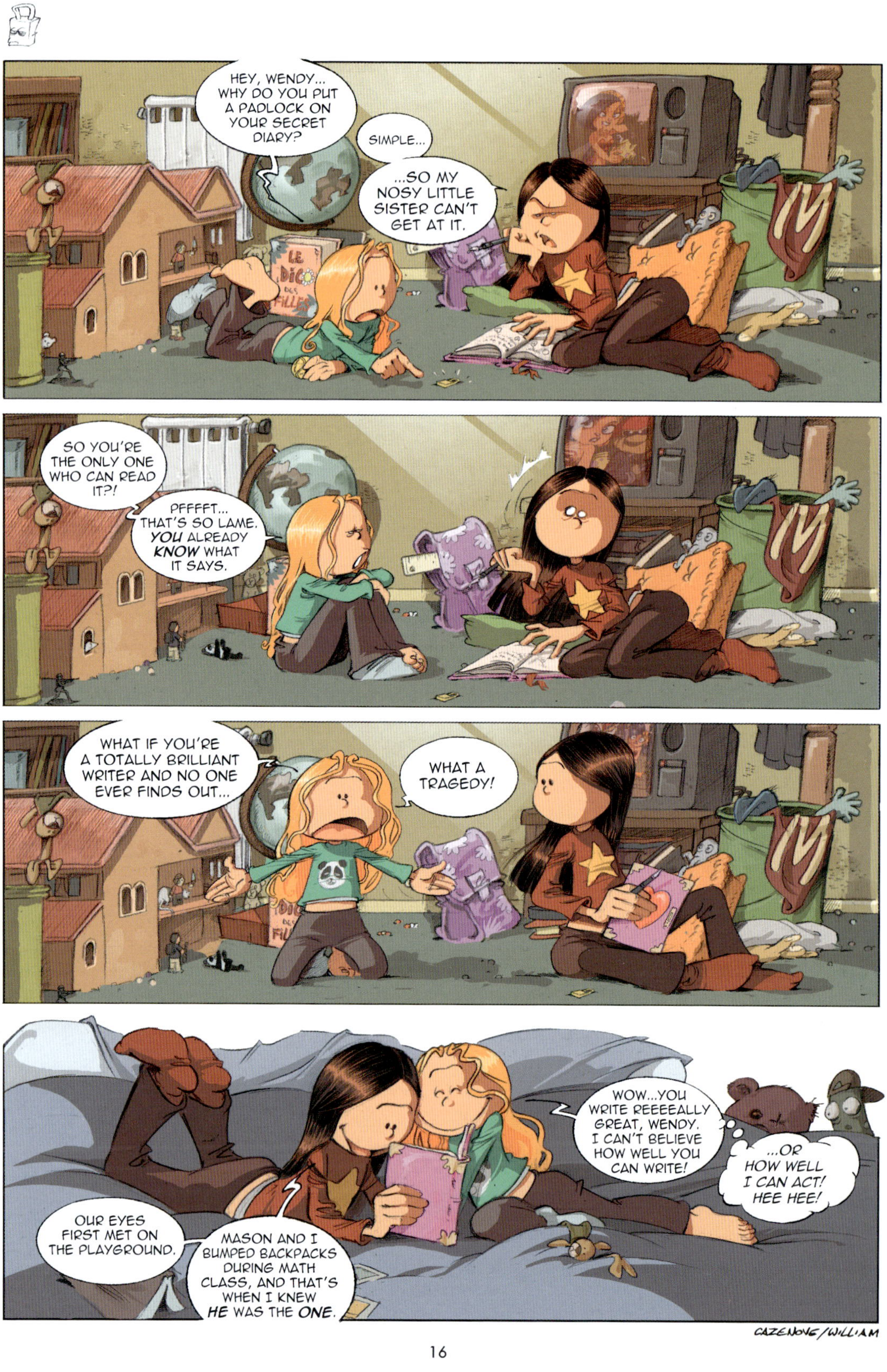
HEY, WENDY... WHY DO YOU PUT A PADLOCK ON YOUR SECRET DIARY?
SIMPLE...
...SO MY NOSY LITTLE SISTER CAN'T GET AT IT.
LE DICO DES FILLES
SO YOU'RE THE ONLY ONE WHO CAN READ IT?!
PFFFFT... THAT'S SO LAME. YOU ALREADY KNOW WHAT IT SAYS.
WHAT IF YOU'RE A TOTALLY BRILLIANT WRITER AND NO ONE EVER FINDS OUT...
WHAT A TRAGEDY!
WOW...YOU WRITE REEEEALLY GREAT, WENDY. I CAN'T BELIEVE HOW WELL YOU CAN WRITE!
...OR HOW WELL I CAN ACT! HEE HEE!
OUR EYES FIRST MET ON THE PLAYGROUND.
MASON AND I BUMPED BACKPACKS DURING MATH CLASS, AND THAT'S WHEN I KNEW HE WAS THE ONE.
CAZENOVE/WILLIAM

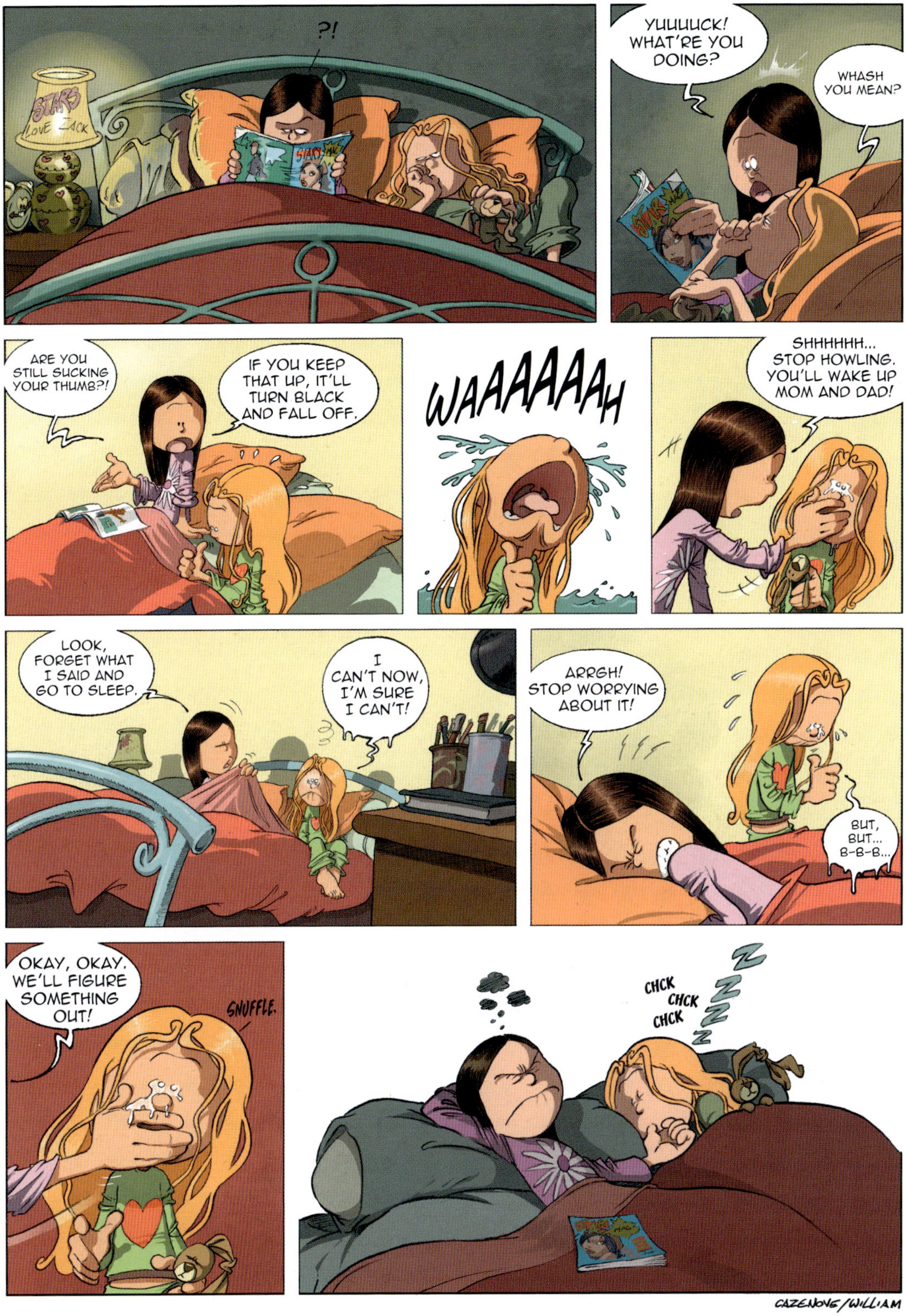
?!
YUUUUCK! WHAT'RE YOU DOING?
WHASH YOU MEAN?
ARE YOU STILL SUCKING YOUR THUMB?!
IF YOU KEEP THAT UP, IT'LL TURN BLACK AND FALL OFF.
WAAAAAAH
SHHHHHH... STOP HOWLING. YOU'LL WAKE UP MOM AND DAD!
LOOK, FORGET WHAT I SAID AND GO TO SLEEP.
I CAN'T NOW, I'M SURE I CAN'T!
ARRGH! STOP WORRYING ABOUT IT!
BUT, BUT... B-B-B...
OKAY, OKAY. WE'LL FIGURE SOMETHING OUT!
SNUFFLE.
CHCK
CHCK
CHCK
CAZENOVE/WILLIAM

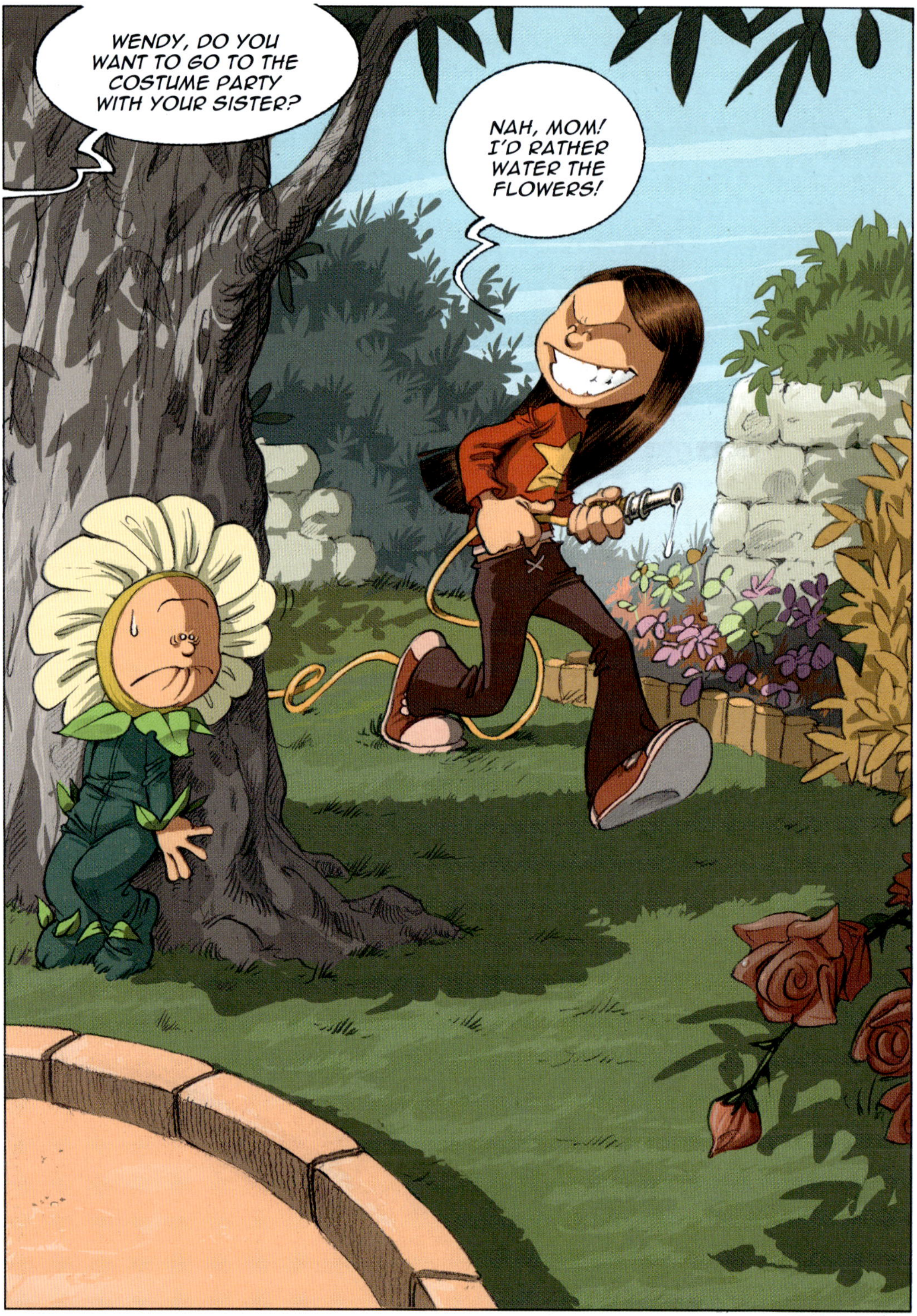
WENDY, DO YOU WANT TO GO TO THE COSTUME PARTY WITH YOUR SISTER?
NAH, MOM! I'D RATHER WATER THE FLOWERS!
CAZENOVE/WILLIAM

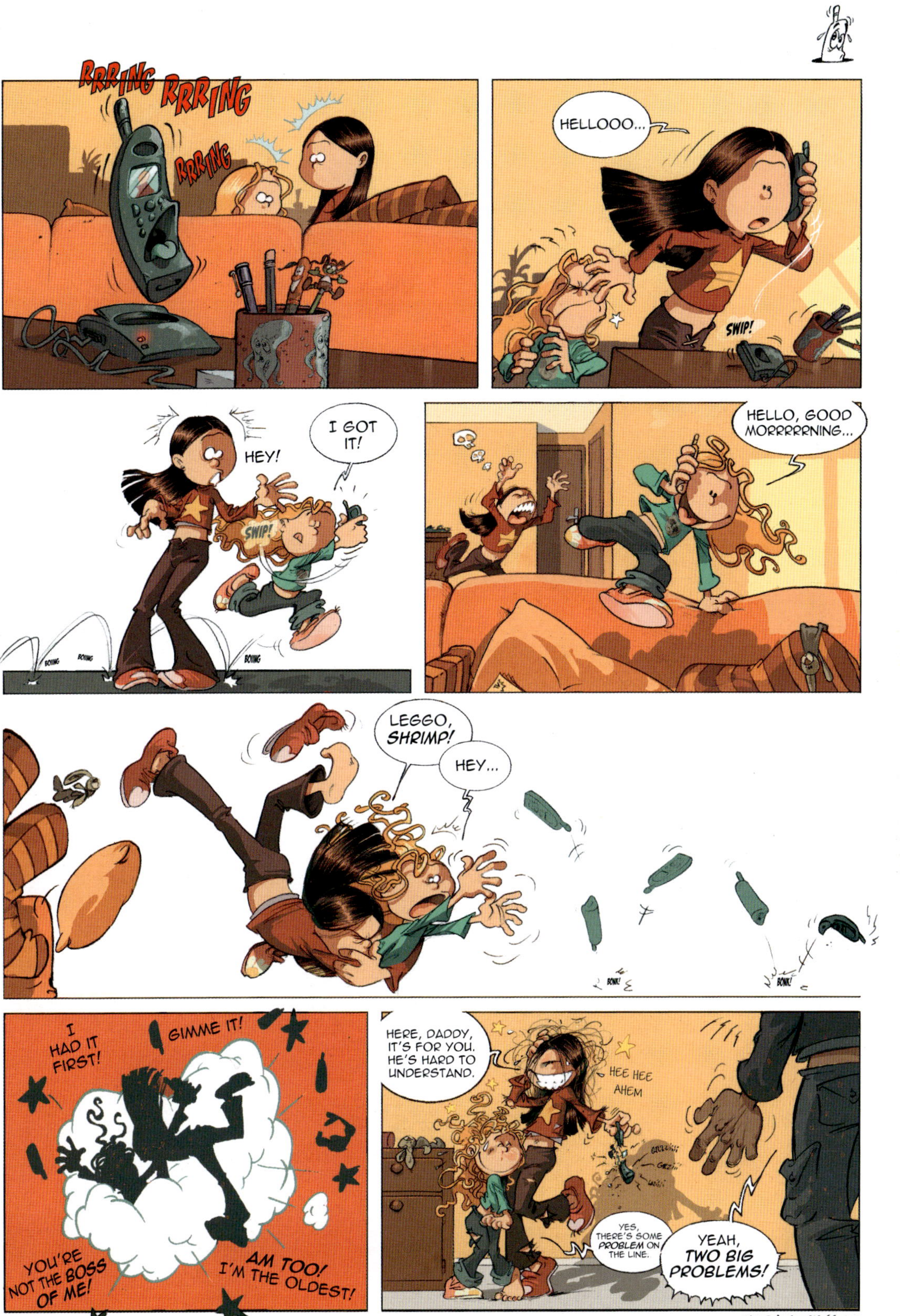
RRRING RRRING
RRRING
HELLOOO...
SWIP!
HEY!
I GOT IT!
SWIP!
HELLO, GOOD MORRRRRNING...
LEGGO, SHRIMP!
HEY...
BONK!
BONK!
I HAD IT FIRST!
GIMME IT!
YOU'RE NOT THE BOSS OF ME!
AM TOO! I'M THE OLDEST!
HERE, DADDY, IT'S FOR YOU. HE'S HARD TO UNDERSTAND.
HEE HEE AHEM
YES, THERE'S SOME PROBLEM ON THE LINE.
YEAH, TWO BIG PROBLEMS!
CAZENOVE/WILLIAM

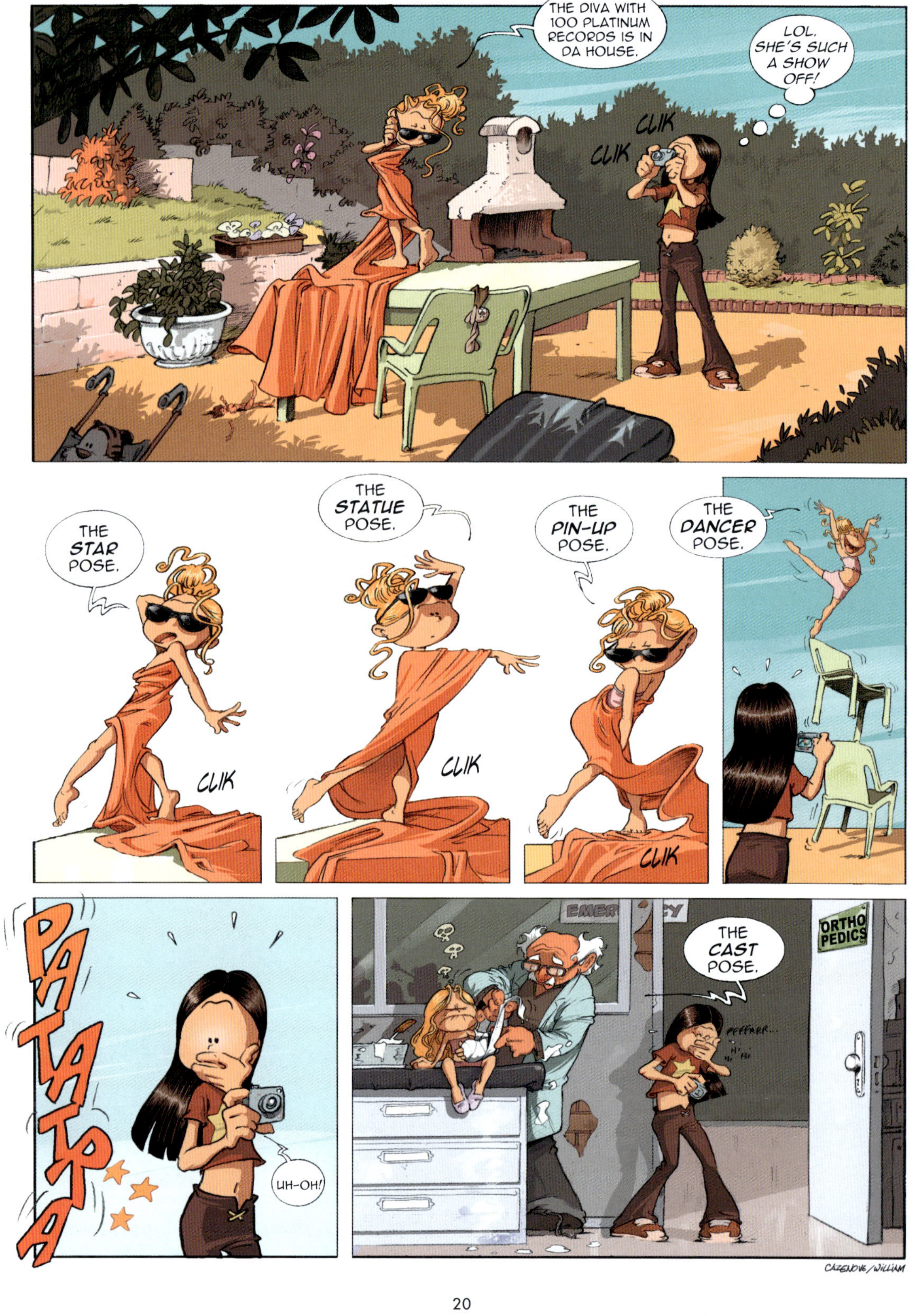
THE DIVA WITH 100 PLATINUM RECORDS IS IN DA HOUSE.
LOL. SHE'S SUCH A SHOW OFF!
CLIK
CLIK
THE STAR POSE.
CLIK
THE STATUE POSE.
CLIK
THE PIN-UP POSE.
CLIK
THE DANCER POSE.
PATATRA
UH-OH!
ORTHO PEDICS
THE CAST POSE.

CAZENOVE/WILLIAM

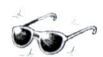

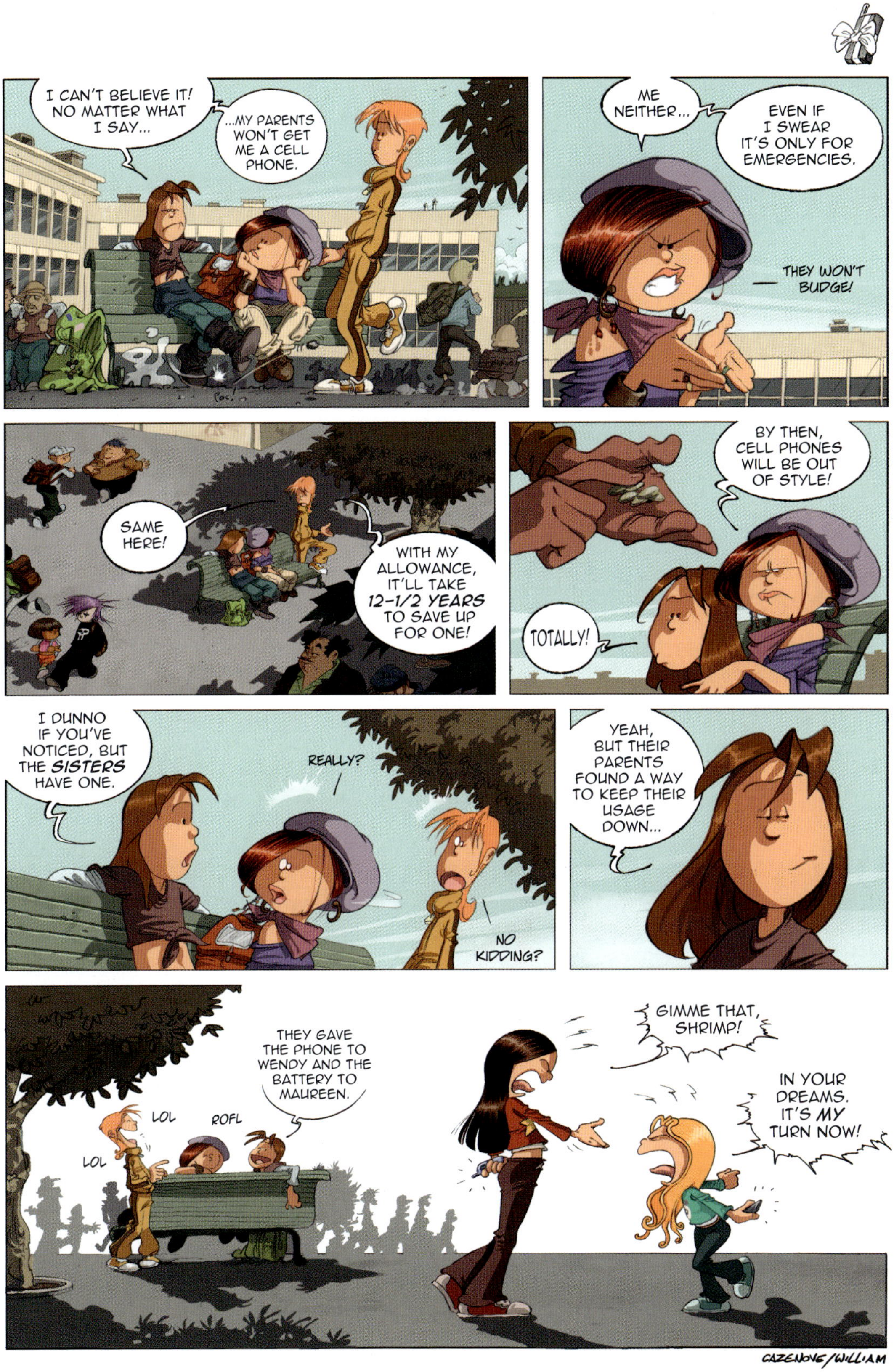
I CAN'T BELIEVE IT! NO MATTER WHAT I SAY...
...MY PARENTS WON'T GET ME A CELL PHONE.
ME NEITHER...
EVEN IF I SWEAR IT'S ONLY FOR EMERGENCIES.
THEY WON'T BUDGE!
SAME HERE!
WITH MY ALLOWANCE, IT'LL TAKE 12-1/2 YEARS TO SAVE UP FOR ONE!
BY THEN, CELL PHONES WILL BE OUT OF STYLE!
TOTALLY!
I DUNNO IF YOU'VE NOTICED, BUT THE SISTERS HAVE ONE.
REALLY?
NO KIDDING?
YEAH, BUT THEIR PARENTS FOUND A WAY TO KEEP THEIR USAGE DOWN...
THEY GAVE THE PHONE TO WENDY AND THE BATTERY TO MAUREEN.
LOL
ROFL
LOL
GIMME THAT, SHRIMP!
IN YOUR DREAMS. IT'S MY TURN NOW!
CAZENOVE/WILLIAM

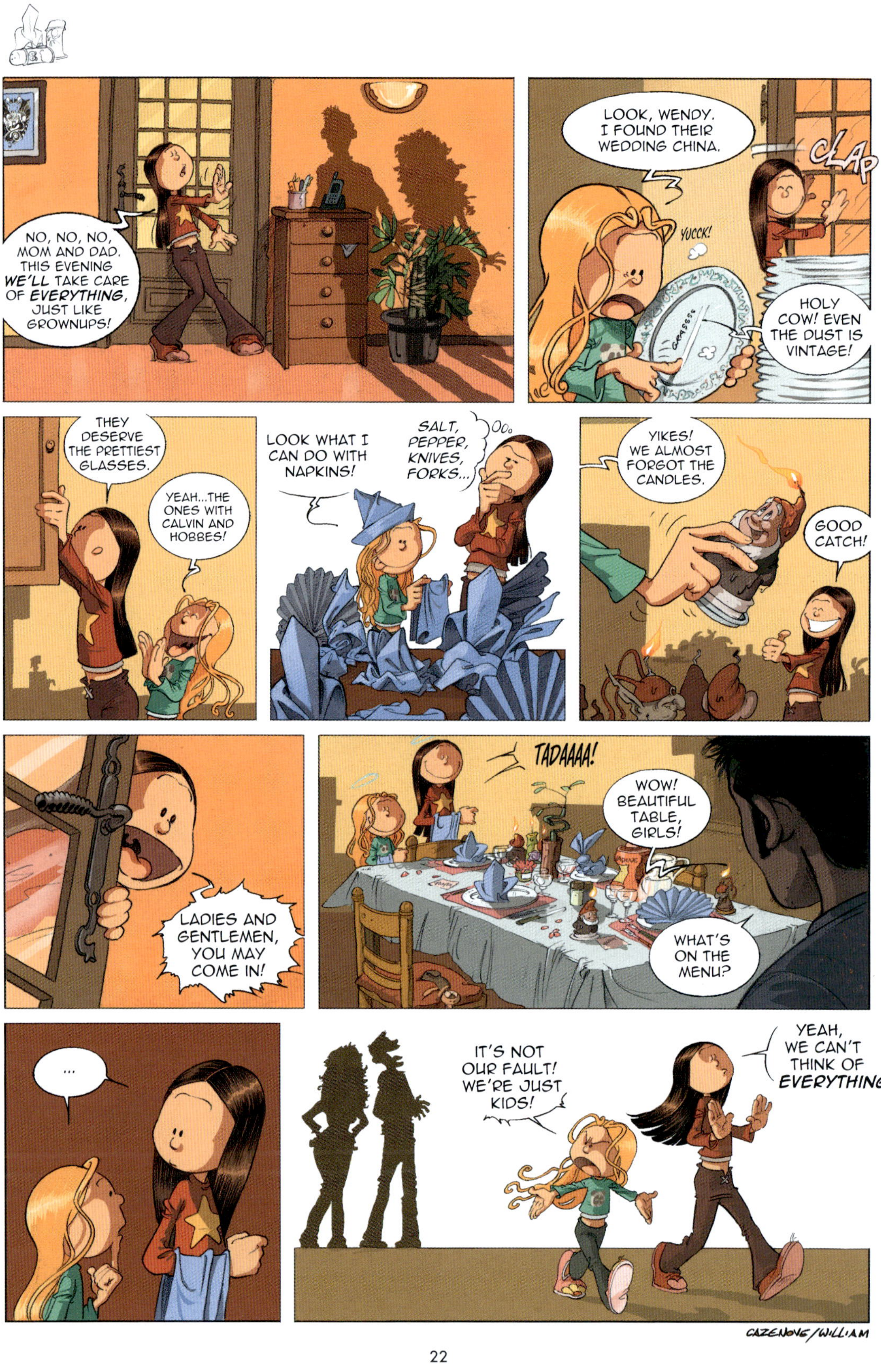
NO, NO, NO, MOM AND DAD. THIS EVENING WE'LL TAKE CARE OF EVERYTHING, JUST LIKE GROWNUPS!
LOOK, WENDY. I FOUND THEIR WEDDING CHINA.
CLAP
YUCCK!
HOLY COW! EVEN THE DUST IS VINTAGE!
THEY DESERVE THE PRETTIEST GLASSES.
YEAH...THE ONES WITH CALVIN AND HOBBES!
LOOK WHAT I CAN DO WITH NAPKINS!
SALT, PEPPER, KNIVES, FORKS...
YIKES! WE ALMOST FORGOT THE CANDLES.
GOOD CATCH!
LADIES AND GENTLEMEN, YOU MAY COME IN!
TADAAAA!
WOW! BEAUTIFUL TABLE, GIRLS!
WHAT'S ON THE MENU?
...
IT'S NOT OUR FAULT! WE'RE JUST KIDS!
YEAH, WE CAN'T THINK OF EVERYTHING
CAZENOVE/WILLIAM

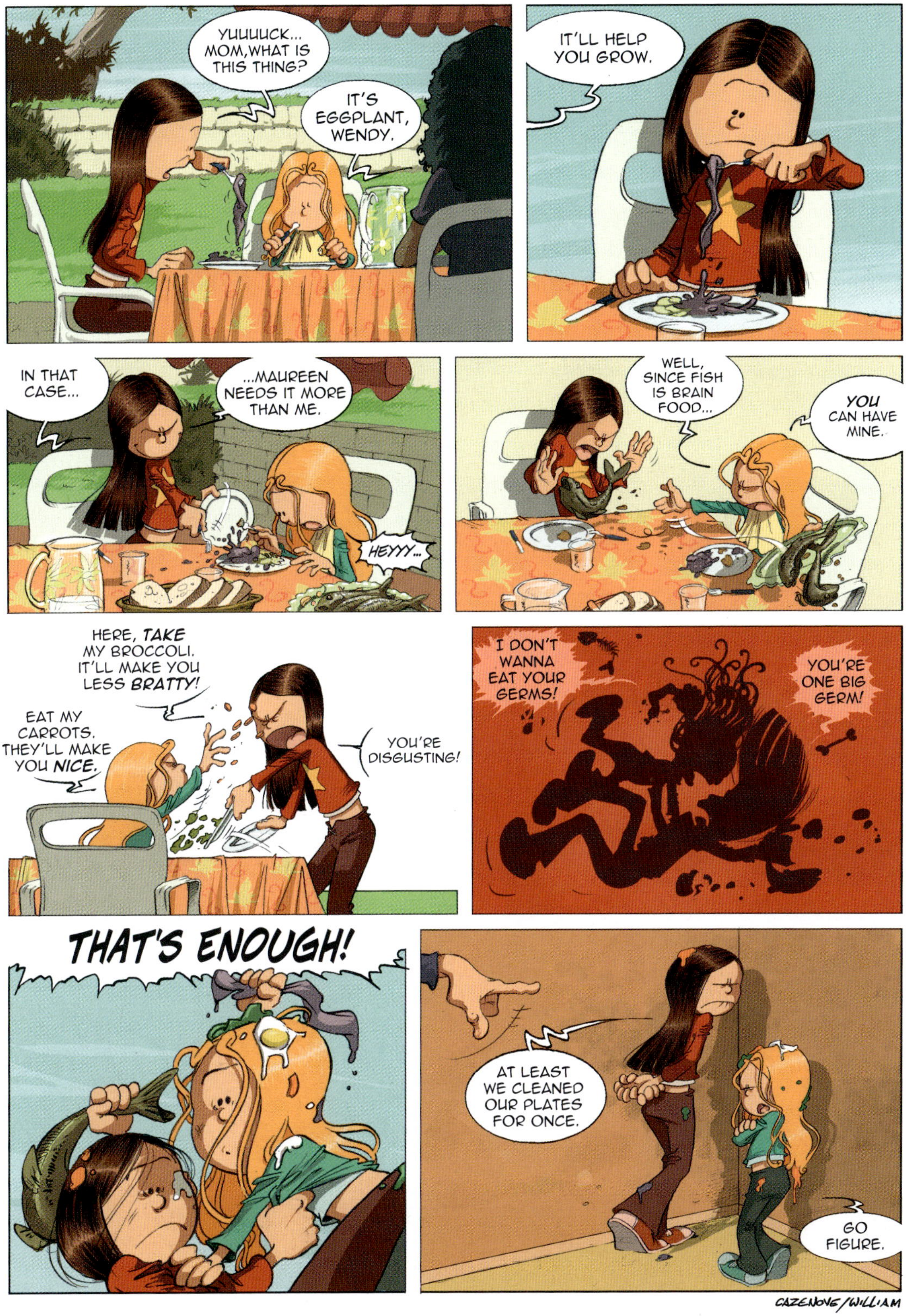
YUUUUCK... MOM, WHAT IS THIS THING?
IT'S EGGPLANT, WENDY.
IT'LL HELP YOU GROW.
IN THAT CASE...
...MAUREEN NEEDS IT MORE THAN ME.
HEYYY...
WELL, SINCE FISH IS BRAIN FOOD...
YOU CAN HAVE MINE.
HERE, TAKE MY BROCCOLI. IT'LL MAKE YOU LESS BRATTY!
EAT MY CARROTS. THEY'LL MAKE YOU NICE.
YOU'RE DISGUSTING!
I DON'T WANNA EAT YOUR GERMS!
YOU'RE ONE BIG GERM!
THAT'S ENOUGH!
AT LEAST WE CLEANED OUR PLATES FOR ONCE.
GO FIGURE.
CAZENOVE/WILLIAM

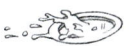

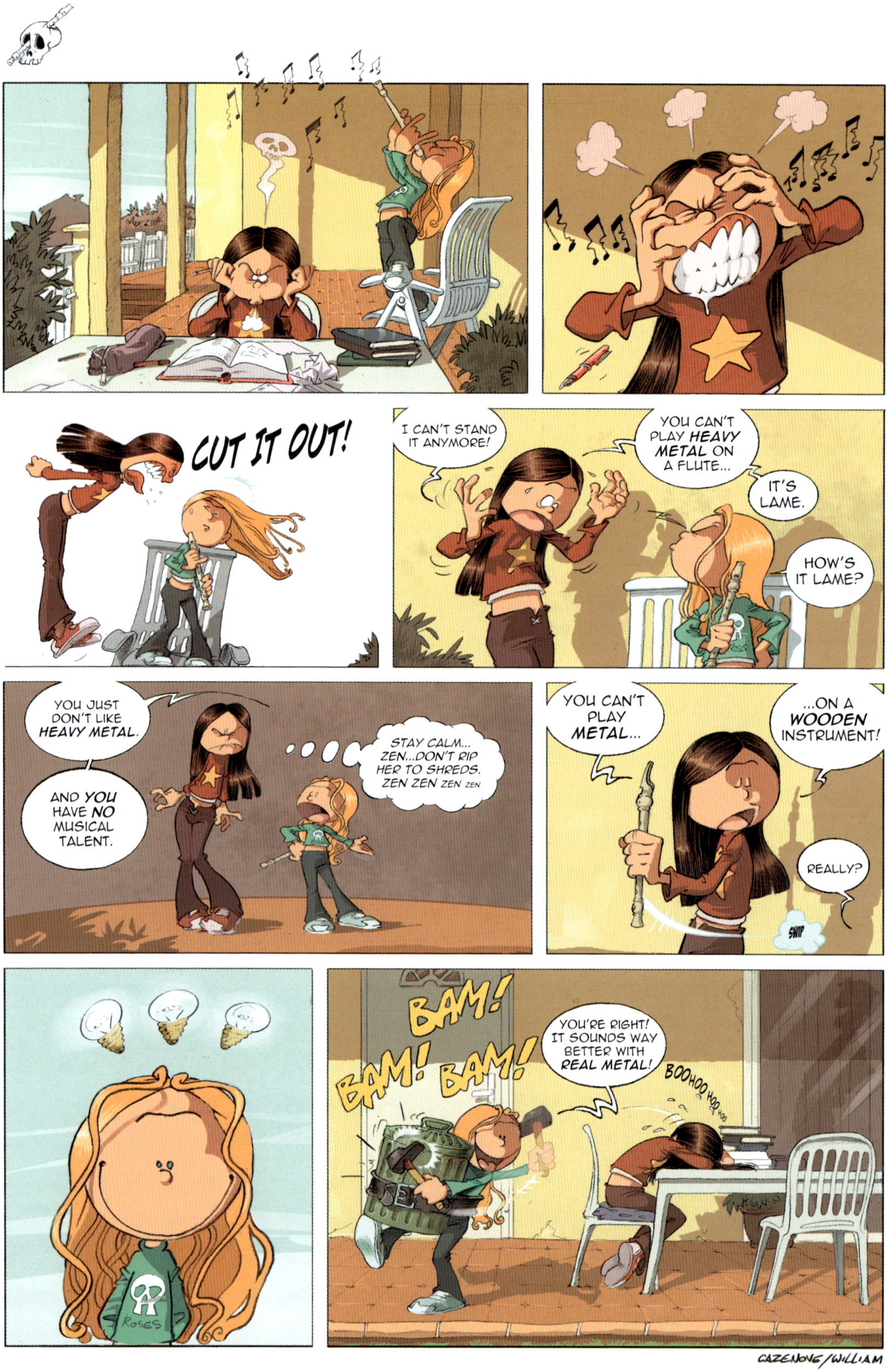

CUT IT OUT!
I CAN'T STAND IT ANYMORE!
YOU CAN'T PLAY HEAVY METAL ON A FLUTE...
IT'S LAME.
HOW'S IT LAME?
YOU JUST DON'T LIKE HEAVY METAL.
AND YOU HAVE NO MUSICAL TALENT.
STAY CALM... ZEN...DON'T RIP HER TO SHREDS. ZEN ZEN ZEN ZEN
YOU CAN'T PLAY METAL...
...ON A WOODEN INSTRUMENT!
REALLY?
SWIP
BAM!
BAM! BAM!
YOU'RE RIGHT! IT SOUNDS WAY BETTER WITH REAL METAL!
BOOHOO HOO HOO
CAZENOVE/WILLIAM

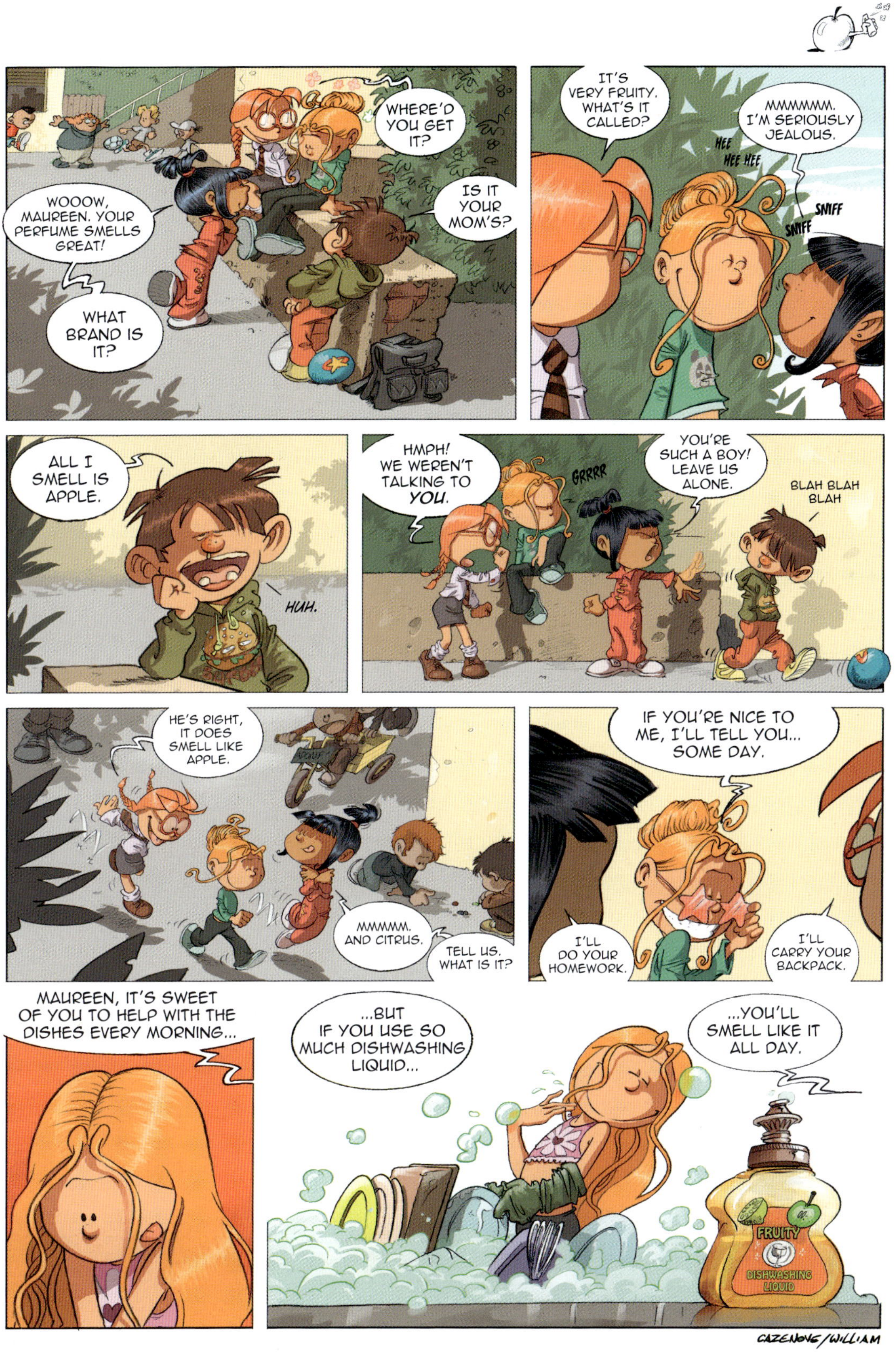
WOOOW, MAUREEN. YOUR PERFUME SMELLS GREAT!
WHAT BRAND IS IT?
WHERE'D YOU GET IT?
IS IT YOUR MOM'S?
IT'S VERY FRUITY. WHAT'S IT CALLED?
MMMMMM. I'M SERIOUSLY JEALOUS.
HEE HEE HEE
SNIFF SNIFF
ALL I SMELL IS APPLE.
HUH.
HMPH! WE WEREN'T TALKING TO *YOU*.
GRRRR
YOU'RE SUCH A BOY! LEAVE US ALONE.
BLAH BLAH BLAH
HE'S RIGHT, IT DOES SMELL LIKE APPLE.
MMMMM. AND CITRUS.
TELL US. WHAT IS IT?
IF YOU'RE NICE TO ME, I'LL TELL YOU... SOME DAY.
I'LL DO YOUR HOMEWORK.
I'LL CARRY YOUR BACKPACK.
MAUREEN, IT'S SWEET OF YOU TO HELP WITH THE DISHES EVERY MORNING...
...BUT IF YOU USE SO MUCH DISHWASHING LIQUID...
...YOU'LL SMELL LIKE IT ALL DAY.
FRUITY
DISHWASHING LIQUID
CAZENOVE/WILLIAM

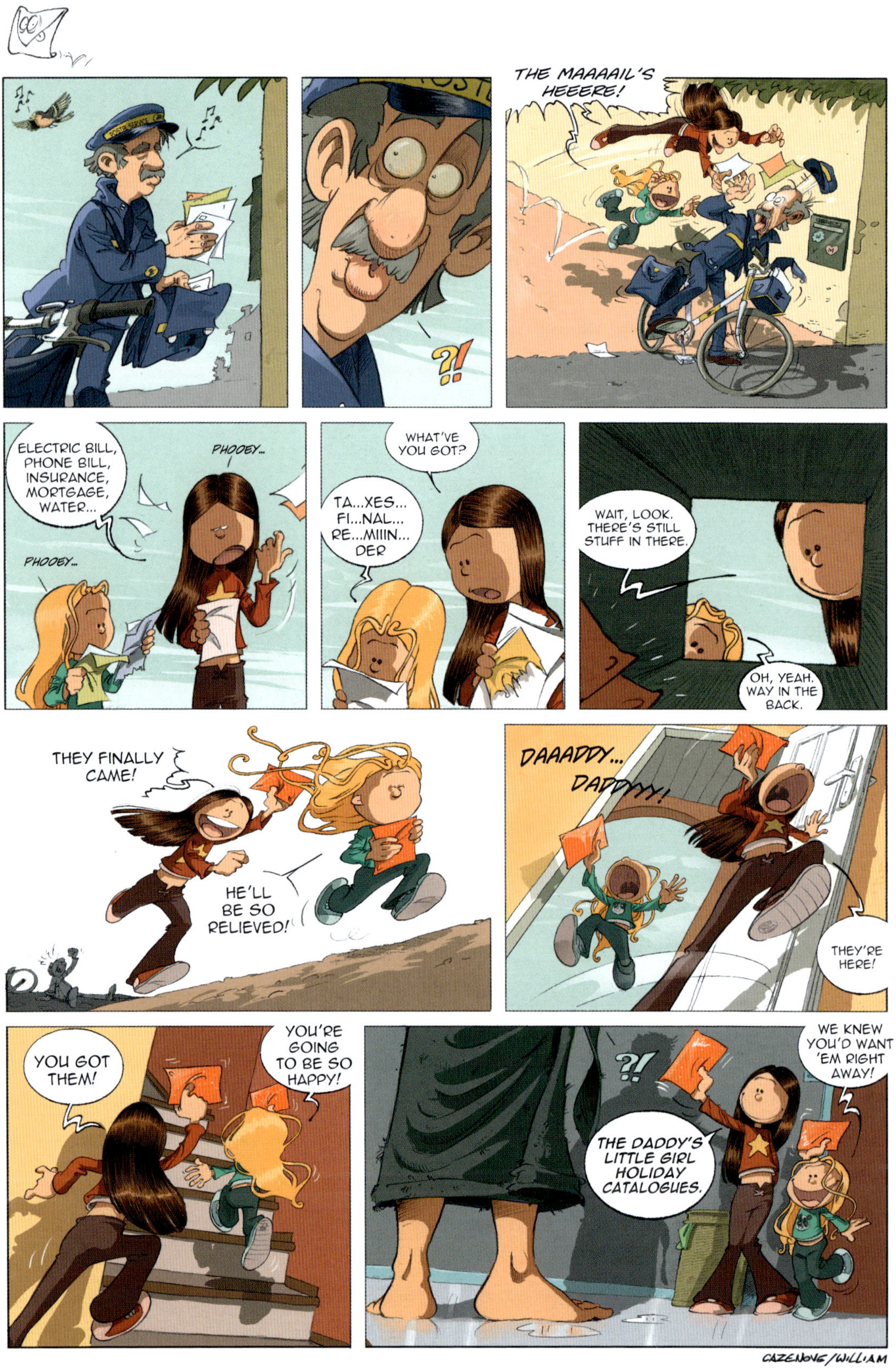
?!
THE MAAAAIL'S HEEERE!
ELECTRIC BILL, PHONE BILL, INSURANCE, MORTGAGE, WATER...
PHOOEY...
PHOOEY...
WHAT'VE YOU GOT?
TA...XES... FI...NAL... RE...MIIIN... DER
WAIT, LOOK. THERE'S STILL STUFF IN THERE.
OH, YEAH. WAY IN THE BACK.
THEY FINALLY CAME!
HE'LL BE SO RELIEVED!
DAAADDY... DADDYYY!
THEY'RE HERE!
YOU GOT THEM!
YOU'RE GOING TO BE SO HAPPY!
?!
WE KNEW YOU'D WANT 'EM RIGHT AWAY!
THE DADDY'S LITTLE GIRL HOLIDAY CATALOGUES.
CAZENOVE/WILLIAM

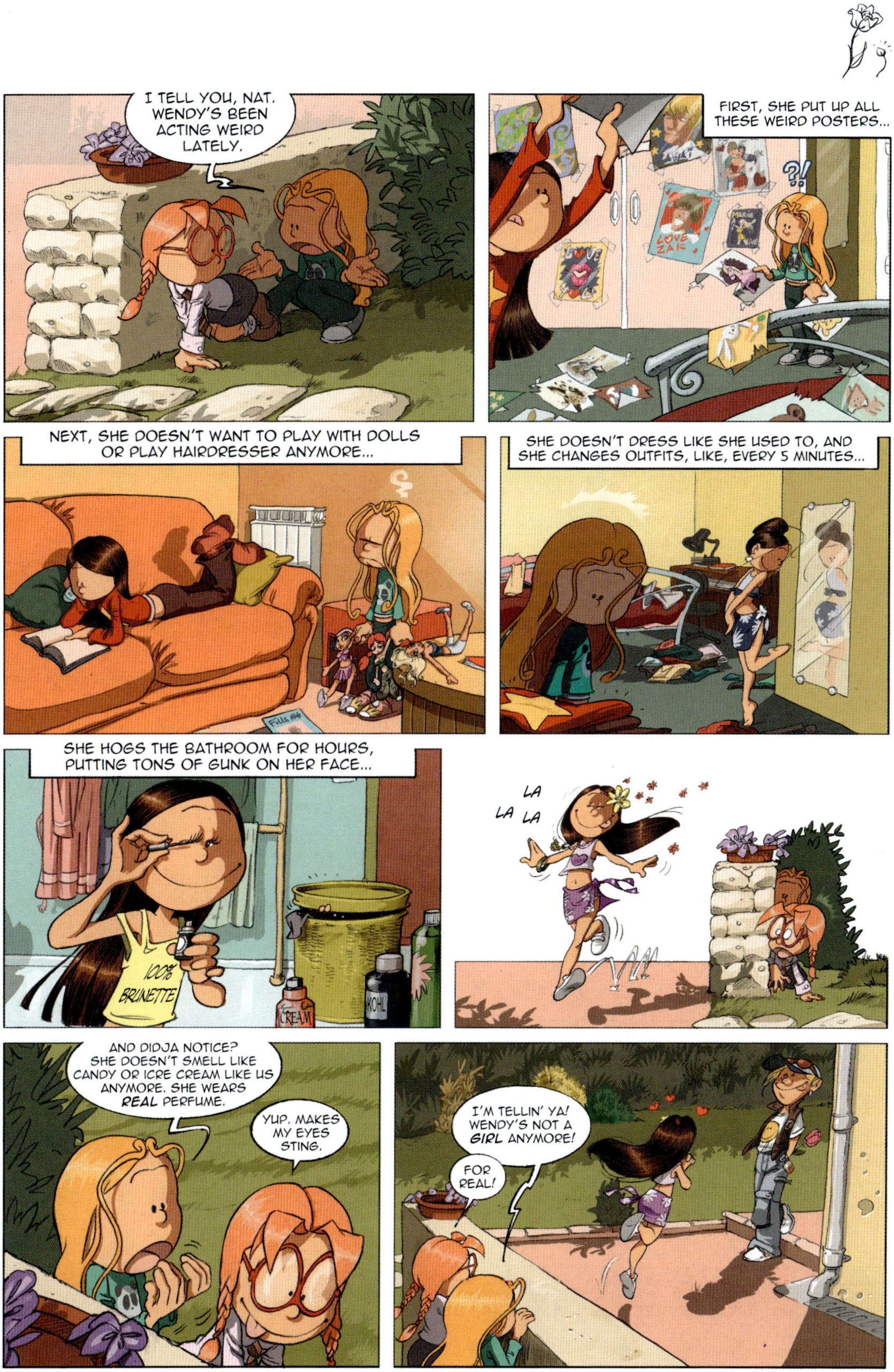

I TELL YOU, NAT. WENDY'S BEEN ACTING WEIRD LATELY.
FIRST, SHE PUT UP ALL THESE WEIRD POSTERS...
?!
NEXT, SHE DOESN'T WANT TO PLAY WITH DOLLS OR PLAY HAIRDRESSER ANYMORE...
SHE DOESN'T DRESS LIKE SHE USED TO, AND SHE CHANGES OUTFITS, LIKE, EVERY 5 MINUTES...
SHE HOGS THE BATHROOM FOR HOURS, PUTTING TONS OF GUNK ON HER FACE...
100% BRUNETTE
CREAM
KOHL
LA LA LA
AND DIDJA NOTICE? SHE DOESN'T SMELL LIKE CANDY OR ICRE CREAM LIKE US ANYMORE. SHE WEARS **REAL** PERFUME.
YUP. MAKES MY EYES STING.
I'M TELLIN' YA! WENDY'S NOT A **GIRL** ANYMORE!
FOR REAL!
CAZENOVE/WILLIAM

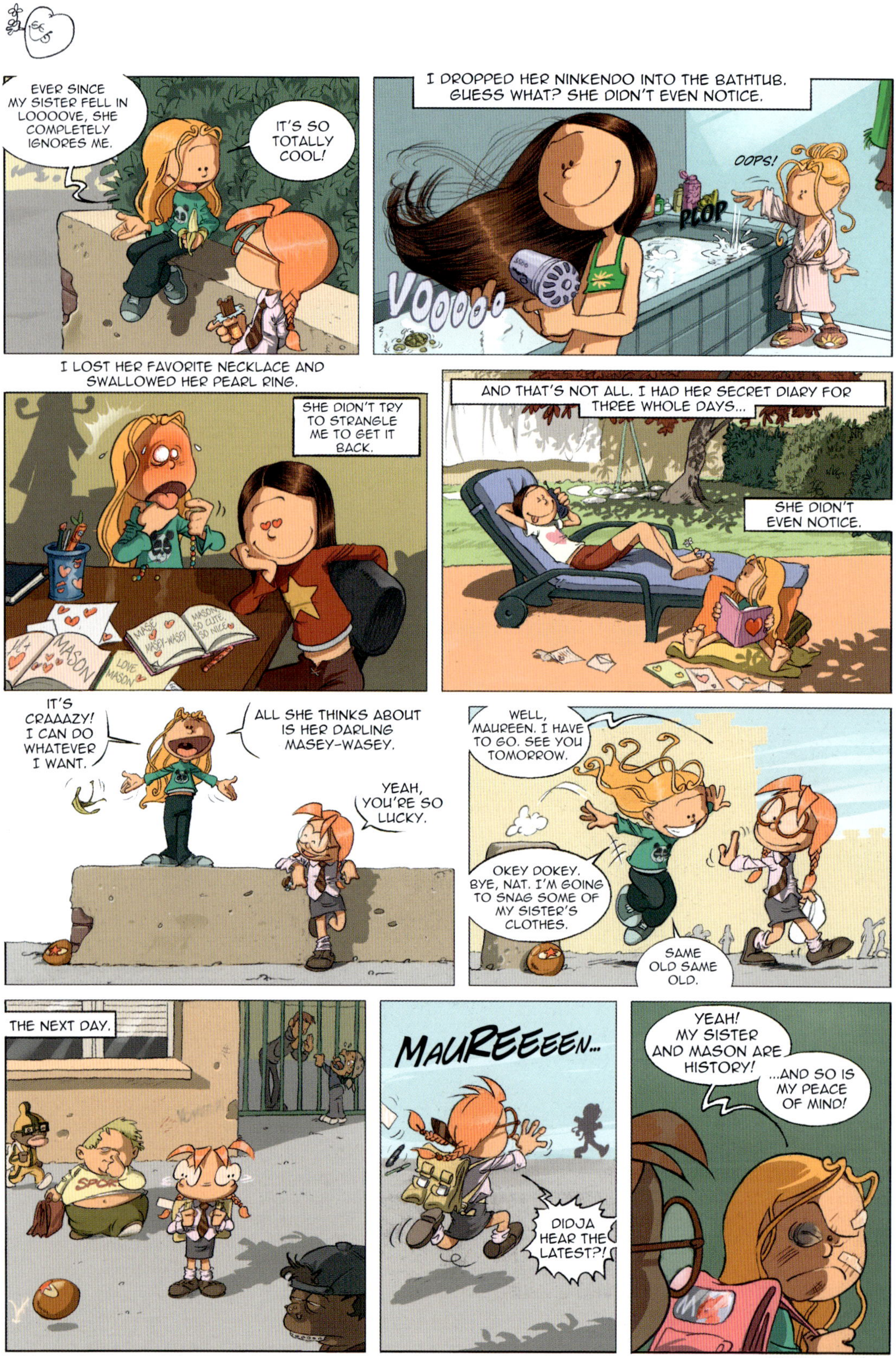
EVER SINCE MY SISTER FELL IN LOOOOVE, SHE COMPLETELY IGNORES ME.
IT'S SO TOTALLY COOL!
I DROPPED HER NINKENDO INTO THE BATHTUB. GUESS WHAT? SHE DIDN'T EVEN NOTICE.
OOPS!
PLOP
VOOOOO
I LOST HER FAVORITE NECKLACE AND SWALLOWED HER PEARL RING.
SHE DIDN'T TRY TO STRANGLE ME TO GET IT BACK.
MASON
LOVE MASON
MASE MASEY-WASEY
MASON SO CUTE, SO NICE
AND THAT'S NOT ALL. I HAD HER SECRET DIARY FOR THREE WHOLE DAYS...
SHE DIDN'T EVEN NOTICE.
IT'S CRAAAZY! I CAN DO WHATEVER I WANT.
ALL SHE THINKS ABOUT IS HER DARLING MASEY-WASEY.
YEAH, YOU'RE SO LUCKY.
WELL, MAUREEN. I HAVE TO GO. SEE YOU TOMORROW.
OKEY DOKEY. BYE, NAT. I'M GOING TO SNAG SOME OF MY SISTER'S CLOTHES.
SAME OLD SAME OLD.
THE NEXT DAY.
MAUREEEEEN...
DIDJA HEAR THE LATEST?!
YEAH! MY SISTER AND MASON ARE HISTORY!
...AND SO IS MY PEACE OF MIND!
CAZENOVE/WILLIAM

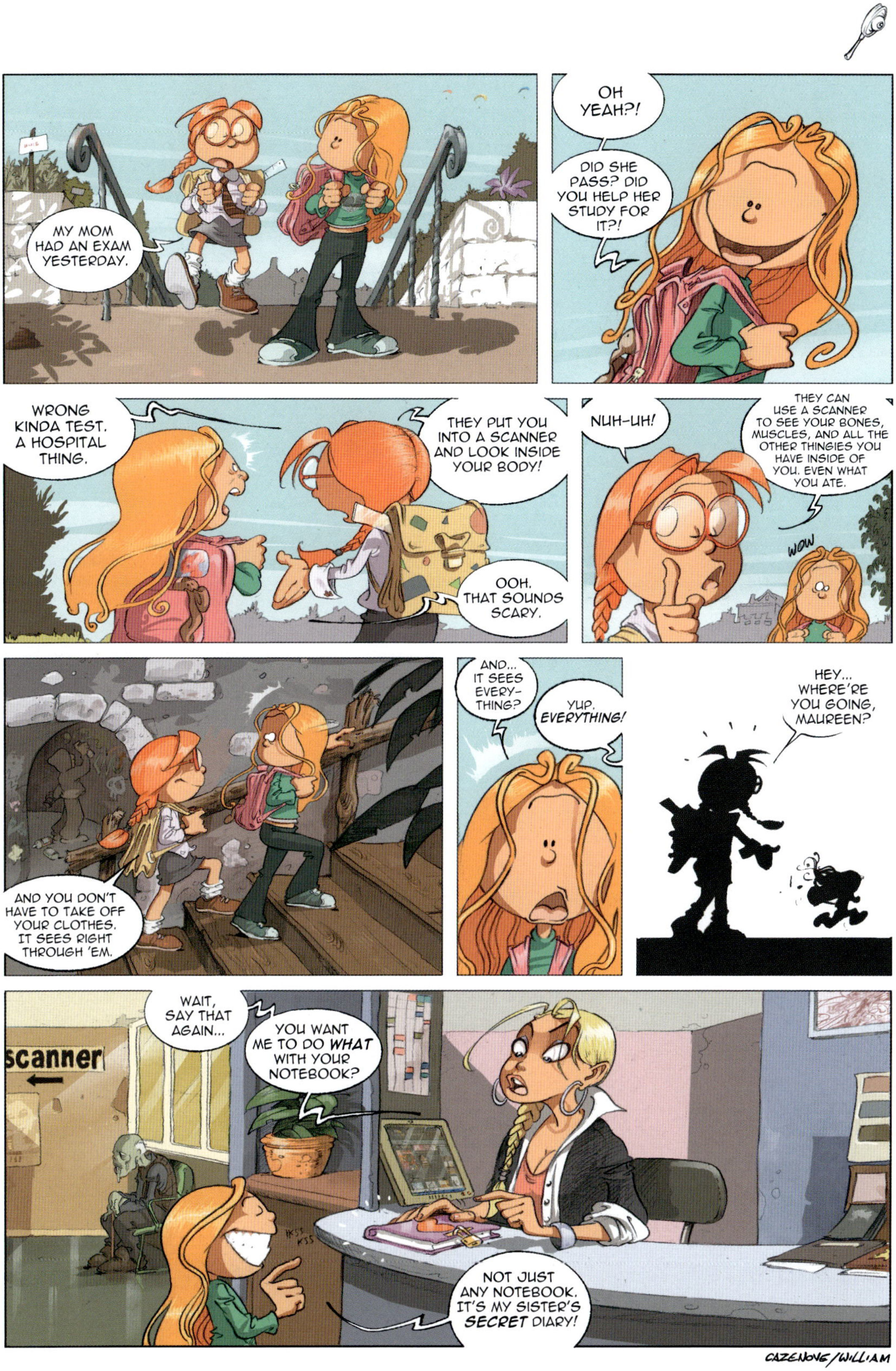
MY MOM HAD AN EXAM YESTERDAY.
OH YEAH?!
DID SHE PASS? DID YOU HELP HER STUDY FOR IT?!
WRONG KINDA TEST. A HOSPITAL THING.
THEY PUT YOU INTO A SCANNER AND LOOK INSIDE YOUR BODY!
OOH. THAT SOUNDS SCARY.
NUH-UH!
THEY CAN USE A SCANNER TO SEE YOUR BONES, MUSCLES, AND ALL THE OTHER THINGIES YOU HAVE INSIDE OF YOU. EVEN WHAT YOU ATE.
WOW
AND YOU DON'T HAVE TO TAKE OFF YOUR CLOTHES. IT SEES RIGHT THROUGH 'EM.
AND... IT SEES EVERY-THING?
YUP. EVERYTHING!
HEY... WHERE'RE YOU GOING, MAUREEN?
scanner
WAIT, SAY THAT AGAIN...
YOU WANT ME TO DO WHAT WITH YOUR NOTEBOOK?
NOT JUST ANY NOTEBOOK. IT'S MY SISTER'S SECRET DIARY!
CAZENOVE/WILLIAM

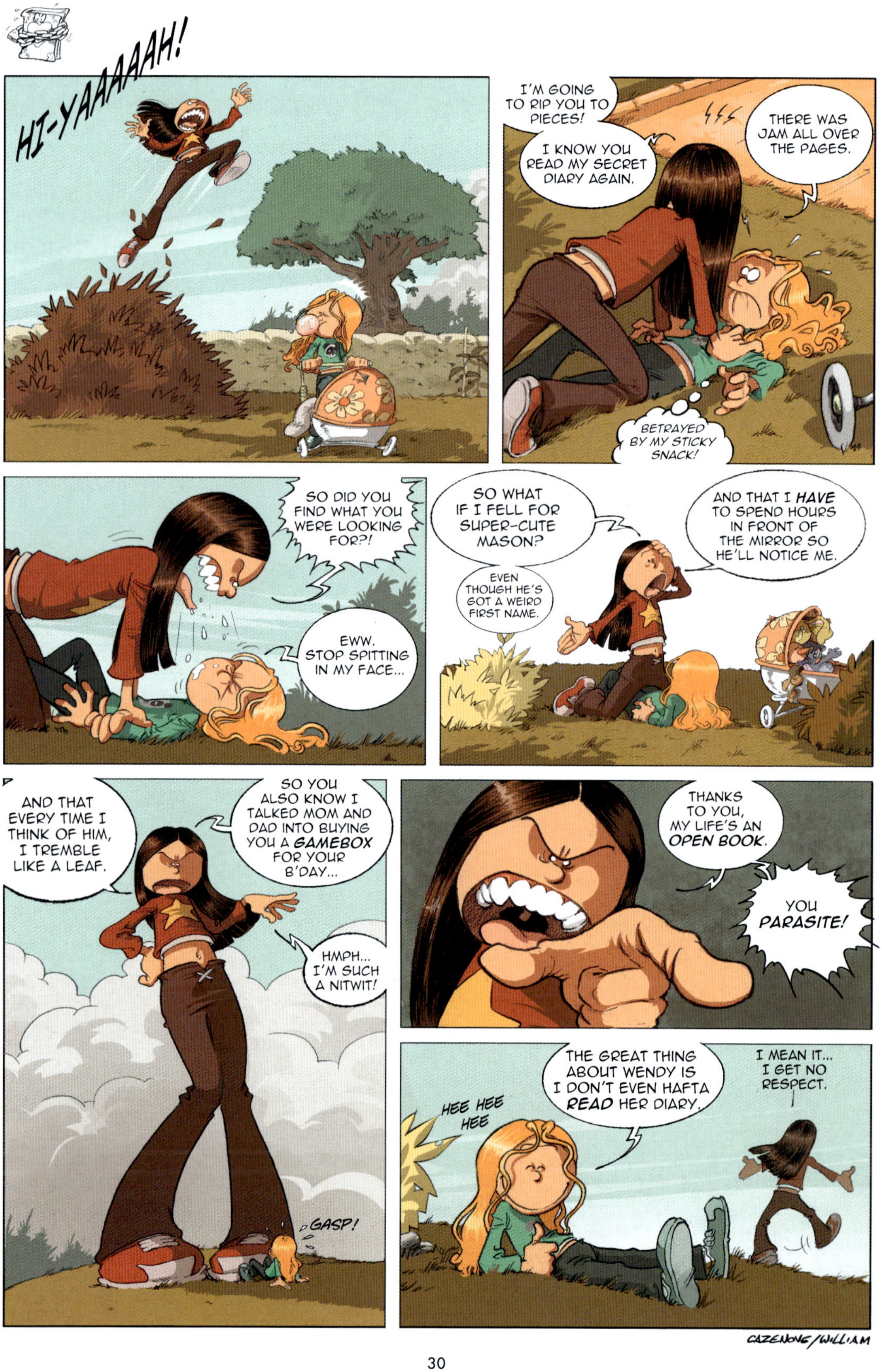
HI-YAAAAAH!
I'M GOING TO RIP YOU TO PIECES!
I KNOW YOU READ MY SECRET DIARY AGAIN.
THERE WAS JAM ALL OVER THE PAGES.
BETRAYED BY MY STICKY SNACK!
SO DID YOU FIND WHAT YOU WERE LOOKING FOR?!
EWW. STOP SPITTING IN MY FACE...
SO WHAT IF I FELL FOR SUPER-CUTE MASON?
EVEN THOUGH HE'S GOT A WEIRD FIRST NAME.
AND THAT I **HAVE** TO SPEND HOURS IN FRONT OF THE MIRROR SO HE'LL NOTICE ME.
AND THAT EVERY TIME I THINK OF HIM, I TREMBLE LIKE A LEAF.
SO YOU ALSO KNOW I TALKED MOM AND DAD INTO BUYING YOU A **GAMEBOX** FOR YOUR B'DAY...
HMPH... I'M SUCH A NITWIT!
GASP!
THANKS TO YOU, MY LIFE'S AN **OPEN BOOK**.
YOU **PARASITE!**
HEE HEE HEE
THE GREAT THING ABOUT WENDY IS I DON'T EVEN HAFTA **READ** HER DIARY.
I MEAN IT... I GET NO RESPECT.
CAZENOVE/WILLIAM

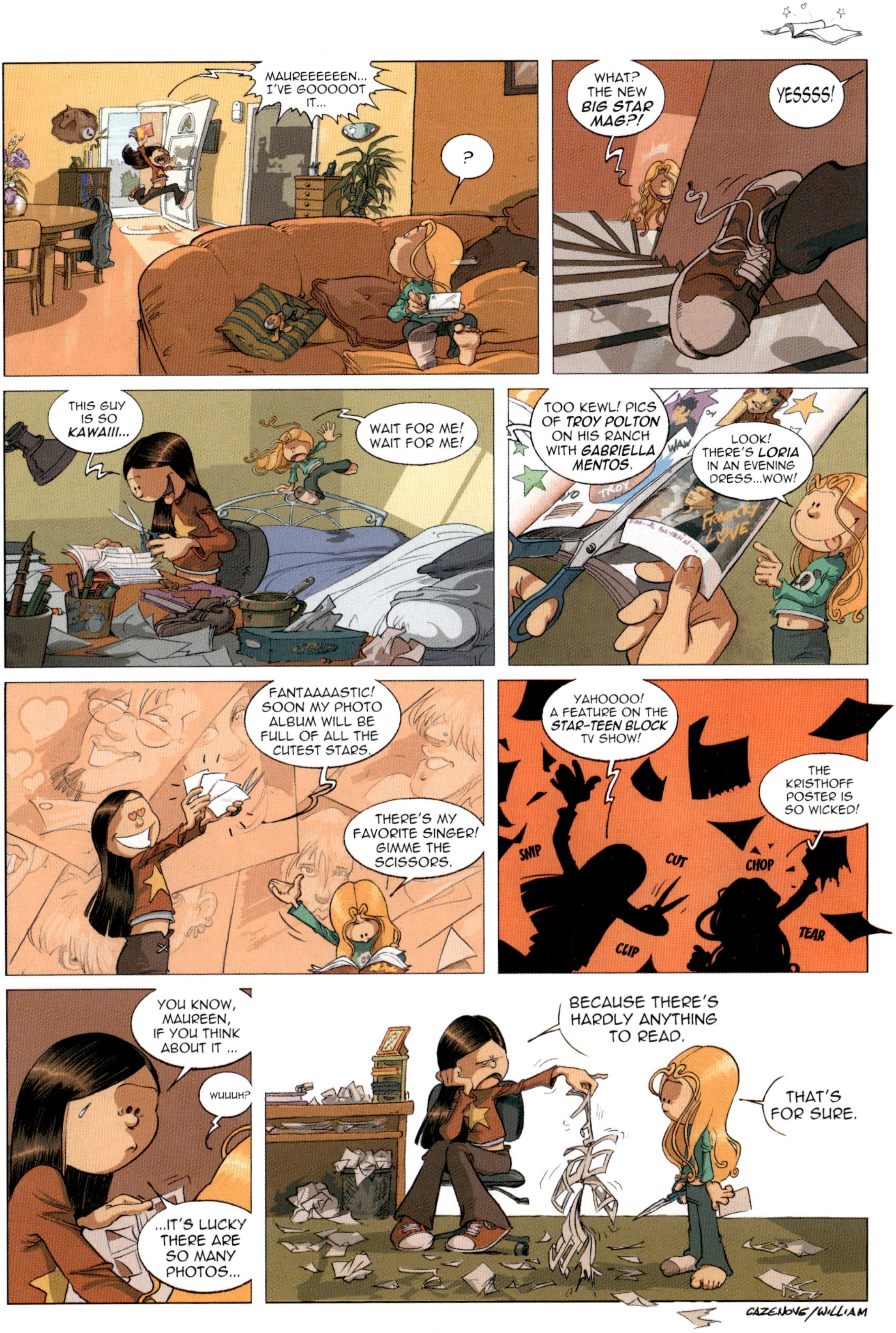
MAUREEEEEEN... I'VE GOOOOOT IT...
?
WHAT? THE NEW BIG STAR MAG?!
YESSSS!
THIS GUY IS SO KAWAIII...
WAIT FOR ME! WAIT FOR ME!
TOO KEWL! PICS OF TROY POLTON ON HIS RANCH WITH GABRIELLA MENTOS.
LOOK! THERE'S LORIA IN AN EVENING DRESS...WOW!
FANTAAAASTIC! SOON MY PHOTO ALBUM WILL BE FULL OF ALL THE CUTEST STARS.
THERE'S MY FAVORITE SINGER! GIMME THE SCISSORS.
YAHOOOO! A FEATURE ON THE STAR-TEEN BLOCK TV SHOW!
THE KRISTHOFF POSTER IS SO WICKED!
SNIP
CUT
CHOP
CLIP
TEAR
YOU KNOW, MAUREEN, IF YOU THINK ABOUT IT ...
WUUUH?
...IT'S LUCKY THERE ARE SO MANY PHOTOS...
BECAUSE THERE'S HARDLY ANYTHING TO READ.
THAT'S FOR SURE.
CAZENOVE/WILLIAM

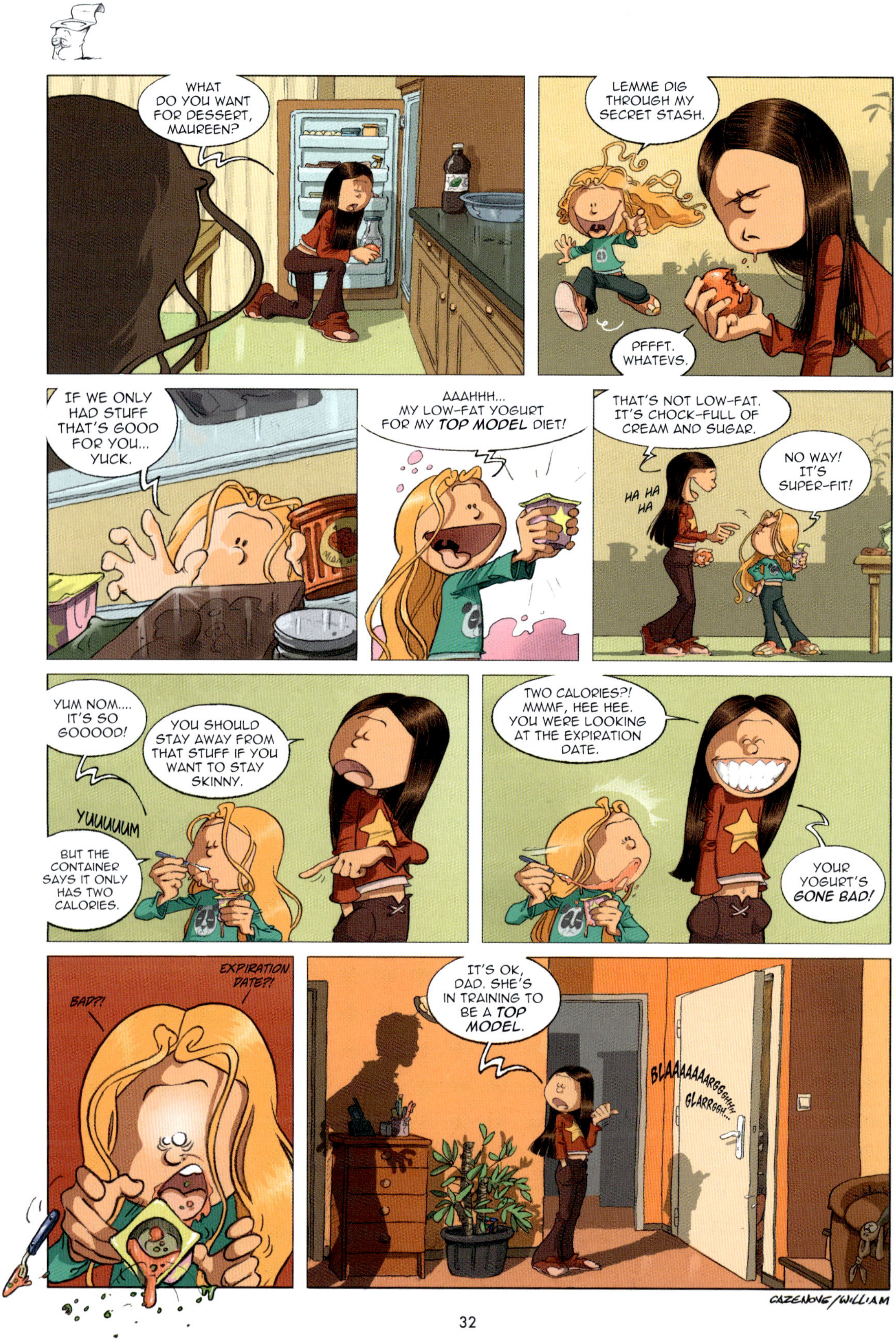
WHAT DO YOU WANT FOR DESSERT, MAUREEN?
LEMME DIG THROUGH MY SECRET STASH.
PFFFT. WHATEVS.
IF WE ONLY HAD STUFF THAT'S GOOD FOR YOU... YUCK.
AAAHHH... MY LOW-FAT YOGURT FOR MY TOP MODEL DIET!
THAT'S NOT LOW-FAT. IT'S CHOCK-FULL OF CREAM AND SUGAR.
HA HA HA
NO WAY! IT'S SUPER-FIT!
YUM NOM.... IT'S SO GOOOOD!
YOU SHOULD STAY AWAY FROM THAT STUFF IF YOU WANT TO STAY SKINNY.
YUUUUUM
BUT THE CONTAINER SAYS IT ONLY HAS TWO CALORIES.
TWO CALORIES?! MMMF, HEE HEE. YOU WERE LOOKING AT THE EXPIRATION DATE.
YOUR YOGURT'S GONE BAD!
BAD?!
EXPIRATION DATE?!
IT'S OK, DAD. SHE'S IN TRAINING TO BE A TOP MODEL.
BLAAAAAAARGGGHHH
GLARRGGH...
CAZENOVE/WILLIAM

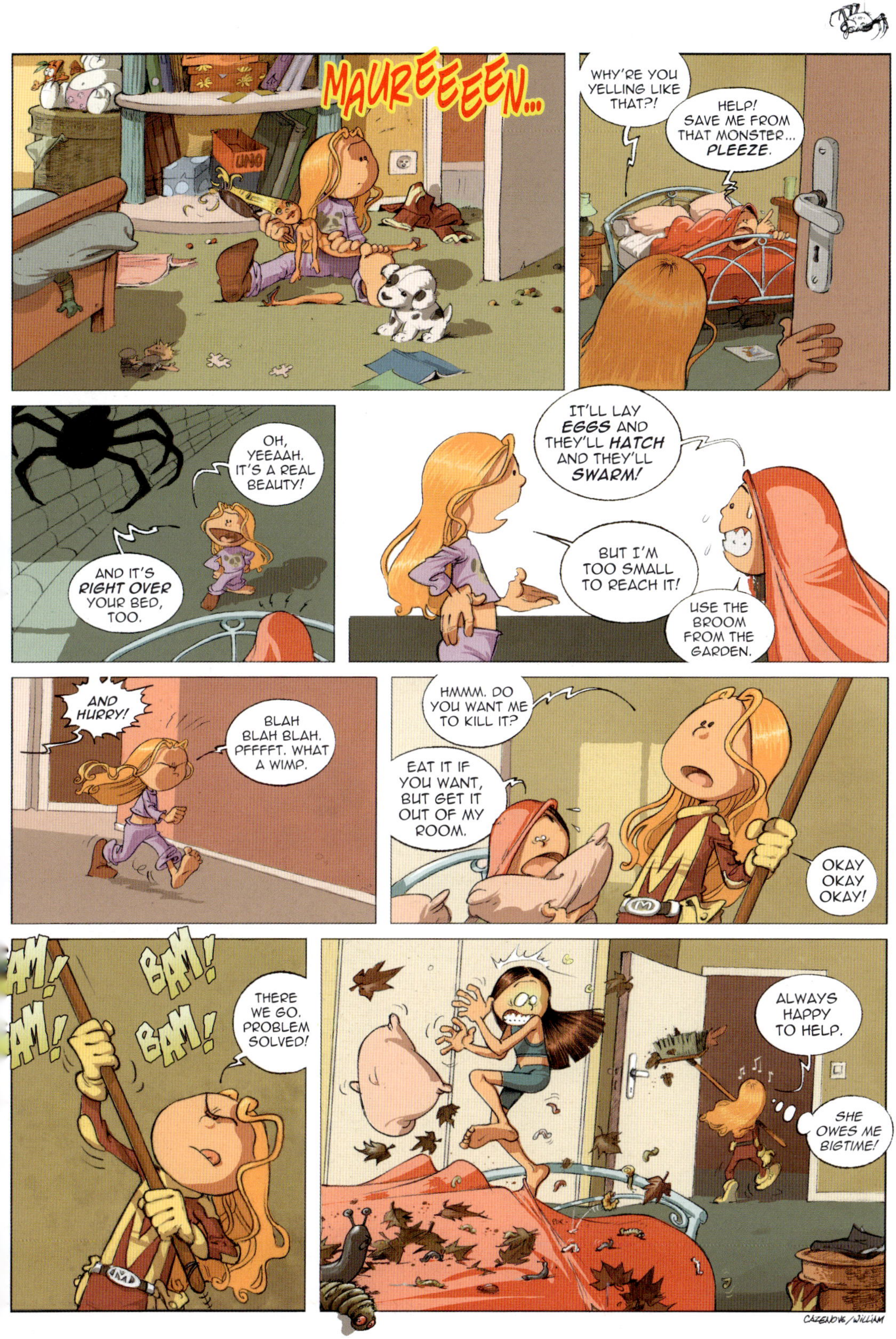
MAUREEEEN...
WHY'RE YOU YELLING LIKE THAT?!
HELP! SAVE ME FROM THAT MONSTER... PLEEZE.
OH, YEEAAH. IT'S A REAL BEAUTY!
AND IT'S RIGHT OVER YOUR BED, TOO.
IT'LL LAY EGGS AND THEY'LL HATCH AND THEY'LL SWARM!
BUT I'M TOO SMALL TO REACH IT!
USE THE BROOM FROM THE GARDEN.
AND HURRY!
BLAH BLAH BLAH. PFFFFT. WHAT A WIMP.
HMMM. DO YOU WANT ME TO KILL IT?
EAT IT IF YOU WANT, BUT GET IT OUT OF MY ROOM.
OKAY OKAY OKAY!
BAM! BAM! BAM! BAM!
THERE WE GO. PROBLEM SOLVED!
ALWAYS HAPPY TO HELP.
SHE OWES ME BIGTIME!
CAZENOVE/WILLIAM

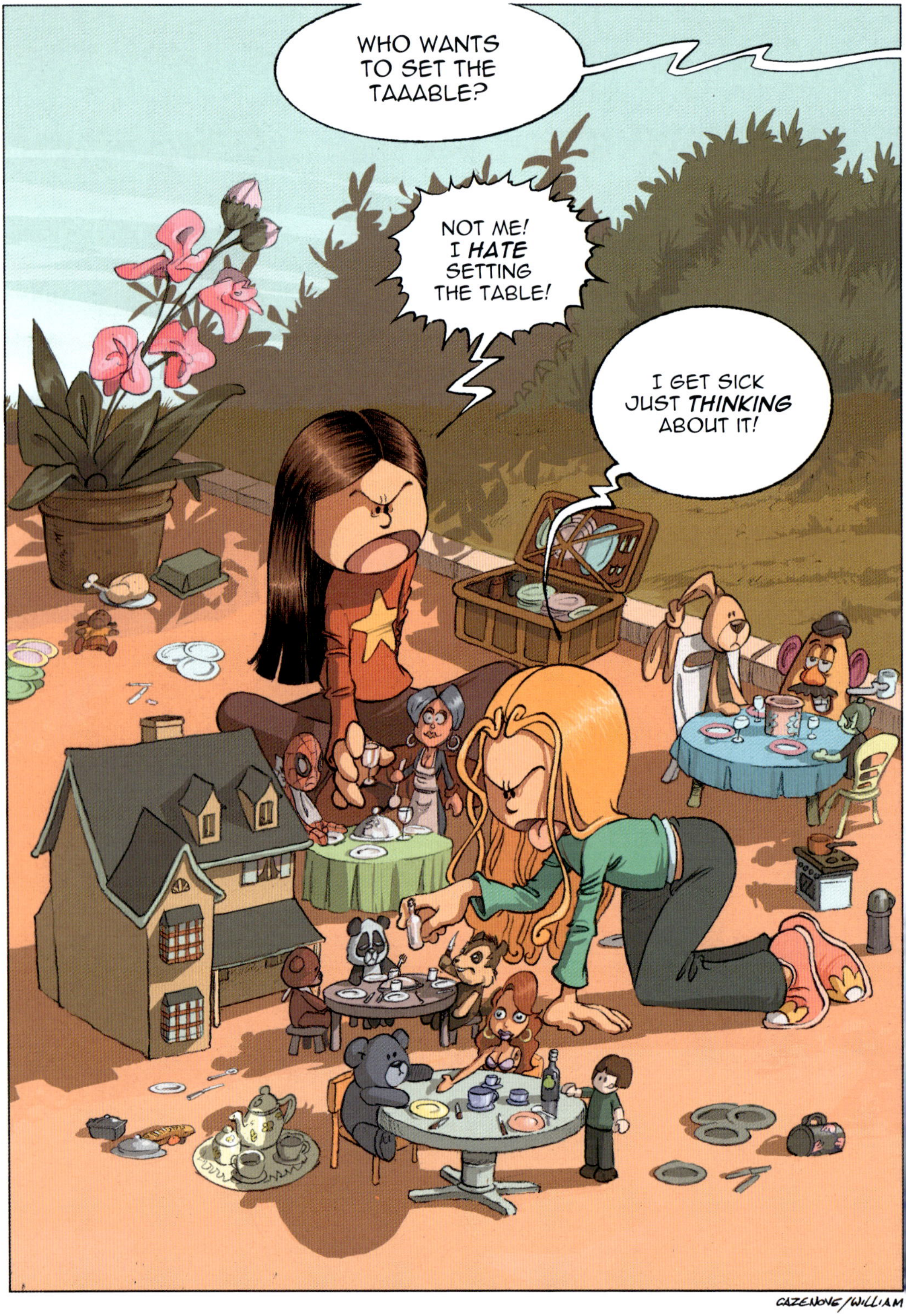
WHO WANTS TO SET THE TAAABLE?
NOT ME! I *HATE* SETTING THE TABLE!
I GET SICK JUST *THINKING* ABOUT IT!

CAZENOVE/WILLIAM

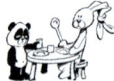

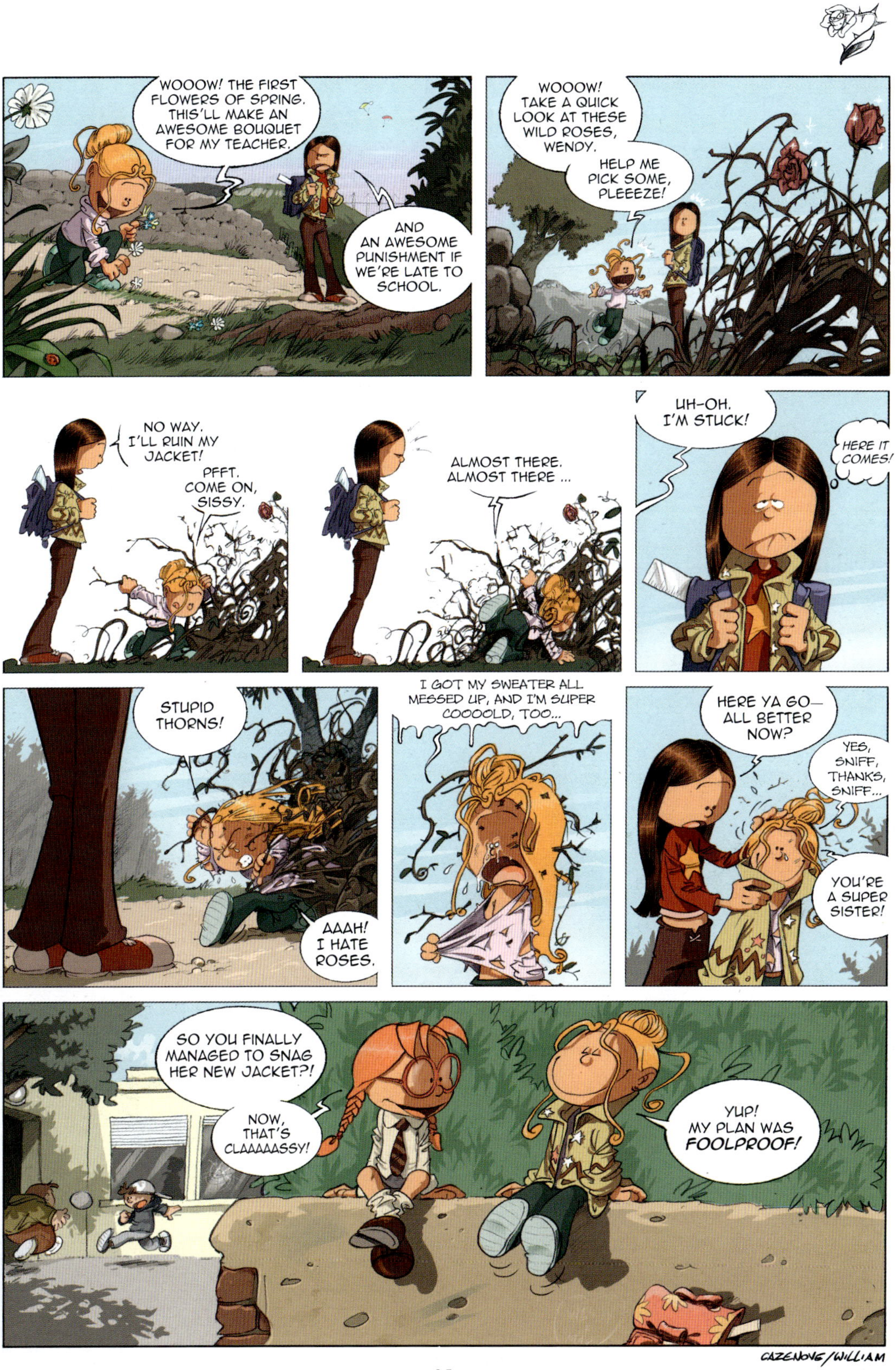
WOOOW! THE FIRST FLOWERS OF SPRING. THIS'LL MAKE AN AWESOME BOUQUET FOR MY TEACHER.
AND AN AWESOME PUNISHMENT IF WE'RE LATE TO SCHOOL.
WOOOW! TAKE A QUICK LOOK AT THESE WILD ROSES, WENDY.
HELP ME PICK SOME, PLEEEZE!
NO WAY. I'LL RUIN MY JACKET!
PFFT. COME ON, SISSY.
ALMOST THERE. ALMOST THERE ...
UH-OH. I'M STUCK!
HERE IT COMES!
STUPID THORNS!
AAAH! I HATE ROSES.
I GOT MY SWEATER ALL MESSED UP, AND I'M SUPER COOOOLD, TOO...
HERE YA GO— ALL BETTER NOW?
YES, SNIFF, THANKS, SNIFF...
YOU'RE A SUPER SISTER!
SO YOU FINALLY MANAGED TO SNAG HER NEW JACKET?!
NOW, THAT'S CLAAAAASSY!
YUP! MY PLAN WAS FOOLPROOF!
CAZENOVE/WILLIAM

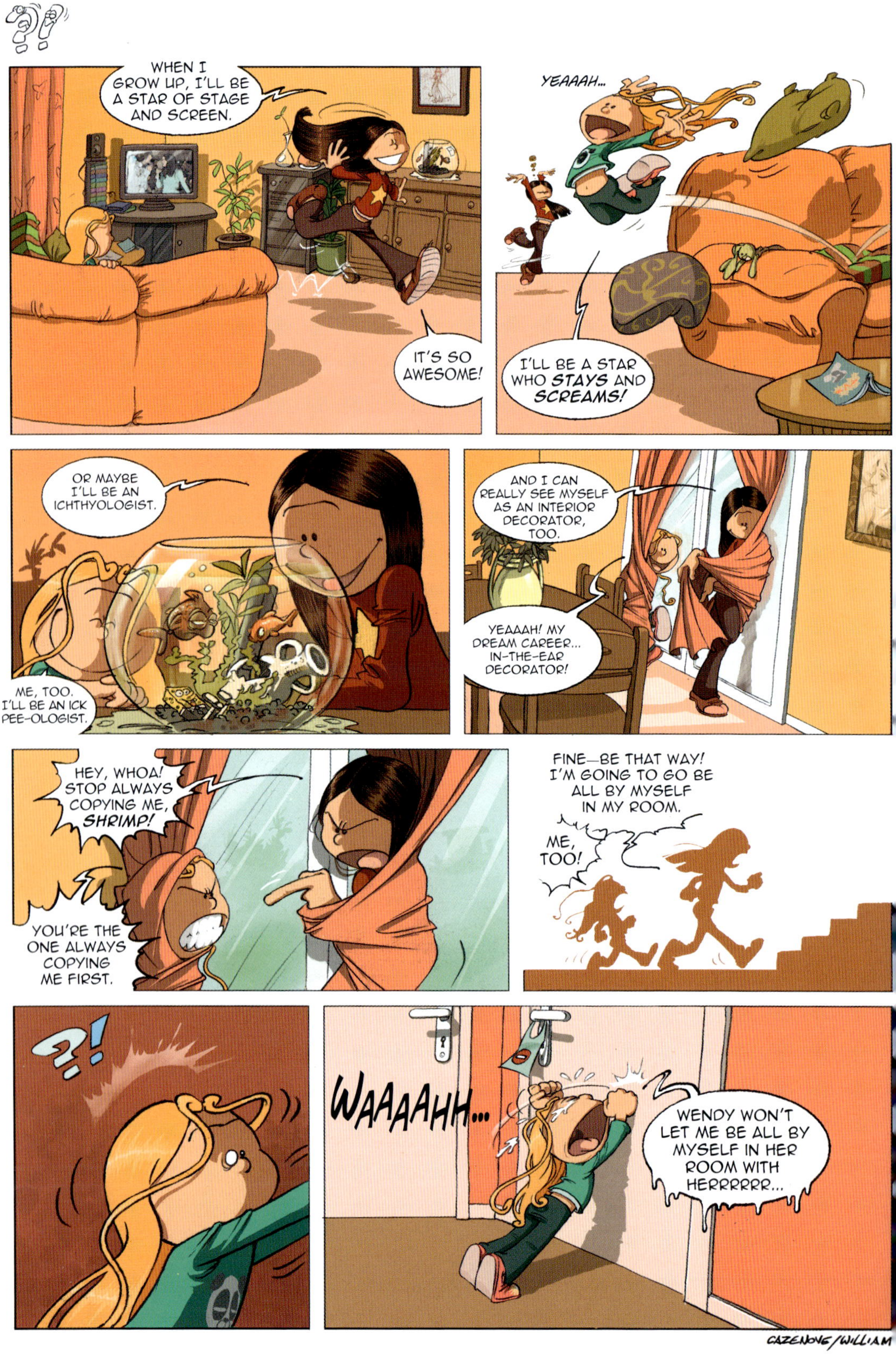
WHEN I GROW UP, I'LL BE A STAR OF STAGE AND SCREEN.
IT'S SO AWESOME!
YEAAAH...
I'LL BE A STAR WHO STAYS AND SCREAMS!
OR MAYBE I'LL BE AN ICHTHYOLOGIST.
ME, TOO. I'LL BE AN ICK PEE-OLOGIST.
AND I CAN REALLY SEE MYSELF AS AN INTERIOR DECORATOR, TOO.
YEAAAH! MY DREAM CAREER... IN-THE-EAR DECORATOR!
HEY, WHOA! STOP ALWAYS COPYING ME, SHRIMP!
YOU'RE THE ONE ALWAYS COPYING ME FIRST.
FINE—BE THAT WAY! I'M GOING TO GO BE ALL BY MYSELF IN MY ROOM.
ME, TOO!
?!
WAAAAHH...
WENDY WON'T LET ME BE ALL BY MYSELF IN HER ROOM WITH HERRRRRR...
CAZENOVE/WILLIAM

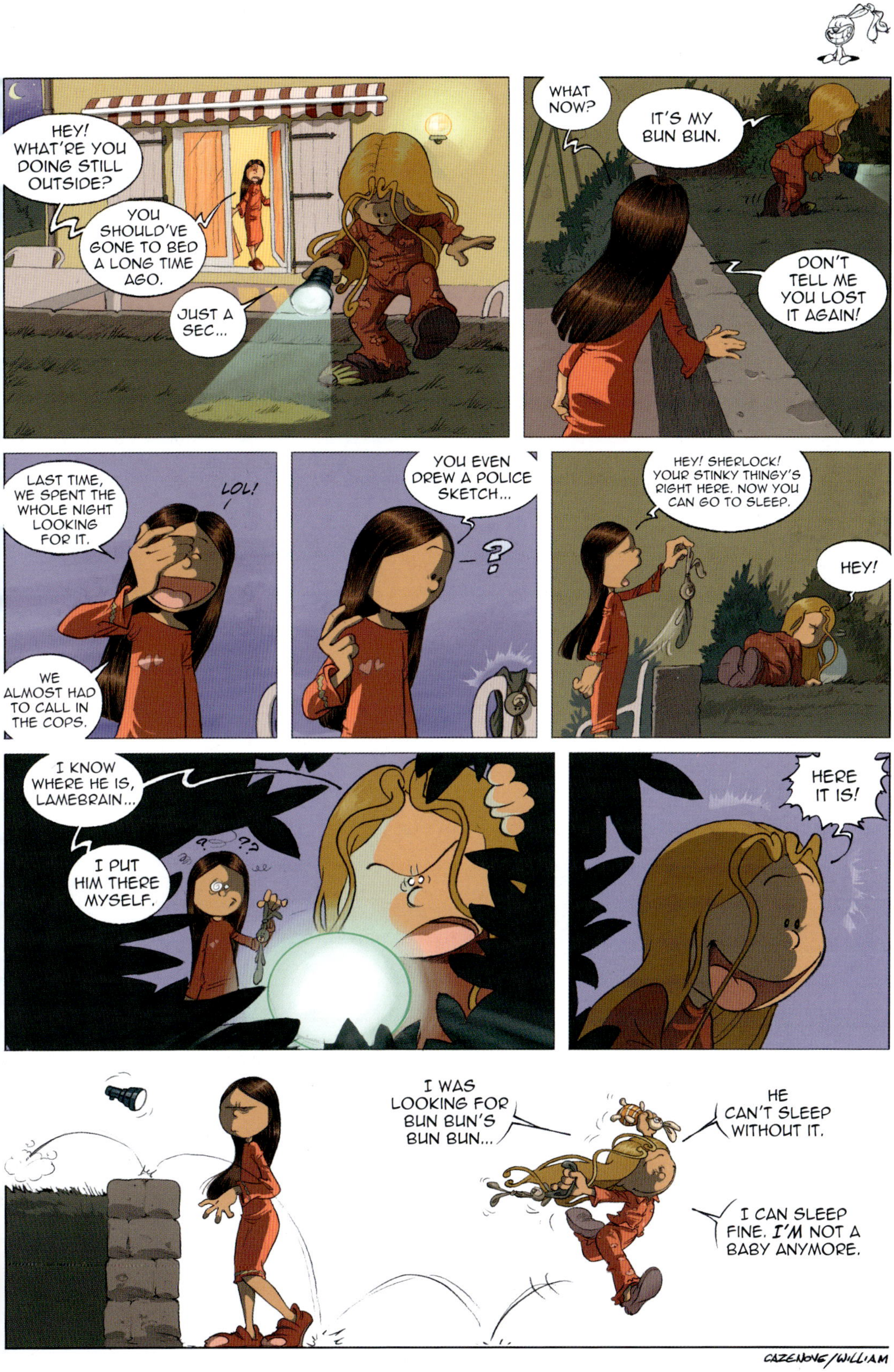
HEY! WHAT'RE YOU DOING STILL OUTSIDE?
YOU SHOULD'VE GONE TO BED A LONG TIME AGO.
JUST A SEC...
WHAT NOW?
IT'S MY BUN BUN.
DON'T TELL ME YOU LOST IT AGAIN!
LAST TIME, WE SPENT THE WHOLE NIGHT LOOKING FOR IT.
LOL!
WE ALMOST HAD TO CALL IN THE COPS.
YOU EVEN DREW A POLICE SKETCH...
?
HEY! SHERLOCK! YOUR STINKY THINGY'S RIGHT HERE. NOW YOU CAN GO TO SLEEP.
HEY!
I KNOW WHERE HE IS, LAMEBRAIN...
I PUT HIM THERE MYSELF.
HERE IT IS!
I WAS LOOKING FOR BUN BUN'S BUN BUN...
HE CAN'T SLEEP WITHOUT IT.
I CAN SLEEP FINE. *I'M* NOT A BABY ANYMORE.
CAZENOVE/WILLIAM

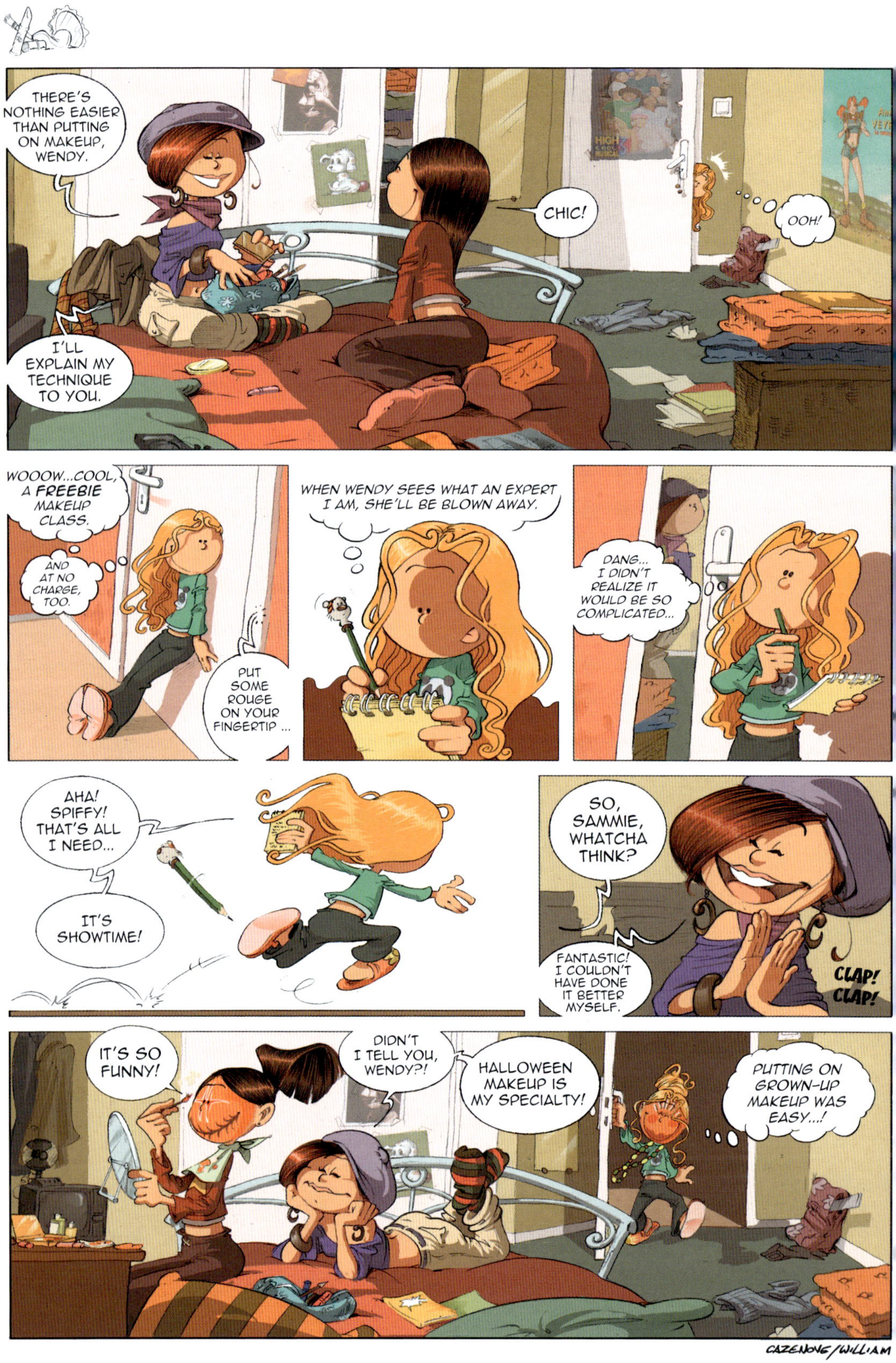
THERE'S NOTHING EASIER THAN PUTTING ON MAKEUP, WENDY.
I'LL EXPLAIN MY TECHNIQUE TO YOU.
CHIC!
OOH!
WOOOW...COOL, A **FREEBIE** MAKEUP CLASS.
AND AT NO CHARGE, TOO.
PUT SOME ROUGE ON YOUR FINGERTIP ...
WHEN WENDY SEES WHAT AN EXPERT I AM, SHE'LL BE BLOWN AWAY.
DANG... I DIDN'T REALIZE IT WOULD BE SO COMPLICATED...
AHA! SPIFFY! THAT'S ALL I NEED...
IT'S SHOWTIME!
SO, SAMMIE, WHATCHA THINK?
FANTASTIC! I COULDN'T HAVE DONE IT BETTER MYSELF.
CLAP! CLAP!
IT'S SO FUNNY!
DIDN'T I TELL YOU, WENDY?!
HALLOWEEN MAKEUP IS MY SPECIALTY!
PUTTING ON GROWN-UP MAKEUP WAS EASY...!
CAZENOVE/WILLIAM

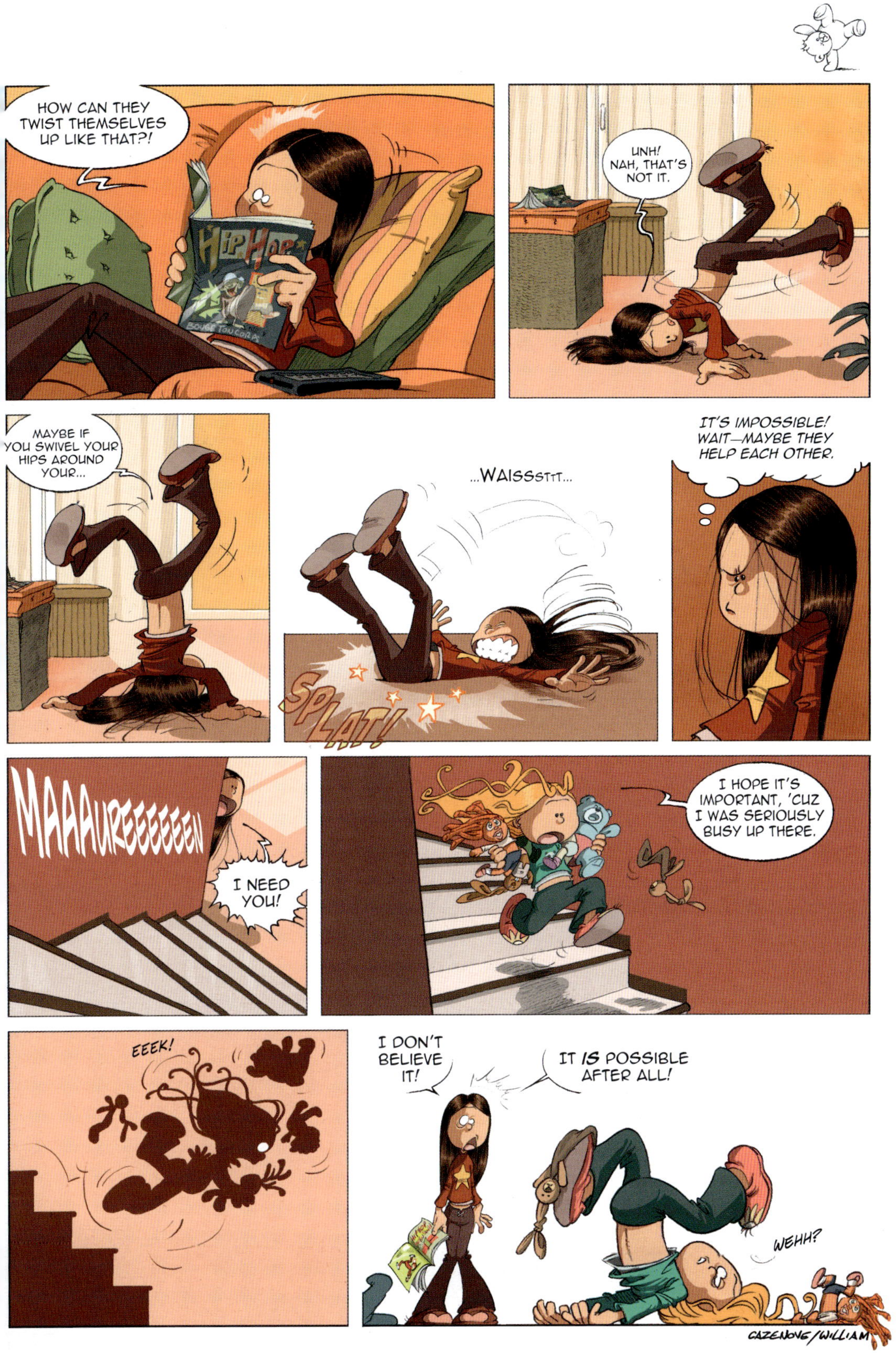
HOW CAN THEY TWIST THEMSELVES UP LIKE THAT?!
BOUGE TON CORPS
UNH! NAH, THAT'S NOT IT.
MAYBE IF YOU SWIVEL YOUR HIPS AROUND YOUR...
...WAISSSTTT...
SPLAT!
IT'S IMPOSSIBLE! WAIT—MAYBE THEY HELP EACH OTHER.
MAAAUREEEEEEN
I NEED YOU!
I HOPE IT'S IMPORTANT, 'CUZ I WAS SERIOUSLY BUSY UP THERE.
EEEK!
I DON'T BELIEVE IT!
IT IS POSSIBLE AFTER ALL!
WEHH?
CAZENOVE/WILLIAM

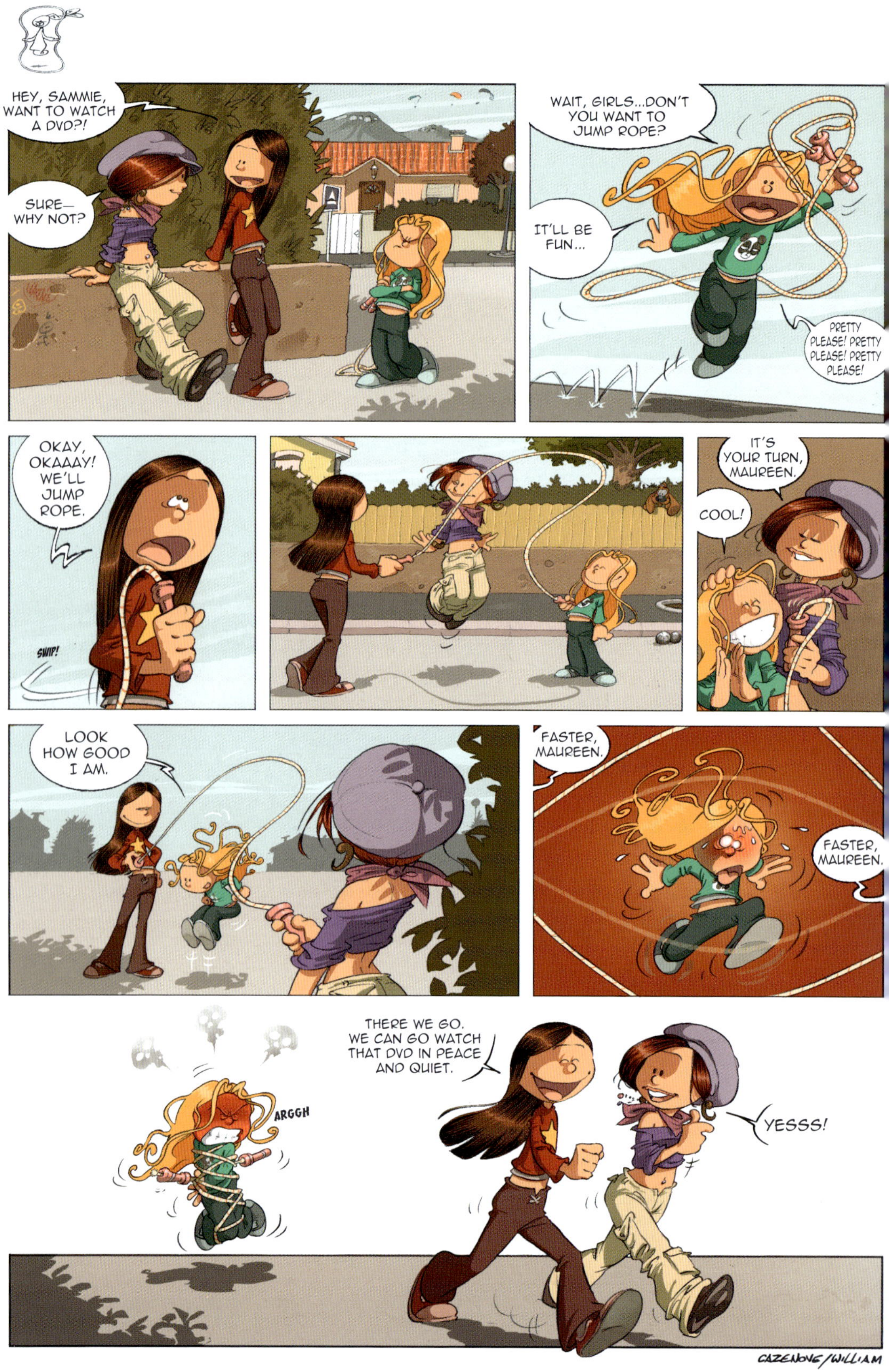
HEY, SAMMIE, WANT TO WATCH A DVD?!
SURE—WHY NOT?
WAIT, GIRLS...DON'T YOU WANT TO JUMP ROPE?
IT'LL BE FUN...
PRETTY PLEASE! PRETTY PLEASE! PRETTY PLEASE!
OKAY, OKAAAY! WE'LL JUMP ROPE.
SWIP!
IT'S YOUR TURN, MAUREEN.
COOL!
LOOK HOW GOOD I AM.
FASTER, MAUREEN.
FASTER, MAUREEN.
ARGGH
THERE WE GO. WE CAN GO WATCH THAT DVD IN PEACE AND QUIET.
YESSS!
CAZENOVE/WILLIAM

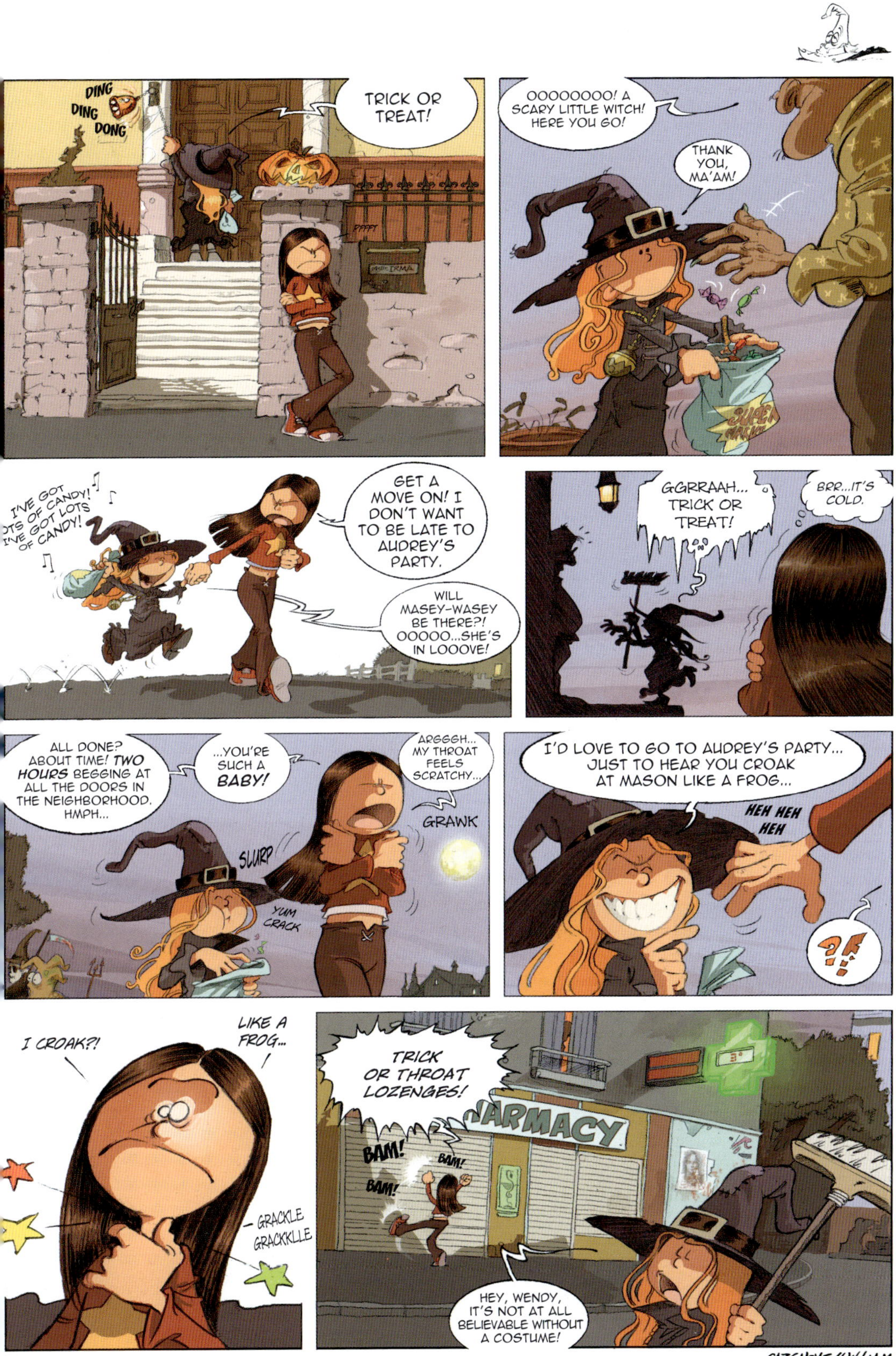
DING
DING
DONG
TRICK OR TREAT!
PFFFT
OOOOOOOO! A SCARY LITTLE WITCH! HERE YOU GO!
THANK YOU, MA'AM!
I'VE GOT LOTS OF CANDY! I'VE GOT LOTS OF CANDY!
GET A MOVE ON! I DON'T WANT TO BE LATE TO AUDREY'S PARTY.
WILL MASEY-WASEY BE THERE?! OOOOO...SHE'S IN LOOOVE!
GGRRAAH... TRICK OR TREAT!
BRR...IT'S COLD.
ALL DONE? ABOUT TIME! **TWO HOURS** BEGGING AT ALL THE DOORS IN THE NEIGHBORHOOD. HMPH...
...YOU'RE SUCH A **BABY!**
ARGGGH... MY THROAT FEELS SCRATCHY...
GRAWK
SLURP
YUM
CRACK
I'D LOVE TO GO TO AUDREY'S PARTY... JUST TO HEAR YOU CROAK AT MASON LIKE A FROG...
HEH HEH HEH
?!
I CROAK?!
LIKE A FROG...
GRACKLE
GRACKKLLE
TRICK OR THROAT LOZENGES!
ARMACY
BAM!
BAM!
BAM!
HEY, WENDY, IT'S NOT AT ALL BELIEVABLE WITHOUT A COSTUME!
CAZENOVE/WILLIAM

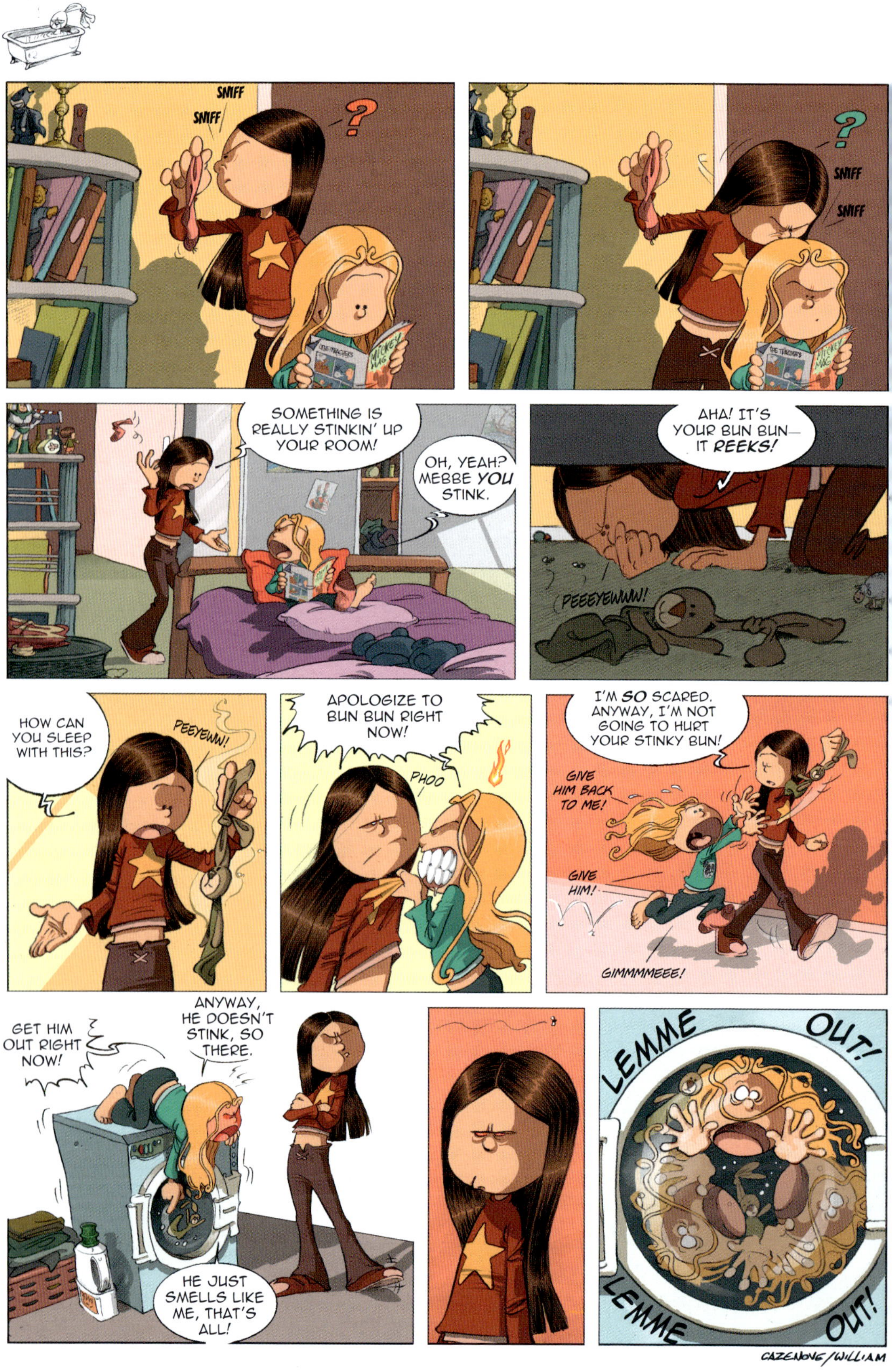
SNIFF
SNIFF
?
?
SNIFF
SNIFF
SOMETHING IS REALLY STINKIN' UP YOUR ROOM!
OH, YEAH? MEBBE **YOU** STINK.
AHA! IT'S YOUR BUN BUN— IT **REEKS!**
PEEEYEWWW!
HOW CAN YOU SLEEP WITH THIS?
PEEYEWW!
APOLOGIZE TO BUN BUN RIGHT NOW!
PHOO
I'M **SO** SCARED. ANYWAY, I'M NOT GOING TO HURT YOUR STINKY BUN!
GIVE HIM BACK TO ME!
GIVE HIM!
GIMMMMEEE!
GET HIM OUT RIGHT NOW!
ANYWAY, HE DOESN'T STINK, SO THERE.
HE JUST SMELLS LIKE ME, THAT'S ALL!
LEMME OUT!
LEMME OUT!
CAZENOVE/WILLIAM

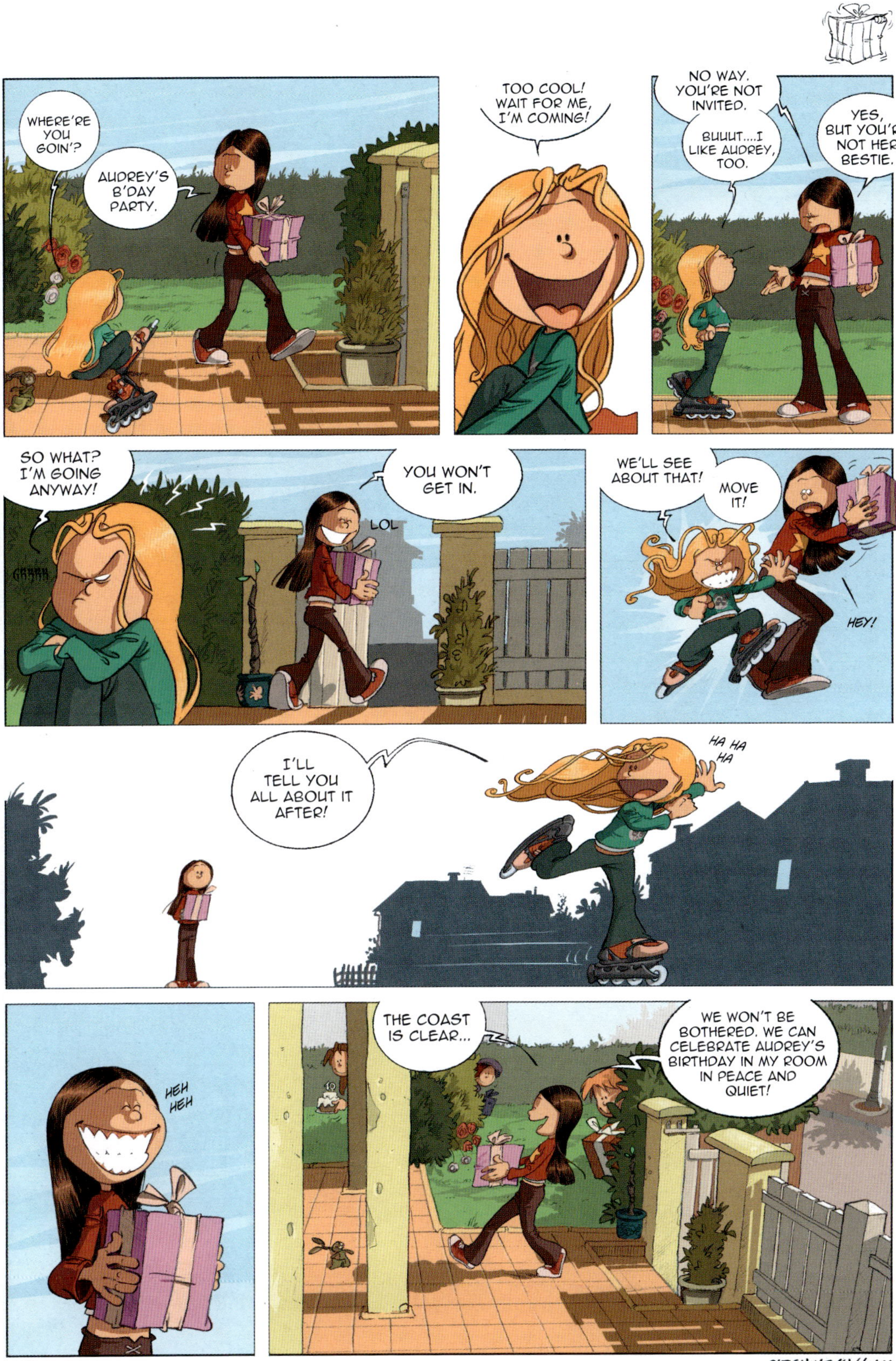

WHERE'RE YOU GOIN'?
AUDREY'S B'DAY PARTY.
TOO COOL! WAIT FOR ME, I'M COMING!
NO WAY. YOU'RE NOT INVITED.
BUUUT....I LIKE AUDREY, TOO.
YES, BUT YOU'RE NOT HER BESTIE.
SO WHAT? I'M GOING ANYWAY!
GRRRR
YOU WON'T GET IN.
LOL
WE'LL SEE ABOUT THAT!
MOVE IT!
HEY!
I'LL TELL YOU ALL ABOUT IT AFTER!
HA HA HA
HEH HEH
THE COAST IS CLEAR...
WE WON'T BE BOTHERED. WE CAN CELEBRATE AUDREY'S BIRTHDAY IN MY ROOM IN PEACE AND QUIET!

CAZENOVE/WILLIAM

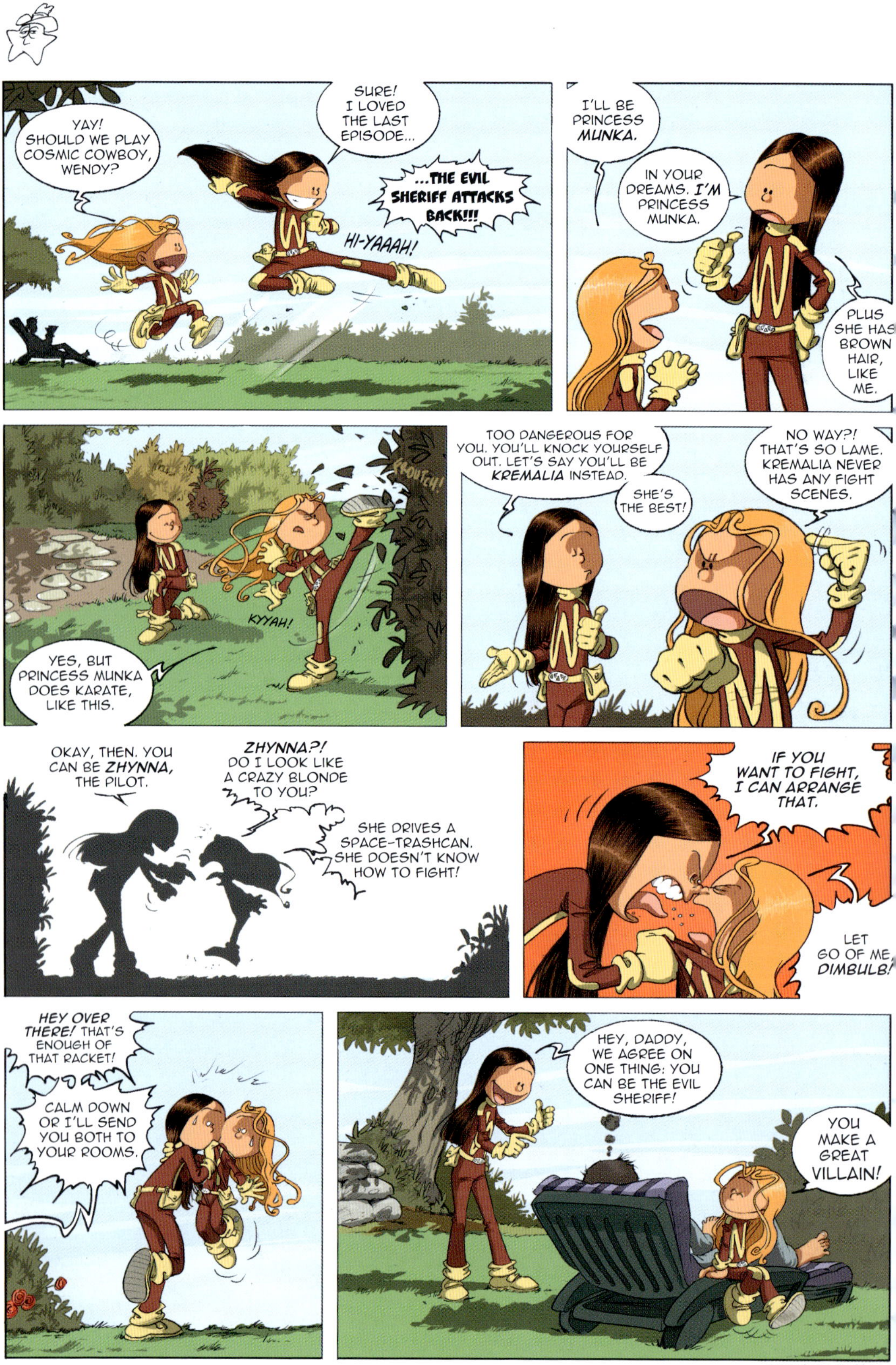
YAY! SHOULD WE PLAY COSMIC COWBOY, WENDY?
SURE! I LOVED THE LAST EPISODE...
...THE EVIL SHERIFF ATTACKS BACK!!!
HI-YAAAH!
I'LL BE PRINCESS MUNKA.
IN YOUR DREAMS. I'M PRINCESS MUNKA.
PLUS SHE HAS BROWN HAIR, LIKE ME.
YES, BUT PRINCESS MUNKA DOES KARATE, LIKE THIS.
KYYAH!
TOO DANGEROUS FOR YOU. YOU'LL KNOCK YOURSELF OUT. LET'S SAY YOU'LL BE KREMALIA INSTEAD.
SHE'S THE BEST!
NO WAY?! THAT'S SO LAME. KREMALIA NEVER HAS ANY FIGHT SCENES.
OKAY, THEN. YOU CAN BE ZHYNNA, THE PILOT.
ZHYNNA?! DO I LOOK LIKE A CRAZY BLONDE TO YOU?
SHE DRIVES A SPACE-TRASHCAN. SHE DOESN'T KNOW HOW TO FIGHT!
IF YOU WANT TO FIGHT, I CAN ARRANGE THAT.
LET GO OF ME, DIMBULB!
HEY OVER THERE! THAT'S ENOUGH OF THAT RACKET!
CALM DOWN OR I'LL SEND YOU BOTH TO YOUR ROOMS.
HEY, DADDY, WE AGREE ON ONE THING: YOU CAN BE THE EVIL SHERIFF!
YOU MAKE A GREAT VILLAIN!
CAZENOVE/WILLIAM

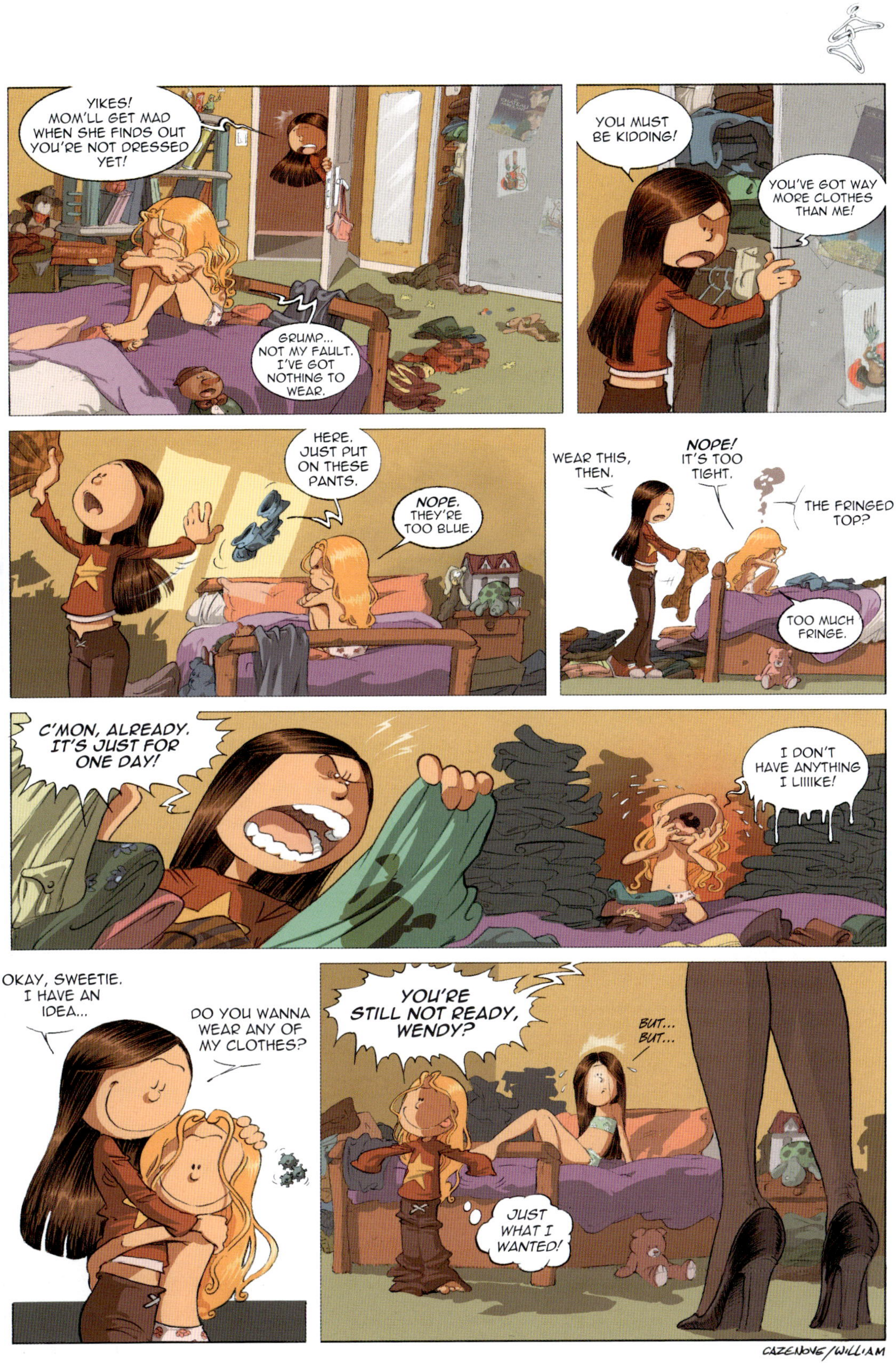
YIKES! MOM'LL GET MAD WHEN SHE FINDS OUT YOU'RE NOT DRESSED YET!
GRUMP... NOT MY FAULT. I'VE GOT NOTHING TO WEAR.
YOU MUST BE KIDDING!
YOU'VE GOT WAY MORE CLOTHES THAN ME!
HERE. JUST PUT ON THESE PANTS.
NOPE. THEY'RE TOO BLUE.
WEAR THIS, THEN.
NOPE! IT'S TOO TIGHT.
THE FRINGED TOP?
TOO MUCH FRINGE.
C'MON, ALREADY. IT'S JUST FOR ONE DAY!
I DON'T HAVE ANYTHING I LIIIIKE!
OKAY, SWEETIE. I HAVE AN IDEA...
DO YOU WANNA WEAR ANY OF MY CLOTHES?
YOU'RE STILL NOT READY, WENDY?
BUT... BUT...
JUST WHAT I WANTED!
CAZENOVE/WILLIAM

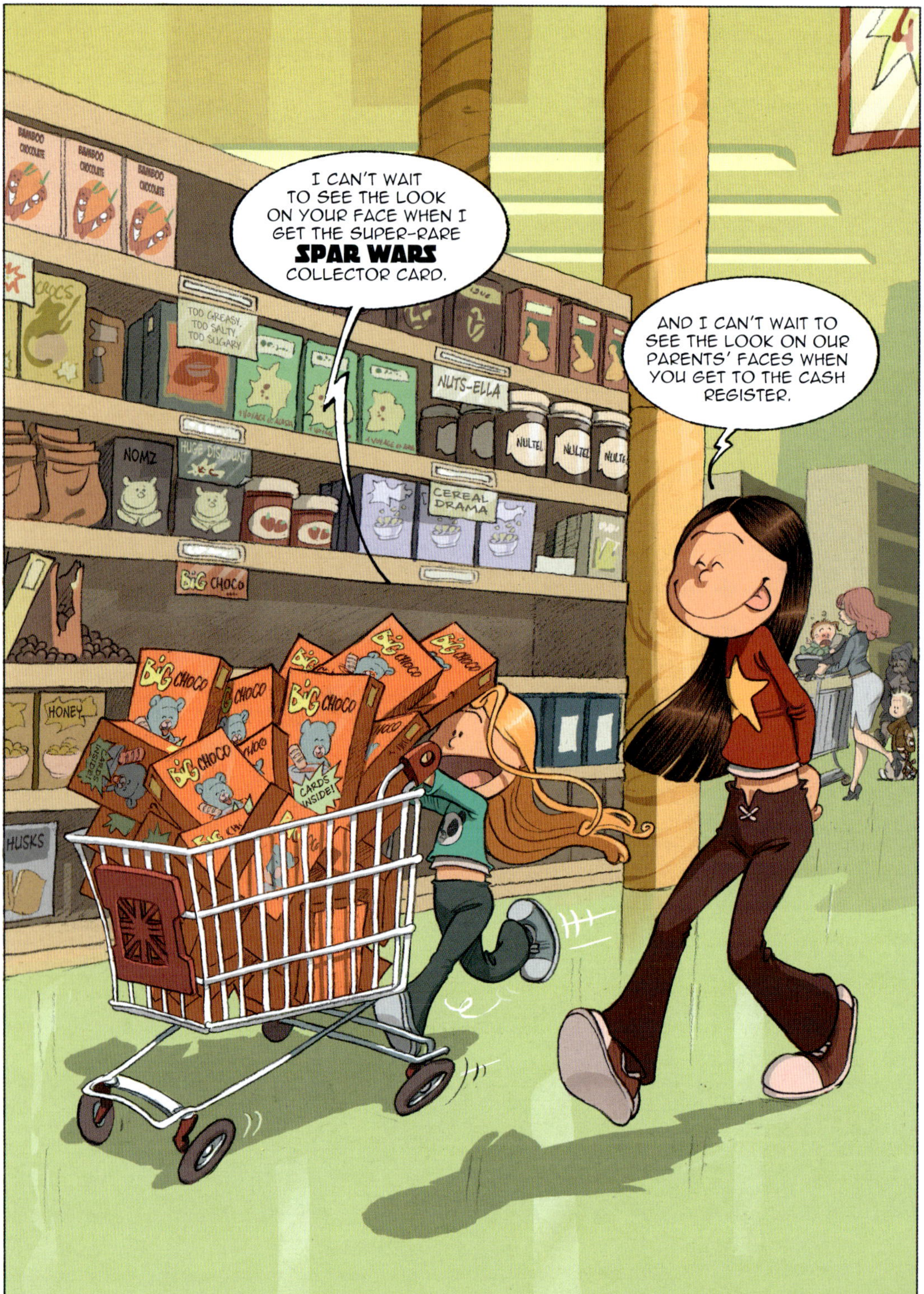
I CAN'T WAIT TO SEE THE LOOK ON YOUR FACE WHEN I GET THE SUPER-RARE **SPAR WARS** COLLECTOR CARD.
AND I CAN'T WAIT TO SEE THE LOOK ON OUR PARENTS' FACES WHEN YOU GET TO THE CASH REGISTER.
TOO GREASY. TOO SALTY. TOO SUGARY
NUTS-ELLA
NOMZ
CEREAL DRAMA
BIG CHOCO
HONEY
HUSKS
CARDS INSIDE!

CAZENOVE/WILLIAM

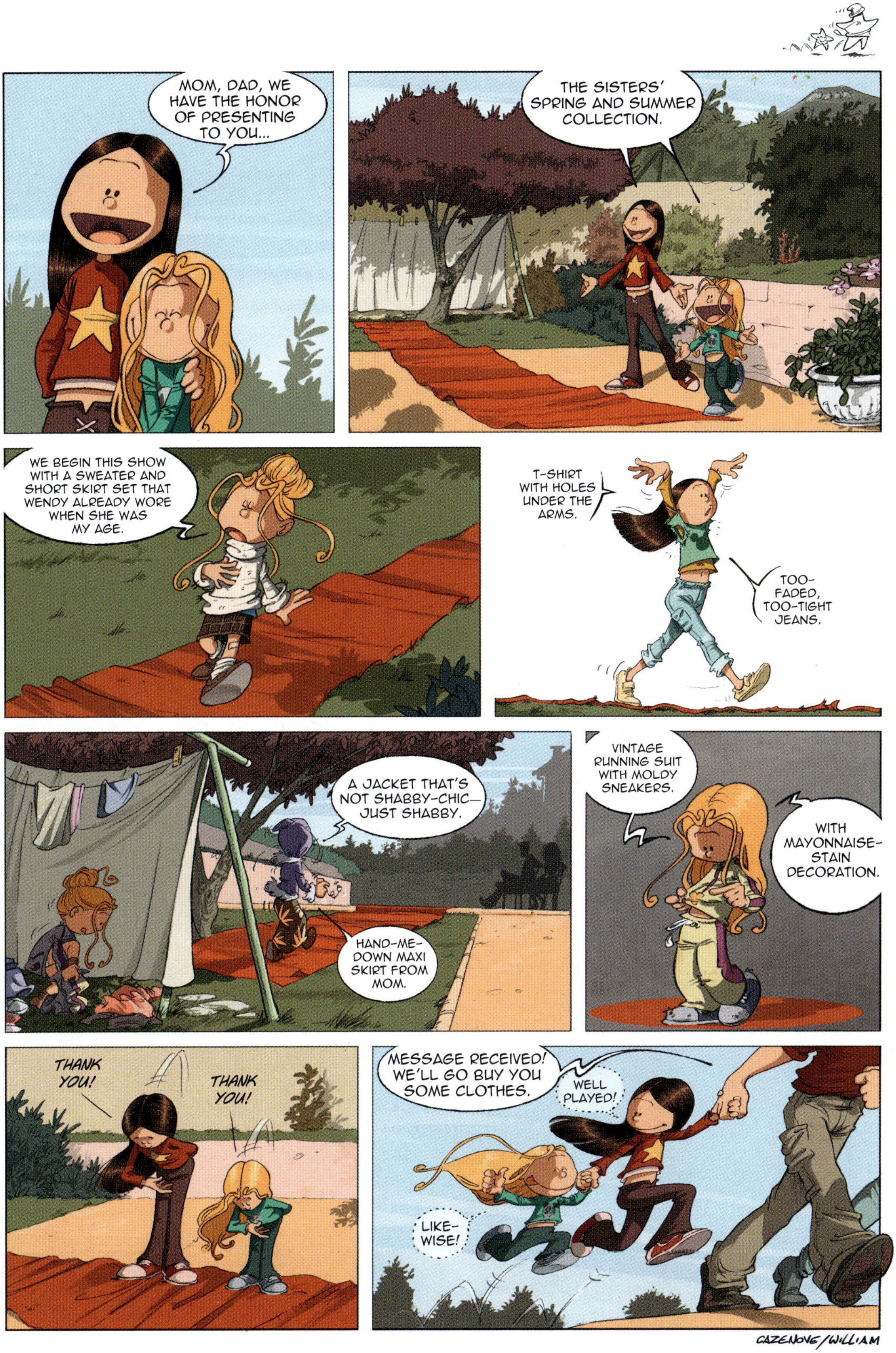
MOM, DAD, WE HAVE THE HONOR OF PRESENTING TO YOU...
THE SISTERS' SPRING AND SUMMER COLLECTION.
WE BEGIN THIS SHOW WITH A SWEATER AND SHORT SKIRT SET THAT WENDY ALREADY WORE WHEN SHE WAS MY AGE.
T-SHIRT WITH HOLES UNDER THE ARMS.
TOO-FADED, TOO-TIGHT JEANS.
A JACKET THAT'S NOT SHABBY-CHIC— JUST SHABBY.
HAND-ME-DOWN MAXI SKIRT FROM MOM.
VINTAGE RUNNING SUIT WITH MOLDY SNEAKERS.
WITH MAYONNAISE-STAIN DECORATION.
THANK YOU!
THANK YOU!
MESSAGE RECEIVED! WE'LL GO BUY YOU SOME CLOTHES.
WELL PLAYED!
LIKE-WISE!
CAZENOVE/WILLIAM

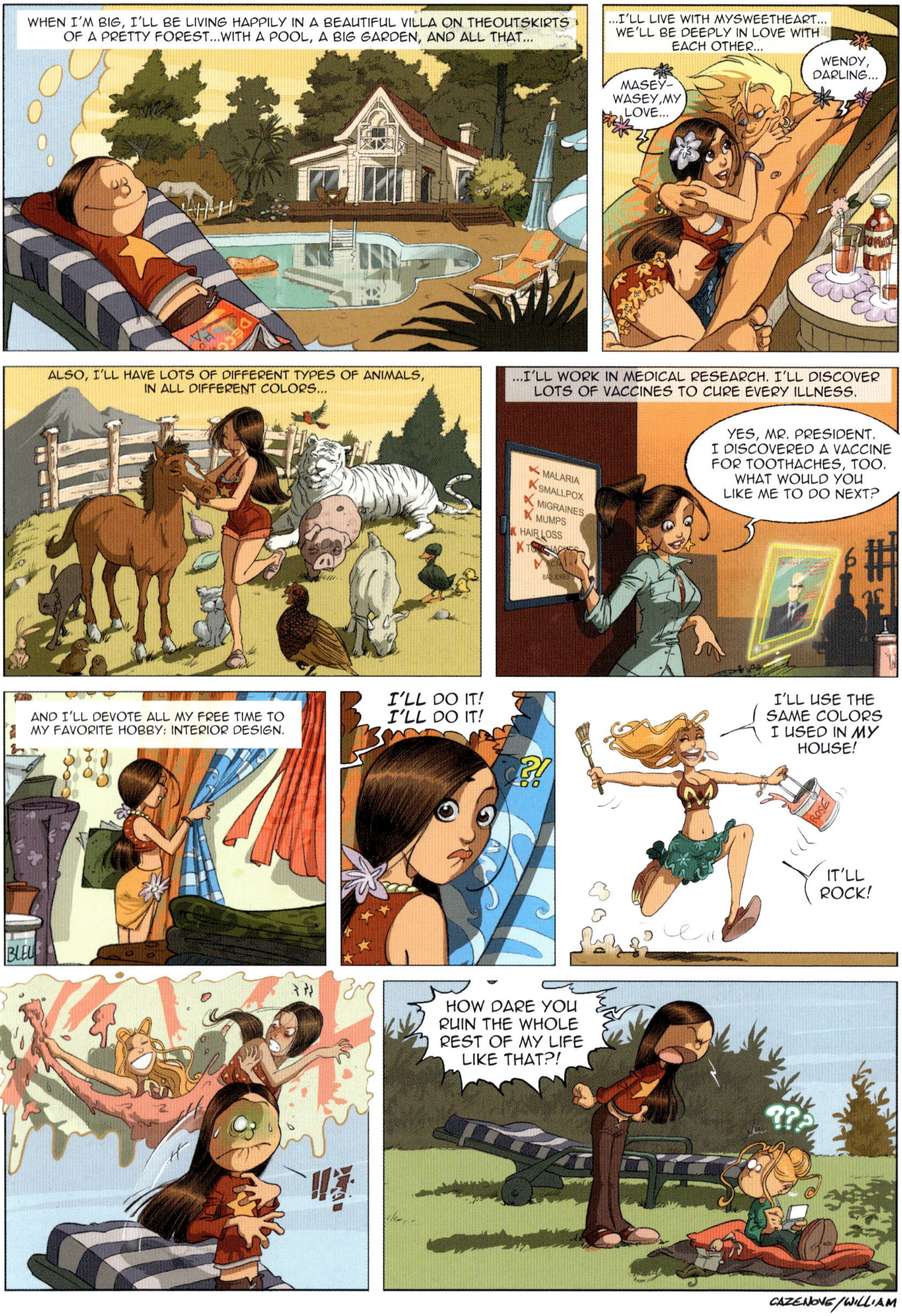
WHEN I'M BIG, I'LL BE LIVING HAPPILY IN A BEAUTIFUL VILLA ON THEOUTSKIRTS OF A PRETTY FOREST...WITH A POOL, A BIG GARDEN, AND ALL THAT...
...I'LL LIVE WITH MYSWEETHEART... WE'LL BE DEEPLY IN LOVE WITH EACH OTHER...
MASEY-WASEY,MY LOVE...
WENDY, DARLING...
ALSO, I'LL HAVE LOTS OF DIFFERENT TYPES OF ANIMALS, IN ALL DIFFERENT COLORS...
...I'LL WORK IN MEDICAL RESEARCH. I'LL DISCOVER LOTS OF VACCINES TO CURE EVERY ILLNESS.
MALARIA
SMALLPOX
MIGRAINES
MUMPS
HAIR LOSS
YES, MR. PRESIDENT. I DISCOVERED A VACCINE FOR TOOTHACHES, TOO. WHAT WOULD YOU LIKE ME TO DO NEXT?
AND I'LL DEVOTE ALL MY FREE TIME TO MY FAVORITE HOBBY: INTERIOR DESIGN.
BLEU
I'LL DO IT! I'LL DO IT!
?!
I'LL USE THE SAME COLORS I USED IN MY HOUSE!
ROSE
IT'LL ROCK!
HOW DARE YOU RUIN THE WHOLE REST OF MY LIFE LIKE THAT?!
???
CAZENOVE/WILLIAM

"A Style Of Our Own"

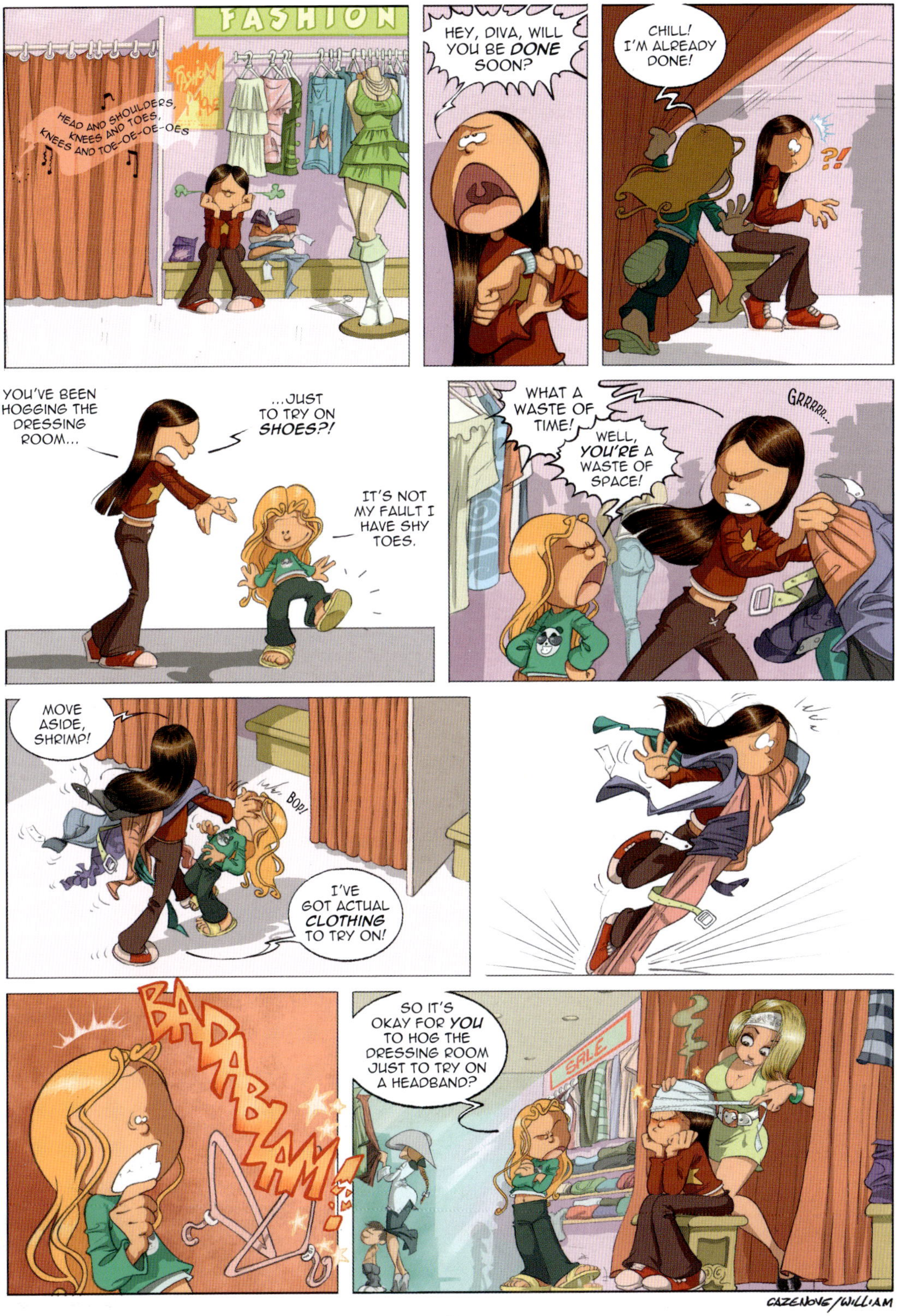

FASHION
HEAD AND SHOULDERS, KNEES AND TOES, KNEES AND TOE-OE-OE-OES
HEY, DIVA, WILL YOU BE DONE SOON?
CHILL! I'M ALREADY DONE!
?!
YOU'VE BEEN HOGGING THE DRESSING ROOM...
...JUST TO TRY ON SHOES?!
IT'S NOT MY FAULT I HAVE SHY TOES.
WHAT A WASTE OF TIME!
WELL, YOU'RE A WASTE OF SPACE!
GRRRRR...
MOVE ASIDE, SHRIMP!
BOP!
I'VE GOT ACTUAL CLOTHING TO TRY ON!
BADABAM!
SO IT'S OKAY FOR YOU TO HOG THE DRESSING ROOM JUST TO TRY ON A HEADBAND?
SALE
CAZENOVE/WILLIAM

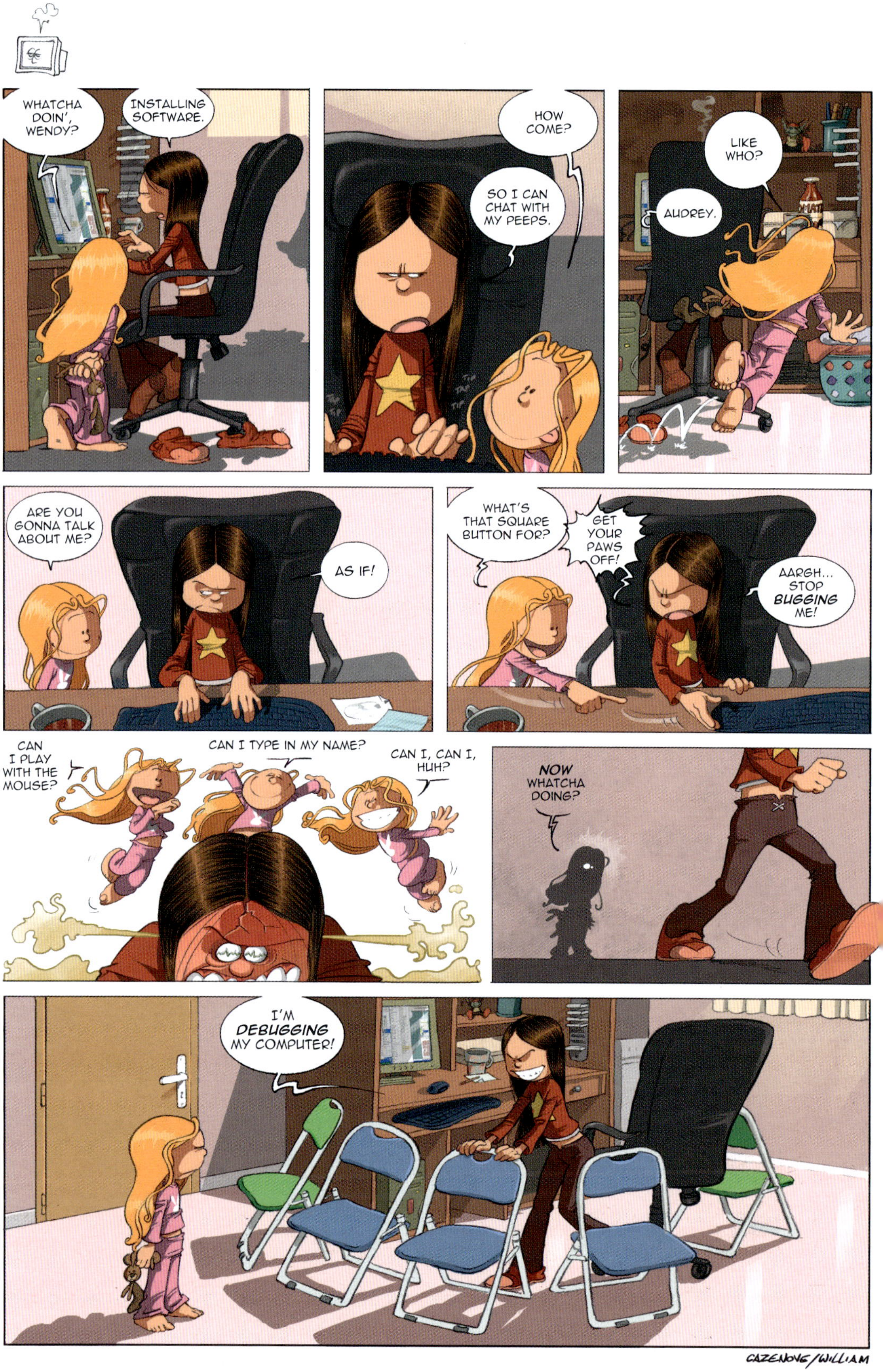
WHATCHA DOIN', WENDY?
INSTALLING SOFTWARE.
HOW COME?
SO I CAN CHAT WITH MY PEEPS.
LIKE WHO?
AUDREY.
ARE YOU GONNA TALK ABOUT ME?
AS IF!
WHAT'S THAT SQUARE BUTTON FOR?
GET YOUR PAWS OFF!
AARGH... STOP BUGGING ME!
CAN I PLAY WITH THE MOUSE?
CAN I TYPE IN MY NAME?
CAN I, CAN I, HUH?
NOW WHATCHA DOING?
I'M DEBUGGING MY COMPUTER!
CAZENOVE/WILLIAM

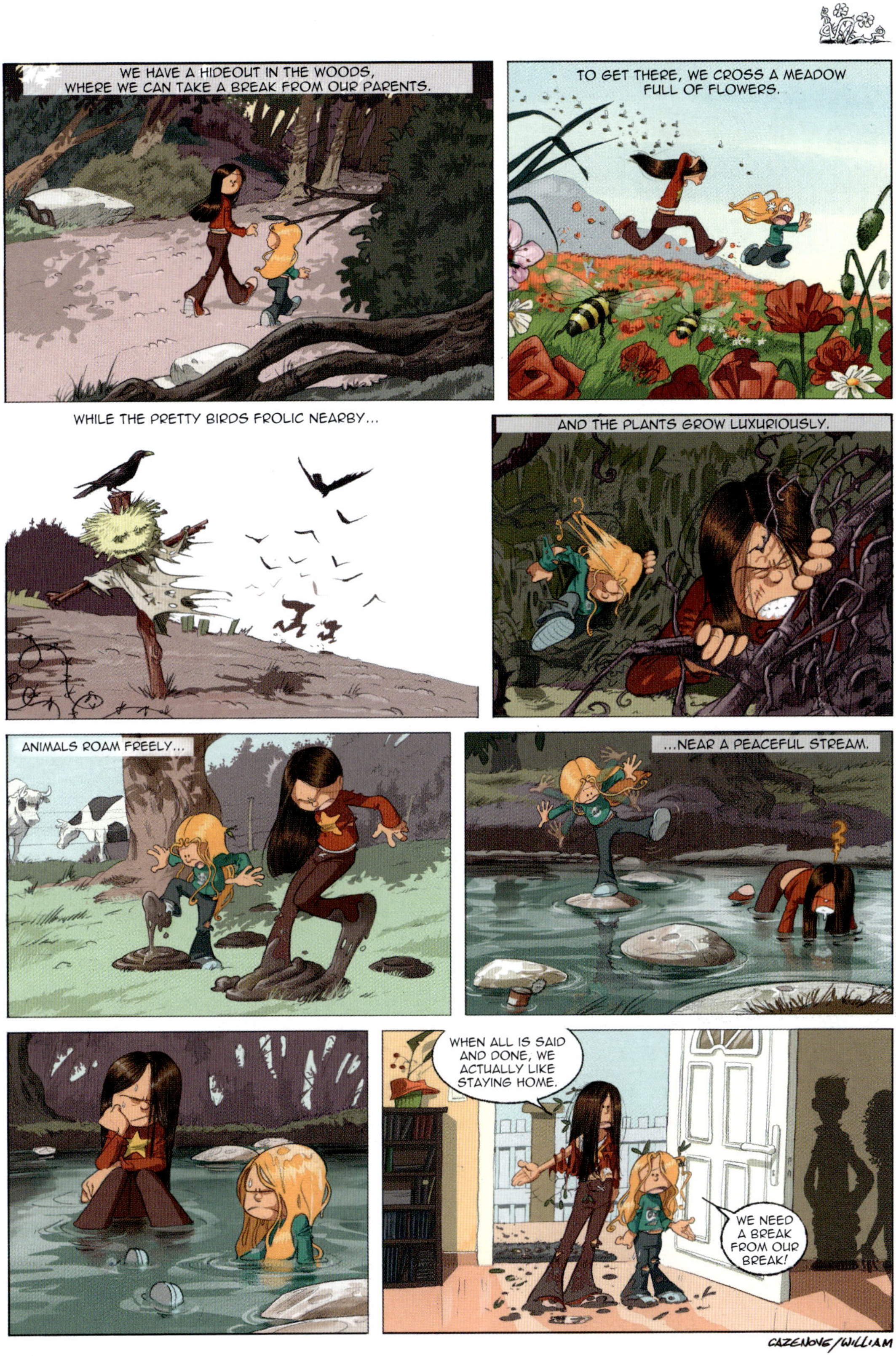
WE HAVE A HIDEOUT IN THE WOODS, WHERE WE CAN TAKE A BREAK FROM OUR PARENTS.
TO GET THERE, WE CROSS A MEADOW FULL OF FLOWERS.
WHILE THE PRETTY BIRDS FROLIC NEARBY...
AND THE PLANTS GROW LUXURIOUSLY.
ANIMALS ROAM FREELY...
...NEAR A PEACEFUL STREAM.
WHEN ALL IS SAID AND DONE, WE ACTUALLY LIKE STAYING HOME.
WE NEED A BREAK FROM OUR BREAK!
CAZENOVE/WILLIAM

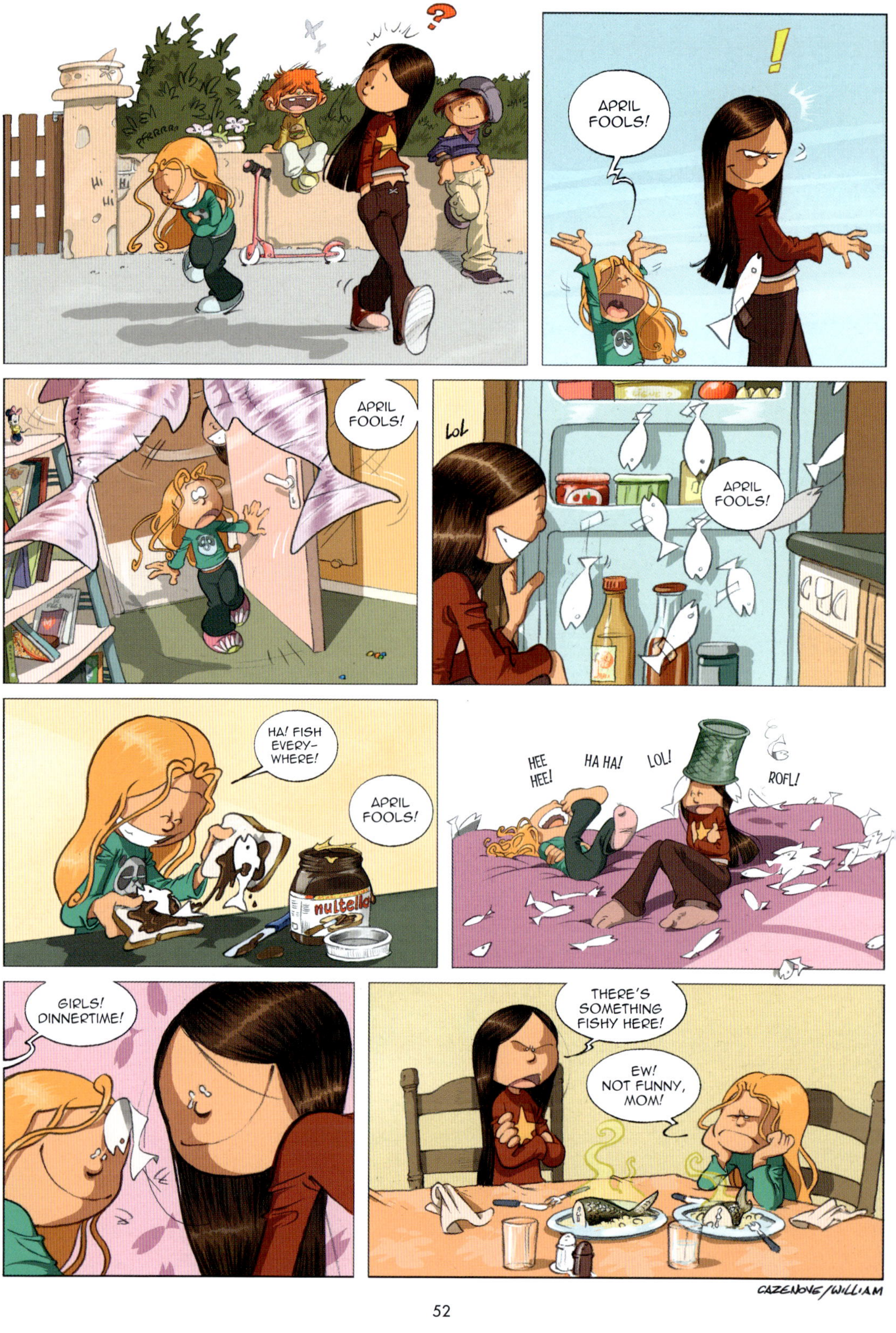
APRIL FOOLS!
APRIL FOOLS!
LOL
APRIL FOOLS!
HA! FISH EVERY-WHERE!
APRIL FOOLS!
HEE HEE!
HA HA!
LOL!
ROFL!
GIRLS! DINNERTIME!
THERE'S SOMETHING FISHY HERE!
EW! NOT FUNNY, MOM!

CAZENOVE/WILLIAM

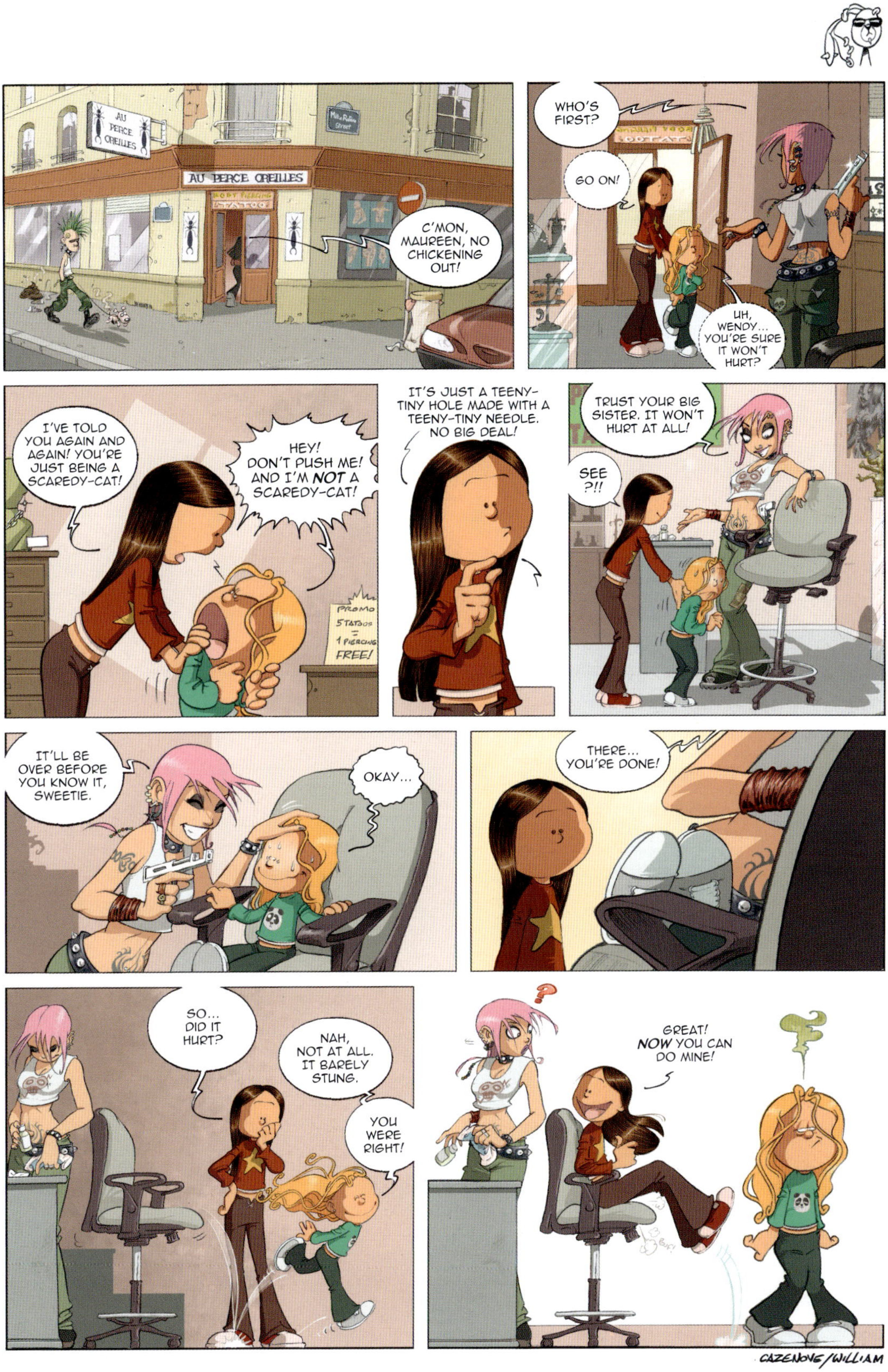
AU PERCE OREILLES
AU PERCE OREILLES
TATOO
C'MON, MAUREEN, NO CHICKENING OUT!
WHO'S FIRST?
GO ON!
UH, WENDY... YOU'RE SURE IT WON'T HURT?
I'VE TOLD YOU AGAIN AND AGAIN! YOU'RE JUST BEING A SCAREDY-CAT!
HEY! DON'T PUSH ME! AND I'M NOT A SCAREDY-CAT!
PROMO 5 TATOOS = 1 PIERCING FREE!
IT'S JUST A TEENY-TINY HOLE MADE WITH A TEENY-TINY NEEDLE. NO BIG DEAL!
TRUST YOUR BIG SISTER. IT WON'T HURT AT ALL!
SEE ?!!
IT'LL BE OVER BEFORE YOU KNOW IT, SWEETIE.
OKAY...
THERE... YOU'RE DONE!
SO... DID IT HURT?
NAH, NOT AT ALL. IT BARELY STUNG.
YOU WERE RIGHT!
GREAT! NOW YOU CAN DO MINE!
CAZENOVE/WILLIAM

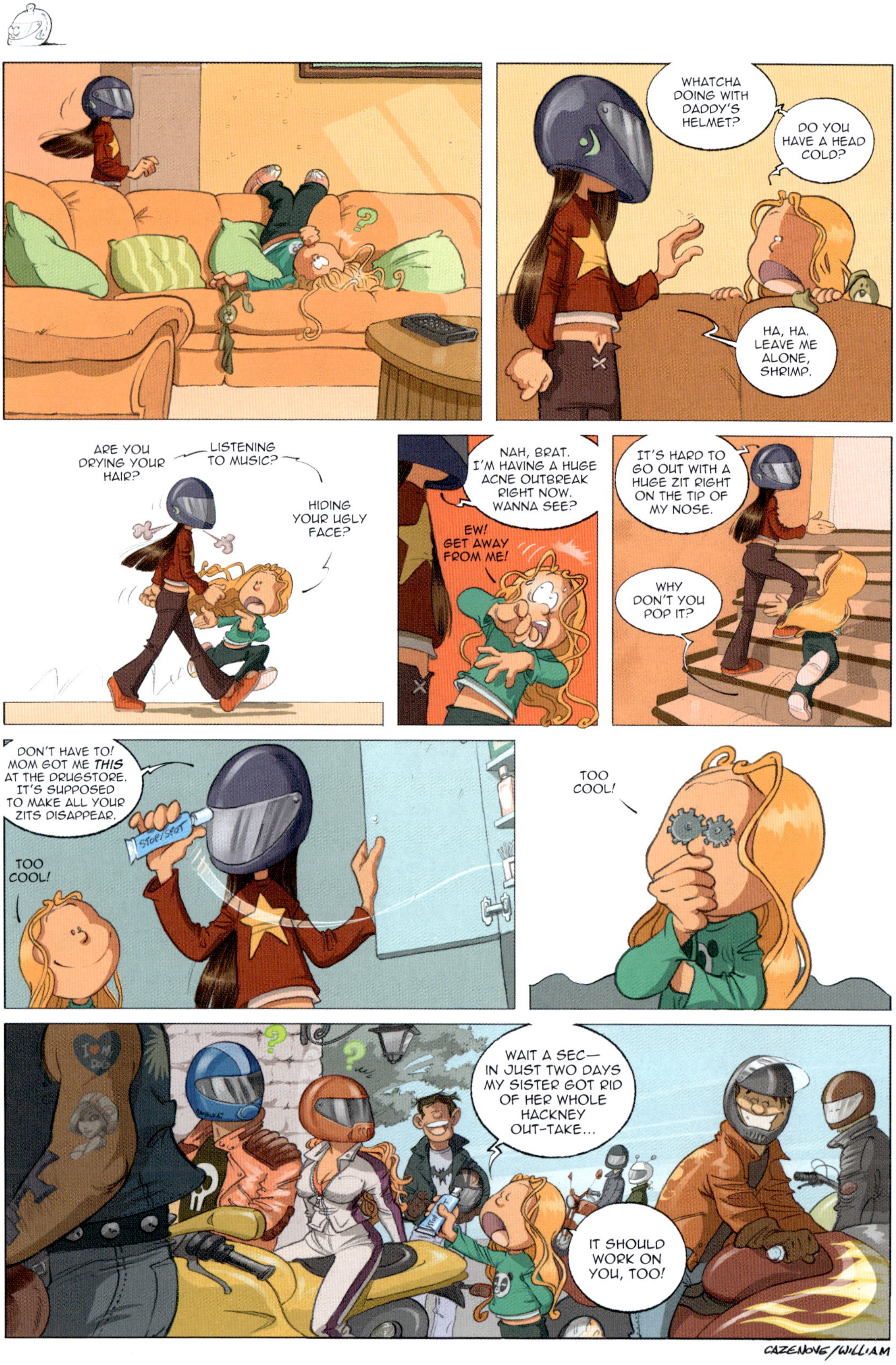
WHATCHA DOING WITH DADDY'S HELMET?
DO YOU HAVE A HEAD COLD?
HA, HA. LEAVE ME ALONE, SHRIMP.
ARE YOU DRYING YOUR HAIR?
LISTENING TO MUSIC?
HIDING YOUR UGLY FACE?
NAH, BRAT. I'M HAVING A HUGE ACNE OUTBREAK RIGHT NOW. WANNA SEE?
EW! GET AWAY FROM ME!
IT'S HARD TO GO OUT WITH A HUGE ZIT RIGHT ON THE TIP OF MY NOSE.
WHY DON'T YOU POP IT?
DON'T HAVE TO! MOM GOT ME *THIS* AT THE DRUGSTORE. IT'S SUPPOSED TO MAKE ALL YOUR ZITS DISAPPEAR.
STOP/SPOT
TOO COOL!
TOO COOL!
WAIT A SEC— IN JUST TWO DAYS MY SISTER GOT RID OF HER WHOLE HACKNEY OUT-TAKE...
IT SHOULD WORK ON YOU, TOO!
CAZENOVE/WILLIAM

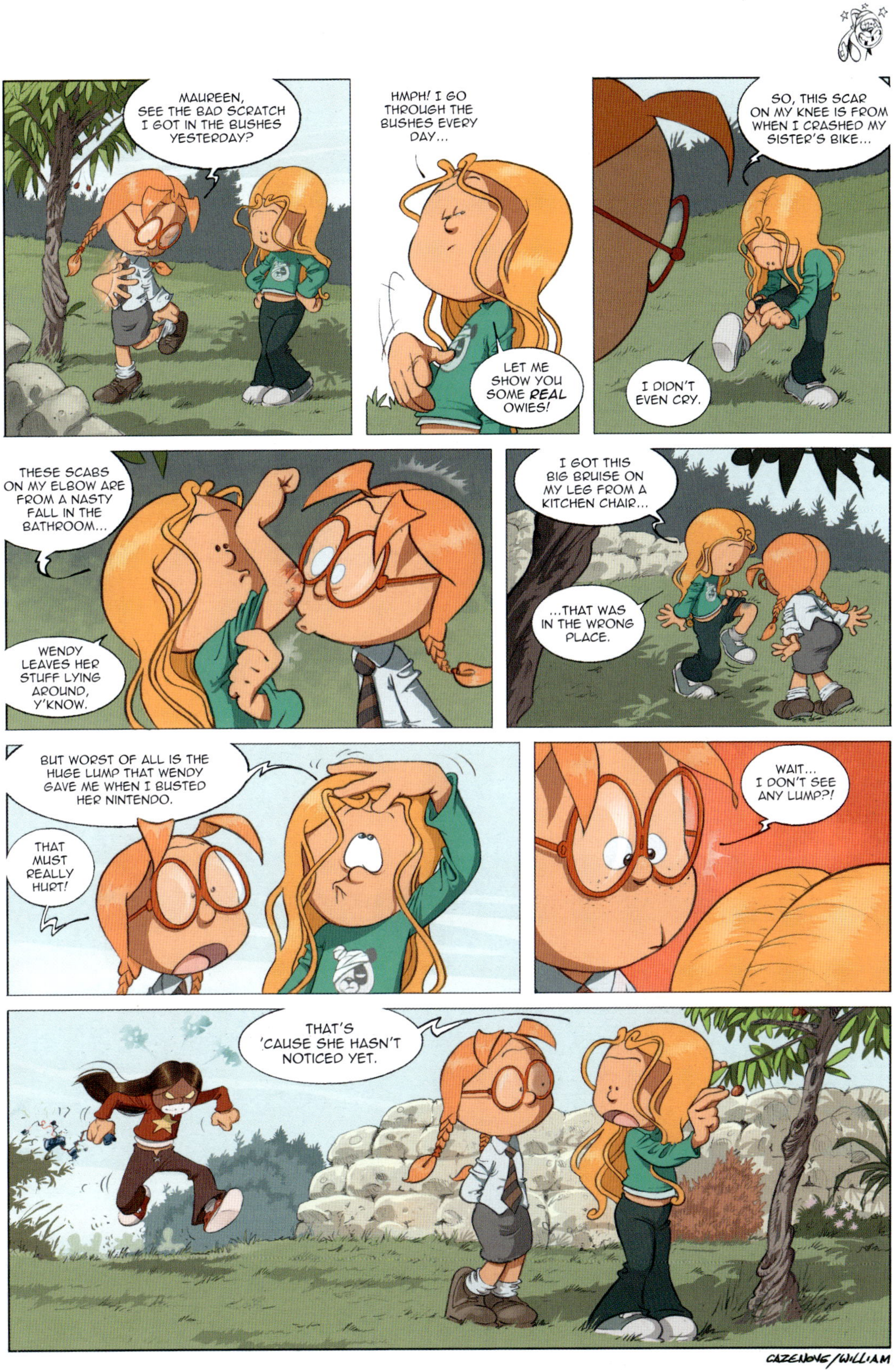
MAUREEN, SEE THE BAD SCRATCH I GOT IN THE BUSHES YESTERDAY?
HMPH! I GO THROUGH THE BUSHES EVERY DAY...
LET ME SHOW YOU SOME **REAL** OWIES!
SO, THIS SCAR ON MY KNEE IS FROM WHEN I CRASHED MY SISTER'S BIKE...
I DIDN'T EVEN CRY.
THESE SCABS ON MY ELBOW ARE FROM A NASTY FALL IN THE BATHROOM...
WENDY LEAVES HER STUFF LYING AROUND, Y'KNOW.
I GOT THIS BIG BRUISE ON MY LEG FROM A KITCHEN CHAIR...
...THAT WAS IN THE WRONG PLACE.
BUT WORST OF ALL IS THE HUGE LUMP THAT WENDY GAVE ME WHEN I BUSTED HER NINTENDO.
THAT MUST REALLY HURT!
WAIT... I DON'T SEE ANY LUMP?!
THAT'S 'CAUSE SHE HASN'T NOTICED YET.
CAZENOVE/WILLIAM

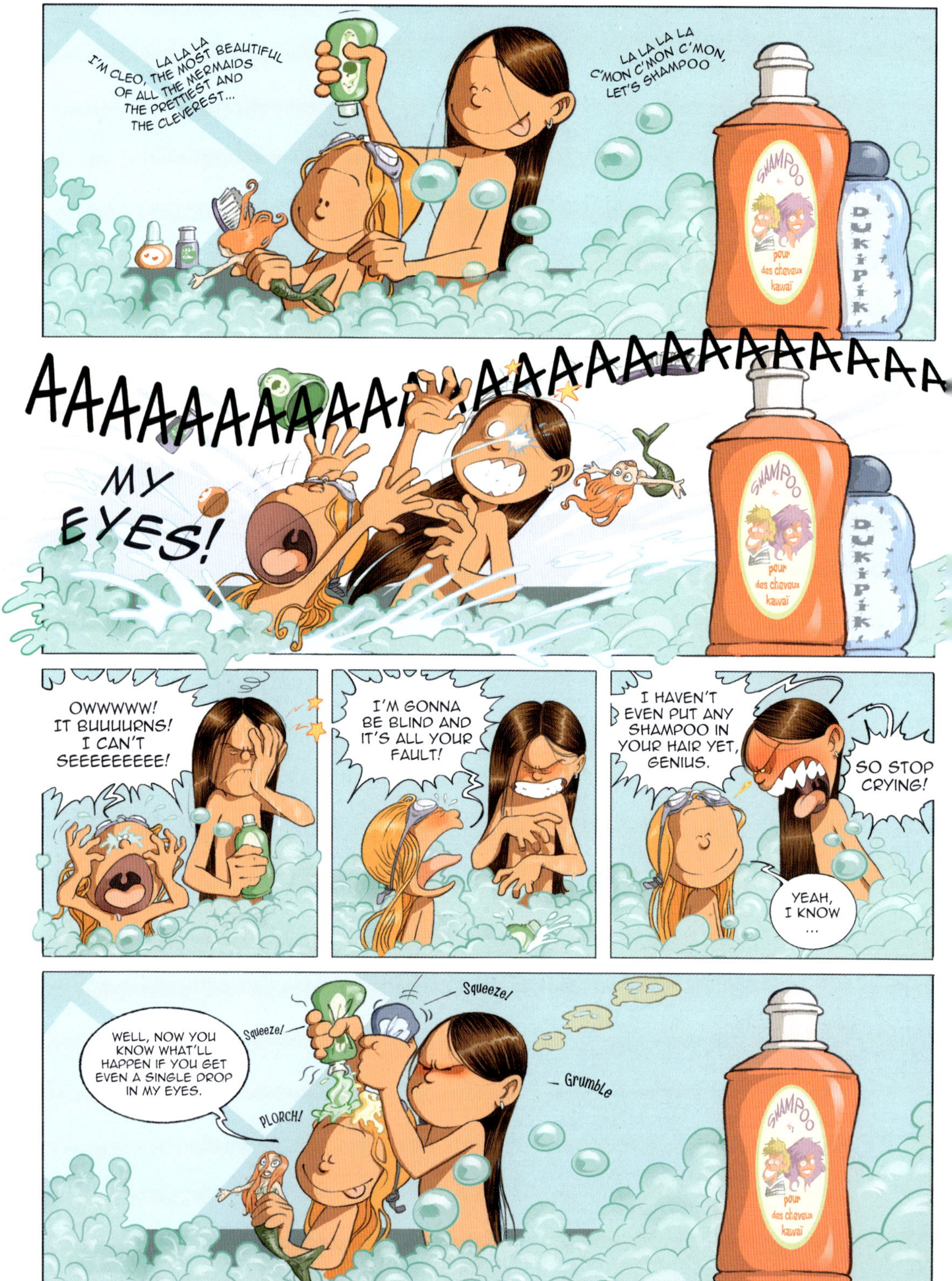
LA LA LA
I'M CLEO, THE MOST BEAUTIFUL OF ALL THE MERMAIDS THE PRETTIEST AND THE CLEVEREST...
LA LA LA LA
C'MON C'MON C'MON, LET'S SHAMPOO
SHAMPOO pour des cheveux kawaï
DUKIPIK
AAAAAAAAAAAAAAAAAAAAAAAAAAAA
MY EYES!
SHAMPOO pour des cheveux kawaï
DUKIPIK
OWWWWW! IT BUUUURNS! I CAN'T SEEEEEEEEE!
I'M GONNA BE BLIND AND IT'S ALL YOUR FAULT!
I HAVEN'T EVEN PUT ANY SHAMPOO IN YOUR HAIR YET, GENIUS.
SO STOP CRYING!
YEAH, I KNOW ...
WELL, NOW YOU KNOW WHAT'LL HAPPEN IF YOU GET EVEN A SINGLE DROP IN MY EYES.
Squeeze!
Squeeze!
PLORCH!
Grumble
SHAMPOO pour des cheveux kawaï

CAZENOVE/WILLIAM

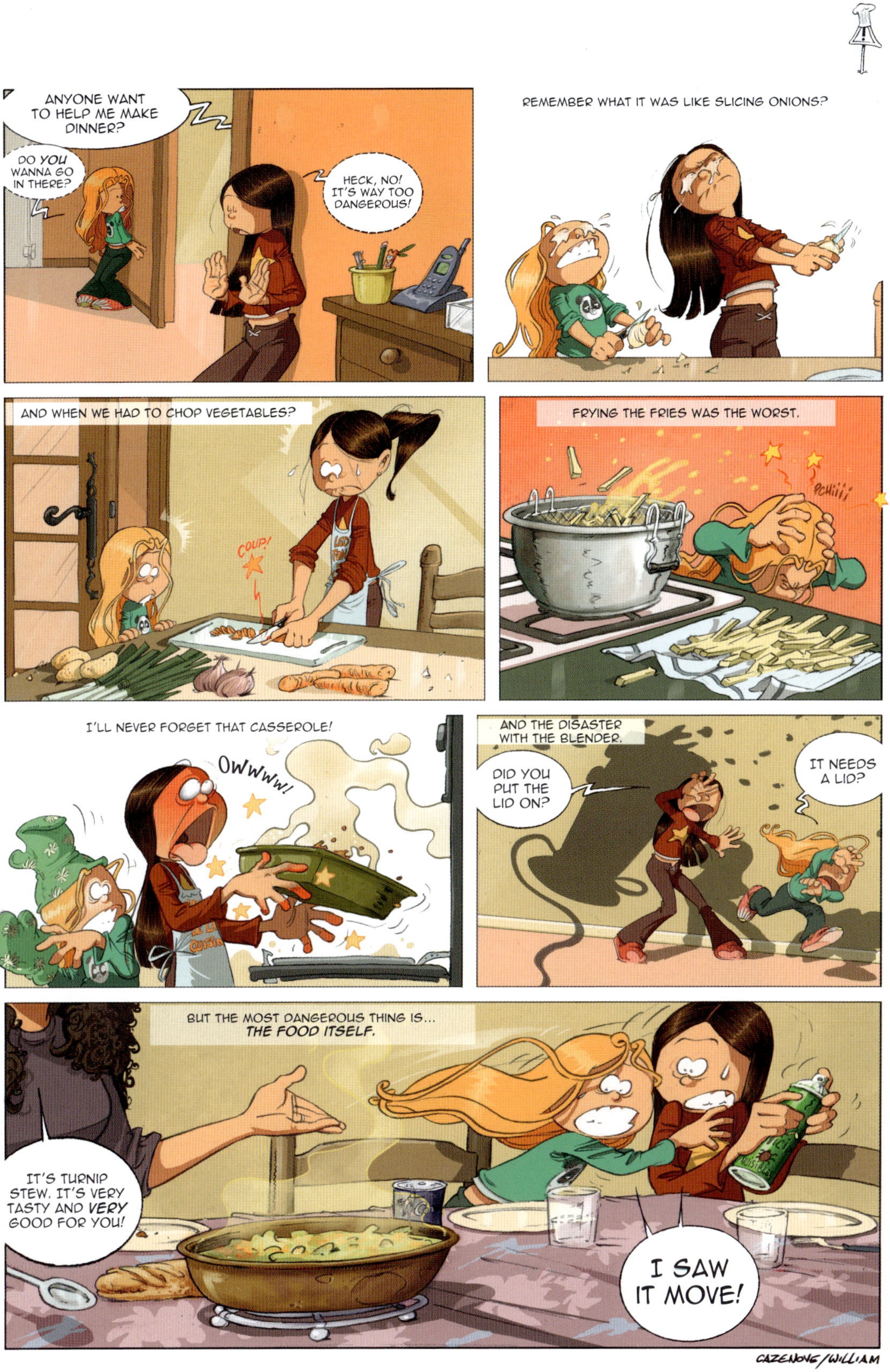

ANYONE WANT TO HELP ME MAKE DINNER?
DO *YOU* WANNA GO IN THERE?
HECK, NO! IT'S WAY TOO DANGEROUS!
REMEMBER WHAT IT WAS LIKE SLICING ONIONS?
AND WHEN WE HAD TO CHOP VEGETABLES?
COUP!
FRYING THE FRIES WAS THE WORST.
I'LL NEVER FORGET THAT CASSEROLE!
OWWWW!
AND THE DISASTER WITH THE BLENDER.
DID YOU PUT THE LID ON?
IT NEEDS A LID?
BUT THE MOST DANGEROUS THING IS... *THE FOOD ITSELF.*
IT'S TURNIP STEW. IT'S VERY TASTY AND *VERY* GOOD FOR YOU!
I SAW IT MOVE!
CAZENOVE/WILLIAM

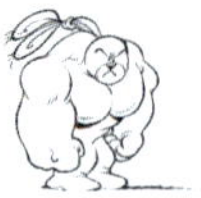

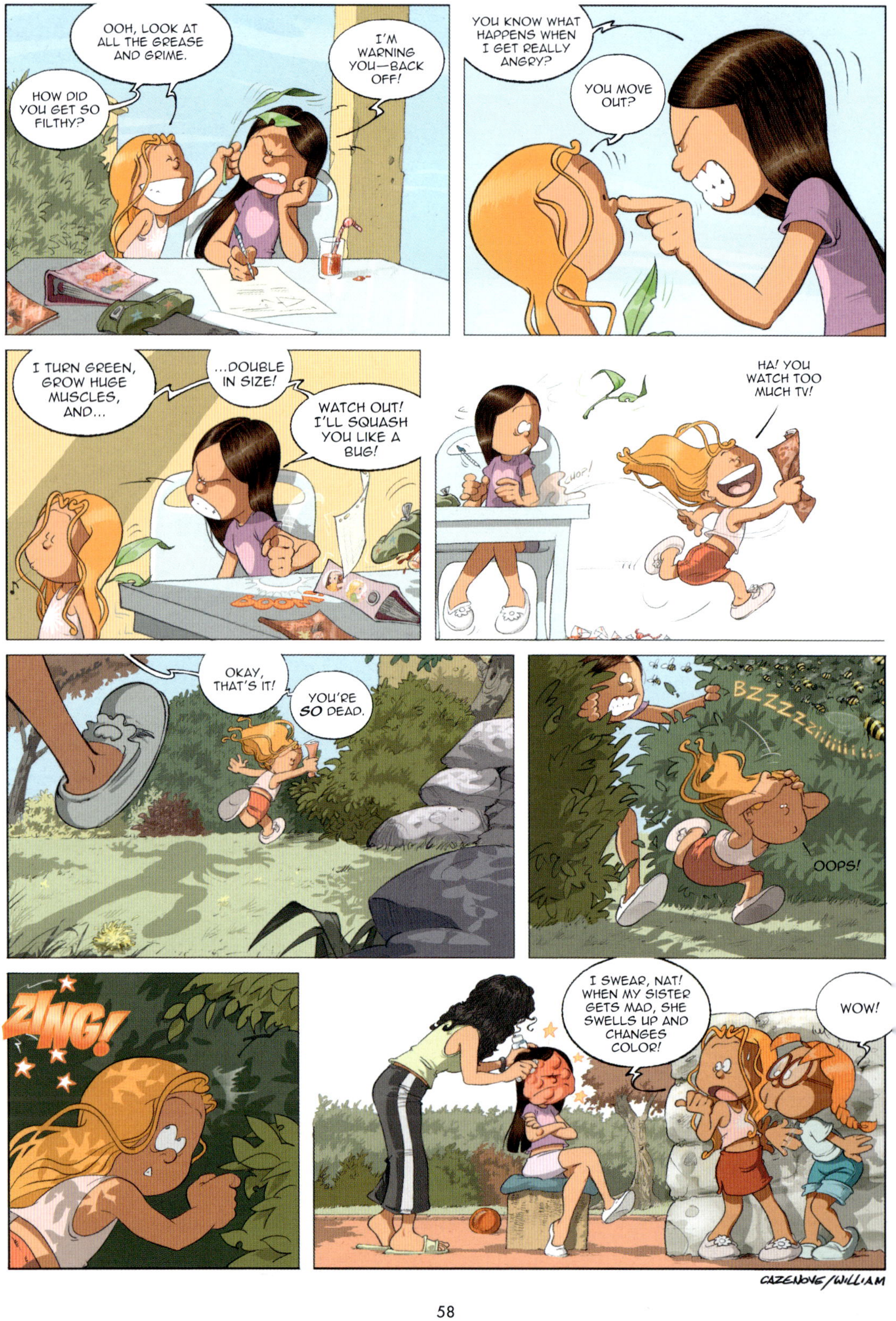

OOH, LOOK AT ALL THE GREASE AND GRIME.
HOW DID YOU GET SO FILTHY?
I'M WARNING YOU—BACK OFF!
YOU KNOW WHAT HAPPENS WHEN I GET REALLY ANGRY?
YOU MOVE OUT?
I TURN GREEN, GROW HUGE MUSCLES, AND...
...DOUBLE IN SIZE!
WATCH OUT! I'LL SQUASH YOU LIKE A BUG!
BOOM!
CHOP!
HA! YOU WATCH TOO MUCH TV!
OKAY, THAT'S IT!
YOU'RE SO DEAD.
BZZZZZ
OOPS!
ZING!
I SWEAR, NAT! WHEN MY SISTER GETS MAD, SHE SWELLS UP AND CHANGES COLOR!
WOW!
CAZENOVE/WILLIAM

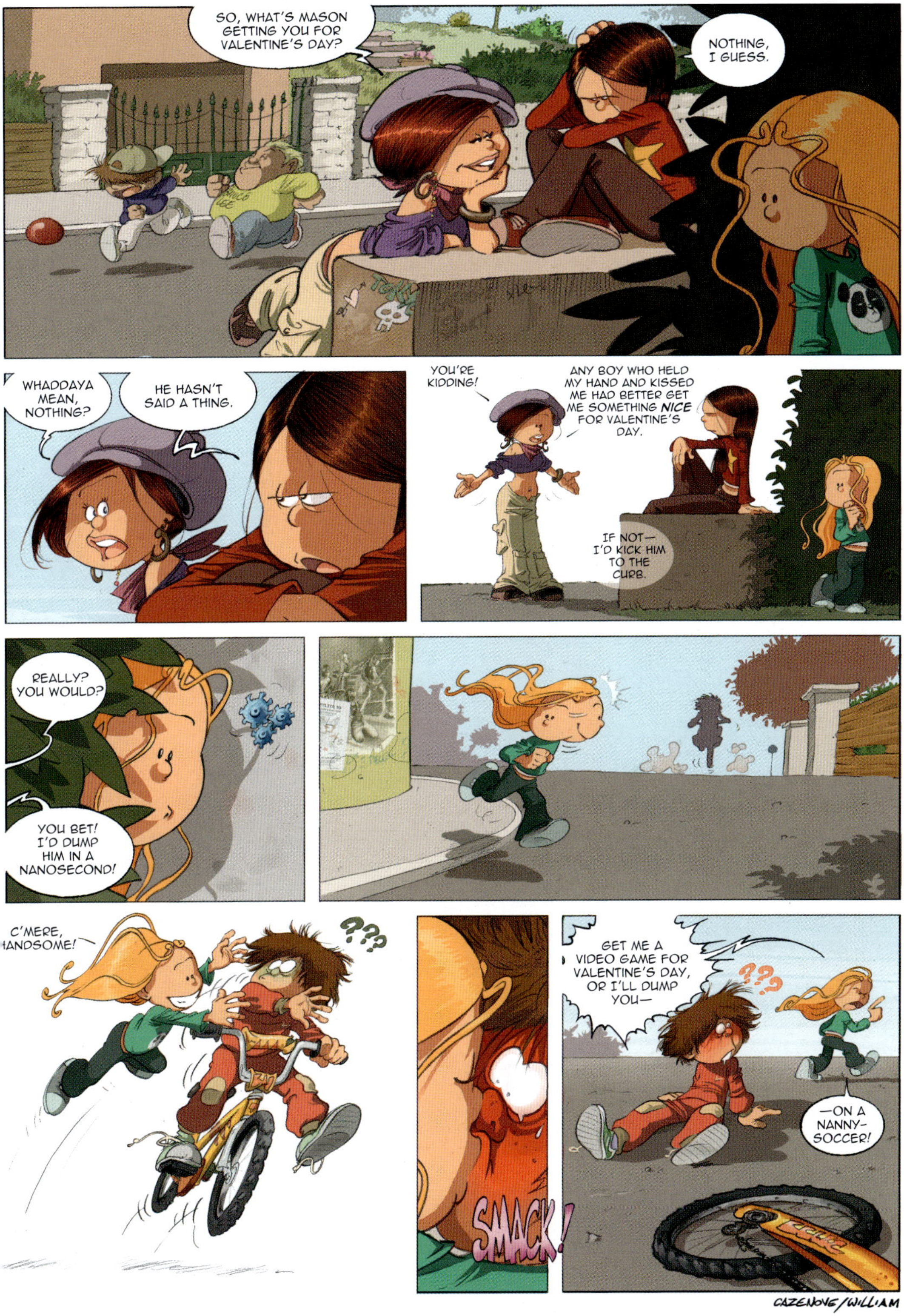
SO, WHAT'S MASON GETTING YOU FOR VALENTINE'S DAY?
NOTHING, I GUESS.
WHADDAYA MEAN, NOTHING?
HE HASN'T SAID A THING.
YOU'RE KIDDING!
ANY BOY WHO HELD MY HAND AND KISSED ME HAD BETTER GET ME SOMETHING NICE FOR VALENTINE'S DAY.
IF NOT— I'D KICK HIM TO THE CURB.
REALLY? YOU WOULD?
YOU BET! I'D DUMP HIM IN A NANOSECOND!
C'MERE, HANDSOME!
???
SMACK!
GET ME A VIDEO GAME FOR VALENTINE'S DAY, OR I'LL DUMP YOU—
???
—ON A NANNY-SOCCER!
CAZENOVE/WILLIAM

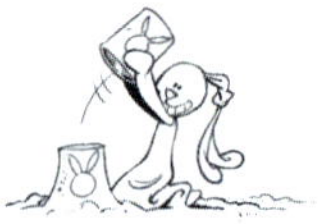

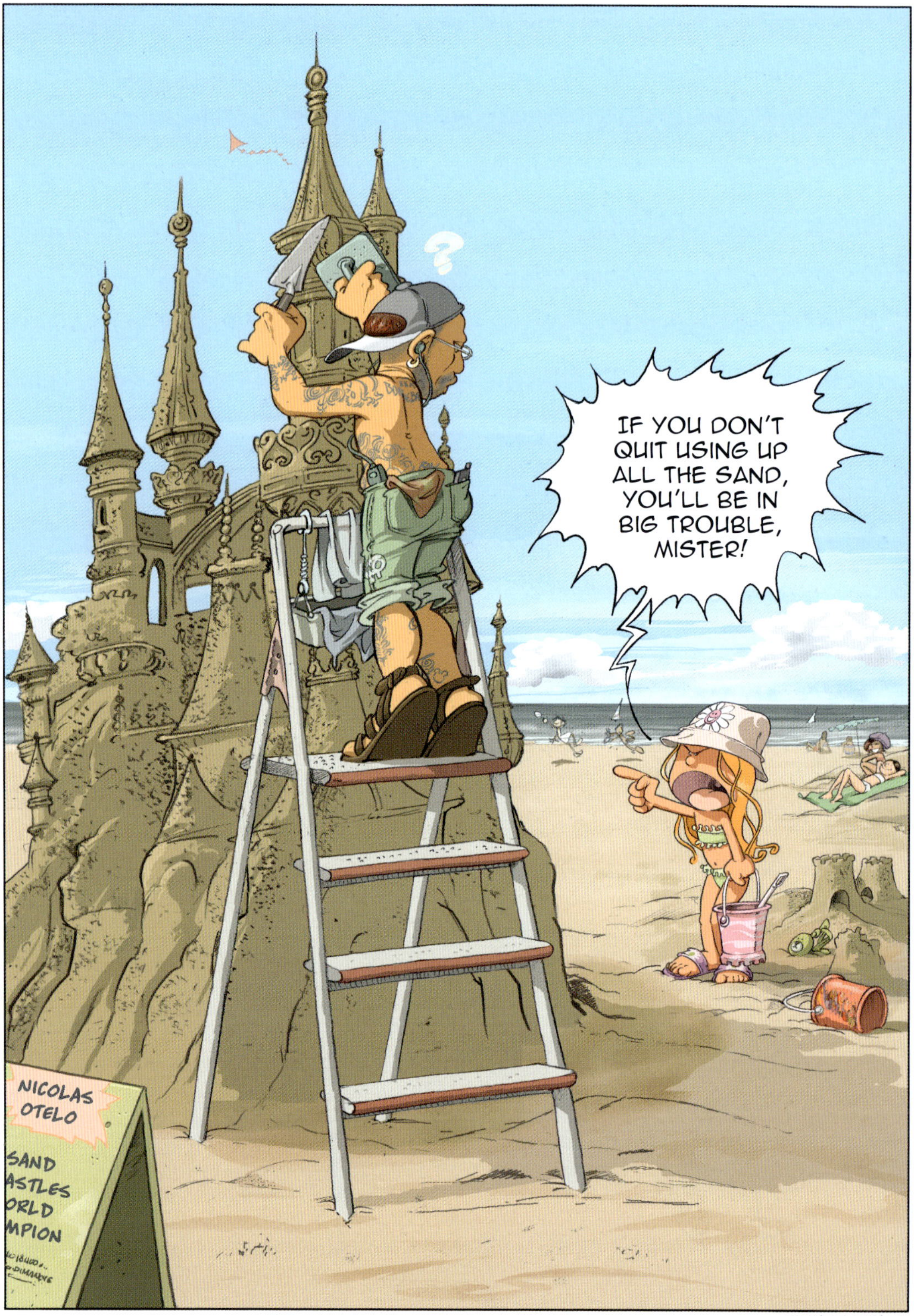
IF YOU DON'T QUIT USING UP ALL THE SAND, YOU'LL BE IN BIG TROUBLE, MISTER!
NICOLAS OTELO
SAND
ASTLES
ORLD
MPION

CAZENOVE/WILLIAM

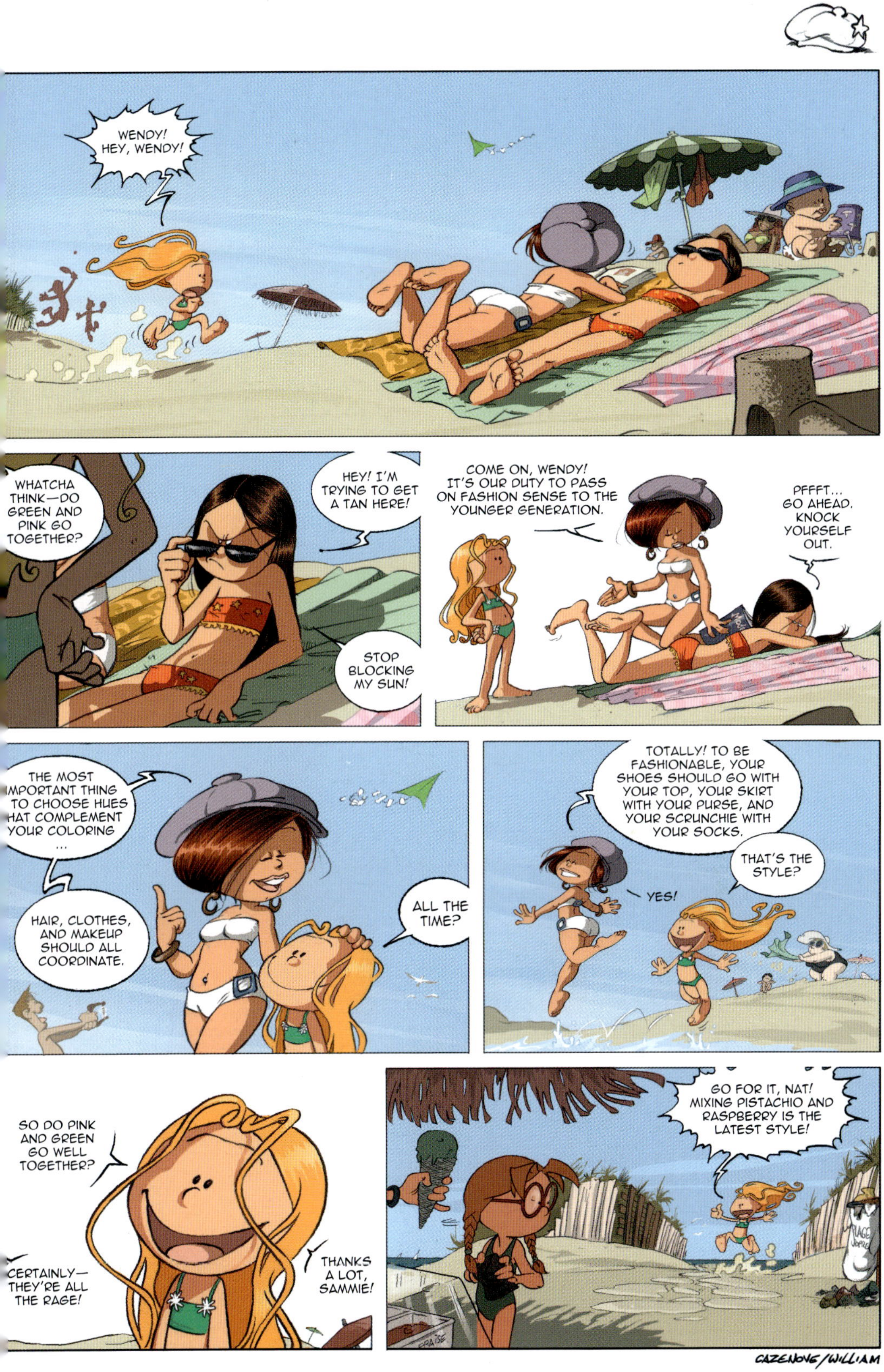
WENDY! HEY, WENDY!
WHATCHA THINK—DO GREEN AND PINK GO TOGETHER?
HEY! I'M TRYING TO GET A TAN HERE!
STOP BLOCKING MY SUN!
COME ON, WENDY! IT'S OUR DUTY TO PASS ON FASHION SENSE TO THE YOUNGER GENERATION.
PFFFT... GO AHEAD. KNOCK YOURSELF OUT.
THE MOST IMPORTANT THING TO CHOOSE HUES THAT COMPLEMENT YOUR COLORING ...
HAIR, CLOTHES, AND MAKEUP SHOULD ALL COORDINATE.
ALL THE TIME?
TOTALLY! TO BE FASHIONABLE, YOUR SHOES SHOULD GO WITH YOUR TOP, YOUR SKIRT WITH YOUR PURSE, AND YOUR SCRUNCHIE WITH YOUR SOCKS.
THAT'S THE STYLE?
YES!
SO DO PINK AND GREEN GO WELL TOGETHER?
CERTAINLY— THEY'RE ALL THE RAGE!
THANKS A LOT, SAMMIE!
GO FOR IT, NAT! MIXING PISTACHIO AND RASPBERRY IS THE LATEST STYLE!
CAZENOVE/WILLIAM

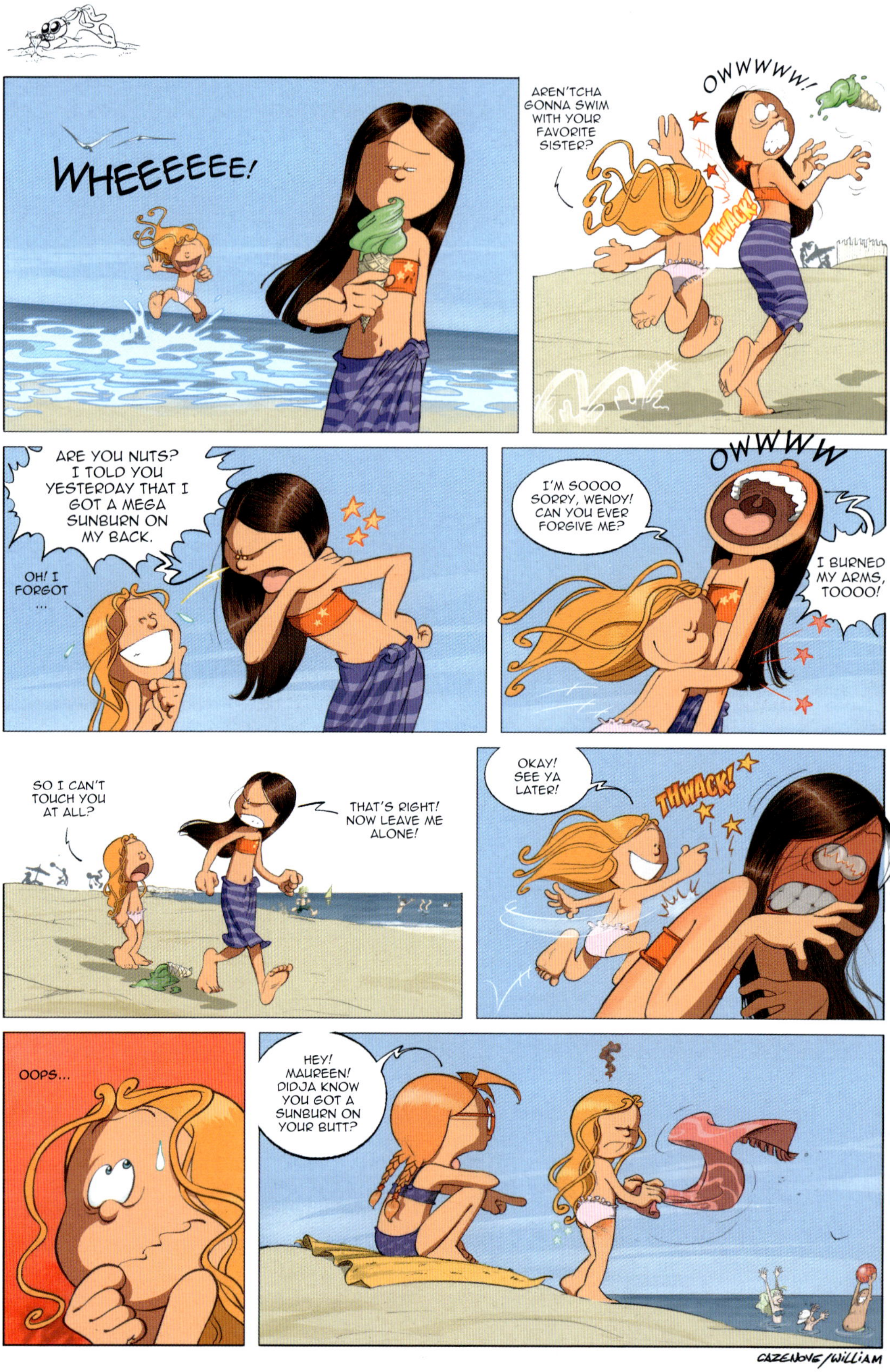

WHEEEEEE!
AREN'TCHA GONNA SWIM WITH YOUR FAVORITE SISTER?
THWACK!
OWWWWW!
ARE YOU NUTS? I TOLD YOU YESTERDAY THAT I GOT A MEGA SUNBURN ON MY BACK.
OH! I FORGOT ...
OWWWW
I'M SOOOO SORRY, WENDY! CAN YOU EVER FORGIVE ME?
I BURNED MY ARMS, TOOOO!
SO I CAN'T TOUCH YOU AT ALL?
THAT'S RIGHT! NOW LEAVE ME ALONE!
OKAY! SEE YA LATER!
THWACK!
OOPS...
HEY! MAUREEN! DIDJA KNOW YOU GOT A SUNBURN ON YOUR BUTT?
CAZENOVE/WILLIAM

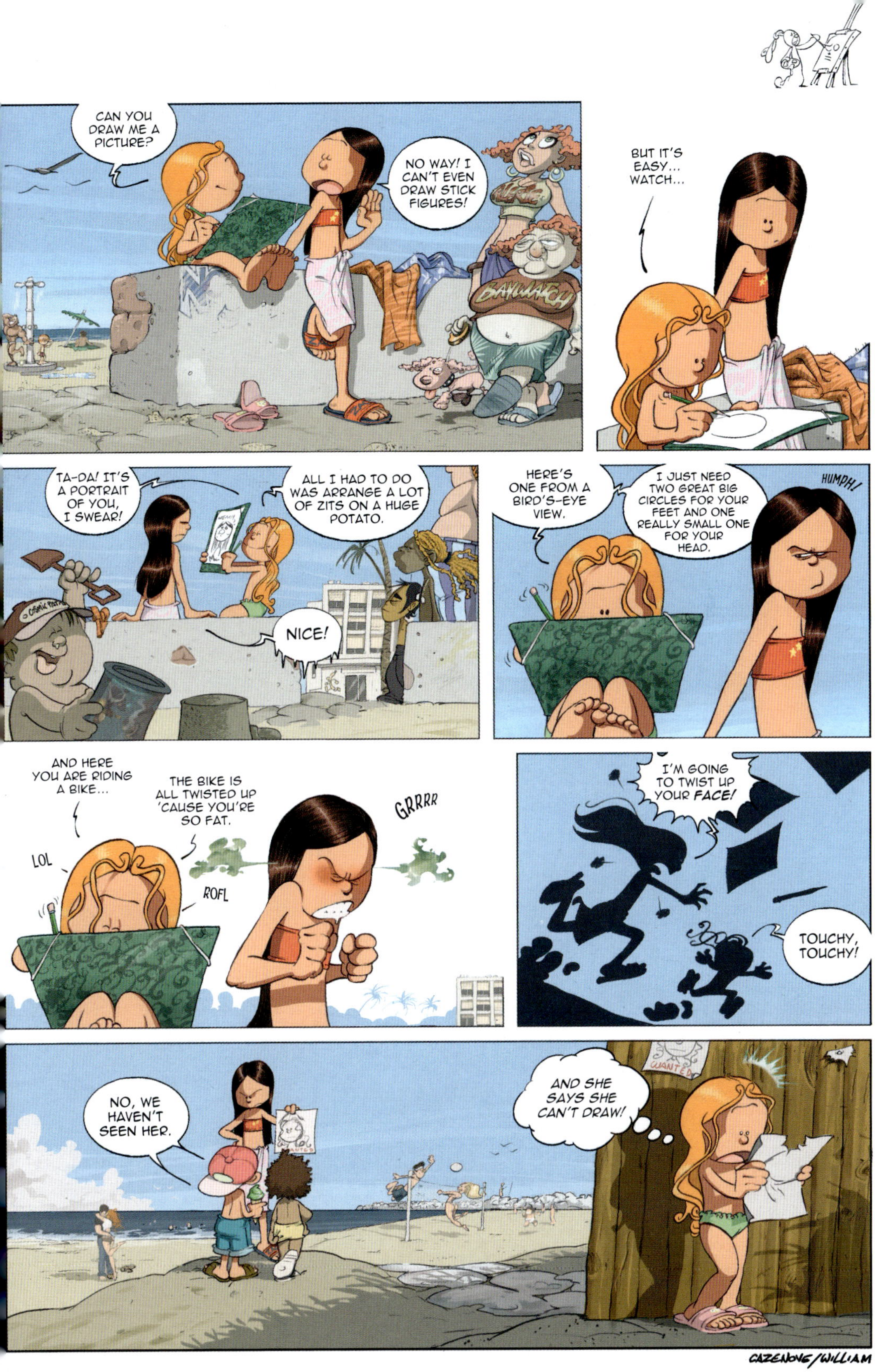
CAN YOU DRAW ME A PICTURE?
NO WAY! I CAN'T EVEN DRAW STICK FIGURES!
BAYWATCH
BUT IT'S EASY... WATCH...
TA-DA! IT'S A PORTRAIT OF YOU, I SWEAR!
ALL I HAD TO DO WAS ARRANGE A LOT OF ZITS ON A HUGE POTATO.
NICE!
HERE'S ONE FROM A BIRD'S-EYE VIEW.
I JUST NEED TWO GREAT BIG CIRCLES FOR YOUR FEET AND ONE REALLY SMALL ONE FOR YOUR HEAD.
HUMPH!
AND HERE YOU ARE RIDING A BIKE...
THE BIKE IS ALL TWISTED UP 'CAUSE YOU'RE SO FAT.
LOL
ROFL
GRRRR
I'M GOING TO TWIST UP YOUR FACE!
TOUCHY, TOUCHY!
NO, WE HAVEN'T SEEN HER.
AND SHE SAYS SHE CAN'T DRAW!
WANTED
CAZENOVE/WILLIAM

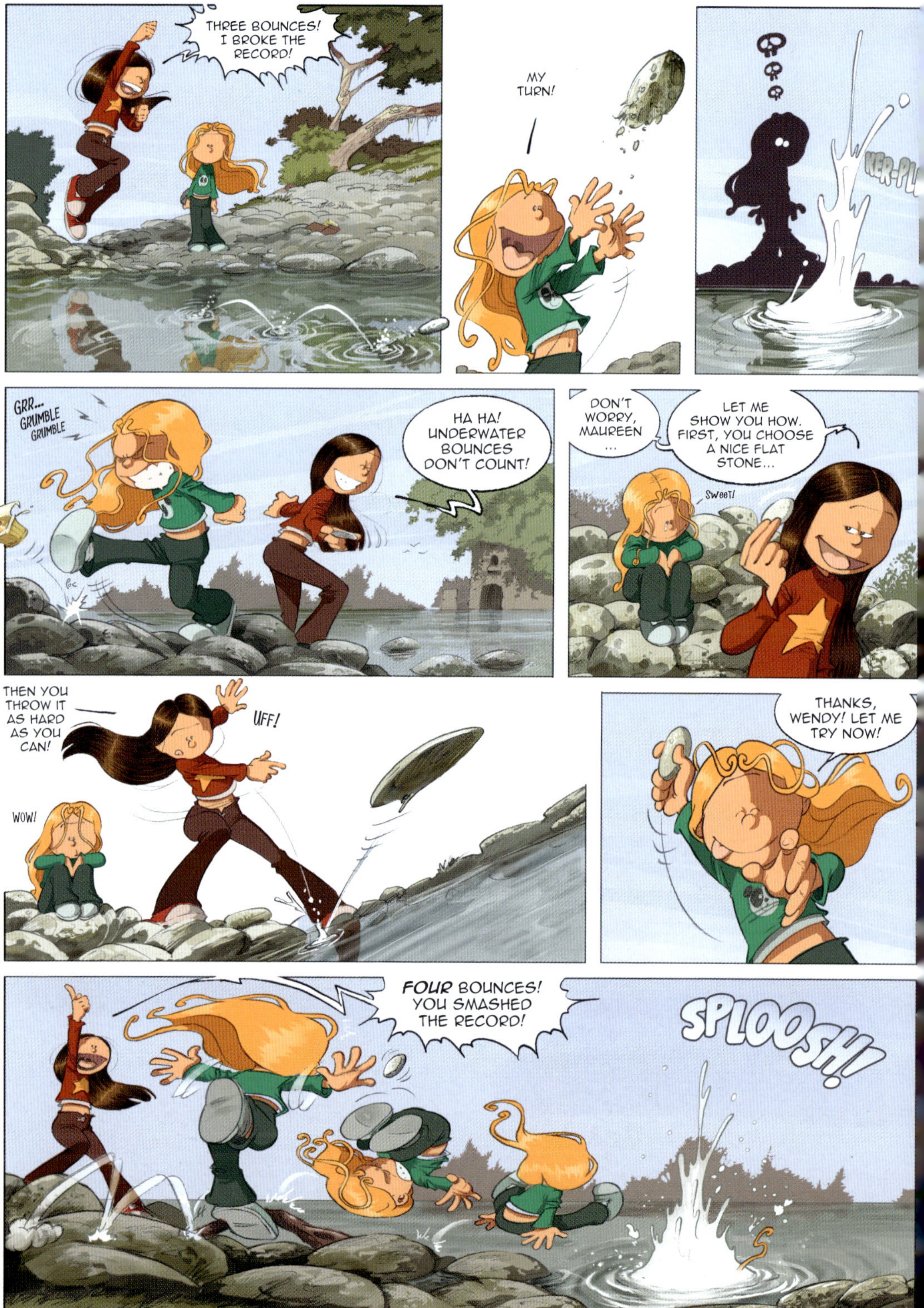
THREE BOUNCES! I BROKE THE RECORD!
MY TURN!
KER-PL
GRR... GRUMBLE GRUMBLE
HA HA! UNDERWATER BOUNCES DON'T COUNT!
DON'T WORRY, MAUREEN ...
LET ME SHOW YOU HOW. FIRST, YOU CHOOSE A NICE FLAT STONE...
SWEET!
THEN YOU THROW IT AS HARD AS YOU CAN!
UFF!
WOW!
THANKS, WENDY! LET ME TRY NOW!
FOUR BOUNCES! YOU SMASHED THE RECORD!
SPLOOSH!

CAZENOVE/WILLIAM

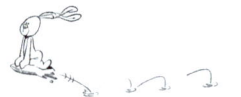

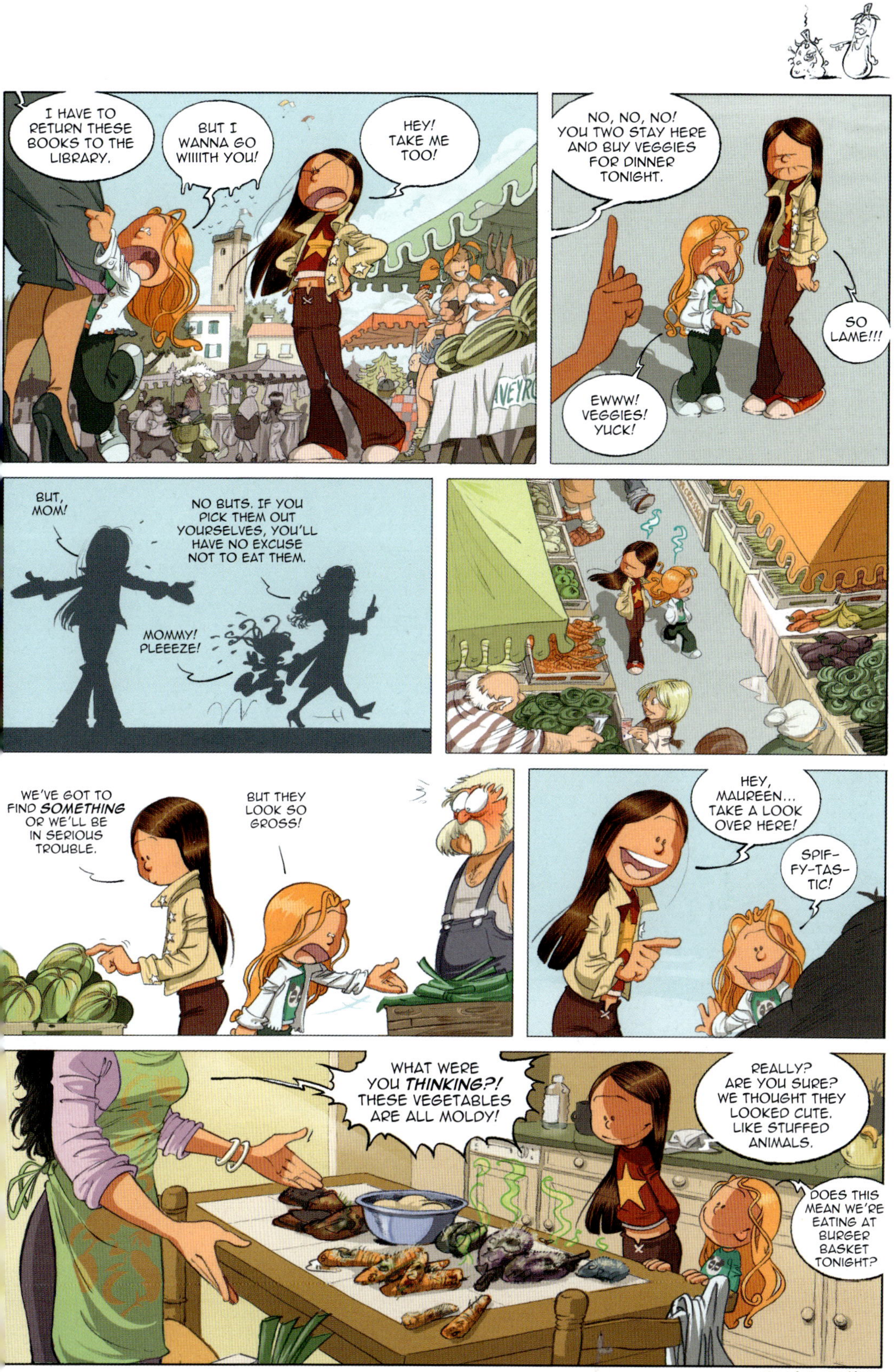
I HAVE TO RETURN THESE BOOKS TO THE LIBRARY.
BUT I WANNA GO WIIIITH YOU!
HEY! TAKE ME TOO!
AVEYR
NO, NO, NO! YOU TWO STAY HERE AND BUY VEGGIES FOR DINNER TONIGHT.
SO LAME!!!
EWWW! VEGGIES! YUCK!
BUT, MOM!
NO BUTS. IF YOU PICK THEM OUT YOURSELVES, YOU'LL HAVE NO EXCUSE NOT TO EAT THEM.
MOMMY! PLEEEZE!
WE'VE GOT TO FIND *SOMETHING* OR WE'LL BE IN SERIOUS TROUBLE.
BUT THEY LOOK SO GROSS!
HEY, MAUREEN... TAKE A LOOK OVER HERE!
SPIF-FY-TAS-TIC!
WHAT WERE YOU *THINKING?!* THESE VEGETABLES ARE ALL MOLDY!
REALLY? ARE YOU SURE? WE THOUGHT THEY LOOKED CUTE. LIKE STUFFED ANIMALS.
DOES THIS MEAN WE'RE EATING AT BURGER BASKET TONIGHT?

CAZENOVE/WILLIAM

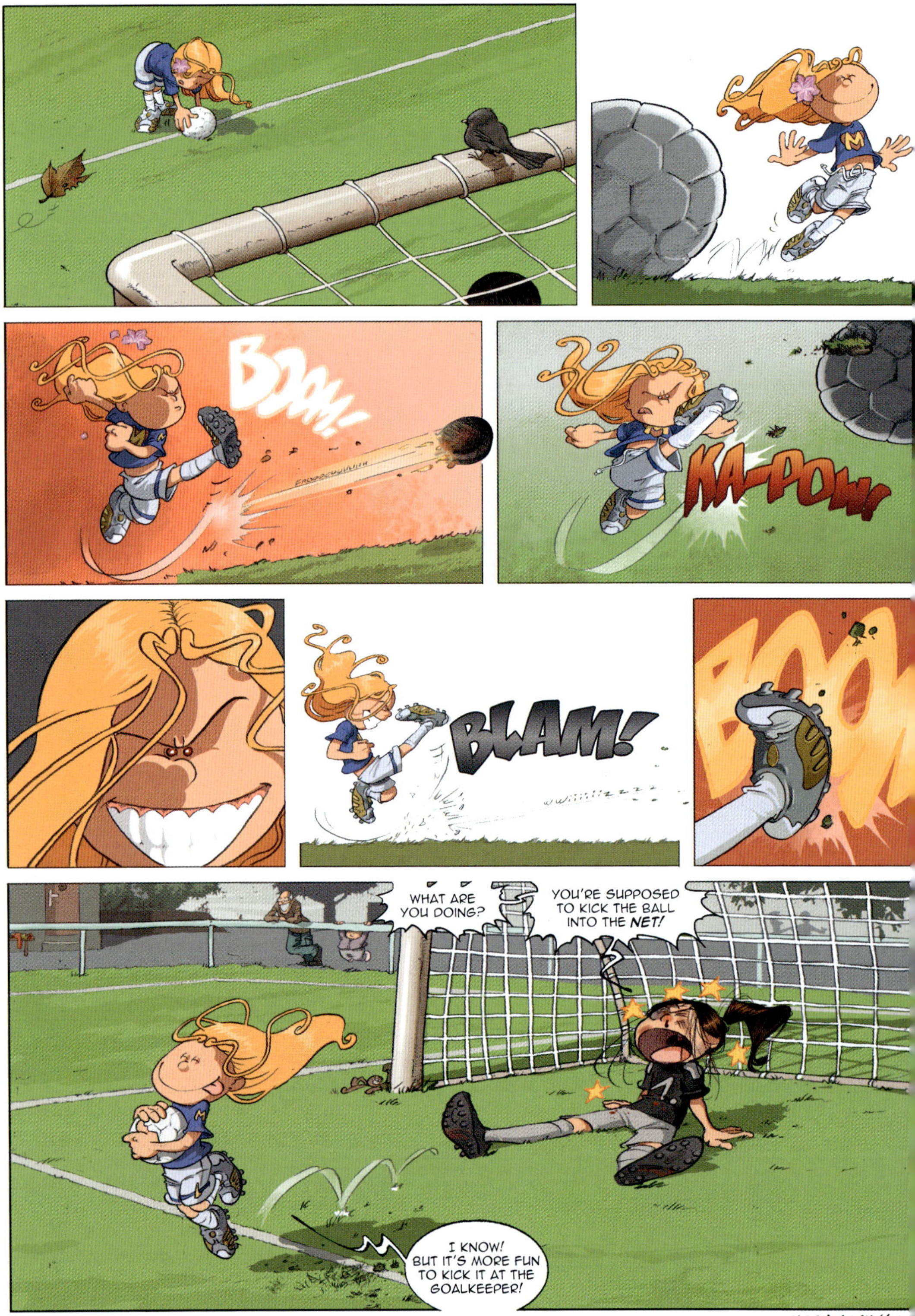
BOOM!
KA-POW!
BLAM!
WHAT ARE YOU DOING?
YOU'RE SUPPOSED TO KICK THE BALL INTO THE **NET!**
I KNOW! BUT IT'S MORE FUN TO KICK IT AT THE GOALKEEPER!

CAZENOVE/WILLIAM

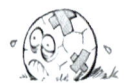

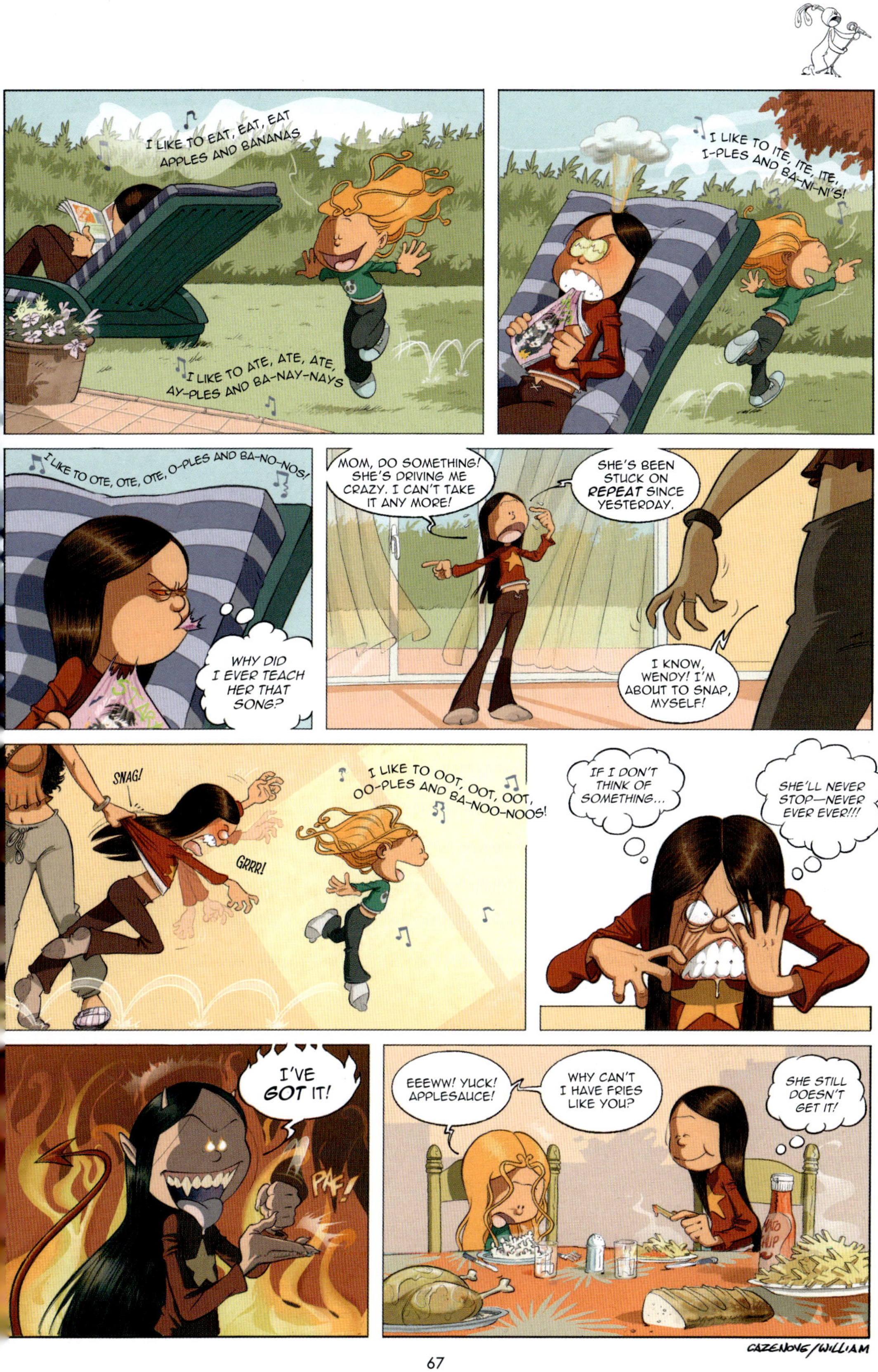

I LIKE TO EAT, EAT, EAT APPLES AND BANANAS
I LIKE TO ATE, ATE, ATE, AY-PLES AND BA-NAY-NAYS
I LIKE TO ITE, ITE, ITE, I-PLES AND BA-NI-NI'S!
I LIKE TO OTE, OTE, OTE, O-PLES AND BA-NO-NOS!
WHY DID I EVER TEACH HER THAT SONG?
MOM, DO SOMETHING! SHE'S DRIVING ME CRAZY. I CAN'T TAKE IT ANY MORE!
SHE'S BEEN STUCK ON **REPEAT** SINCE YESTERDAY.
I KNOW, WENDY! I'M ABOUT TO SNAP, MYSELF!
SNAG!
GRRR!
I LIKE TO OOT, OOT, OOT, OO-PLES AND BA-NOO-NOOS!
IF I DON'T THINK OF SOMETHING...
SHE'LL NEVER STOP—NEVER EVER EVER!!!
I'VE **GOT** IT!
PAF!
EEEWW! YUCK! APPLESAUCE!
WHY CAN'T I HAVE FRIES LIKE YOU?
SHE STILL DOESN'T GET IT!
CAZENOVE/WILLIAM

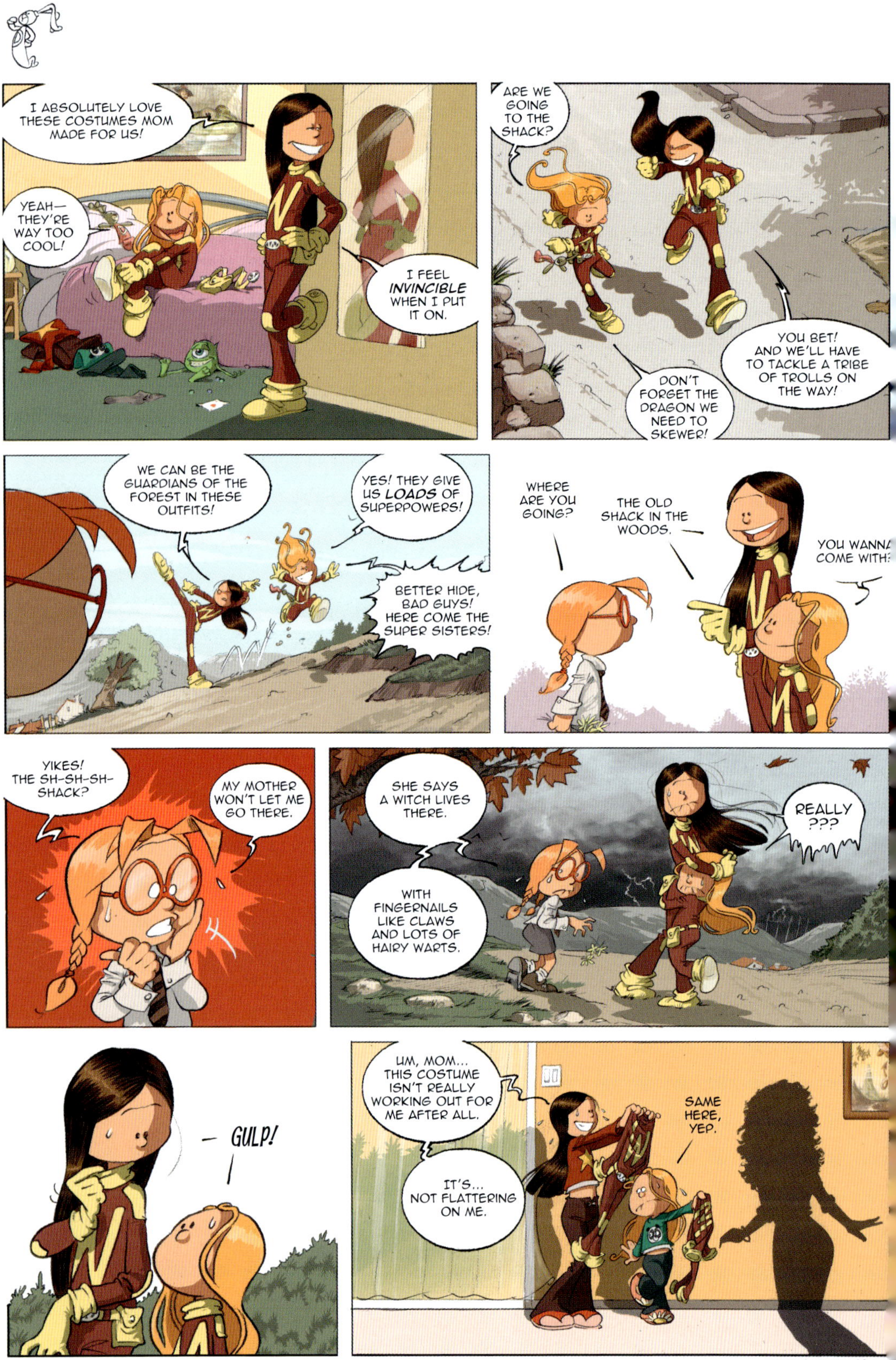
I ABSOLUTELY LOVE THESE COSTUMES MOM MADE FOR US!
YEAH— THEY'RE WAY TOO COOL!
I FEEL *INVINCIBLE* WHEN I PUT IT ON.
ARE WE GOING TO THE SHACK?
YOU BET! AND WE'LL HAVE TO TACKLE A TRIBE OF TROLLS ON THE WAY!
DON'T FORGET THE DRAGON WE NEED TO SKEWER!
WE CAN BE THE GUARDIANS OF THE FOREST IN THESE OUTFITS!
YES! THEY GIVE US *LOADS* OF SUPERPOWERS!
BETTER HIDE, BAD GUYS! HERE COME THE SUPER SISTERS!
WHERE ARE YOU GOING?
THE OLD SHACK IN THE WOODS.
YOU WANNA COME WITH?
YIKES! THE SH-SH-SH-SHACK?
MY MOTHER WON'T LET ME GO THERE.
SHE SAYS A WITCH LIVES THERE.
WITH FINGERNAILS LIKE CLAWS AND LOTS OF HAIRY WARTS.
REALLY ???
GULP!
UM, MOM... THIS COSTUME ISN'T REALLY WORKING OUT FOR ME AFTER ALL.
IT'S... NOT FLATTERING ON ME.
SAME HERE, YEP.

CAZENOVE/WILLIAM

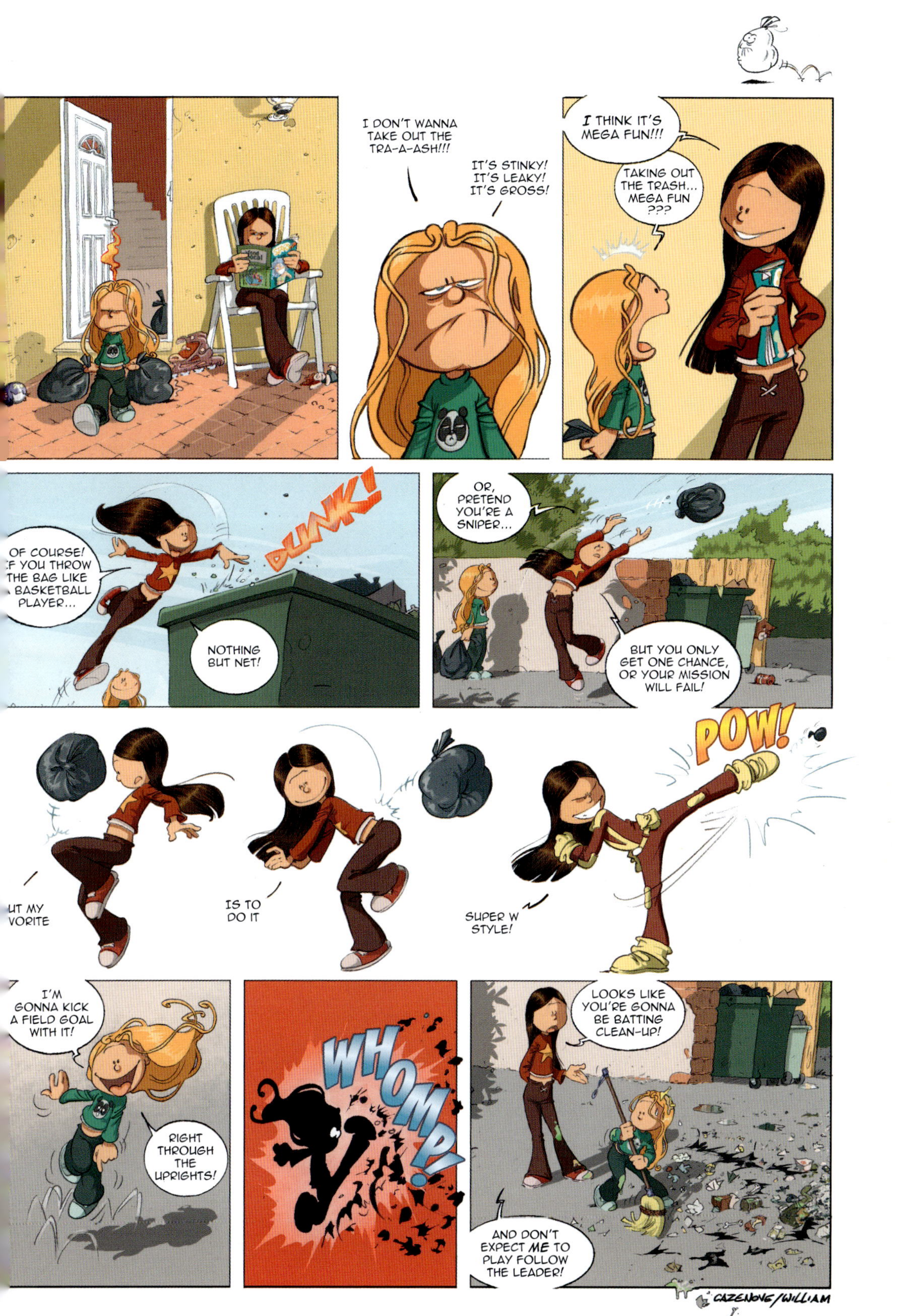
I DON'T WANNA TAKE OUT THE TRA-A-ASH!!!
IT'S STINKY! IT'S LEAKY! IT'S GROSS!
I THINK IT'S MEGA FUN!!!
TAKING OUT THE TRASH... MEGA FUN ???
OF COURSE! IF YOU THROW THE BAG LIKE A BASKETBALL PLAYER...
DUNK!
NOTHING BUT NET!
OR, PRETEND YOU'RE A SNIPER...
BUT YOU ONLY GET ONE CHANCE, OR YOUR MISSION WILL FAIL!
UT MY VORITE
IS TO DO IT
SUPER W STYLE!
POW!
I'M GONNA KICK A FIELD GOAL WITH IT!
RIGHT THROUGH THE UPRIGHTS!
WHOMP!
LOOKS LIKE YOU'RE GONNA BE BATTING CLEAN-UP!
AND DON'T EXPECT ME TO PLAY FOLLOW THE LEADER!
CAZENOVE/WILLIAM

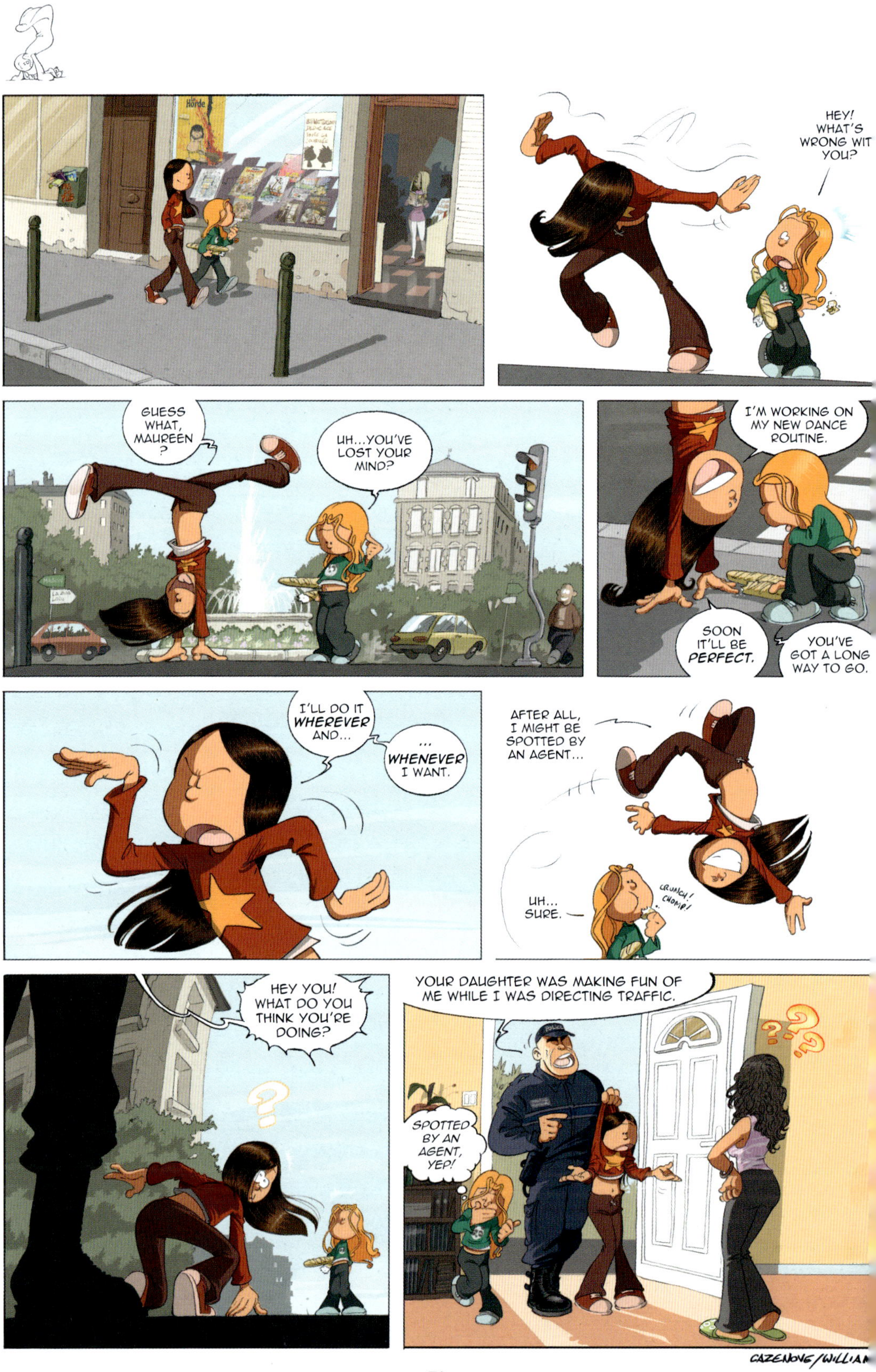
HEY!
WHAT'S
WRONG WIT
YOU?
GUESS
WHAT,
MAUREEN
?
UH...YOU'VE
LOST YOUR
MIND?
I'M WORKING ON
MY NEW DANCE
ROUTINE.
SOON
IT'LL BE
PERFECT.
YOU'VE
GOT A LONG
WAY TO GO.
I'LL DO IT
WHEREVER
AND...
...
WHENEVER
I WANT.
AFTER ALL,
I MIGHT BE
SPOTTED BY
AN AGENT...
UH...
SURE.
CRUNCH!
CHOMP!
HEY YOU!
WHAT DO YOU
THINK YOU'RE
DOING?
YOUR DAUGHTER WAS MAKING FUN OF
ME WHILE I WAS DIRECTING TRAFFIC.
SPOTTED
BY AN
AGENT,
YEP!
CAZENOVE/WILLIAM

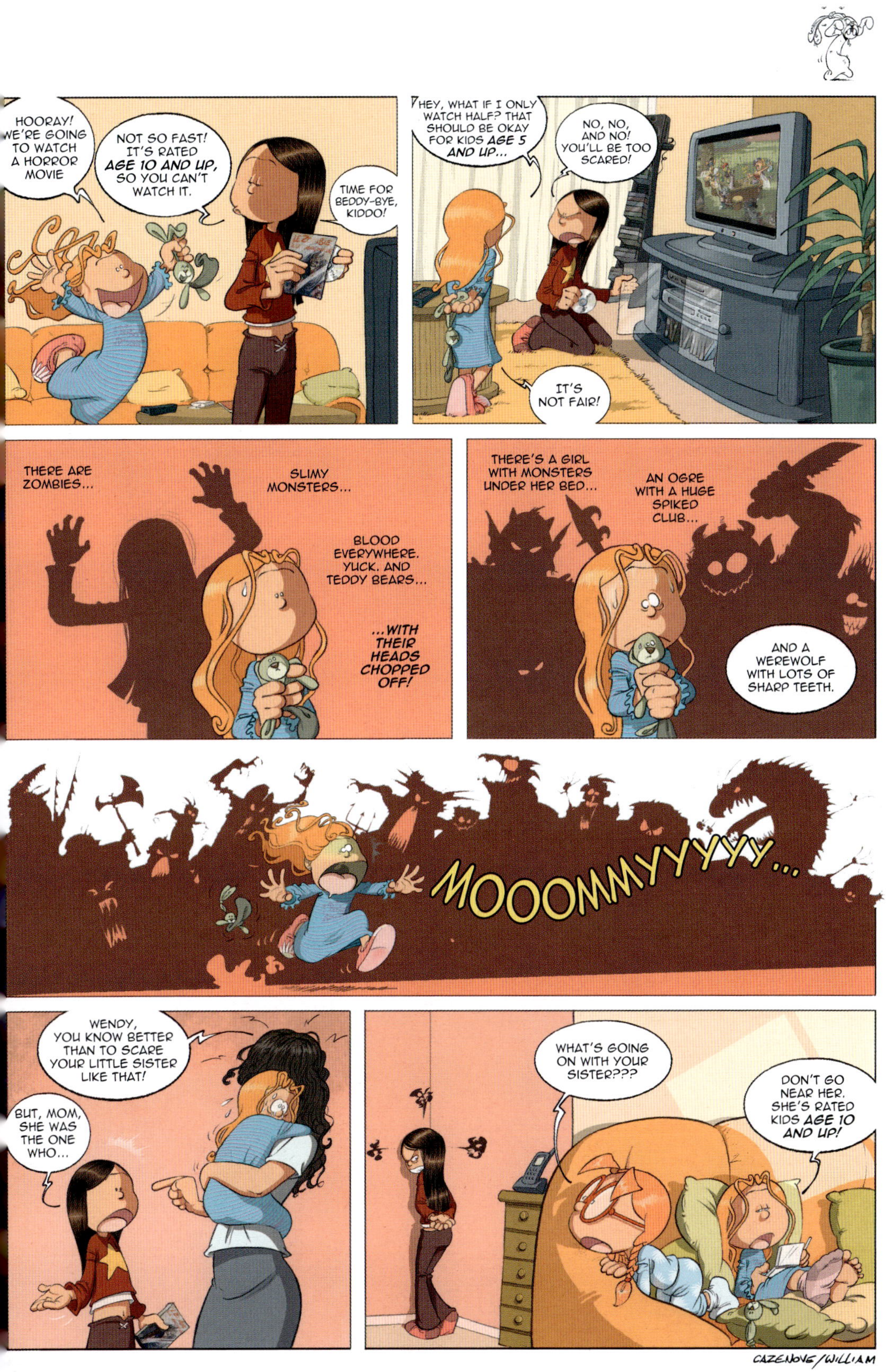
HOORAY! WE'RE GOING TO WATCH A HORROR MOVIE
NOT SO FAST! IT'S RATED AGE 10 AND UP, SO YOU CAN'T WATCH IT.
TIME FOR BEDDY-BYE, KIDDO!
HEY, WHAT IF I ONLY WATCH HALF? THAT SHOULD BE OKAY FOR KIDS AGE 5 AND UP...
NO, NO, AND NO! YOU'LL BE TOO SCARED!
IT'S NOT FAIR!
THERE ARE ZOMBIES...
SLIMY MONSTERS...
BLOOD EVERYWHERE. YUCK. AND TEDDY BEARS...
...WITH THEIR HEADS CHOPPED OFF!
THERE'S A GIRL WITH MONSTERS UNDER HER BED...
AN OGRE WITH A HUGE SPIKED CLUB...
AND A WEREWOLF WITH LOTS OF SHARP TEETH.
MOOOMMYYYYY...
WENDY, YOU KNOW BETTER THAN TO SCARE YOUR LITTLE SISTER LIKE THAT!
BUT, MOM, SHE WAS THE ONE WHO...
WHAT'S GOING ON WITH YOUR SISTER???
DON'T GO NEAR HER. SHE'S RATED KIDS AGE 10 AND UP!
CAZENOVE/WILLIAM

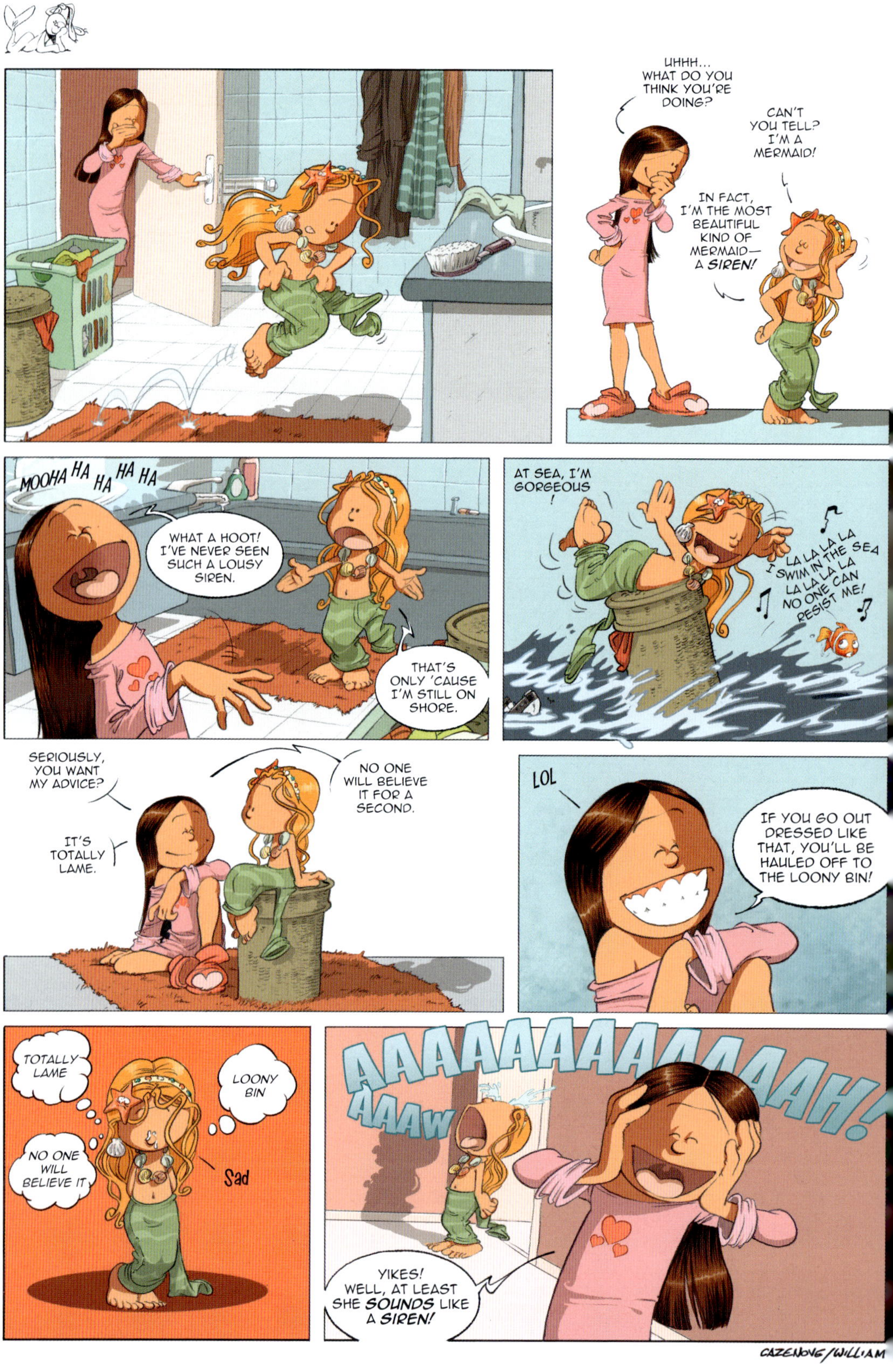
UHHH... WHAT DO YOU THINK YOU'RE DOING?
CAN'T YOU TELL? I'M A MERMAID!
IN FACT, I'M THE MOST BEAUTIFUL KIND OF MERMAID— A SIREN!
MOOHA HA HA HA HA
WHAT A HOOT! I'VE NEVER SEEN SUCH A LOUSY SIREN.
THAT'S ONLY 'CAUSE I'M STILL ON SHORE.
AT SEA, I'M GORGEOUS!
LA LA LA LA I SWIM IN THE SEA LA LA LA LA NO ONE CAN RESIST ME!
SERIOUSLY, YOU WANT MY ADVICE?
IT'S TOTALLY LAME.
NO ONE WILL BELIEVE IT FOR A SECOND.
LOL
IF YOU GO OUT DRESSED LIKE THAT, YOU'LL BE HAULED OFF TO THE LOONY BIN!
TOTALLY LAME
LOONY BIN
NO ONE WILL BELIEVE IT
Sad
AAAAAAAAAAAAAAH!
AAAW
YIKES! WELL, AT LEAST SHE SOUNDS LIKE A SIREN!
CAZENOVE/WILLIAM

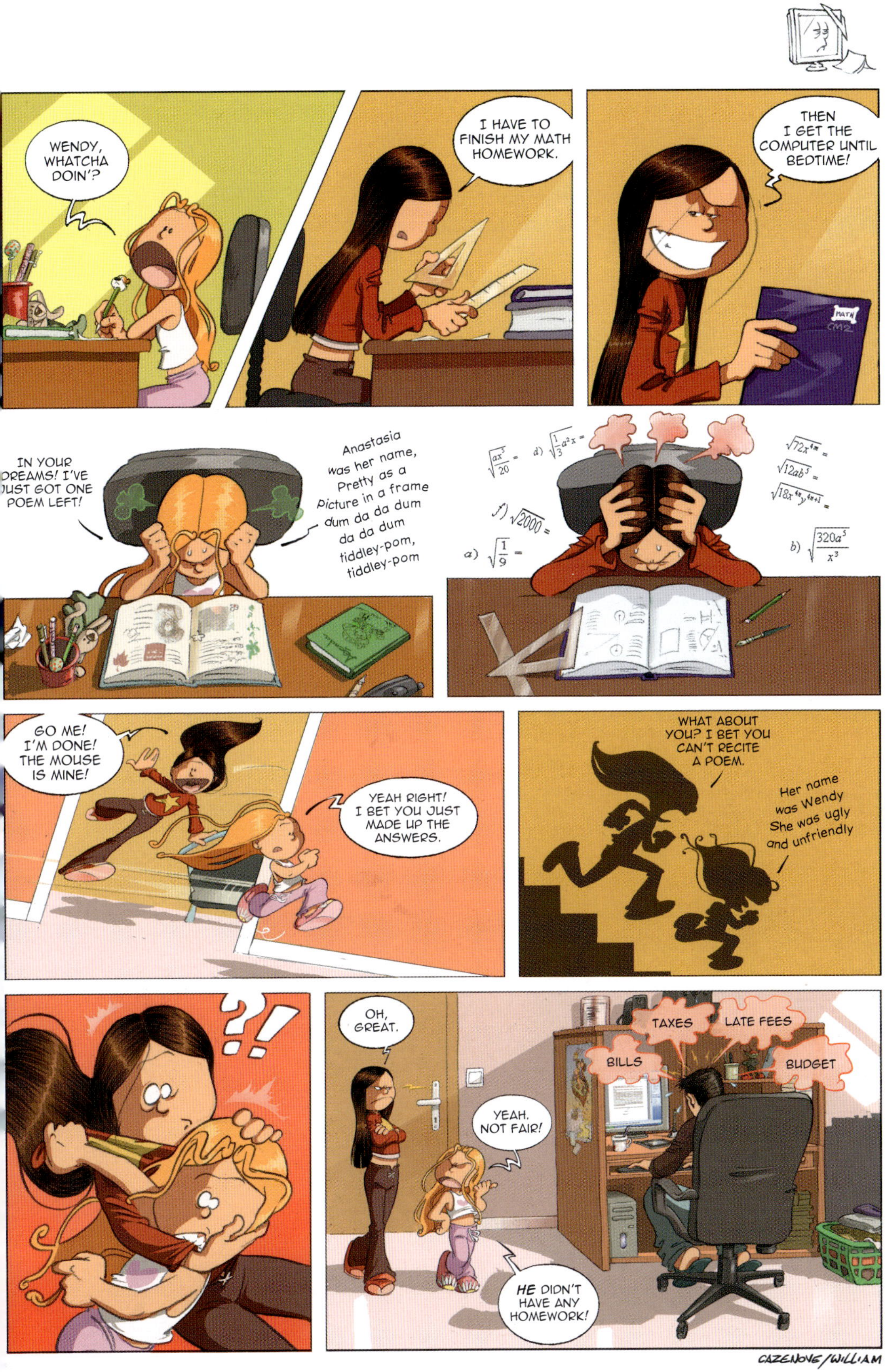
WENDY, WHATCHA DOIN'?
I HAVE TO FINISH MY MATH HOMEWORK.
THEN I GET THE COMPUTER UNTIL BEDTIME!
MATH CM2
IN YOUR DREAMS! I'VE JUST GOT ONE POEM LEFT!
Anastasia was her name, Pretty as a picture in a frame dum da da dum da da dum tiddley-pom, tiddley-pom
$\sqrt{\frac{ax^3}{20}} =$
d) $\sqrt{\frac{1}{3}a^2x} =$
f) $\sqrt{2000} =$
a) $\sqrt{\frac{1}{9}} =$
$\sqrt{72x^{4m}} =$
$\sqrt{12ab^5} =$
$\sqrt{18x^{4n}y^{4n+1}} =$
b) $\sqrt{\frac{320a^5}{x^3}}$
GO ME! I'M DONE! THE MOUSE IS MINE!
YEAH RIGHT! I BET YOU JUST MADE UP THE ANSWERS.
WHAT ABOUT YOU? I BET YOU CAN'T RECITE A POEM.
Her name was Wendy She was ugly and unfriendly
?!
OH, GREAT.
TAXES
LATE FEES
BILLS
BUDGET
YEAH. NOT FAIR!
HE DIDN'T HAVE ANY HOMEWORK!
CAZENOVE/WILLIAM

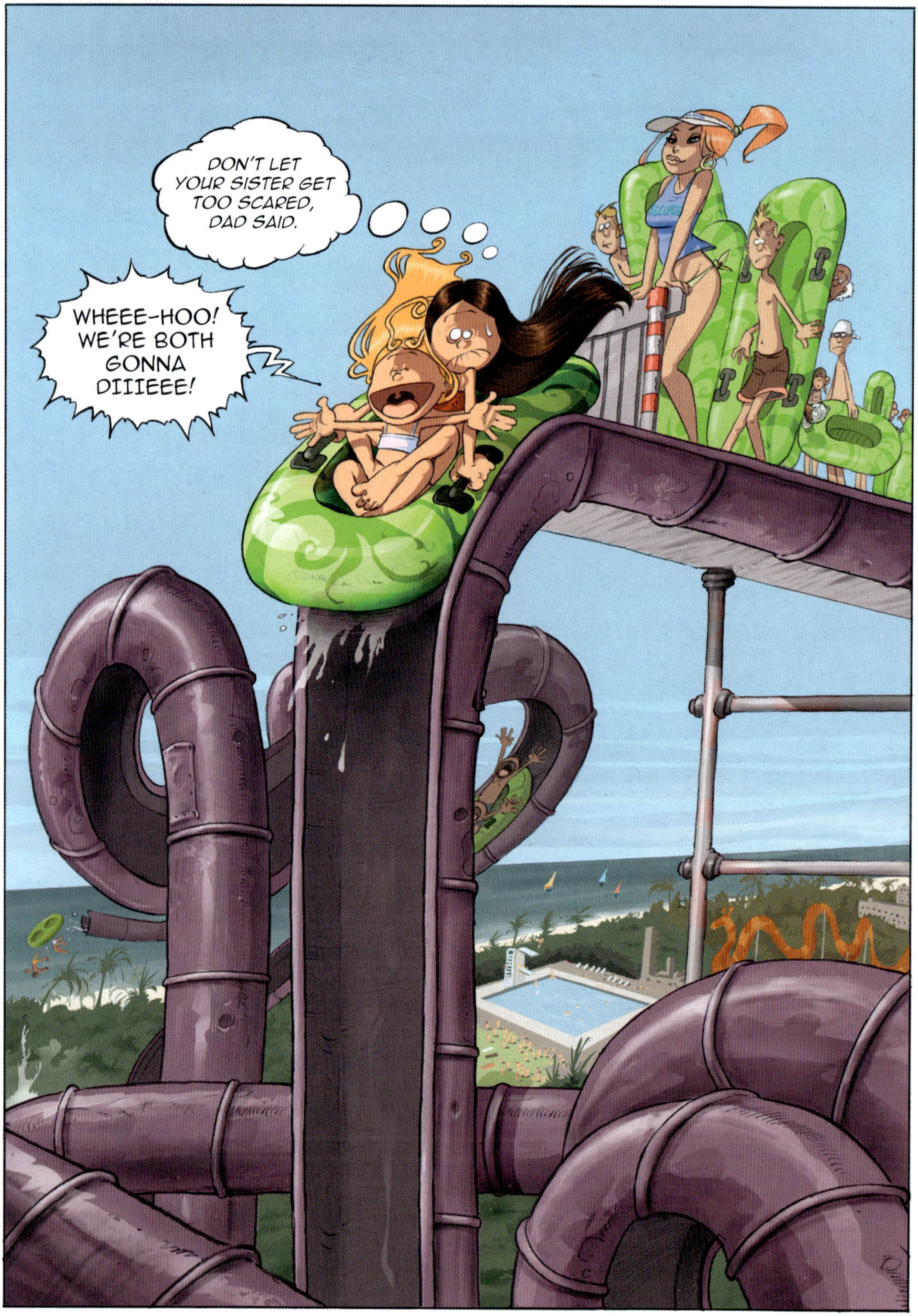
DON'T LET YOUR SISTER GET TOO SCARED, DAD SAID.
WHEEE-HOO! WE'RE BOTH GONNA DIIIEEE!

CAZENOVE/WILLIAM

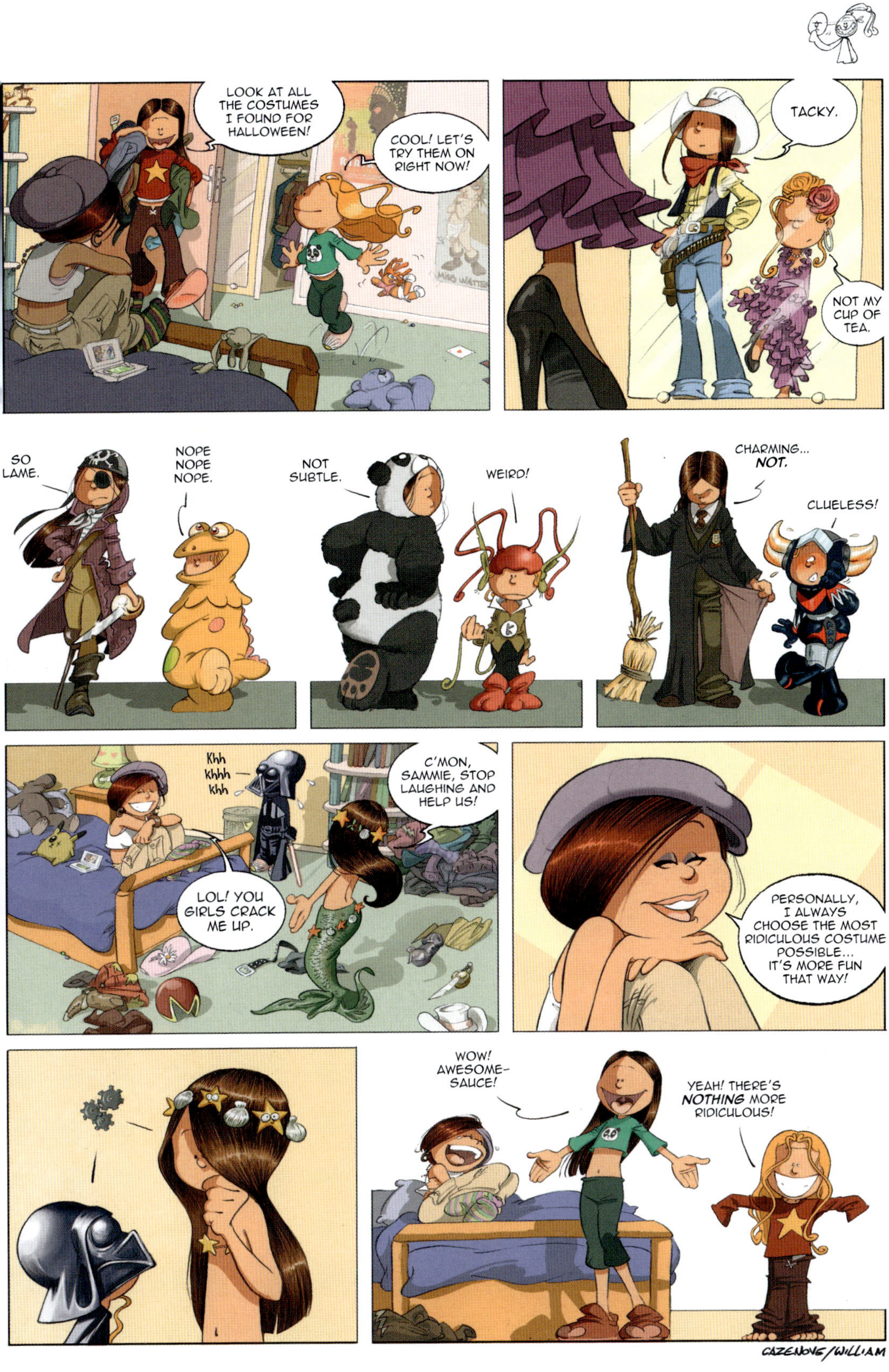

LOOK AT ALL THE COSTUMES I FOUND FOR HALLOWEEN!
COOL! LET'S TRY THEM ON RIGHT NOW!
TACKY.
NOT MY CUP OF TEA.
SO LAME.
NOPE NOPE NOPE.
NOT SUBTLE.
WEIRD!
CHARMING... NOT.
CLUELESS!
Khh khhh khh
C'MON, SAMMIE, STOP LAUGHING AND HELP US!
LOL! YOU GIRLS CRACK ME UP.
PERSONALLY, I ALWAYS CHOOSE THE MOST RIDICULOUS COSTUME POSSIBLE... IT'S MORE FUN THAT WAY!
WOW! AWESOME-SAUCE!
YEAH! THERE'S NOTHING MORE RIDICULOUS!
CAZENOVE/WILLIAM

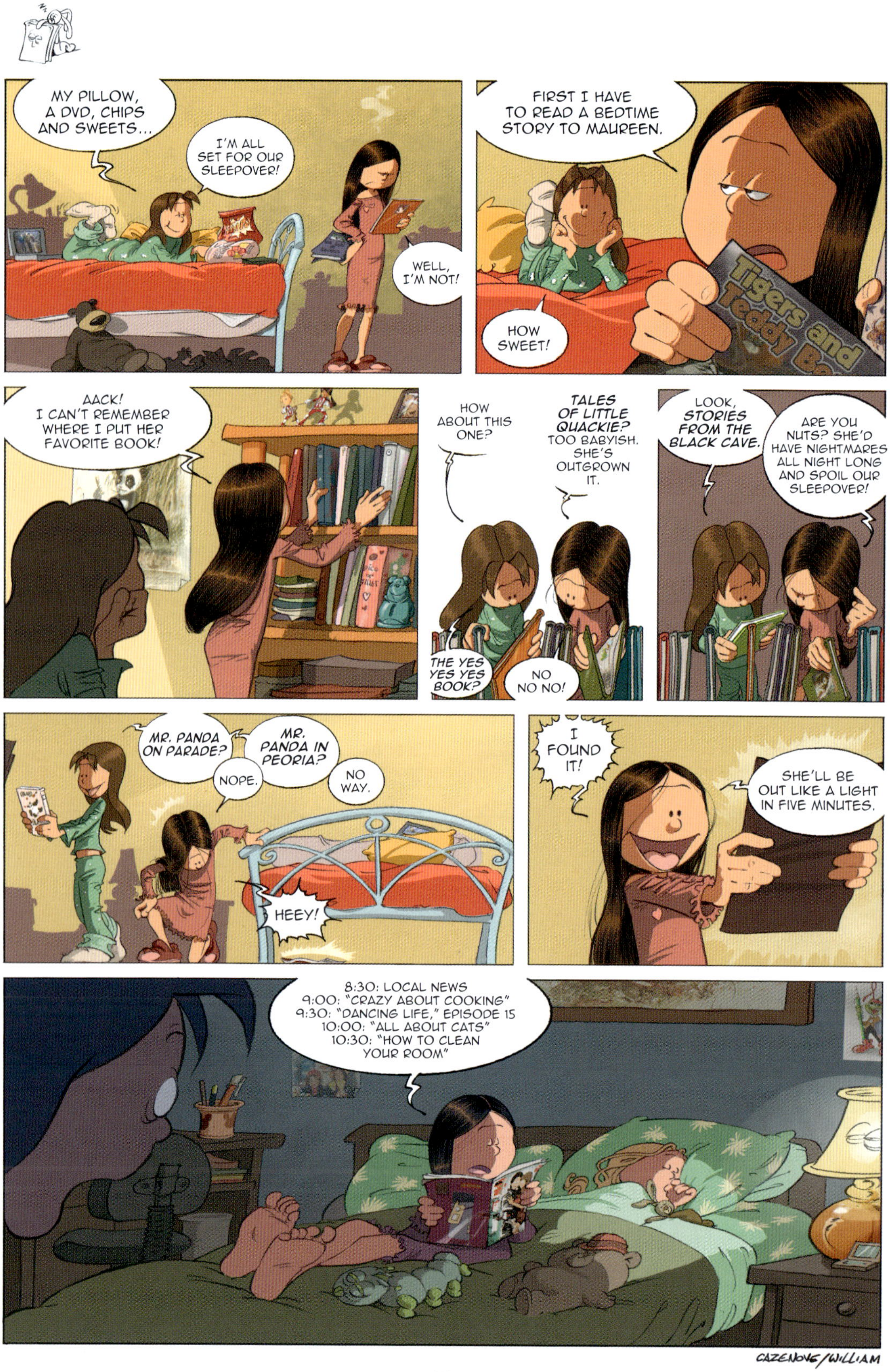
MY PILLOW, A DVD, CHIPS AND SWEETS...
I'M ALL SET FOR OUR SLEEPOVER!
WELL, I'M NOT!
FIRST I HAVE TO READ A BEDTIME STORY TO MAUREEN.
HOW SWEET!
AACK! I CAN'T REMEMBER WHERE I PUT HER FAVORITE BOOK!
HOW ABOUT THIS ONE?
TALES OF LITTLE QUACKIE? TOO BABYISH. SHE'S OUTGROWN IT.
THE YES YES YES BOOK?
NO NO NO!
LOOK, STORIES FROM THE BLACK CAVE.
ARE YOU NUTS? SHE'D HAVE NIGHTMARES ALL NIGHT LONG AND SPOIL OUR SLEEPOVER!
MR. PANDA ON PARADE?
NOPE.
MR. PANDA IN PEORIA?
NO WAY.
HEEY!
I FOUND IT!
SHE'LL BE OUT LIKE A LIGHT IN FIVE MINUTES.
8:30: LOCAL NEWS
9:00: "CRAZY ABOUT COOKING"
9:30: "DANCING LIFE," EPISODE 15
10:00: "ALL ABOUT CATS"
10:30: "HOW TO CLEAN YOUR ROOM"
CAZENOVE/WILLIAM

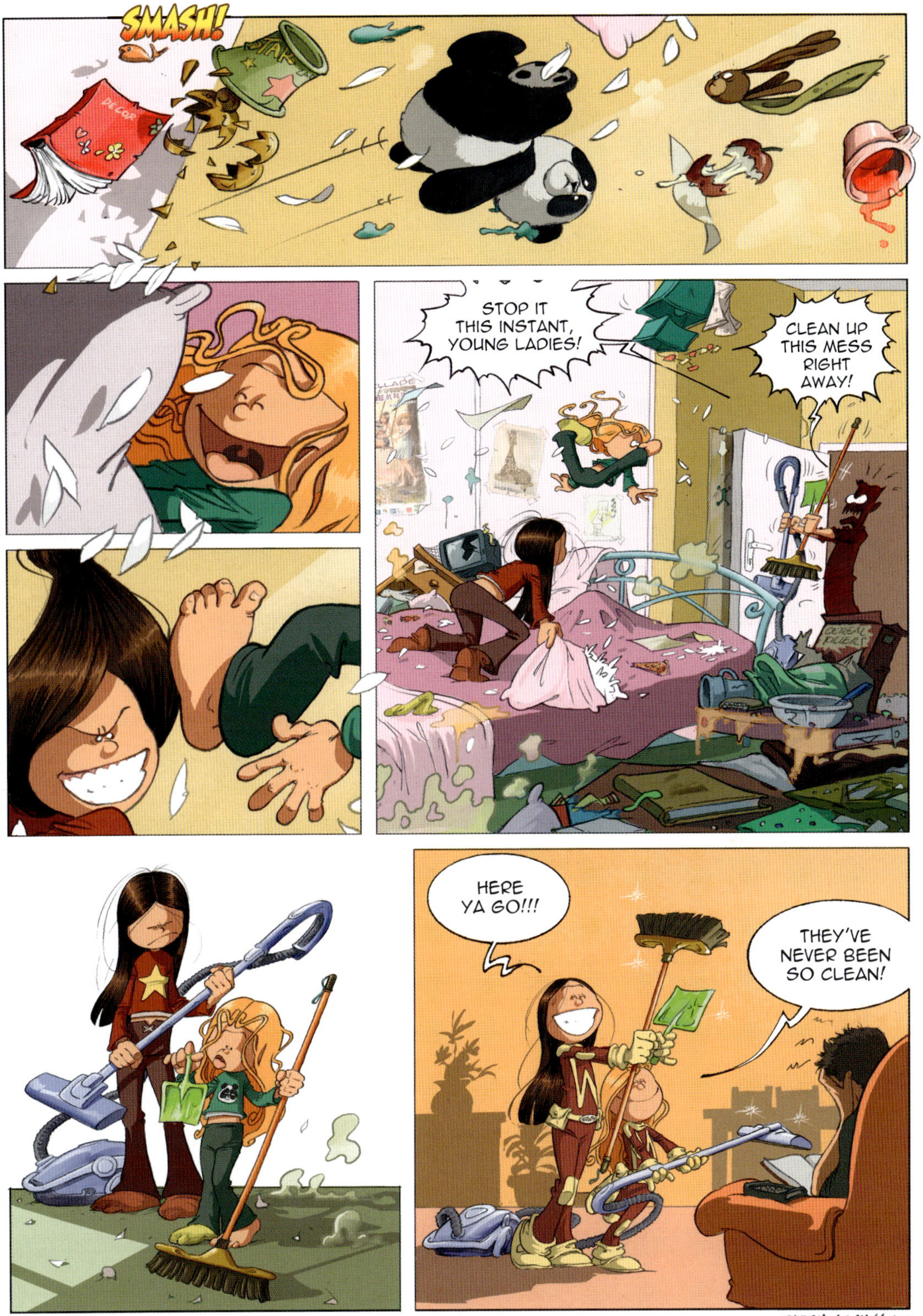
SMASH!
DECOR
STOP IT THIS INSTANT, YOUNG LADIES!
CLEAN UP THIS MESS RIGHT AWAY!
CEREAL KILLERS
HERE YA GO!!!
THEY'VE NEVER BEEN SO CLEAN!

CAZENOVE/WILLIAM

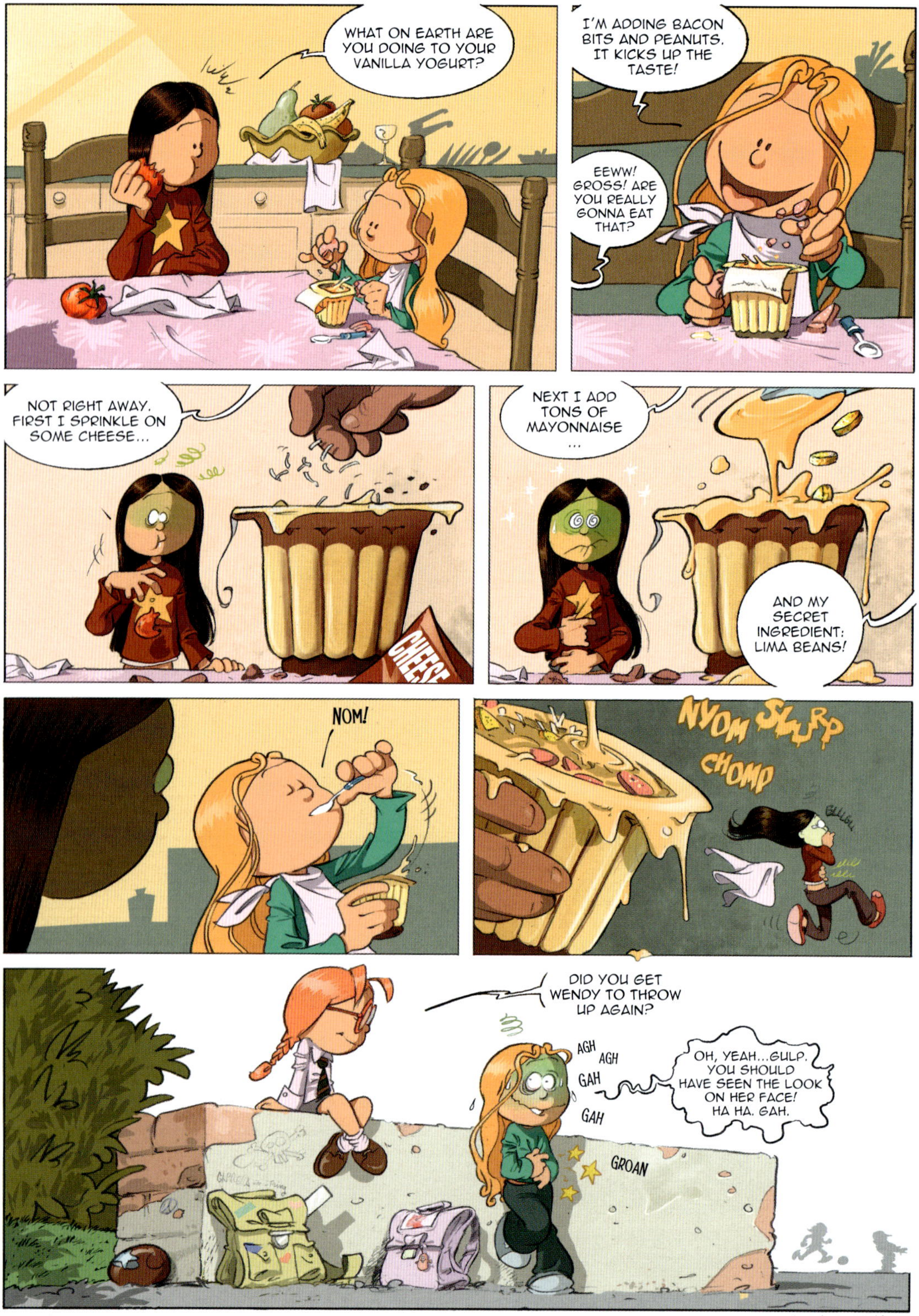
WHAT ON EARTH ARE YOU DOING TO YOUR VANILLA YOGURT?
I'M ADDING BACON BITS AND PEANUTS. IT KICKS UP THE TASTE!
EEWW! GROSS! ARE YOU REALLY GONNA EAT THAT?
NOT RIGHT AWAY. FIRST I SPRINKLE ON SOME CHEESE...
CHEESE
NEXT I ADD TONS OF MAYONNAISE ...
AND MY SECRET INGREDIENT: LIMA BEANS!
NOM!
NYOM SLURP
CHOMP
DID YOU GET WENDY TO THROW UP AGAIN?
AGH AGH GAH GAH
OH, YEAH...GULP. YOU SHOULD HAVE SEEN THE LOOK ON HER FACE! HA HA. GAH.
GROAN

CAZENOVE/WILLIAM

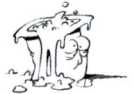

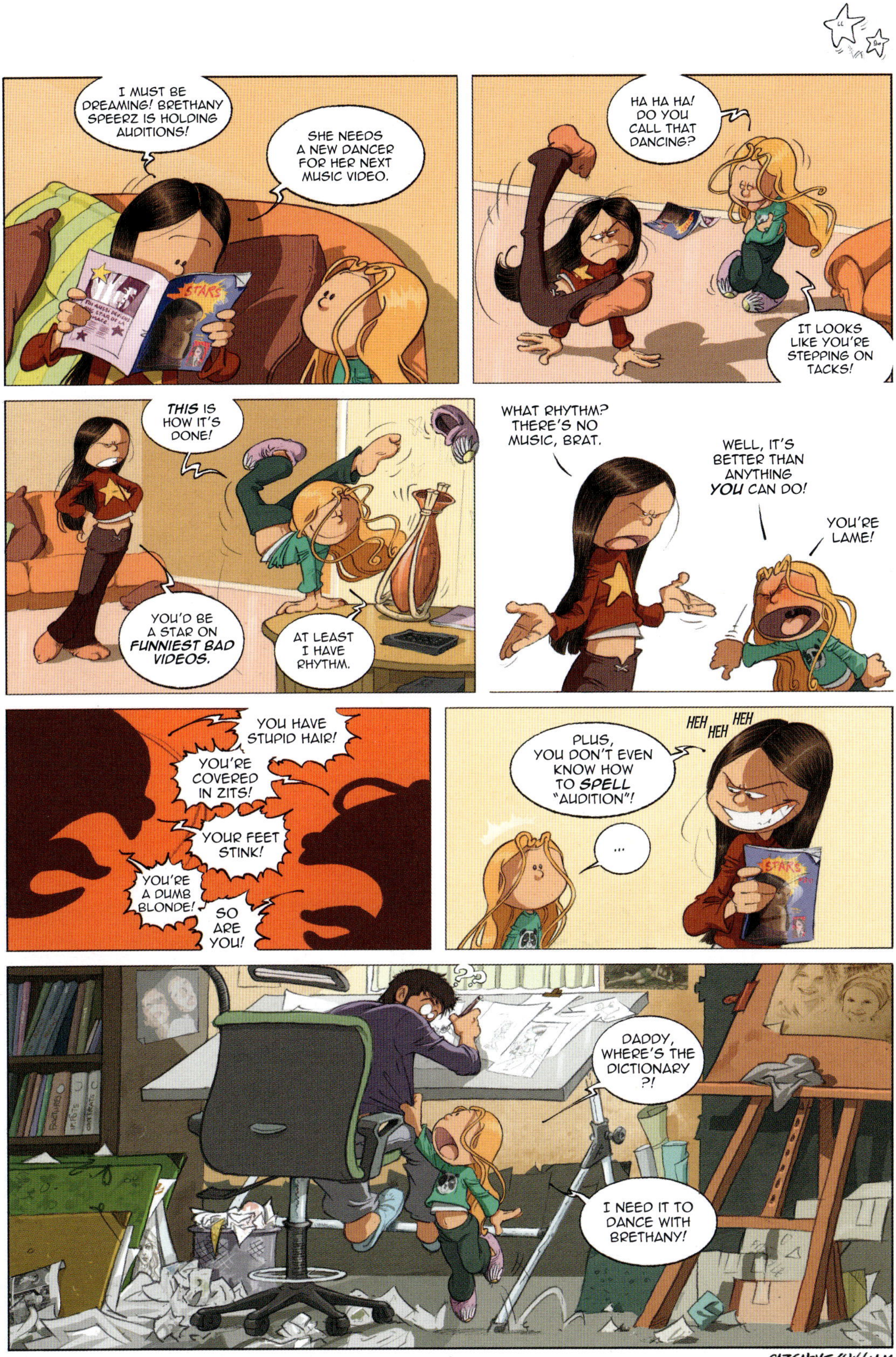
I MUST BE DREAMING! BRETHANY SPEERZ IS HOLDING AUDITIONS!
SHE NEEDS A NEW DANCER FOR HER NEXT MUSIC VIDEO.
STARS
HA HA HA! DO YOU CALL THAT DANCING?
IT LOOKS LIKE YOU'RE STEPPING ON TACKS!
THIS IS HOW IT'S DONE!
YOU'D BE A STAR ON ***FUNNIEST BAD VIDEOS.***
AT LEAST I HAVE RHYTHM.
WHAT RHYTHM? THERE'S NO MUSIC, BRAT.
WELL, IT'S BETTER THAN ANYTHING ***YOU*** CAN DO!
YOU'RE LAME!
YOU HAVE STUPID HAIR!
YOU'RE COVERED IN ZITS!
YOUR FEET STINK!
YOU'RE A DUMB BLONDE!
SO ARE YOU!
HEH HEH HEH
PLUS, YOU DON'T EVEN KNOW HOW TO **SPELL** "AUDITION"!
...
STARS
DADDY, WHERE'S THE DICTIONARY ?!
I NEED IT TO DANCE WITH BRETHANY!

CAZENOVE/WILLIAM

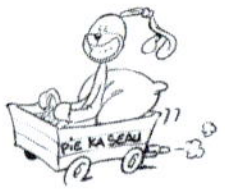

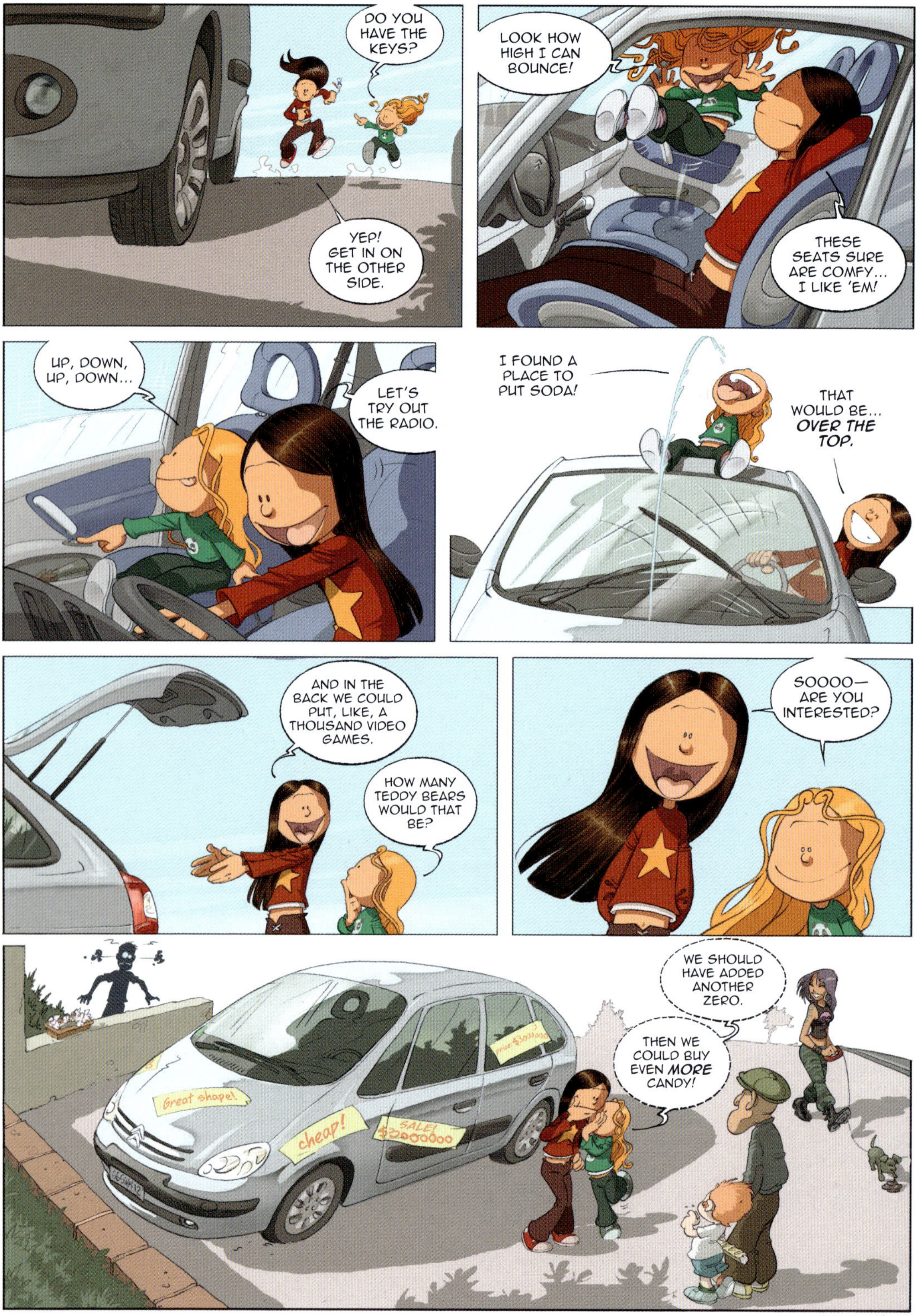
DO YOU HAVE THE KEYS?
YEP! GET IN ON THE OTHER SIDE.
LOOK HOW HIGH I CAN BOUNCE!
THESE SEATS SURE ARE COMFY... I LIKE 'EM!
UP, DOWN, UP, DOWN...
LET'S TRY OUT THE RADIO.
I FOUND A PLACE TO PUT SODA!
THAT WOULD BE... **OVER THE TOP.**
AND IN THE BACK WE COULD PUT, LIKE, A THOUSAND VIDEO GAMES.
HOW MANY TEDDY BEARS WOULD THAT BE?
SOOOO— ARE YOU INTERESTED?
Great shape!
cheap!
SALE!
WE SHOULD HAVE ADDED ANOTHER ZERO.
THEN WE COULD BUY EVEN **MORE** CANDY!

CAZENOVE/WILLIAM

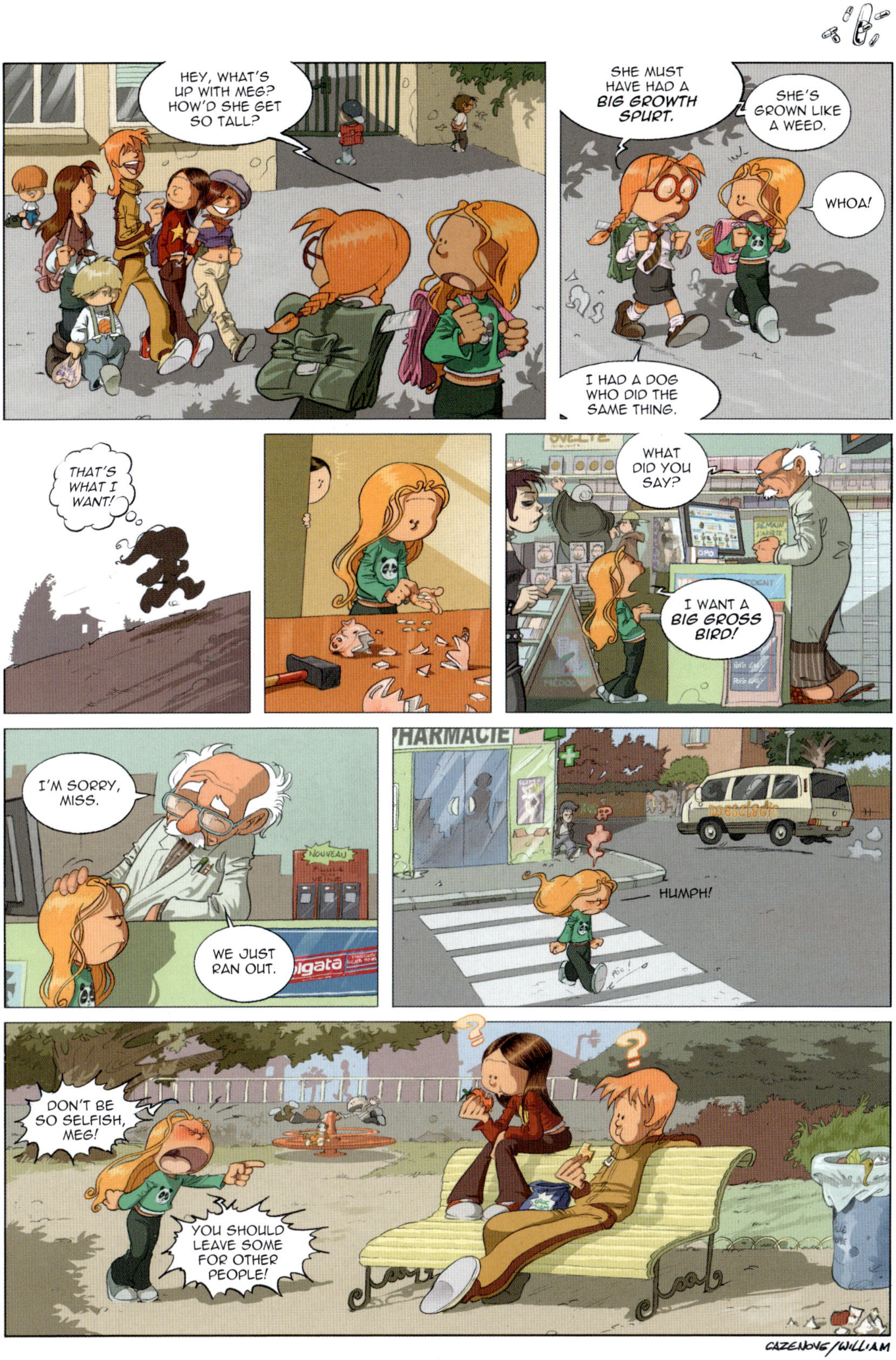
HEY, WHAT'S UP WITH MEG? HOW'D SHE GET SO TALL?
SHE MUST HAVE HAD A BIG GROWTH SPURT.
SHE'S GROWN LIKE A WEED.
WHOA!
I HAD A DOG WHO DID THE SAME THING.
THAT'S WHAT I WANT!
WHAT DID YOU SAY?
I WANT A BIG GROSS BIRD!
I'M SORRY, MISS.
WE JUST RAN OUT.
PHARMACIE
HUMPH!
DON'T BE SO SELFISH, MEG!
YOU SHOULD LEAVE SOME FOR OTHER PEOPLE!
CAZENOVE/WILLIAM

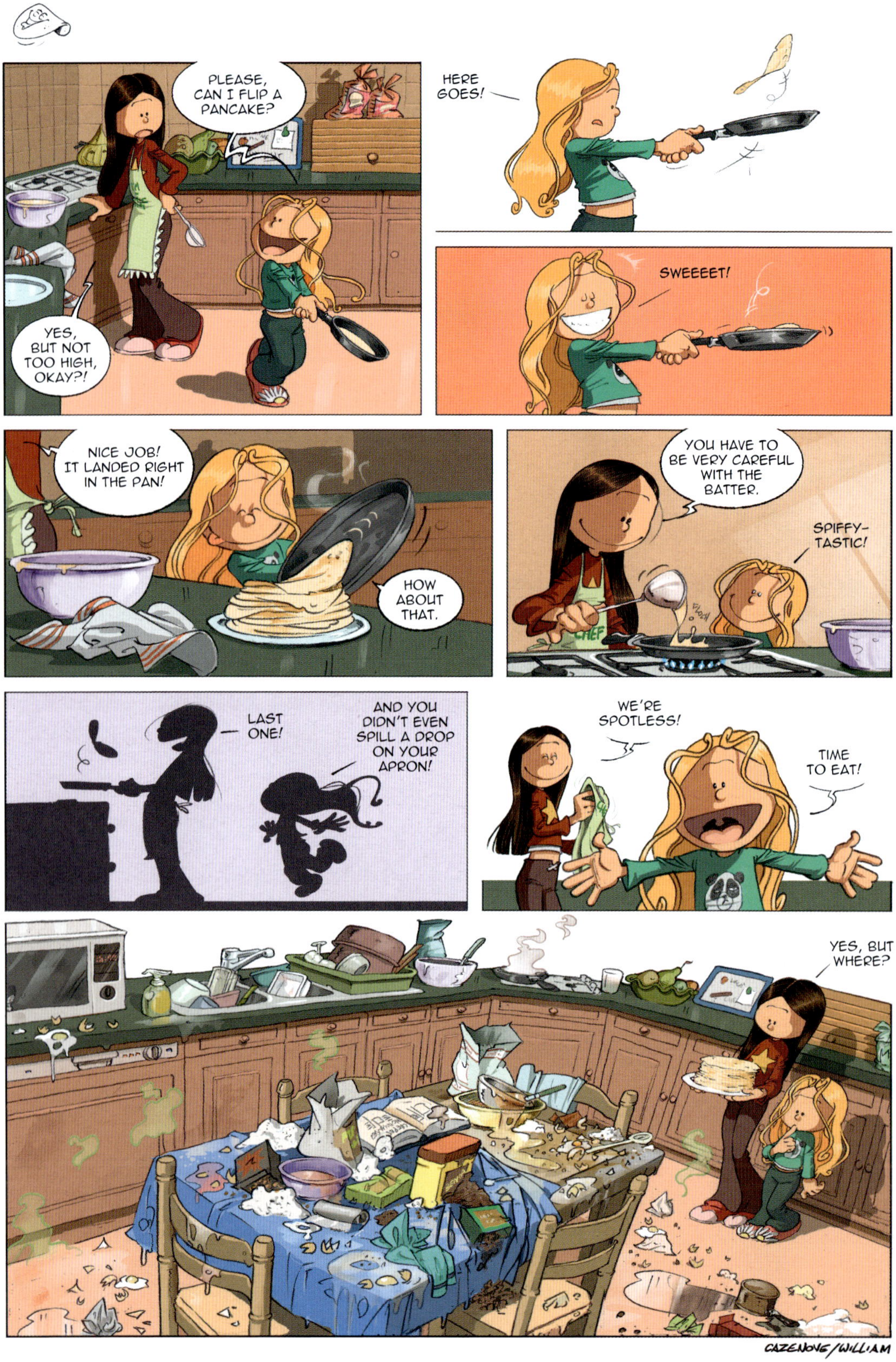
PLEASE, CAN I FLIP A PANCAKE?
YES, BUT NOT TOO HIGH, OKAY?!
HERE GOES!
SWEEEET!
NICE JOB! IT LANDED RIGHT IN THE PAN!
HOW ABOUT THAT.
YOU HAVE TO BE VERY CAREFUL WITH THE BATTER.
SPIFFY-TASTIC!
LAST ONE!
AND YOU DIDN'T EVEN SPILL A DROP ON YOUR APRON!
WE'RE SPOTLESS!
TIME TO EAT!
YES, BUT WHERE?
CAZENOVE/WILLIAM

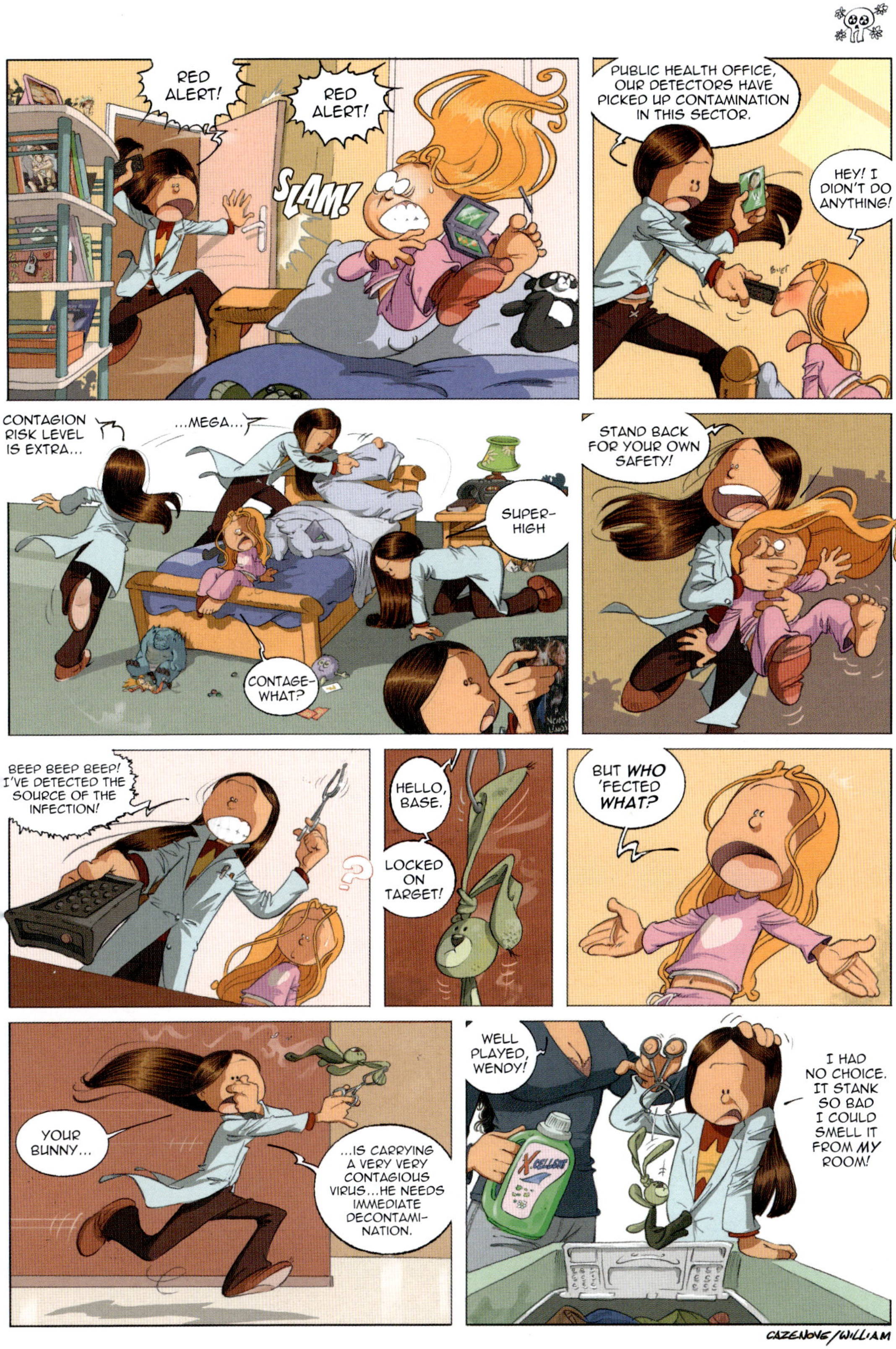

RED ALERT!
RED ALERT!
SLAM!
PUBLIC HEALTH OFFICE, OUR DETECTORS HAVE PICKED UP CONTAMINATION IN THIS SECTOR.
HEY! I DIDN'T DO ANYTHING!
CONTAGION RISK LEVEL IS EXTRA...
...MEGA...
SUPER-HIGH
CONTAGE-WHAT?
STAND BACK FOR YOUR OWN SAFETY!
BEEP BEEP BEEP! I'VE DETECTED THE SOURCE OF THE INFECTION!
HELLO, BASE.
LOCKED ON TARGET!
BUT WHO 'FECTED WHAT?
YOUR BUNNY...
...IS CARRYING A VERY VERY CONTAGIOUS VIRUS...HE NEEDS IMMEDIATE DECONTAMI-NATION.
WELL PLAYED, WENDY!
I HAD NO CHOICE. IT STANK SO BAD I COULD SMELL IT FROM MY ROOM!
CAZENOVE/WILLIAM

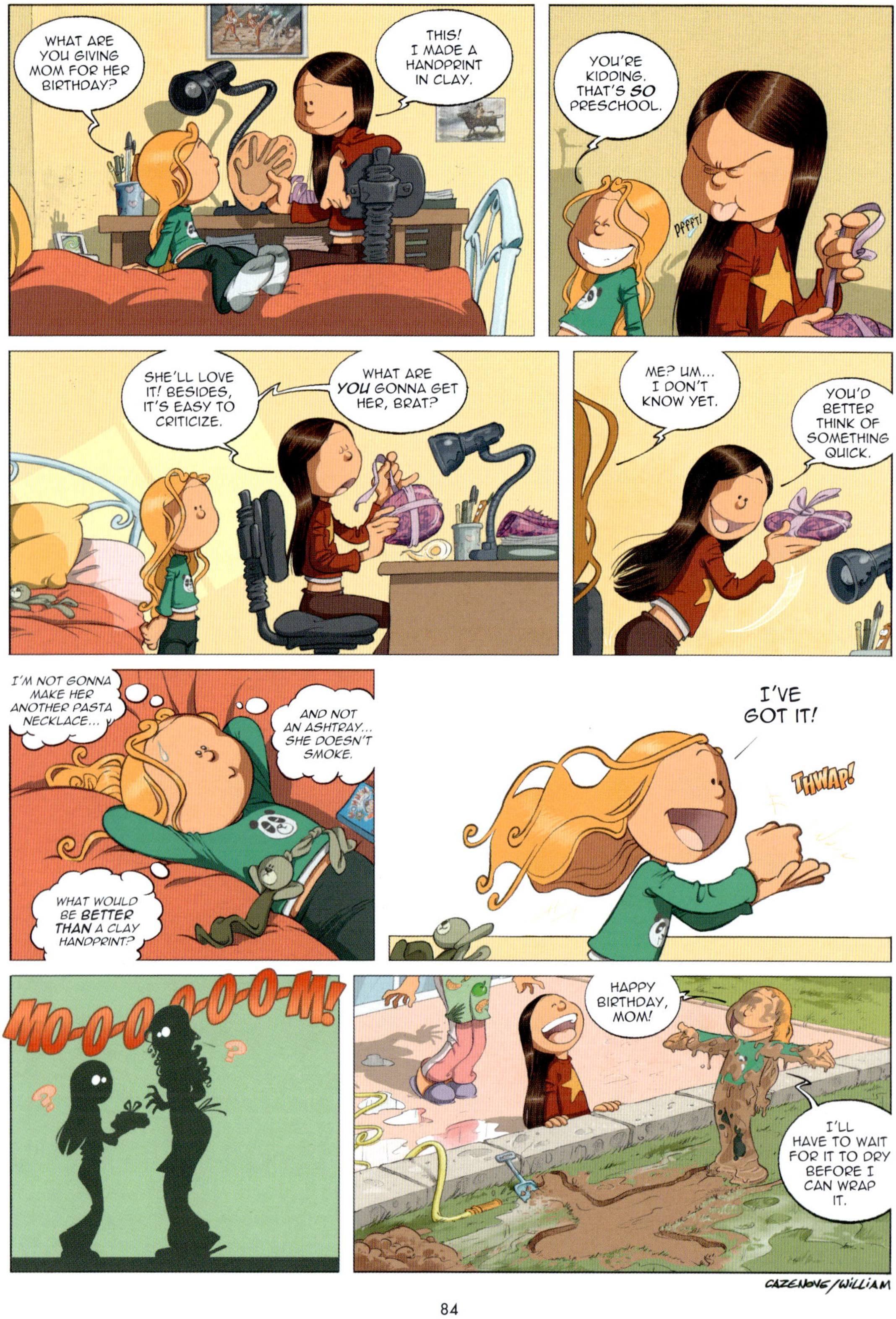
WHAT ARE YOU GIVING MOM FOR HER BIRTHDAY?
THIS! I MADE A HANDPRINT IN CLAY.
YOU'RE KIDDING. THAT'S SO PRESCHOOL.
PFFFT!
SHE'LL LOVE IT! BESIDES, IT'S EASY TO CRITICIZE.
WHAT ARE YOU GONNA GET HER, BRAT?
ME? UM... I DON'T KNOW YET.
YOU'D BETTER THINK OF SOMETHING QUICK.
I'M NOT GONNA MAKE HER ANOTHER PASTA NECKLACE...
AND NOT AN ASHTRAY... SHE DOESN'T SMOKE.
WHAT WOULD BE BETTER THAN A CLAY HANDPRINT?
I'VE GOT IT!
THWAP!
MO-O-O-O-O-O-M!
HAPPY BIRTHDAY, MOM!
I'LL HAVE TO WAIT FOR IT TO DRY BEFORE I CAN WRAP IT.

CAZENOVE/WILLIAM

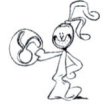

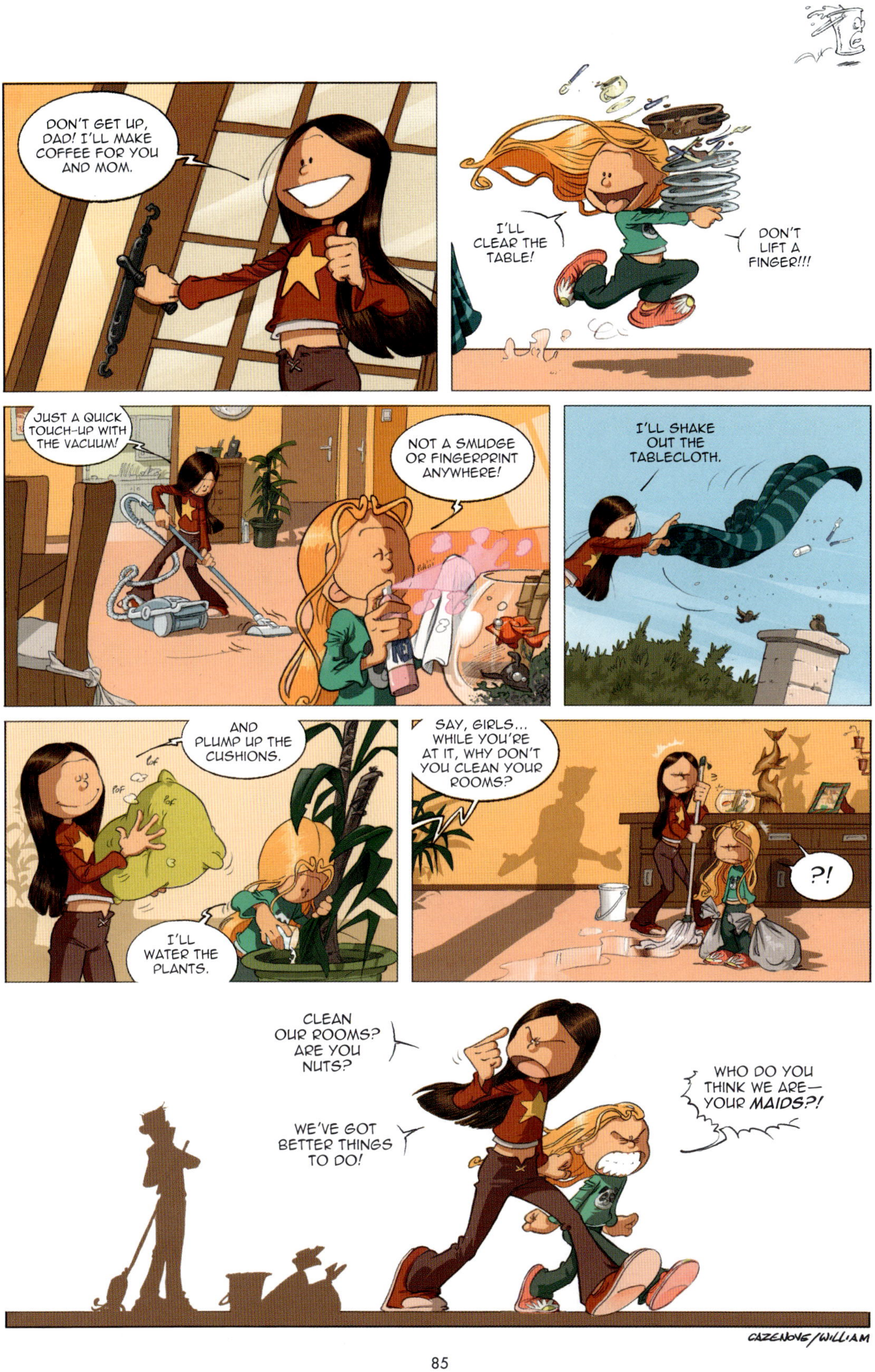
DON'T GET UP, DAD! I'LL MAKE COFFEE FOR YOU AND MOM.
I'LL CLEAR THE TABLE!
DON'T LIFT A FINGER!!!
JUST A QUICK TOUCH-UP WITH THE VACUUM!
NOT A SMUDGE OR FINGERPRINT ANYWHERE!
I'LL SHAKE OUT THE TABLECLOTH.
AND PLUMP UP THE CUSHIONS.
POF
POF
POF
I'LL WATER THE PLANTS.
SAY, GIRLS... WHILE YOU'RE AT IT, WHY DON'T YOU CLEAN YOUR ROOMS?
?!
CLEAN OUR ROOMS? ARE YOU NUTS?
WE'VE GOT BETTER THINGS TO DO!
WHO DO YOU THINK WE ARE— YOUR *MAIDS?!*
CAZENOVE/WILLIAM

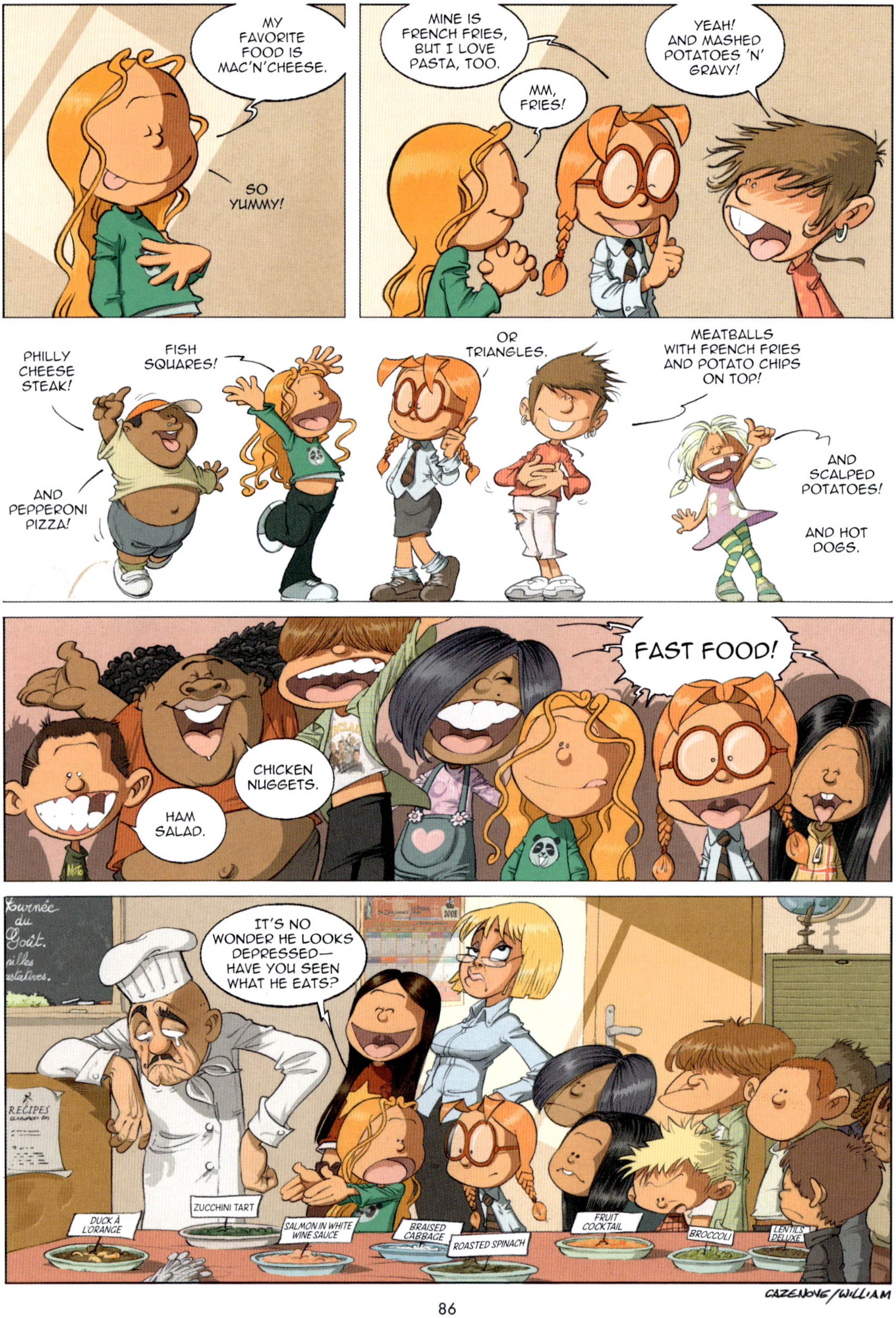

MY FAVORITE FOOD IS MAC'N'CHEESE.
SO YUMMY!
MINE IS FRENCH FRIES, BUT I LOVE PASTA, TOO.
MM, FRIES!
YEAH! AND MASHED POTATOES 'N' GRAVY!
PHILLY CHEESE STEAK!
AND PEPPERONI PIZZA!
FISH SQUARES!
OR TRIANGLES.
MEATBALLS WITH FRENCH FRIES AND POTATO CHIPS ON TOP!
AND SCALPED POTATOES!
AND HOT DOGS.
FAST FOOD!
CHICKEN NUGGETS.
HAM SALAD.
IT'S NO WONDER HE LOOKS DEPRESSED— HAVE YOU SEEN WHAT HE EATS?
RECIPES
DUCK À L'ORANGE
ZUCCHINI TART
SALMON IN WHITE WINE SAUCE
BRAISED CABBAGE
ROASTED SPINACH
FRUIT COCKTAIL
BROCCOLI
LENTILS DELUXE
CAZENOVE/WILLIAM

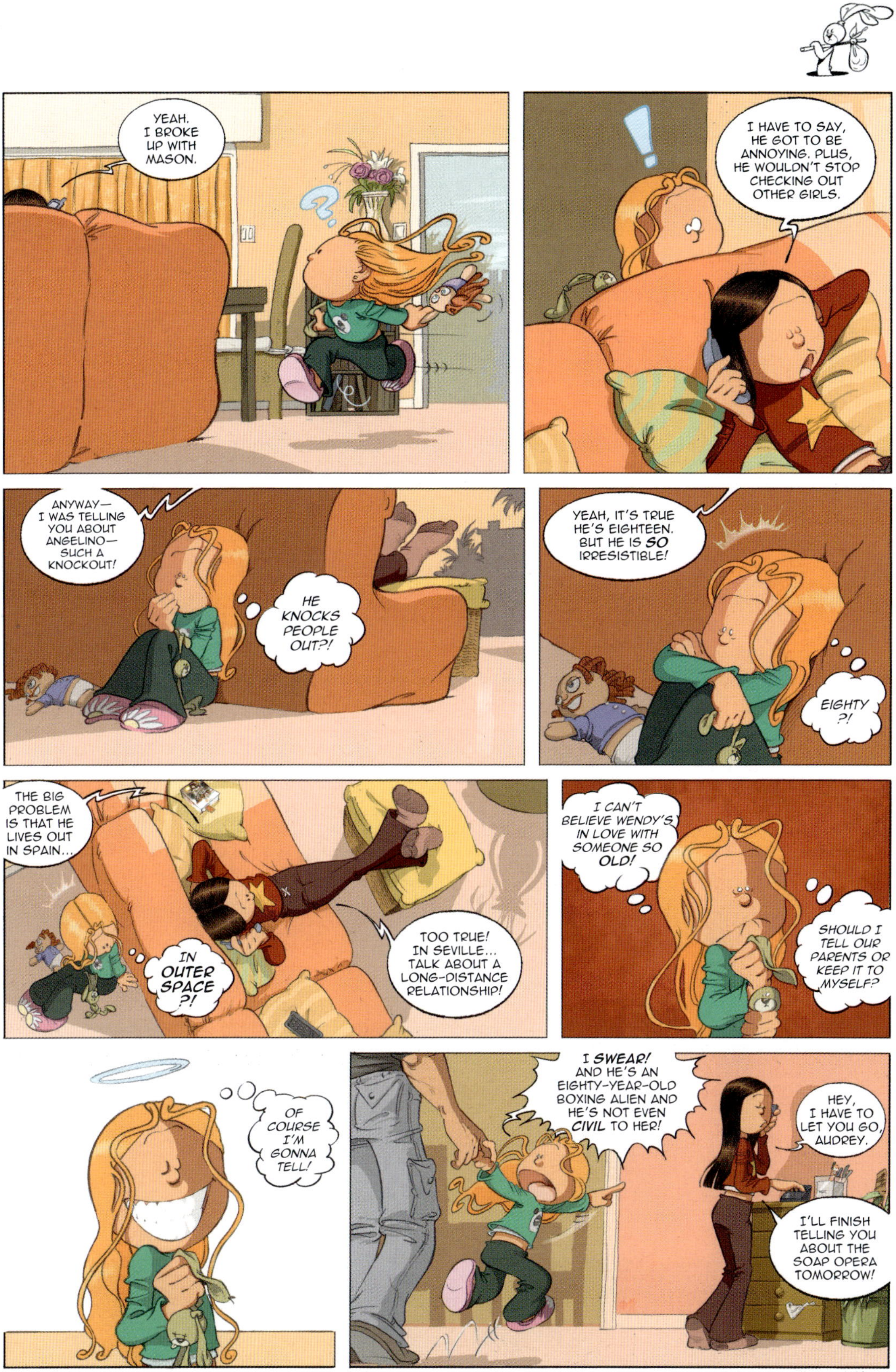
YEAH. I BROKE UP WITH MASON.
I HAVE TO SAY, HE GOT TO BE ANNOYING. PLUS, HE WOULDN'T STOP CHECKING OUT OTHER GIRLS.
ANYWAY— I WAS TELLING YOU ABOUT ANGELINO— SUCH A KNOCKOUT!
HE KNOCKS PEOPLE OUT?!
YEAH, IT'S TRUE HE'S EIGHTEEN. BUT HE IS SO IRRESISTIBLE!
EIGHTY ?!
THE BIG PROBLEM IS THAT HE LIVES OUT IN SPAIN...
IN OUTER SPACE ?!
TOO TRUE! IN SEVILLE... TALK ABOUT A LONG-DISTANCE RELATIONSHIP!
I CAN'T BELIEVE WENDY'S IN LOVE WITH SOMEONE SO OLD!
SHOULD I TELL OUR PARENTS OR KEEP IT TO MYSELF?
OF COURSE I'M GONNA TELL!
I SWEAR! AND HE'S AN EIGHTY-YEAR-OLD BOXING ALIEN AND HE'S NOT EVEN CIVIL TO HER!
HEY, I HAVE TO LET YOU GO, AUDREY.
I'LL FINISH TELLING YOU ABOUT THE SOAP OPERA TOMORROW!
CAZENOVE/WILLIAM

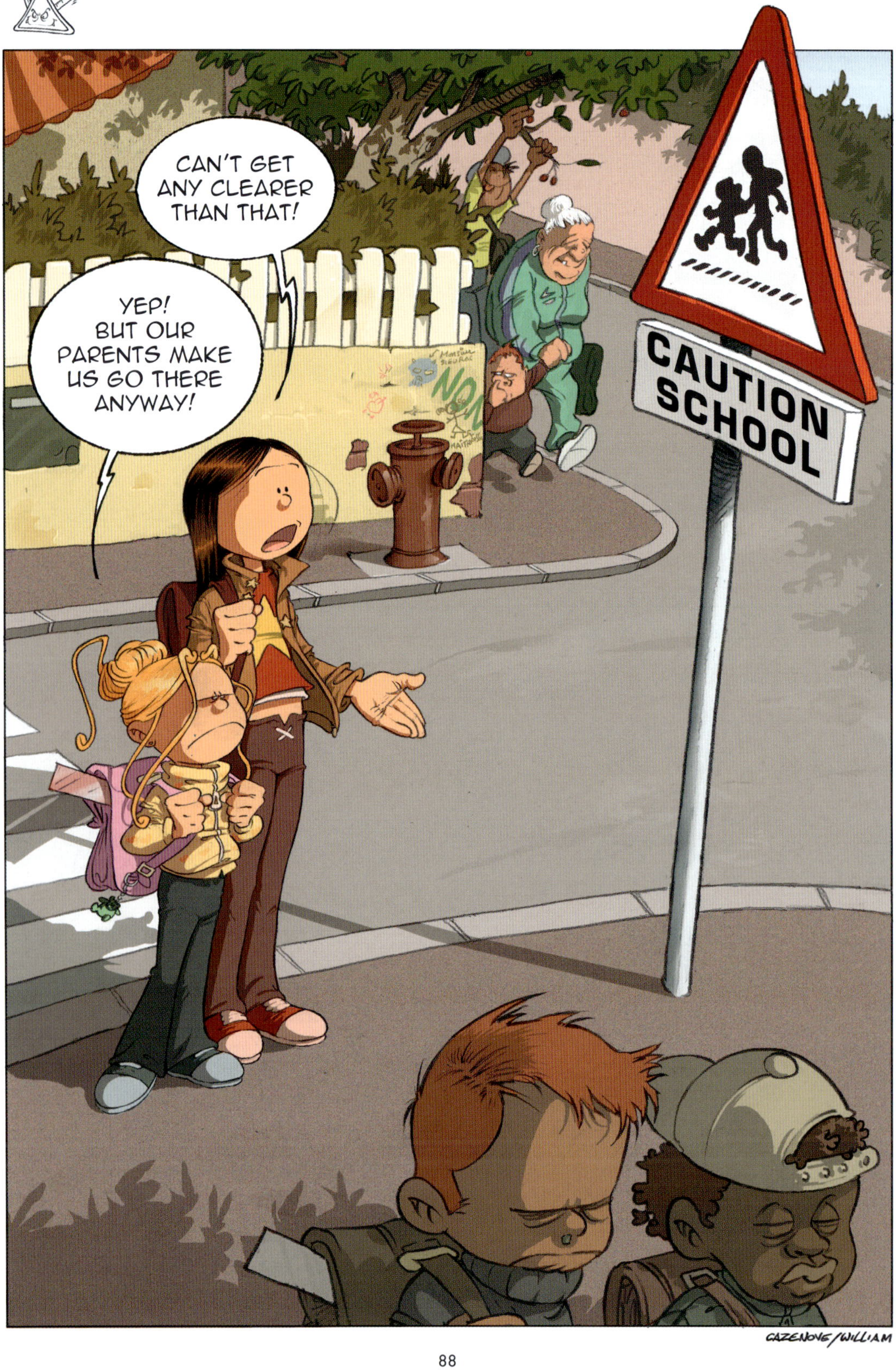
YEP! BUT OUR PARENTS MAKE US GO THERE ANYWAY!
CAN'T GET ANY CLEARER THAN THAT!
CAUTION SCHOOL
CAZENOVE/WILLIAM

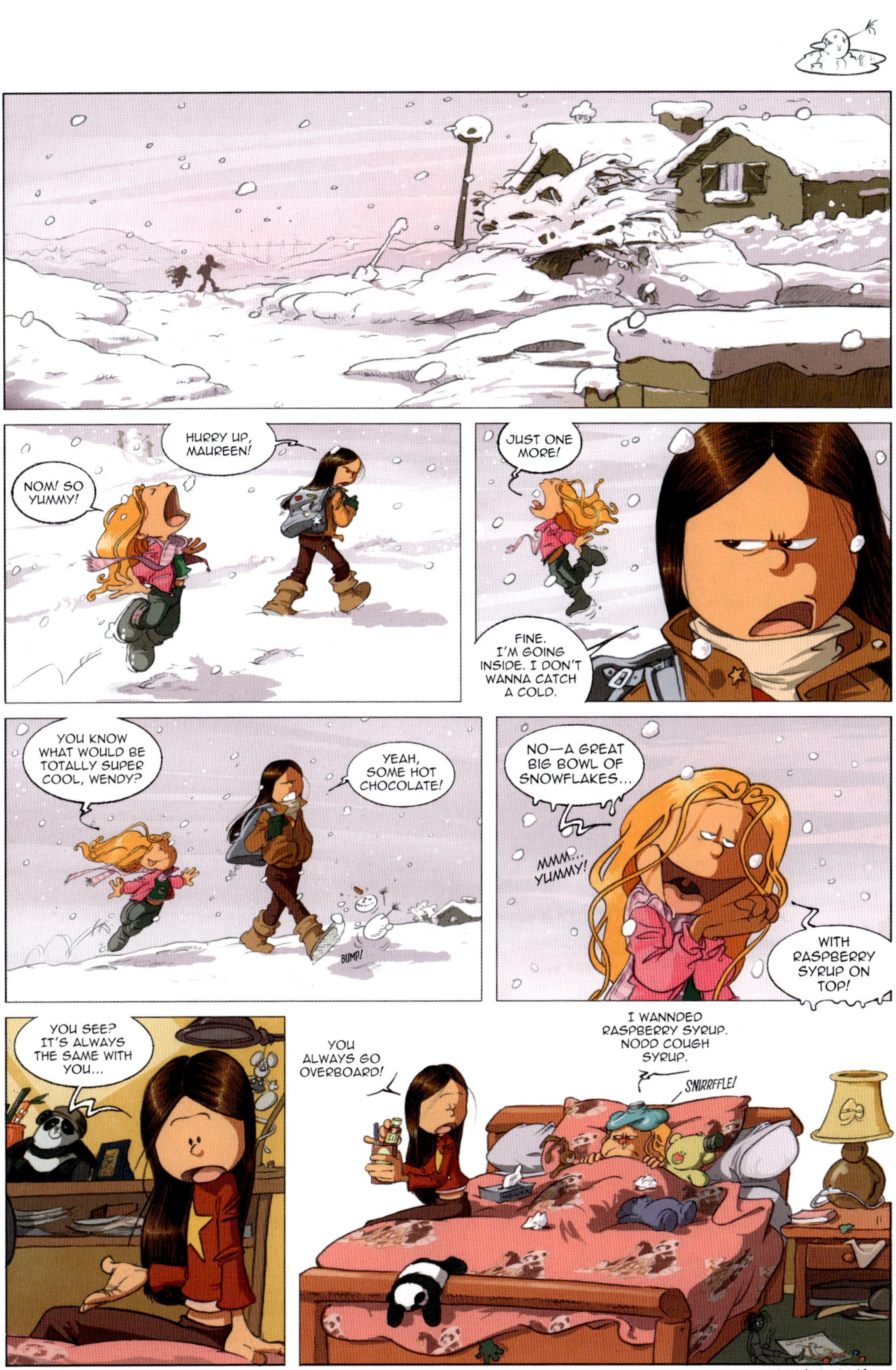
HURRY UP, MAUREEN!
NOM! SO YUMMY!
JUST ONE MORE!
FINE. I'M GOING INSIDE. I DON'T WANNA CATCH A COLD.
YOU KNOW WHAT WOULD BE TOTALLY SUPER COOL, WENDY?
YEAH, SOME HOT CHOCOLATE!
BUMP!
NO—A GREAT BIG BOWL OF SNOWFLAKES...
MMM... YUMMY!
WITH RASPBERRY SYRUP ON TOP!
YOU SEE? IT'S ALWAYS THE SAME WITH YOU...
YOU ALWAYS GO OVERBOARD!
I WANNDED RASPBERRY SYRUP. NODD COUGH SYRUP.
SNIRRFFLE!
CAZENOVE/WILLIAM

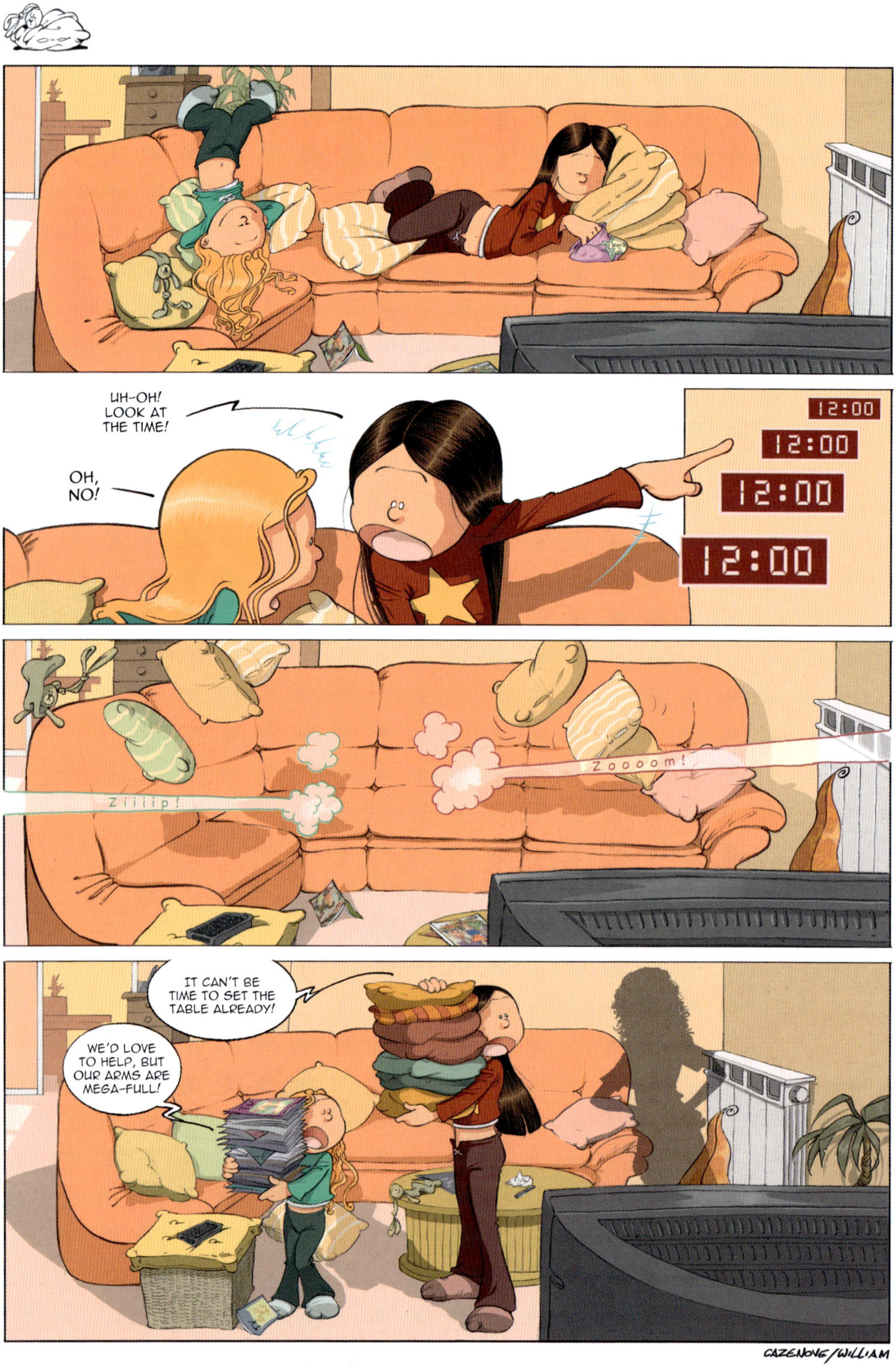
UH-OH! LOOK AT THE TIME!
OH, NO!
12:00
12:00
12:00
12:00
Ziiiip!
Zoooom!
IT CAN'T BE TIME TO SET THE TABLE ALREADY!
WE'D LOVE TO HELP, BUT OUR ARMS ARE MEGA-FULL!
CAZENOVE/WILLIAM

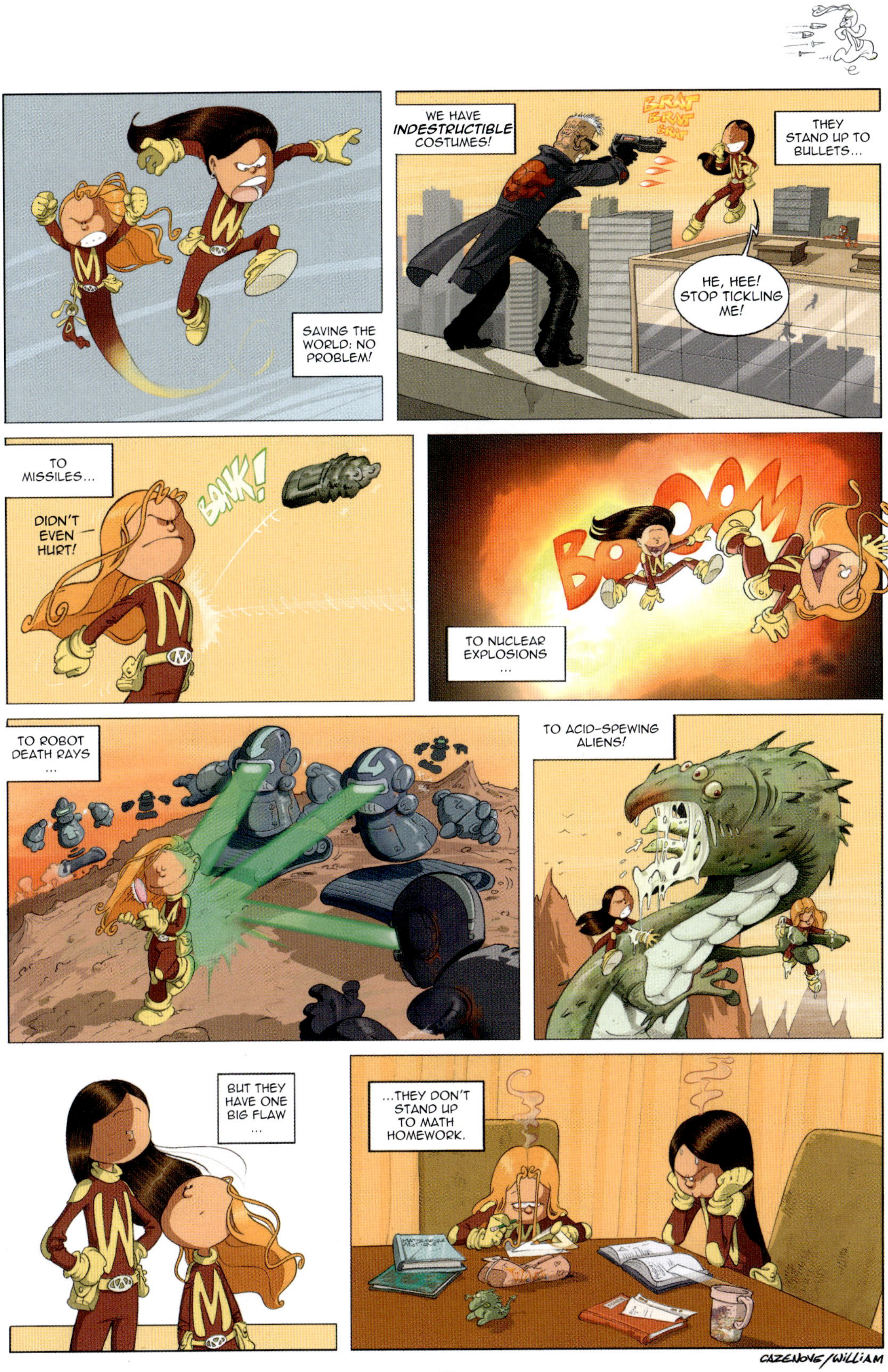

SAVING THE WORLD: NO PROBLEM!
WE HAVE INDESTRUCTIBLE COSTUMES!
BRAT BRAT BRAT
THEY STAND UP TO BULLETS...
HE, HEE! STOP TICKLING ME!
TO MISSILES...
DIDN'T EVEN HURT!
BONK!
BOOOM
TO NUCLEAR EXPLOSIONS ...
TO ROBOT DEATH RAYS ...
TO ACID-SPEWING ALIENS!
BUT THEY HAVE ONE BIG FLAW ...
...THEY DON'T STAND UP TO MATH HOMEWORK.
CAZENOVE/WILLIAM

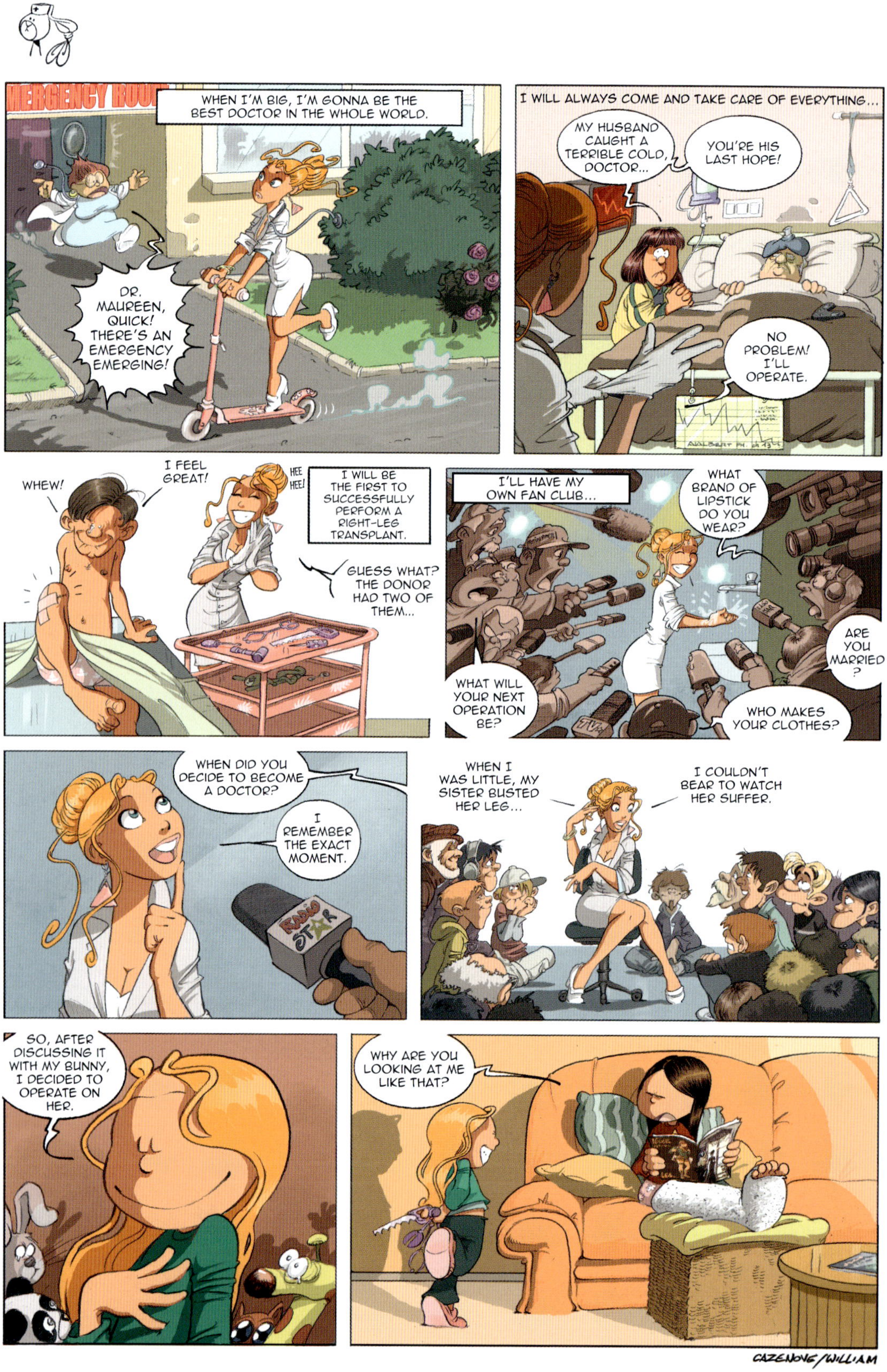
WHEN I'M BIG, I'M GONNA BE THE BEST DOCTOR IN THE WHOLE WORLD.
DR. MAUREEN, QUICK! THERE'S AN EMERGENCY EMERGING!
I WILL ALWAYS COME AND TAKE CARE OF EVERYTHING...
MY HUSBAND CAUGHT A TERRIBLE COLD, DOCTOR...
YOU'RE HIS LAST HOPE!
NO PROBLEM! I'LL OPERATE.
WHEW!
I FEEL GREAT!
HEE HEE!
I WILL BE THE FIRST TO SUCCESSFULLY PERFORM A RIGHT-LEG TRANSPLANT.
GUESS WHAT? THE DONOR HAD TWO OF THEM...
I'LL HAVE MY OWN FAN CLUB...
WHAT BRAND OF LIPSTICK DO YOU WEAR?
ARE YOU MARRIED?
WHAT WILL YOUR NEXT OPERATION BE?
WHO MAKES YOUR CLOTHES?
WHEN DID YOU DECIDE TO BECOME A DOCTOR?
I REMEMBER THE EXACT MOMENT.
RADIO STAR
WHEN I WAS LITTLE, MY SISTER BUSTED HER LEG...
I COULDN'T BEAR TO WATCH HER SUFFER.
SO, AFTER DISCUSSING IT WITH MY BUNNY, I DECIDED TO OPERATE ON HER.
WHY ARE YOU LOOKING AT ME LIKE THAT?
CAZENOVE/WILLIAM

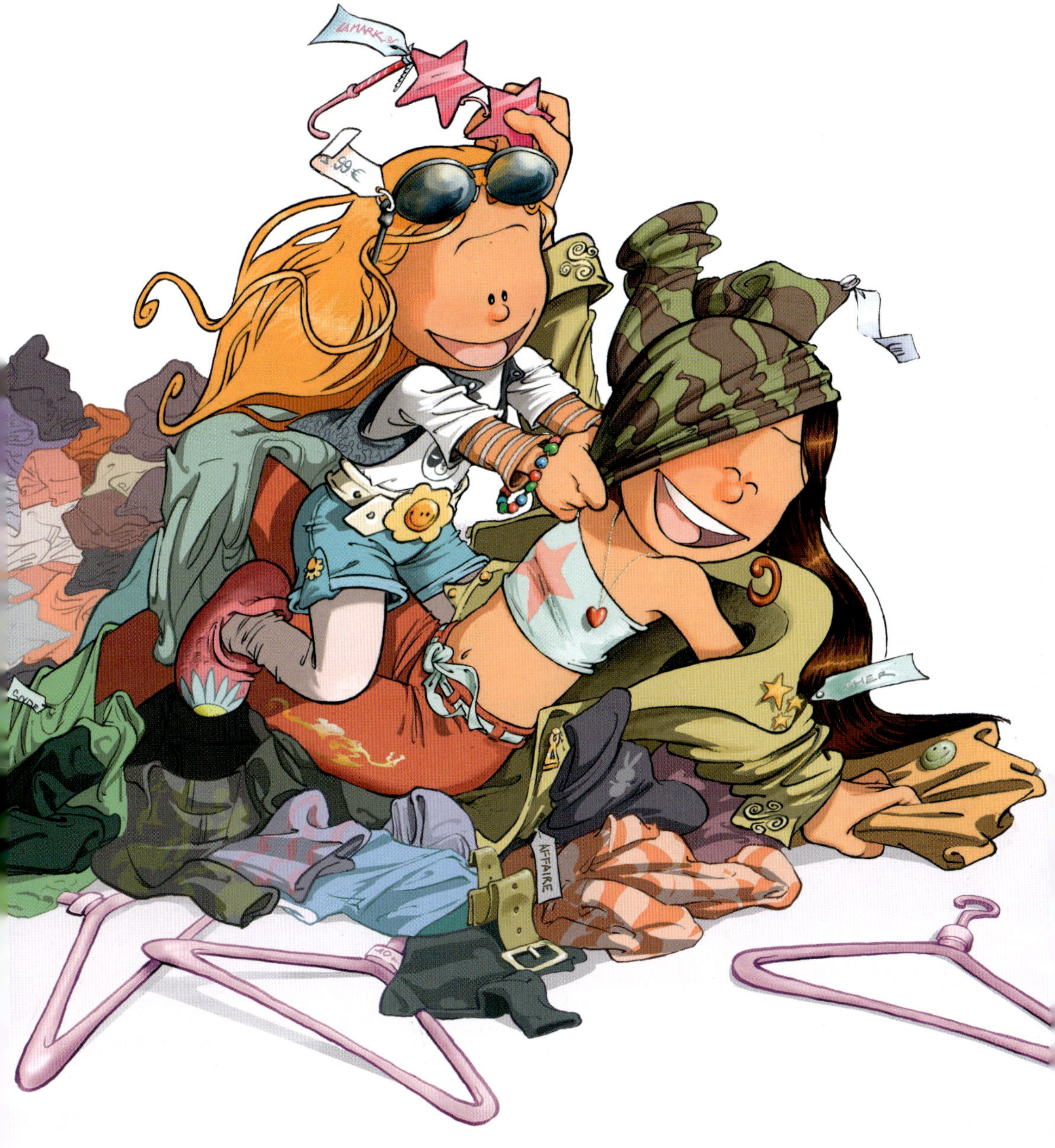
AFFAIRE
CHER

"Doing It Our Way"

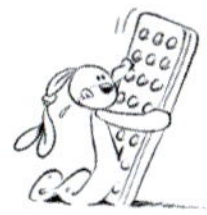
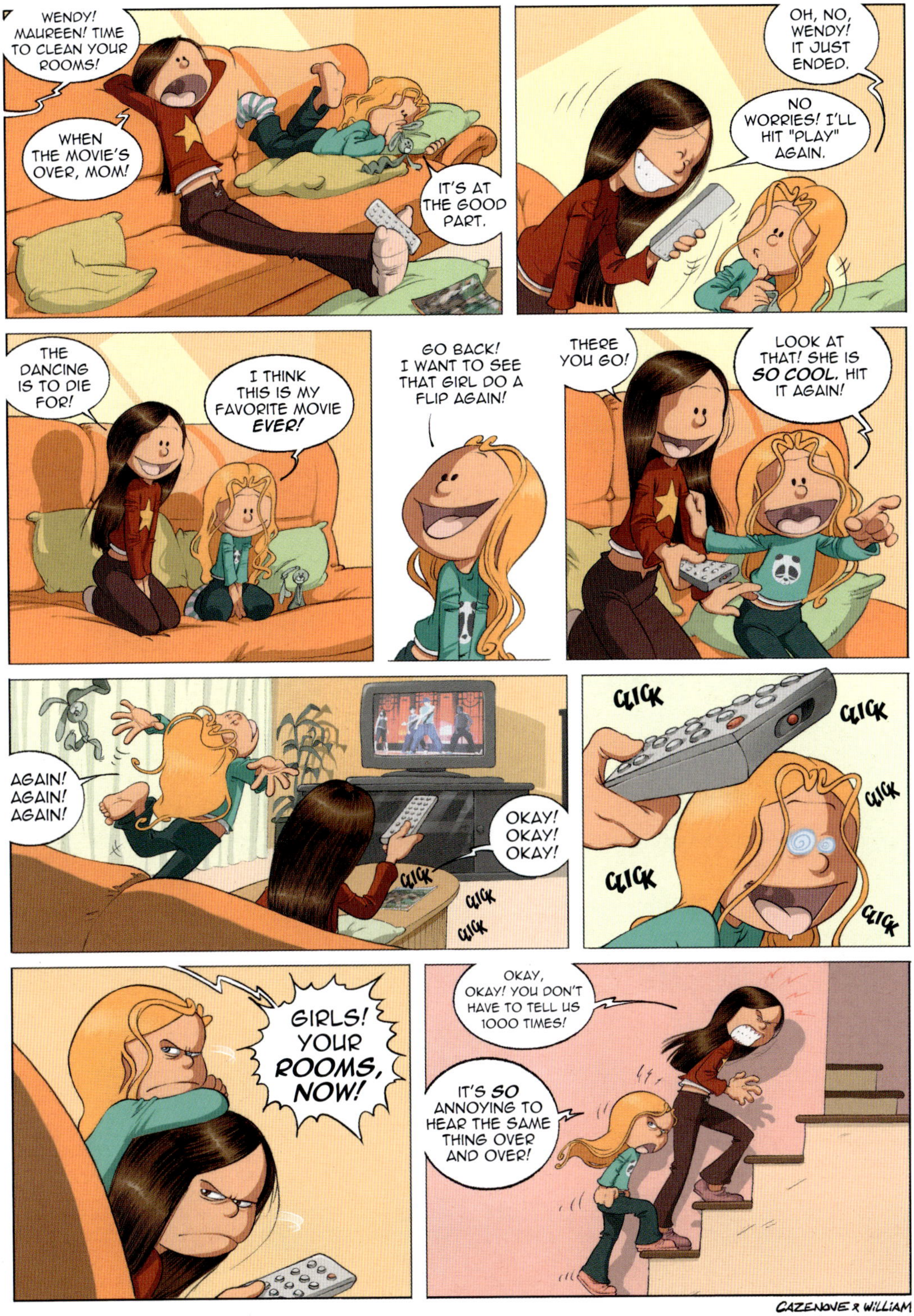
WENDY! MAUREEN! TIME TO CLEAN YOUR ROOMS!
WHEN THE MOVIE'S OVER, MOM!
IT'S AT THE GOOD PART.
OH, NO, WENDY! IT JUST ENDED.
NO WORRIES! I'LL HIT "PLAY" AGAIN.
THE DANCING IS TO DIE FOR!
I THINK THIS IS MY FAVORITE MOVIE **EVER!**
GO BACK! I WANT TO SEE THAT GIRL DO A FLIP AGAIN!
THERE YOU GO!
LOOK AT THAT! SHE IS **SO COOL.** HIT IT AGAIN!
AGAIN! AGAIN! AGAIN!
OKAY! OKAY! OKAY!
CLICK
CLICK
CLICK
CLICK
CLICK
CLICK
CLICK
CLICK
CLICK
GIRLS! YOUR **ROOMS, NOW!**
OKAY, OKAY! YOU DON'T HAVE TO TELL US 1000 TIMES!
IT'S **SO** ANNOYING TO HEAR THE SAME THING OVER AND OVER!
CAZENOVE & WILLIAM

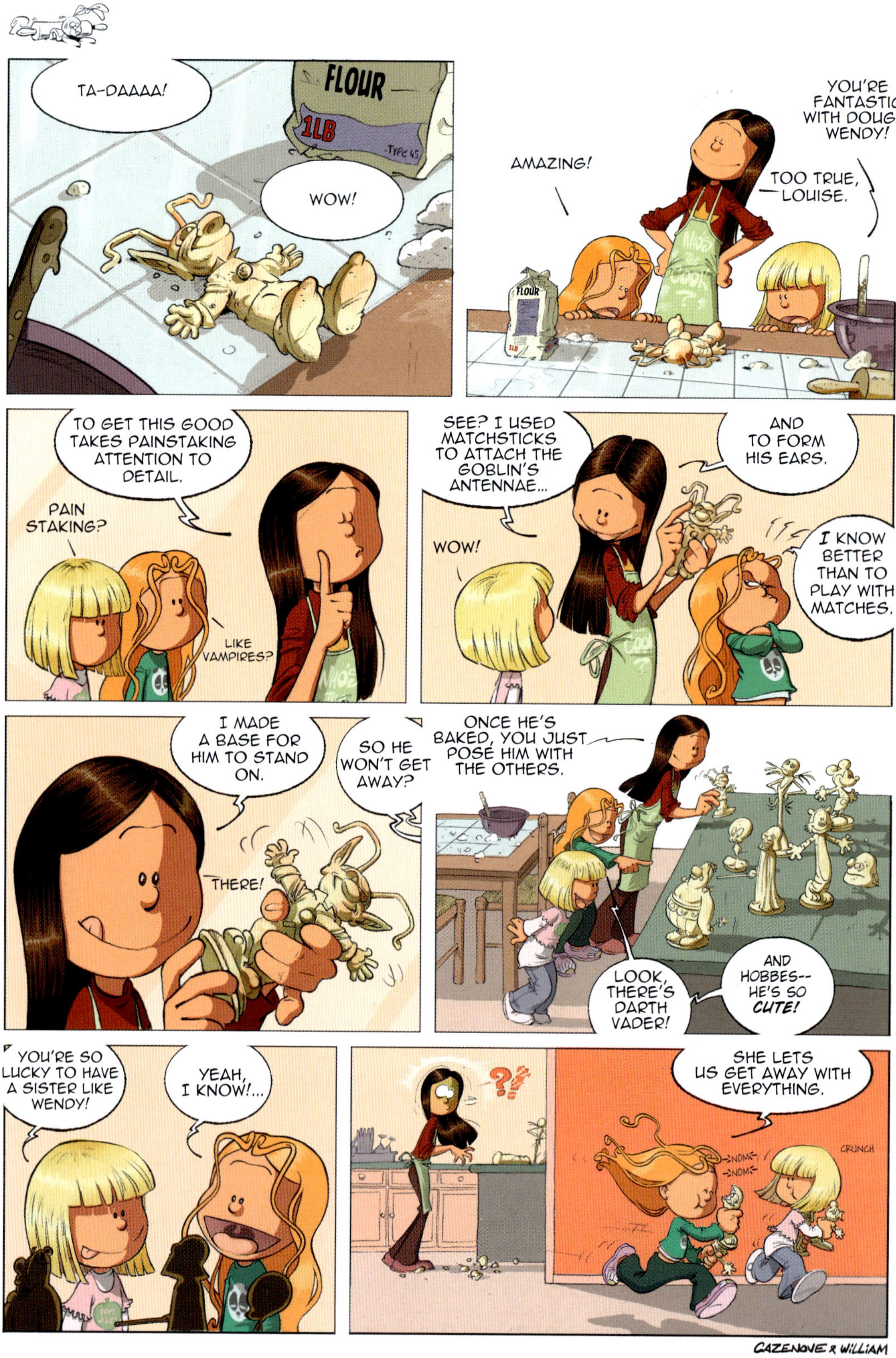
TA-DAAAA!
FLOUR
1LB
WOW!
AMAZING!
YOU'RE FANTASTIC WITH DOUGH WENDY!
TOO TRUE, LOUISE.
TO GET THIS GOOD TAKES PAINSTAKING ATTENTION TO DETAIL.
PAIN STAKING?
LIKE VAMPIRES?
SEE? I USED MATCHSTICKS TO ATTACH THE GOBLIN'S ANTENNAE...
AND TO FORM HIS EARS.
WOW!
I KNOW BETTER THAN TO PLAY WITH MATCHES.
I MADE A BASE FOR HIM TO STAND ON.
SO HE WON'T GET AWAY?
THERE!
ONCE HE'S BAKED, YOU JUST POSE HIM WITH THE OTHERS.
LOOK, THERE'S DARTH VADER!
AND HOBBES-- HE'S SO *CUTE!*
YOU'RE SO LUCKY TO HAVE A SISTER LIKE WENDY!
YEAH, I KNOW!...
?!
SHE LETS US GET AWAY WITH EVERYTHING.
NOM
NOM
CRUNCH

CAZENOVE & WILLIAM

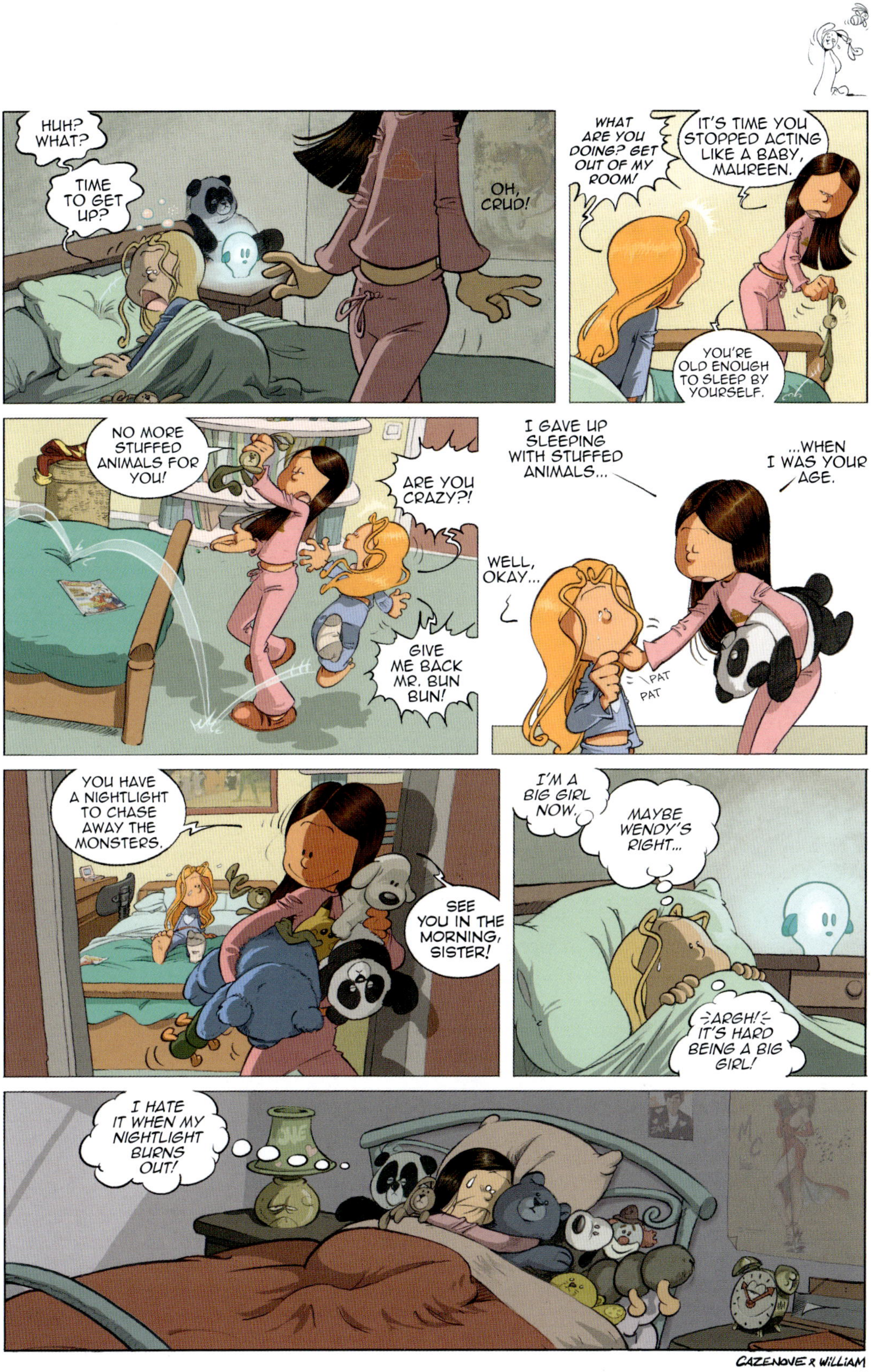
HUH? WHAT?
TIME TO GET UP?
OH, CRUD!
WHAT ARE YOU DOING? GET OUT OF MY ROOM!
IT'S TIME YOU STOPPED ACTING LIKE A BABY, MAUREEN.
YOU'RE OLD ENOUGH TO SLEEP BY YOURSELF.
NO MORE STUFFED ANIMALS FOR YOU!
ARE YOU CRAZY?!
GIVE ME BACK MR. BUN BUN!
I GAVE UP SLEEPING WITH STUFFED ANIMALS...
...WHEN I WAS YOUR AGE.
WELL, OKAY...
PAT
PAT
YOU HAVE A NIGHTLIGHT TO CHASE AWAY THE MONSTERS.
SEE YOU IN THE MORNING, SISTER!
I'M A BIG GIRL NOW.
MAYBE WENDY'S RIGHT...
ARGH! IT'S HARD BEING A BIG GIRL!
I HATE IT WHEN MY NIGHTLIGHT BURNS OUT!
CAZENOVE & WILLIAM

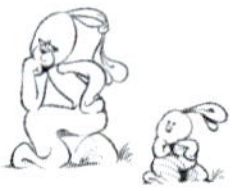

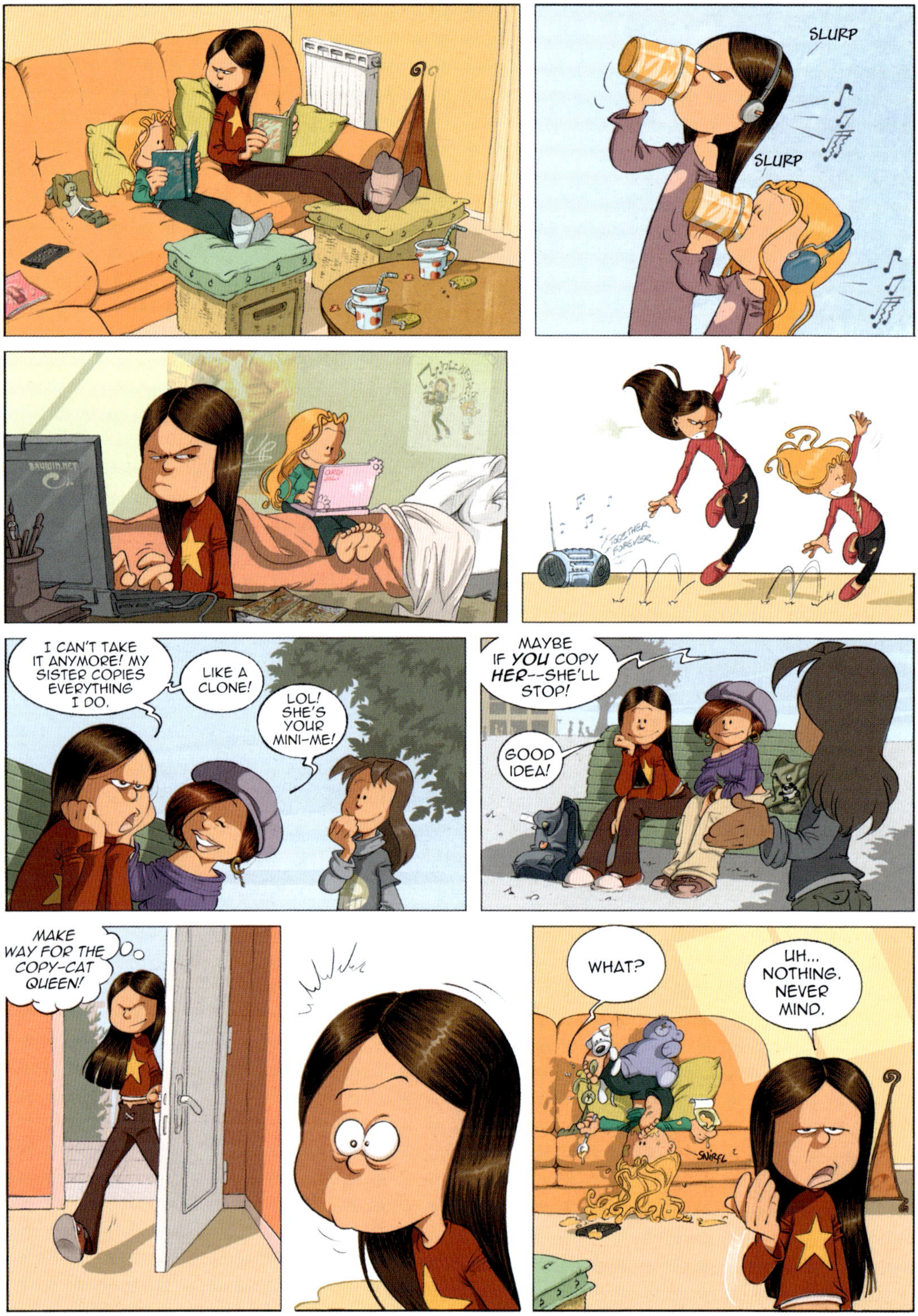
SLURP
SLURP
BAYWIN.NET
TOGETHER FOREVER...
I CAN'T TAKE IT ANYMORE! MY SISTER COPIES EVERYTHING I DO.
LIKE A CLONE!
LOL! SHE'S YOUR MINI-ME!
MAYBE IF ***YOU*** COPY ***HER***--SHE'LL STOP!
GOOD IDEA!
MAKE WAY FOR THE COPY-CAT QUEEN!
WHAT?
UH... NOTHING. NEVER MIND.
SNIRFL

CAZENOVE & WILLIAM

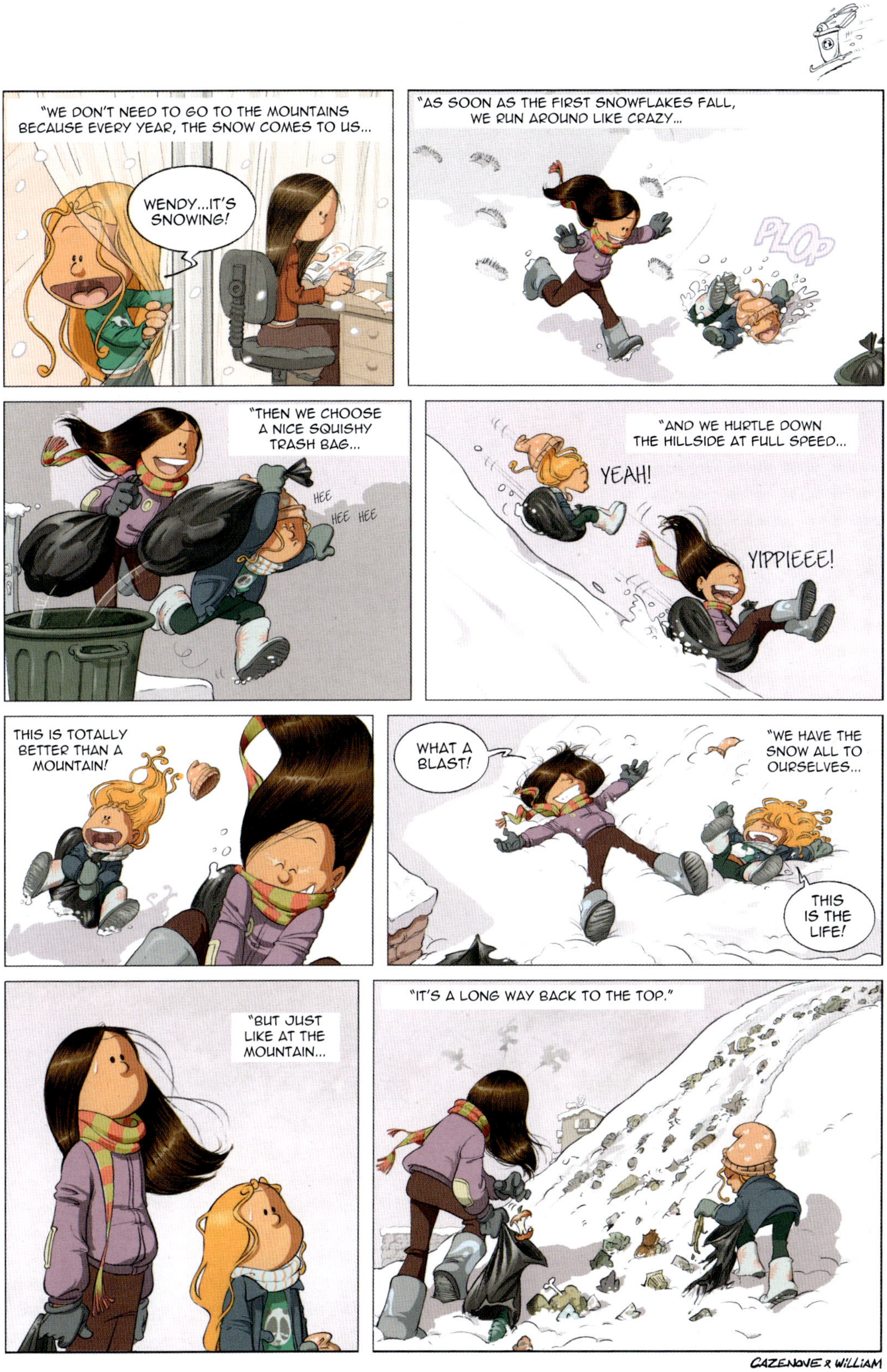
"WE DON'T NEED TO GO TO THE MOUNTAINS BECAUSE EVERY YEAR, THE SNOW COMES TO US...
WENDY...IT'S SNOWING!
"AS SOON AS THE FIRST SNOWFLAKES FALL, WE RUN AROUND LIKE CRAZY...
PLOP
"THEN WE CHOOSE A NICE SQUISHY TRASH BAG...
HEE
HEE HEE
"AND WE HURTLE DOWN THE HILLSIDE AT FULL SPEED...
YEAH!
YIPPIEEE!
THIS IS TOTALLY BETTER THAN A MOUNTAIN!
WHAT A BLAST!
"WE HAVE THE SNOW ALL TO OURSELVES...
THIS IS THE LIFE!
"BUT JUST LIKE AT THE MOUNTAIN...
"IT'S A LONG WAY BACK TO THE TOP."
CAZENOVE & WILLIAM

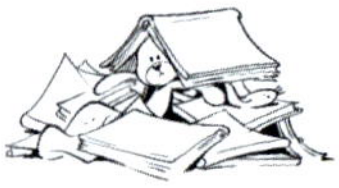

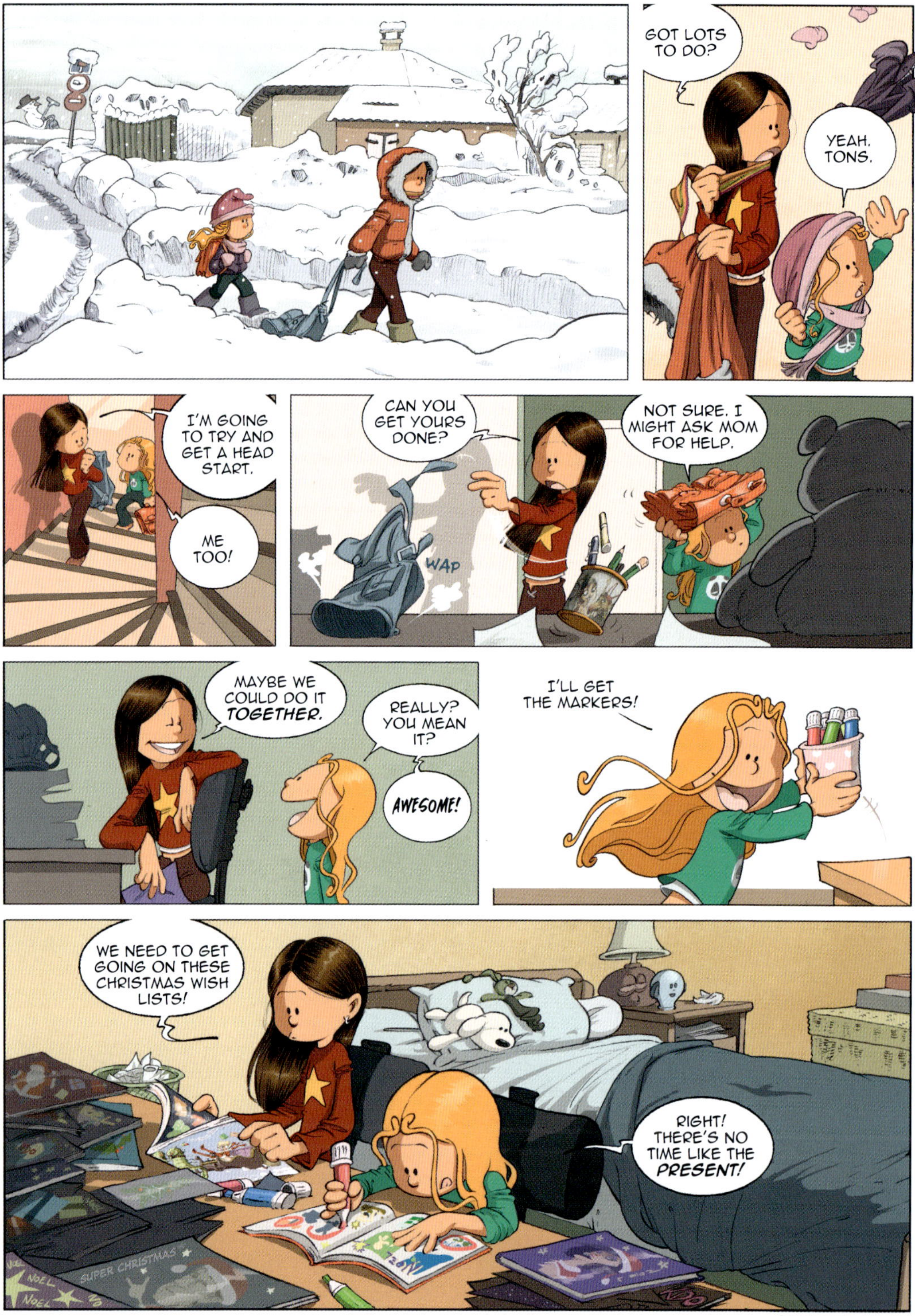
GOT LOTS TO DO?
YEAH. TONS.
I'M GOING TO TRY AND GET A HEAD START.
ME TOO!
CAN YOU GET YOURS DONE?
WAP
NOT SURE. I MIGHT ASK MOM FOR HELP.
MAYBE WE COULD DO IT *TOGETHER.*
REALLY? YOU MEAN IT?
AWESOME!
I'LL GET THE MARKERS!
WE NEED TO GET GOING ON THESE CHRISTMAS WISH LISTS!
RIGHT! THERE'S NO TIME LIKE THE *PRESENT!*
SUPER CHRISTMAS
NOEL

CAZENOVE & WILLIAM

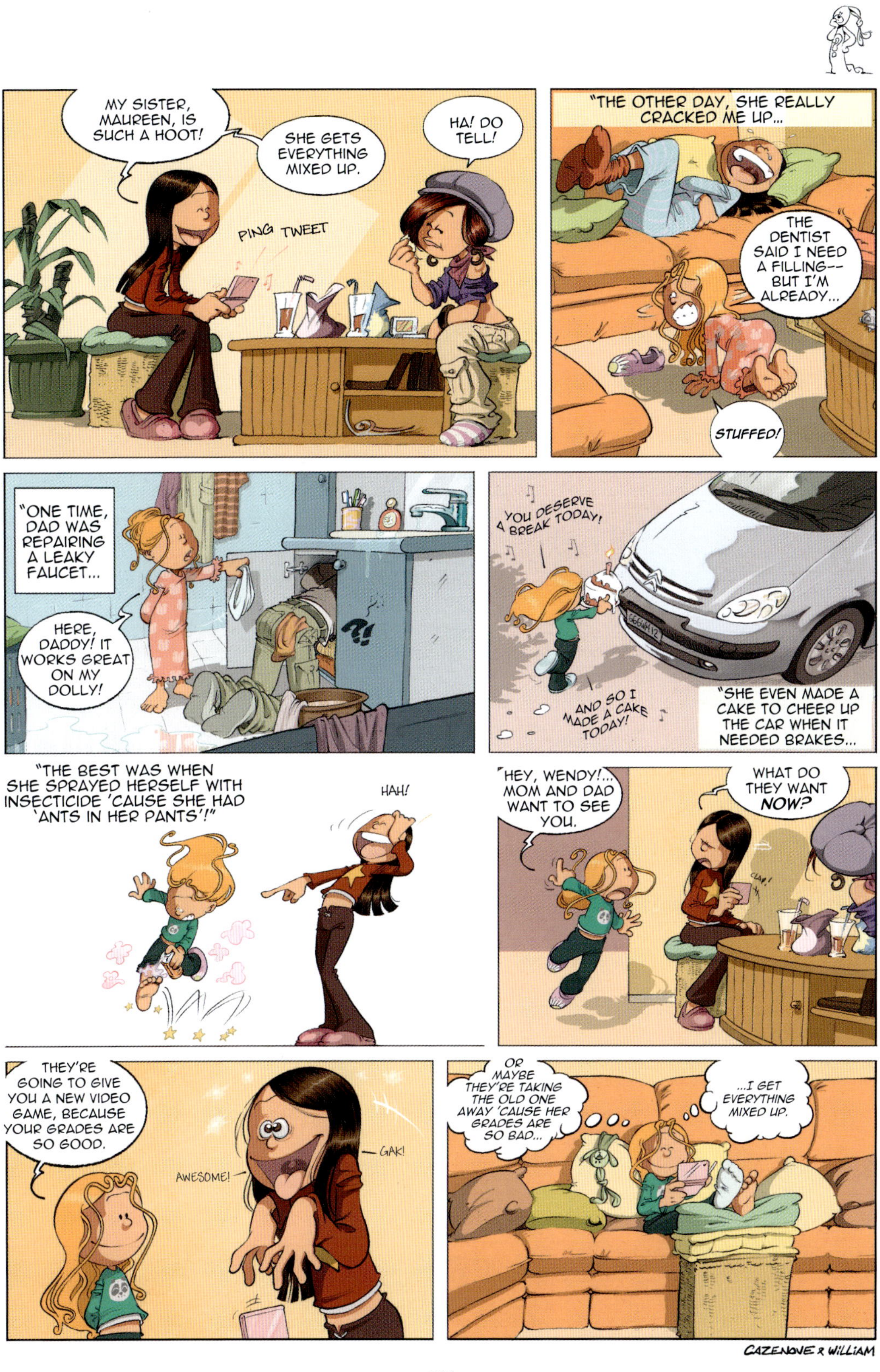
MY SISTER, MAUREEN, IS SUCH A HOOT!
SHE GETS EVERYTHING MIXED UP.
HA! DO TELL!
PING TWEET
"THE OTHER DAY, SHE REALLY CRACKED ME UP...
THE DENTIST SAID I NEED A FILLING-- BUT I'M ALREADY...
STUFFED!
"ONE TIME, DAD WAS REPAIRING A LEAKY FAUCET...
HERE, DADDY! IT WORKS GREAT ON MY DOLLY!
?!
YOU DESERVE A BREAK TODAY!
AND SO I MADE A CAKE TODAY!
"SHE EVEN MADE A CAKE TO CHEER UP THE CAR WHEN IT NEEDED BRAKES...
"THE BEST WAS WHEN SHE SPRAYED HERSELF WITH INSECTICIDE 'CAUSE SHE HAD 'ANTS IN HER PANTS'!"
HAH!
"HEY, WENDY!... MOM AND DAD WANT TO SEE YOU.
WHAT DO THEY WANT NOW?
THEY'RE GOING TO GIVE YOU A NEW VIDEO GAME, BECAUSE YOUR GRADES ARE SO GOOD.
AWESOME!
GAK!
OR MAYBE THEY'RE TAKING THE OLD ONE AWAY 'CAUSE HER GRADES ARE SO BAD...
...I GET EVERYTHING MIXED UP.
CAZENOVE & WILLIAM

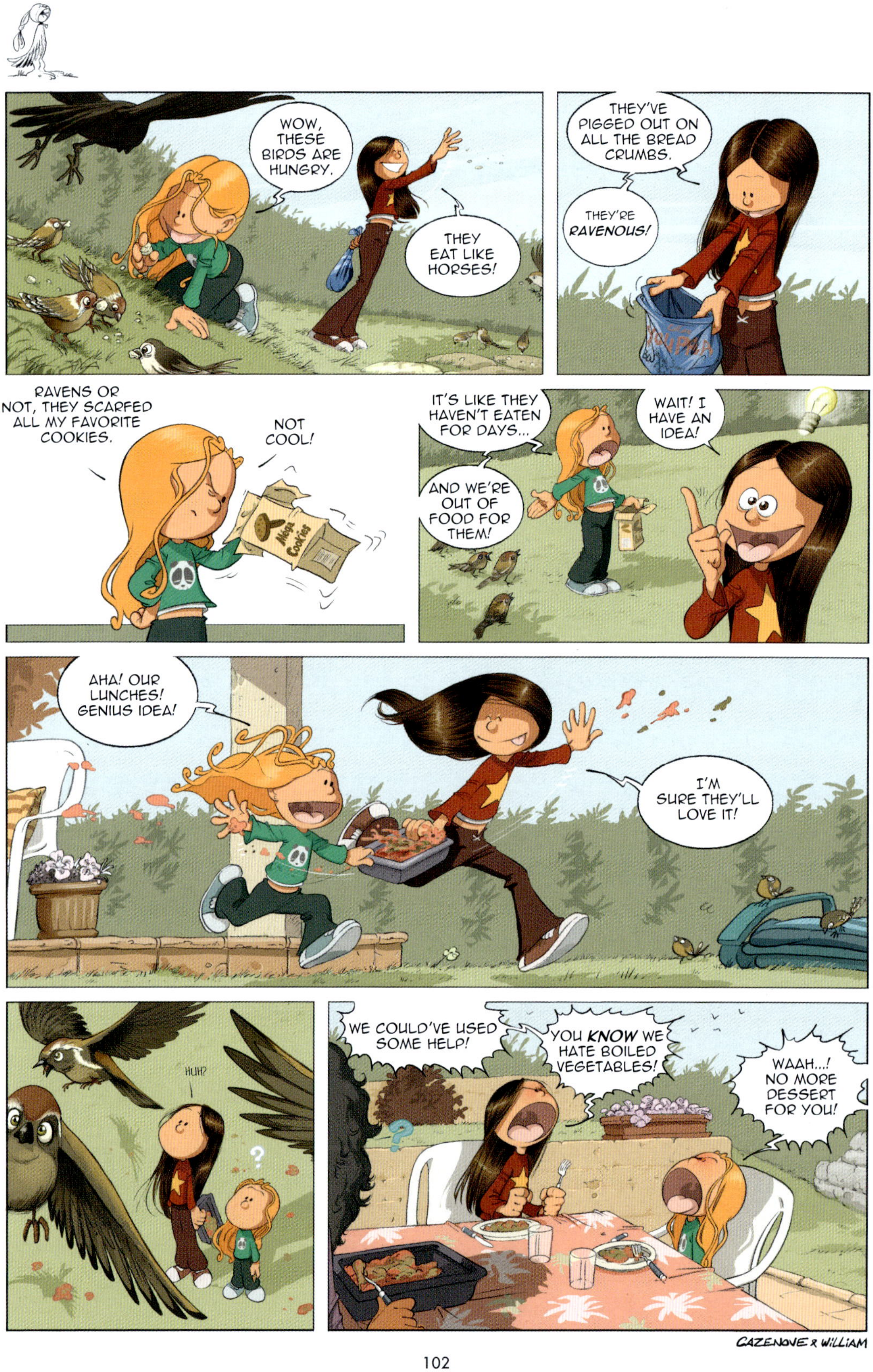
WOW, THESE BIRDS ARE HUNGRY.
THEY EAT LIKE HORSES!
THEY'VE PIGGED OUT ON ALL THE BREAD CRUMBS.
THEY'RE *RAVENOUS!*
RAVENS OR NOT, THEY SCARFED ALL MY FAVORITE COOKIES.
NOT COOL!
Méga Cookies
IT'S LIKE THEY HAVEN'T EATEN FOR DAYS...
AND WE'RE OUT OF FOOD FOR THEM!
WAIT! I HAVE AN IDEA!
AHA! OUR LUNCHES! GENIUS IDEA!
I'M SURE THEY'LL LOVE IT!
HUH?
WE COULD'VE USED SOME HELP!
YOU **KNOW** WE HATE BOILED VEGETABLES!
WAAH...! NO MORE DESSERT FOR YOU!
CAZENOVE & WILLIAM

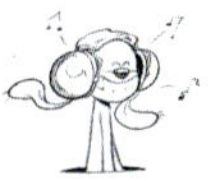

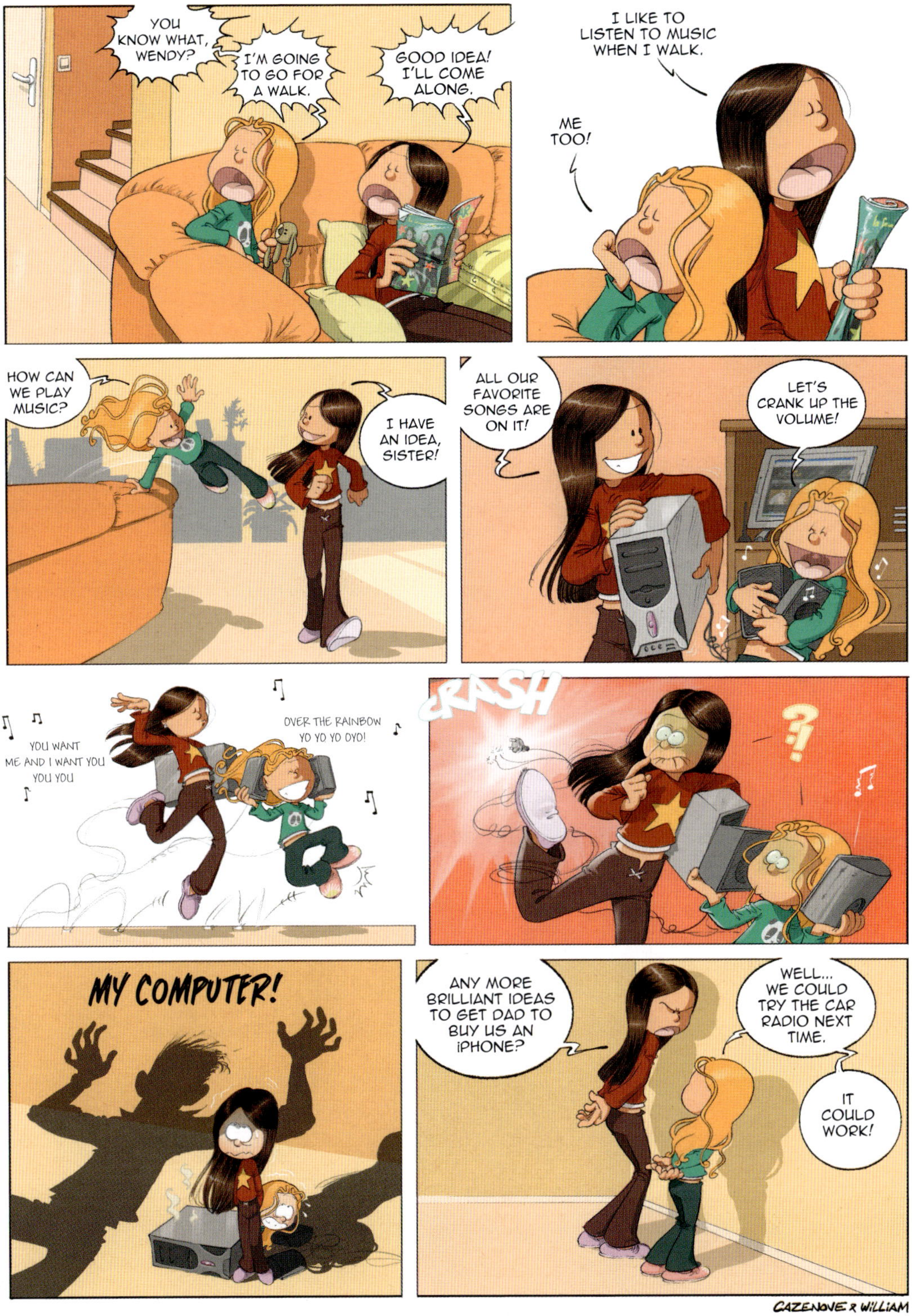

YOU KNOW WHAT, WENDY?
I'M GOING TO GO FOR A WALK.
GOOD IDEA! I'LL COME ALONG.
I LIKE TO LISTEN TO MUSIC WHEN I WALK.
ME TOO!
HOW CAN WE PLAY MUSIC?
I HAVE AN IDEA, SISTER!
ALL OUR FAVORITE SONGS ARE ON IT!
LET'S CRANK UP THE VOLUME!
YOU WANT ME AND I WANT YOU YOU YOU
OVER THE RAINBOW YO YO YO OYO!
CRASH
MY COMPUTER!
ANY MORE BRILLIANT IDEAS TO GET DAD TO BUY US AN iPHONE?
WELL... WE COULD TRY THE CAR RADIO NEXT TIME.
IT COULD WORK!

CAZENOVE & WILLIAM

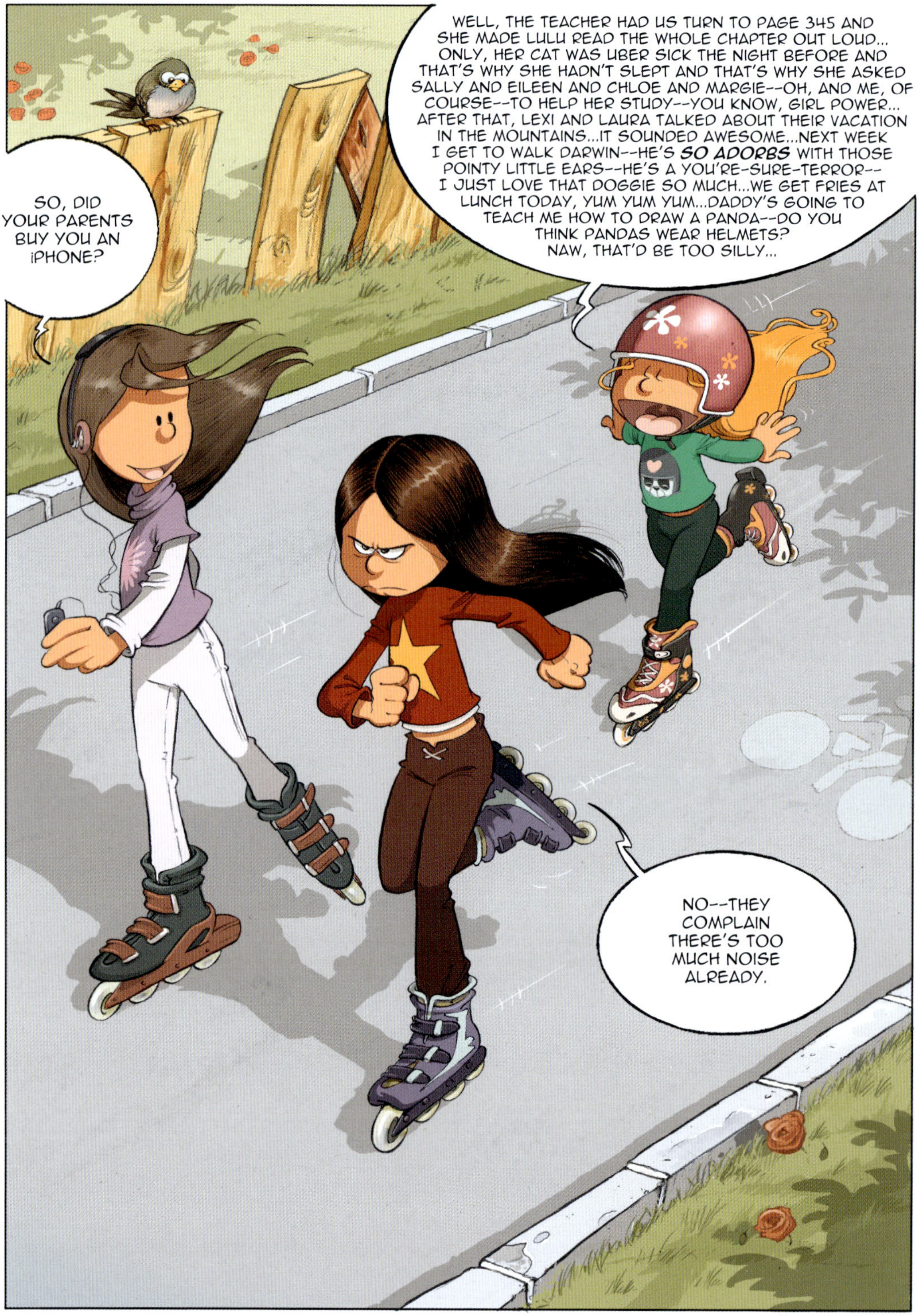
SO, DID YOUR PARENTS BUY YOU AN iPHONE?
WELL, THE TEACHER HAD US TURN TO PAGE 345 AND SHE MADE LULU READ THE WHOLE CHAPTER OUT LOUD... ONLY, HER CAT WAS UBER SICK THE NIGHT BEFORE AND THAT'S WHY SHE HADN'T SLEPT AND THAT'S WHY SHE ASKED SALLY AND EILEEN AND CHLOE AND MARGIE--OH, AND ME, OF COURSE--TO HELP HER STUDY--YOU KNOW, GIRL POWER... AFTER THAT, LEXI AND LAURA TALKED ABOUT THEIR VACATION IN THE MOUNTAINS...IT SOUNDED AWESOME...NEXT WEEK I GET TO WALK DARWIN--HE'S SO ADORBS WITH THOSE POINTY LITTLE EARS--HE'S A YOU'RE-SURE-TERROR--I JUST LOVE THAT DOGGIE SO MUCH...WE GET FRIES AT LUNCH TODAY, YUM YUM YUM...DADDY'S GOING TO TEACH ME HOW TO DRAW A PANDA--DO YOU THINK PANDAS WEAR HELMETS? NAW, THAT'D BE TOO SILLY...
NO--THEY COMPLAIN THERE'S TOO MUCH NOISE ALREADY.
CAZENOVE & WILLIAM

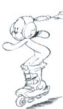

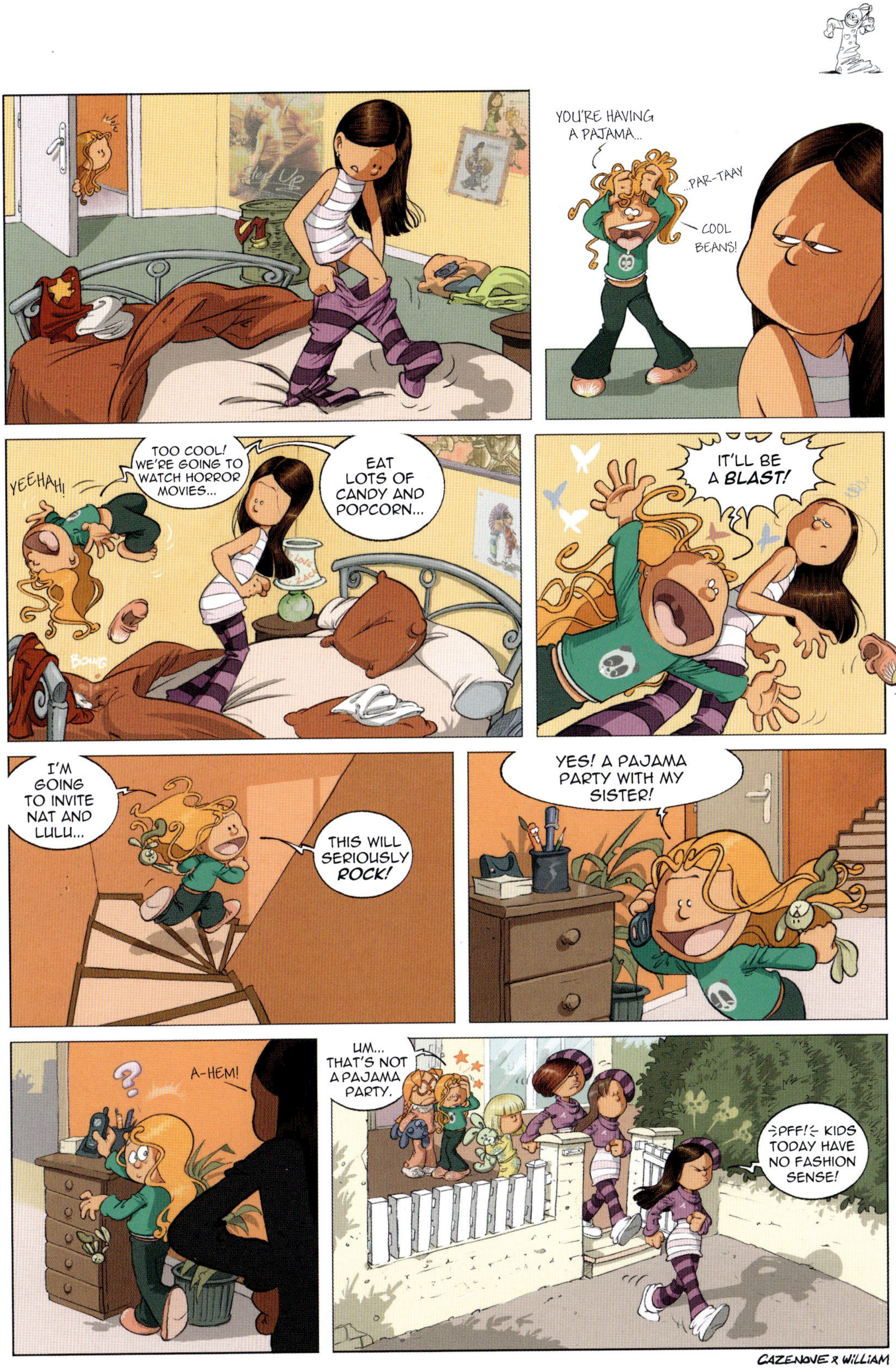

YOU'RE HAVING A PAJAMA...
...PAR-TAAY
COOL BEANS!
YEEHAH!
TOO COOL! WE'RE GOING TO WATCH HORROR MOVIES...
EAT LOTS OF CANDY AND POPCORN...
BOING
IT'LL BE A BLAST!
I'M GOING TO INVITE NAT AND LULU...
THIS WILL SERIOUSLY ROCK!
YES! A PAJAMA PARTY WITH MY SISTER!
A-HEM!
UM... THAT'S NOT A PAJAMA PARTY.
PFF! KIDS TODAY HAVE NO FASHION SENSE!
CAZENOVE & WILLIAM

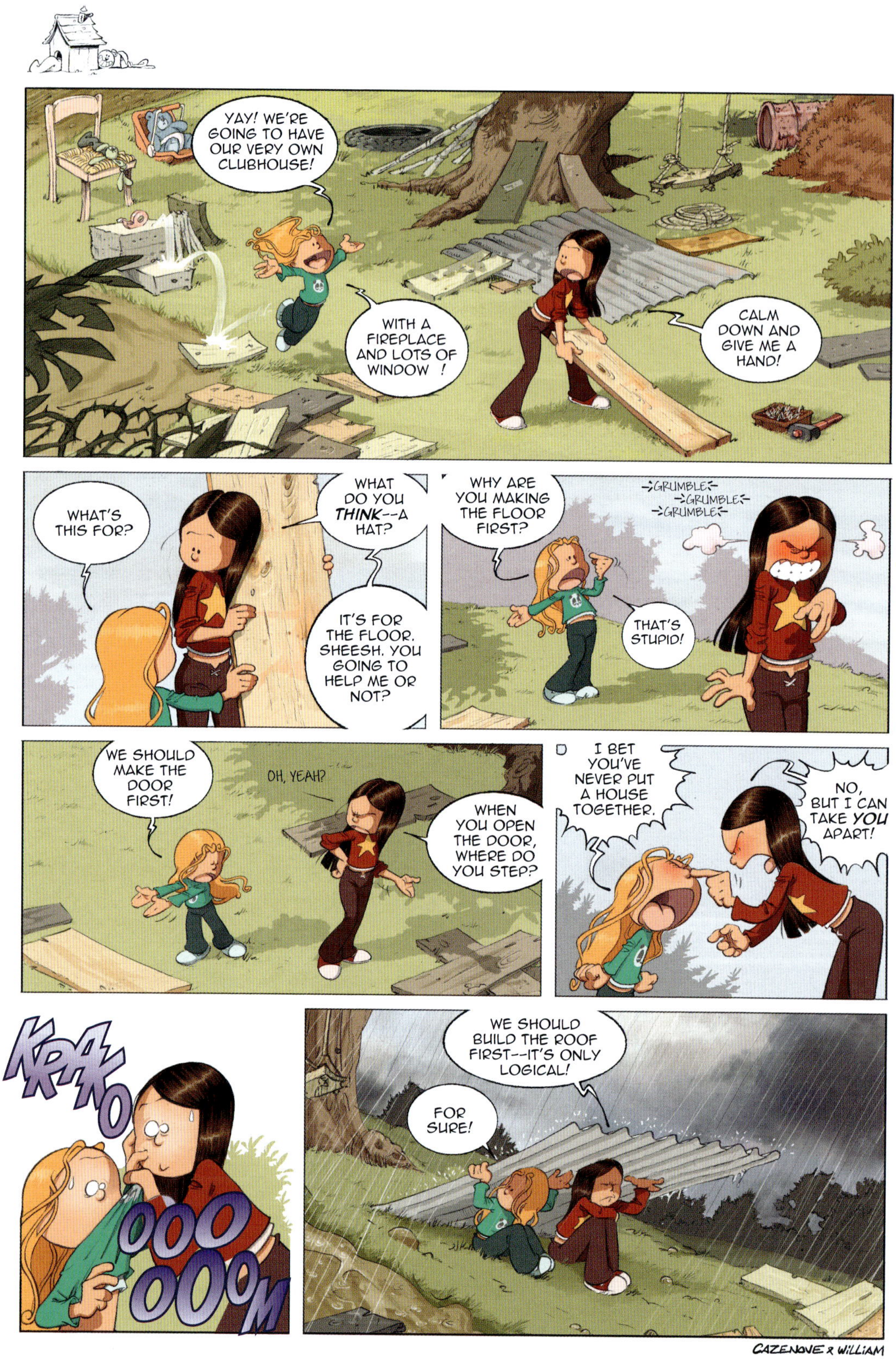
YAY! WE'RE GOING TO HAVE OUR VERY OWN CLUBHOUSE!
WITH A FIREPLACE AND LOTS OF WINDOW !
CALM DOWN AND GIVE ME A HAND!
WHAT'S THIS FOR?
WHAT DO YOU THINK--A HAT?
IT'S FOR THE FLOOR. SHEESH. YOU GOING TO HELP ME OR NOT?
WHY ARE YOU MAKING THE FLOOR FIRST?
GRUMBLE GRUMBLE GRUMBLE
THAT'S STUPID!
WE SHOULD MAKE THE DOOR FIRST!
OH, YEAH?
WHEN YOU OPEN THE DOOR, WHERE DO YOU STEP?
I BET YOU'VE NEVER PUT A HOUSE TOGETHER.
NO, BUT I CAN TAKE YOU APART!
KRAKOOOOOOOM
WE SHOULD BUILD THE ROOF FIRST--IT'S ONLY LOGICAL!
FOR SURE!
CAZENOVE & WILLIAM

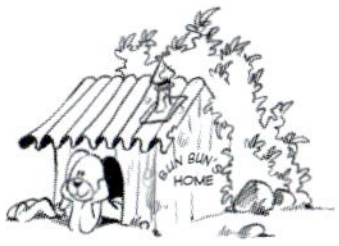
BUN BUN'S HOME

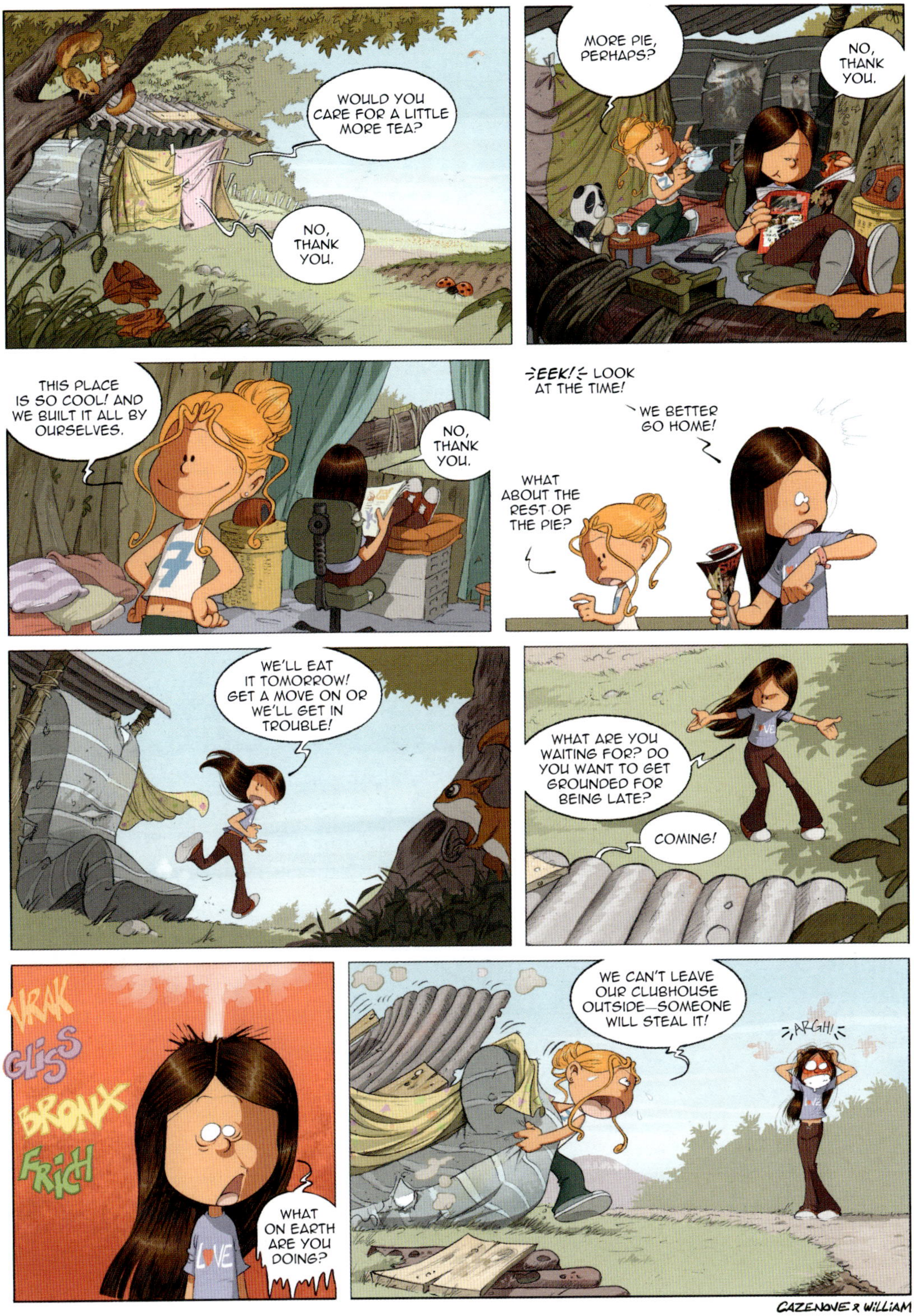
WOULD YOU CARE FOR A LITTLE MORE TEA?
NO, THANK YOU.
MORE PIE, PERHAPS?
NO, THANK YOU.
THIS PLACE IS SO COOL! AND WE BUILT IT ALL BY OURSELVES.
NO, THANK YOU.
EEK! LOOK AT THE TIME!
WE BETTER GO HOME!
WHAT ABOUT THE REST OF THE PIE?
WE'LL EAT IT TOMORROW! GET A MOVE ON OR WE'LL GET IN TROUBLE!
WHAT ARE YOU WAITING FOR? DO YOU WANT TO GET GROUNDED FOR BEING LATE?
COMING!
VRAK
GLISS
BRONX
FRICH
WHAT ON EARTH ARE YOU DOING?
WE CAN'T LEAVE OUR CLUBHOUSE OUTSIDE—SOMEONE WILL STEAL IT!
ARGH!

CAZENOVE & WILLIAM

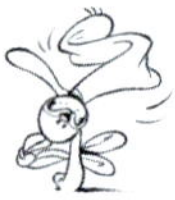

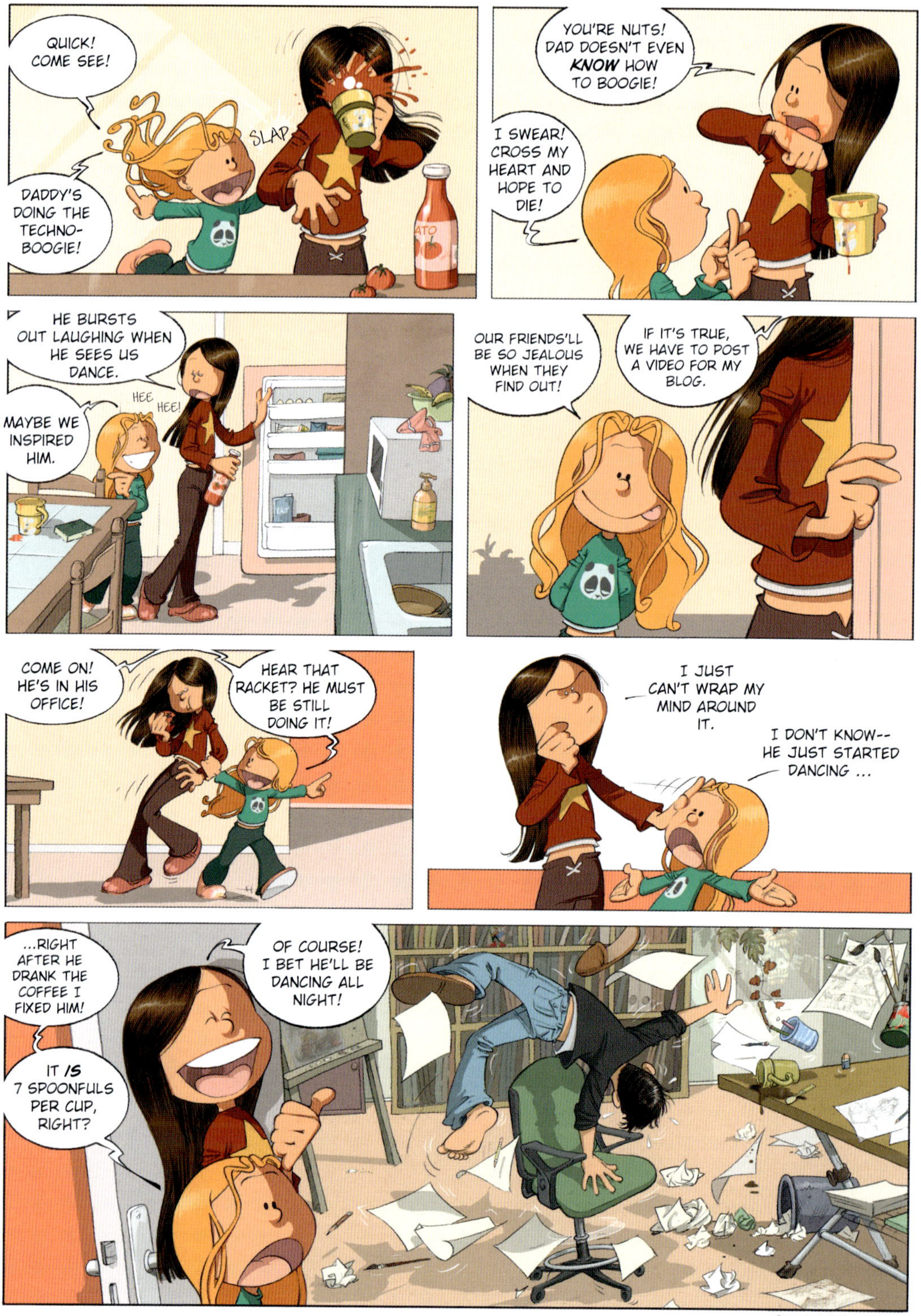
QUICK! COME SEE!
DADDY'S DOING THE TECHNO-BOOGIE!
SLAP
YOU'RE NUTS! DAD DOESN'T EVEN **KNOW** HOW TO BOOGIE!
I SWEAR! CROSS MY HEART AND HOPE TO DIE!
HE BURSTS OUT LAUGHING WHEN HE SEES US DANCE.
MAYBE WE INSPIRED HIM.
HEE HEE!
IF IT'S TRUE, WE HAVE TO POST A VIDEO FOR MY BLOG.
OUR FRIENDS'LL BE SO JEALOUS WHEN THEY FIND OUT!
COME ON! HE'S IN HIS OFFICE!
HEAR THAT RACKET? HE MUST BE STILL DOING IT!
I JUST CAN'T WRAP MY MIND AROUND IT.
I DON'T KNOW-- HE JUST STARTED DANCING ...
...RIGHT AFTER HE DRANK THE COFFEE I FIXED HIM!
OF COURSE! I BET HE'LL BE DANCING ALL NIGHT!
IT *IS* 7 SPOONFULS PER CUP, RIGHT?

CAZENOVE & WILLIAM

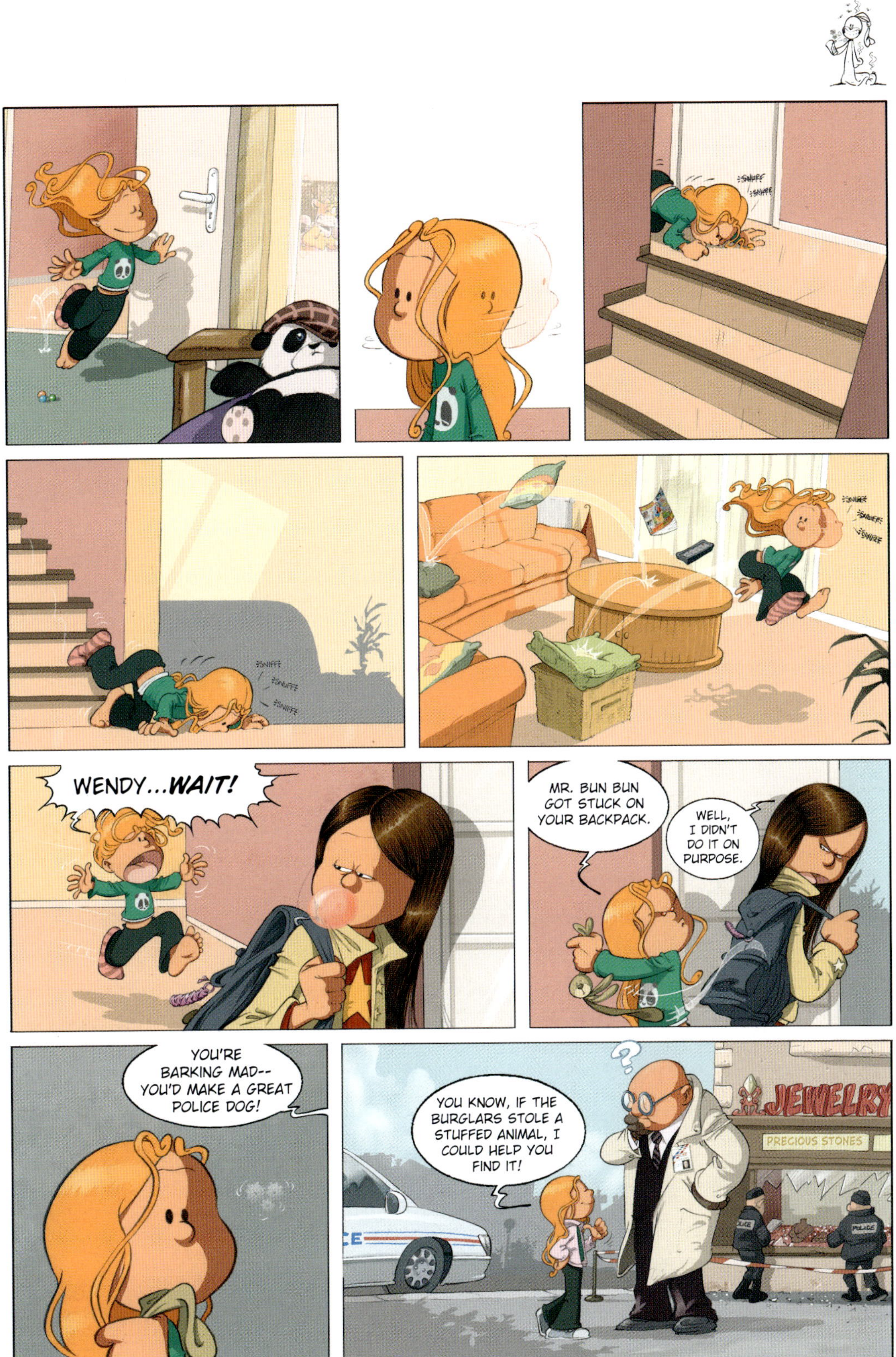
SNIFF
SNIFF
SNIFF
SNIFF
SNIFF
SNIFF
SNIFF
SNIFF
WENDY...WAIT!
MR. BUN BUN GOT STUCK ON YOUR BACKPACK.
WELL, I DIDN'T DO IT ON PURPOSE.
YOU'RE BARKING MAD-- YOU'D MAKE A GREAT POLICE DOG!
YOU KNOW, IF THE BURGLARS STOLE A STUFFED ANIMAL, I COULD HELP YOU FIND IT!
JEWELRY
PRECIOUS STONES
POLICE

CAZENOVE & WILLIAM

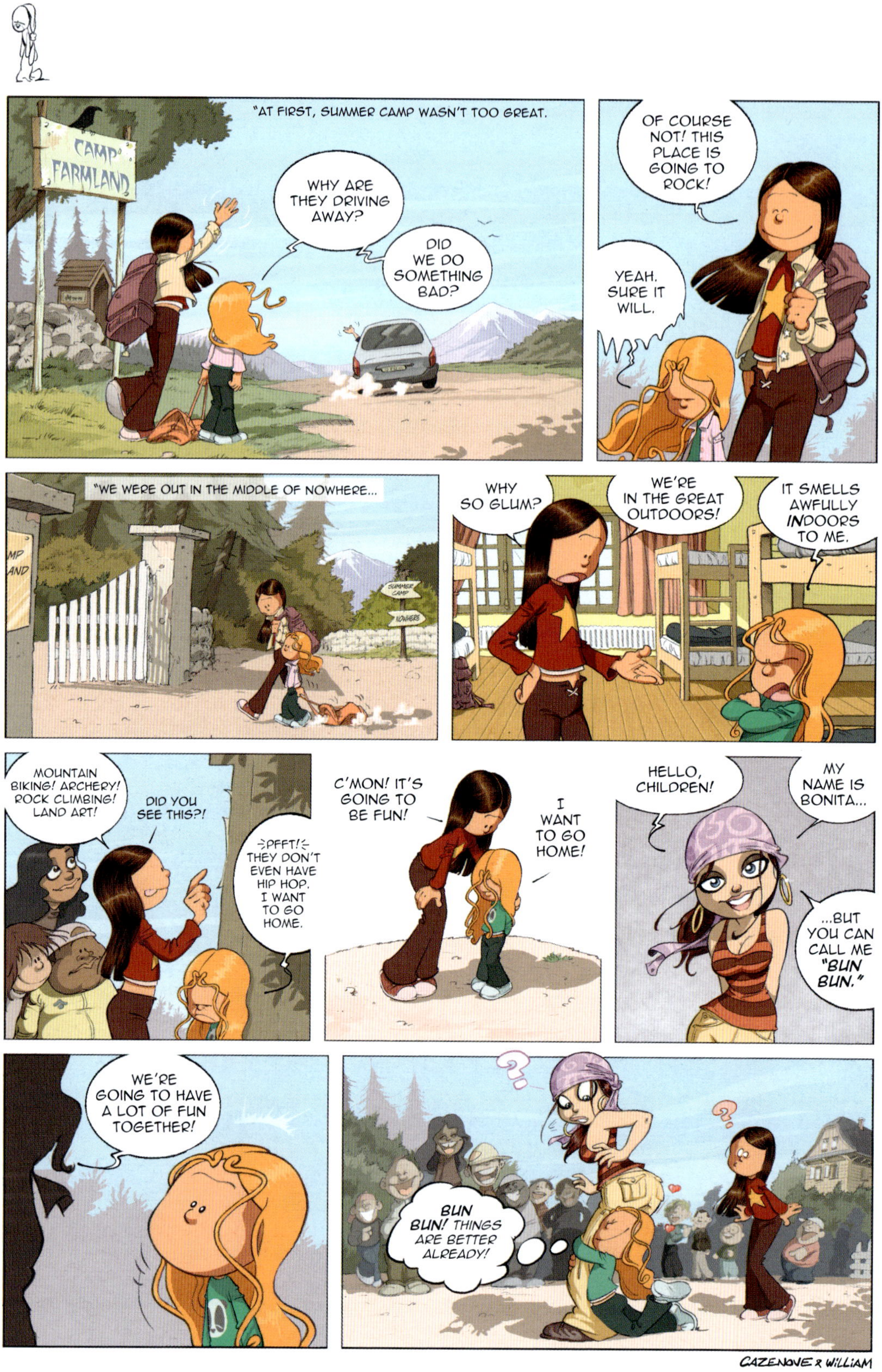
CAMP FARMLAND
"AT FIRST, SUMMER CAMP WASN'T TOO GREAT.
WHY ARE THEY DRIVING AWAY?
DID WE DO SOMETHING BAD?
OF COURSE NOT! THIS PLACE IS GOING TO ROCK!
YEAH. SURE IT WILL.
"WE WERE OUT IN THE MIDDLE OF NOWHERE...
SUMMER CAMP
NOWHERE
WHY SO GLUM?
WE'RE IN THE GREAT OUTDOORS!
IT SMELLS AWFULLY INDOORS TO ME.
MOUNTAIN BIKING! ARCHERY! ROCK CLIMBING! LAND ART!
DID YOU SEE THIS?!
PFFT! THEY DON'T EVEN HAVE HIP HOP. I WANT TO GO HOME.
C'MON! IT'S GOING TO BE FUN!
I WANT TO GO HOME!
HELLO, CHILDREN!
MY NAME IS BONITA...
...BUT YOU CAN CALL ME "BUN BUN."
WE'RE GOING TO HAVE A LOT OF FUN TOGETHER!
BUN BUN! THINGS ARE BETTER ALREADY!

CAZENOVE & WILLIAM

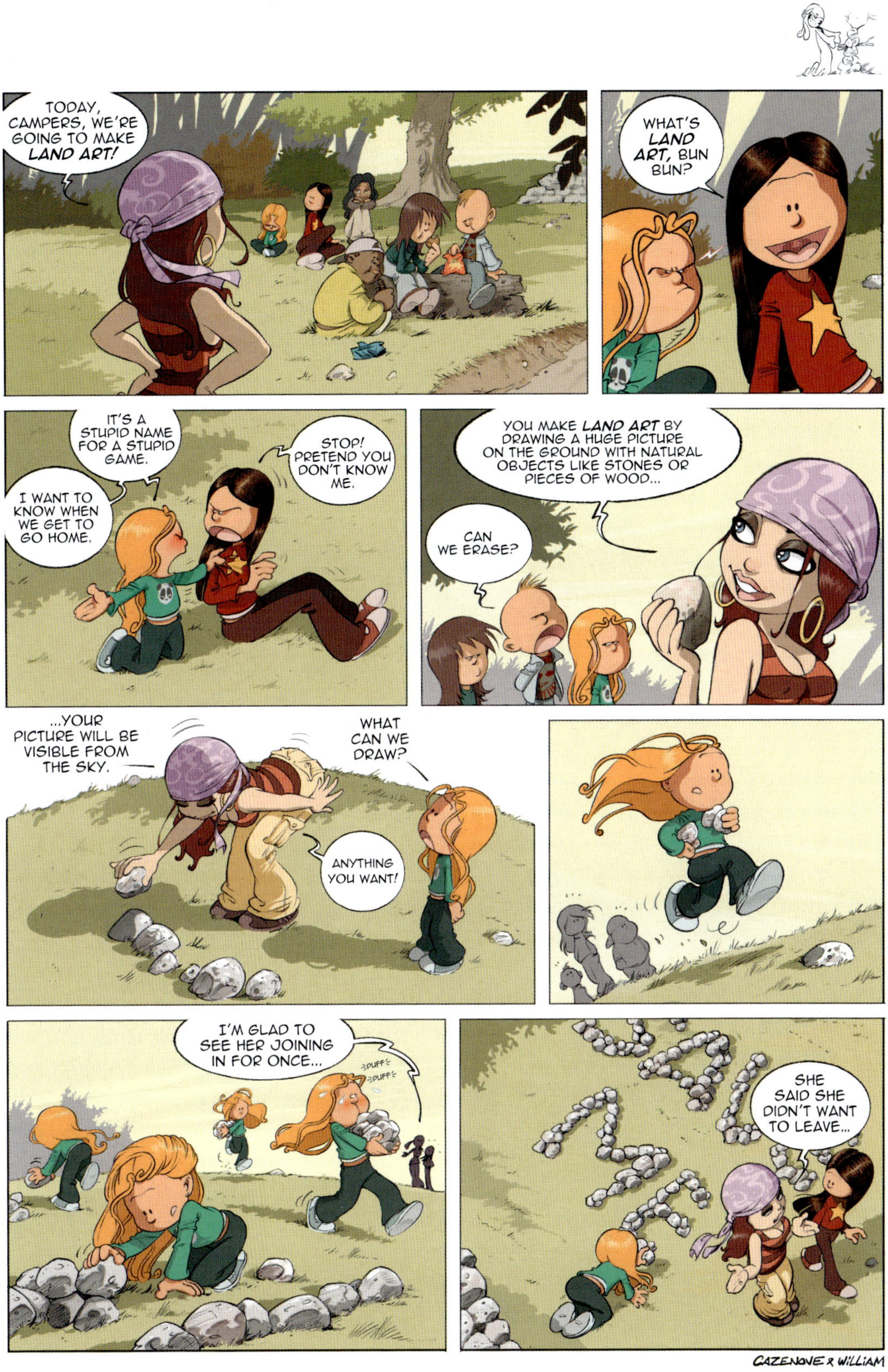
TODAY, CAMPERS, WE'RE GOING TO MAKE LAND ART!
WHAT'S LAND ART, BUN BUN?
IT'S A STUPID NAME FOR A STUPID GAME.
I WANT TO KNOW WHEN WE GET TO GO HOME.
STOP! PRETEND YOU DON'T KNOW ME.
YOU MAKE LAND ART BY DRAWING A HUGE PICTURE ON THE GROUND WITH NATURAL OBJECTS LIKE STONES OR PIECES OF WOOD...
CAN WE ERASE?
...YOUR PICTURE WILL BE VISIBLE FROM THE SKY.
WHAT CAN WE DRAW?
ANYTHING YOU WANT!
I'M GLAD TO SEE HER JOINING IN FOR ONCE...
PUFF
PUFF
SHE SAID SHE DIDN'T WANT TO LEAVE...
CAZENOVE & WILLIAM

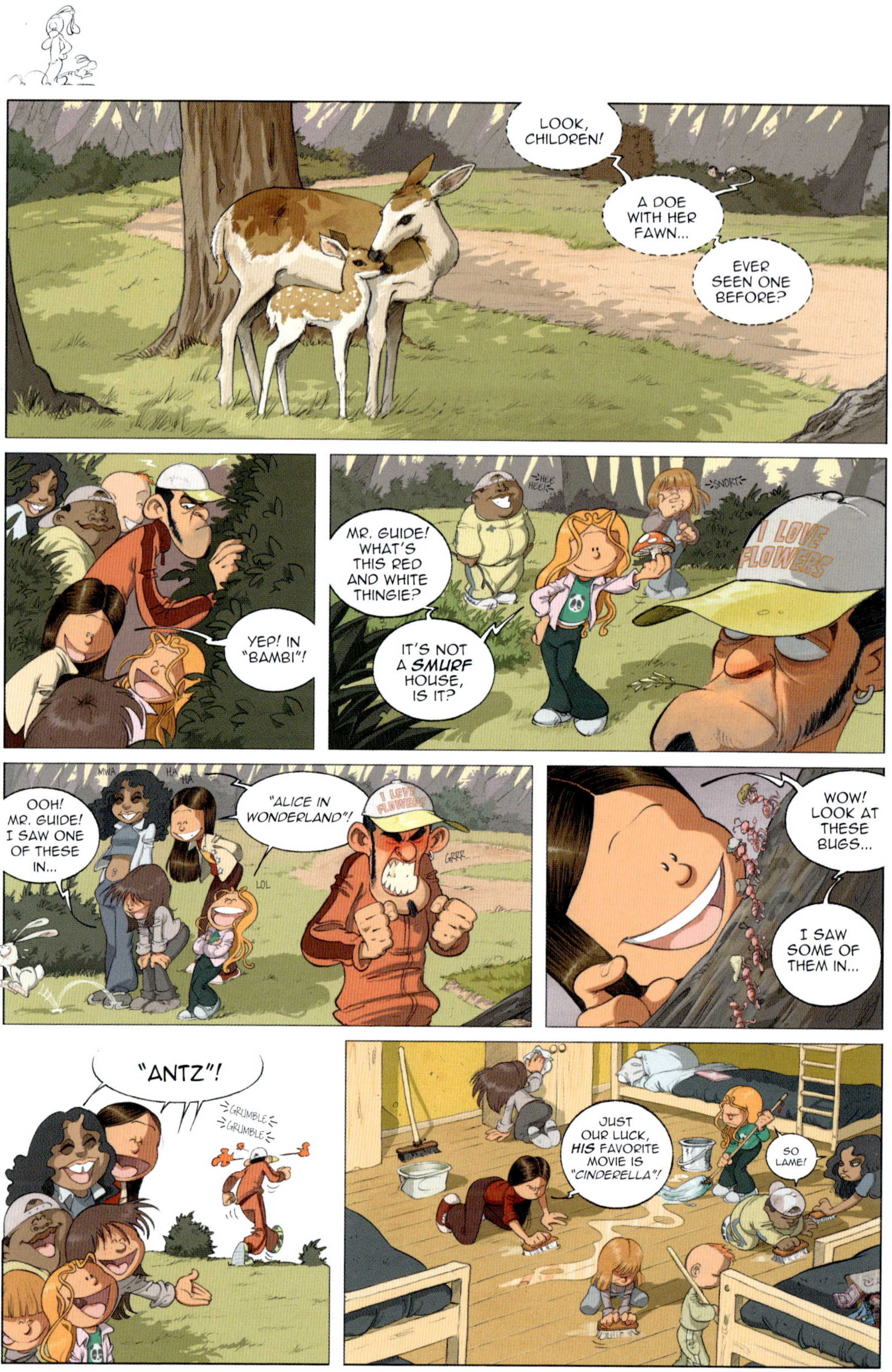

LOOK, CHILDREN!
A DOE WITH HER FAWN...
EVER SEEN ONE BEFORE?
YEP! IN "BAMBI"!
HEE HEE!
SNORT
MR. GUIDE! WHAT'S THIS RED AND WHITE THINGIE?
IT'S NOT A **SMURF** HOUSE, IS IT?
I LOVE FLOWERS
MWA HA HA
OOH! MR. GUIDE! I SAW ONE OF THESE IN...
"ALICE IN WONDERLAND"!
LOL
I LOVE FLOWERS
GRRR...
WOW! LOOK AT THESE BUGS...
I SAW SOME OF THEM IN...
"ANTZ"!
GRUMBLE GRUMBLE
JUST OUR LUCK, **HIS** FAVORITE MOVIE IS "CINDERELLA"!
SO LAME!

CAZENOVE & WILLIAM

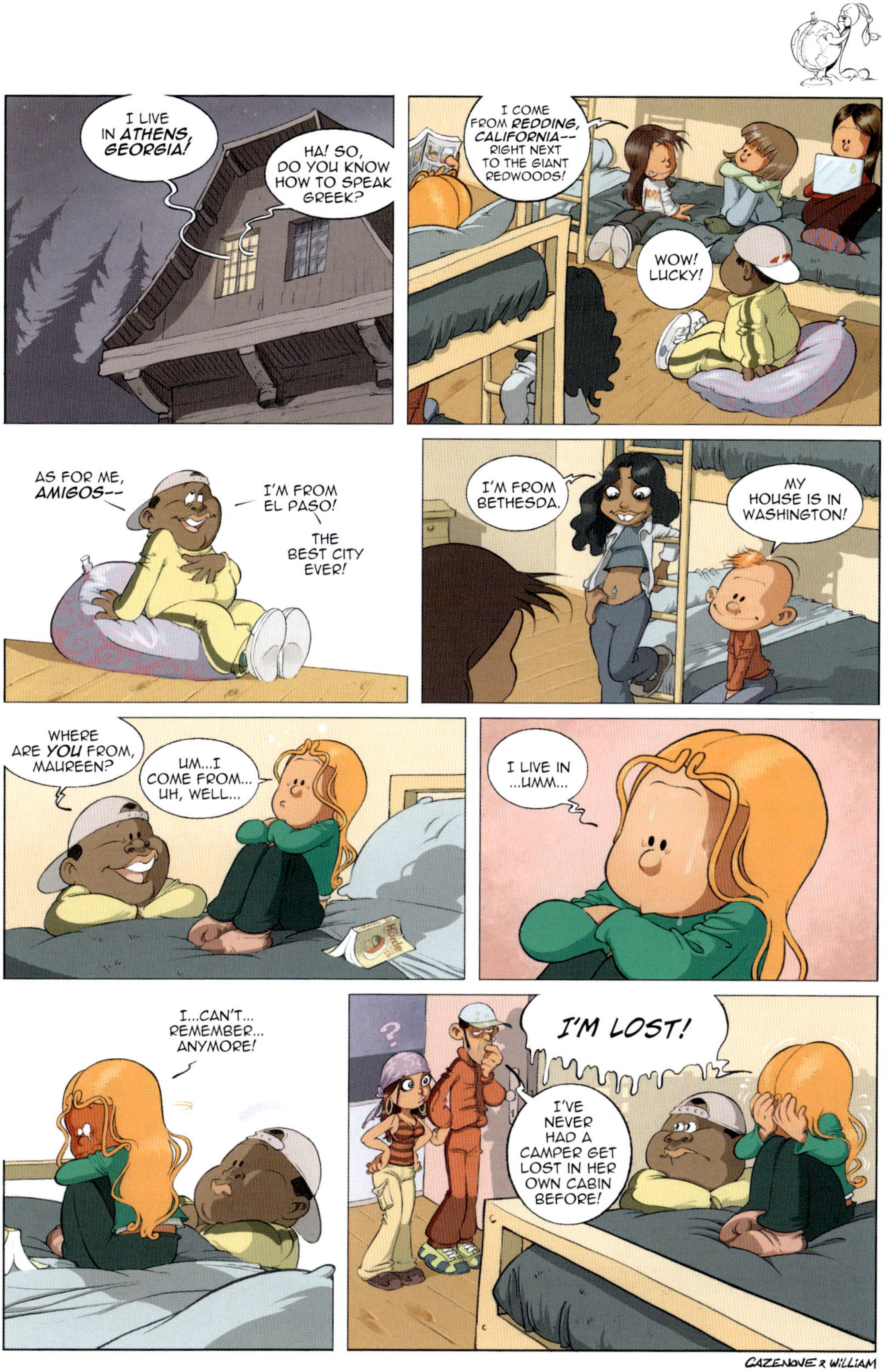
I LIVE IN ATHENS, GEORGIA!
HA! SO, DO YOU KNOW HOW TO SPEAK GREEK?
I COME FROM REDDING, CALIFORNIA-- RIGHT NEXT TO THE GIANT REDWOODS!
WOW! LUCKY!
AS FOR ME, AMIGOS--
I'M FROM EL PASO!
THE BEST CITY EVER!
I'M FROM BETHESDA.
MY HOUSE IS IN WASHINGTON!
WHERE ARE YOU FROM, MAUREEN?
UM...I COME FROM... UH, WELL...
I LIVE IN ...UMM...
I...CAN'T... REMEMBER... ANYMORE!
I'M LOST!
I'VE NEVER HAD A CAMPER GET LOST IN HER OWN CABIN BEFORE!
CAZENOVE & WILLIAM

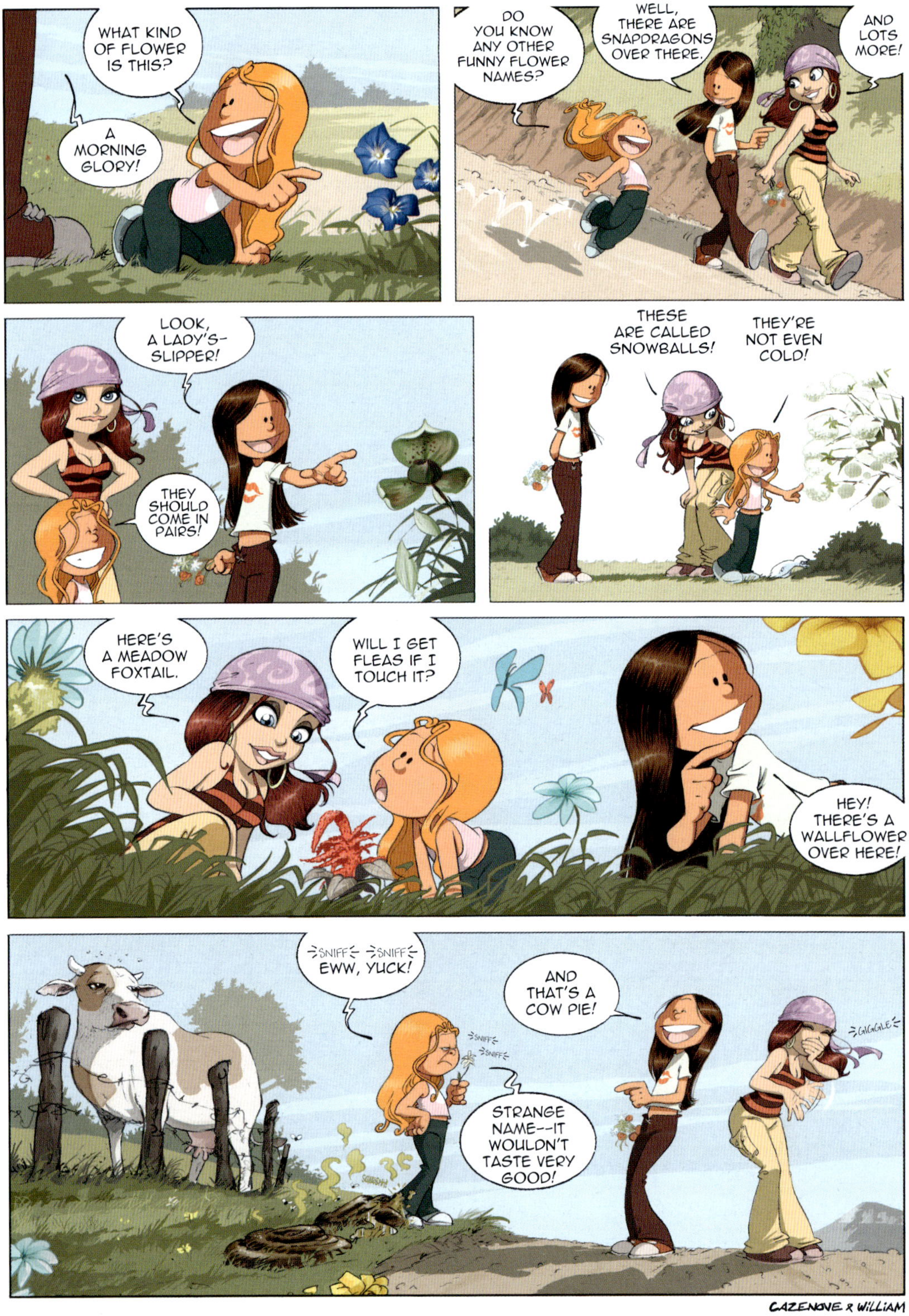
WHAT KIND OF FLOWER IS THIS?
A MORNING GLORY!
DO YOU KNOW ANY OTHER FUNNY FLOWER NAMES?
WELL, THERE ARE SNAPDRAGONS OVER THERE.
AND LOTS MORE!
LOOK, A LADY'S-SLIPPER!
THEY SHOULD COME IN PAIRS!
THESE ARE CALLED SNOWBALLS!
THEY'RE NOT EVEN COLD!
HERE'S A MEADOW FOXTAIL.
WILL I GET FLEAS IF I TOUCH IT?
HEY! THERE'S A WALLFLOWER OVER HERE!
SNIFF SNIFF
EWW, YUCK!
SNIFF SNIFF
AND THAT'S A COW PIE!
GIGGLE
STRANGE NAME--IT WOULDN'T TASTE VERY GOOD!
CAZENOVE & WILLIAM

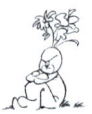

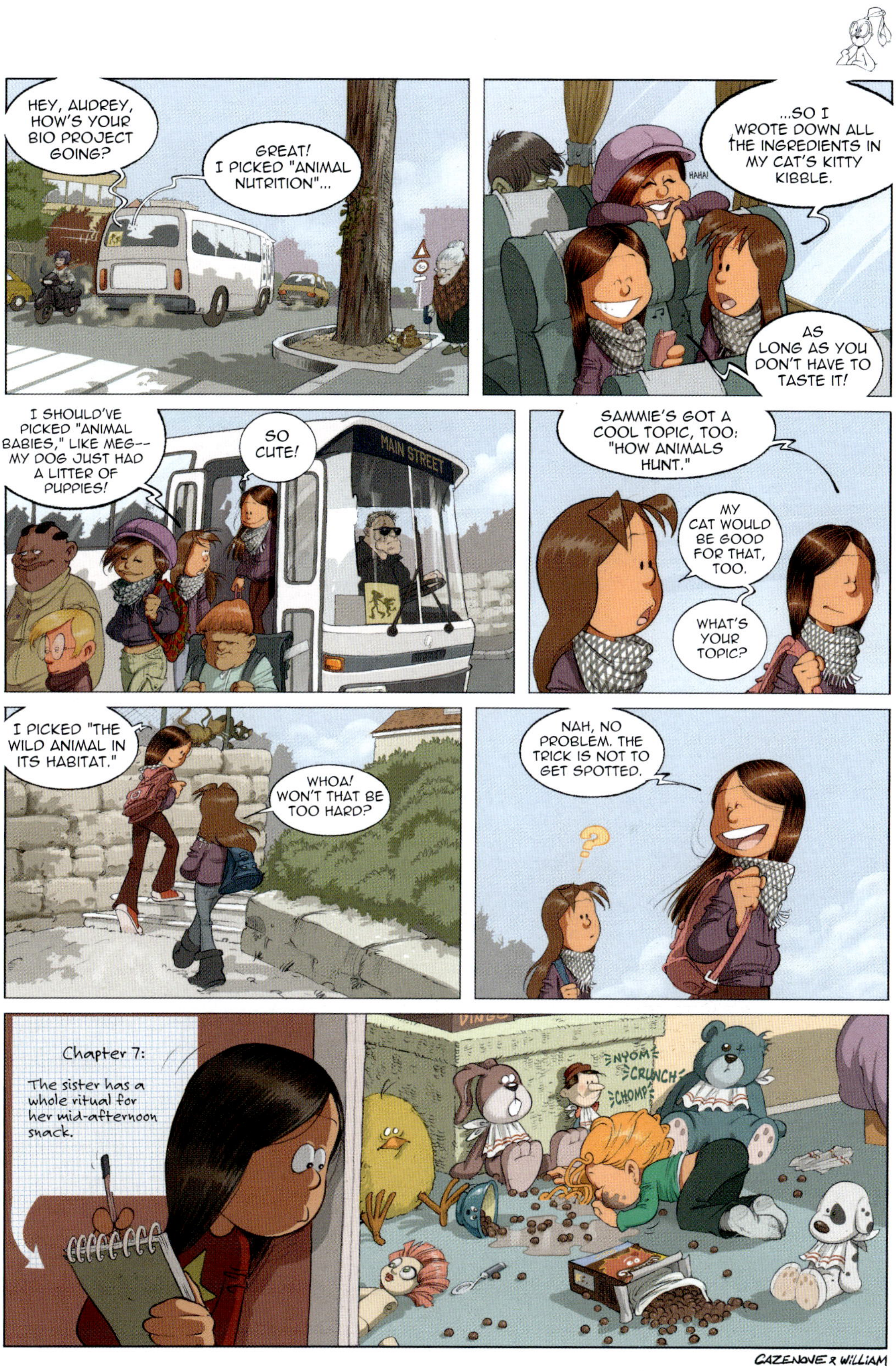
HEY, AUDREY, HOW'S YOUR BIO PROJECT GOING?
GREAT! I PICKED "ANIMAL NUTRITION"...
...SO I WROTE DOWN ALL THE INGREDIENTS IN MY CAT'S KITTY KIBBLE.
HAHA!
AS LONG AS YOU DON'T HAVE TO TASTE IT!
I SHOULD'VE PICKED "ANIMAL BABIES," LIKE MEG-- MY DOG JUST HAD A LITTER OF PUPPIES!
SO CUTE!
MAIN STREET
SAMMIE'S GOT A COOL TOPIC, TOO: "HOW ANIMALS HUNT."
MY CAT WOULD BE GOOD FOR THAT, TOO.
WHAT'S YOUR TOPIC?
I PICKED "THE WILD ANIMAL IN ITS HABITAT."
WHOA! WON'T THAT BE TOO HARD?
NAH, NO PROBLEM. THE TRICK IS NOT TO GET SPOTTED.
Chapter 7:
The sister has a whole ritual for her mid-afternoon snack.
NYOM
CRUNCH
CHOMP
CAZENOVE & WILLIAM

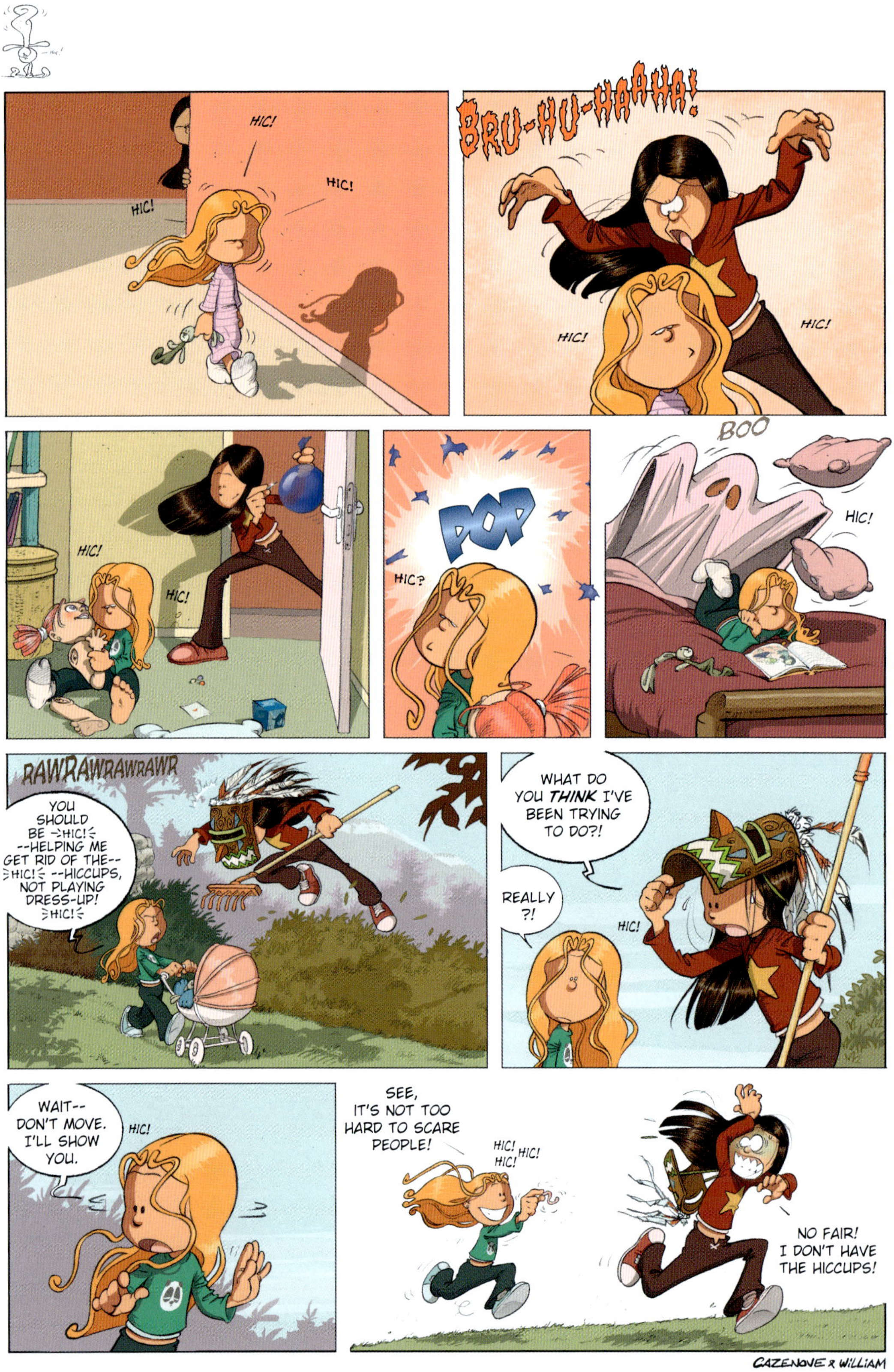
HIC!
HIC!
HIC!
BRU-HU-HAAHA!
HIC!
HIC!
HIC!
HIC!
POP
HIC?
BOO
HIC!
RAWRAWRAWRAWR
YOU SHOULD BE -HIC!- --HELPING ME GET RID OF THE-- -HIC!- --HICCUPS, NOT PLAYING DRESS-UP! -HIC!-
WHAT DO YOU THINK I'VE BEEN TRYING TO DO?!
REALLY ?!
HIC!
WAIT-- DON'T MOVE. I'LL SHOW YOU.
HIC!
SEE, IT'S NOT TOO HARD TO SCARE PEOPLE!
HIC! HIC! HIC!
NO FAIR! I DON'T HAVE THE HICCUPS!
CAZENOVE & WILLIAM

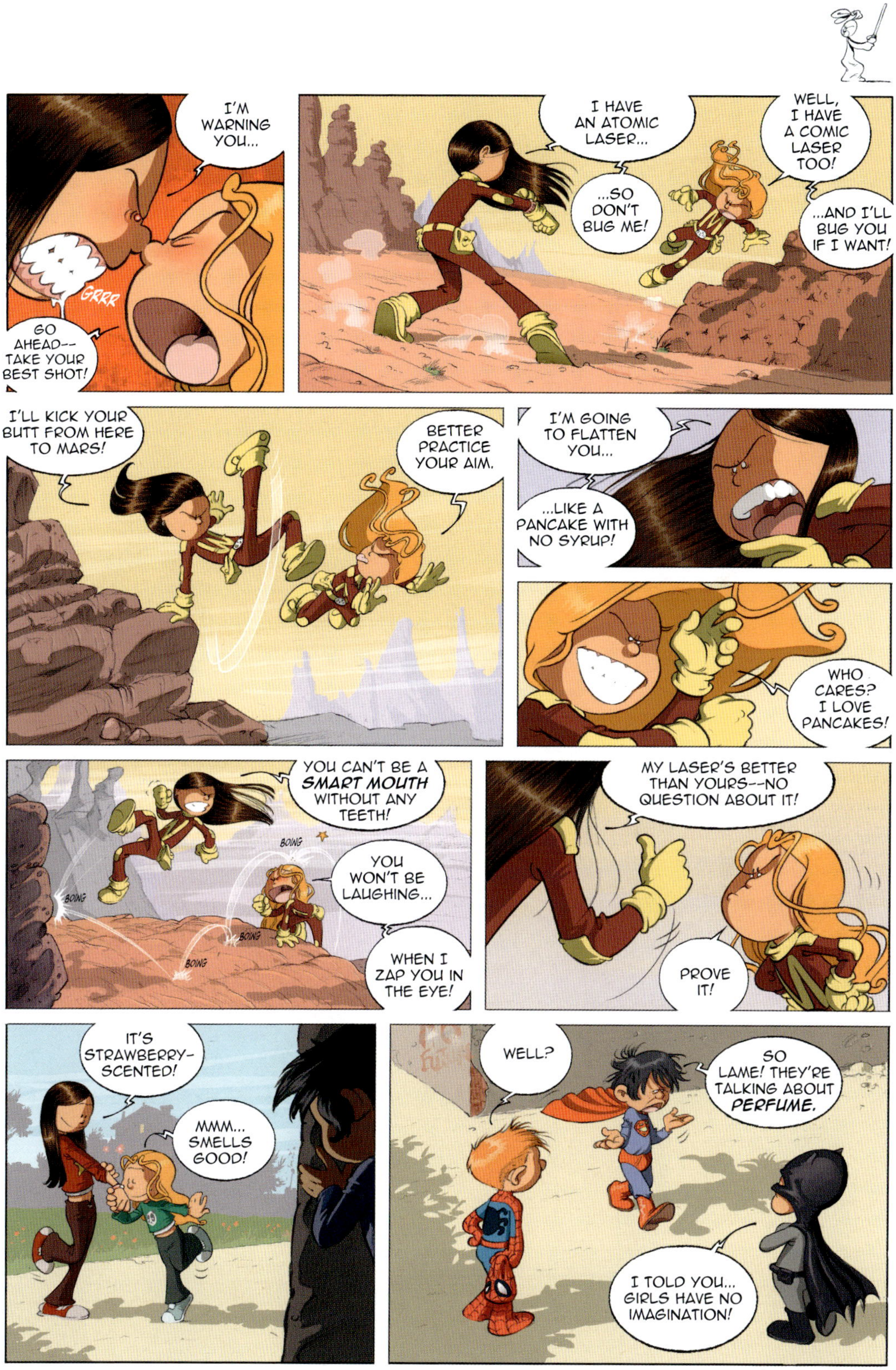
I'M WARNING YOU...
GRRR
GO AHEAD-- TAKE YOUR BEST SHOT!
I HAVE AN ATOMIC LASER...
...SO DON'T BUG ME!
WELL, I HAVE A COMIC LASER TOO!
...AND I'LL BUG YOU IF I WANT!
I'LL KICK YOUR BUTT FROM HERE TO MARS!
BETTER PRACTICE YOUR AIM.
I'M GOING TO FLATTEN YOU...
...LIKE A PANCAKE WITH NO SYRUP!
WHO CARES? I LOVE PANCAKES!
YOU CAN'T BE A SMART MOUTH WITHOUT ANY TEETH!
BOING
YOU WON'T BE LAUGHING...
WHEN I ZAP YOU IN THE EYE!
MY LASER'S BETTER THAN YOURS--NO QUESTION ABOUT IT!
PROVE IT!
IT'S STRAWBERRY-SCENTED!
MMM... SMELLS GOOD!
WELL?
SO LAME! THEY'RE TALKING ABOUT PERFUME.
I TOLD YOU... GIRLS HAVE NO IMAGINATION!

CAZENOVE & WILLIAM

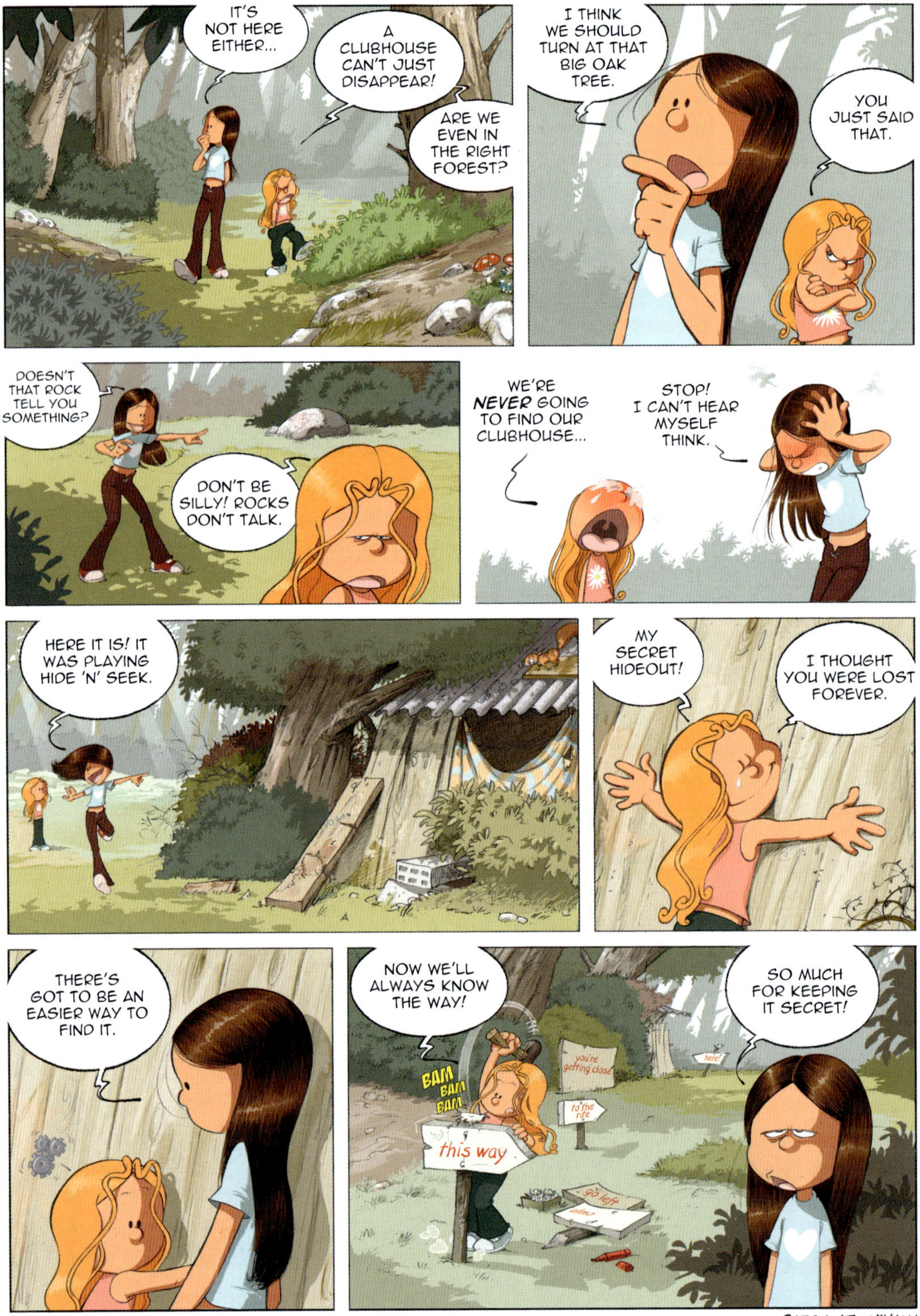
IT'S NOT HERE EITHER...
A CLUBHOUSE CAN'T JUST DISAPPEAR!
ARE WE EVEN IN THE RIGHT FOREST?
I THINK WE SHOULD TURN AT THAT BIG OAK TREE.
YOU JUST SAID THAT.
DOESN'T THAT ROCK TELL YOU SOMETHING?
DON'T BE SILLY! ROCKS DON'T TALK.
WE'RE **NEVER** GOING TO FIND OUR CLUBHOUSE...
STOP! I CAN'T HEAR MYSELF THINK.
HERE IT IS! IT WAS PLAYING HIDE 'N' SEEK.
MY SECRET HIDEOUT!
I THOUGHT YOU WERE LOST FOREVER.
THERE'S GOT TO BE AN EASIER WAY TO FIND IT.
NOW WE'LL ALWAYS KNOW THE WAY!
BAM BAM BAM
you're getting close
here!
this way
SO MUCH FOR KEEPING IT SECRET!

CAZENOVE & WILLIAM

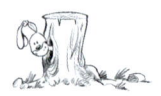

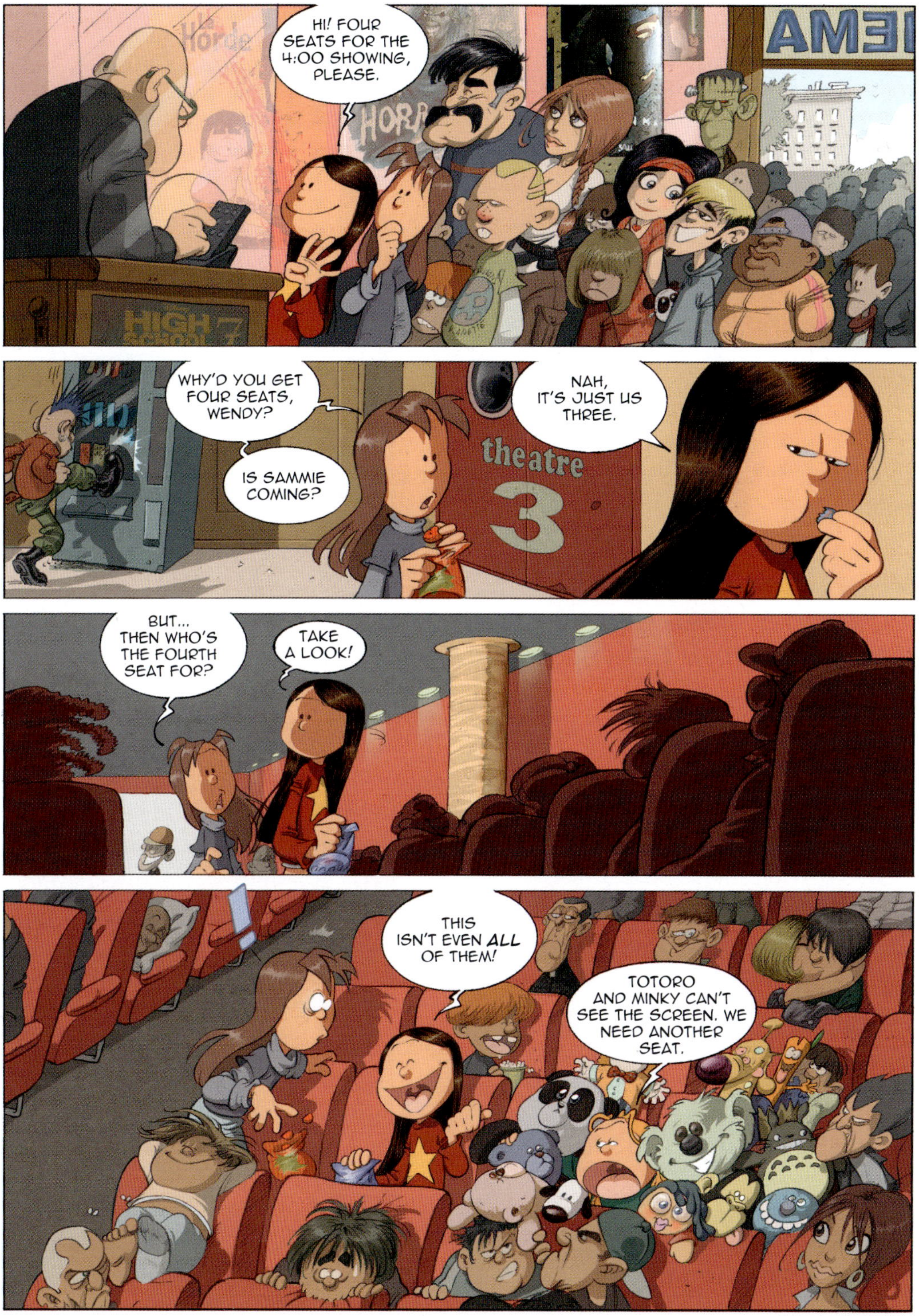
HI! FOUR SEATS FOR THE 4:00 SHOWING, PLEASE.
WHY'D YOU GET FOUR SEATS, WENDY?
IS SAMMIE COMING?
theatre 3
NAH, IT'S JUST US THREE.
BUT... THEN WHO'S THE FOURTH SEAT FOR?
TAKE A LOOK!
THIS ISN'T EVEN **ALL** OF THEM!
TOTORO AND MINKY CAN'T SEE THE SCREEN. WE NEED ANOTHER SEAT.

CAZENOVE & WILLIAM

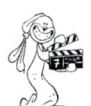

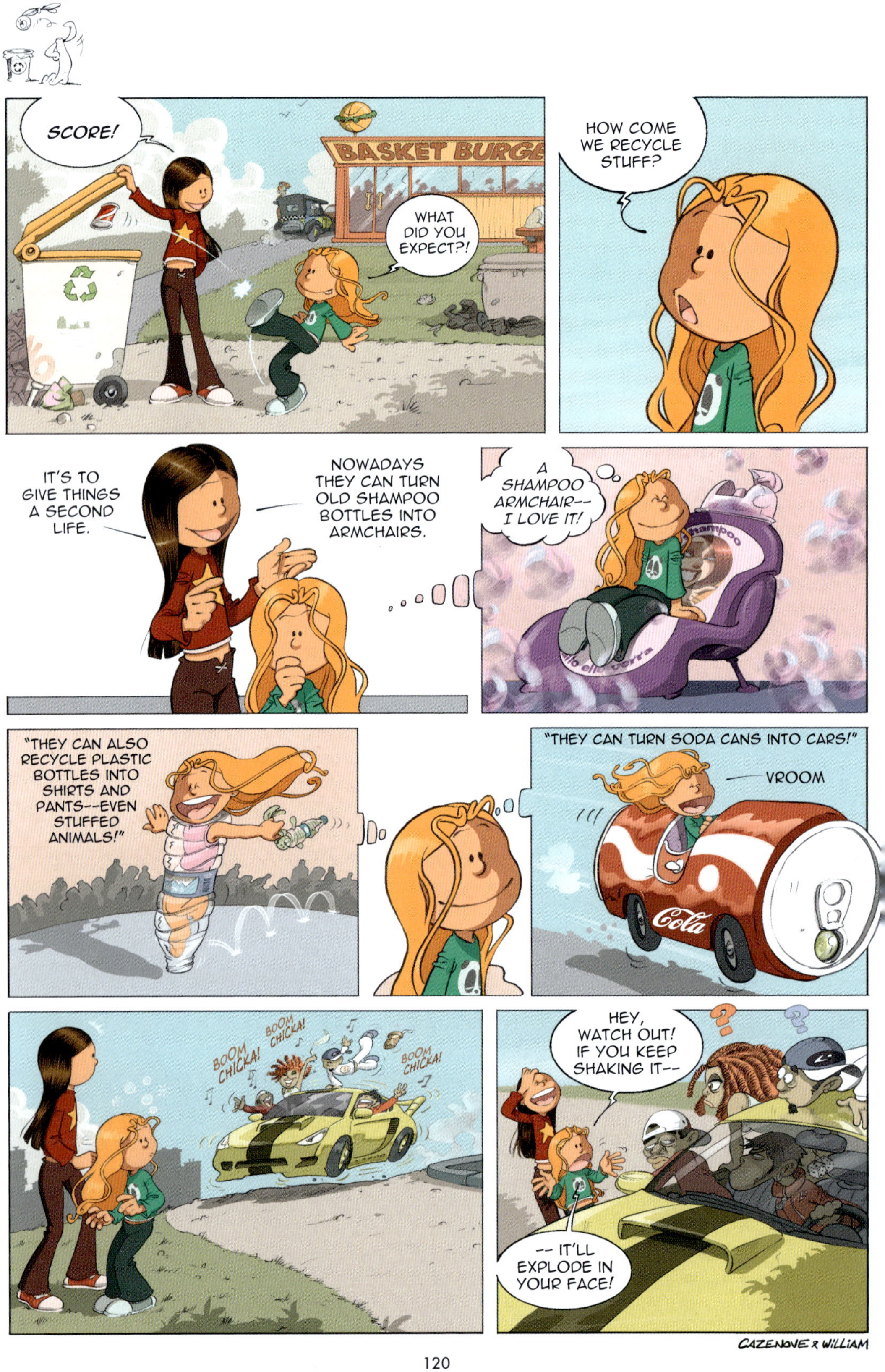
SCORE!
BASKET BURGE
WHAT DID YOU EXPECT?!
HOW COME WE RECYCLE STUFF?
IT'S TO GIVE THINGS A SECOND LIFE.
NOWADAYS THEY CAN TURN OLD SHAMPOO BOTTLES INTO ARMCHAIRS.
A SHAMPOO ARMCHAIR-- I LOVE IT!
"THEY CAN ALSO RECYCLE PLASTIC BOTTLES INTO SHIRTS AND PANTS--EVEN STUFFED ANIMALS!"
"THEY CAN TURN SODA CANS INTO CARS!"
VROOM
Cola
BOOM CHICKA!
BOOM CHICKA!
BOOM CHICKA!
HEY, WATCH OUT! IF YOU KEEP SHAKING IT--
-- IT'LL EXPLODE IN YOUR FACE!
CAZENOVE & WILLIAM

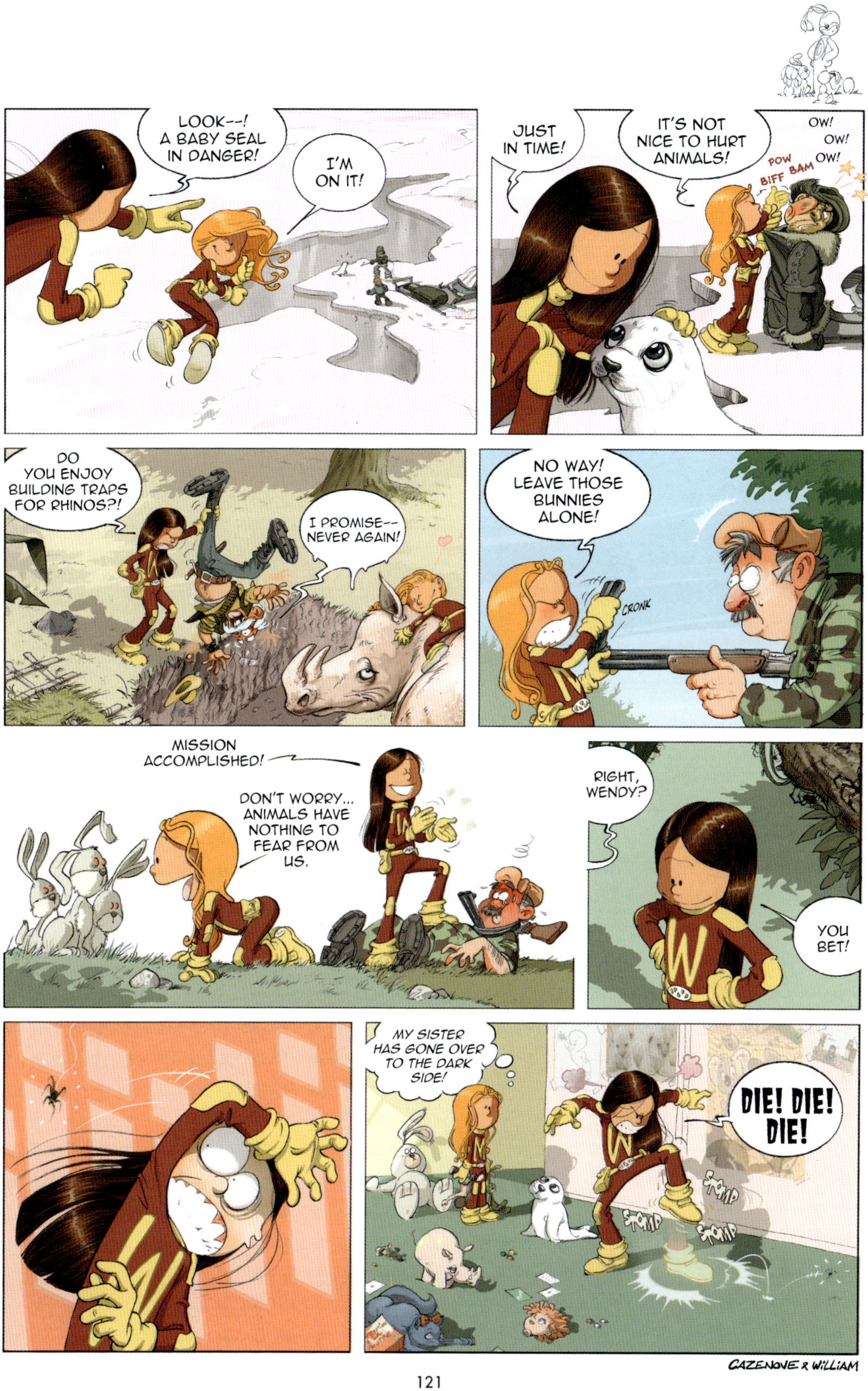
LOOK--! A BABY SEAL IN DANGER!
I'M ON IT!
JUST IN TIME!
IT'S NOT NICE TO HURT ANIMALS!
OW! OW! OW!
POW BIFF BAM
DO YOU ENJOY BUILDING TRAPS FOR RHINOS?!
I PROMISE-- NEVER AGAIN!
NO WAY! LEAVE THOSE BUNNIES ALONE!
CRONK
MISSION ACCOMPLISHED!
DON'T WORRY... ANIMALS HAVE NOTHING TO FEAR FROM US.
RIGHT, WENDY?
YOU BET!
MY SISTER HAS GONE OVER TO THE DARK SIDE!
DIE! DIE! DIE!
STOMP
STOMP
STOMP
CAZENOVE & WILLIAM

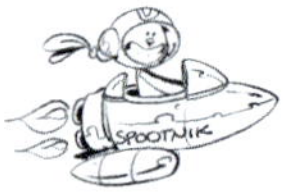
SPOOTNIK

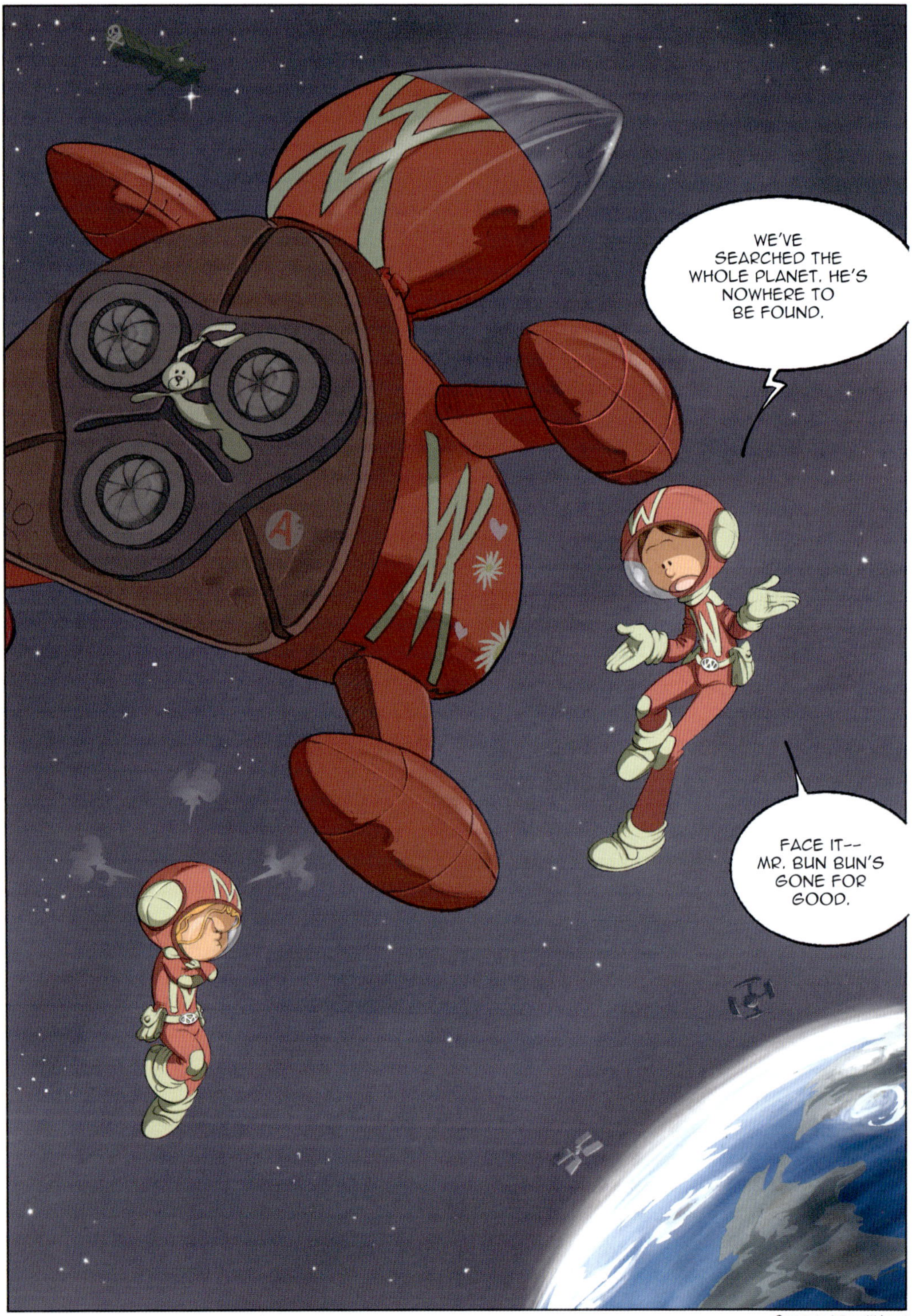
WE'VE SEARCHED THE WHOLE PLANET. HE'S NOWHERE TO BE FOUND.
FACE IT-- MR. BUN BUN'S GONE FOR GOOD.

CAZENOVE & WILLIAM

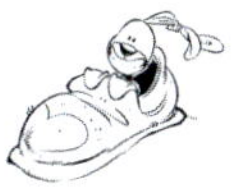

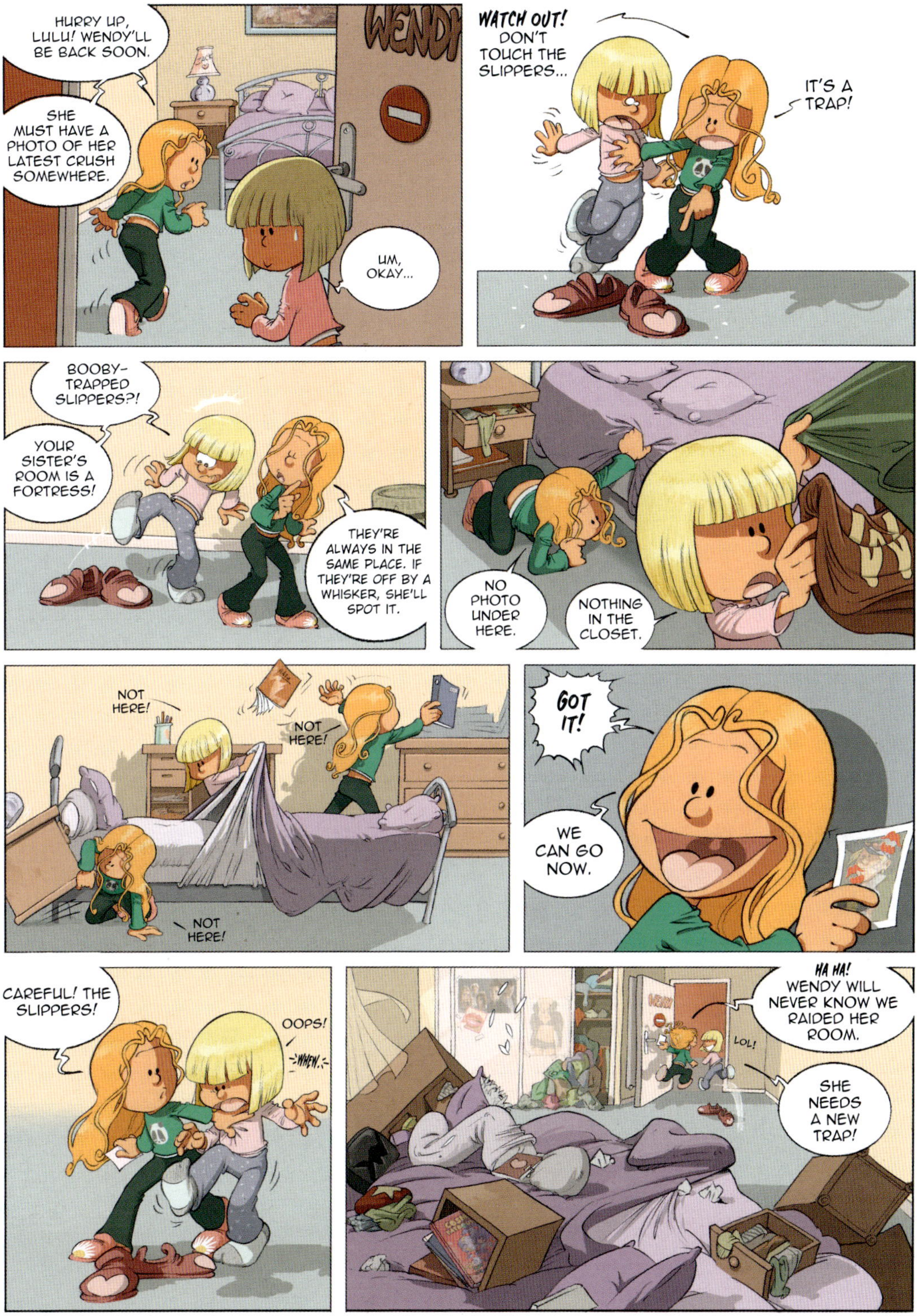
HURRY UP, LULU! WENDY'LL BE BACK SOON.
SHE MUST HAVE A PHOTO OF HER LATEST CRUSH SOMEWHERE.
WENDY
UM, OKAY...
WATCH OUT! DON'T TOUCH THE SLIPPERS...
IT'S A TRAP!
BOOBY-TRAPPED SLIPPERS?!
YOUR SISTER'S ROOM IS A FORTRESS!
THEY'RE ALWAYS IN THE SAME PLACE. IF THEY'RE OFF BY A WHISKER, SHE'LL SPOT IT.
NO PHOTO UNDER HERE.
NOTHING IN THE CLOSET.
NOT HERE!
NOT HERE!
NOT HERE!
GOT IT!
WE CAN GO NOW.
CAREFUL! THE SLIPPERS!
OOPS!
WHEW.
HA HA! WENDY WILL NEVER KNOW WE RAIDED HER ROOM.
LOL!
SHE NEEDS A NEW TRAP!

CAZENOVE & WILLIAM

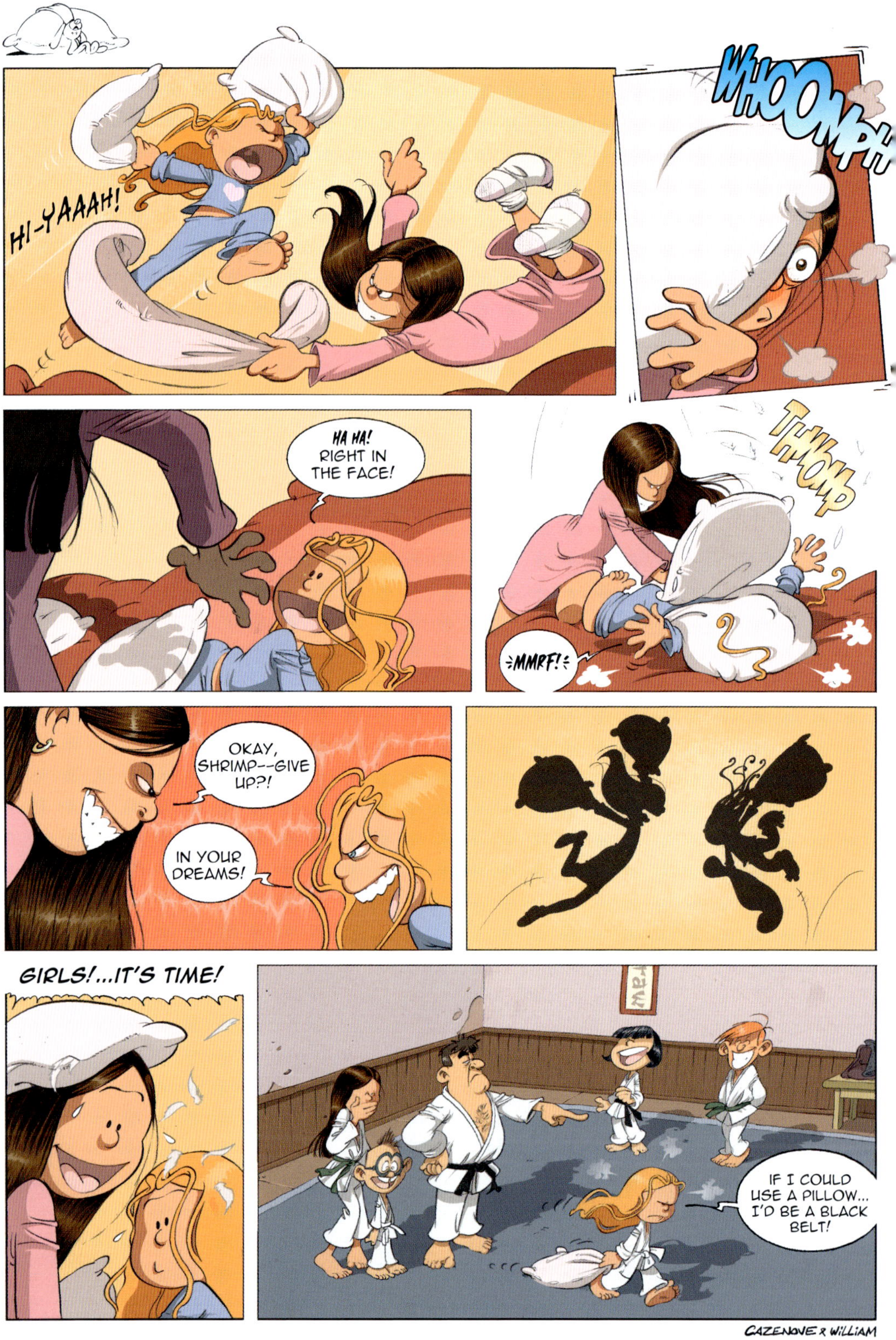
HI-YAAAH!
WHOOOMPH
HA HA! RIGHT IN THE FACE!
THWOMP
MMRF!
OKAY, SHRIMP--GIVE UP?!
IN YOUR DREAMS!
GIRLS!...IT'S TIME!
IF I COULD USE A PILLOW... I'D BE A BLACK BELT!
CAZENOVE & WILLIAM

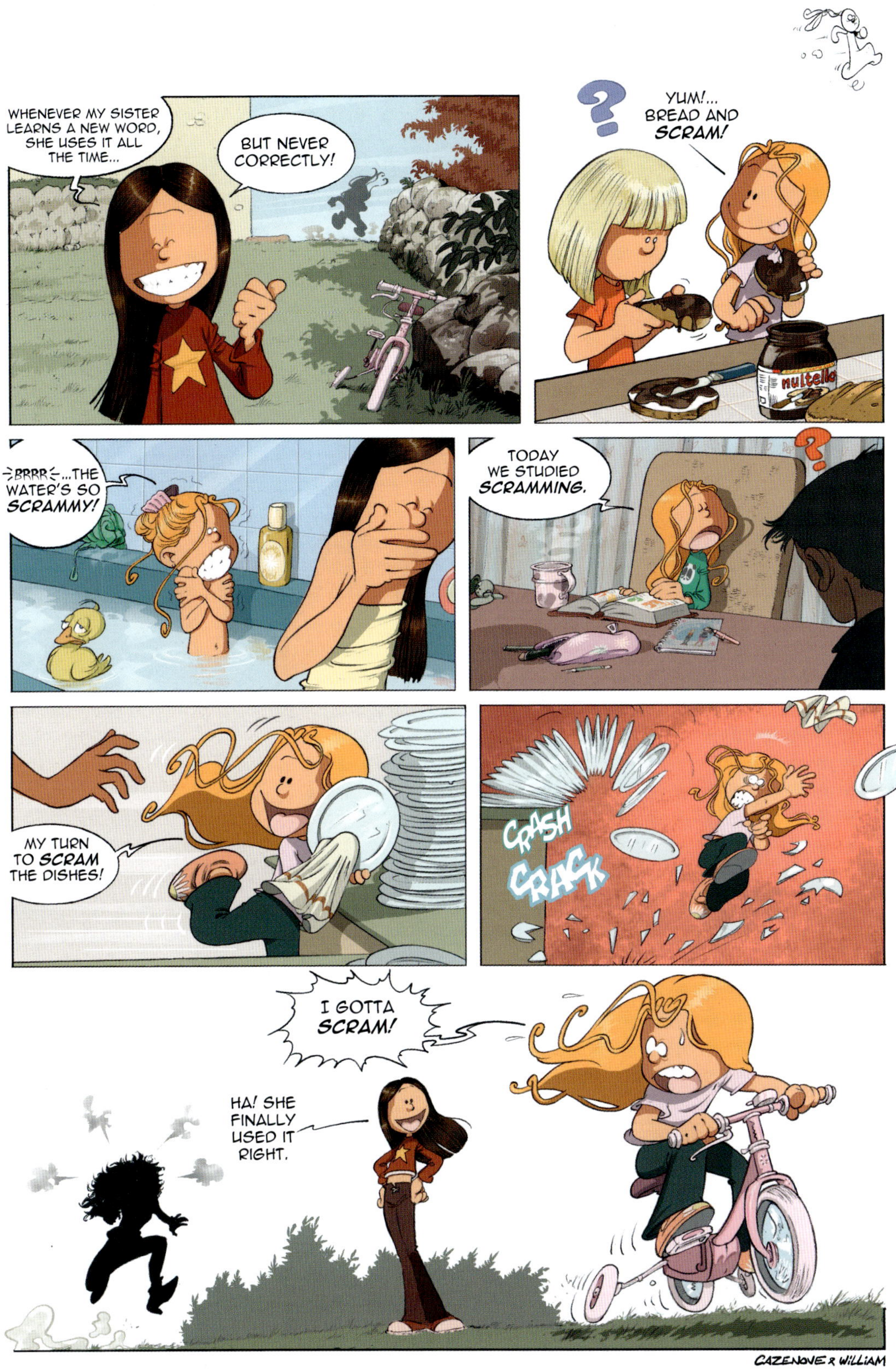
WHENEVER MY SISTER LEARNS A NEW WORD, SHE USES IT ALL THE TIME...
BUT NEVER CORRECTLY!
YUM!... BREAD AND SCRAM!
BRRR ...THE WATER'S SO SCRAMMY!
TODAY WE STUDIED SCRAMMING.
MY TURN TO SCRAM THE DISHES!
CRASH
CRACK
I GOTTA SCRAM!
HA! SHE FINALLY USED IT RIGHT.
CAZENOVE & WILLIAM

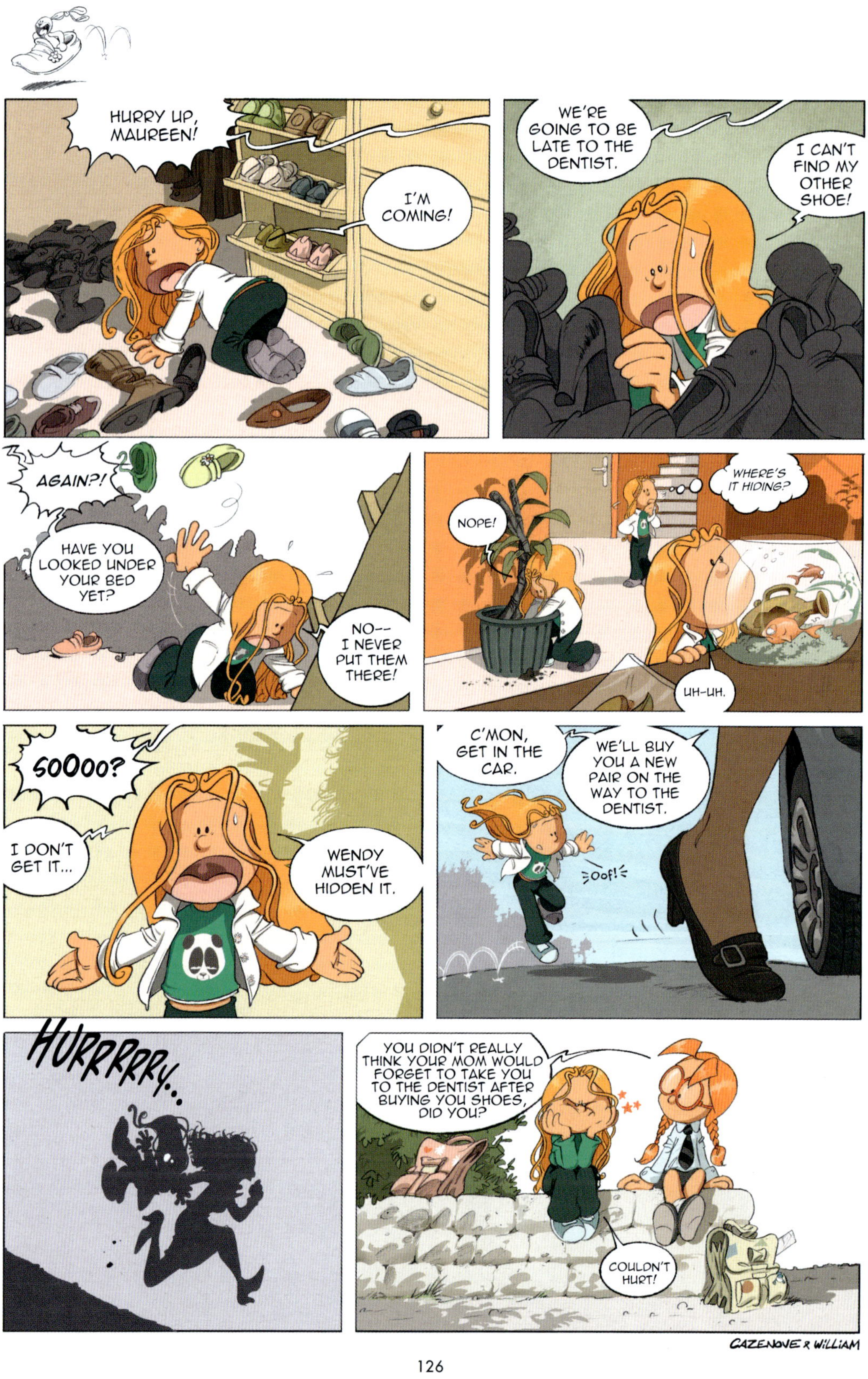
HURRY UP, MAUREEN!
I'M COMING!
WE'RE GOING TO BE LATE TO THE DENTIST.
I CAN'T FIND MY OTHER SHOE!
AGAIN?!
HAVE YOU LOOKED UNDER YOUR BED YET?
NO-- I NEVER PUT THEM THERE!
WHERE'S IT HIDING?
NOPE!
UH-UH.
SOOOO?
I DON'T GET IT...
WENDY MUST'VE HIDDEN IT.
C'MON, GET IN THE CAR.
WE'LL BUY YOU A NEW PAIR ON THE WAY TO THE DENTIST.
OOF!
HURRRRRY...
YOU DIDN'T REALLY THINK YOUR MOM WOULD FORGET TO TAKE YOU TO THE DENTIST AFTER BUYING YOU SHOES, DID YOU?
COULDN'T HURT!
CAZENOVE & WILLIAM

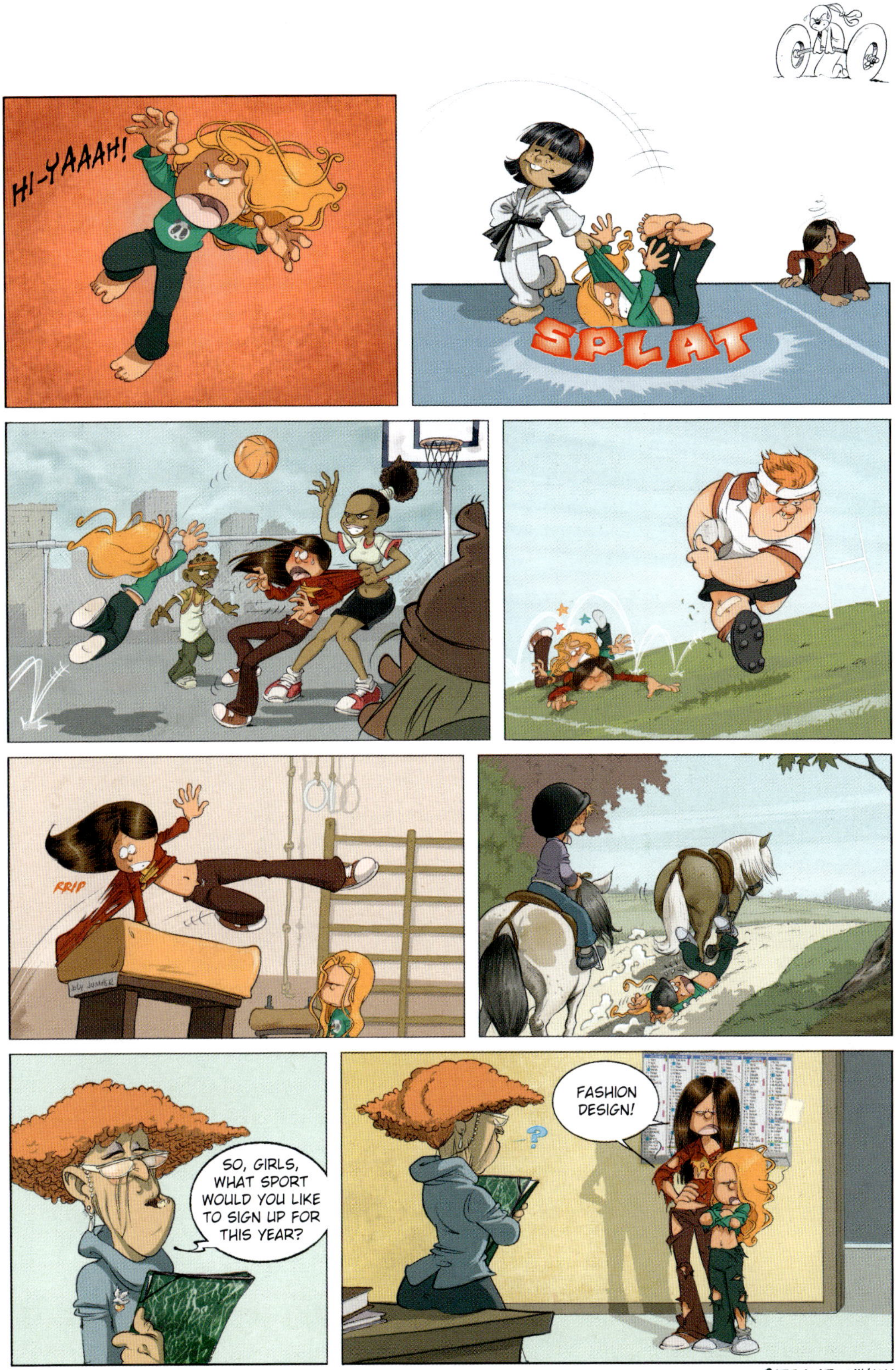
HI-YAAAH!
SPLAT
RRIP
SO, GIRLS, WHAT SPORT WOULD YOU LIKE TO SIGN UP FOR THIS YEAR?
FASHION DESIGN!

CAZENOVE & WILLIAM

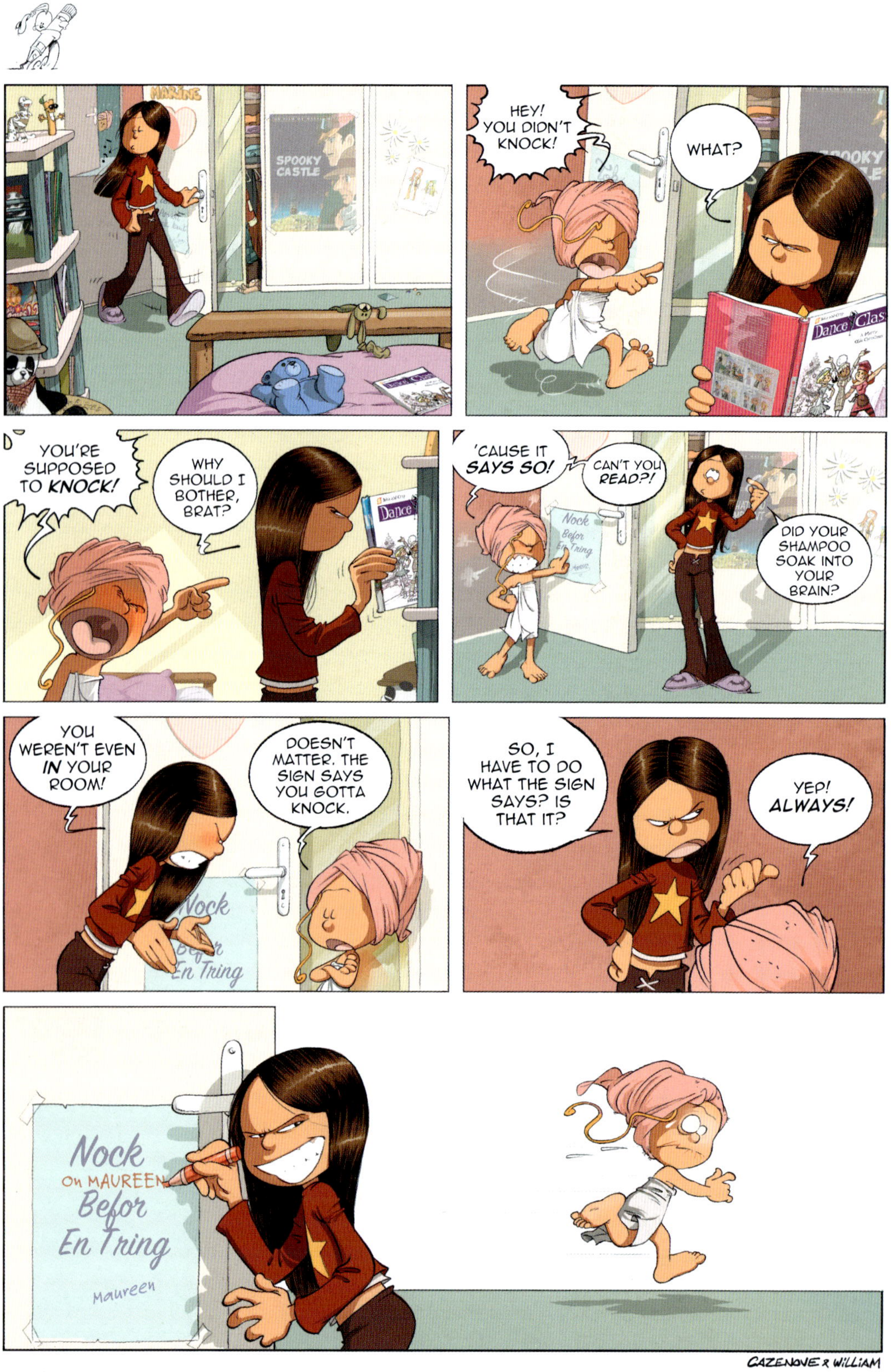
MARINE
SPOOKY CASTLE
HEY! YOU DIDN'T KNOCK!
WHAT?
Dance Class
YOU'RE SUPPOSED TO **KNOCK!**
WHY SHOULD I BOTHER, BRAT?
'CAUSE IT ***SAYS SO!***
CAN'T YOU *READ?!*
Nock Befor En Tring
DID YOUR SHAMPOO SOAK INTO YOUR BRAIN?
YOU WEREN'T EVEN ***IN*** YOUR ROOM!
DOESN'T MATTER. THE SIGN SAYS YOU GOTTA KNOCK.
SO, I HAVE TO DO WHAT THE SIGN SAYS? IS THAT IT?
YEP! ***ALWAYS!***
Nock On MAUREEN Befor En Tring
Maureen
CAZENOVE & WILLIAM

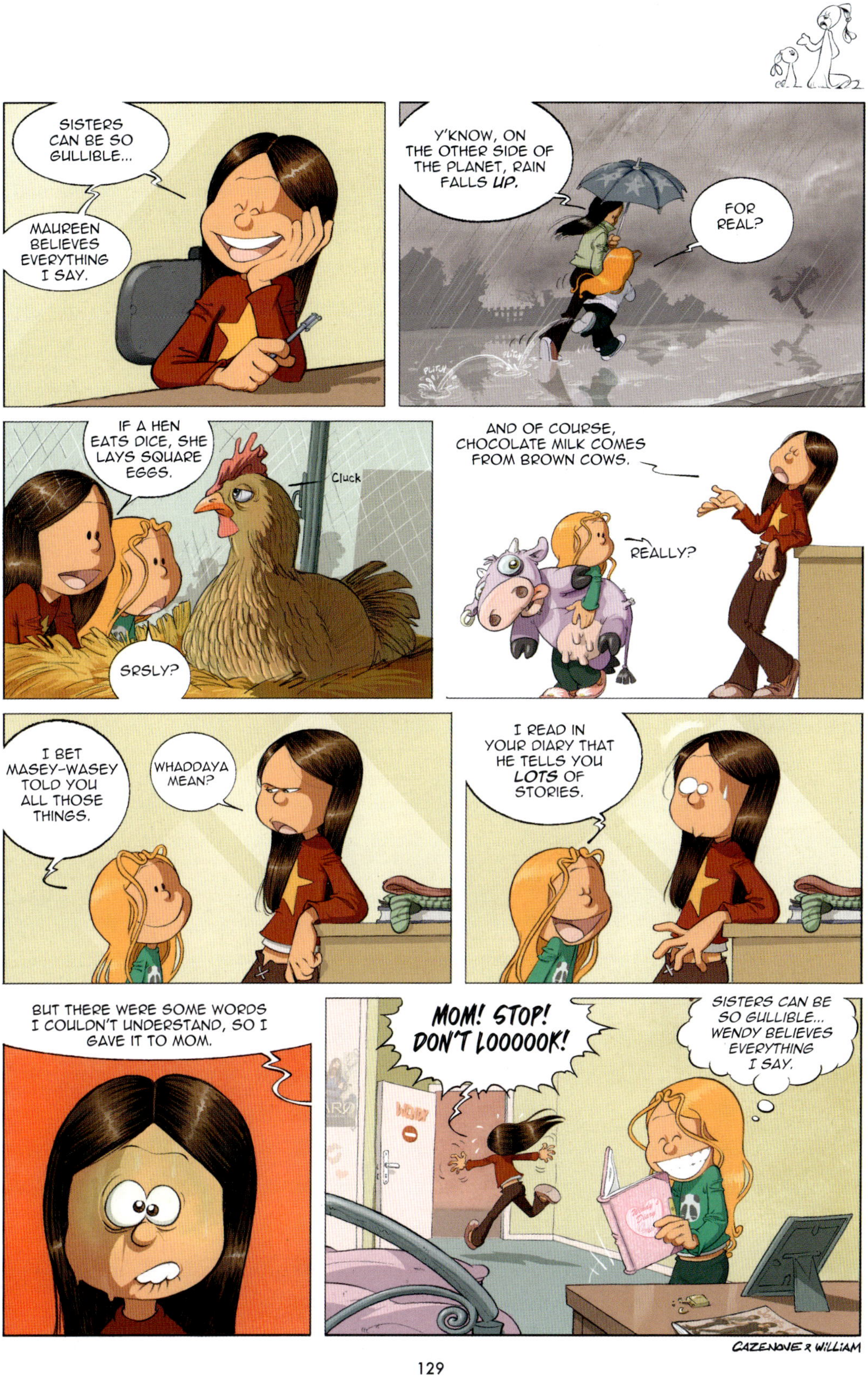
SISTERS CAN BE SO GULLIBLE...
MAUREEN BELIEVES EVERYTHING I SAY.
Y'KNOW, ON THE OTHER SIDE OF THE PLANET, RAIN FALLS *UP.*
FOR REAL?
PLITCH
PLITCH
IF A HEN EATS DICE, SHE LAYS SQUARE EGGS.
Cluck
SRSLY?
AND OF COURSE, CHOCOLATE MILK COMES FROM BROWN COWS.
REALLY?
I BET MASEY-WASEY TOLD YOU ALL THOSE THINGS.
WHADDAYA MEAN?
I READ IN YOUR DIARY THAT HE TELLS YOU *LOTS* OF STORIES.
BUT THERE WERE SOME WORDS I COULDN'T UNDERSTAND, SO I GAVE IT TO MOM.
MOM! STOP! DON'T LOOOOOK!
SISTERS CAN BE SO GULLIBLE... WENDY BELIEVES EVERYTHING I SAY.
CAZENOVE & WILLIAM

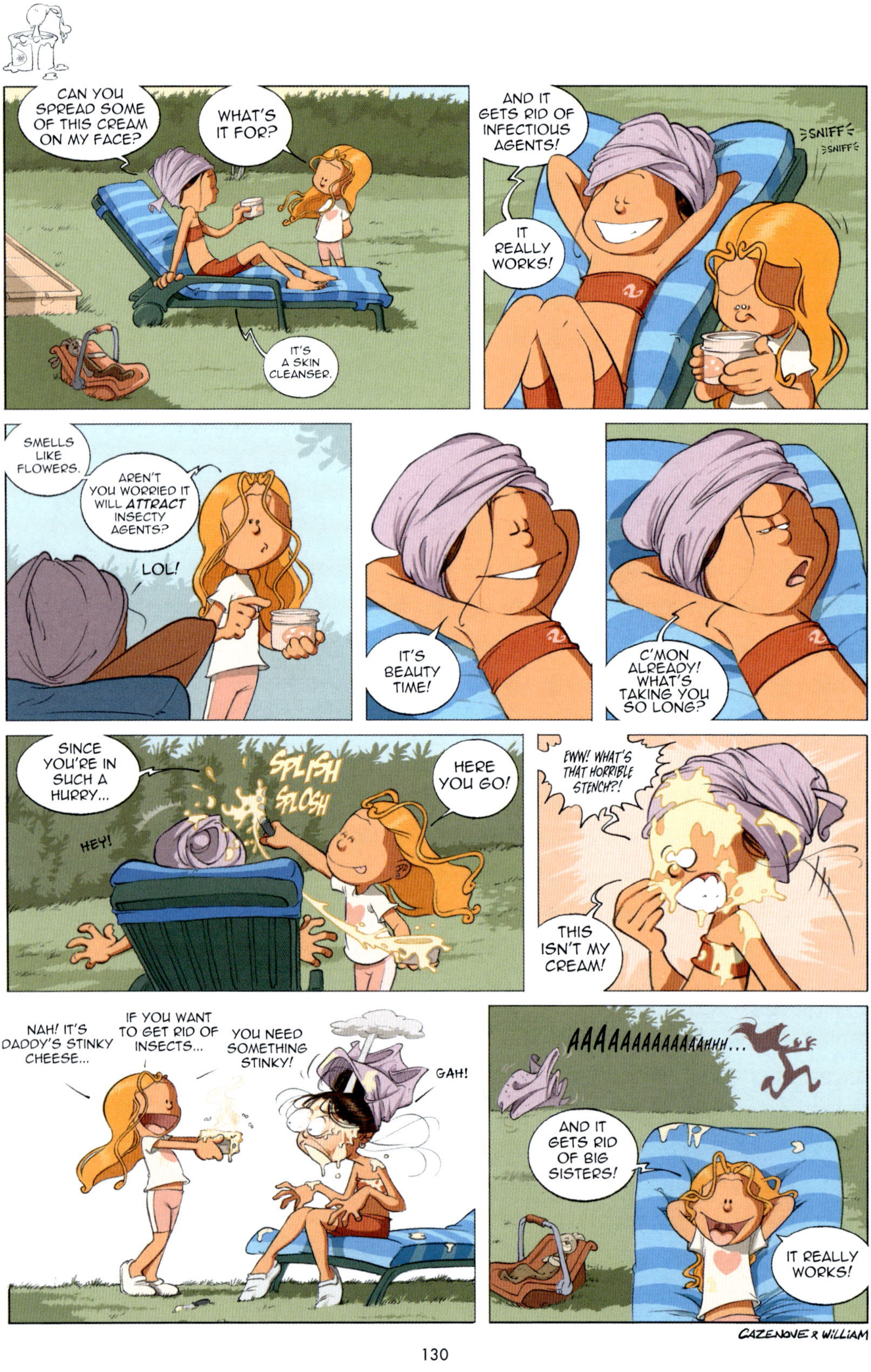
CAN YOU SPREAD SOME OF THIS CREAM ON MY FACE?
WHAT'S IT FOR?
IT'S A SKIN CLEANSER.
AND IT GETS RID OF INFECTIOUS AGENTS!
IT REALLY WORKS!
SNIFF
SNIFF
SMELLS LIKE FLOWERS.
AREN'T YOU WORRIED IT WILL ATTRACT INSECTY AGENTS?
LOL!
IT'S BEAUTY TIME!
C'MON ALREADY! WHAT'S TAKING YOU SO LONG?
SINCE YOU'RE IN SUCH A HURRY...
SPLISH
SPLOSH
HERE YOU GO!
HEY!
EWW! WHAT'S THAT HORRIBLE STENCH?!
THIS ISN'T MY CREAM!
NAH! IT'S DADDY'S STINKY CHEESE...
IF YOU WANT TO GET RID OF INSECTS...
YOU NEED SOMETHING STINKY!
GAH!
AAAAAAAAAAAAAHHH...
AND IT GETS RID OF BIG SISTERS!
IT REALLY WORKS!
CAZENOVE & WILLIAM

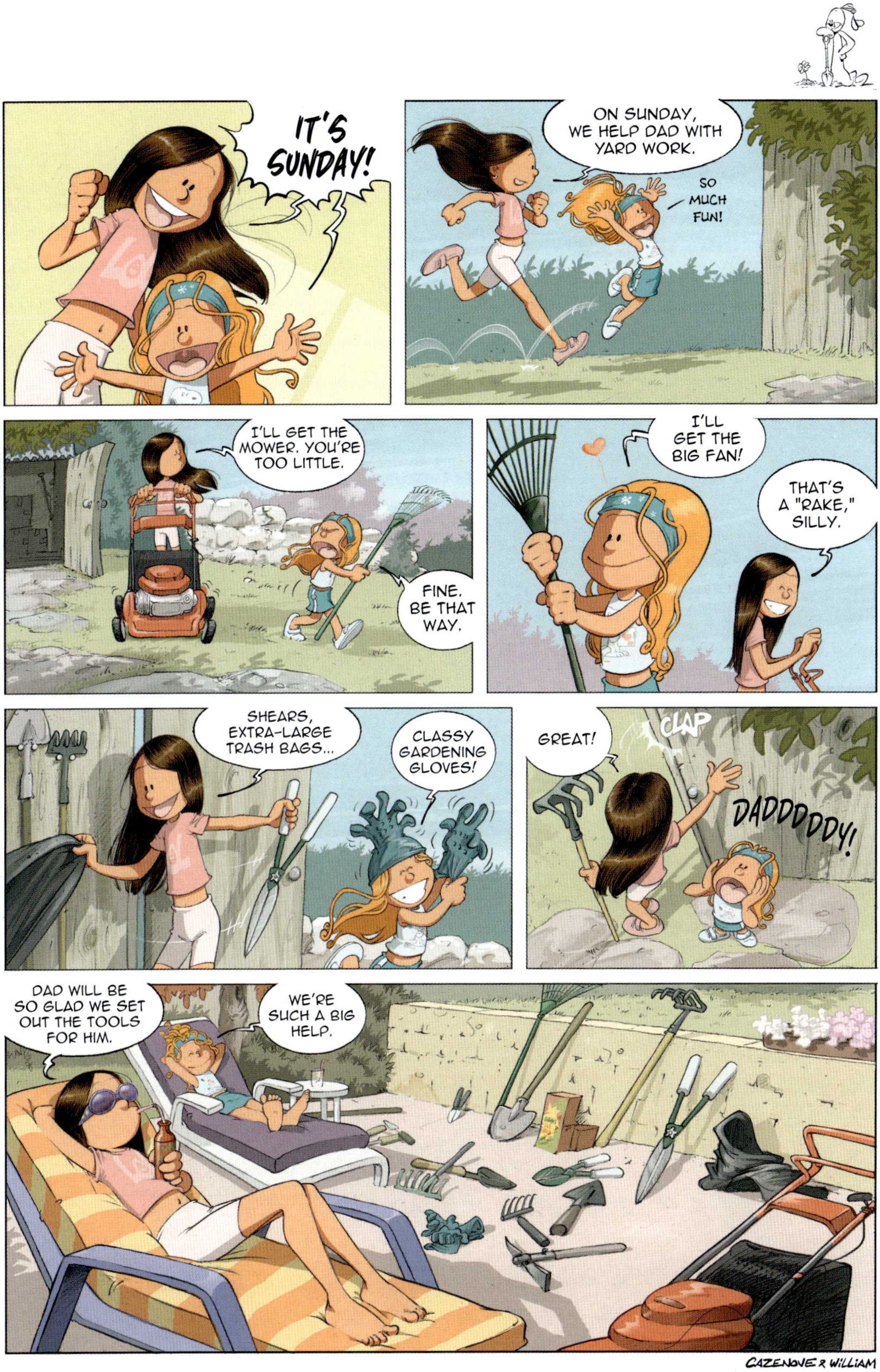
IT'S SUNDAY!
ON SUNDAY, WE HELP DAD WITH YARD WORK.
SO MUCH FUN!
I'LL GET THE MOWER. YOU'RE TOO LITTLE.
FINE. BE THAT WAY.
I'LL GET THE BIG FAN!
THAT'S A "RAKE," SILLY.
SHEARS, EXTRA-LARGE TRASH BAGS...
CLASSY GARDENING GLOVES!
GREAT!
CLAP
DADDDDDY!
DAD WILL BE SO GLAD WE SET OUT THE TOOLS FOR HIM.
WE'RE SUCH A BIG HELP.
CAZENOVE & WILLIAM

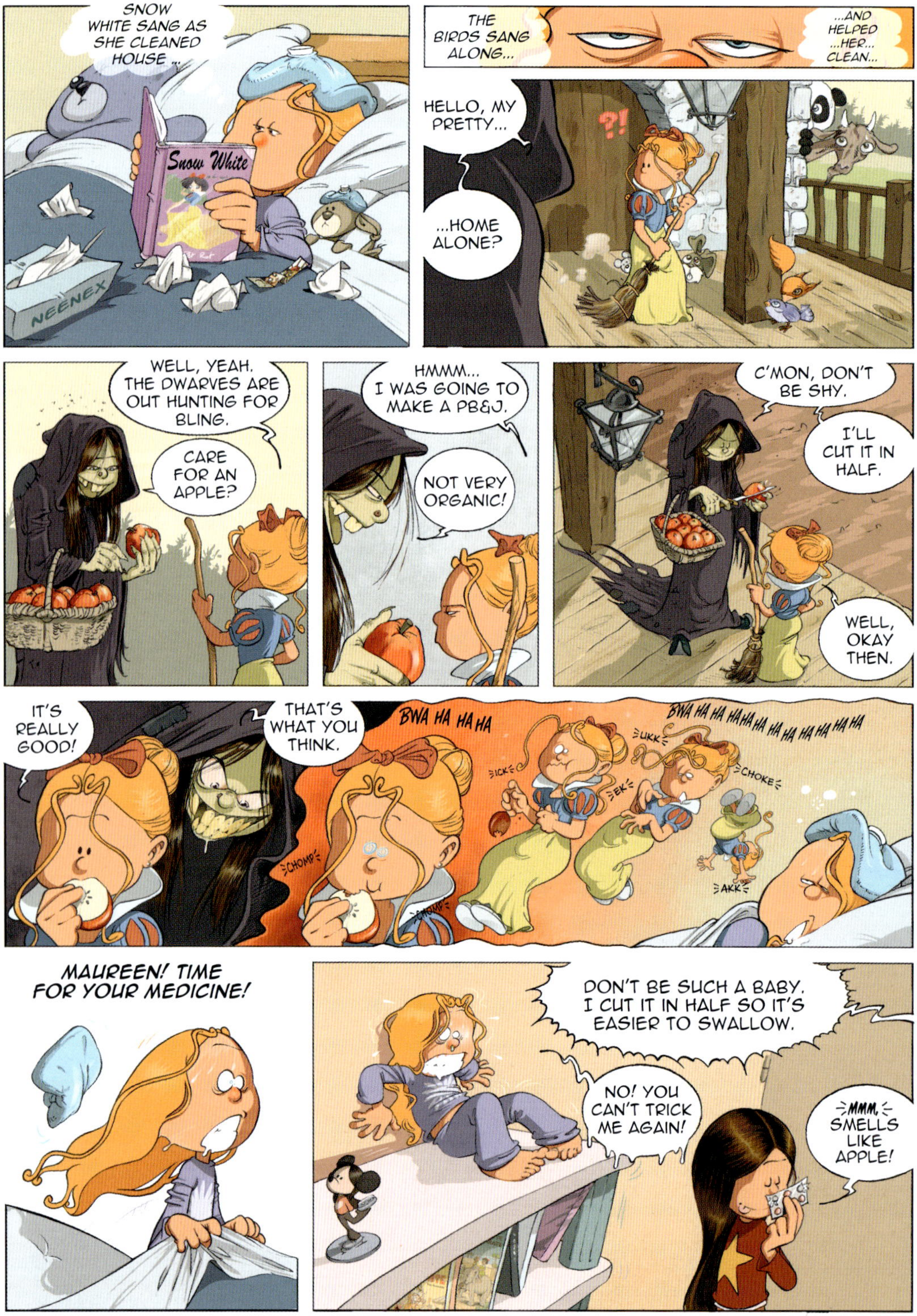

SNOW WHITE SANG AS SHE CLEANED HOUSE ...
Snow White
NEENEX
THE BIRDS SANG ALONG...
...AND HELPED ...HER... CLEAN...
HELLO, MY PRETTY...
...HOME ALONE?
?!
WELL, YEAH. THE DWARVES ARE OUT HUNTING FOR BLING.
CARE FOR AN APPLE?
HMMM... I WAS GOING TO MAKE A PB&J.
NOT VERY ORGANIC!
C'MON, DON'T BE SHY.
I'LL CUT IT IN HALF.
WELL, OKAY THEN.
IT'S REALLY GOOD!
THAT'S WHAT YOU THINK.
BWA HA HA HA
CHOMP
CHOMP
BWA HA HA HA HA HA HA HA HA HA HA HA HA
ICK
UKK
EK
CHOKE
AKK
MAUREEN! TIME FOR YOUR MEDICINE!
DON'T BE SUCH A BABY. I CUT IT IN HALF SO IT'S EASIER TO SWALLOW.
NO! YOU CAN'T TRICK ME AGAIN!
MMM, SMELLS LIKE APPLE!

CAZENOVE & WILLIAM

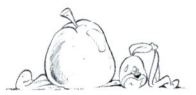

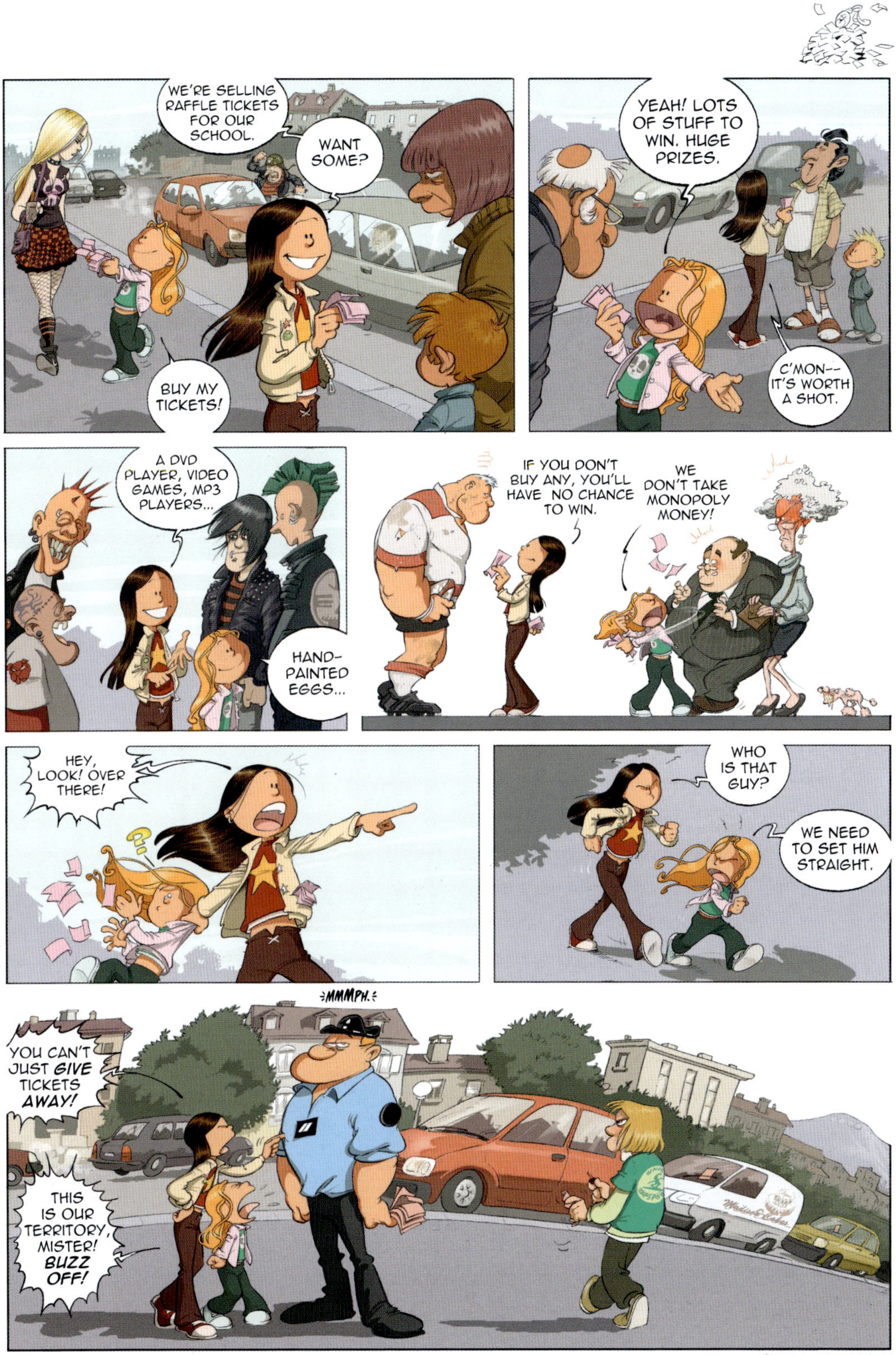

WE'RE SELLING RAFFLE TICKETS FOR OUR SCHOOL.
WANT SOME?
BUY MY TICKETS!
YEAH! LOTS OF STUFF TO WIN. HUGE PRIZES.
C'MON-- IT'S WORTH A SHOT.
A DVD PLAYER, VIDEO GAMES, MP3 PLAYERS...
HAND-PAINTED EGGS...
IF YOU DON'T BUY ANY, YOU'LL HAVE NO CHANCE TO WIN.
WE DON'T TAKE MONOPOLY MONEY!
HEY, LOOK! OVER THERE!
WHO IS THAT GUY?
WE NEED TO SET HIM STRAIGHT.
MMMPH.
YOU CAN'T JUST GIVE TICKETS AWAY!
THIS IS OUR TERRITORY, MISTER! BUZZ OFF!
CAZENOVE & WILLIAM

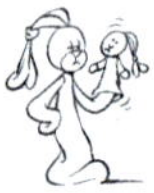

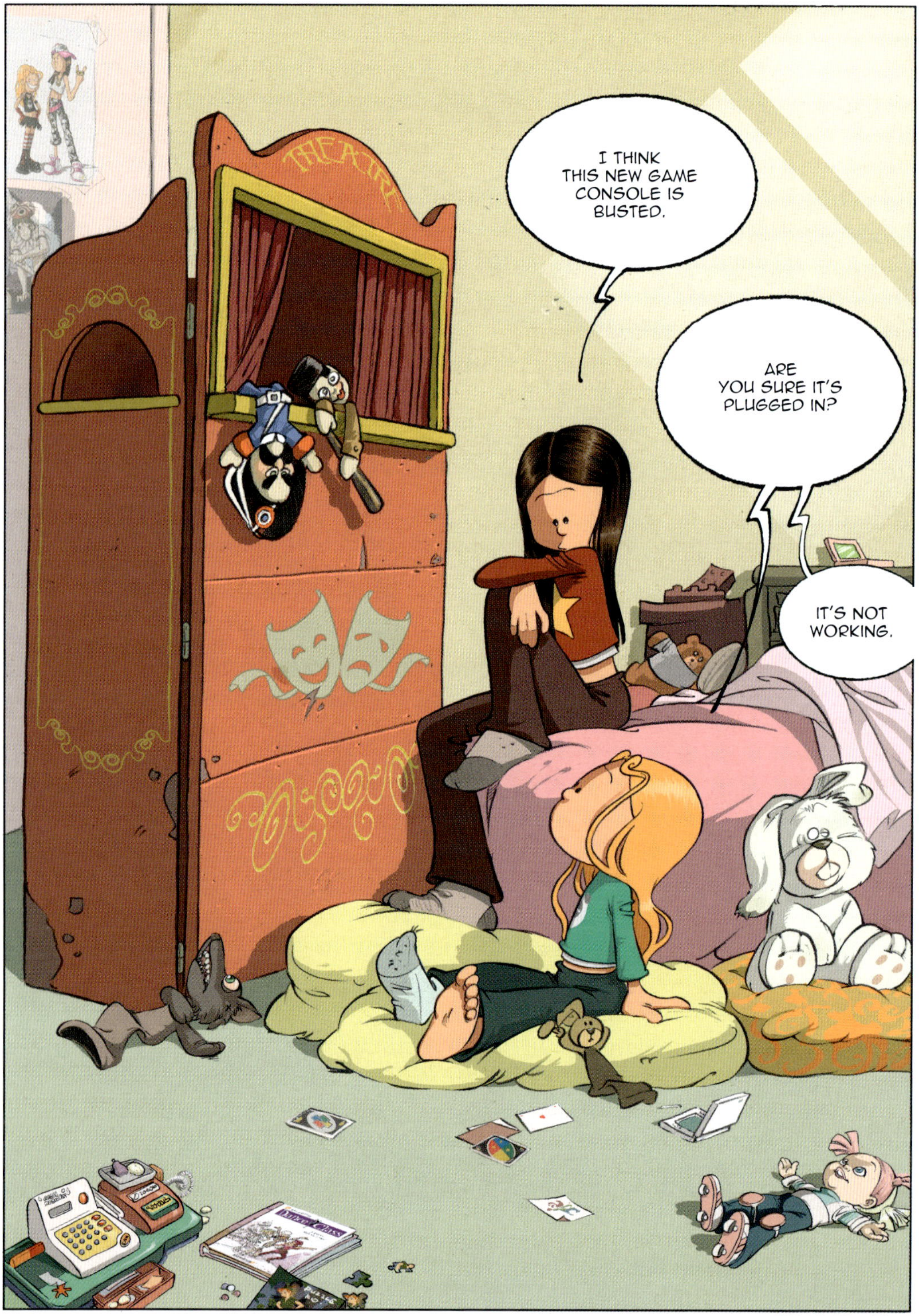
I THINK THIS NEW GAME CONSOLE IS BUSTED.
ARE YOU SURE IT'S PLUGGED IN?
IT'S NOT WORKING.

CAZENOVE & WILLIAM

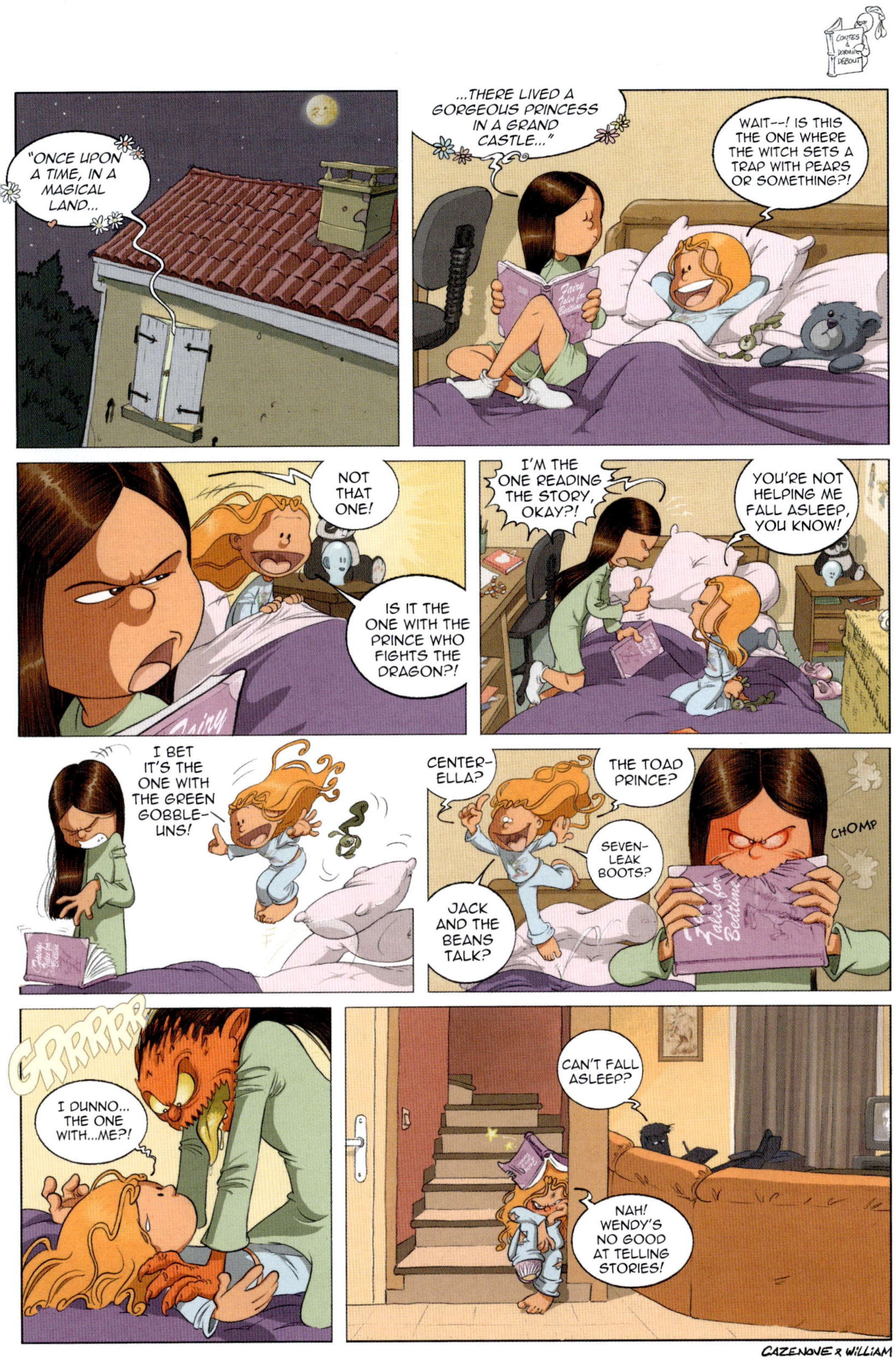
"ONCE UPON A TIME, IN A MAGICAL LAND...
...THERE LIVED A GORGEOUS PRINCESS IN A GRAND CASTLE..."
WAIT--! IS THIS THE ONE WHERE THE WITCH SETS A TRAP WITH PEARS OR SOMETHING?!
NOT THAT ONE!
IS IT THE ONE WITH THE PRINCE WHO FIGHTS THE DRAGON?!
I'M THE ONE READING THE STORY, OKAY?!
YOU'RE NOT HELPING ME FALL ASLEEP, YOU KNOW!
I BET IT'S THE ONE WITH THE GREEN GOBBLE-UNS!
CENTER-ELLA?
THE TOAD PRINCE?
SEVEN-LEAK BOOTS?
JACK AND THE BEANS TALK?
CHOMP
GRRRRR
I DUNNO... THE ONE WITH...ME?!
CAN'T FALL ASLEEP?
NAH! WENDY'S NO GOOD AT TELLING STORIES!
CAZENOVE & WILLIAM

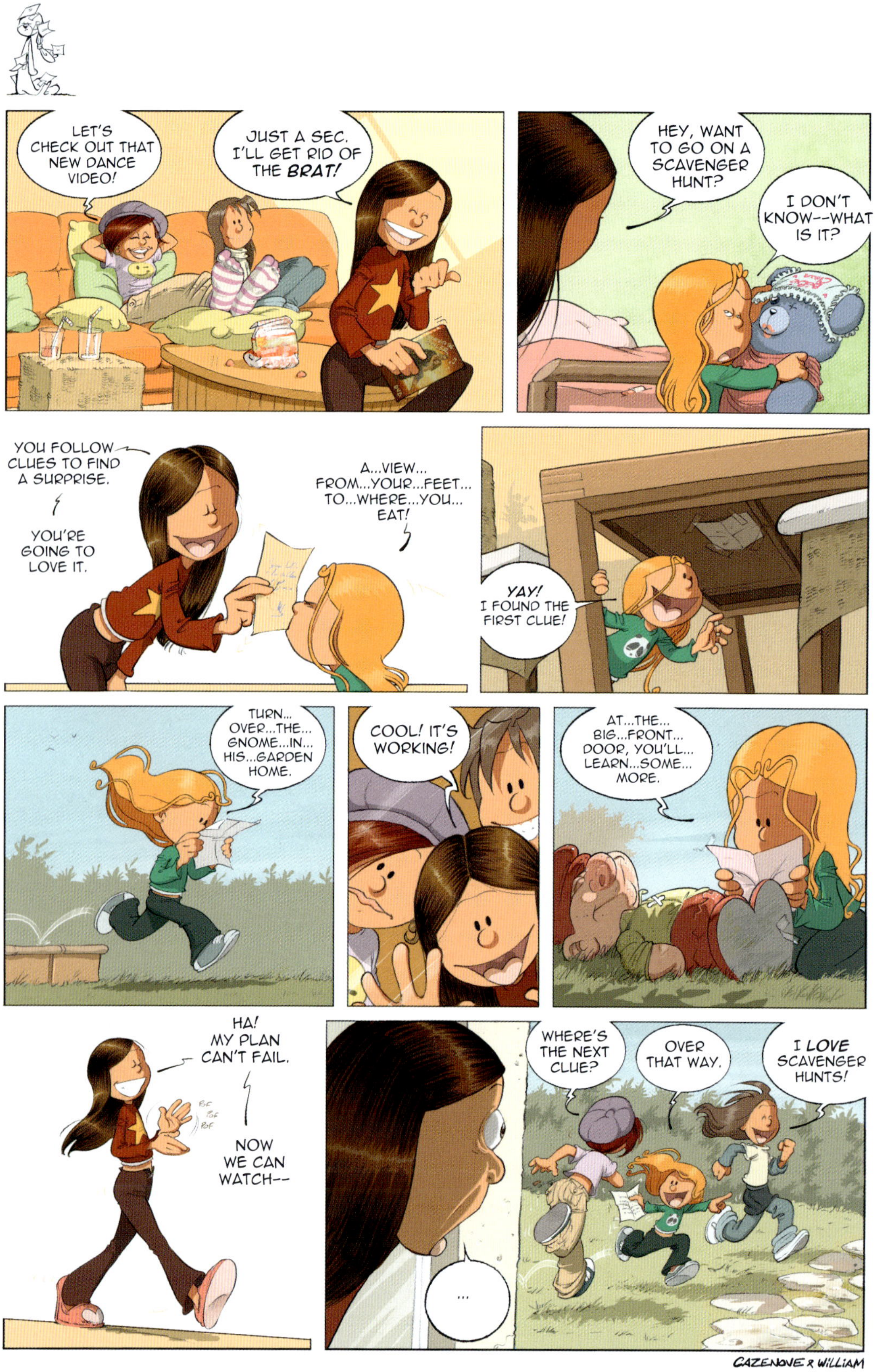
LET'S CHECK OUT THAT NEW DANCE VIDEO!
JUST A SEC. I'LL GET RID OF THE *BRAT!*
HEY, WANT TO GO ON A SCAVENGER HUNT?
I DON'T KNOW--WHAT IS IT?
YOU FOLLOW CLUES TO FIND A SURPRISE.
YOU'RE GOING TO LOVE IT.
A...VIEW... FROM...YOUR...FEET... TO...WHERE...YOU... EAT!
YAY! I FOUND THE FIRST CLUE!
TURN... OVER...THE... GNOME...IN... HIS...GARDEN HOME.
COOL! IT'S WORKING!
AT...THE... BIG...FRONT... DOOR, YOU'LL... LEARN...SOME... MORE.
HA! MY PLAN CAN'T FAIL.
NOW WE CAN WATCH--
...
WHERE'S THE NEXT CLUE?
OVER THAT WAY.
I *LOVE* SCAVENGER HUNTS!
CAZENOVE & WILLIAM

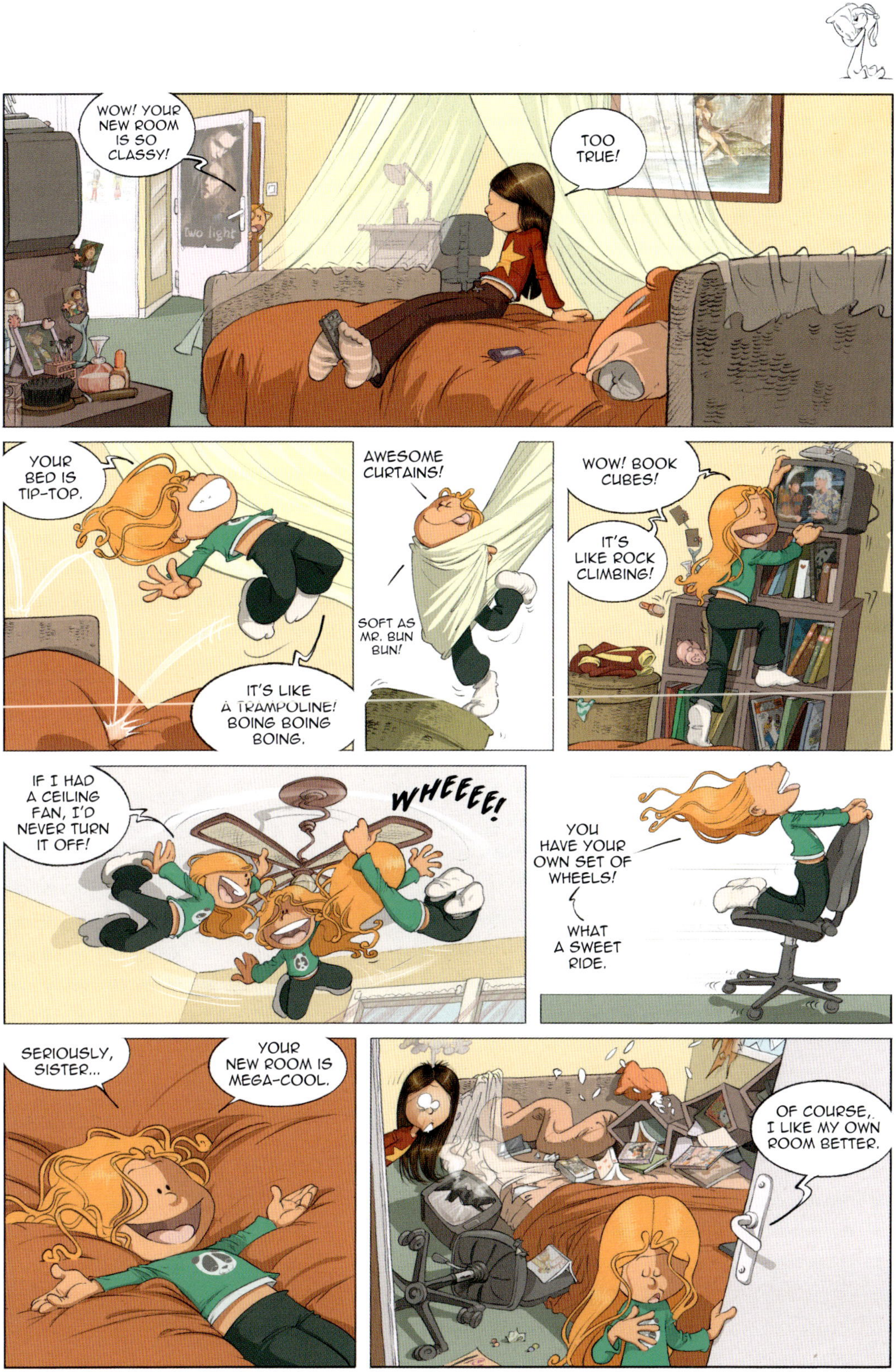

WOW! YOUR NEW ROOM IS SO CLASSY!
TOO TRUE!
two light
YOUR BED IS TIP-TOP.
IT'S LIKE A TRAMPOLINE! BOING BOING BOING.
AWESOME CURTAINS!
SOFT AS MR. BUN BUN!
WOW! BOOK CUBES!
IT'S LIKE ROCK CLIMBING!
IF I HAD A CEILING FAN, I'D NEVER TURN IT OFF!
WHEEEE!
YOU HAVE YOUR OWN SET OF WHEELS!
WHAT A SWEET RIDE.
SERIOUSLY, SISTER...
YOUR NEW ROOM IS MEGA-COOL.
OF COURSE, I LIKE MY OWN ROOM BETTER.
CAZENOVE & WILLIAM

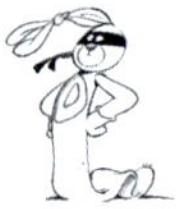

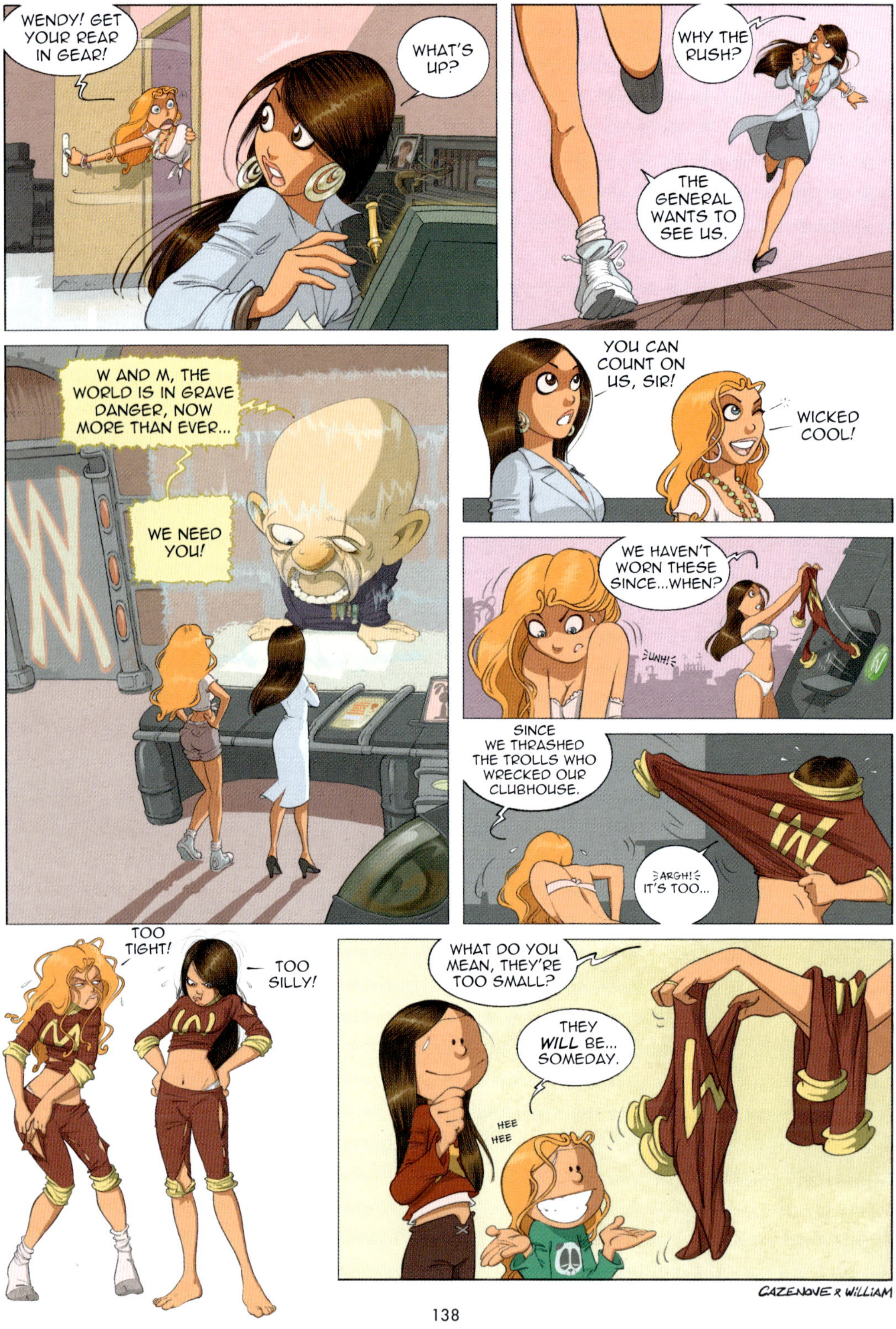

WENDY! GET YOUR REAR IN GEAR!
WHAT'S UP?
WHY THE RUSH?
THE GENERAL WANTS TO SEE US.
W AND M, THE WORLD IS IN GRAVE DANGER, NOW MORE THAN EVER...
WE NEED YOU!
YOU CAN COUNT ON US, SIR!
WICKED COOL!
WE HAVEN'T WORN THESE SINCE...WHEN?
UNH!
SINCE WE THRASHED THE TROLLS WHO WRECKED OUR CLUBHOUSE.
ARGH! IT'S TOO...
TOO TIGHT!
TOO SILLY!
WHAT DO YOU MEAN, THEY'RE TOO SMALL?
THEY *WILL* BE... SOMEDAY.
HEE HEE

CAZENOVE & WILLIAM

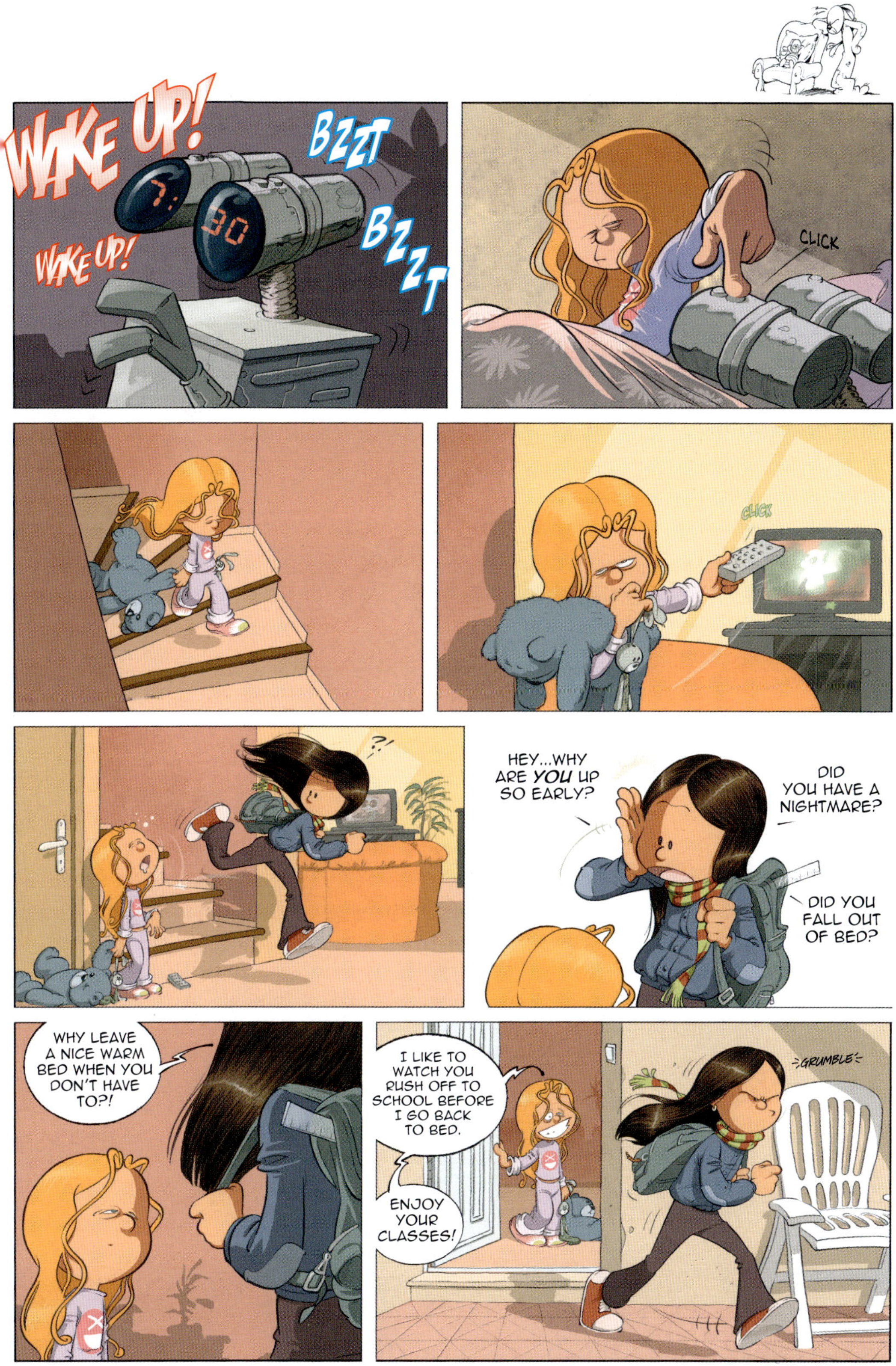
WAKE UP!
BZZT
7:30
WAKE UP!
BZZT
CLICK
CLICK
?!
HEY...WHY ARE YOU UP SO EARLY?
DID YOU HAVE A NIGHTMARE?
DID YOU FALL OUT OF BED?
WHY LEAVE A NICE WARM BED WHEN YOU DON'T HAVE TO?!
I LIKE TO WATCH YOU RUSH OFF TO SCHOOL BEFORE I GO BACK TO BED.
ENJOY YOUR CLASSES!
GRUMBLE

CAZENOVE & WILLIAM

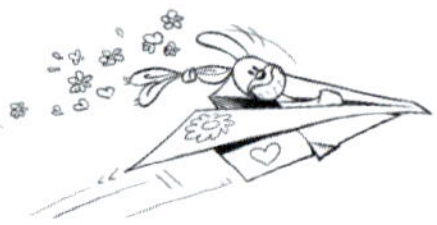

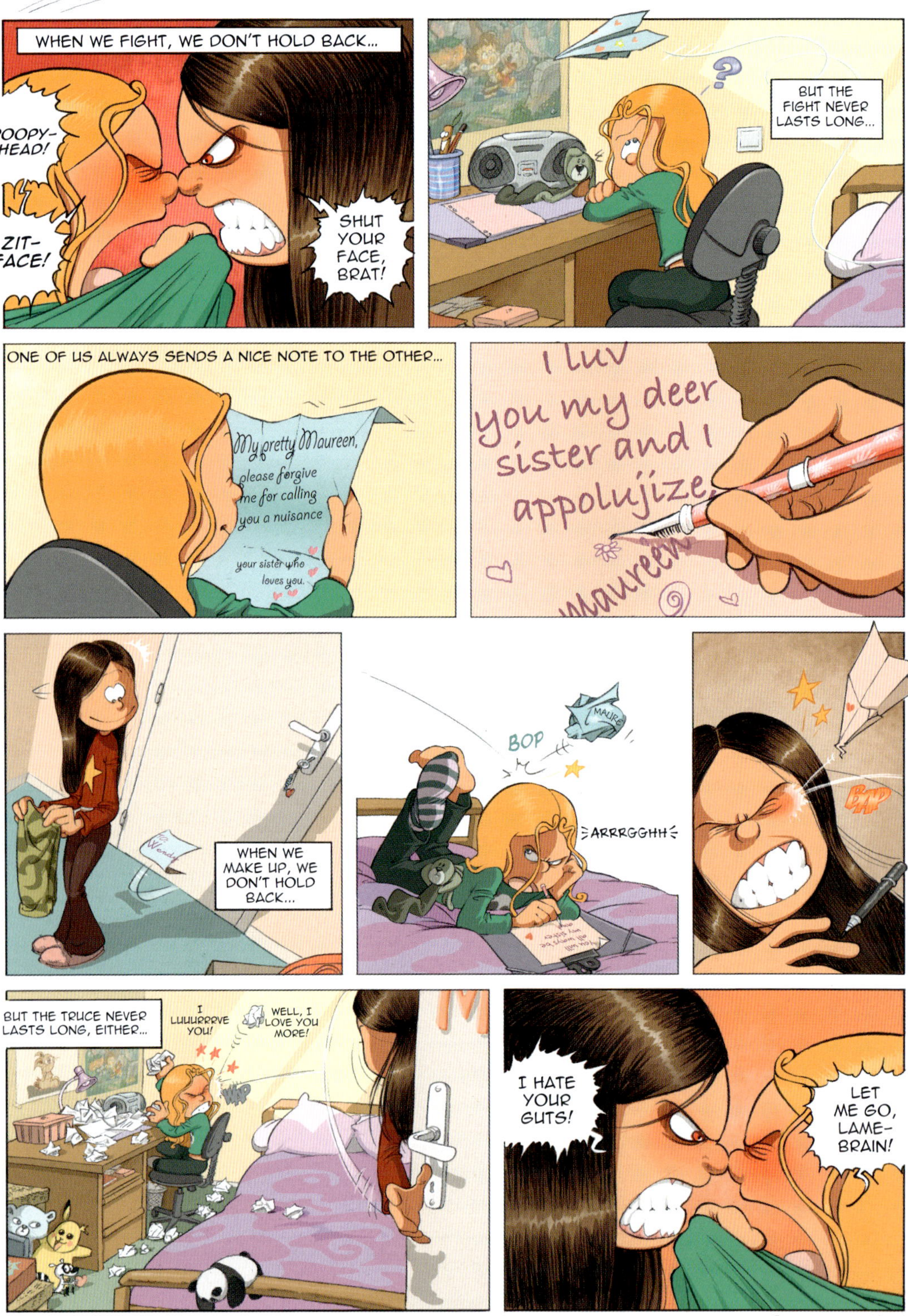

WHEN WE FIGHT, WE DON'T HOLD BACK...
POOPY-HEAD!
ZIT-FACE!
SHUT YOUR FACE, BRAT!
BUT THE FIGHT NEVER LASTS LONG...
ONE OF US ALWAYS SENDS A NICE NOTE TO THE OTHER...
My pretty Maureen,
please forgive me for calling you a nuisance
your sister who loves you.
I luv you my deer sister and I appolujize,
maureen
WHEN WE MAKE UP, WE DON'T HOLD BACK...
BOP
ARRRGGHH
BAP
BUT THE TRUCE NEVER LASTS LONG, EITHER...
I LUUURRRVE YOU!
WELL, I LOVE YOU MORE!
WAP
I HATE YOUR GUTS!
LET ME GO, LAME-BRAIN!

CAZENOVE & WILLIAM

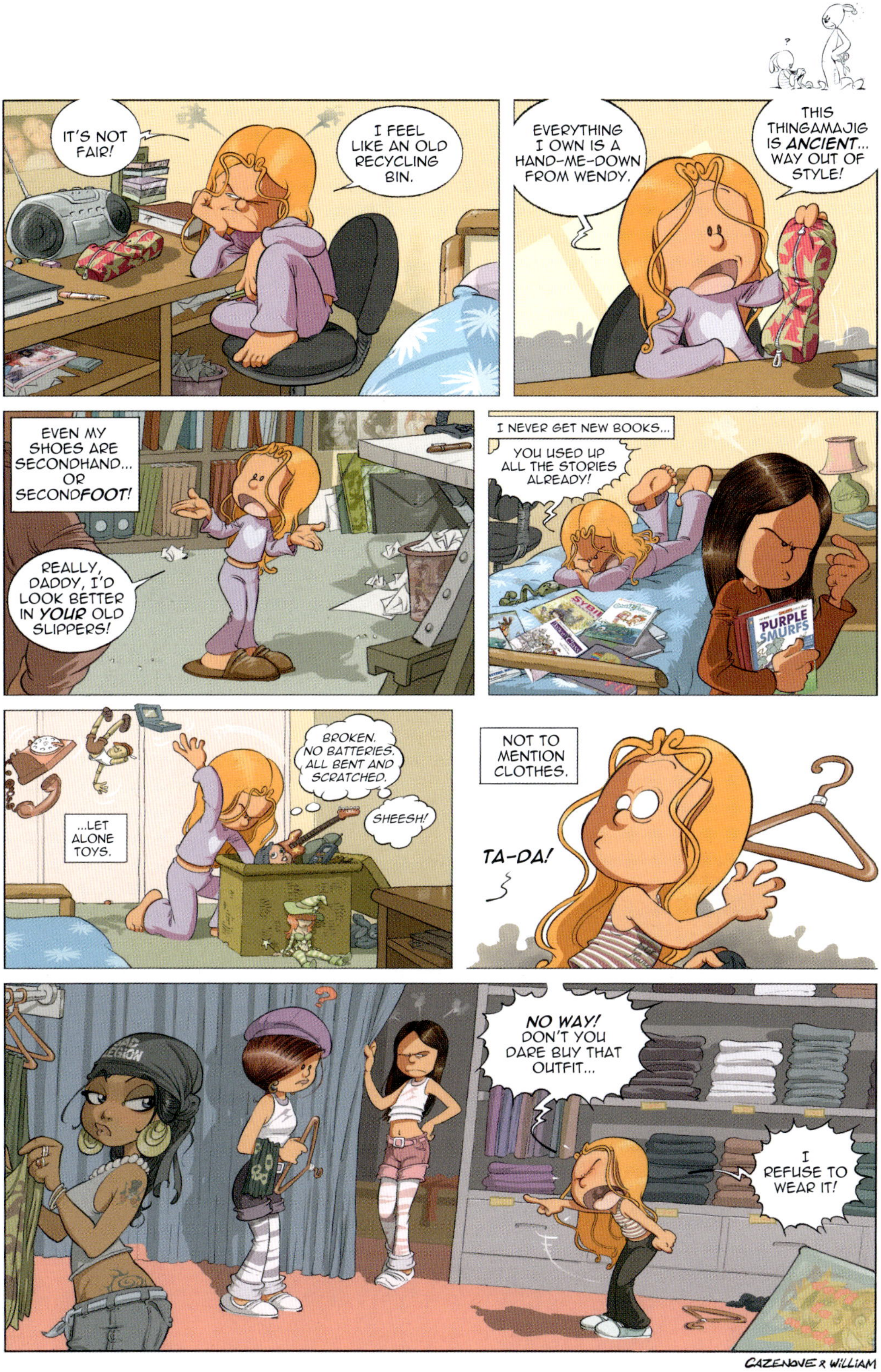
IT'S NOT FAIR!
I FEEL LIKE AN OLD RECYCLING BIN.
EVERYTHING I OWN IS A HAND-ME-DOWN FROM WENDY.
THIS THINGAMAJIG IS *ANCIENT*... WAY OUT OF STYLE!
EVEN MY SHOES ARE SECONDHAND... OR SECOND*FOOT*!
REALLY, DADDY, I'D LOOK BETTER IN *YOUR* OLD SLIPPERS!
I NEVER GET NEW BOOKS...
YOU USED UP ALL THE STORIES ALREADY!
PURPLE SMURFS
...LET ALONE TOYS.
BROKEN. NO BATTERIES. ALL BENT AND SCRATCHED.
SHEESH!
NOT TO MENTION CLOTHES.
TA-DA!
NO WAY! DON'T YOU DARE BUY THAT OUTFIT...
I REFUSE TO WEAR IT!
CAZENOVE & WILLIAM

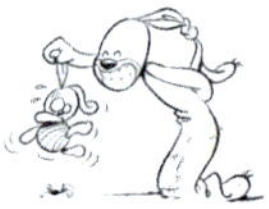

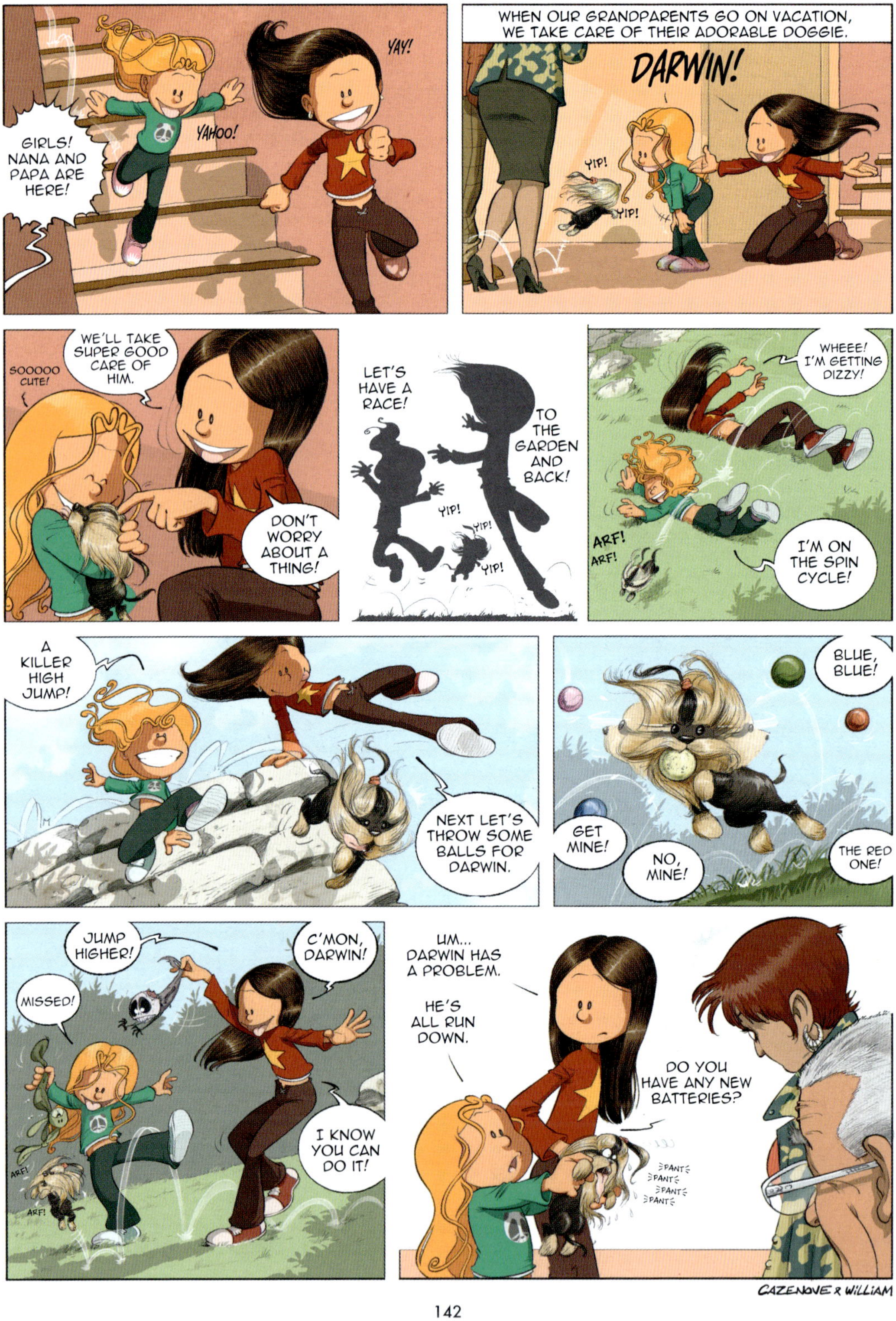
GIRLS! NANA AND PAPA ARE HERE!
YAHOO!
YAY!
WHEN OUR GRANDPARENTS GO ON VACATION, WE TAKE CARE OF THEIR ADORABLE DOGGIE.
DARWIN!
YIP!
YIP!
SOOOOO CUTE!
WE'LL TAKE SUPER GOOD CARE OF HIM.
DON'T WORRY ABOUT A THING!
LET'S HAVE A RACE!
TO THE GARDEN AND BACK!
YIP!
YIP!
YIP!
WHEEE! I'M GETTING DIZZY!
ARF!
ARF!
I'M ON THE SPIN CYCLE!
A KILLER HIGH JUMP!
NEXT LET'S THROW SOME BALLS FOR DARWIN.
BLUE, BLUE!
GET MINE!
NO, MINE!
THE RED ONE!
JUMP HIGHER!
C'MON, DARWIN!
MISSED!
ARF!
ARF!
I KNOW YOU CAN DO IT!
UM... DARWIN HAS A PROBLEM.
HE'S ALL RUN DOWN.
DO YOU HAVE ANY NEW BATTERIES?
PANT
PANT
PANT
PANT
CAZENOVE & WILLIAM

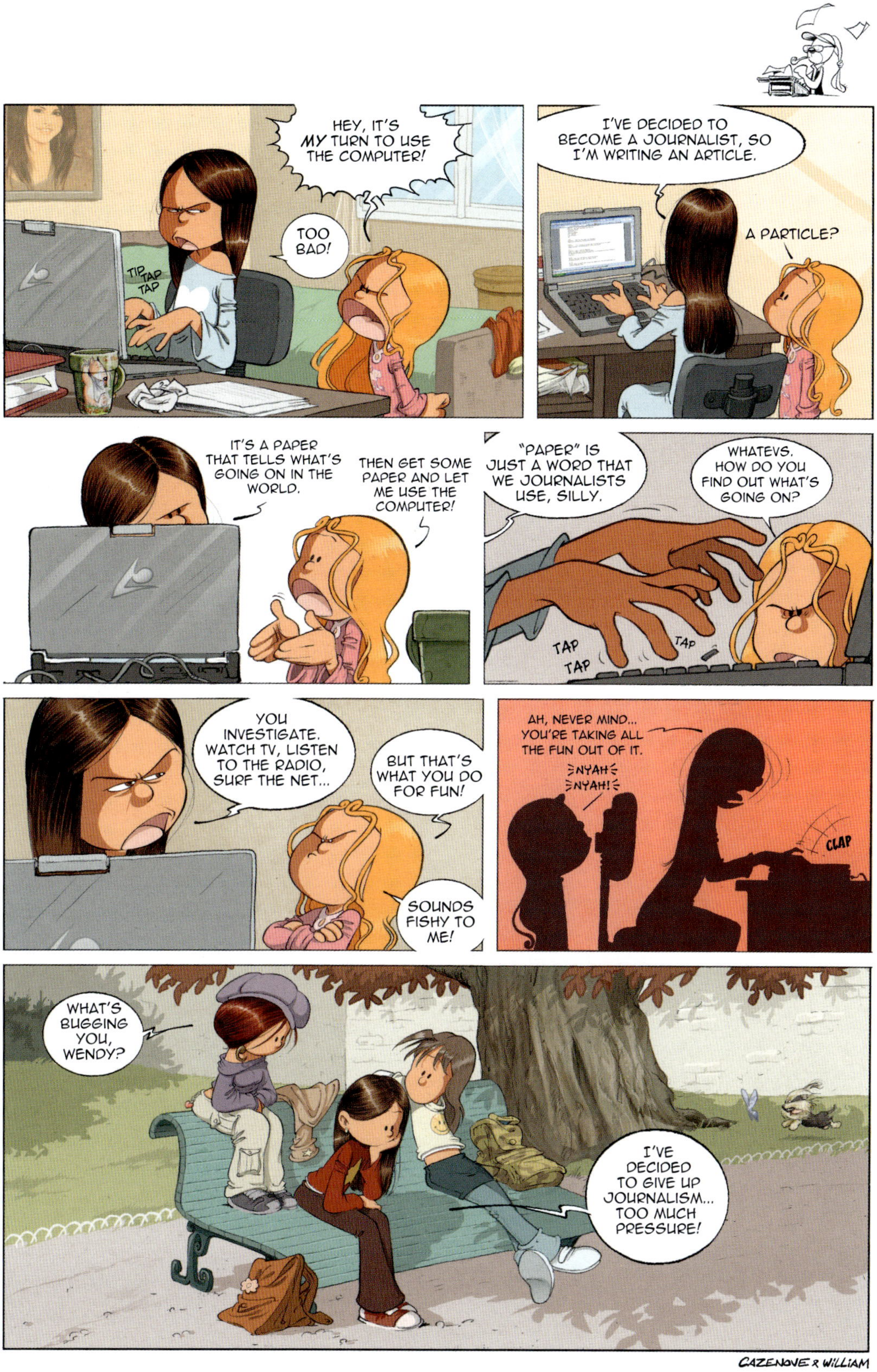
HEY, IT'S MY TURN TO USE THE COMPUTER!
TOO BAD!
TIP TAP TAP
I'VE DECIDED TO BECOME A JOURNALIST, SO I'M WRITING AN ARTICLE.
A PARTICLE?
IT'S A PAPER THAT TELLS WHAT'S GOING ON IN THE WORLD.
THEN GET SOME PAPER AND LET ME USE THE COMPUTER!
"PAPER" IS JUST A WORD THAT WE JOURNALISTS USE, SILLY.
WHATEVS. HOW DO YOU FIND OUT WHAT'S GOING ON?
TAP TAP TAP
YOU INVESTIGATE. WATCH TV, LISTEN TO THE RADIO, SURF THE NET...
BUT THAT'S WHAT YOU DO FOR FUN!
SOUNDS FISHY TO ME!
AH, NEVER MIND... YOU'RE TAKING ALL THE FUN OUT OF IT.
NYAH NYAH!
CLAP
WHAT'S BUGGING YOU, WENDY?
I'VE DECIDED TO GIVE UP JOURNALISM... TOO MUCH PRESSURE!
CAZENOVE & WILLIAM

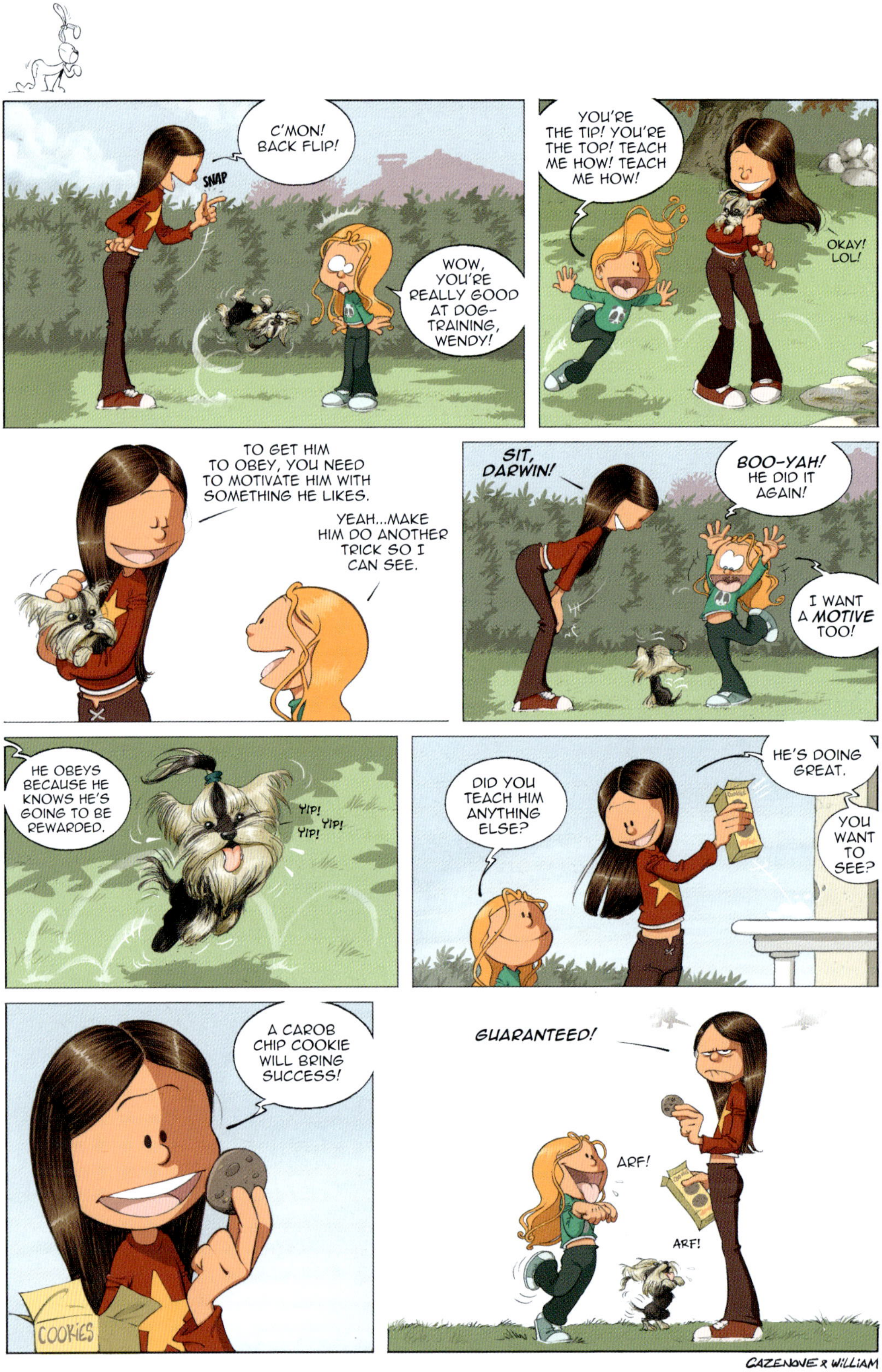
C'MON! BACK FLIP!
SNAP
WOW, YOU'RE REALLY GOOD AT DOG-TRAINING, WENDY!
YOU'RE THE TIP! YOU'RE THE TOP! TEACH ME HOW! TEACH ME HOW!
OKAY! LOL!
TO GET HIM TO OBEY, YOU NEED TO MOTIVATE HIM WITH SOMETHING HE LIKES.
YEAH...MAKE HIM DO ANOTHER TRICK SO I CAN SEE.
SIT, DARWIN!
BOO-YAH! HE DID IT AGAIN!
I WANT A MOTIVE TOO!
HE OBEYS BECAUSE HE KNOWS HE'S GOING TO BE REWARDED.
YIP! YIP! YIP!
HE'S DOING GREAT.
DID YOU TEACH HIM ANYTHING ELSE?
YOU WANT TO SEE?
A CAROB CHIP COOKIE WILL BRING SUCCESS!
COOKIES
GUARANTEED!
ARF!
ARF!

CAZENOVE & WILLIAM

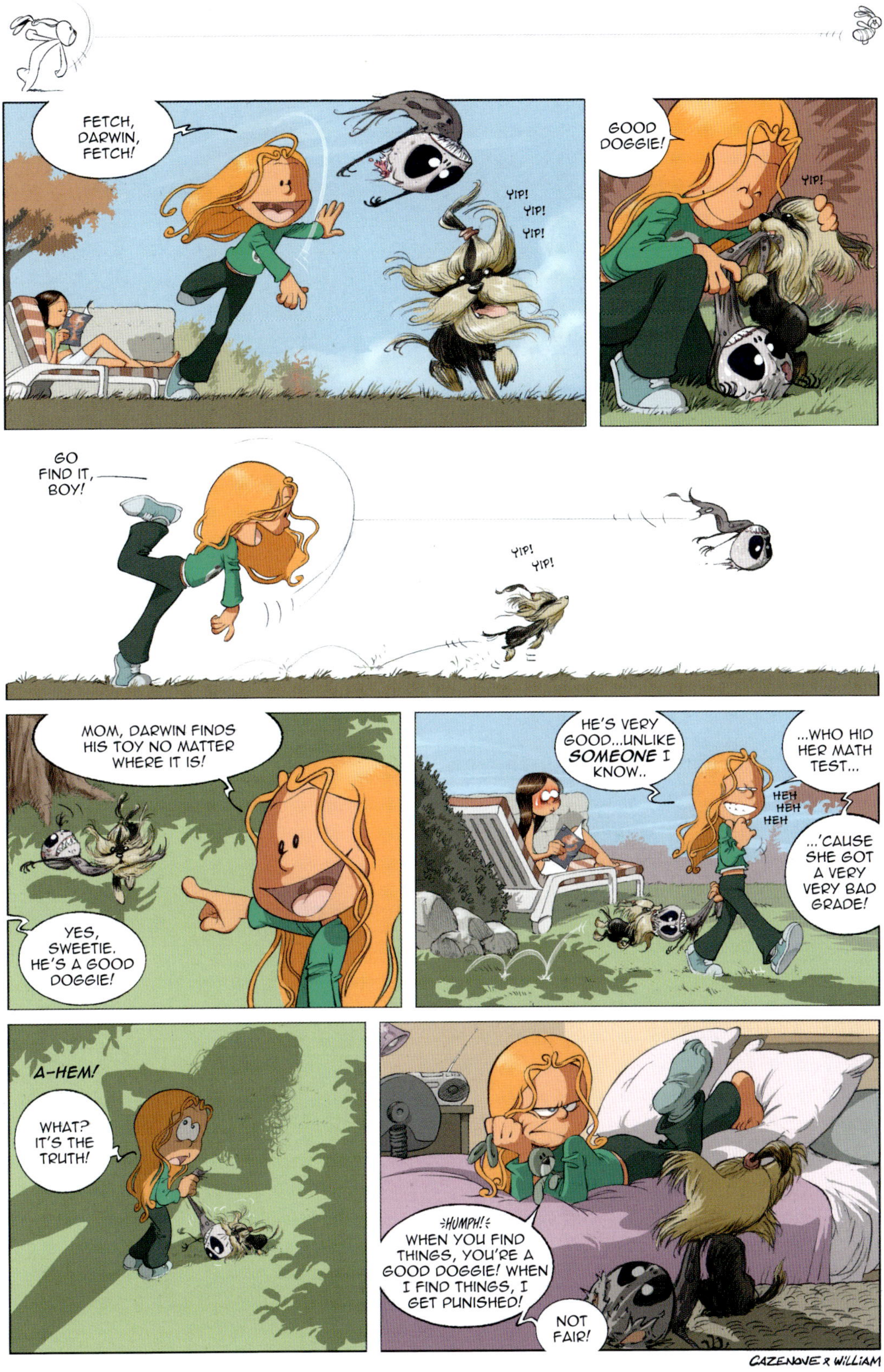
FETCH, DARWIN, FETCH!
YIP! YIP! YIP!
GOOD DOGGIE!
YIP!
GO FIND IT, BOY!
YIP! YIP!
MOM, DARWIN FINDS HIS TOY NO MATTER WHERE IT IS!
YES, SWEETIE. HE'S A GOOD DOGGIE!
HE'S VERY GOOD...UNLIKE SOMEONE I KNOW..
...WHO HID HER MATH TEST...
HEH HEH HEH
...'CAUSE SHE GOT A VERY VERY BAD GRADE!
A-HEM!
WHAT? IT'S THE TRUTH!
HUMPH!
WHEN YOU FIND THINGS, YOU'RE A GOOD DOGGIE! WHEN I FIND THINGS, I GET PUNISHED!
NOT FAIR!
CAZENOVE & WILLIAM

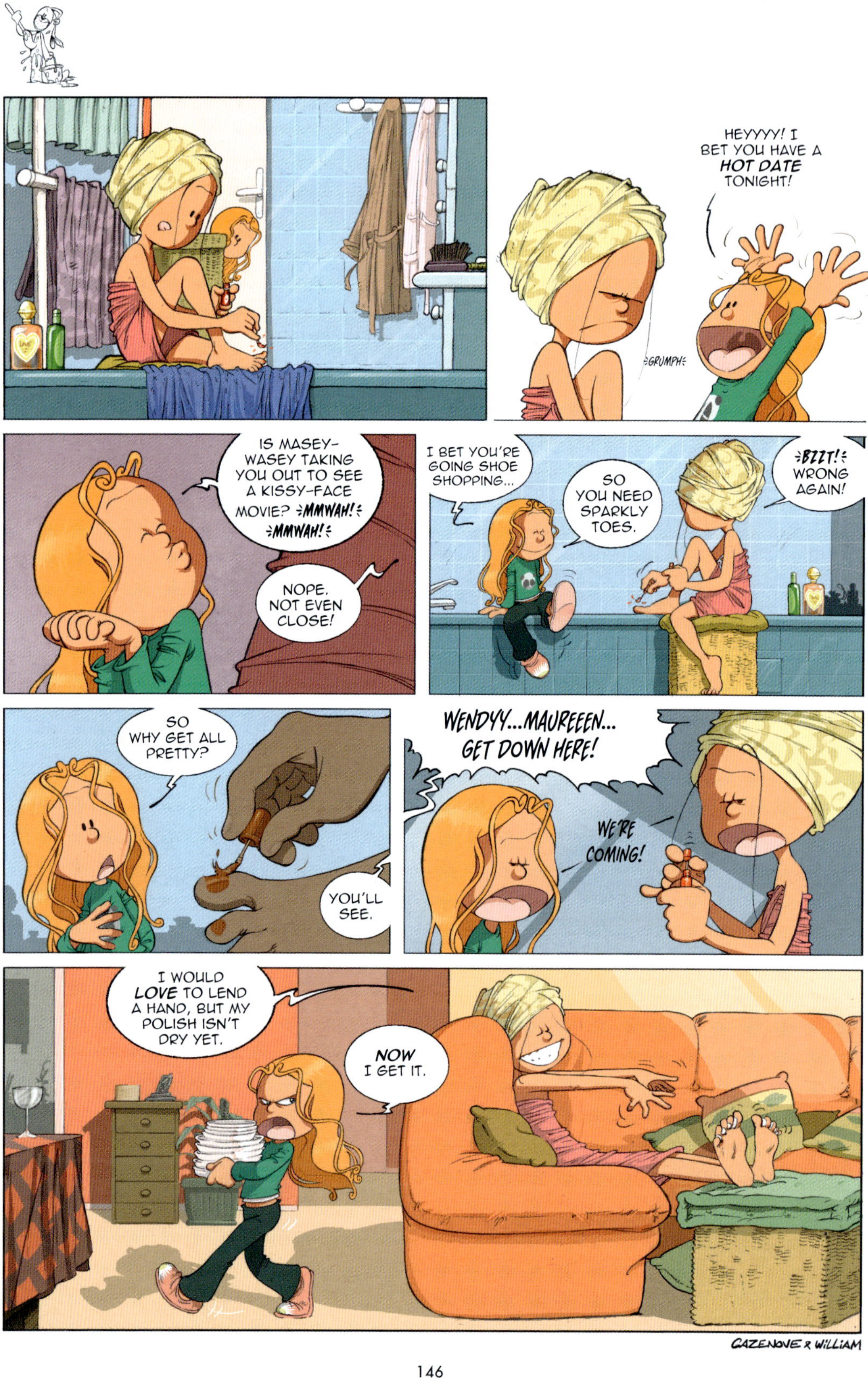
HEYYYY! I BET YOU HAVE A **HOT DATE** TONIGHT!
GRUMPH
IS MASEY-WASEY TAKING YOU OUT TO SEE A KISSY-FACE MOVIE? MMWAH! MMWAH!
NOPE. NOT EVEN CLOSE!
I BET YOU'RE GOING SHOE SHOPPING...
SO YOU NEED SPARKLY TOES.
BZZT! WRONG AGAIN!
SO WHY GET ALL PRETTY?
YOU'LL SEE.
WENDYY...MAUREEEN... GET DOWN HERE!
WE'RE COMING!
I WOULD **LOVE** TO LEND A HAND, BUT MY POLISH ISN'T DRY YET.
NOW I GET IT.
CAZENOVE & WILLIAM

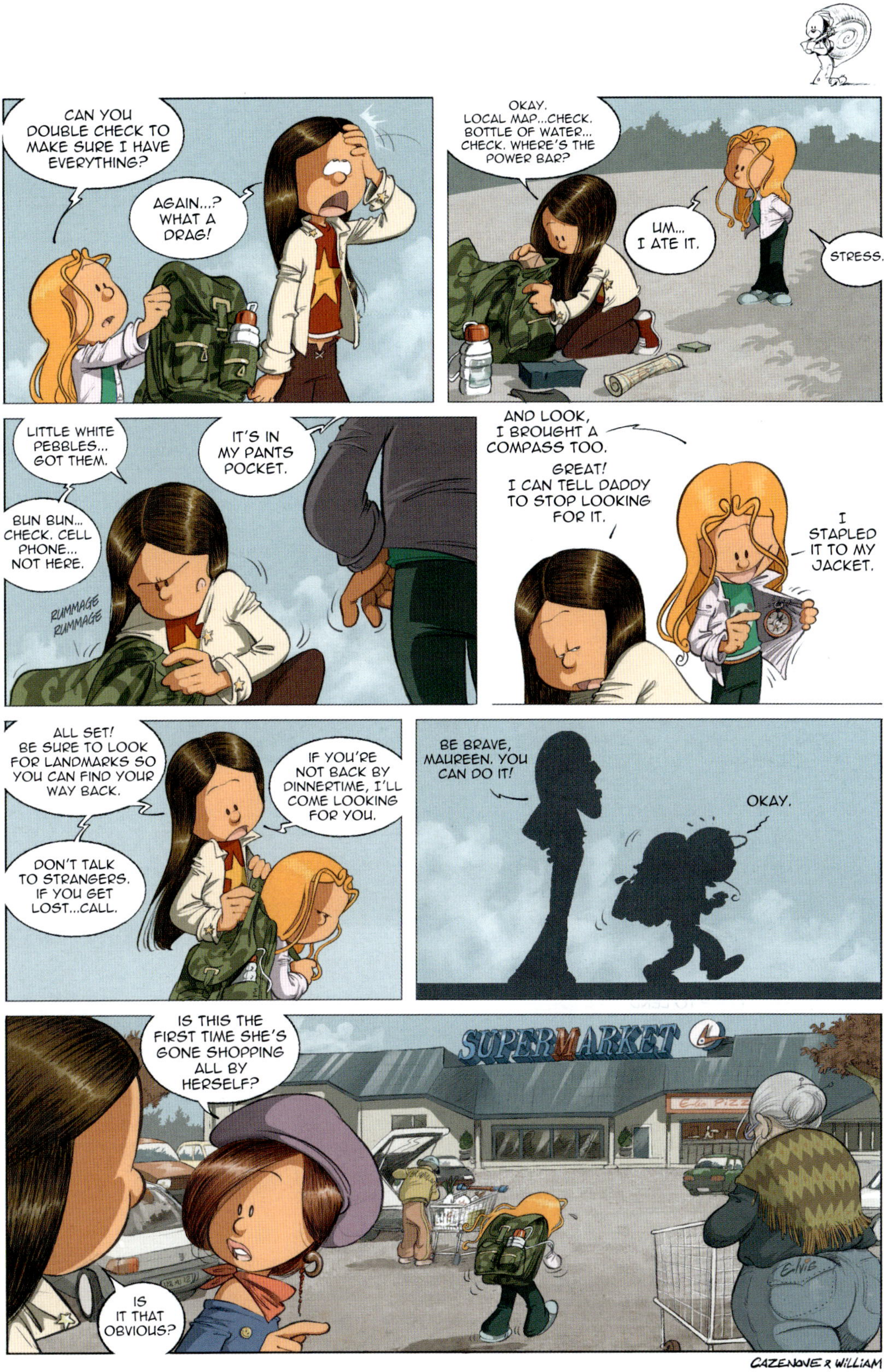
CAN YOU DOUBLE CHECK TO MAKE SURE I HAVE EVERYTHING?
AGAIN...? WHAT A DRAG!
OKAY. LOCAL MAP...CHECK. BOTTLE OF WATER... CHECK. WHERE'S THE POWER BAR?
UM... I ATE IT.
STRESS.
LITTLE WHITE PEBBLES... GOT THEM.
IT'S IN MY PANTS POCKET.
BUN BUN... CHECK. CELL PHONE... NOT HERE.
RUMMAGE RUMMAGE
AND LOOK, I BROUGHT A COMPASS TOO.
GREAT! I CAN TELL DADDY TO STOP LOOKING FOR IT.
I STAPLED IT TO MY JACKET.
ALL SET! BE SURE TO LOOK FOR LANDMARKS SO YOU CAN FIND YOUR WAY BACK.
IF YOU'RE NOT BACK BY DINNERTIME, I'LL COME LOOKING FOR YOU.
DON'T TALK TO STRANGERS. IF YOU GET LOST...CALL.
BE BRAVE, MAUREEN. YOU CAN DO IT!
OKAY.
IS THIS THE FIRST TIME SHE'S GONE SHOPPING ALL BY HERSELF?
SUPERMARKET
IS IT THAT OBVIOUS?
CAZENOVE & WILLIAM

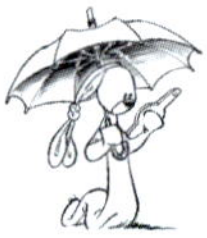

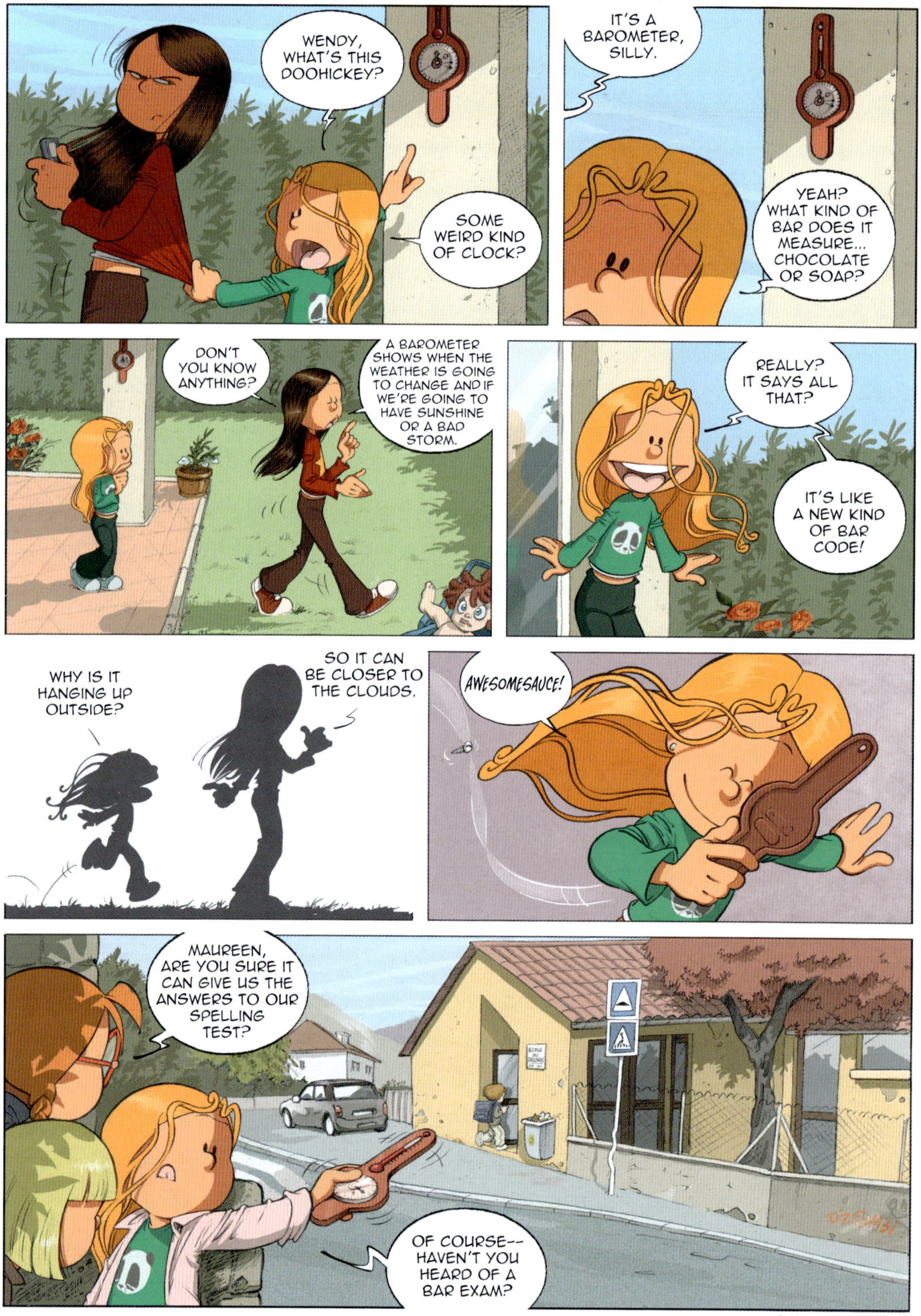

WENDY, WHAT'S THIS DOOHICKEY?
SOME WEIRD KIND OF CLOCK?
IT'S A BAROMETER, SILLY.
YEAH? WHAT KIND OF BAR DOES IT MEASURE... CHOCOLATE OR SOAP?
DON'T YOU KNOW ANYTHING?
A BAROMETER SHOWS WHEN THE WEATHER IS GOING TO CHANGE AND IF WE'RE GOING TO HAVE SUNSHINE OR A BAD STORM.
REALLY? IT SAYS ALL THAT?
IT'S LIKE A NEW KIND OF BAR CODE!
WHY IS IT HANGING UP OUTSIDE?
SO IT CAN BE CLOSER TO THE CLOUDS.
AWESOMESAUCE!
MAUREEN, ARE YOU SURE IT CAN GIVE US THE ANSWERS TO OUR SPELLING TEST?
OF COURSE-- HAVEN'T YOU HEARD OF A BAR EXAM?

CAZENOVE & WILLIAM

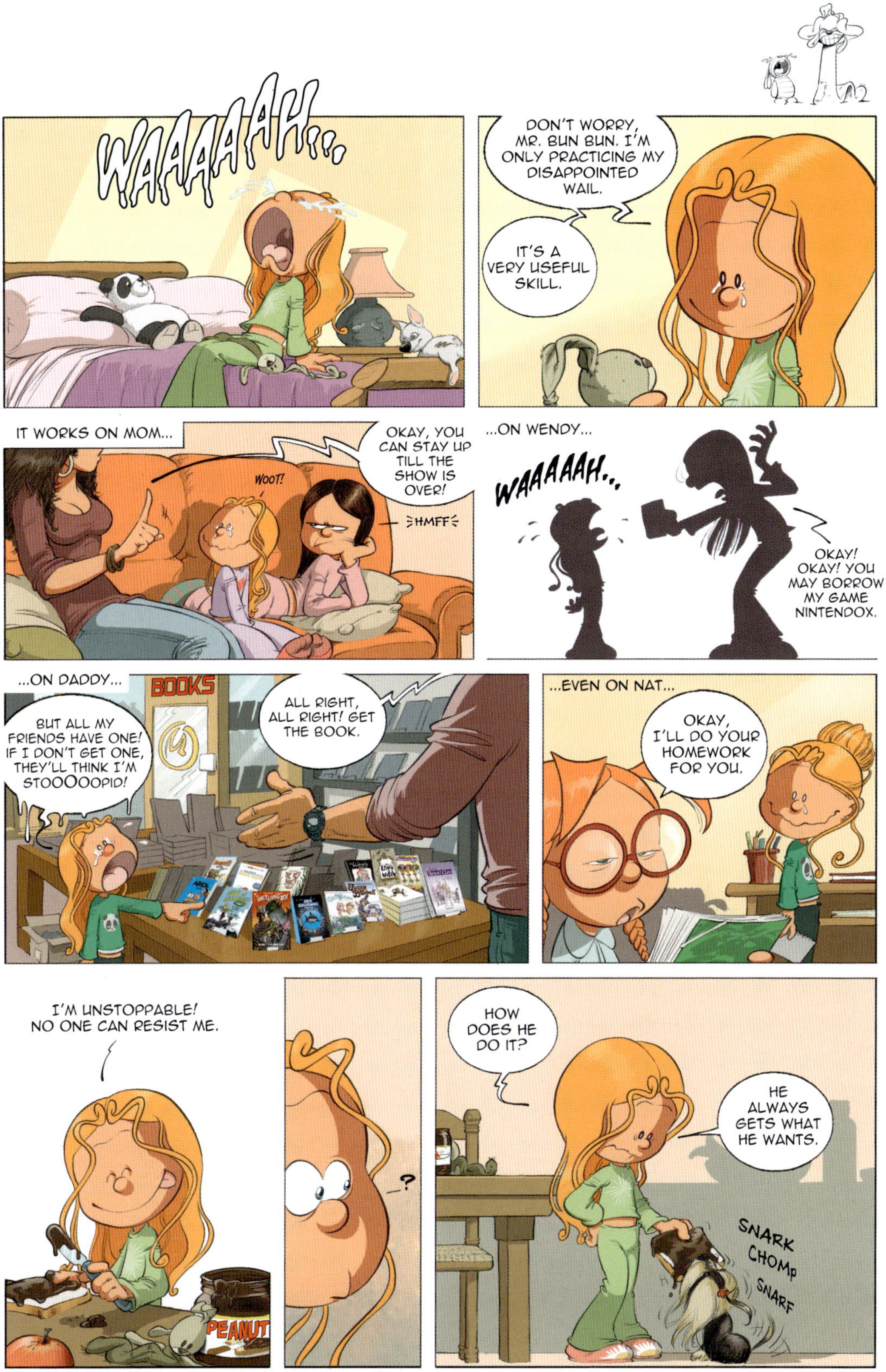
WAAAAAH...
DON'T WORRY, MR. BUN BUN. I'M ONLY PRACTICING MY DISAPPOINTED WAIL.
IT'S A VERY USEFUL SKILL.
IT WORKS ON MOM...
OKAY, YOU CAN STAY UP TILL THE SHOW IS OVER!
WOOT!
HMFF
...ON WENDY...
WAAAAAH...
OKAY! OKAY! YOU MAY BORROW MY GAME NINTENDOX.
...ON DADDY...
BOOKS
BUT ALL MY FRIENDS HAVE ONE! IF I DON'T GET ONE, THEY'LL THINK I'M STOOOOOPID!
ALL RIGHT, ALL RIGHT! GET THE BOOK.
...EVEN ON NAT...
OKAY, I'LL DO YOUR HOMEWORK FOR YOU.
I'M UNSTOPPABLE! NO ONE CAN RESIST ME.
PEANUT
?
HOW DOES HE DO IT?
HE ALWAYS GETS WHAT HE WANTS.
SNARK
CHOMP
SNARF

WARNING: Never feed any human food, especially anything containing chocolate, to a dog. It could be fatal.

CAZENOVE & WILLIAM

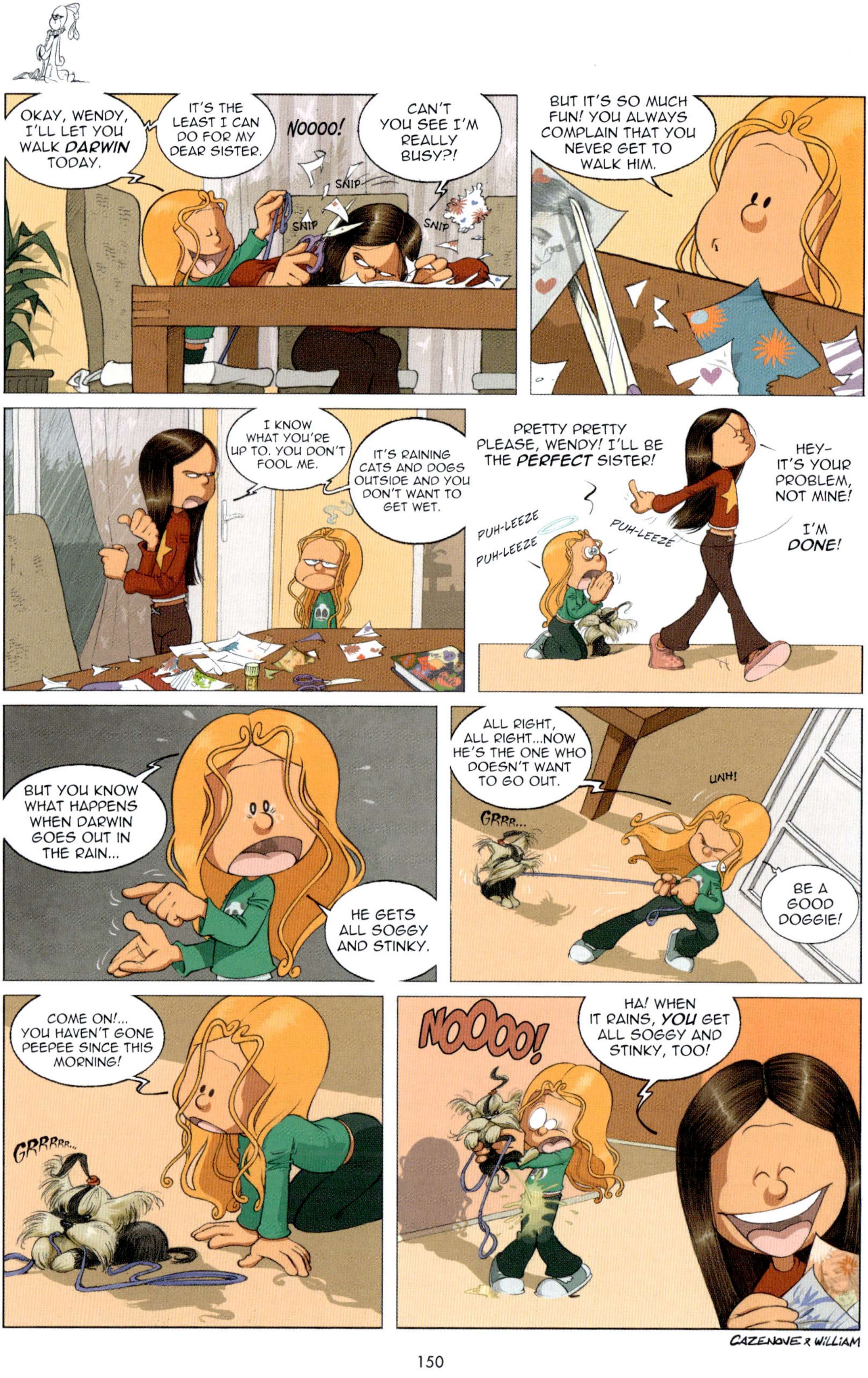
OKAY, WENDY, I'LL LET YOU WALK **DARWIN** TODAY.
IT'S THE LEAST I CAN DO FOR MY DEAR SISTER.
NOOOO!
CAN'T YOU SEE I'M REALLY BUSY?!
SNIP
SNIP
SNIP
BUT IT'S SO MUCH FUN! YOU ALWAYS COMPLAIN THAT YOU NEVER GET TO WALK HIM.
I KNOW WHAT YOU'RE UP TO. YOU DON'T FOOL ME.
IT'S RAINING CATS AND DOGS OUTSIDE AND YOU DON'T WANT TO GET WET.
PRETTY PRETTY PLEASE, WENDY! I'LL BE THE **PERFECT** SISTER!
PUH-LEEZE
PUH-LEEZE
PUH-LEEZE
HEY- IT'S YOUR PROBLEM, NOT MINE!
I'M **DONE**!
BUT YOU KNOW WHAT HAPPENS WHEN DARWIN GOES OUT IN THE RAIN...
HE GETS ALL SOGGY AND STINKY.
ALL RIGHT, ALL RIGHT...NOW HE'S THE ONE WHO DOESN'T WANT TO GO OUT.
UNH!
GRRR...
BE A GOOD DOGGIE!
COME ON!... YOU HAVEN'T GONE PEEPEE SINCE THIS MORNING!
GRRRRR...
NOOOO!
HA! WHEN IT RAINS, **YOU** GET ALL SOGGY AND STINKY, TOO!
CAZENOVE & WILLIAM

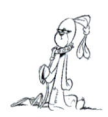

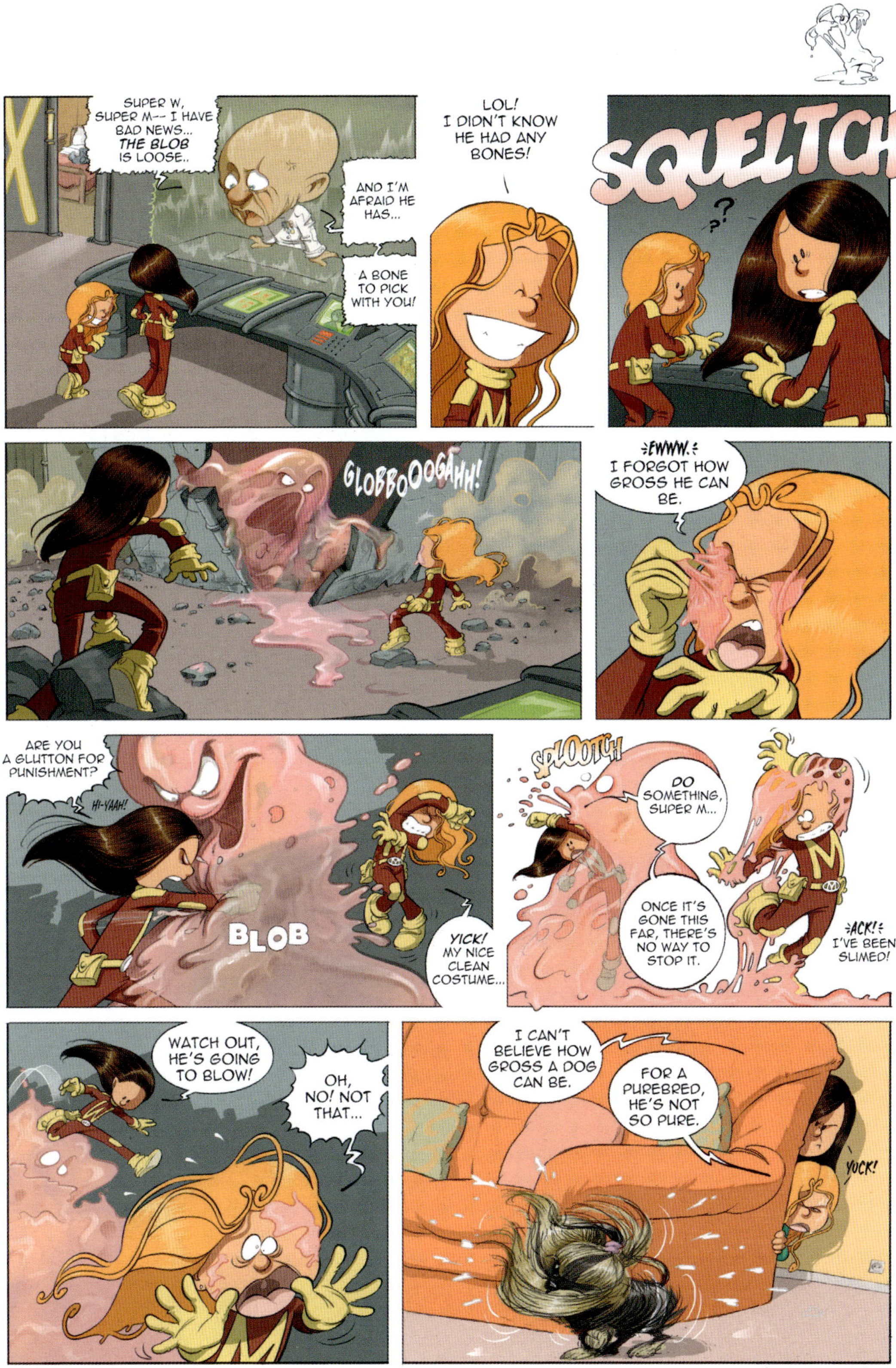

SUPER W, SUPER M-- I HAVE BAD NEWS... THE BLOB IS LOOSE..
AND I'M AFRAID HE HAS...
A BONE TO PICK WITH YOU!
LOL! I DIDN'T KNOW HE HAD ANY BONES!
SQUELTCH
?
?
GLOBBOOOGAHH!
EWWW.
I FORGOT HOW GROSS HE CAN BE.
ARE YOU A GLUTTON FOR PUNISHMENT?
HI-YAAH!
BLOB
YICK! MY NICE CLEAN COSTUME...
SPLOOTCH
DO SOMETHING, SUPER M...
ONCE IT'S GONE THIS FAR, THERE'S NO WAY TO STOP IT.
ACK!
I'VE BEEN SLIMED!
WATCH OUT, HE'S GOING TO BLOW!
OH, NO! NOT THAT...
I CAN'T BELIEVE HOW GROSS A DOG CAN BE.
FOR A PUREBRED, HE'S NOT SO PURE.
YUCK!
CAZENOVE & WILLIAM

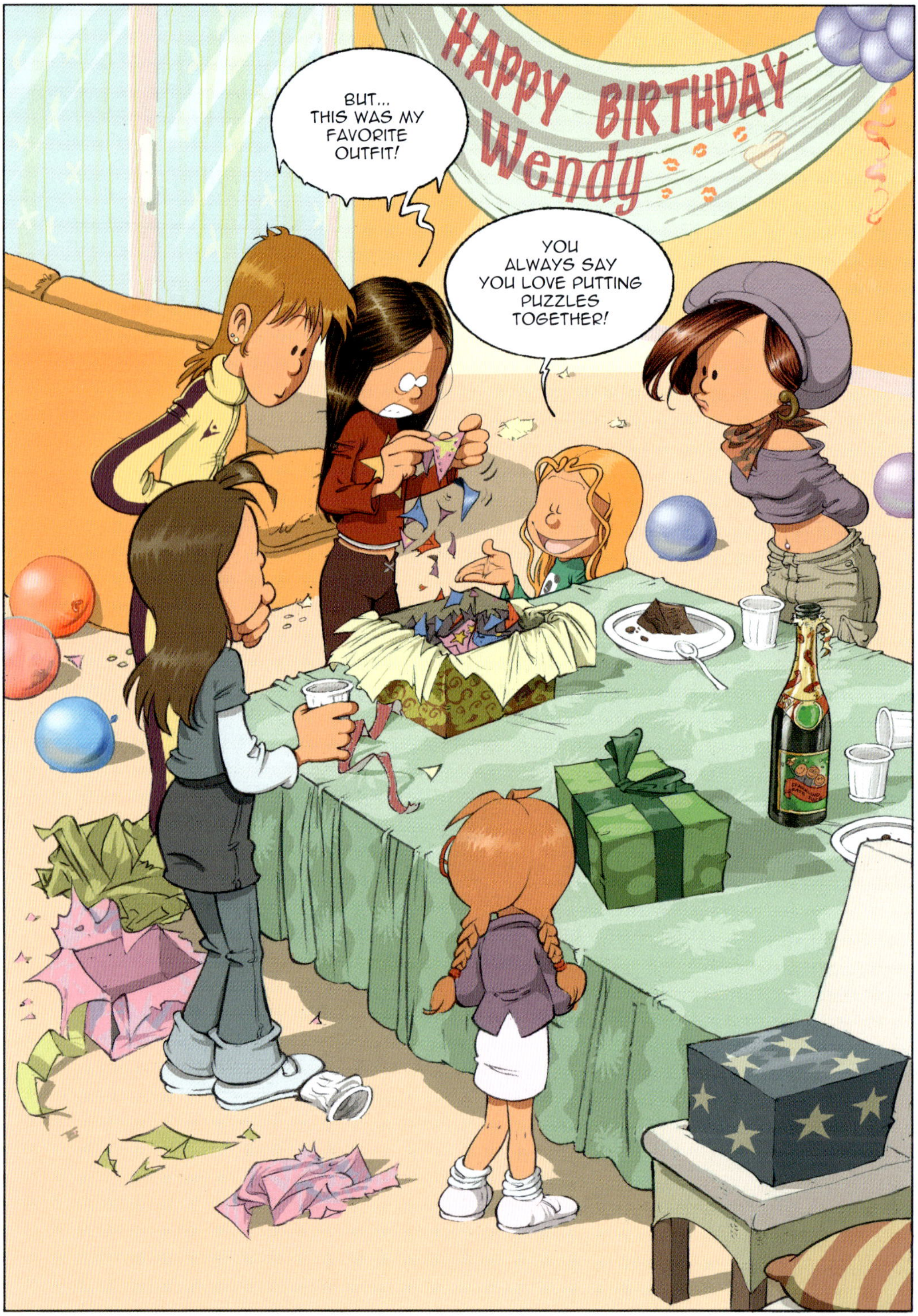
HAPPY BIRTHDAY Wendy
BUT... THIS WAS MY FAVORITE OUTFIT!
YOU ALWAYS SAY YOU LOVE PUTTING PUZZLES TOGETHER!

CAZENOVE & WILLIAM

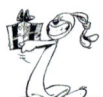

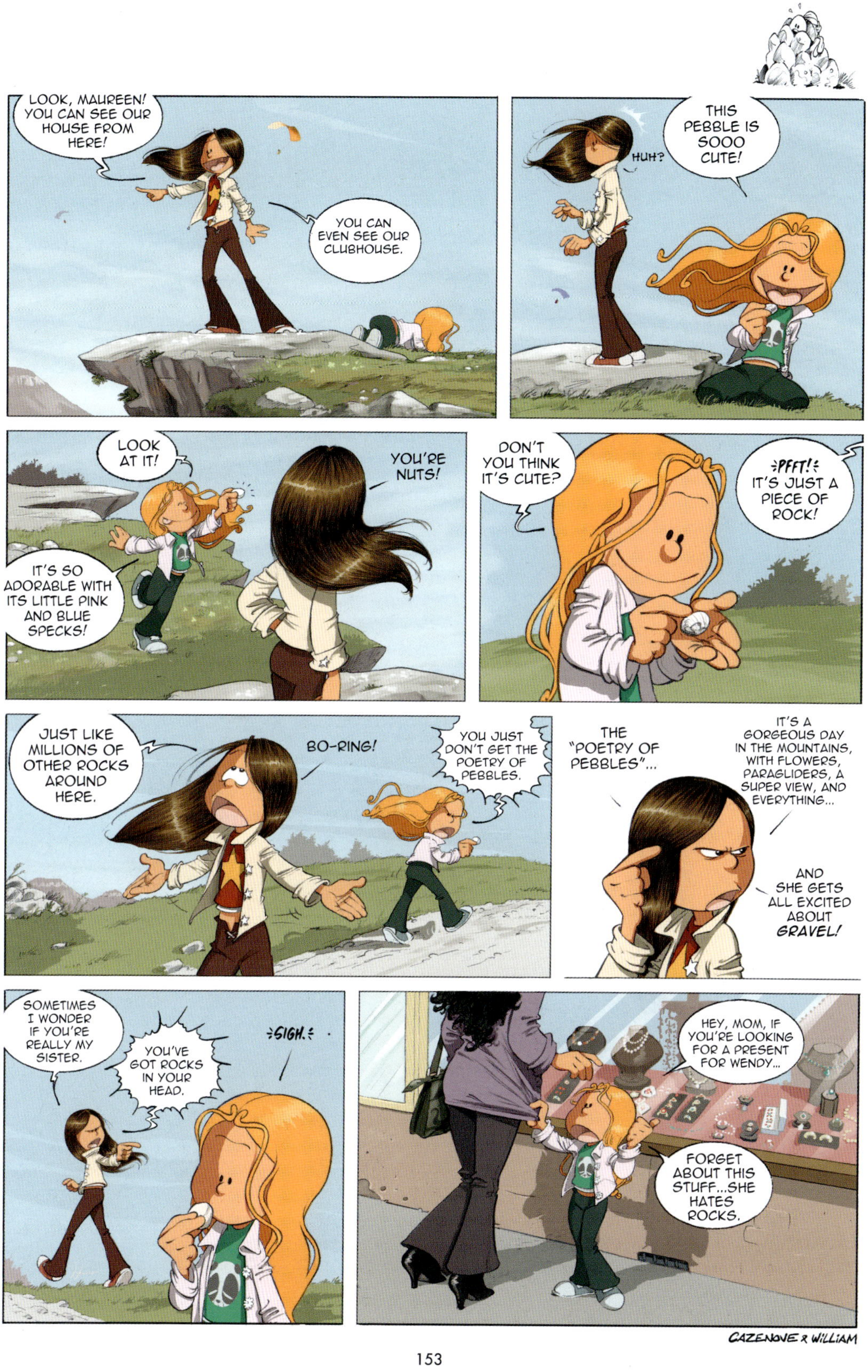
LOOK, MAUREEN! YOU CAN SEE OUR HOUSE FROM HERE!
YOU CAN EVEN SEE OUR CLUBHOUSE.
HUH?
THIS PEBBLE IS SOOO CUTE!
LOOK AT IT!
IT'S SO ADORABLE WITH ITS LITTLE PINK AND BLUE SPECKS!
YOU'RE NUTS!
DON'T YOU THINK IT'S CUTE?
PFFT! IT'S JUST A PIECE OF ROCK!
JUST LIKE MILLIONS OF OTHER ROCKS AROUND HERE.
BO-RING!
YOU JUST DON'T GET THE POETRY OF PEBBLES.
THE "POETRY OF PEBBLES"...
IT'S A GORGEOUS DAY IN THE MOUNTAINS, WITH FLOWERS, PARAGLIDERS, A SUPER VIEW, AND EVERYTHING...
AND SHE GETS ALL EXCITED ABOUT GRAVEL!
SOMETIMES I WONDER IF YOU'RE REALLY MY SISTER.
YOU'VE GOT ROCKS IN YOUR HEAD.
SIGH.
HEY, MOM, IF YOU'RE LOOKING FOR A PRESENT FOR WENDY...
FORGET ABOUT THIS STUFF...SHE HATES ROCKS.
CAZENOVE & WILLIAM

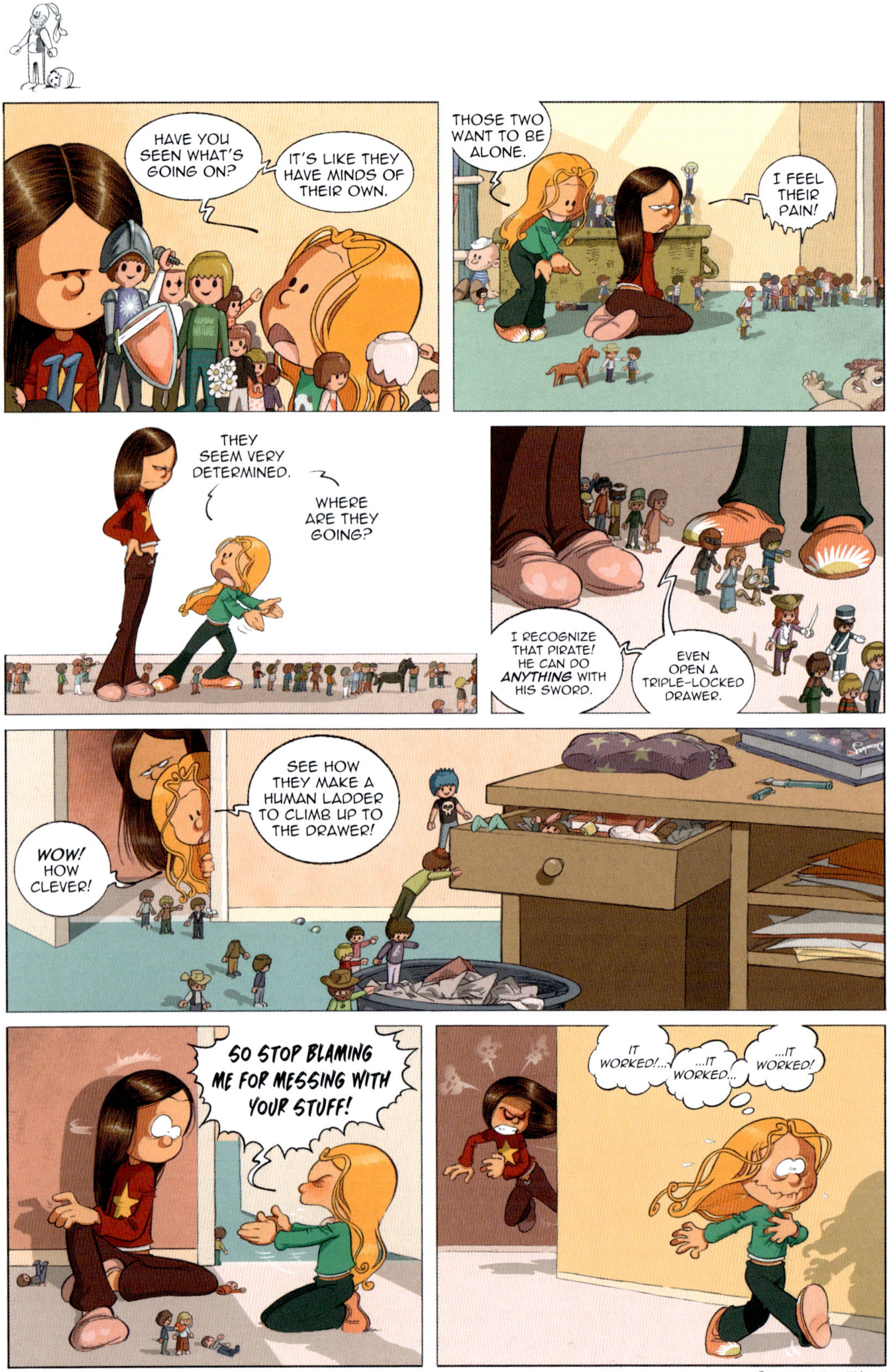
HAVE YOU SEEN WHAT'S GOING ON?
IT'S LIKE THEY HAVE MINDS OF THEIR OWN.
THOSE TWO WANT TO BE ALONE.
I FEEL THEIR PAIN!
THEY SEEM VERY DETERMINED.
WHERE ARE THEY GOING?
I RECOGNIZE THAT PIRATE! HE CAN DO ANYTHING WITH HIS SWORD.
EVEN OPEN A TRIPLE-LOCKED DRAWER.
SEE HOW THEY MAKE A HUMAN LADDER TO CLIMB UP TO THE DRAWER!
WOW! HOW CLEVER!
SO STOP BLAMING ME FOR MESSING WITH YOUR STUFF!
IT WORKED!...
...IT WORKED...
...IT WORKED!

CAZENOVE & WILLIAM

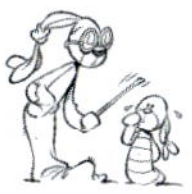

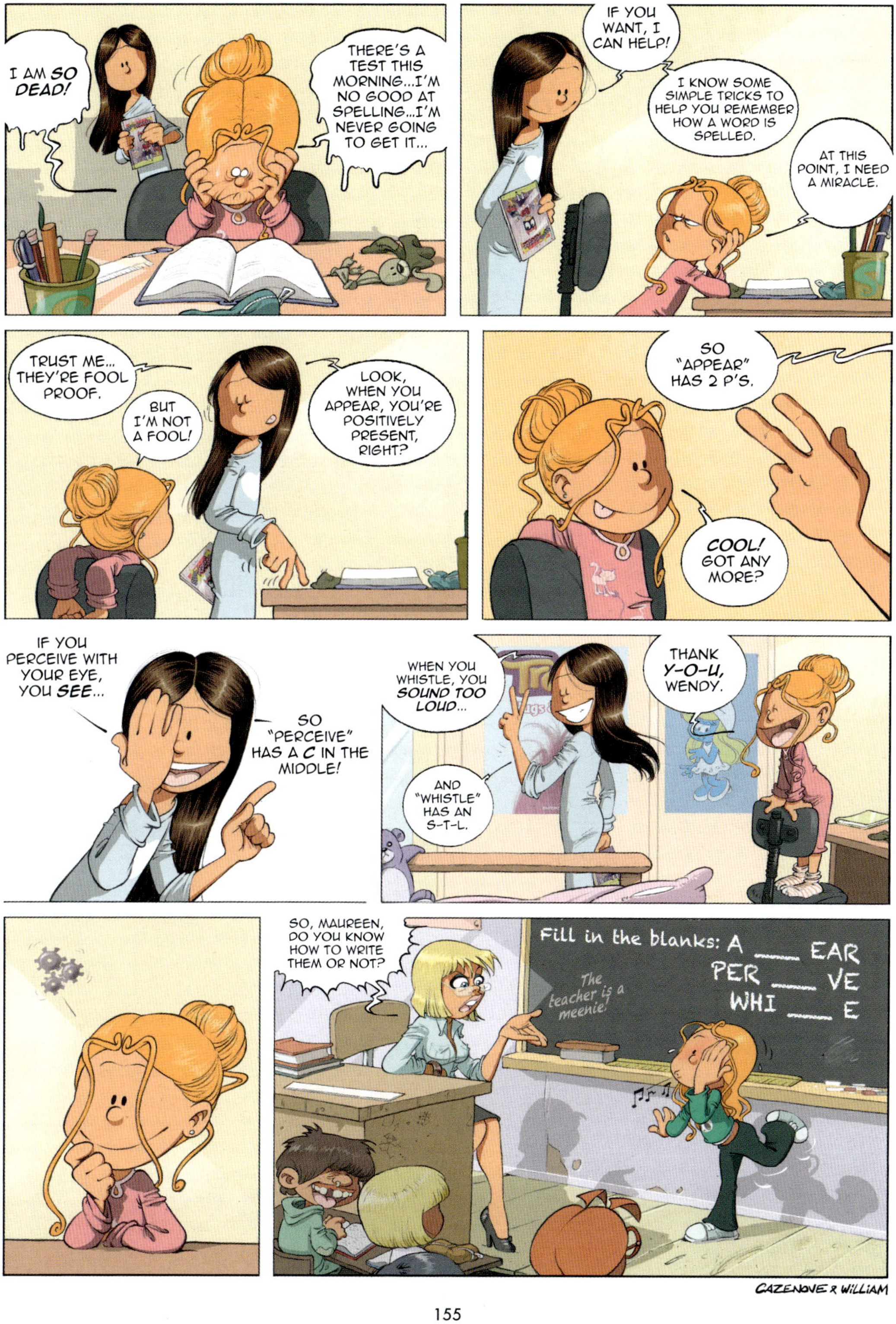

I AM **SO DEAD!**
THERE'S A TEST THIS MORNING...I'M NO GOOD AT SPELLING...I'M NEVER GOING TO GET IT...
IF YOU WANT, I CAN HELP!
I KNOW SOME SIMPLE TRICKS TO HELP YOU REMEMBER HOW A WORD IS SPELLED.
AT THIS POINT, I NEED A MIRACLE.
TRUST ME... THEY'RE FOOL PROOF.
BUT I'M NOT A FOOL!
LOOK, WHEN YOU APPEAR, YOU'RE POSITIVELY PRESENT, RIGHT?
SO "APPEAR" HAS 2 P'S.
COOL! GOT ANY MORE?
IF YOU PERCEIVE WITH YOUR EYE, YOU **SEE**...
SO "PERCEIVE" HAS A **C** IN THE MIDDLE!
WHEN YOU WHISTLE, YOU **SOUND TOO LOUD**...
AND "WHISTLE" HAS AN S-T-L.
THANK **Y-O-U,** WENDY.
SO, MAUREEN, DO YOU KNOW HOW TO WRITE THEM OR NOT?
Fill in the blanks: A ___ EAR
PER ___ VE
WHI ___ E
The teacher is a meenie!

CAZENOVE & WILLIAM

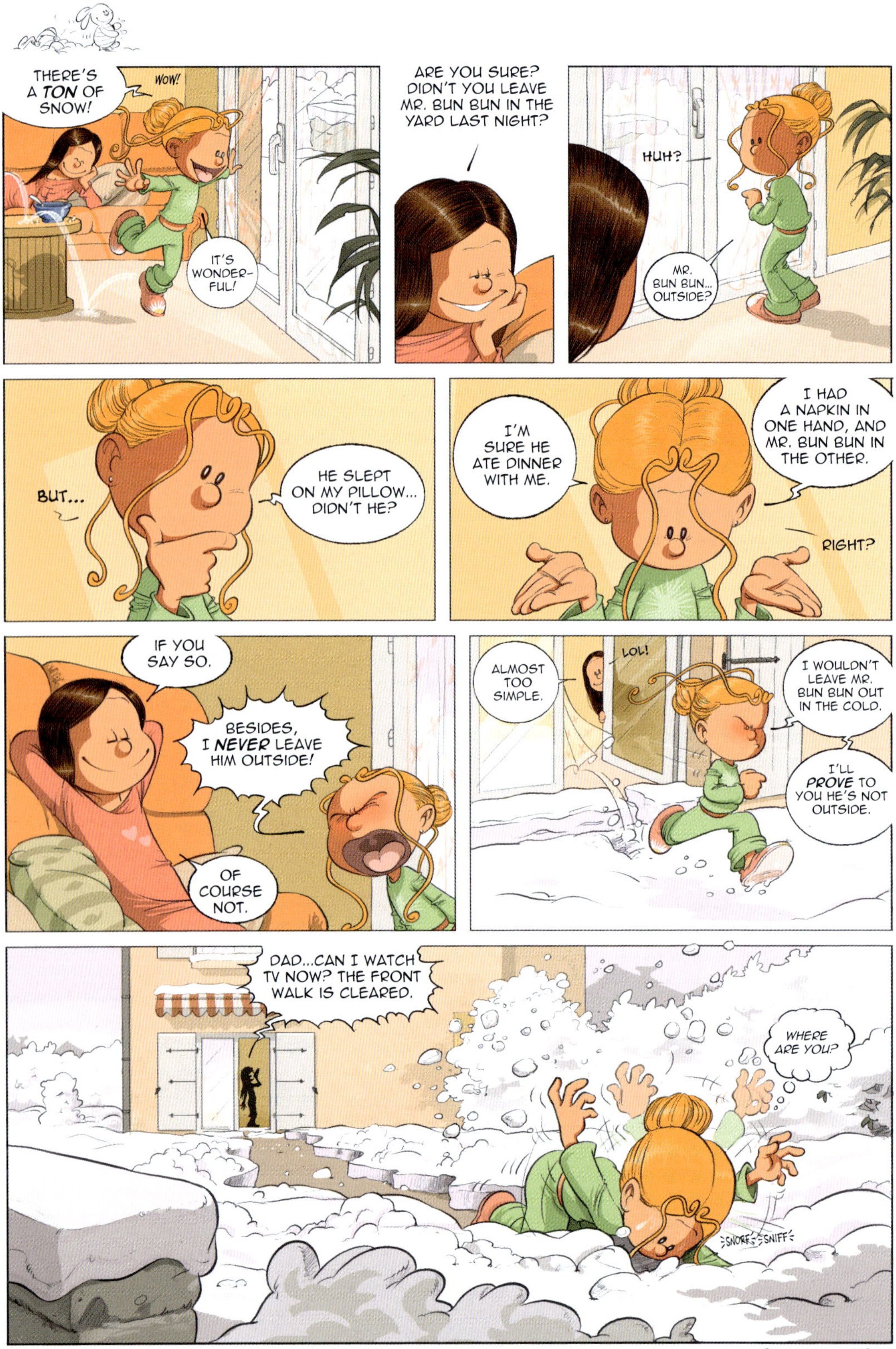
THERE'S A TON OF SNOW!
WOW!
IT'S WONDERFUL!
ARE YOU SURE? DIDN'T YOU LEAVE MR. BUN BUN IN THE YARD LAST NIGHT?
HUH?
MR. BUN BUN... OUTSIDE?
BUT...
HE SLEPT ON MY PILLOW... DIDN'T HE?
I'M SURE HE ATE DINNER WITH ME.
I HAD A NAPKIN IN ONE HAND, AND MR. BUN BUN IN THE OTHER.
RIGHT?
IF YOU SAY SO.
BESIDES, I NEVER LEAVE HIM OUTSIDE!
OF COURSE NOT.
ALMOST TOO SIMPLE.
LOL!
I WOULDN'T LEAVE MR. BUN BUN OUT IN THE COLD.
I'LL PROVE TO YOU HE'S NOT OUTSIDE.
DAD...CAN I WATCH TV NOW? THE FRONT WALK IS CLEARED.
WHERE ARE YOU?
SNORF SNIFF

CAZENOVE & WILLIAM

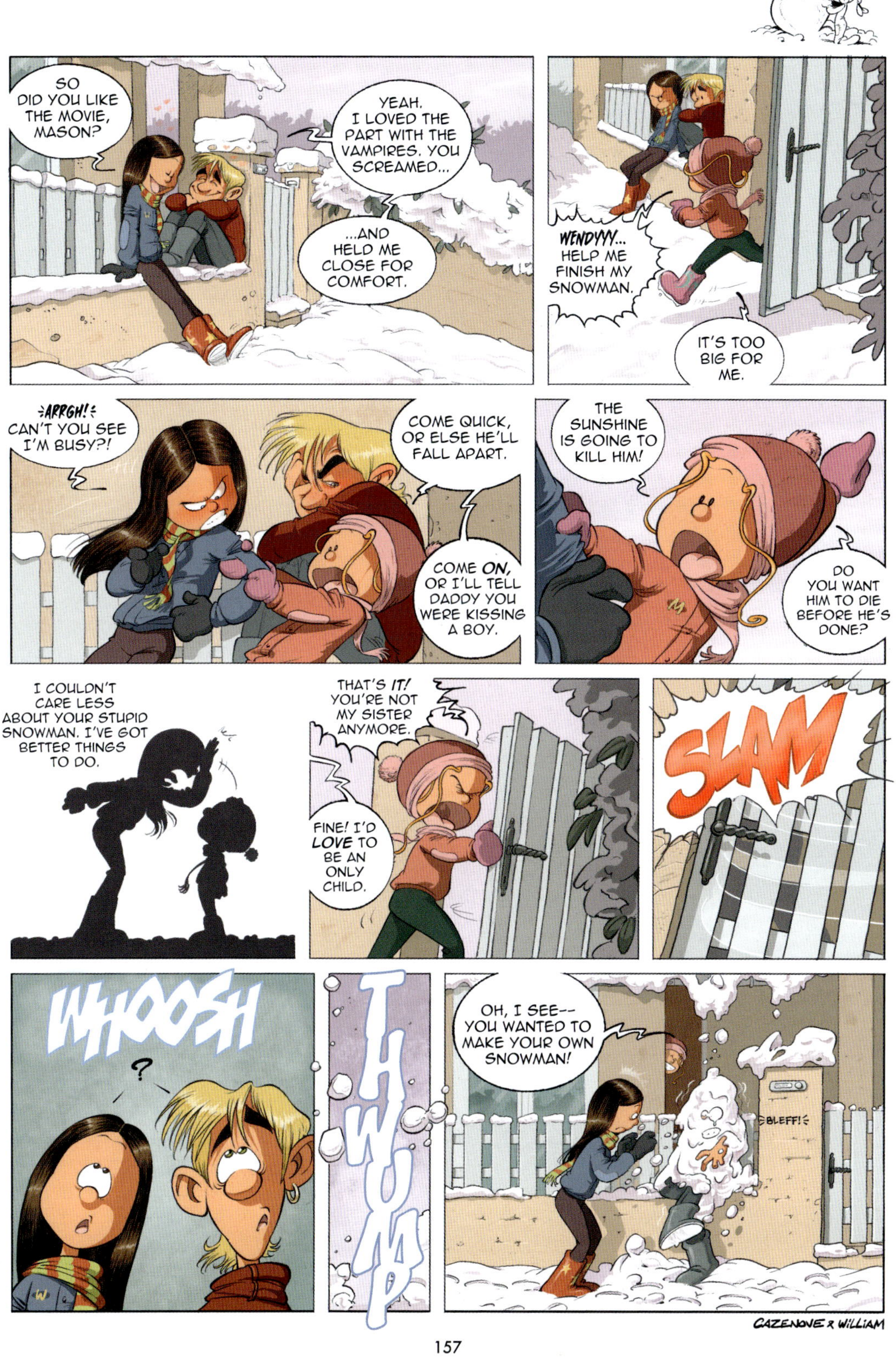

SO DID YOU LIKE THE MOVIE, MASON?
YEAH. I LOVED THE PART WITH THE VAMPIRES. YOU SCREAMED...
...AND HELD ME CLOSE FOR COMFORT.
WENDYYY... HELP ME FINISH MY SNOWMAN.
IT'S TOO BIG FOR ME.
ARRGH! CAN'T YOU SEE I'M BUSY?!
COME QUICK, OR ELSE HE'LL FALL APART.
COME ON, OR I'LL TELL DADDY YOU WERE KISSING A BOY.
THE SUNSHINE IS GOING TO KILL HIM!
DO YOU WANT HIM TO DIE BEFORE HE'S DONE?
I COULDN'T CARE LESS ABOUT YOUR STUPID SNOWMAN. I'VE GOT BETTER THINGS TO DO.
THAT'S IT! YOU'RE NOT MY SISTER ANYMORE.
FINE! I'D LOVE TO BE AN ONLY CHILD.
SLAM
WHOOSH
?
THWUMP
OH, I SEE-- YOU WANTED TO MAKE YOUR OWN SNOWMAN!
BLEFF!
CAZENOVE & WILLIAM

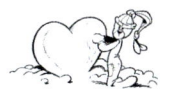

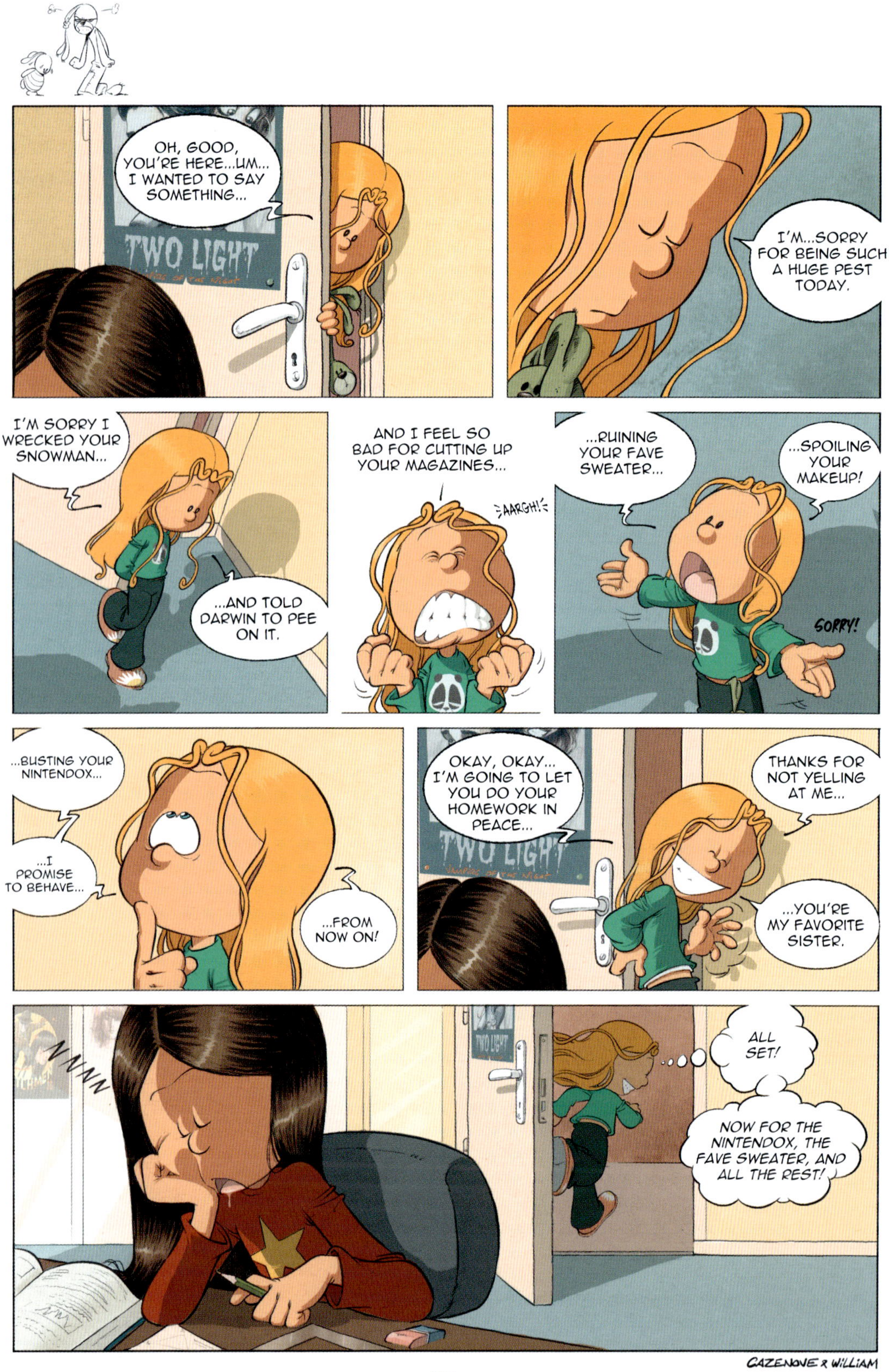

OH, GOOD, YOU'RE HERE...UM... I WANTED TO SAY SOMETHING...
TWO LIGHT
I'M...SORRY FOR BEING SUCH A HUGE PEST TODAY.
I'M SORRY I WRECKED YOUR SNOWMAN...
...AND TOLD DARWIN TO PEE ON IT.
AND I FEEL SO BAD FOR CUTTING UP YOUR MAGAZINES...
AARGH!
...RUINING YOUR FAVE SWEATER...
...SPOILING YOUR MAKEUP!
SORRY!
...BUSTING YOUR NINTENDOX...
...I PROMISE TO BEHAVE...
...FROM NOW ON!
OKAY, OKAY... I'M GOING TO LET YOU DO YOUR HOMEWORK IN PEACE...
THANKS FOR NOT YELLING AT ME...
...YOU'RE MY FAVORITE SISTER.
NNNN
TWO LIGHT
ALL SET!
NOW FOR THE NINTENDOX, THE FAVE SWEATER, AND ALL THE REST!
CAZENOVE & WILLIAM

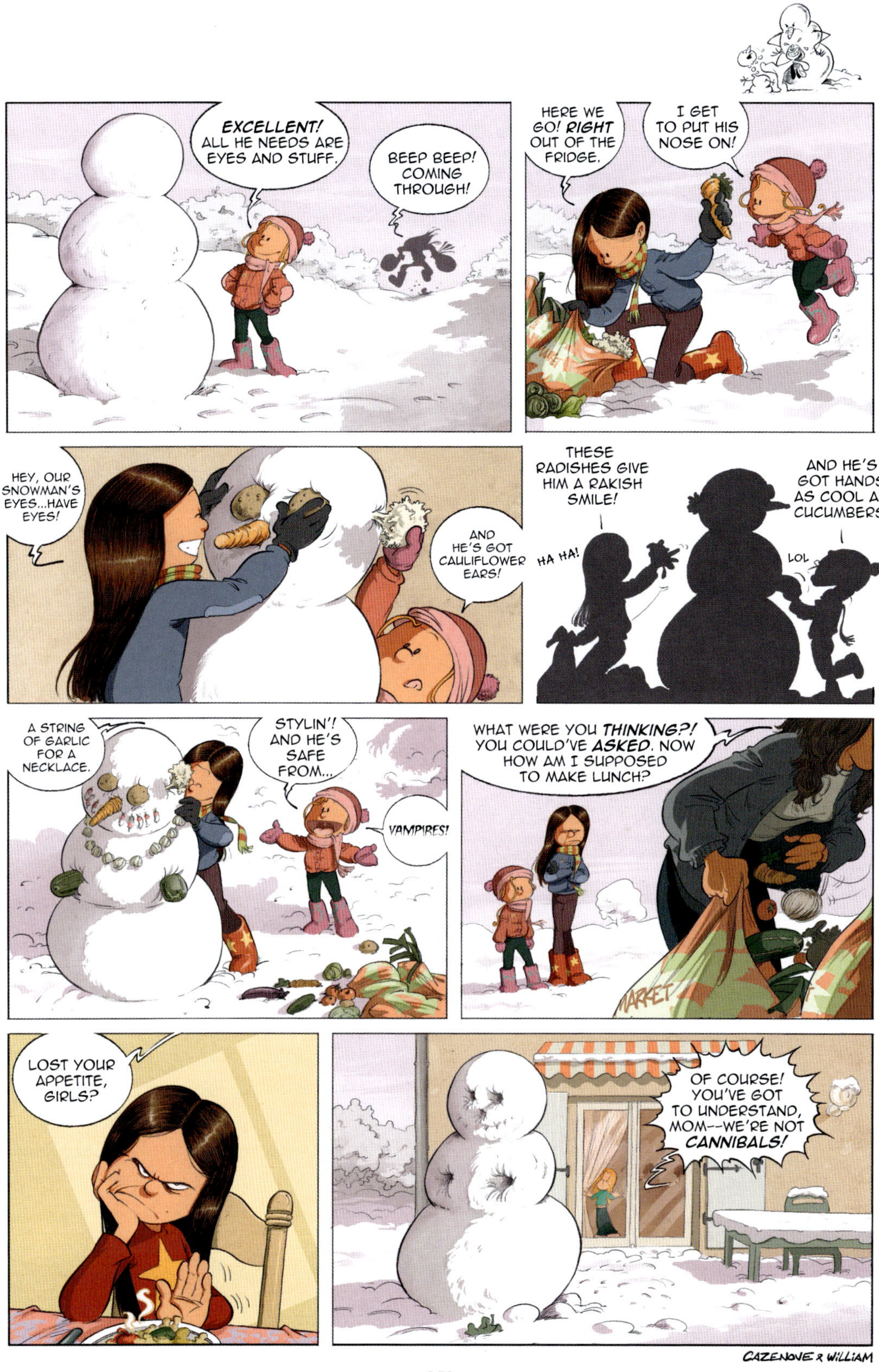
EXCELLENT! ALL HE NEEDS ARE EYES AND STUFF.
BEEP BEEP! COMING THROUGH!
HERE WE GO! RIGHT OUT OF THE FRIDGE.
I GET TO PUT HIS NOSE ON!
HEY, OUR SNOWMAN'S EYES...HAVE EYES!
AND HE'S GOT CAULIFLOWER EARS!
THESE RADISHES GIVE HIM A RAKISH SMILE!
HA HA!
AND HE'S GOT HANDS AS COOL AS CUCUMBERS.
LOL
A STRING OF GARLIC FOR A NECKLACE.
STYLIN'! AND HE'S SAFE FROM...
VAMPIRES!
WHAT WERE YOU THINKING?! YOU COULD'VE ASKED. NOW HOW AM I SUPPOSED TO MAKE LUNCH?
MARKET
LOST YOUR APPETITE, GIRLS?
OF COURSE! YOU'VE GOT TO UNDERSTAND, MOM--WE'RE NOT CANNIBALS!
CAZENOVE & WILLIAM

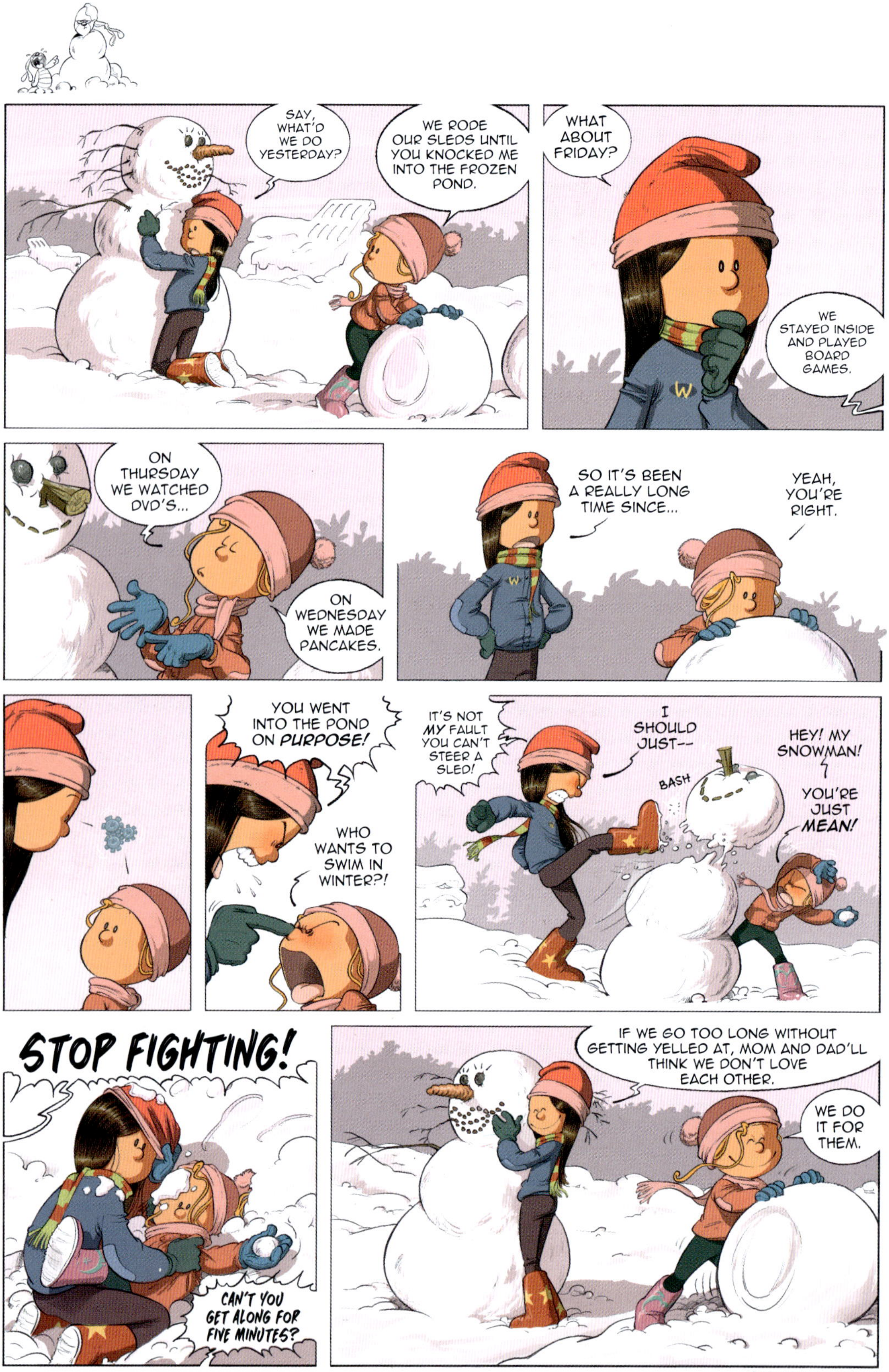
SAY, WHAT'D WE DO YESTERDAY?
WE RODE OUR SLEDS UNTIL YOU KNOCKED ME INTO THE FROZEN POND.
WHAT ABOUT FRIDAY?
WE STAYED INSIDE AND PLAYED BOARD GAMES.
ON THURSDAY WE WATCHED DVD'S...
ON WEDNESDAY WE MADE PANCAKES.
SO IT'S BEEN A REALLY LONG TIME SINCE...
YEAH, YOU'RE RIGHT.
YOU WENT INTO THE POND ON *PURPOSE!*
WHO WANTS TO SWIM IN WINTER?!
IT'S NOT *MY* FAULT YOU CAN'T STEER A SLED!
I SHOULD JUST--
BASH
HEY! MY SNOWMAN!
YOU'RE JUST *MEAN!*
STOP FIGHTING!
CAN'T YOU GET ALONG FOR FIVE MINUTES?
IF WE GO TOO LONG WITHOUT GETTING YELLED AT, MOM AND DAD'LL THINK WE DON'T LOVE EACH OTHER.
WE DO IT FOR THEM.
CAZENOVE & WILLIAM

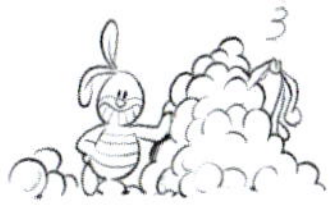

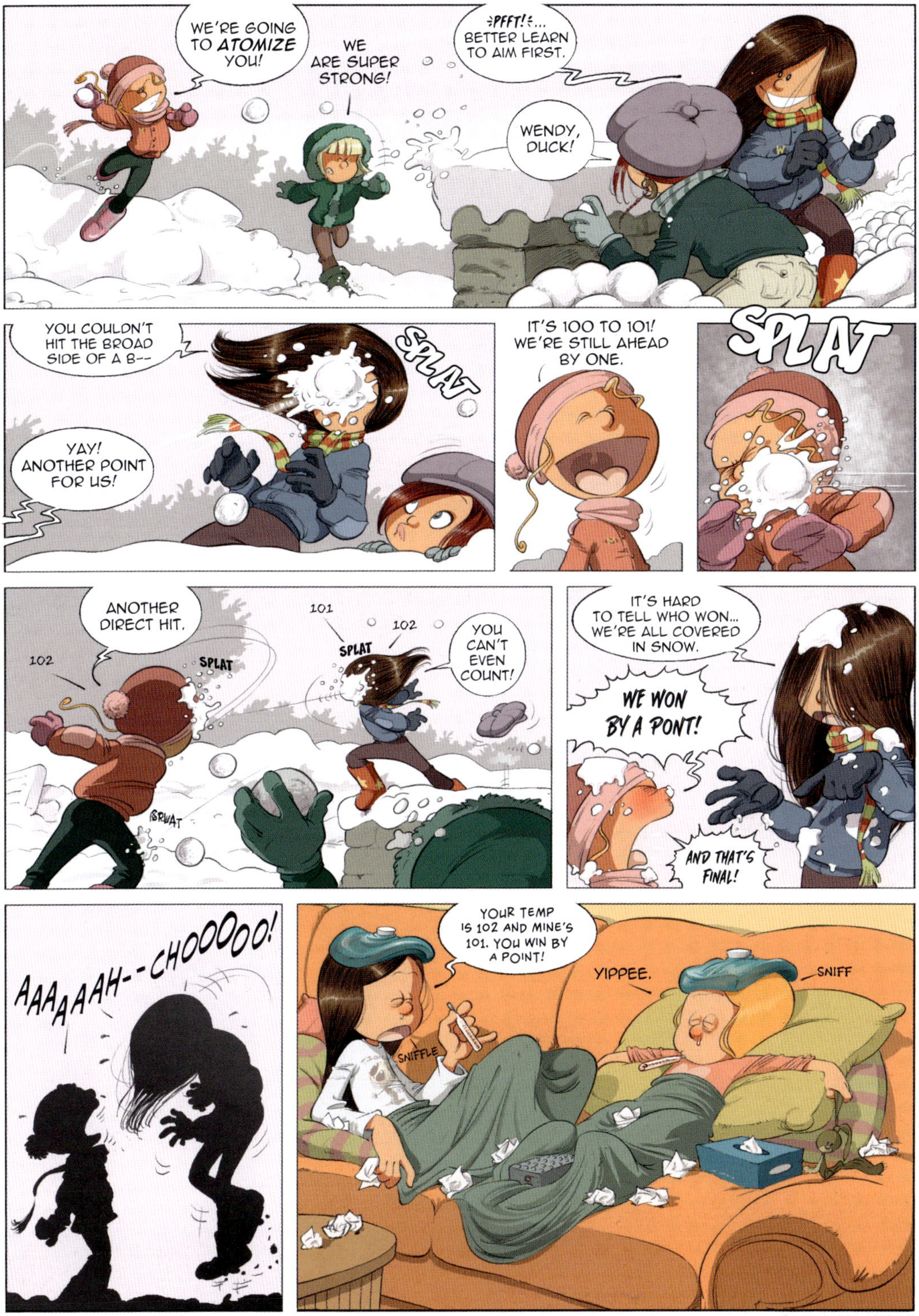

WE'RE GOING TO ATOMIZE YOU!
WE ARE SUPER STRONG!
PFFT!... BETTER LEARN TO AIM FIRST.
WENDY, DUCK!
YOU COULDN'T HIT THE BROAD SIDE OF A B--
SPLAT
YAY! ANOTHER POINT FOR US!
IT'S 100 TO 101! WE'RE STILL AHEAD BY ONE.
SPLAT
ANOTHER DIRECT HIT.
102
SPLAT
101
SPLAT
102
YOU CAN'T EVEN COUNT!
SPLAT
IT'S HARD TO TELL WHO WON... WE'RE ALL COVERED IN SNOW.
WE WON BY A POINT!
AND THAT'S FINAL!
AAAAAAH--CHOOOOO!
YOUR TEMP IS 102 AND MINE'S 101. YOU WIN BY A POINT!
SNIFFLE
YIPPEE.
SNIFF

CAZENOVE & WILLIAM

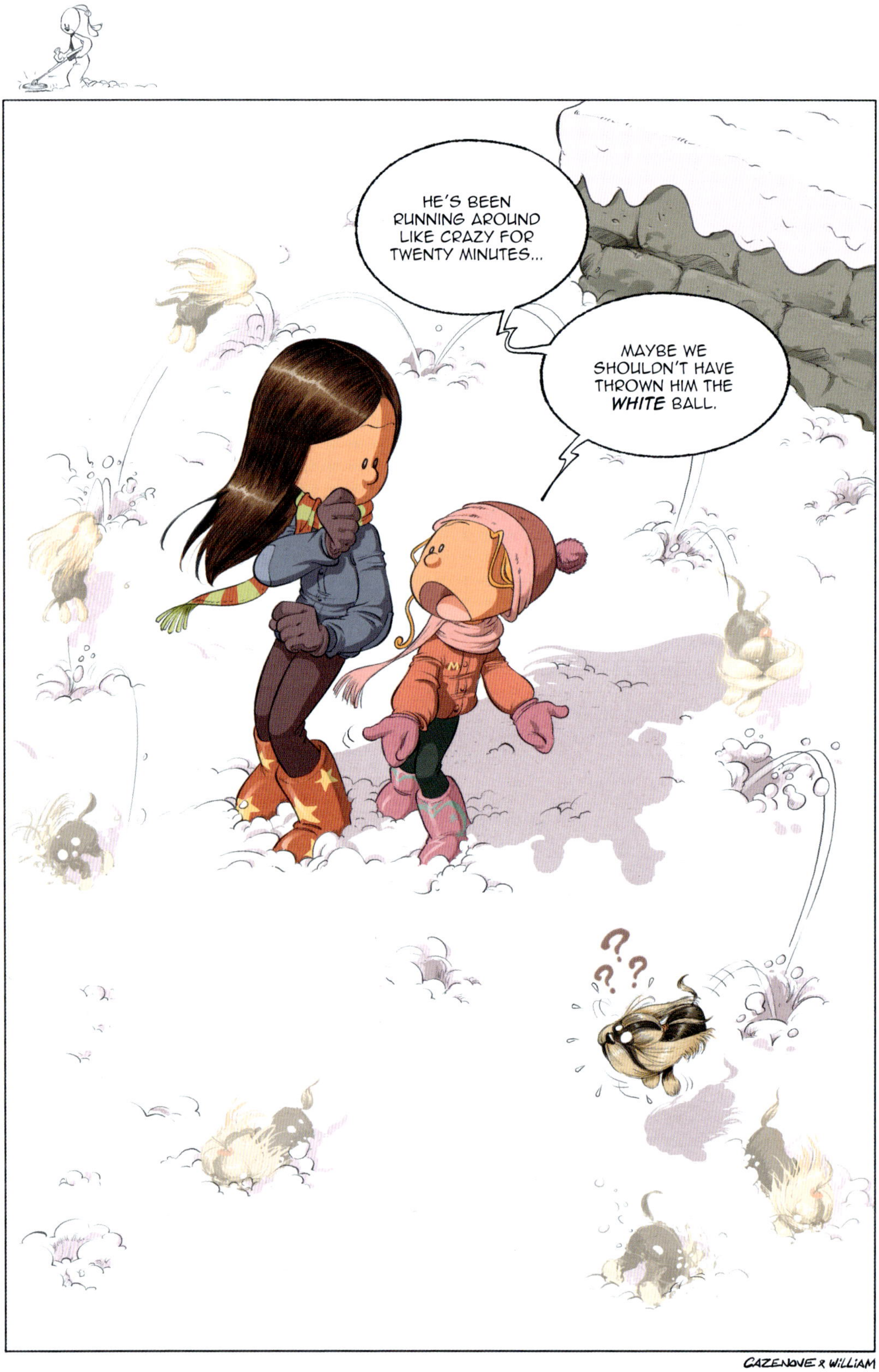
HE'S BEEN RUNNING AROUND LIKE CRAZY FOR TWENTY MINUTES...
MAYBE WE SHOULDN'T HAVE THROWN HIM THE *WHITE* BALL.
??
?

CAZENOVE & WILLIAM

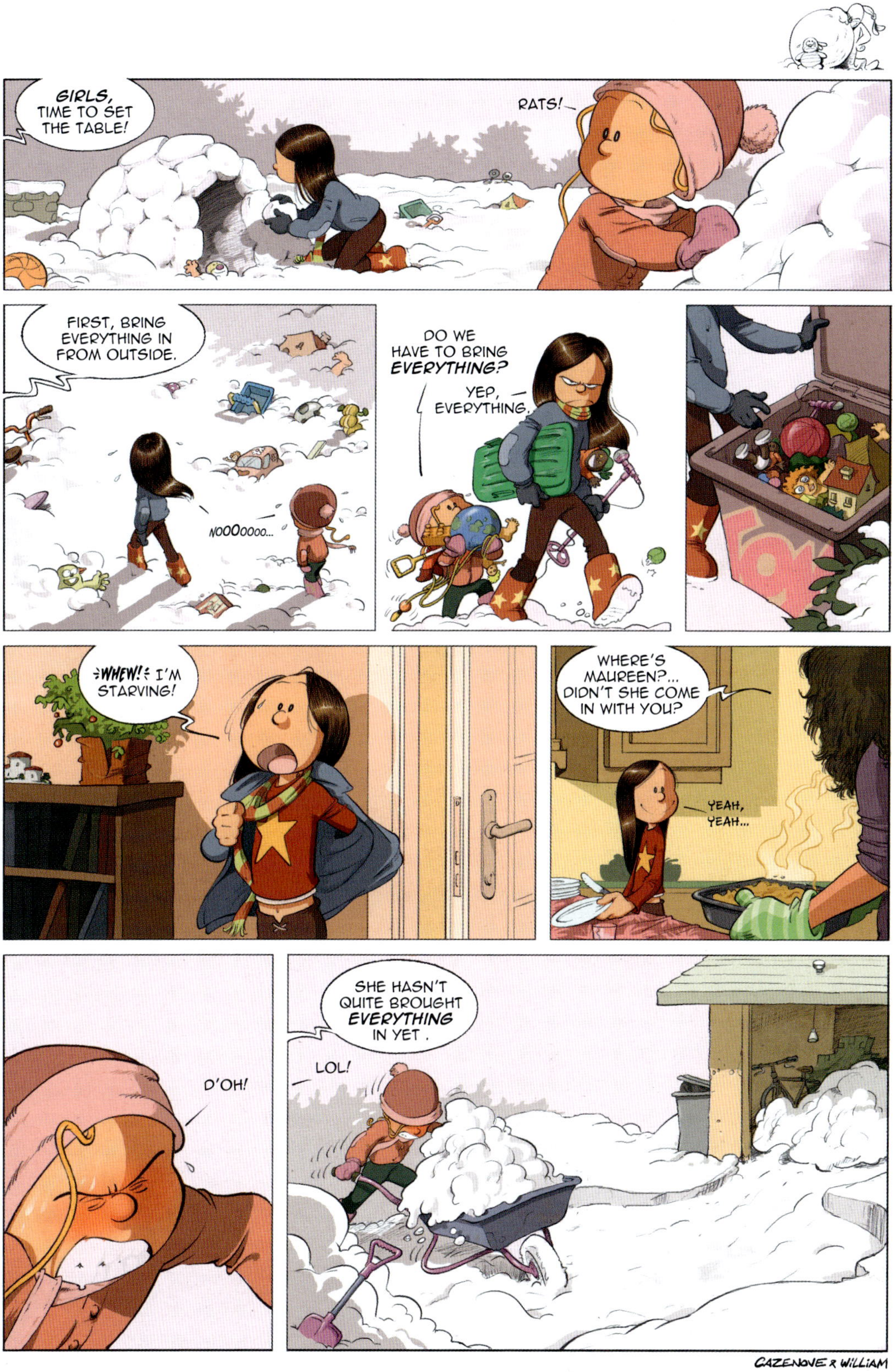
GIRLS, TIME TO SET THE TABLE!
RATS!
FIRST, BRING EVERYTHING IN FROM OUTSIDE.
NOOOoooo...
DO WE HAVE TO BRING EVERYTHING?
YEP, EVERYTHING.
WHEW! I'M STARVING!
WHERE'S MAUREEN?... DIDN'T SHE COME IN WITH YOU?
YEAH, YEAH...
D'OH!
SHE HASN'T QUITE BROUGHT EVERYTHING IN YET .
LOL!
CAZENOVE & WILLIAM

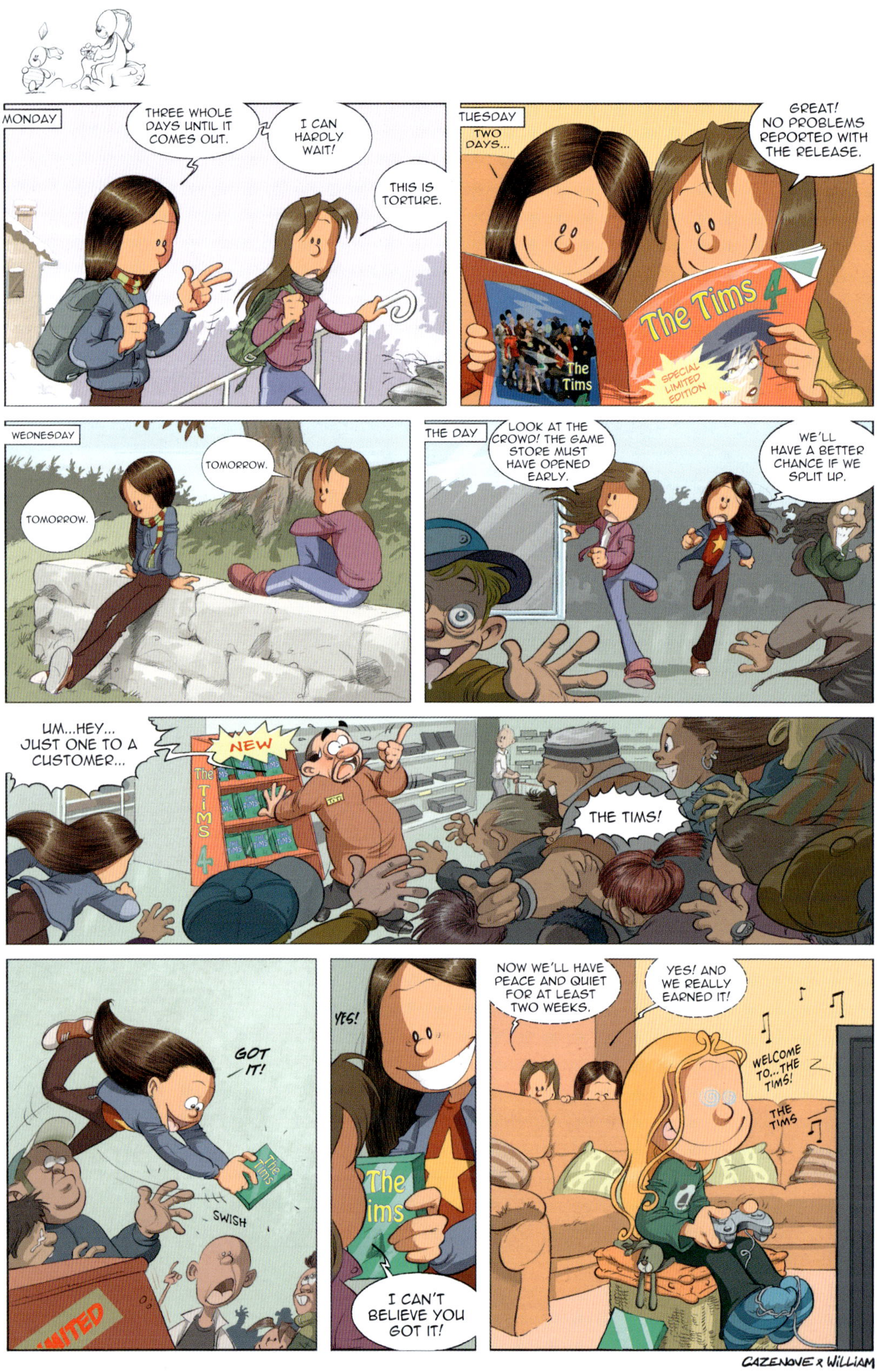
MONDAY
THREE WHOLE DAYS UNTIL IT COMES OUT.
I CAN HARDLY WAIT!
THIS IS TORTURE.
TUESDAY
TWO DAYS...
GREAT! NO PROBLEMS REPORTED WITH THE RELEASE.
The Tims 4
SPECIAL LIMITED EDITION
The Tims
WEDNESDAY
TOMORROW.
TOMORROW.
THE DAY
LOOK AT THE CROWD! THE GAME STORE MUST HAVE OPENED EARLY.
WE'LL HAVE A BETTER CHANCE IF WE SPLIT UP.
UM...HEY... JUST ONE TO A CUSTOMER...
NEW
The Tims 4
THE TIMS!
GOT IT!
SWISH
YES!
I CAN'T BELIEVE YOU GOT IT!
NOW WE'LL HAVE PEACE AND QUIET FOR AT LEAST TWO WEEKS.
YES! AND WE REALLY EARNED IT!
WELCOME TO...THE TIMS!
THE TIMS
CAZENOVE & WILLIAM

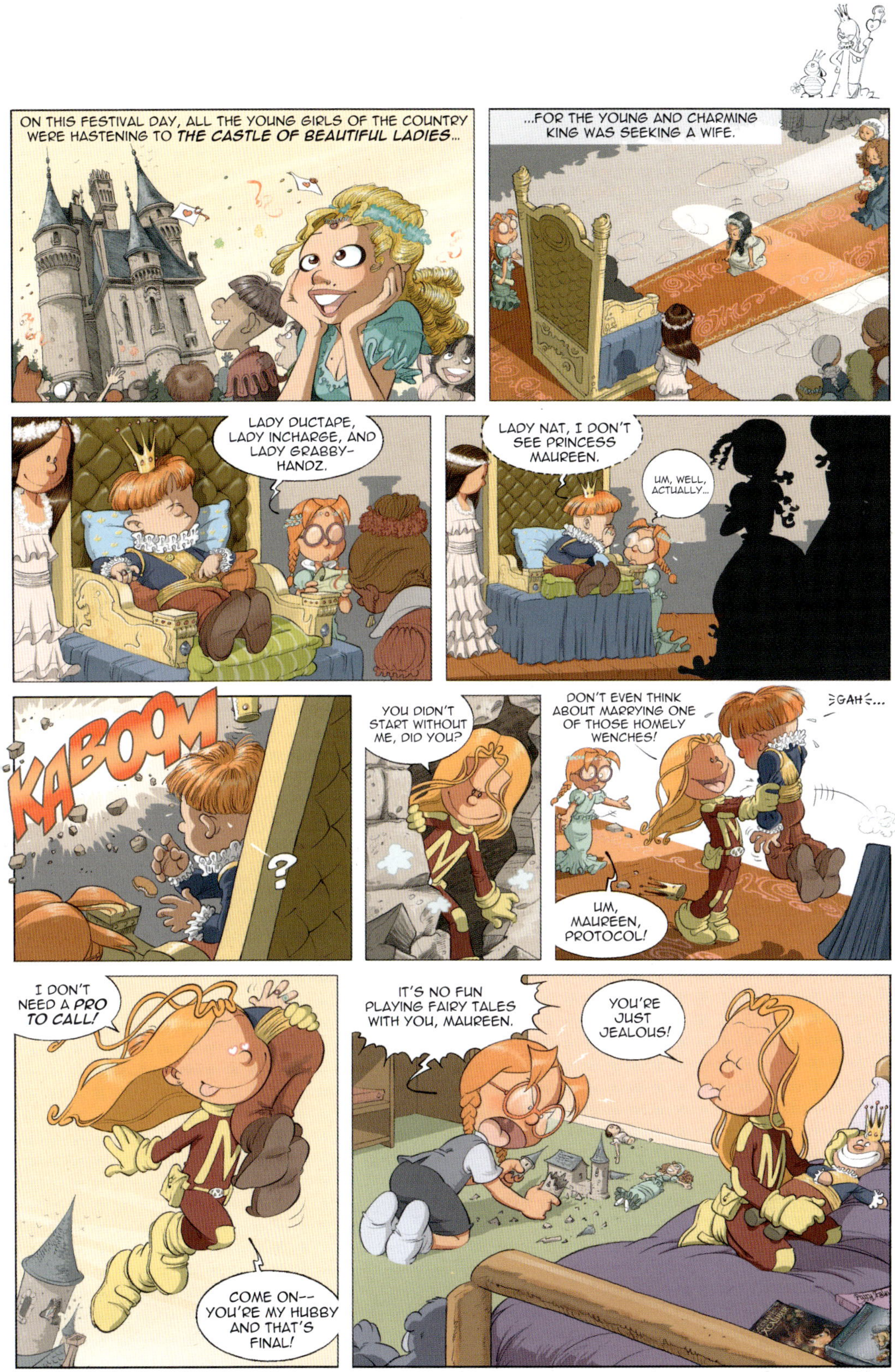

ON THIS FESTIVAL DAY, ALL THE YOUNG GIRLS OF THE COUNTRY WERE HASTENING TO THE CASTLE OF BEAUTIFUL LADIES...
...FOR THE YOUNG AND CHARMING KING WAS SEEKING A WIFE.
LADY DUCTAPE, LADY INCHARGE, AND LADY GRABBY-HANDZ.
LADY NAT, I DON'T SEE PRINCESS MAUREEN.
UM, WELL, ACTUALLY...
KABOOM
?
YOU DIDN'T START WITHOUT ME, DID YOU?
DON'T EVEN THINK ABOUT MARRYING ONE OF THOSE HOMELY WENCHES!
GAH...
UM, MAUREEN, PROTOCOL!
I DON'T NEED A PRO TO CALL!
COME ON-- YOU'RE MY HUBBY AND THAT'S FINAL!
IT'S NO FUN PLAYING FAIRY TALES WITH YOU, MAUREEN.
YOU'RE JUST JEALOUS!

CAZENOVE & WILLIAM

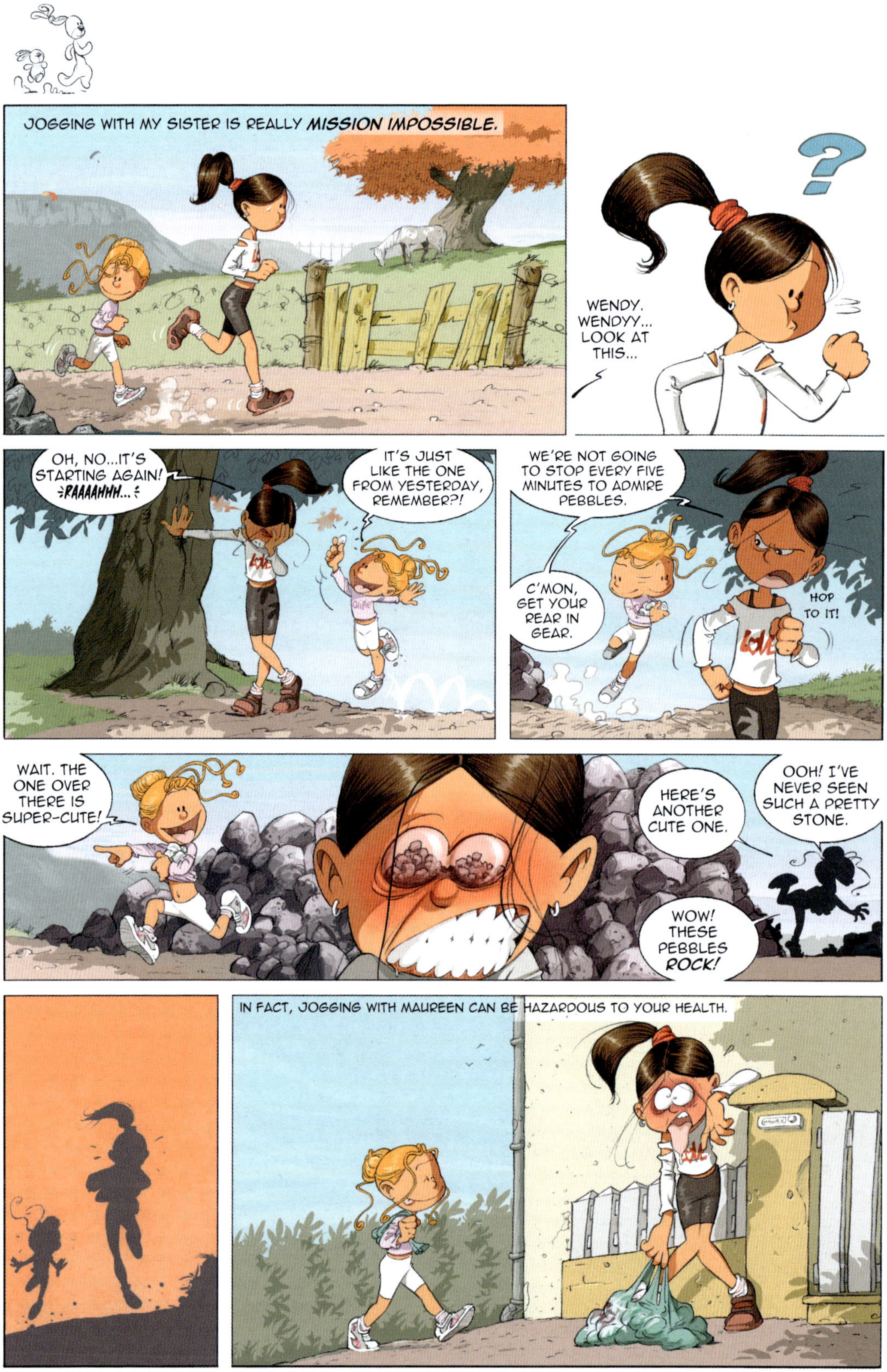
JOGGING WITH MY SISTER IS REALLY MISSION IMPOSSIBLE.
WENDY. WENDYY... LOOK AT THIS...
OH, NO...IT'S STARTING AGAIN! RAAAAHHH...
IT'S JUST LIKE THE ONE FROM YESTERDAY, REMEMBER?!
WE'RE NOT GOING TO STOP EVERY FIVE MINUTES TO ADMIRE PEBBLES.
C'MON, GET YOUR REAR IN GEAR.
HOP TO IT!
WAIT. THE ONE OVER THERE IS SUPER-CUTE!
HERE'S ANOTHER CUTE ONE.
OOH! I'VE NEVER SEEN SUCH A PRETTY STONE.
WOW! THESE PEBBLES ROCK!
IN FACT, JOGGING WITH MAUREEN CAN BE HAZARDOUS TO YOUR HEALTH.
CAZENOVE & WILLIAM

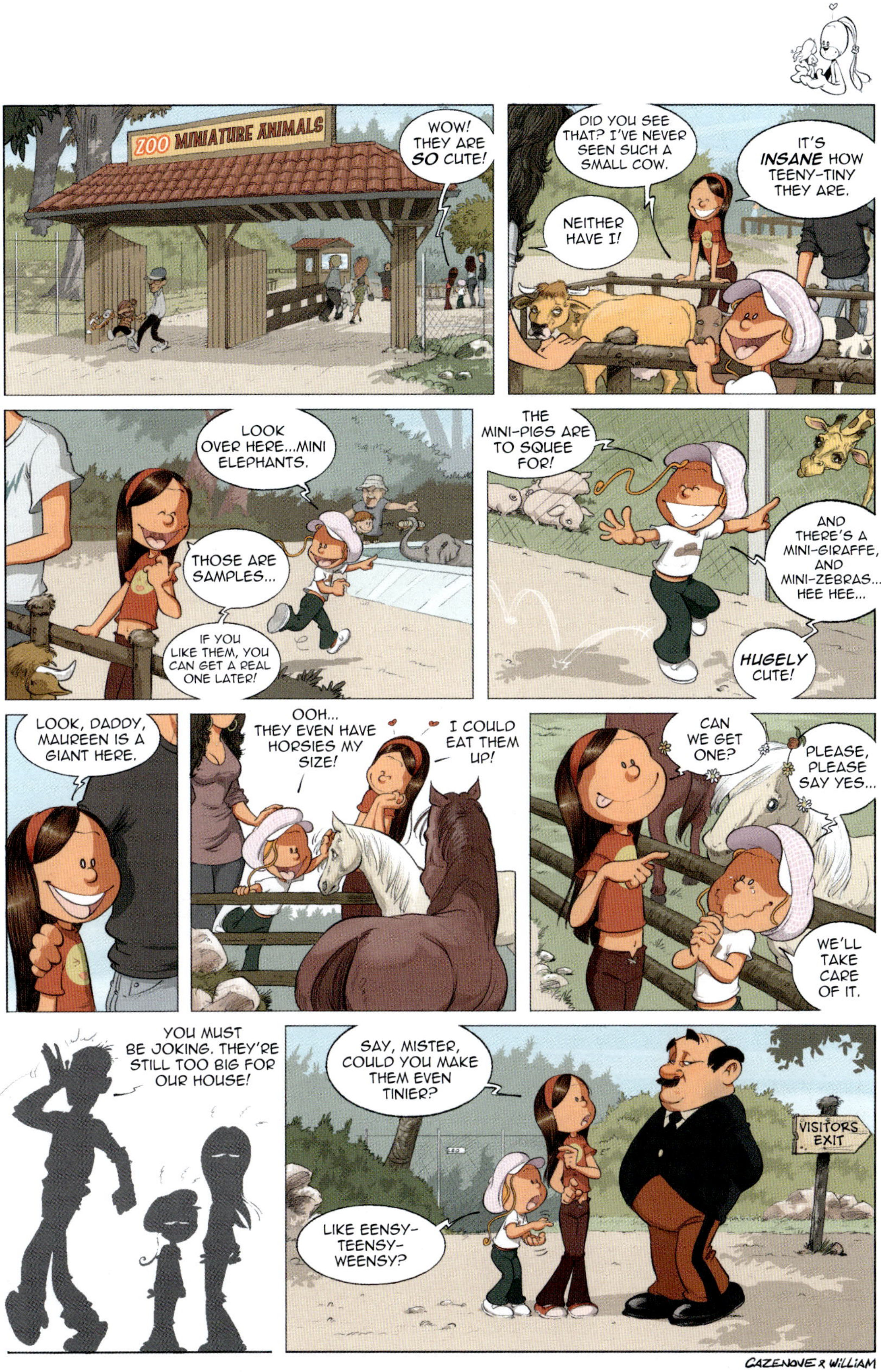
ZOO MINIATURE ANIMALS
WOW! THEY ARE SO CUTE!
DID YOU SEE THAT? I'VE NEVER SEEN SUCH A SMALL COW.
NEITHER HAVE I!
IT'S INSANE HOW TEENY-TINY THEY ARE.
LOOK OVER HERE...MINI ELEPHANTS.
THOSE ARE SAMPLES...
IF YOU LIKE THEM, YOU CAN GET A REAL ONE LATER!
THE MINI-PIGS ARE TO SQUEE FOR!
AND THERE'S A MINI-GIRAFFE, AND MINI-ZEBRAS... HEE HEE...
HUGELY CUTE!
LOOK, DADDY, MAUREEN IS A GIANT HERE.
OOH... THEY EVEN HAVE HORSIES MY SIZE!
I COULD EAT THEM UP!
CAN WE GET ONE?
PLEASE, PLEASE SAY YES...
WE'LL TAKE CARE OF IT.
YOU MUST BE JOKING. THEY'RE STILL TOO BIG FOR OUR HOUSE!
SAY, MISTER, COULD YOU MAKE THEM EVEN TINIER?
LIKE EENSY-TEENSY-WEENSY?
VISITORS EXIT
CAZENOVE & WILLIAM

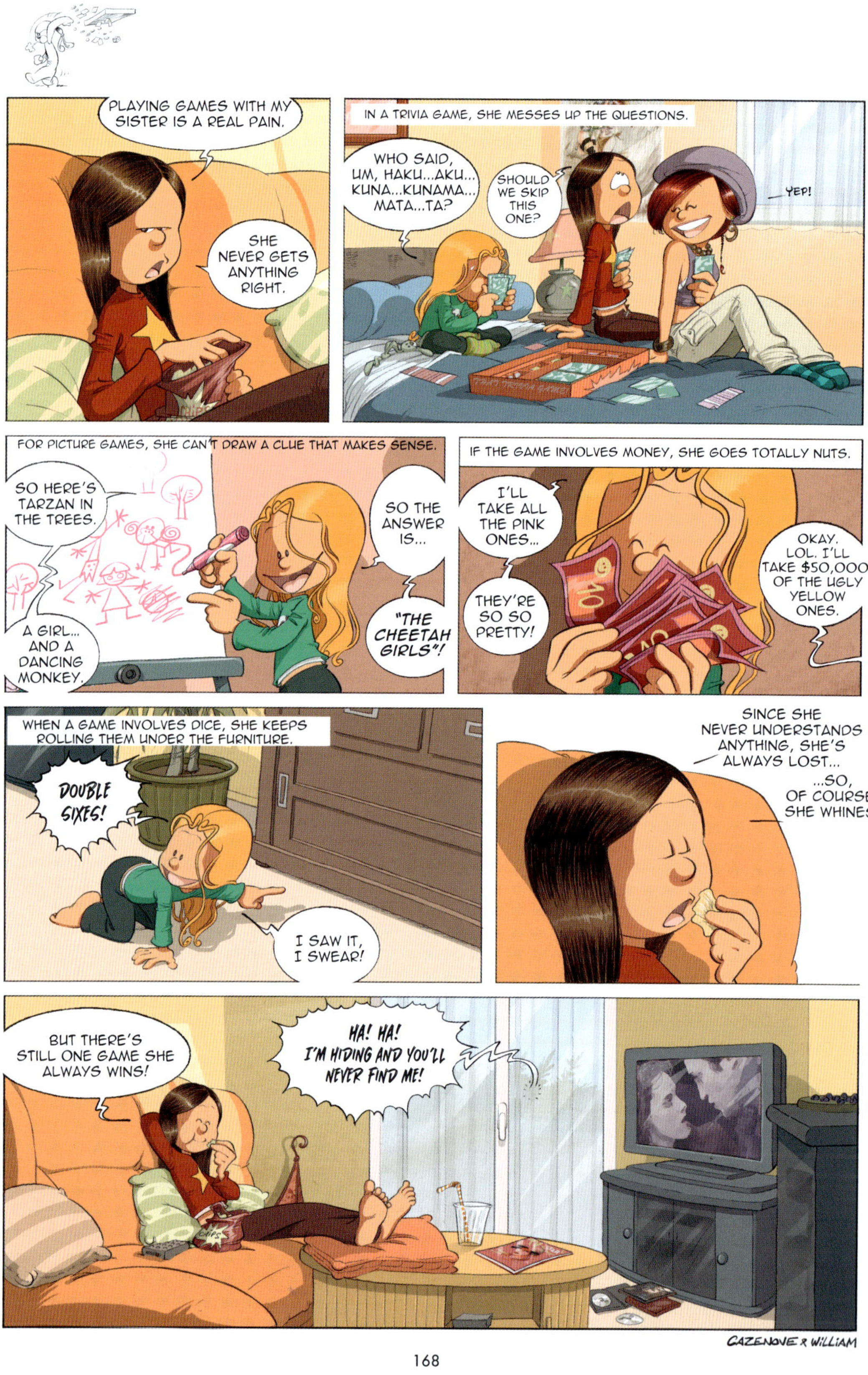
PLAYING GAMES WITH MY SISTER IS A REAL PAIN.
SHE NEVER GETS ANYTHING RIGHT.
IN A TRIVIA GAME, SHE MESSES UP THE QUESTIONS.
WHO SAID, UM, HAKU...AKU... KUNA...KUNAMA... MATA...TA?
SHOULD WE SKIP THIS ONE?
YEP!
FOR PICTURE GAMES, SHE CAN'T DRAW A CLUE THAT MAKES SENSE.
SO HERE'S TARZAN IN THE TREES.
A GIRL... AND A DANCING MONKEY.
SO THE ANSWER IS...
"THE CHEETAH GIRLS"!
IF THE GAME INVOLVES MONEY, SHE GOES TOTALLY NUTS.
I'LL TAKE ALL THE PINK ONES...
THEY'RE SO SO PRETTY!
OKAY. LOL. I'LL TAKE $50,000 OF THE UGLY YELLOW ONES.
WHEN A GAME INVOLVES DICE, SHE KEEPS ROLLING THEM UNDER THE FURNITURE.
DOUBLE SIXES!
I SAW IT, I SWEAR!
SINCE SHE NEVER UNDERSTANDS ANYTHING, SHE'S ALWAYS LOST...
...SO, OF COURSE SHE WHINES
BUT THERE'S STILL ONE GAME SHE ALWAYS WINS!
HA! HA! I'M HIDING AND YOU'LL NEVER FIND ME!
CAZENOVE & WILLIAM

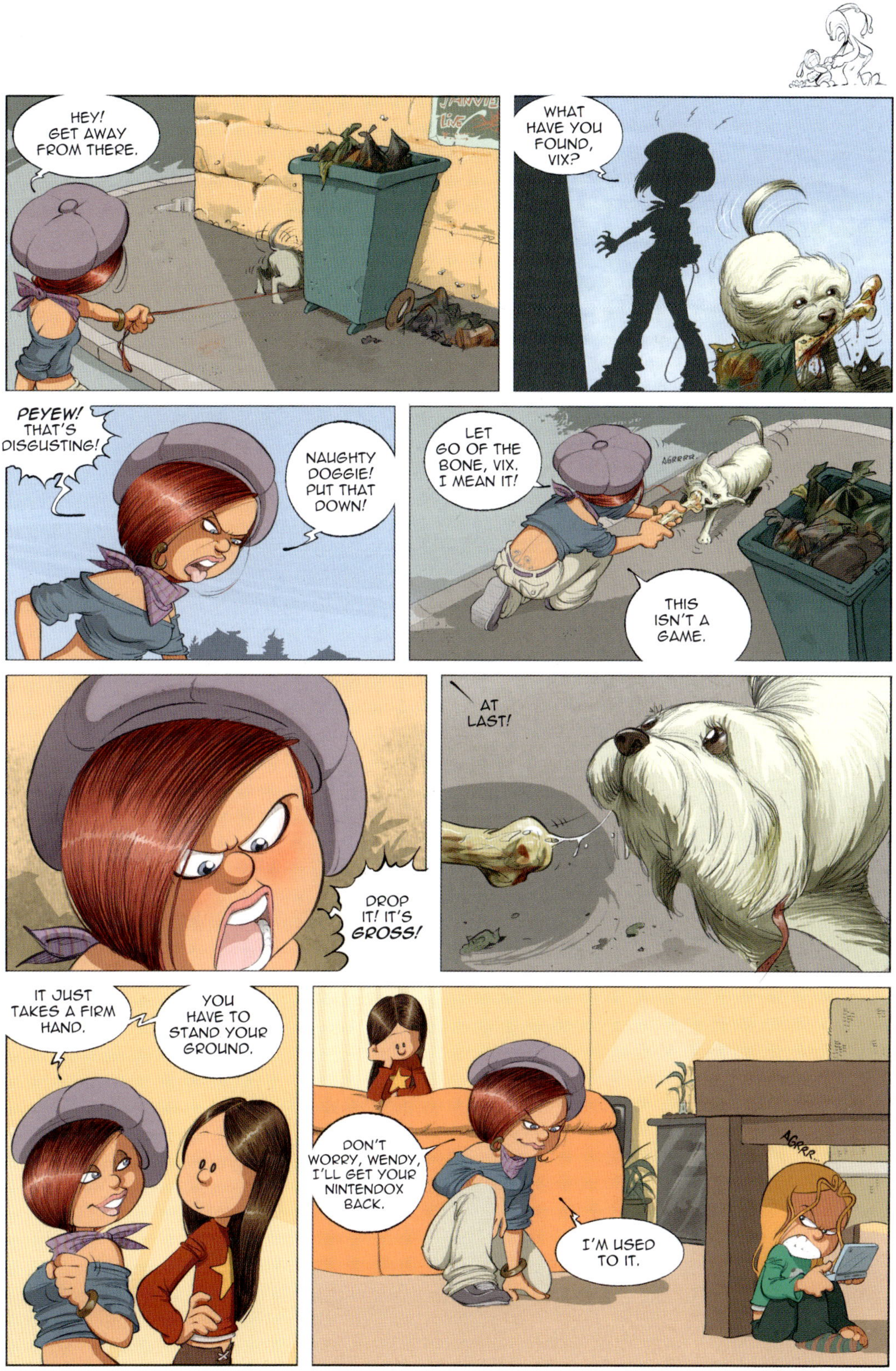
HEY! GET AWAY FROM THERE.
WHAT HAVE YOU FOUND, VIX?
PEYEW! THAT'S DISGUSTING!
NAUGHTY DOGGIE! PUT THAT DOWN!
LET GO OF THE BONE, VIX. I MEAN IT!
AGRRR
THIS ISN'T A GAME.
DROP IT! IT'S GROSS!
AT LAST!
IT JUST TAKES A FIRM HAND.
YOU HAVE TO STAND YOUR GROUND.
DON'T WORRY, WENDY, I'LL GET YOUR NINTENDOX BACK.
AGRRR...
I'M USED TO IT.
CAZENOVE & WILLIAM

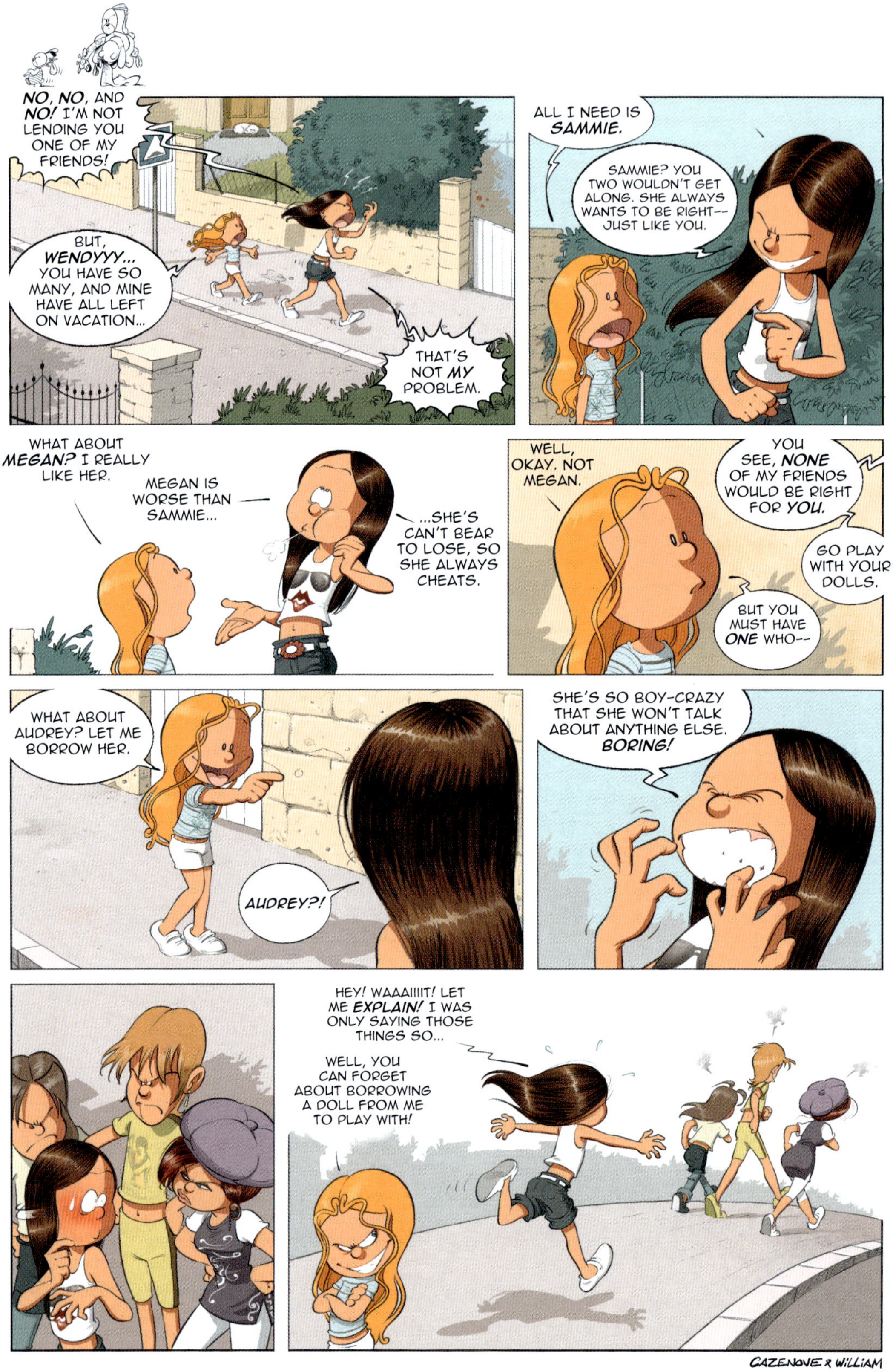

NO, NO, AND NO! I'M NOT LENDING YOU ONE OF MY FRIENDS!
BUT, WENDYYY... YOU HAVE SO MANY, AND MINE HAVE ALL LEFT ON VACATION...
THAT'S NOT MY PROBLEM.
ALL I NEED IS SAMMIE.
SAMMIE? YOU TWO WOULDN'T GET ALONG. SHE ALWAYS WANTS TO BE RIGHT-- JUST LIKE YOU.
WHAT ABOUT MEGAN? I REALLY LIKE HER.
MEGAN IS WORSE THAN SAMMIE...
...SHE'S CAN'T BEAR TO LOSE, SO SHE ALWAYS CHEATS.
WELL, OKAY. NOT MEGAN.
YOU SEE, NONE OF MY FRIENDS WOULD BE RIGHT FOR YOU.
BUT YOU MUST HAVE ONE WHO--
GO PLAY WITH YOUR DOLLS.
WHAT ABOUT AUDREY? LET ME BORROW HER.
AUDREY?!
SHE'S SO BOY-CRAZY THAT SHE WON'T TALK ABOUT ANYTHING ELSE. BORING!
HEY! WAAAIIIIT! LET ME EXPLAIN! I WAS ONLY SAYING THOSE THINGS SO...
WELL, YOU CAN FORGET ABOUT BORROWING A DOLL FROM ME TO PLAY WITH!
CAZENOVE & WILLIAM

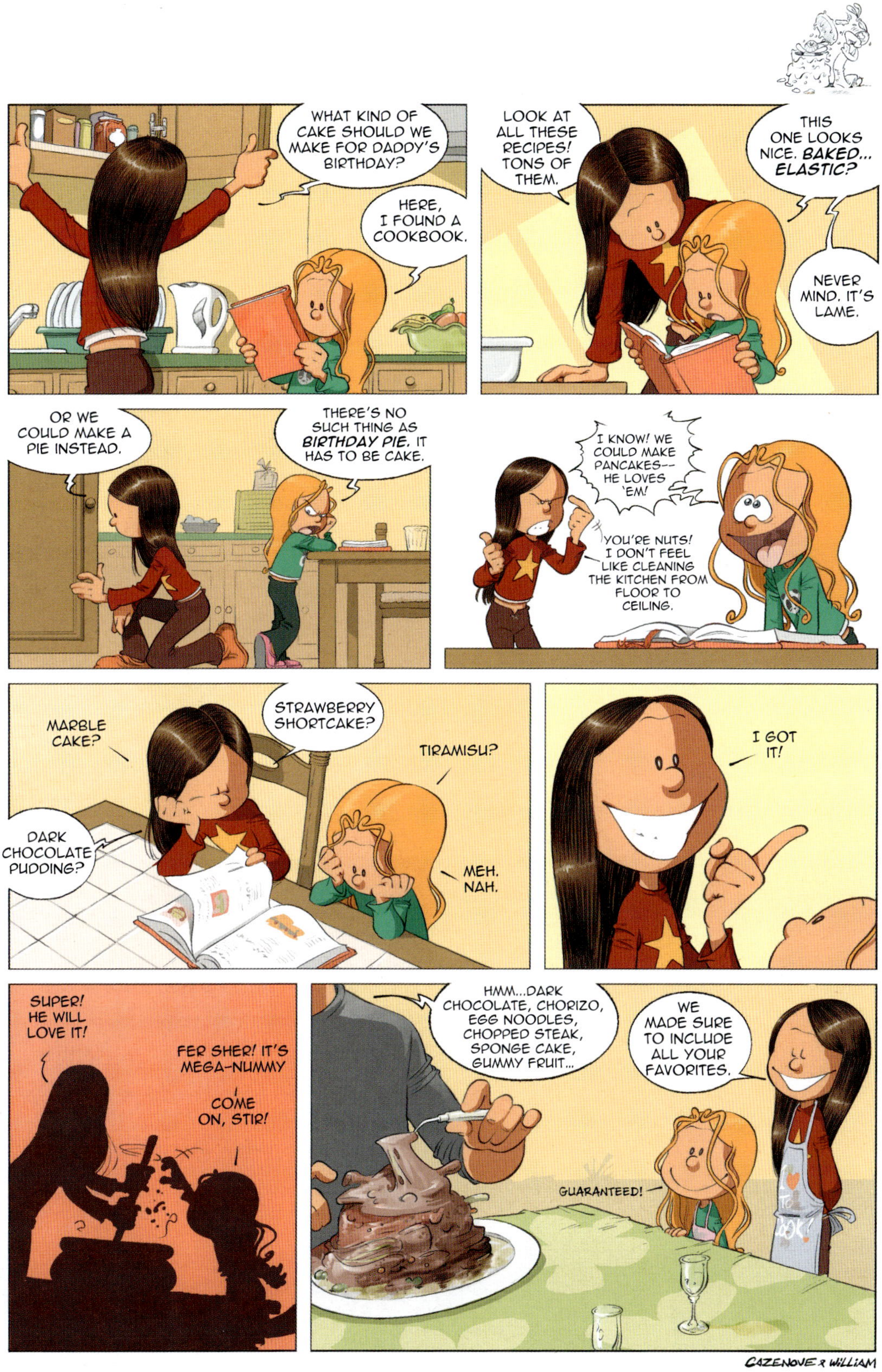
WHAT KIND OF CAKE SHOULD WE MAKE FOR DADDY'S BIRTHDAY?
HERE, I FOUND A COOKBOOK.
LOOK AT ALL THESE RECIPES! TONS OF THEM.
THIS ONE LOOKS NICE. BAKED... ELASTIC?
NEVER MIND. IT'S LAME.
OR WE COULD MAKE A PIE INSTEAD.
THERE'S NO SUCH THING AS BIRTHDAY PIE. IT HAS TO BE CAKE.
I KNOW! WE COULD MAKE PANCAKES-- HE LOVES 'EM!
YOU'RE NUTS! I DON'T FEEL LIKE CLEANING THE KITCHEN FROM FLOOR TO CEILING.
MARBLE CAKE?
STRAWBERRY SHORTCAKE?
TIRAMISU?
DARK CHOCOLATE PUDDING?
MEH. NAH.
I GOT IT!
SUPER! HE WILL LOVE IT!
FER SHER! IT'S MEGA-NUMMY
COME ON, STIR!
HMM...DARK CHOCOLATE, CHORIZO, EGG NOODLES, CHOPPED STEAK, SPONGE CAKE, GUMMY FRUIT...
WE MADE SURE TO INCLUDE ALL YOUR FAVORITES.
GUARANTEED!
CAZENOVE & WILLIAM

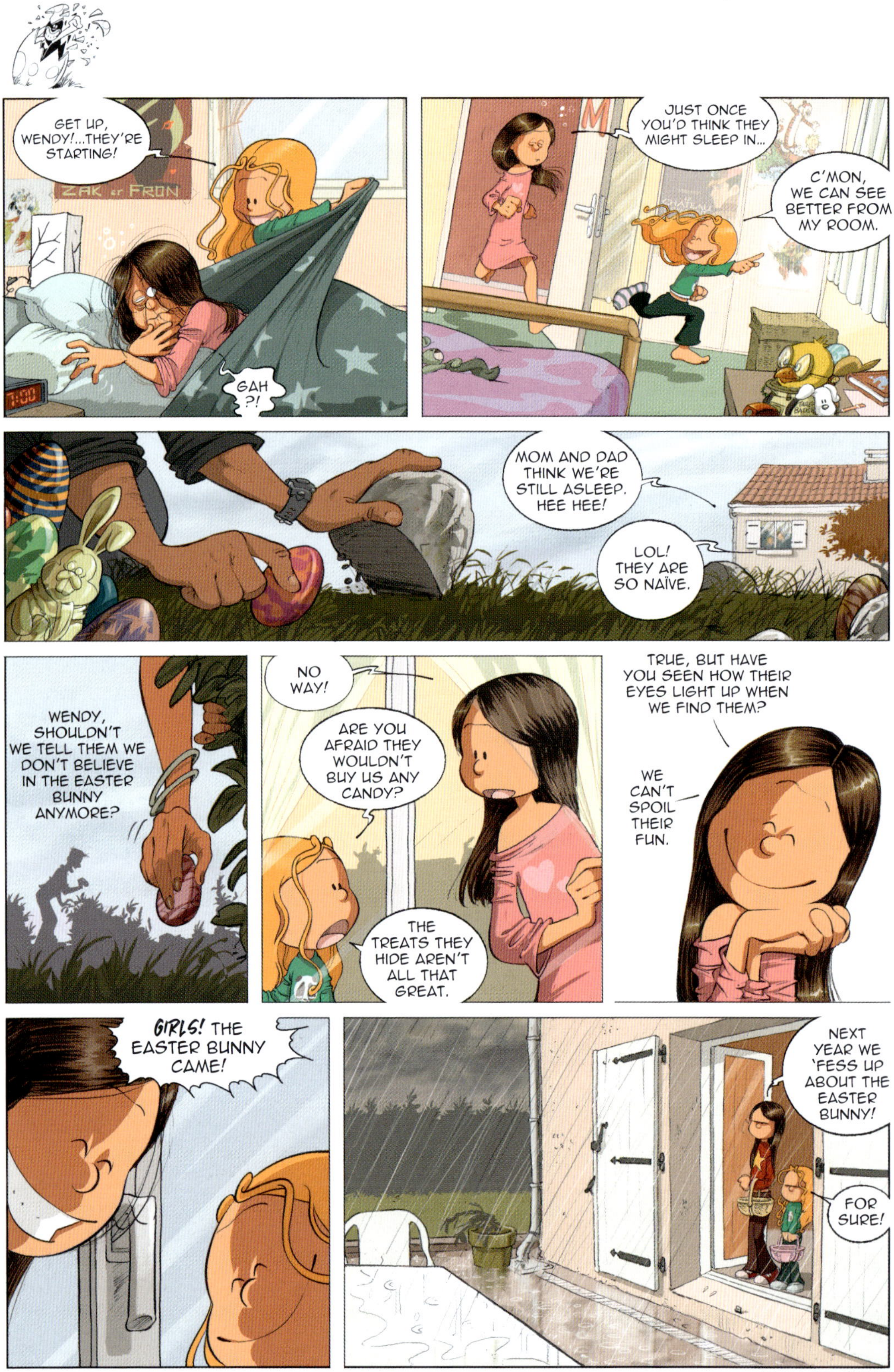
GET UP, WENDY!...THEY'RE STARTING!
GAH ?!
JUST ONCE YOU'D THINK THEY MIGHT SLEEP IN...
C'MON, WE CAN SEE BETTER FROM MY ROOM.
MOM AND DAD THINK WE'RE STILL ASLEEP. HEE HEE!
LOL! THEY ARE SO NAÏVE.
WENDY, SHOULDN'T WE TELL THEM WE DON'T BELIEVE IN THE EASTER BUNNY ANYMORE?
NO WAY!
ARE YOU AFRAID THEY WOULDN'T BUY US ANY CANDY?
THE TREATS THEY HIDE AREN'T ALL THAT GREAT.
TRUE, BUT HAVE YOU SEEN HOW THEIR EYES LIGHT UP WHEN WE FIND THEM?
WE CAN'T SPOIL THEIR FUN.
GIRLS! THE EASTER BUNNY CAME!
NEXT YEAR WE 'FESS UP ABOUT THE EASTER BUNNY!
FOR SURE!
CAZENOVE & WILLIAM

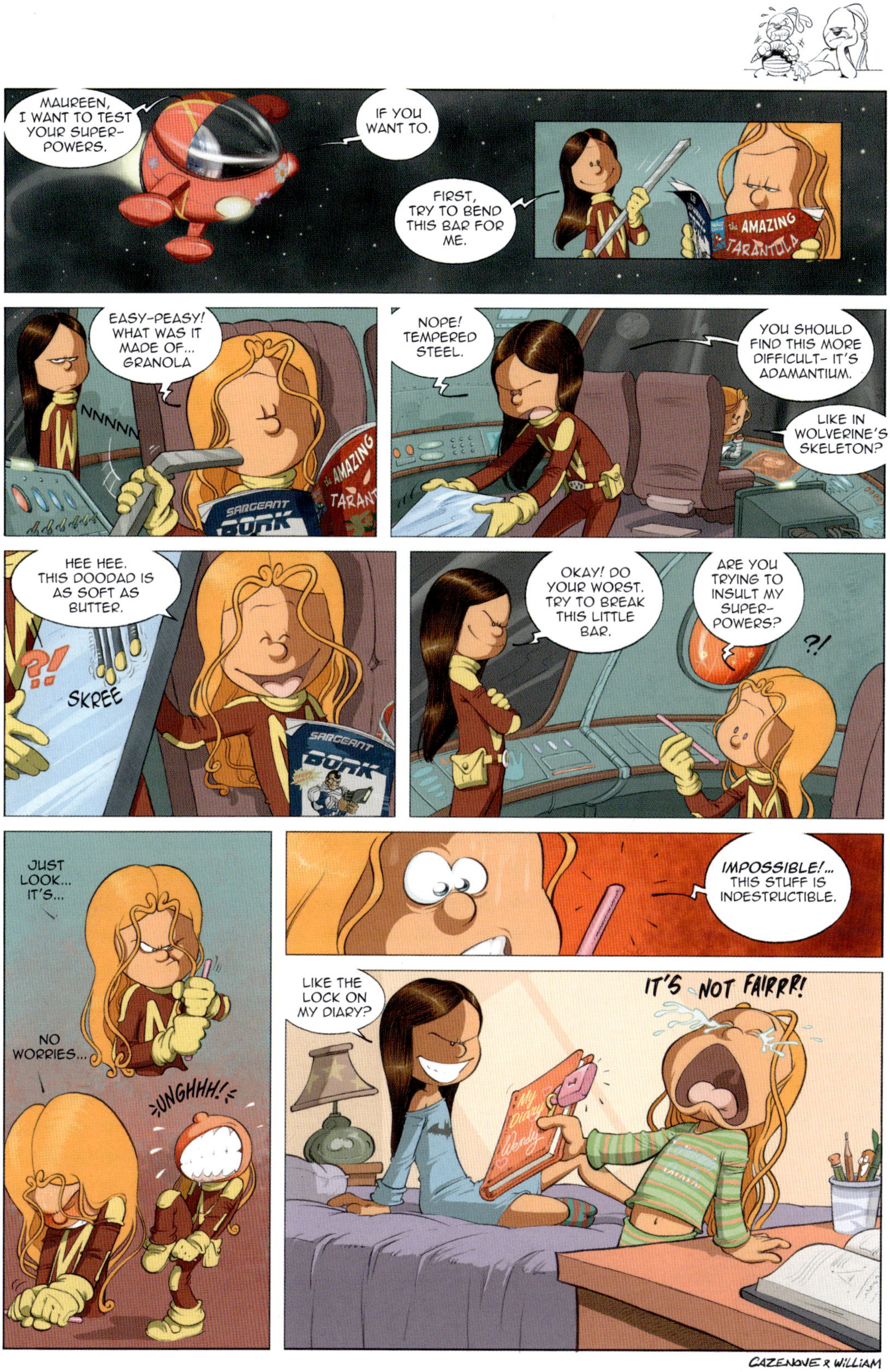
MAUREEN, I WANT TO TEST YOUR SUPER-POWERS.
IF YOU WANT TO.
FIRST, TRY TO BEND THIS BAR FOR ME.
the AMAZING TARANTULA
EASY-PEASY! WHAT WAS IT MADE OF... GRANOLA
NNNNN
SARGEANT BORK
NOPE! TEMPERED STEEL.
YOU SHOULD FIND THIS MORE DIFFICULT- IT'S ADAMANTIUM.
LIKE IN WOLVERINE'S SKELETON?
HEE HEE. THIS DOODAD IS AS SOFT AS BUTTER.
?!
SKREE
OKAY! DO YOUR WORST. TRY TO BREAK THIS LITTLE BAR.
ARE YOU TRYING TO INSULT MY SUPER-POWERS?
?!
JUST LOOK... IT'S...
NO WORRIES...
UNGHHH!
IMPOSSIBLE!... THIS STUFF IS INDESTRUCTIBLE.
LIKE THE LOCK ON MY DIARY?
IT'S NOT FAIRRR!
My Diary Wendy
CAZENOVE & WILLIAM

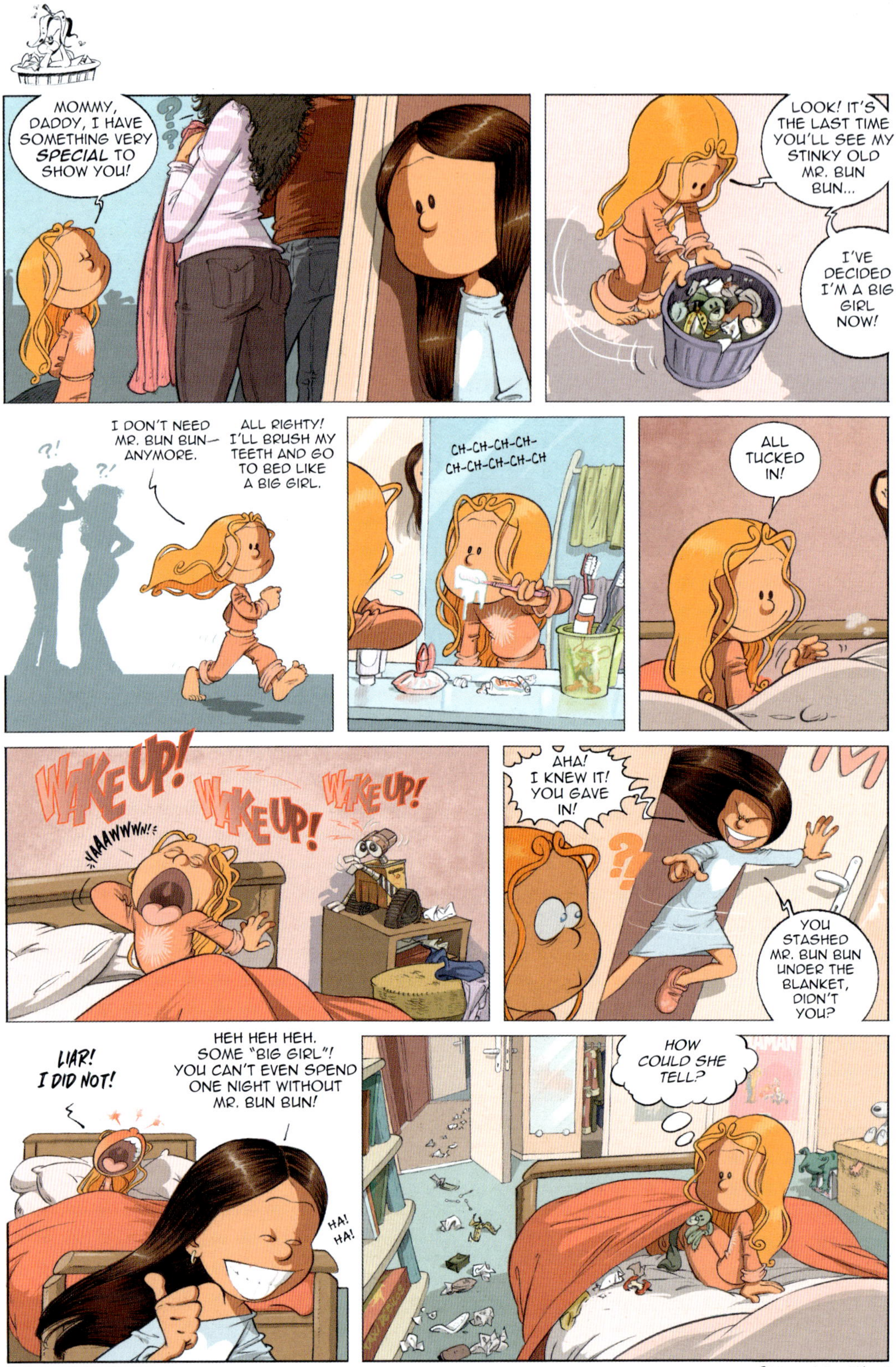
MOMMY, DADDY, I HAVE SOMETHING VERY SPECIAL TO SHOW YOU!
LOOK! IT'S THE LAST TIME YOU'LL SEE MY STINKY OLD MR. BUN BUN...
I'VE DECIDED I'M A BIG GIRL NOW!
?!
?!
I DON'T NEED MR. BUN BUN— ANYMORE.
ALL RIGHTY! I'LL BRUSH MY TEETH AND GO TO BED LIKE A BIG GIRL.
CH-CH-CH-CH-
CH-CH-CH-CH-CH
ALL TUCKED IN!
WAKE UP!
WAKE UP!
WAKE UP!
YAAAWWWN!
AHA! I KNEW IT! YOU GAVE IN!
YOU STASHED MR. BUN BUN UNDER THE BLANKET, DIDN'T YOU?
LIAR! I DID NOT!
HEH HEH HEH. SOME "BIG GIRL"! YOU CAN'T EVEN SPEND ONE NIGHT WITHOUT MR. BUN BUN!
HA! HA!
HOW COULD SHE TELL?
CAZENOVE & WILLIAM

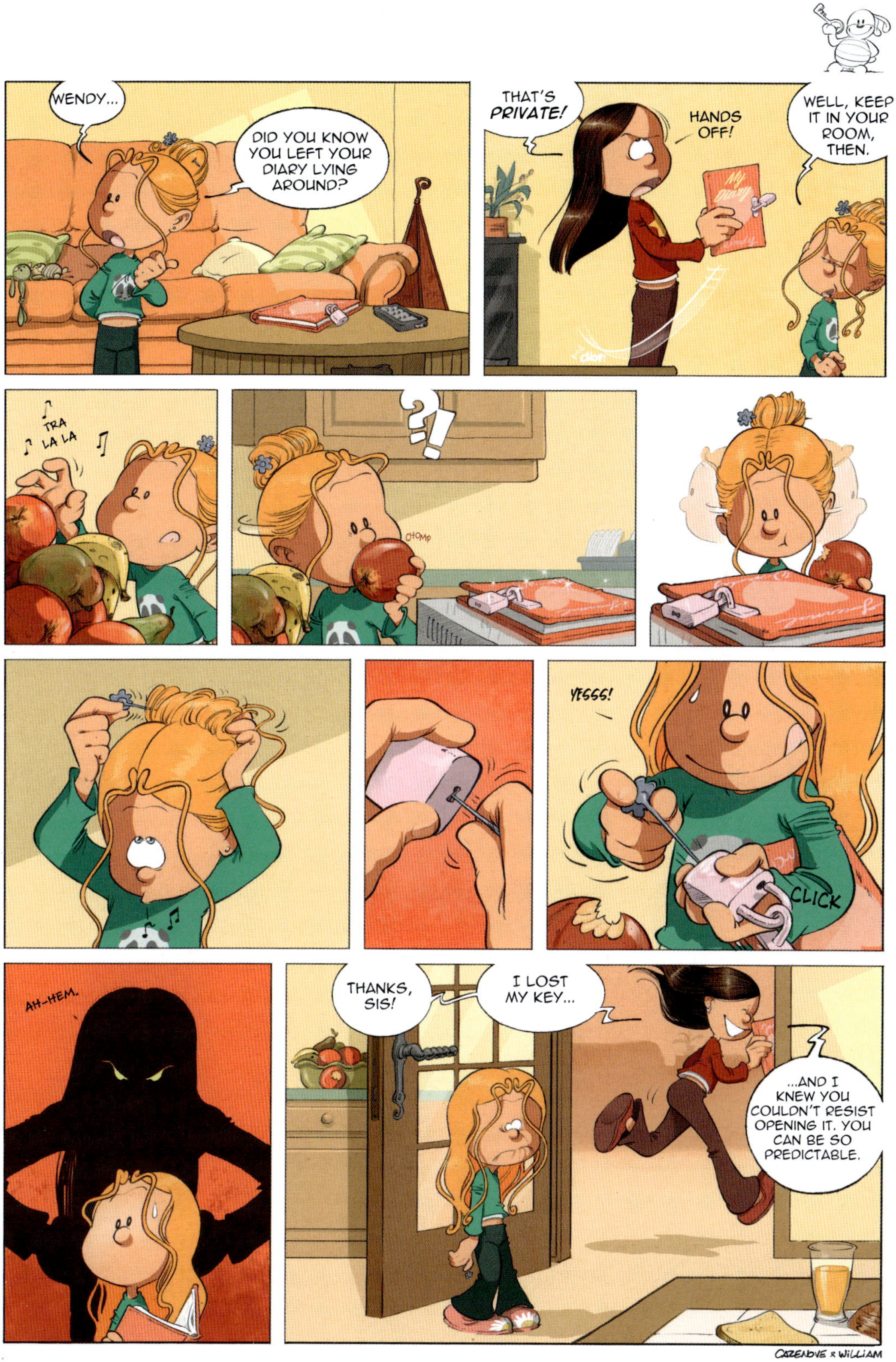
WENDY...
DID YOU KNOW YOU LEFT YOUR DIARY LYING AROUND?
THAT'S *PRIVATE!*
HANDS OFF!
My Diary
WELL, KEEP IT IN YOUR ROOM, THEN.
TRA LA LA
CHOMP
YESSS!
CLICK
AH-HEM.
THANKS, SIS!
I LOST MY KEY...
...AND I KNEW YOU COULDN'T RESIST OPENING IT. YOU CAN BE SO PREDICTABLE.
CAZENOVE & WILLIAM

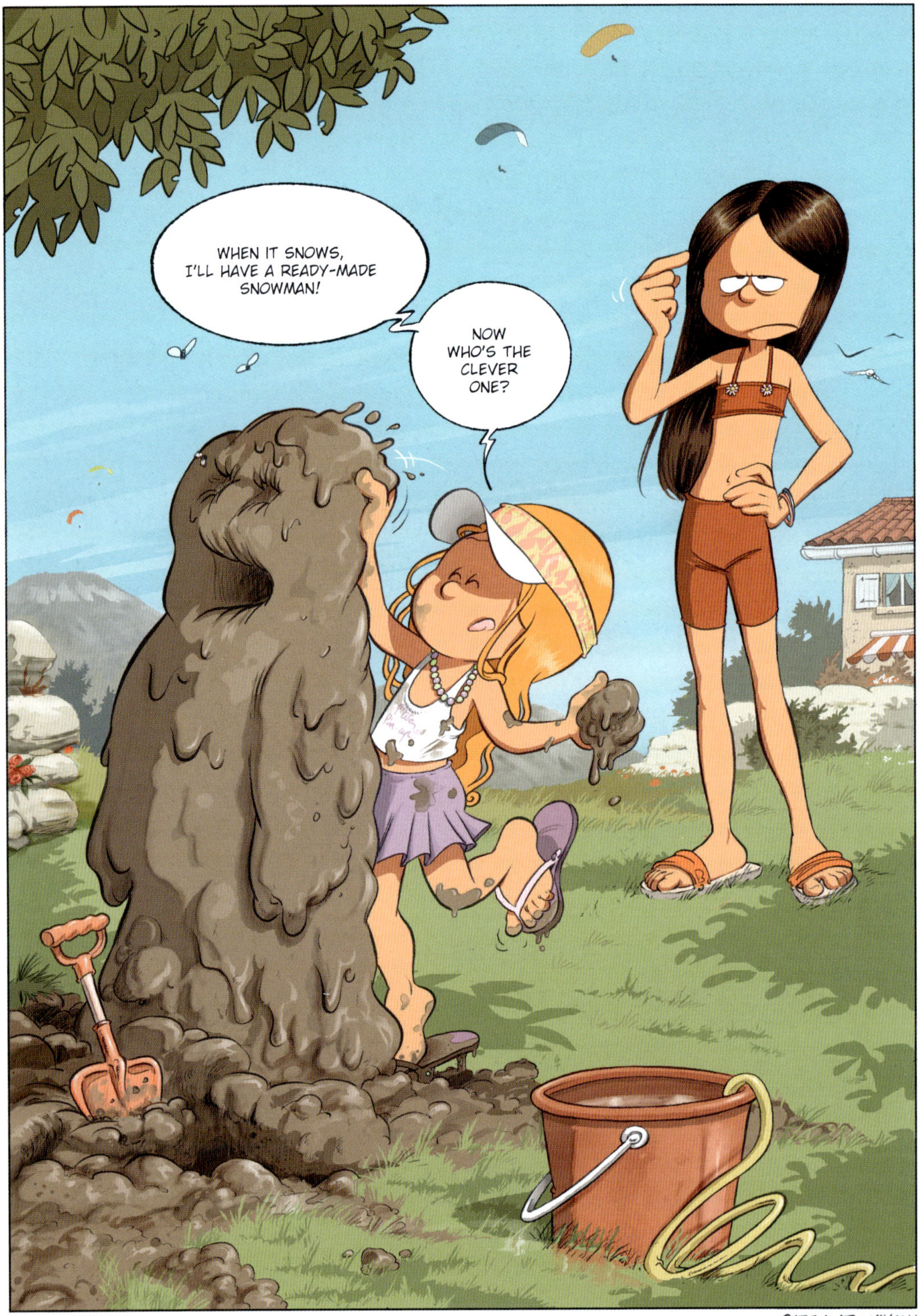
WHEN IT SNOWS, I'LL HAVE A READY-MADE SNOWMAN!
NOW WHO'S THE CLEVER ONE?

CAZENOVE & WILLIAM

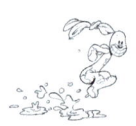

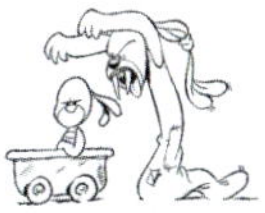

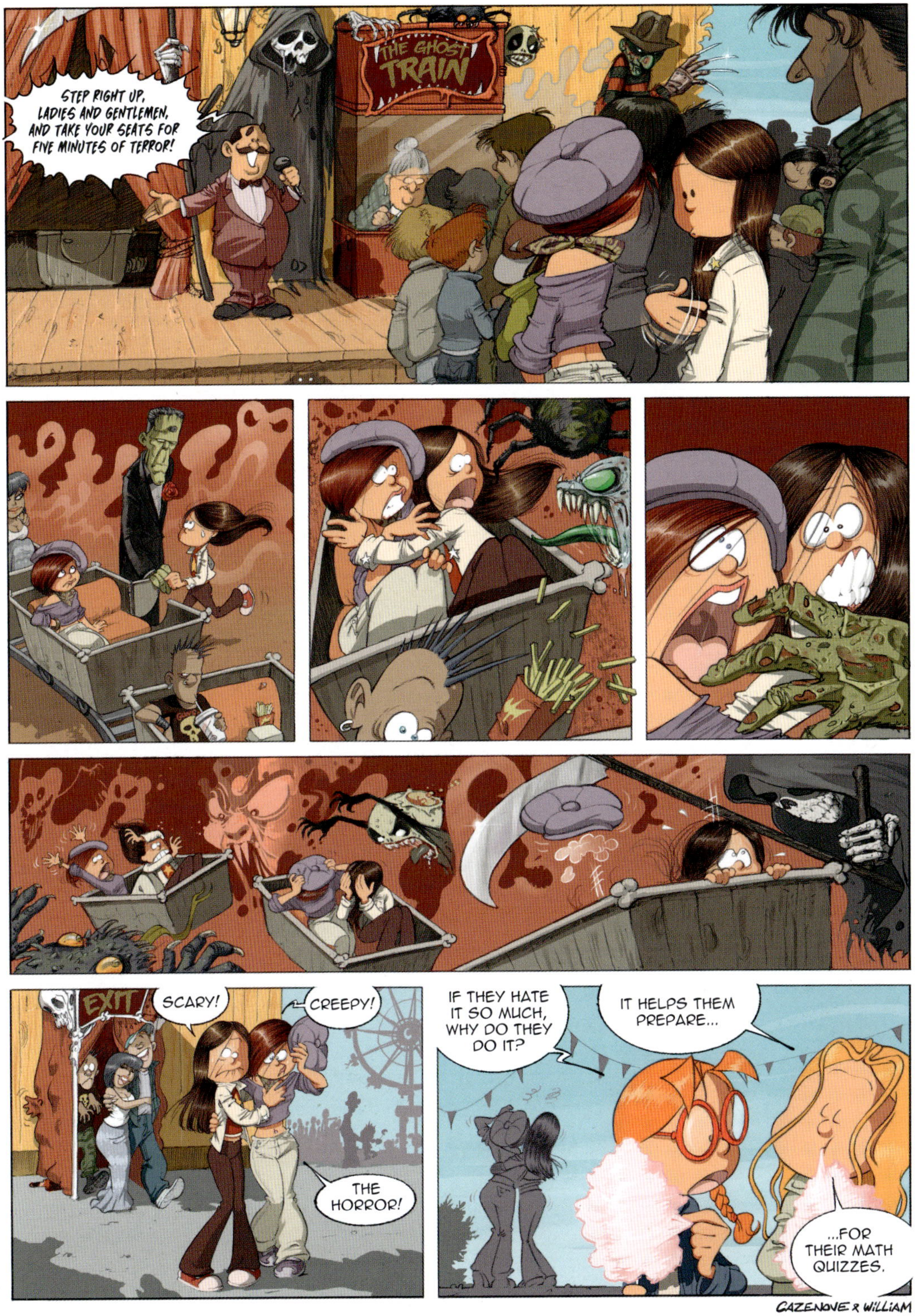
STEP RIGHT UP, LADIES AND GENTLEMEN, AND TAKE YOUR SEATS FOR FIVE MINUTES OF TERROR!
THE GHOST TRAIN
EXIT
SCARY!
CREEPY!
THE HORROR!
IF THEY HATE IT SO MUCH, WHY DO THEY DO IT?
IT HELPS THEM PREPARE...
...FOR THEIR MATH QUIZZES.
CAZENOVE & WILLIAM

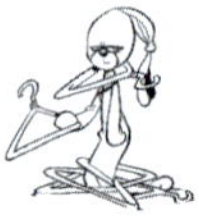
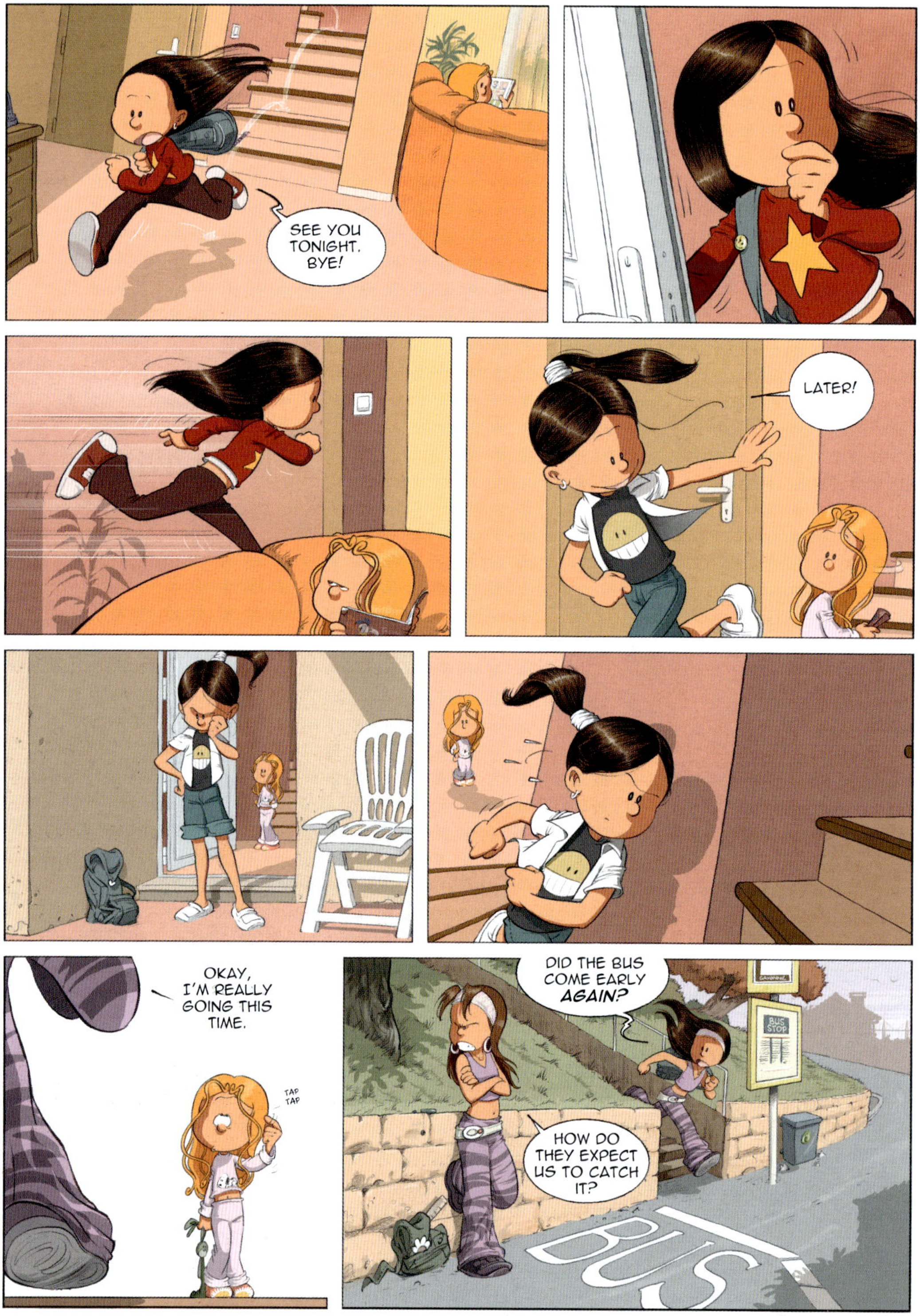
SEE YOU TONIGHT. BYE!
LATER!
OKAY, I'M REALLY GOING THIS TIME.
TAP TAP
DID THE BUS COME EARLY *AGAIN?*
HOW DO THEY EXPECT US TO CATCH IT?
BUS STOP
BUS
CAZENOVE & WILLIAM

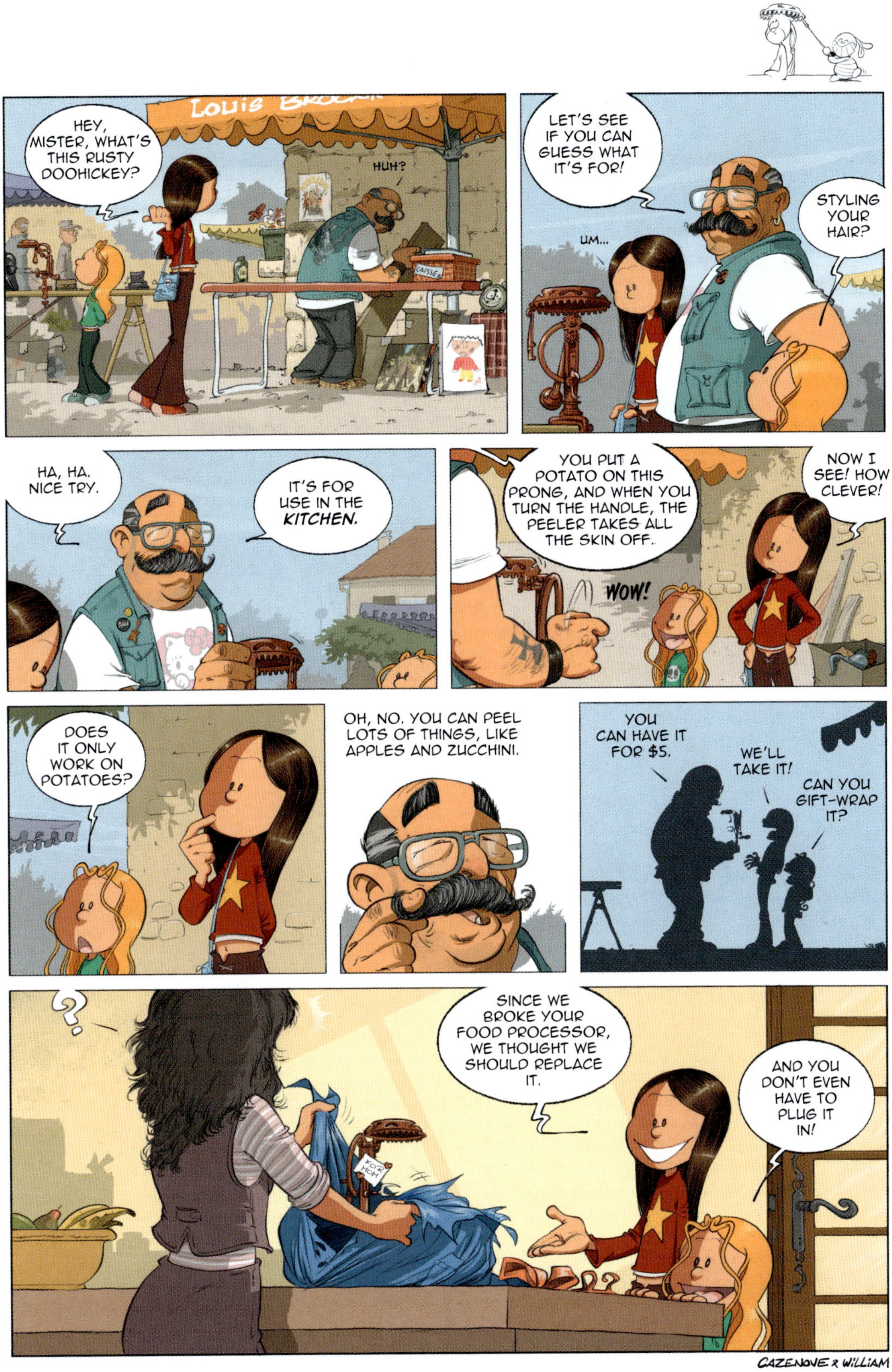
LOUIS BROC
HEY, MISTER, WHAT'S THIS RUSTY DOOHICKEY?
HUH?
LET'S SEE IF YOU CAN GUESS WHAT IT'S FOR!
UM...
STYLING YOUR HAIR?
HA, HA. NICE TRY.
IT'S FOR USE IN THE KITCHEN.
YOU PUT A POTATO ON THIS PRONG, AND WHEN YOU TURN THE HANDLE, THE PEELER TAKES ALL THE SKIN OFF.
WOW!
NOW I SEE! HOW CLEVER!
DOES IT ONLY WORK ON POTATOES?
OH, NO. YOU CAN PEEL LOTS OF THINGS, LIKE APPLES AND ZUCCHINI.
YOU CAN HAVE IT FOR $5.
WE'LL TAKE IT!
CAN YOU GIFT-WRAP IT?
?
FOR MOM
SINCE WE BROKE YOUR FOOD PROCESSOR, WE THOUGHT WE SHOULD REPLACE IT.
AND YOU DON'T EVEN HAVE TO PLUG IT IN!
CAZENOVE & WILLIAM

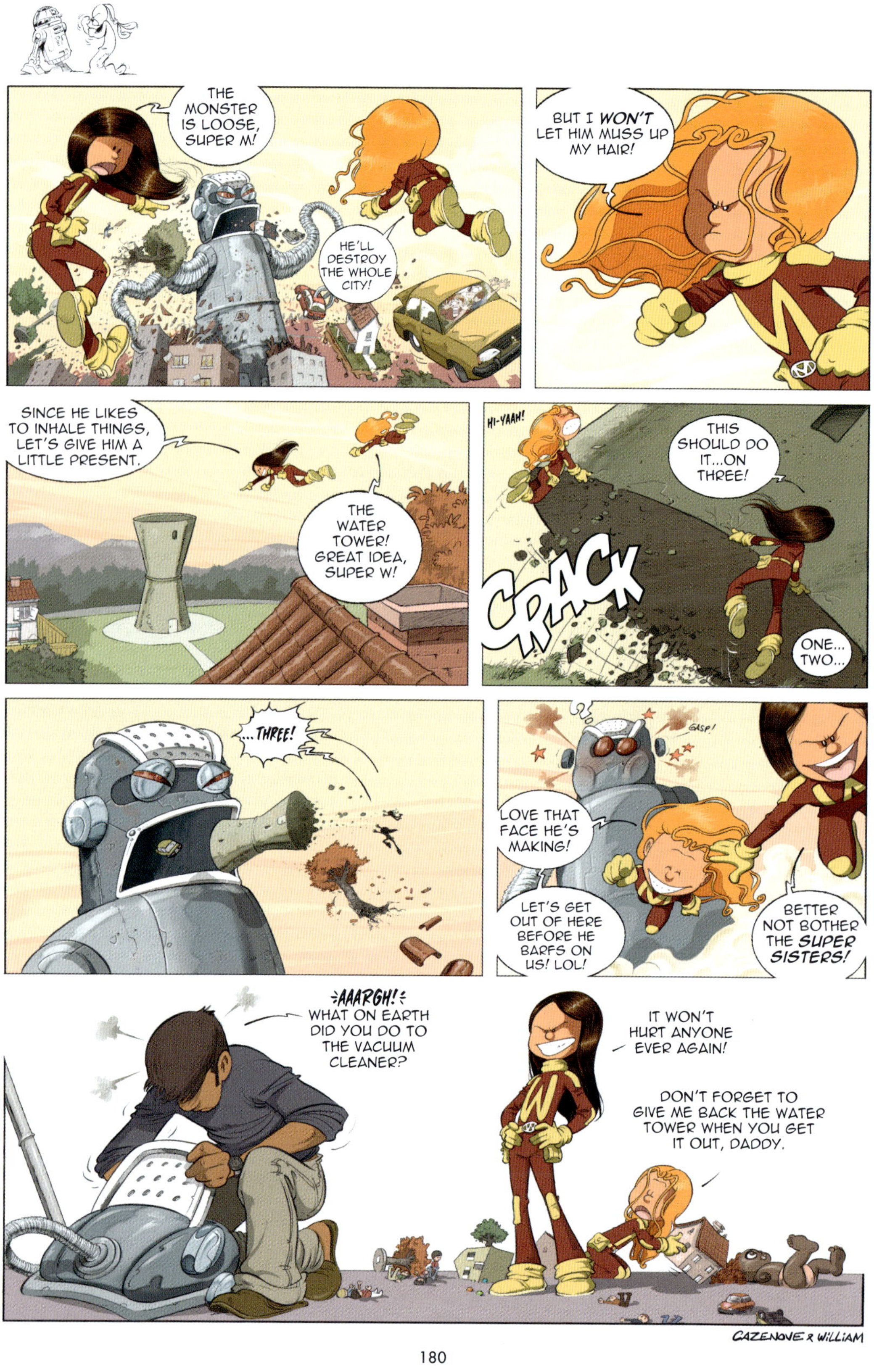
THE MONSTER IS LOOSE, SUPER M!
HE'LL DESTROY THE WHOLE CITY!
BUT I WON'T LET HIM MUSS UP MY HAIR!
SINCE HE LIKES TO INHALE THINGS, LET'S GIVE HIM A LITTLE PRESENT.
THE WATER TOWER! GREAT IDEA, SUPER W!
HI-YAAH!
THIS SHOULD DO IT...ON THREE!
CRACK
ONE... TWO...
...THREE!
GASP!
LOVE THAT FACE HE'S MAKING!
LET'S GET OUT OF HERE BEFORE HE BARFS ON US! LOL!
BETTER NOT BOTHER THE SUPER SISTERS!
AAARGH! WHAT ON EARTH DID YOU DO TO THE VACUUM CLEANER?
IT WON'T HURT ANYONE EVER AGAIN!
DON'T FORGET TO GIVE ME BACK THE WATER TOWER WHEN YOU GET IT OUT, DADDY.
CAZENOVE & WILLIAM

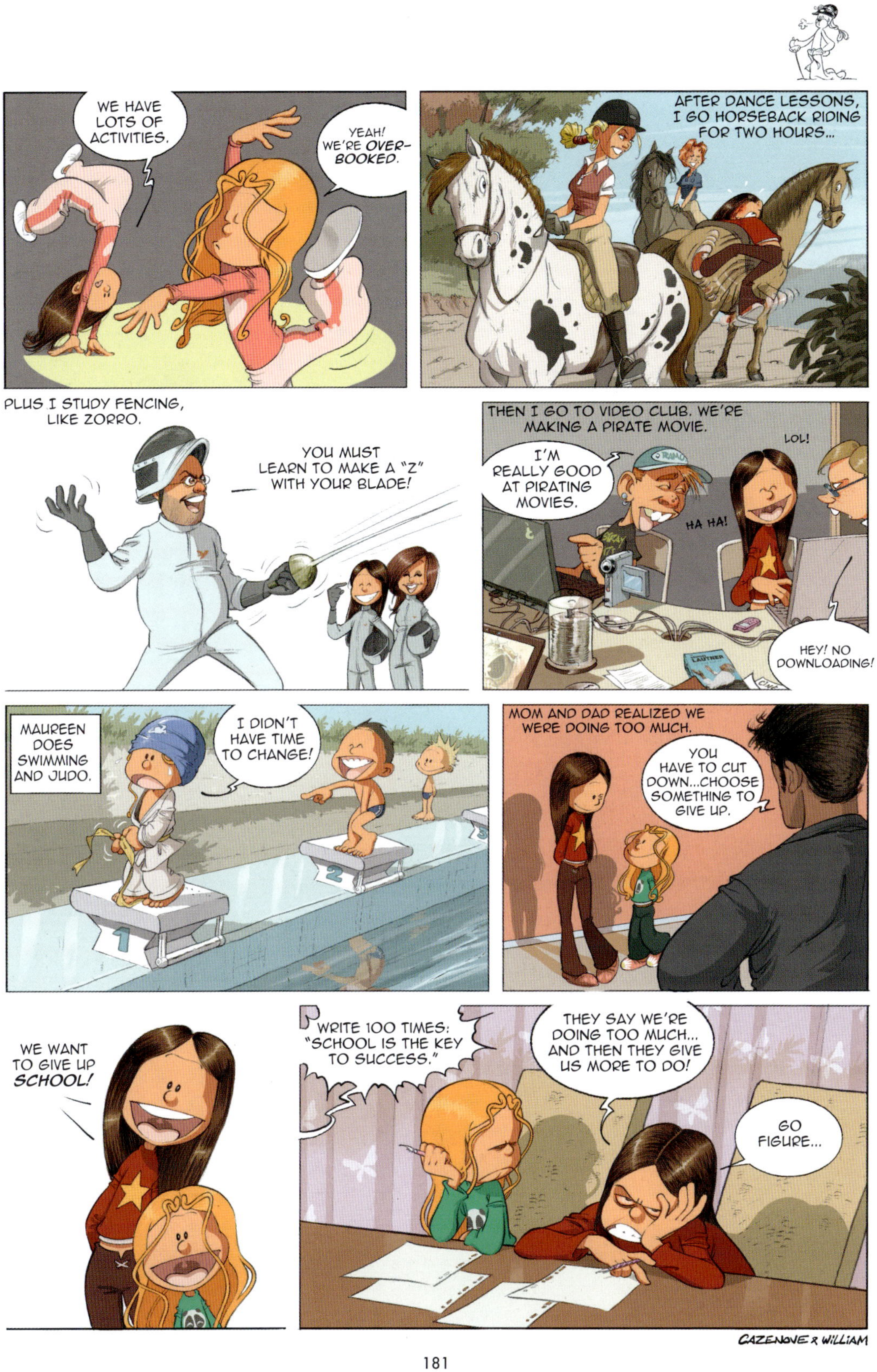
WE HAVE LOTS OF ACTIVITIES.
YEAH! WE'RE OVER-BOOKED.
AFTER DANCE LESSONS, I GO HORSEBACK RIDING FOR TWO HOURS...
PLUS I STUDY FENCING, LIKE ZORRO.
YOU MUST LEARN TO MAKE A "Z" WITH YOUR BLADE!
THEN I GO TO VIDEO CLUB. WE'RE MAKING A PIRATE MOVIE.
I'M REALLY GOOD AT PIRATING MOVIES.
LOL!
HA HA!
HEY! NO DOWNLOADING!
MAUREEN DOES SWIMMING AND JUDO.
I DIDN'T HAVE TIME TO CHANGE!
MOM AND DAD REALIZED WE WERE DOING TOO MUCH.
YOU HAVE TO CUT DOWN...CHOOSE SOMETHING TO GIVE UP.
WE WANT TO GIVE UP SCHOOL!
WRITE 100 TIMES: "SCHOOL IS THE KEY TO SUCCESS."
THEY SAY WE'RE DOING TOO MUCH... AND THEN THEY GIVE US MORE TO DO!
GO FIGURE...
CAZENOVE & WILLIAM

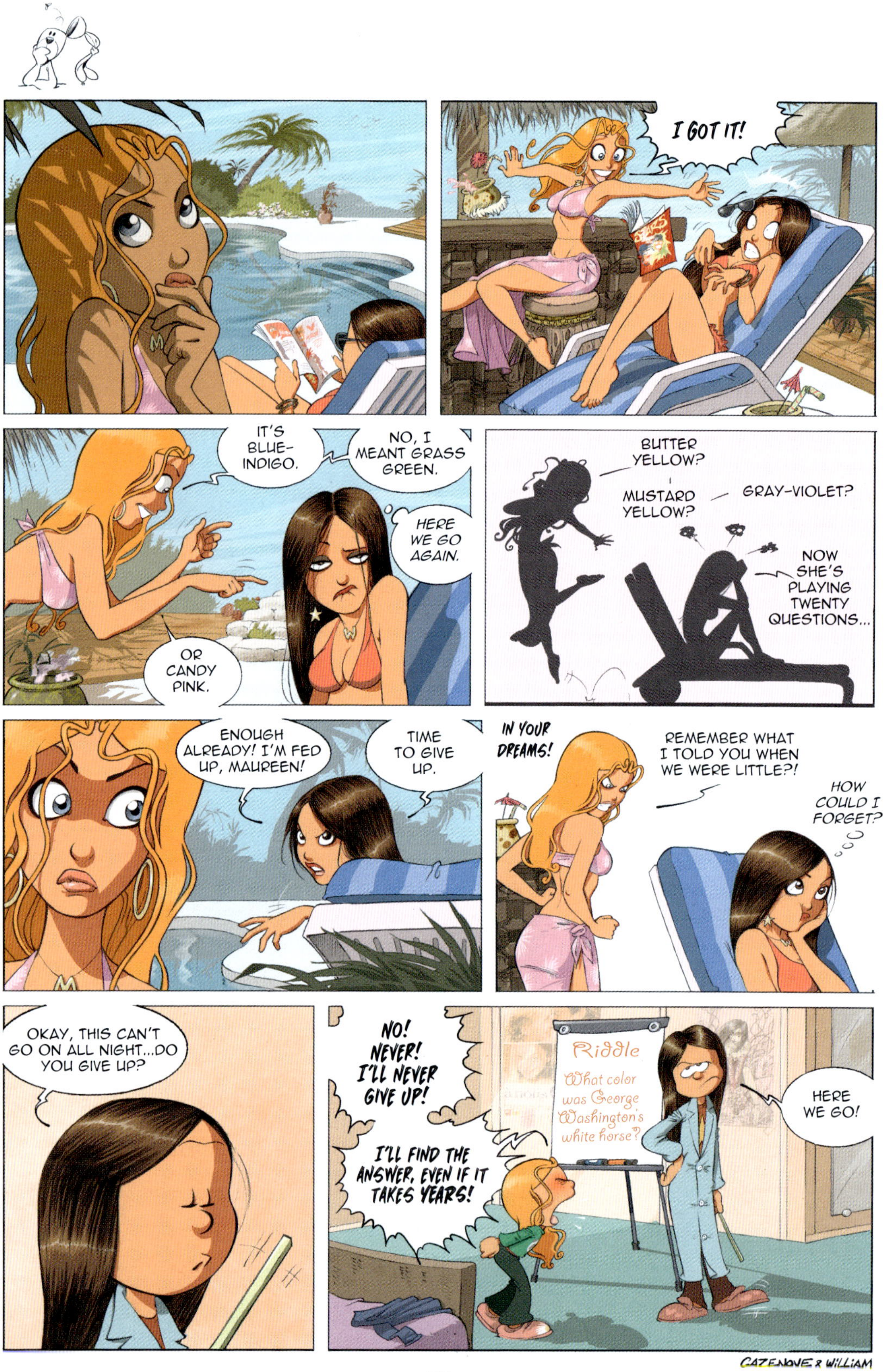
I GOT IT!
IT'S BLUE-INDIGO.
NO, I MEANT GRASS GREEN.
HERE WE GO AGAIN.
OR CANDY PINK.
BUTTER YELLOW?
MUSTARD YELLOW?
GRAY-VIOLET?
NOW SHE'S PLAYING TWENTY QUESTIONS...
ENOUGH ALREADY! I'M FED UP, MAUREEN!
TIME TO GIVE UP.
IN YOUR DREAMS!
REMEMBER WHAT I TOLD YOU WHEN WE WERE LITTLE?!
HOW COULD I FORGET?
OKAY, THIS CAN'T GO ON ALL NIGHT...DO YOU GIVE UP?
NO! NEVER! I'LL NEVER GIVE UP!
I'LL FIND THE ANSWER, EVEN IF IT TAKES YEARS!
Riddle
What color was George Washington's white horse?
HERE WE GO!
CAZENOVE & WILLIAM

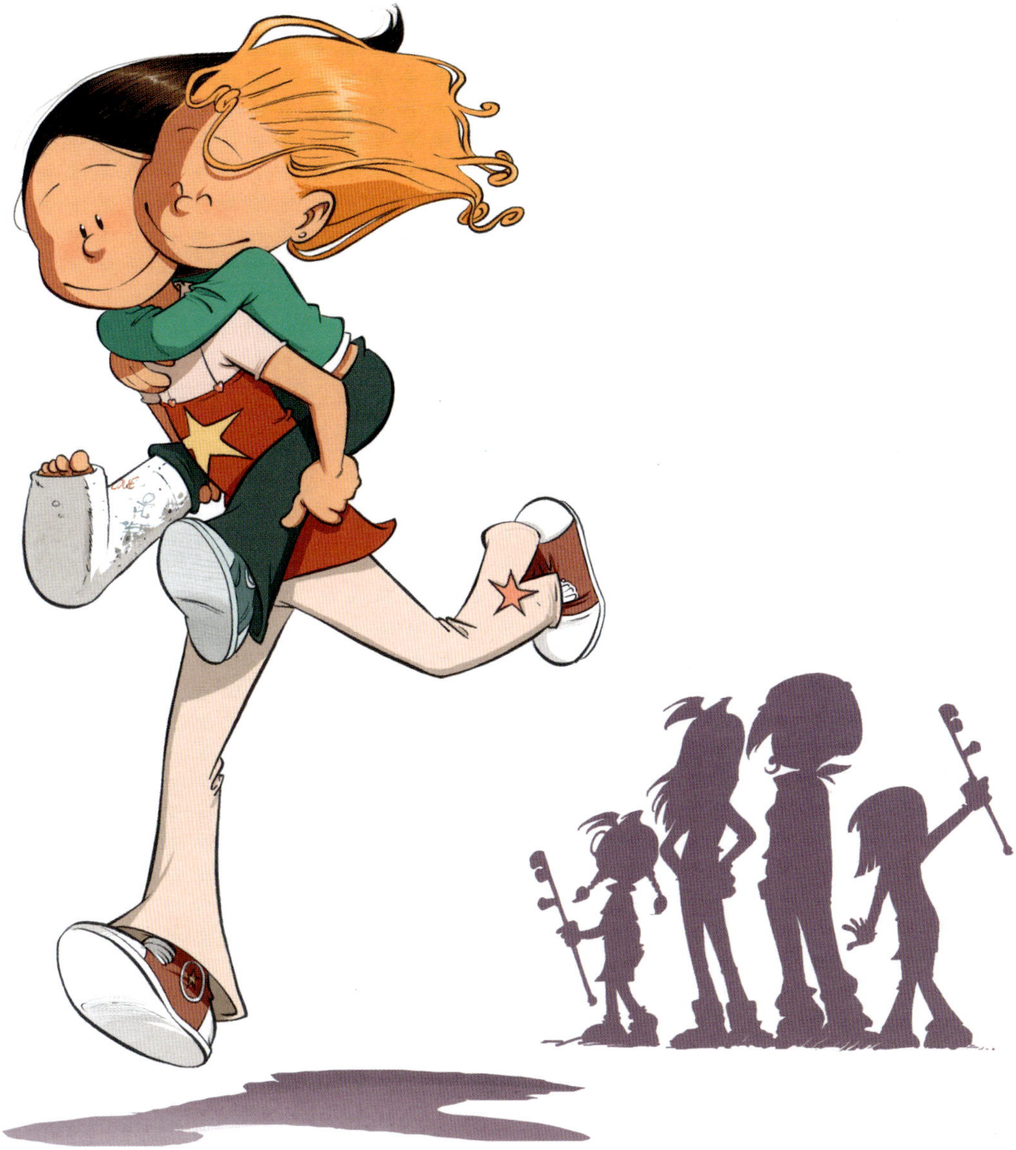

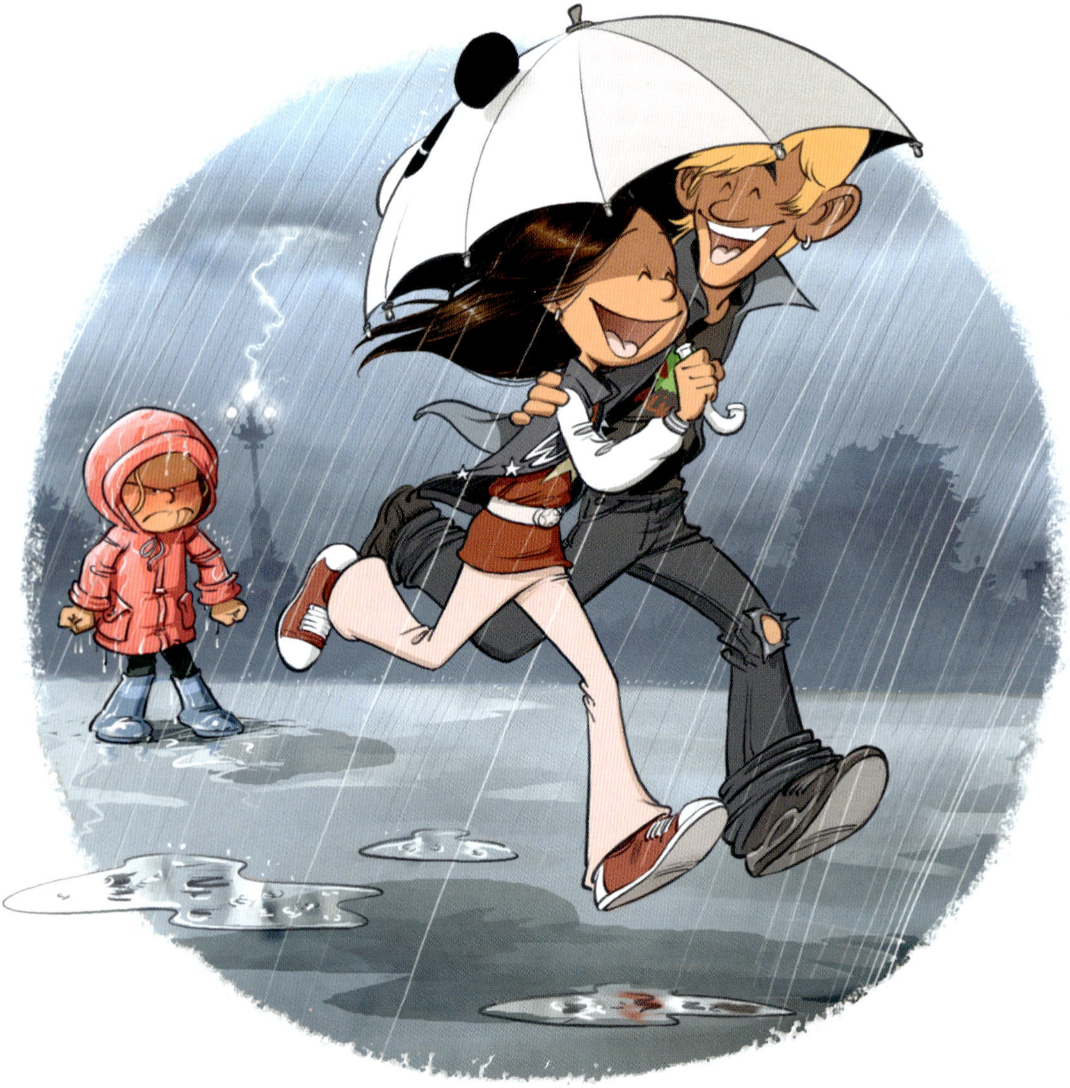

"Honestly, I Love My Sister"

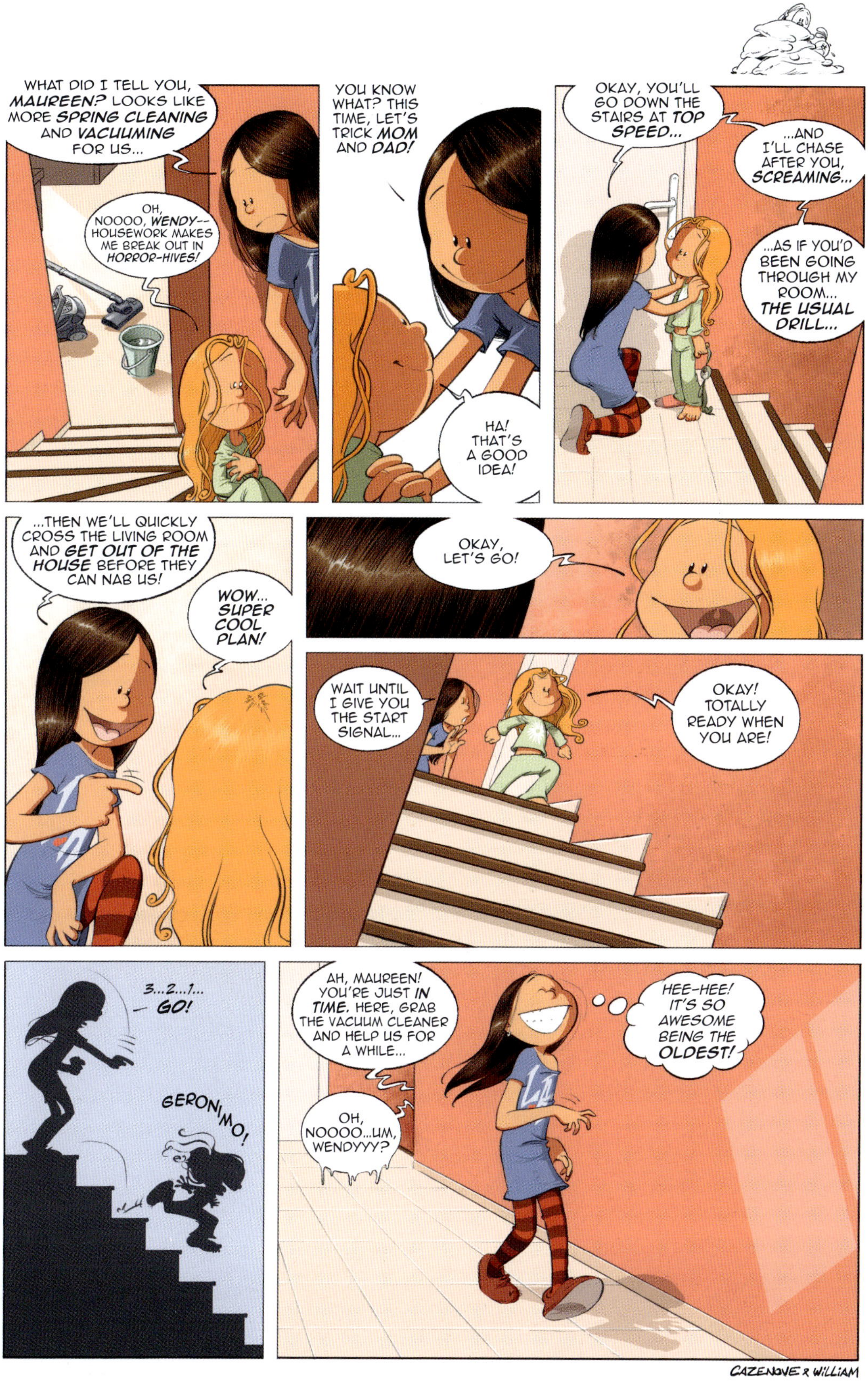
WHAT DID I TELL YOU, MAUREEN? LOOKS LIKE MORE SPRING CLEANING AND VACUUMING FOR US...
OH, NOOOO, WENDY-- HOUSEWORK MAKES ME BREAK OUT IN HORROR-HIVES!
YOU KNOW WHAT? THIS TIME, LET'S TRICK MOM AND DAD!
HA! THAT'S A GOOD IDEA!
OKAY, YOU'LL GO DOWN THE STAIRS AT TOP SPEED...
...AND I'LL CHASE AFTER YOU, SCREAMING...
...AS IF YOU'D BEEN GOING THROUGH MY ROOM... THE USUAL DRILL...
...THEN WE'LL QUICKLY CROSS THE LIVING ROOM AND GET OUT OF THE HOUSE BEFORE THEY CAN NAB US!
WOW... SUPER COOL PLAN!
OKAY, LET'S GO!
WAIT UNTIL I GIVE YOU THE START SIGNAL...
OKAY! TOTALLY READY WHEN YOU ARE!
3...2...1... GO!
GERONIMO!
AH, MAUREEN! YOU'RE JUST IN TIME. HERE, GRAB THE VACUUM CLEANER AND HELP US FOR A WHILE...
OH, NOOOO...UM, WENDYYY?
HEE-HEE! IT'S SO AWESOME BEING THE OLDEST!
CAZENOVE & WILLIAM

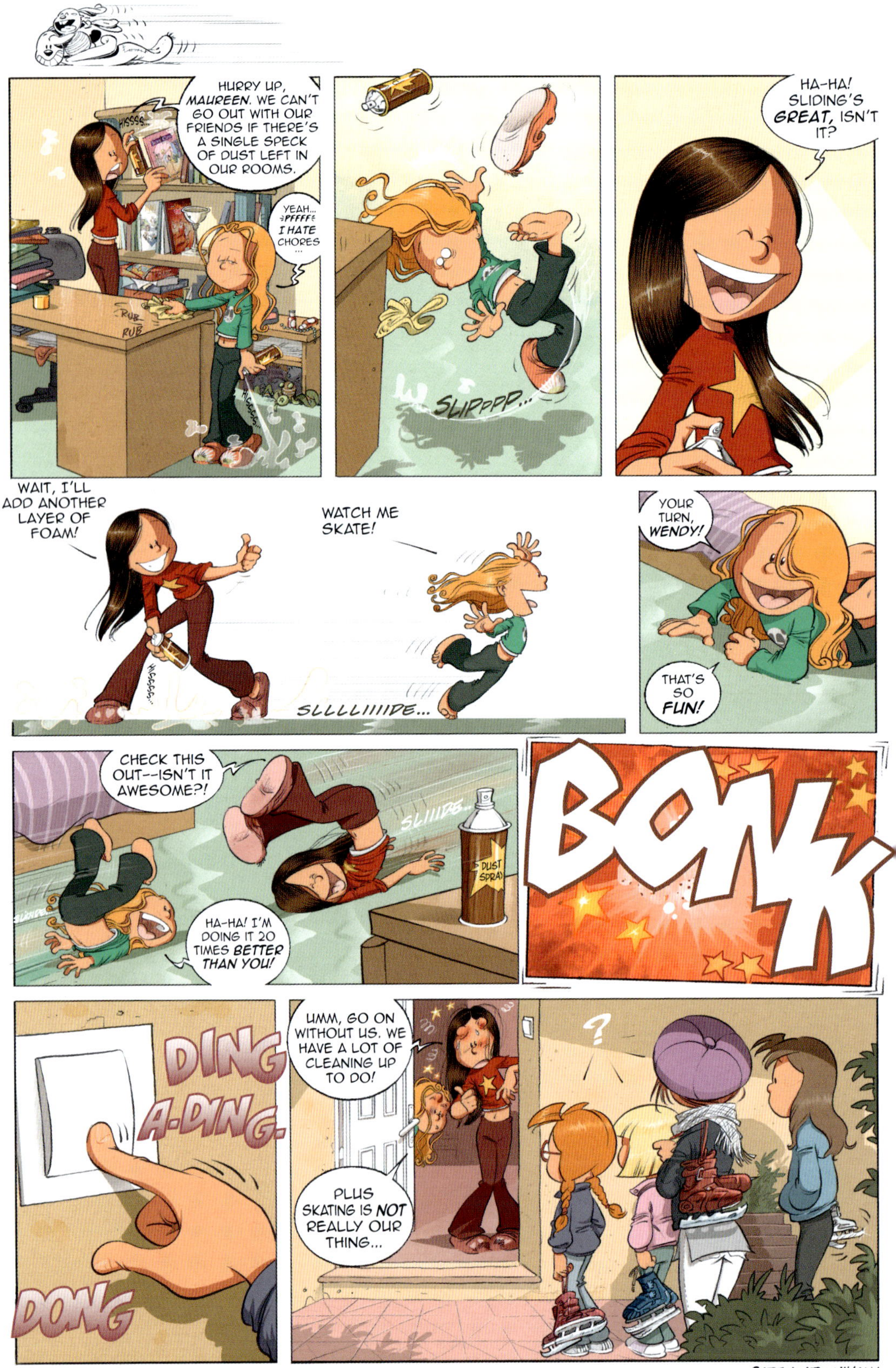
HISSSS...
HURRY UP, MAUREEN. WE CAN'T GO OUT WITH OUR FRIENDS IF THERE'S A SINGLE SPECK OF DUST LEFT IN OUR ROOMS.
YEAH... PFFFF... I HATE CHORES...
RUB RUB
SLIPPPP...
HA-HA! SLIDING'S GREAT, ISN'T IT?
WAIT, I'LL ADD ANOTHER LAYER OF FOAM!
WATCH ME SKATE!
SLLLLIIIIDE...
YOUR TURN, WENDY!
THAT'S SO FUN!
CHECK THIS OUT--ISN'T IT AWESOME?!
SLIIIDE...
DUST SPRAY
HA-HA! I'M DOING IT 20 TIMES BETTER THAN YOU!
BONK
DING A-DING-
DONG
UMM, GO ON WITHOUT US. WE HAVE A LOT OF CLEANING UP TO DO!
PLUS SKATING IS NOT REALLY OUR THING...
?

CAZENOVE & WILLIAM

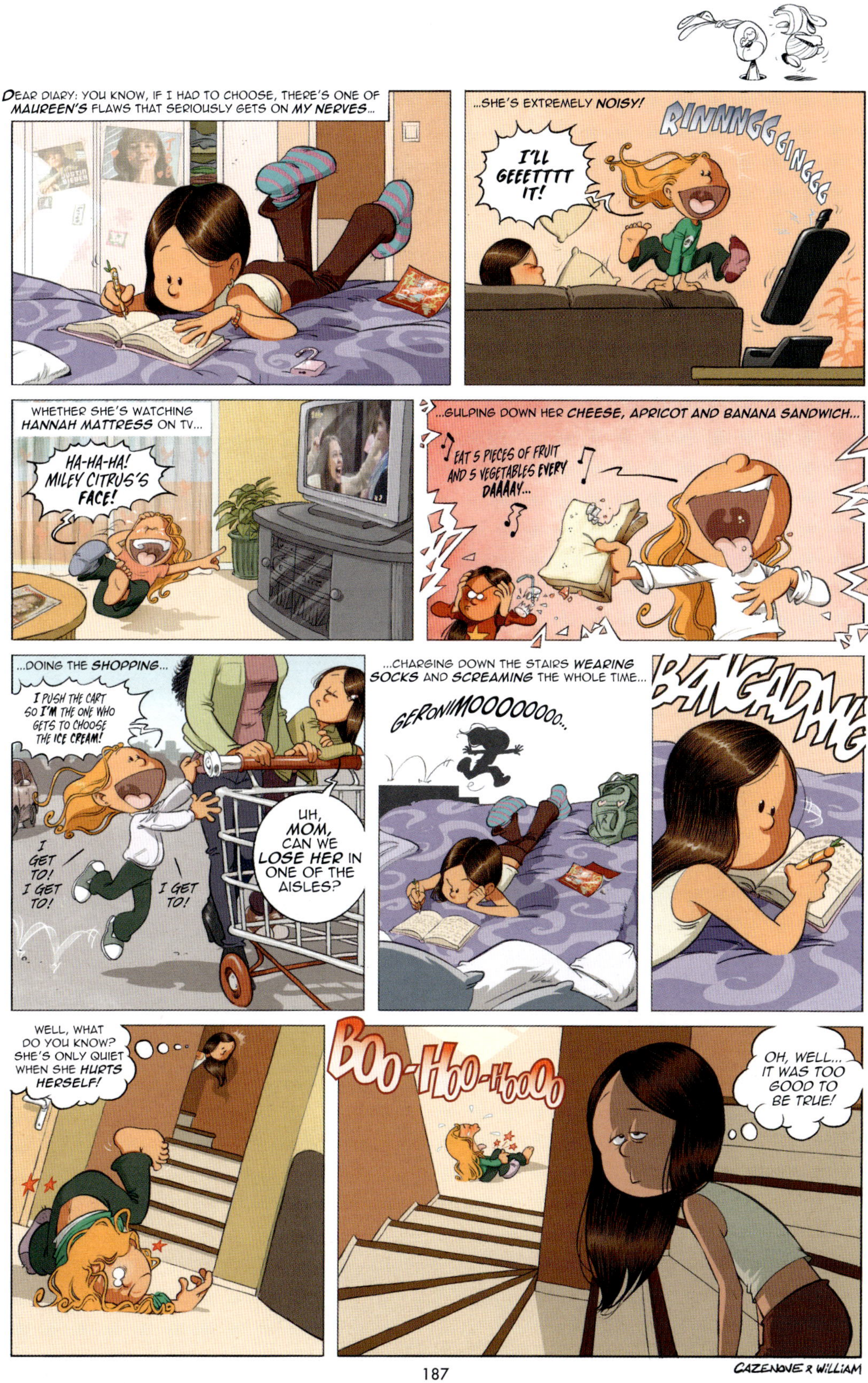

DEAR DIARY: YOU KNOW, IF I HAD TO CHOOSE, THERE'S ONE OF MAUREEN'S FLAWS THAT SERIOUSLY GETS ON MY NERVES...
...SHE'S EXTREMELY NOISY!
RINNNGGGINGGG
I'LL GEEETTTT IT!
WHETHER SHE'S WATCHING HANNAH MATTRESS ON TV...
HA-HA-HA! MILEY CITRUS'S FACE!
...GULPING DOWN HER CHEESE, APRICOT AND BANANA SANDWICH...
EAT 5 PIECES OF FRUIT AND 5 VEGETABLES EVERY DAAAAY...
...DOING THE SHOPPING...
I PUSH THE CART SO I'M THE ONE WHO GETS TO CHOOSE THE ICE CREAM!
I GET TO! I GET TO!
I GET TO!
UH, MOM, CAN WE LOSE HER IN ONE OF THE AISLES?
...CHARGING DOWN THE STAIRS WEARING SOCKS AND SCREAMING THE WHOLE TIME...
GERONIMOOOOOOOO...
BANGADANG
WELL, WHAT DO YOU KNOW? SHE'S ONLY QUIET WHEN SHE HURTS HERSELF!
BOO-HOO-HOOOO
OH, WELL... IT WAS TOO GOOD TO BE TRUE!
CAZENOVE & WILLIAM

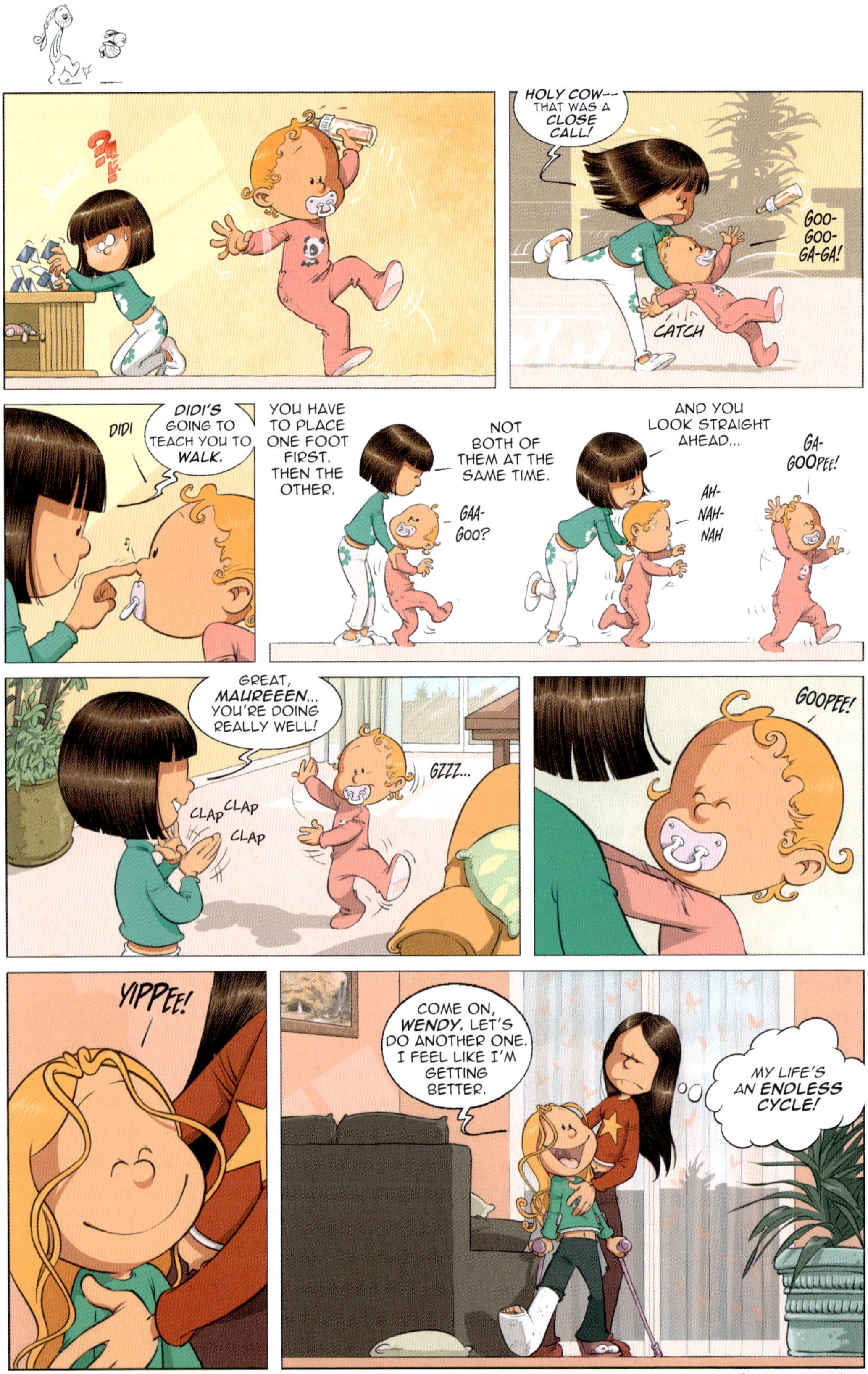

HOLY COW-- THAT WAS A CLOSE CALL!
GOO-GOO-GA-GA!
CATCH
DIDI
DIDI'S GOING TO TEACH YOU TO WALK.
YOU HAVE TO PLACE ONE FOOT FIRST. THEN THE OTHER.
NOT BOTH OF THEM AT THE SAME TIME.
GAA-GOO?
AND YOU LOOK STRAIGHT AHEAD...
AH-NAH-NAH
GA-GOOPEE!
GREAT, MAUREEEN... YOU'RE DOING REALLY WELL!
CLAP CLAP CLAP
GZZZ...
GOOPEE!
YIPPEE!
COME ON, WENDY. LET'S DO ANOTHER ONE. I FEEL LIKE I'M GETTING BETTER.
MY LIFE'S AN ENDLESS CYCLE!

CAZENOVE & WILLIAM

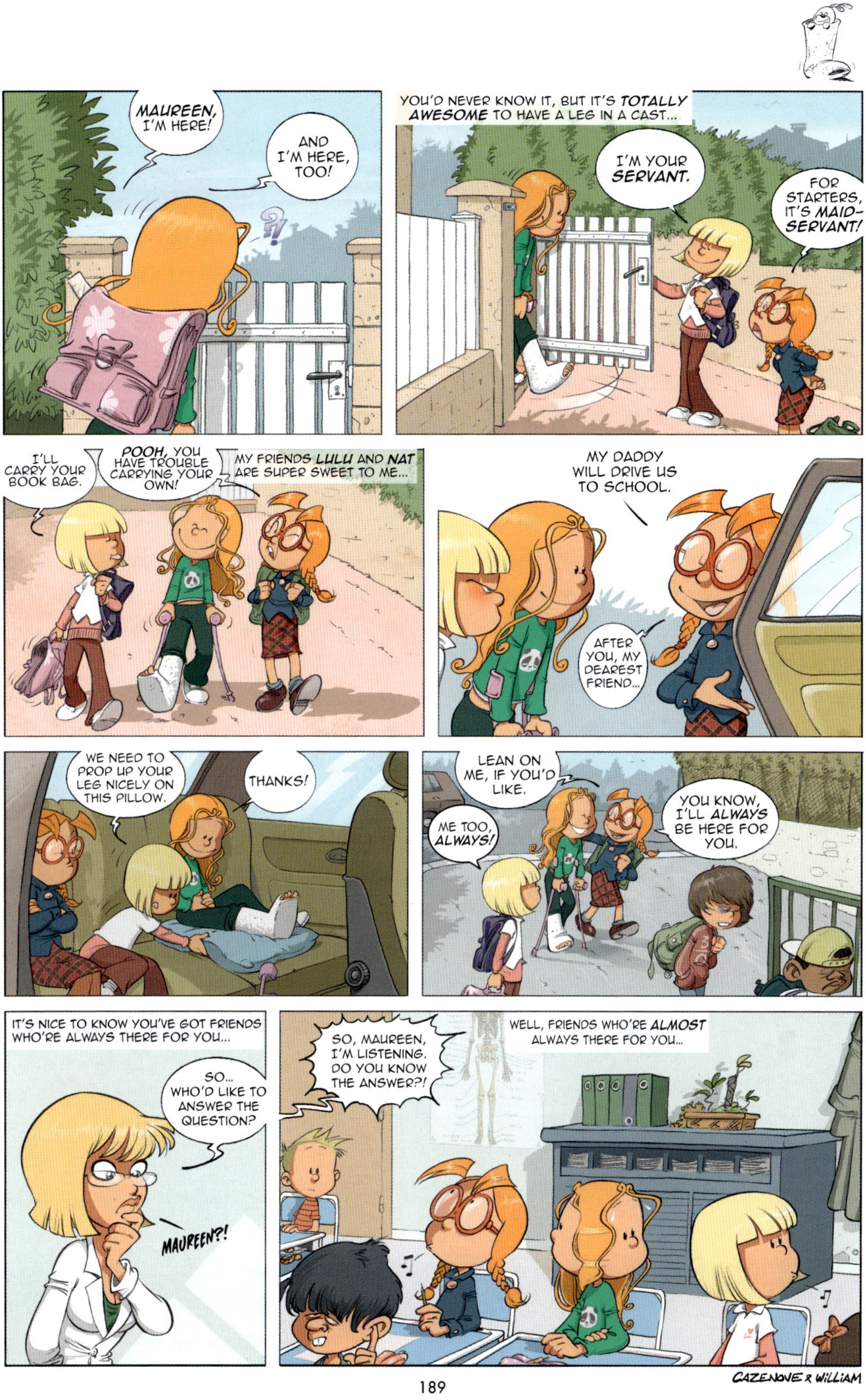
MAUREEN, I'M HERE!
AND I'M HERE, TOO!
YOU'D NEVER KNOW IT, BUT IT'S TOTALLY AWESOME TO HAVE A LEG IN A CAST...
I'M YOUR SERVANT.
FOR STARTERS, IT'S MAID-SERVANT!
I'LL CARRY YOUR BOOK BAG.
POOH, YOU HAVE TROUBLE CARRYING YOUR OWN!
MY FRIENDS LULU AND NAT ARE SUPER SWEET TO ME...
MY DADDY WILL DRIVE US TO SCHOOL.
AFTER YOU, MY DEAREST FRIEND...
WE NEED TO PROP UP YOUR LEG NICELY ON THIS PILLOW.
THANKS!
LEAN ON ME, IF YOU'D LIKE.
ME TOO, ALWAYS!
YOU KNOW, I'LL ALWAYS BE HERE FOR YOU.
IT'S NICE TO KNOW YOU'VE GOT FRIENDS WHO'RE ALWAYS THERE FOR YOU...
SO... WHO'D LIKE TO ANSWER THE QUESTION?
MAUREEN?!
SO, MAUREEN, I'M LISTENING. DO YOU KNOW THE ANSWER?!
WELL, FRIENDS WHO'RE ALMOST ALWAYS THERE FOR YOU...
CAZENOVE & WILLIAM

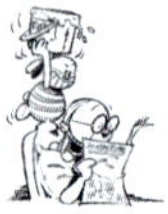

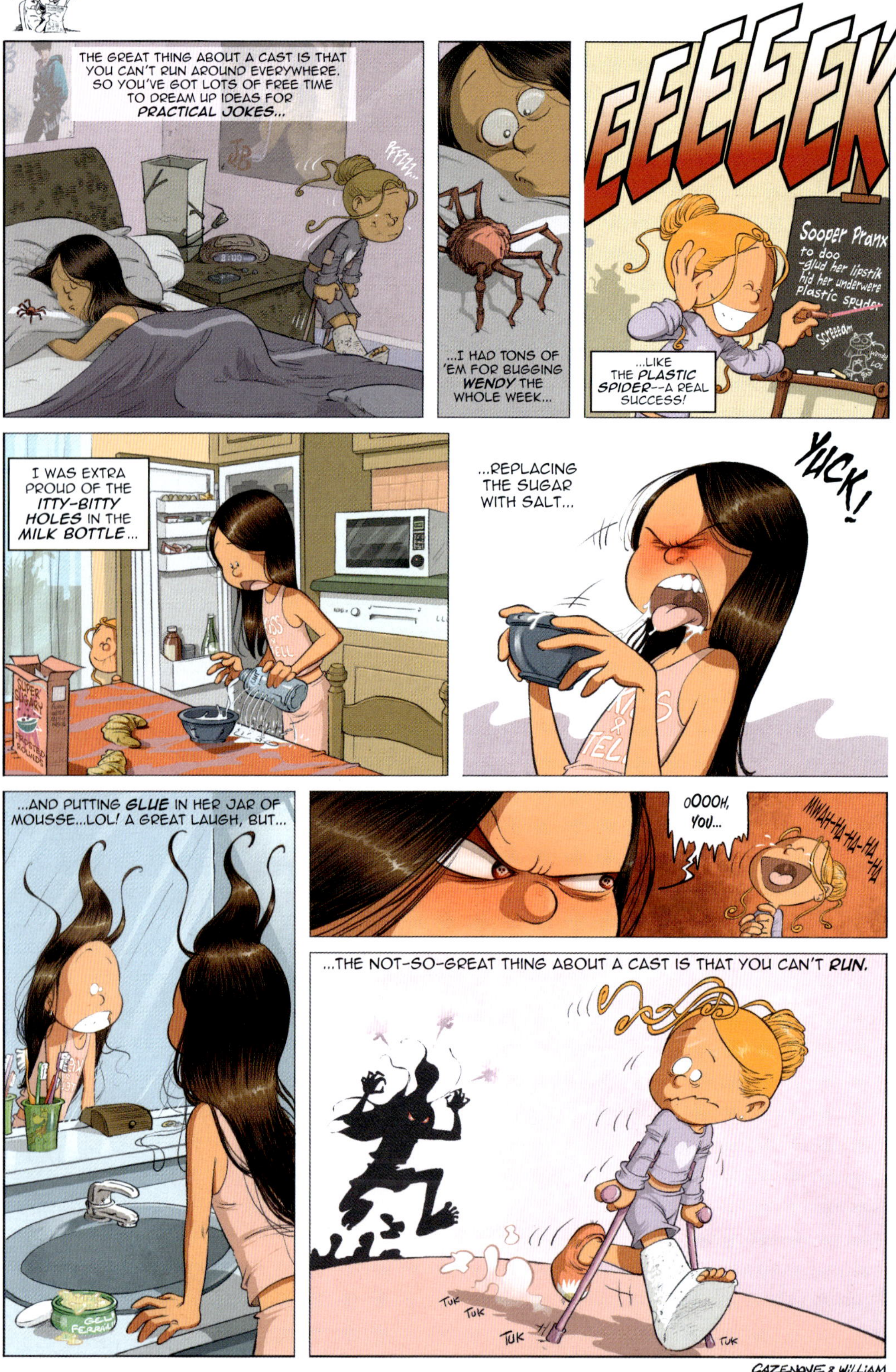

THE GREAT THING ABOUT A CAST IS THAT YOU CAN'T RUN AROUND EVERYWHERE. SO YOU'VE GOT LOTS OF FREE TIME TO DREAM UP IDEAS FOR PRACTICAL JOKES...
PFFZZZ...
...I HAD TONS OF 'EM FOR BUGGING WENDY THE WHOLE WEEK...
EEEEEK
Sooper Pranx
to doo
-glud her lipstik
hid her underwere
plastic spyder
Screeeam
...LIKE THE PLASTIC SPIDER--A REAL SUCCESS!
I WAS EXTRA PROUD OF THE ITTY-BITTY HOLES IN THE MILK BOTTLE...
...REPLACING THE SUGAR WITH SALT...
YUCK!
...AND PUTTING GLUE IN HER JAR OF MOUSSE...LOL! A GREAT LAUGH, BUT...
OOOOH, YOU...
MWAH-HA-HA-HA-HA
...THE NOT-SO-GREAT THING ABOUT A CAST IS THAT YOU CAN'T RUN.
TUK
TUK
TUK
TUK

CAZENOVE & WILLIAM

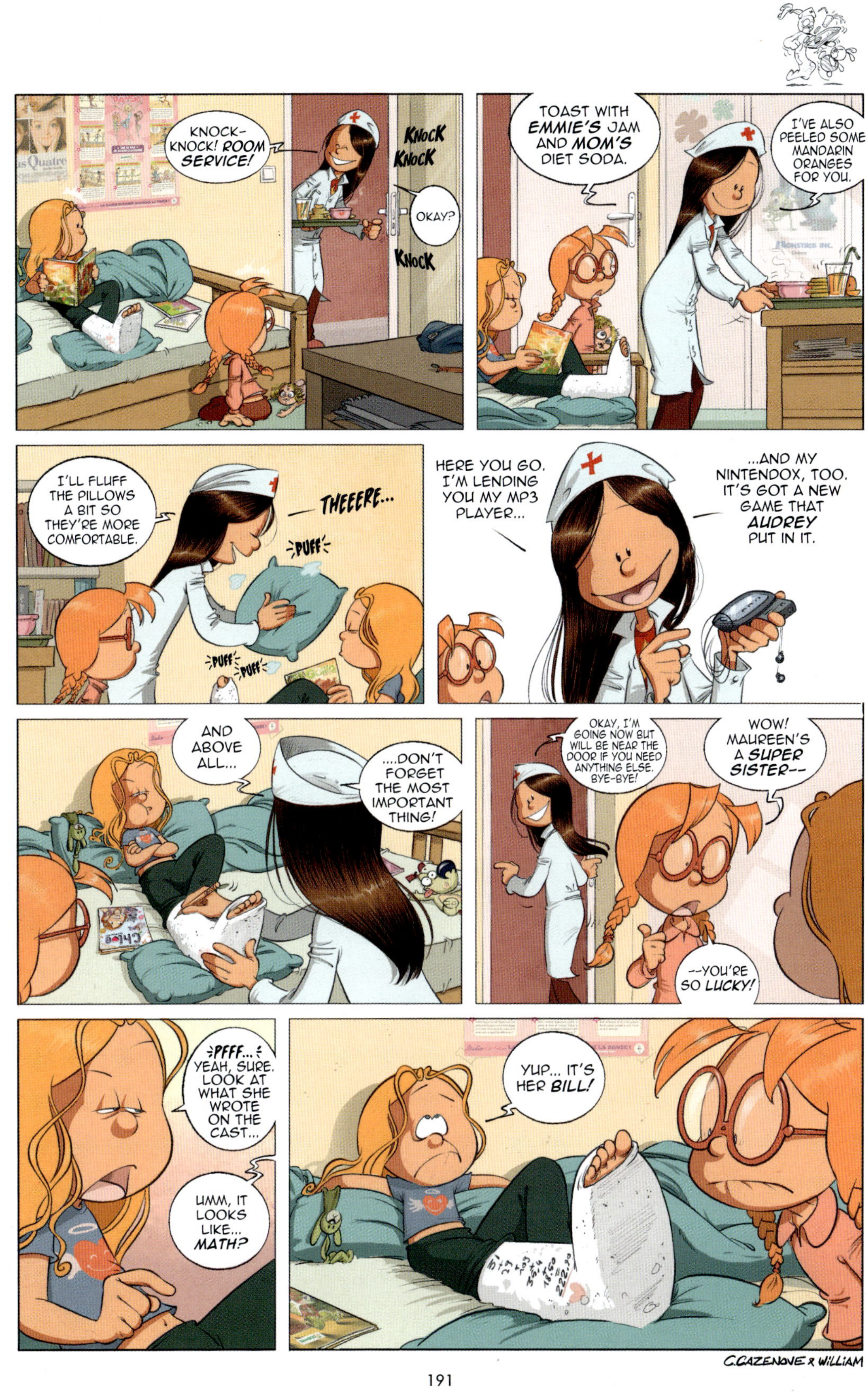
KNOCK-KNOCK! ROOM SERVICE!
KNOCK KNOCK
OKAY?
KNOCK
TOAST WITH EMMIE'S JAM AND MOM'S DIET SODA.
I'VE ALSO PEELED SOME MANDARIN ORANGES FOR YOU.
I'LL FLUFF THE PILLOWS A BIT SO THEY'RE MORE COMFORTABLE.
THEEERE...
PUFF
PUFF PUFF
HERE YOU GO. I'M LENDING YOU MY MP3 PLAYER...
...AND MY NINTENDOX, TOO. IT'S GOT A NEW GAME THAT AUDREY PUT IN IT.
AND ABOVE ALL...
...DON'T FORGET THE MOST IMPORTANT THING!
OKAY, I'M GOING NOW BUT WILL BE NEAR THE DOOR IF YOU NEED ANYTHING ELSE. BYE-BYE!
WOW! MAUREEN'S A SUPER SISTER--
--YOU'RE SO LUCKY!
PFFF... YEAH, SURE. LOOK AT WHAT SHE WROTE ON THE CAST...
UMM, IT LOOKS LIKE... MATH?
YUP... IT'S HER BILL!
C.CAZENOVE & WILLIAM

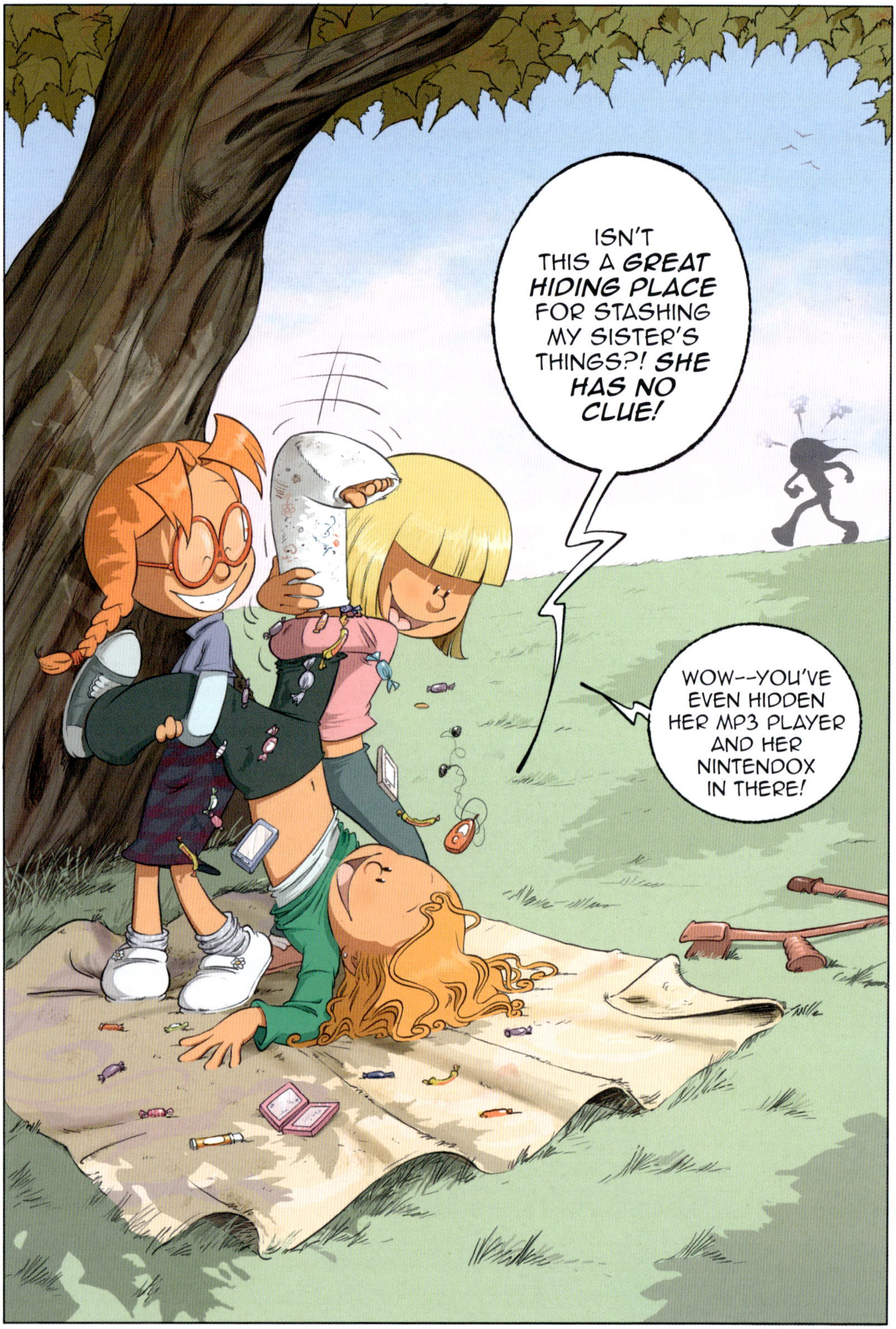
ISN'T THIS A **GREAT HIDING PLACE** FOR STASHING MY SISTER'S THINGS?! **SHE HAS NO CLUE!**
WOW--YOU'VE EVEN HIDDEN HER MP3 PLAYER AND HER NINTENDOX IN THERE!
CAZENOVE & WILLIAM

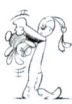

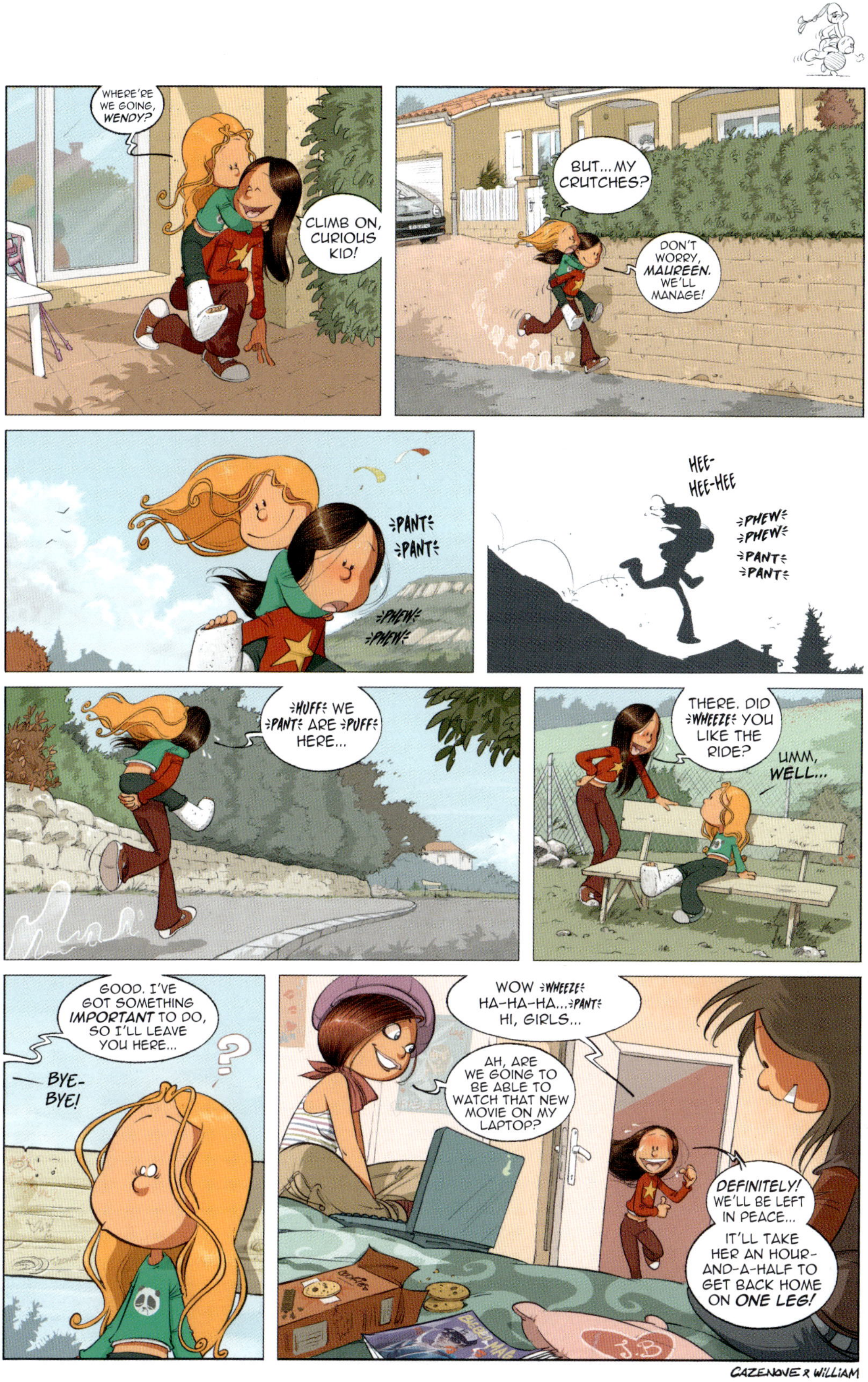
WHERE'RE WE GOING, WENDY?
CLIMB ON, CURIOUS KID!
BUT... MY CRUTCHES?
DON'T WORRY, MAUREEN. WE'LL MANAGE!
PANT PANT
PHEW PHEW
HEE- HEE-HEE
PHEW PHEW PANT PANT
HUFF WE PANT ARE PUFF HERE...
THERE. DID WHEEZE YOU LIKE THE RIDE?
UMM, WELL...
GOOD. I'VE GOT SOMETHING IMPORTANT TO DO, SO I'LL LEAVE YOU HERE...
BYE-BYE!
?
WOW WHEEZE HA-HA-HA... PANT HI, GIRLS...
AH, ARE WE GOING TO BE ABLE TO WATCH THAT NEW MOVIE ON MY LAPTOP?
DEFINITELY! WE'LL BE LEFT IN PEACE...
IT'LL TAKE HER AN HOUR-AND-A-HALF TO GET BACK HOME ON ONE LEG!
CAZENOVE & WILLIAM

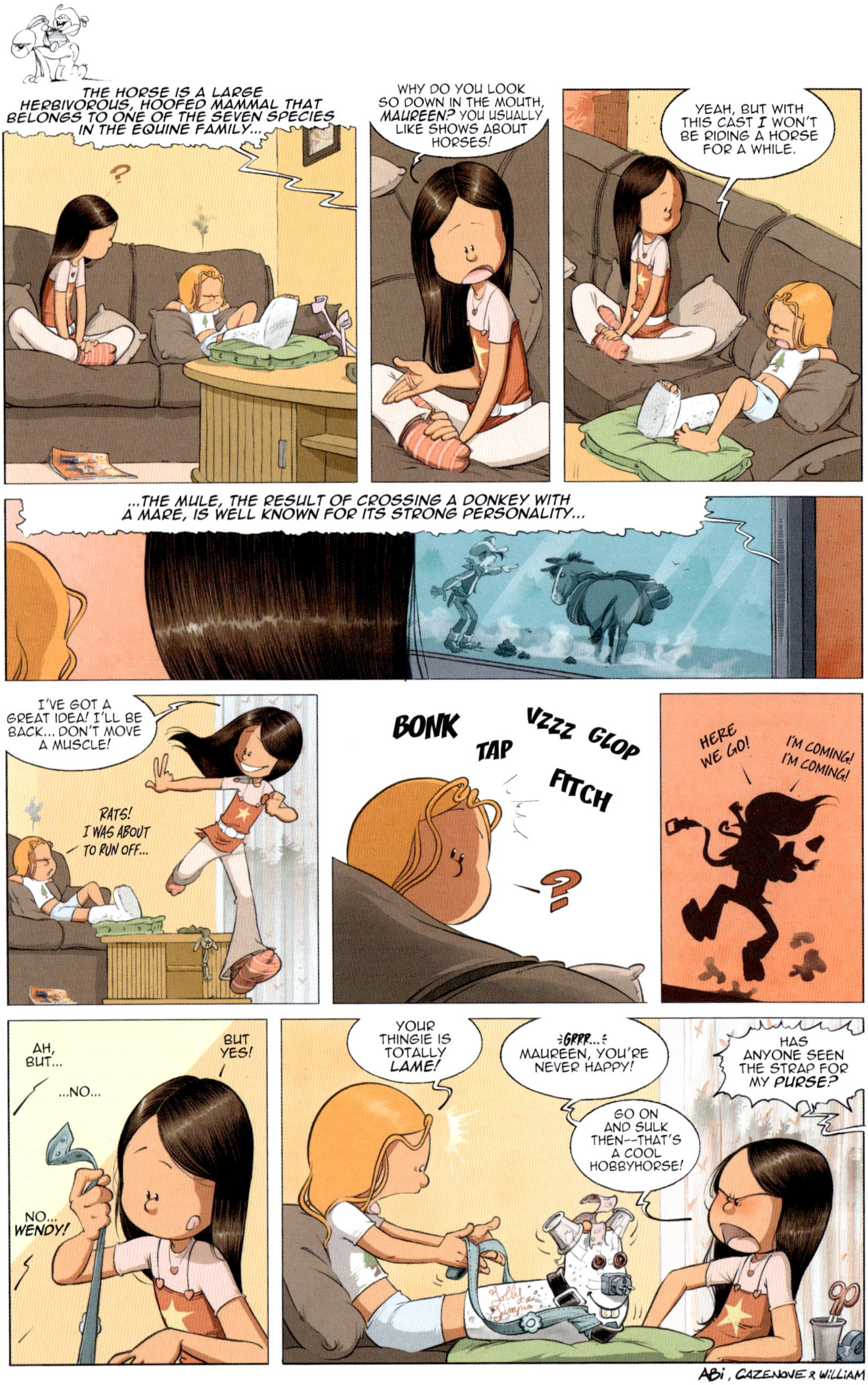

THE HORSE IS A LARGE HERBIVOROUS, HOOFED MAMMAL THAT BELONGS TO ONE OF THE SEVEN SPECIES IN THE EQUINE FAMILY...
?
WHY DO YOU LOOK SO DOWN IN THE MOUTH, MAUREEN? YOU USUALLY LIKE SHOWS ABOUT HORSES!
YEAH, BUT WITH THIS CAST I WON'T BE RIDING A HORSE FOR A WHILE.
...THE MULE, THE RESULT OF CROSSING A DONKEY WITH A MARE, IS WELL KNOWN FOR ITS STRONG PERSONALITY...
I'VE GOT A GREAT IDEA! I'LL BE BACK... DON'T MOVE A MUSCLE!
RATS! I WAS ABOUT TO RUN OFF...
BONK
TAP
VZZZ
GLOP
FITCH
?
HERE WE GO!
I'M COMING! I'M COMING!
AH, BUT...
BUT YES!
...NO...
NO... WENDY!
YOUR THINGIE IS TOTALLY LAME!
GRRR... MAUREEN, YOU'RE NEVER HAPPY!
HAS ANYONE SEEN THE STRAP FOR MY PURSE?
GO ON AND SULK THEN--THAT'S A COOL HOBBYHORSE!

ABi, CAZENOVE & WILLIAM

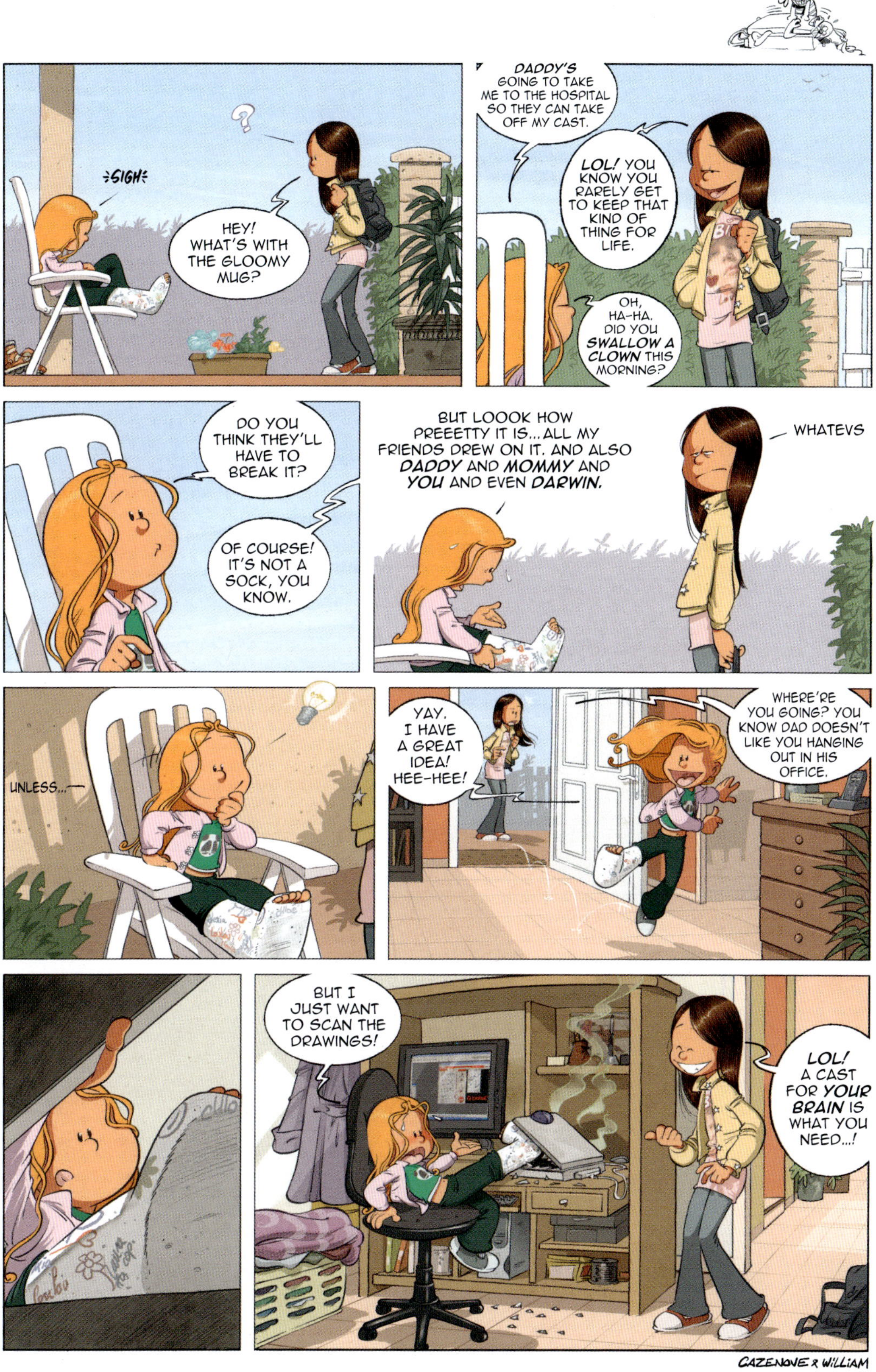

SIGH
?
HEY! WHAT'S WITH THE GLOOMY MUG?
DADDY'S GOING TO TAKE ME TO THE HOSPITAL SO THEY CAN TAKE OFF MY CAST.
LOL! YOU KNOW YOU RARELY GET TO KEEP THAT KIND OF THING FOR LIFE.
OH, HA-HA. DID YOU SWALLOW A CLOWN THIS MORNING?
DO YOU THINK THEY'LL HAVE TO BREAK IT?
OF COURSE! IT'S NOT A SOCK, YOU KNOW.
BUT LOOOK HOW PREEETTY IT IS... ALL MY FRIENDS DREW ON IT. AND ALSO DADDY AND MOMMY AND YOU AND EVEN DARWIN.
WHATEVS
UNLESS...
YAY. I HAVE A GREAT IDEA! HEE-HEE!
WHERE'RE YOU GOING? YOU KNOW DAD DOESN'T LIKE YOU HANGING OUT IN HIS OFFICE.
BUT I JUST WANT TO SCAN THE DRAWINGS!
LOL! A CAST FOR YOUR BRAIN IS WHAT YOU NEED...!
CAZENOVE & WILLIAM

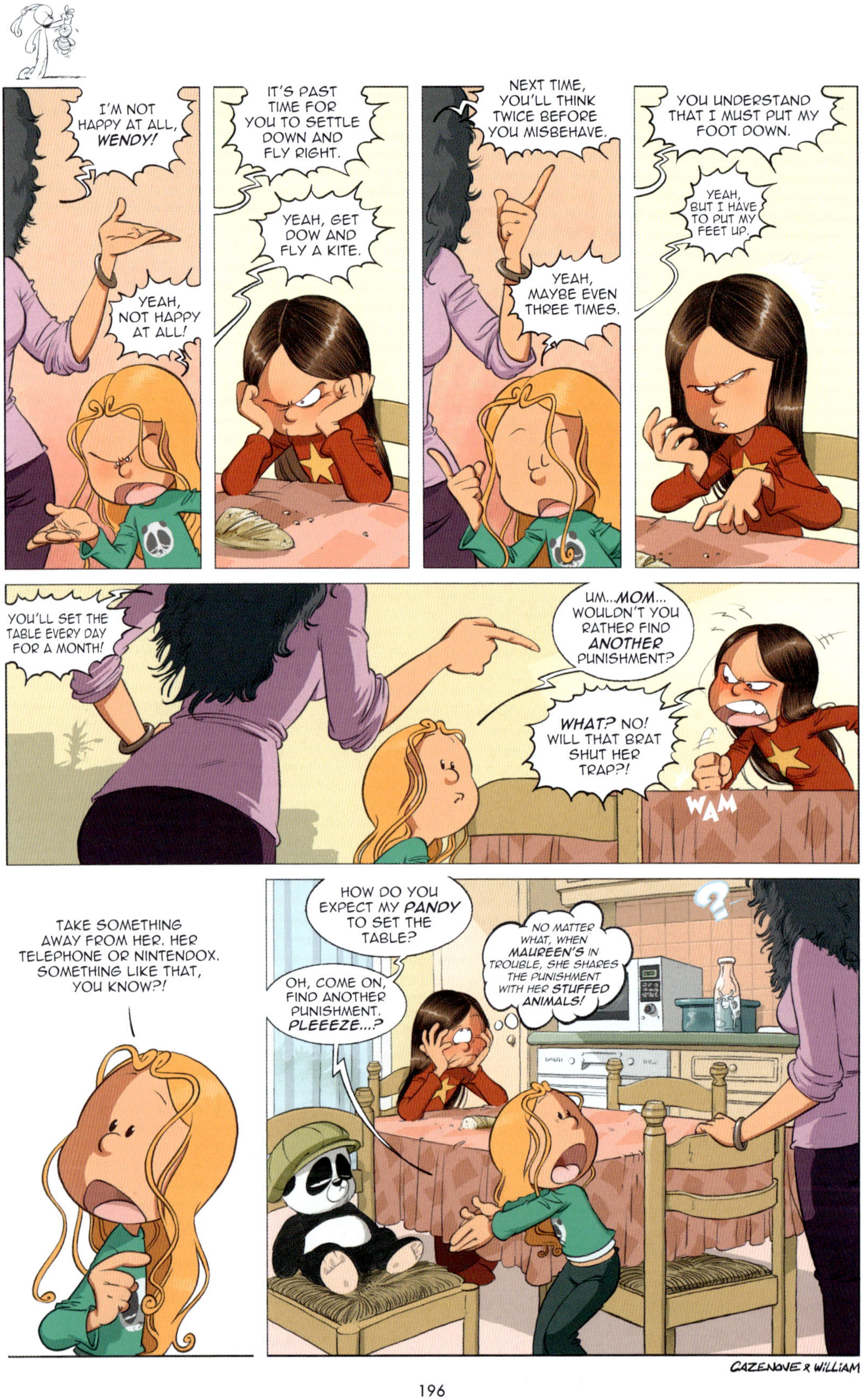

I'M NOT HAPPY AT ALL, WENDY!
YEAH, NOT HAPPY AT ALL!
IT'S PAST TIME FOR YOU TO SETTLE DOWN AND FLY RIGHT.
YEAH, GET DOW AND FLY A KITE.
NEXT TIME, YOU'LL THINK TWICE BEFORE YOU MISBEHAVE.
YEAH, MAYBE EVEN THREE TIMES.
YOU UNDERSTAND THAT I MUST PUT MY FOOT DOWN.
YEAH, BUT I HAVE TO PUT MY FEET UP.
YOU'LL SET THE TABLE EVERY DAY FOR A MONTH!
UM...MOM... WOULDN'T YOU RATHER FIND ANOTHER PUNISHMENT?
WHAT? NO! WILL THAT BRAT SHUT HER TRAP?!
WAM
TAKE SOMETHING AWAY FROM HER. HER TELEPHONE OR NINTENDOX. SOMETHING LIKE THAT, YOU KNOW?!
HOW DO YOU EXPECT MY PANDY TO SET THE TABLE?
OH, COME ON, FIND ANOTHER PUNISHMENT. PLEEEZE...?
NO MATTER WHAT, WHEN MAUREEN'S IN TROUBLE, SHE SHARES THE PUNISHMENT WITH HER STUFFED ANIMALS!
?
CAZENOVE & WILLIAM

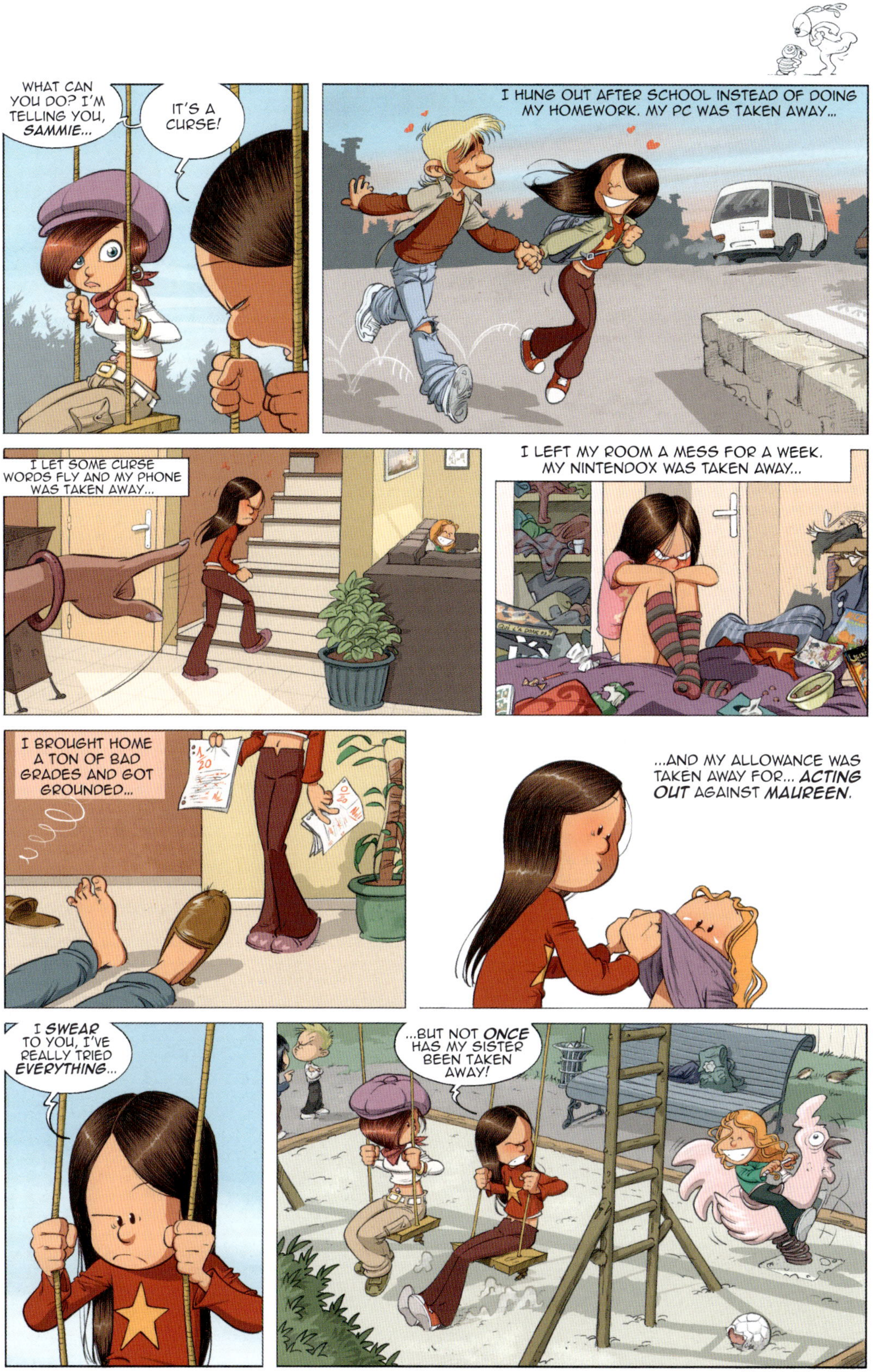
WHAT CAN YOU DO? I'M TELLING YOU, SAMMIE...
IT'S A CURSE!
I HUNG OUT AFTER SCHOOL INSTEAD OF DOING MY HOMEWORK. MY PC WAS TAKEN AWAY...
I LET SOME CURSE WORDS FLY AND MY PHONE WAS TAKEN AWAY...
I LEFT MY ROOM A MESS FOR A WEEK. MY NINTENDOX WAS TAKEN AWAY...
I BROUGHT HOME A TON OF BAD GRADES AND GOT GROUNDED...
...AND MY ALLOWANCE WAS TAKEN AWAY FOR... ACTING OUT AGAINST MAUREEN.
I SWEAR TO YOU, I'VE REALLY TRIED EVERYTHING...
...BUT NOT ONCE HAS MY SISTER BEEN TAKEN AWAY!
CAZENOVE & WILLIAM

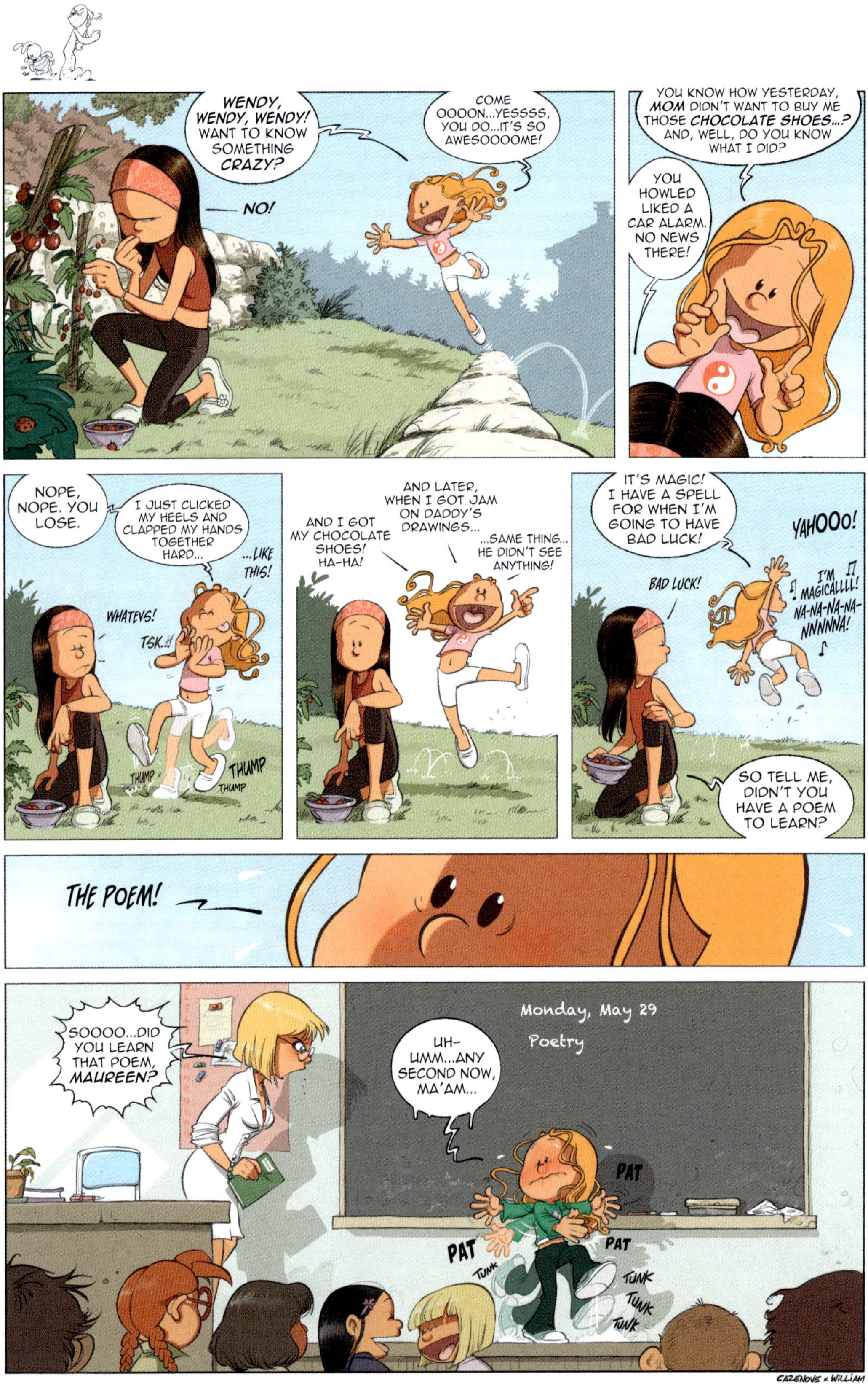
WENDY, WENDY, WENDY! WANT TO KNOW SOMETHING CRAZY?
NO!
COME OOOON...YESSSS, YOU DO...IT'S SO AWESOOOOME!
YOU KNOW HOW YESTERDAY, MOM DIDN'T WANT TO BUY ME THOSE CHOCOLATE SHOES...? AND, WELL, DO YOU KNOW WHAT I DID?
YOU HOWLED LIKED A CAR ALARM. NO NEWS THERE!
NOPE, NOPE. YOU LOSE.
I JUST CLICKED MY HEELS AND CLAPPED MY HANDS TOGETHER HARD...
...LIKE THIS!
WHATEVS!
TSK..!
THUMP
THUMP
THUMP
AND I GOT MY CHOCOLATE SHOES! HA-HA!
AND LATER, WHEN I GOT JAM ON DADDY'S DRAWINGS...
...SAME THING... HE DIDN'T SEE ANYTHING!
IT'S MAGIC! I HAVE A SPELL FOR WHEN I'M GOING TO HAVE BAD LUCK!
YAHOOO!
BAD LUCK!
I'M MAGICALLLL! NA-NA-NA-NA-NNNNNA!
SO TELL ME, DIDN'T YOU HAVE A POEM TO LEARN?
THE POEM!
SOOOO...DID YOU LEARN THAT POEM, MAUREEN?
Monday, May 29
Poetry
UH-UMM...ANY SECOND NOW, MA'AM...
PAT
PAT
PAT
TUNK
TUNK
TUNK
TUNK
CAZENOVE & WILLIAM

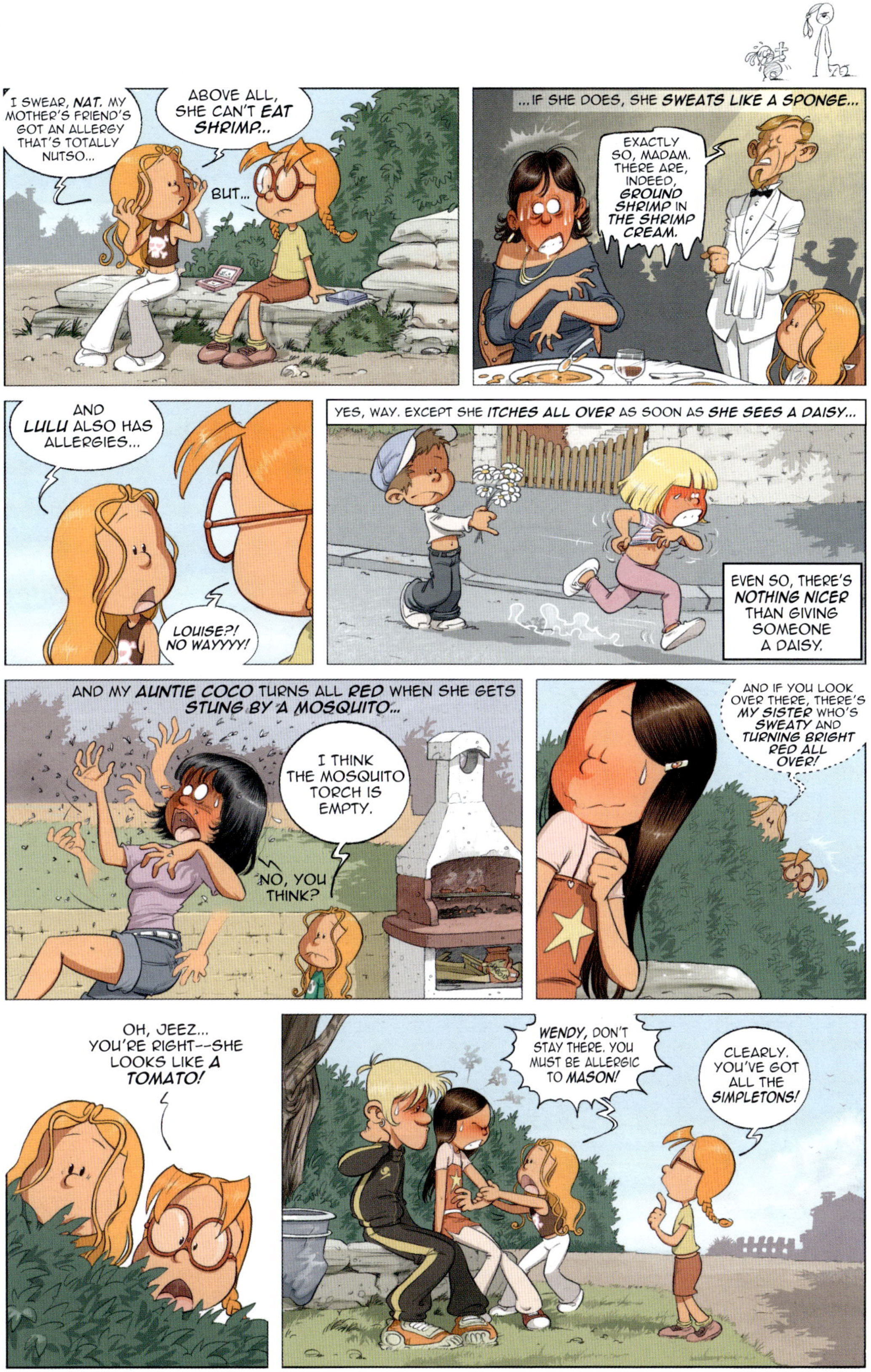

I SWEAR, NAT. MY MOTHER'S FRIEND'S GOT AN ALLERGY THAT'S TOTALLY NUTSO...
ABOVE ALL, SHE CAN'T EAT SHRIMP...
BUT...
...IF SHE DOES, SHE SWEATS LIKE A SPONGE...
EXACTLY SO, MADAM. THERE ARE, INDEED, GROUND SHRIMP IN THE SHRIMP CREAM.
AND LULU ALSO HAS ALLERGIES...
LOUISE?! NO WAYYYY!
YES, WAY. EXCEPT SHE ITCHES ALL OVER AS SOON AS SHE SEES A DAISY...
EVEN SO, THERE'S NOTHING NICER THAN GIVING SOMEONE A DAISY.
AND MY AUNTIE COCO TURNS ALL RED WHEN SHE GETS STUNG BY A MOSQUITO...
I THINK THE MOSQUITO TORCH IS EMPTY.
NO, YOU THINK?
AND IF YOU LOOK OVER THERE, THERE'S MY SISTER WHO'S SWEATY AND TURNING BRIGHT RED ALL OVER!
OH, JEEZ... YOU'RE RIGHT--SHE LOOKS LIKE A TOMATO!
WENDY, DON'T STAY THERE. YOU MUST BE ALLERGIC TO MASON!
CLEARLY, YOU'VE GOT ALL THE SIMPLETONS!
CAZENOVE & WILLIAM

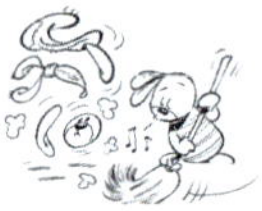

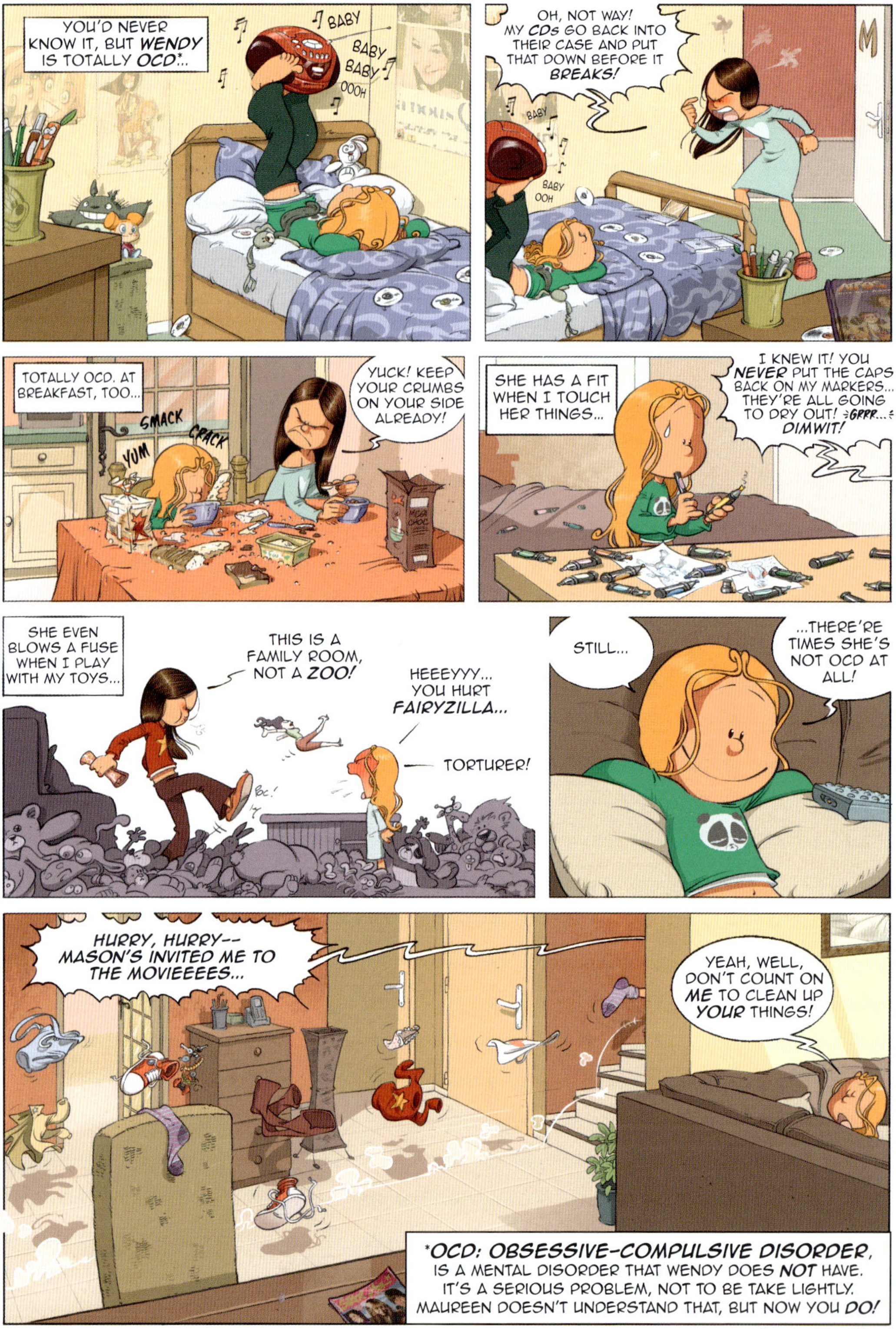

YOU'D NEVER KNOW IT, BUT WENDY IS TOTALLY OCD*...
BABY
BABY
BABY
OOOH
OH, NOT WAY! MY CDs GO BACK INTO THEIR CASE AND PUT THAT DOWN BEFORE IT BREAKS!
BABY
BABY
OOH
TOTALLY OCD. AT BREAKFAST, TOO...
SMACK
CRACK
YUM
YUCK! KEEP YOUR CRUMBS ON YOUR SIDE ALREADY!
SHE HAS A FIT WHEN I TOUCH HER THINGS...
I KNEW IT! YOU NEVER PUT THE CAPS BACK ON MY MARKERS... THEY'RE ALL GOING TO DRY OUT! GRRR... DIMWIT!
SHE EVEN BLOWS A FUSE WHEN I PLAY WITH MY TOYS...
THIS IS A FAMILY ROOM, NOT A ZOO!
HEEEYYY... YOU HURT FAIRYZILLA...
TORTURER!
STILL...
...THERE'RE TIMES SHE'S NOT OCD AT ALL!
HURRY, HURRY-- MASON'S INVITED ME TO THE MOVIEEEES...
YEAH, WELL, DON'T COUNT ON ME TO CLEAN UP YOUR THINGS!
*OCD: OBSESSIVE-COMPULSIVE DISORDER, IS A MENTAL DISORDER THAT WENDY DOES NOT HAVE. IT'S A SERIOUS PROBLEM, NOT TO BE TAKE LIGHTLY. MAUREEN DOESN'T UNDERSTAND THAT, BUT NOW YOU DO!

CAZENOVE & WILLIAM

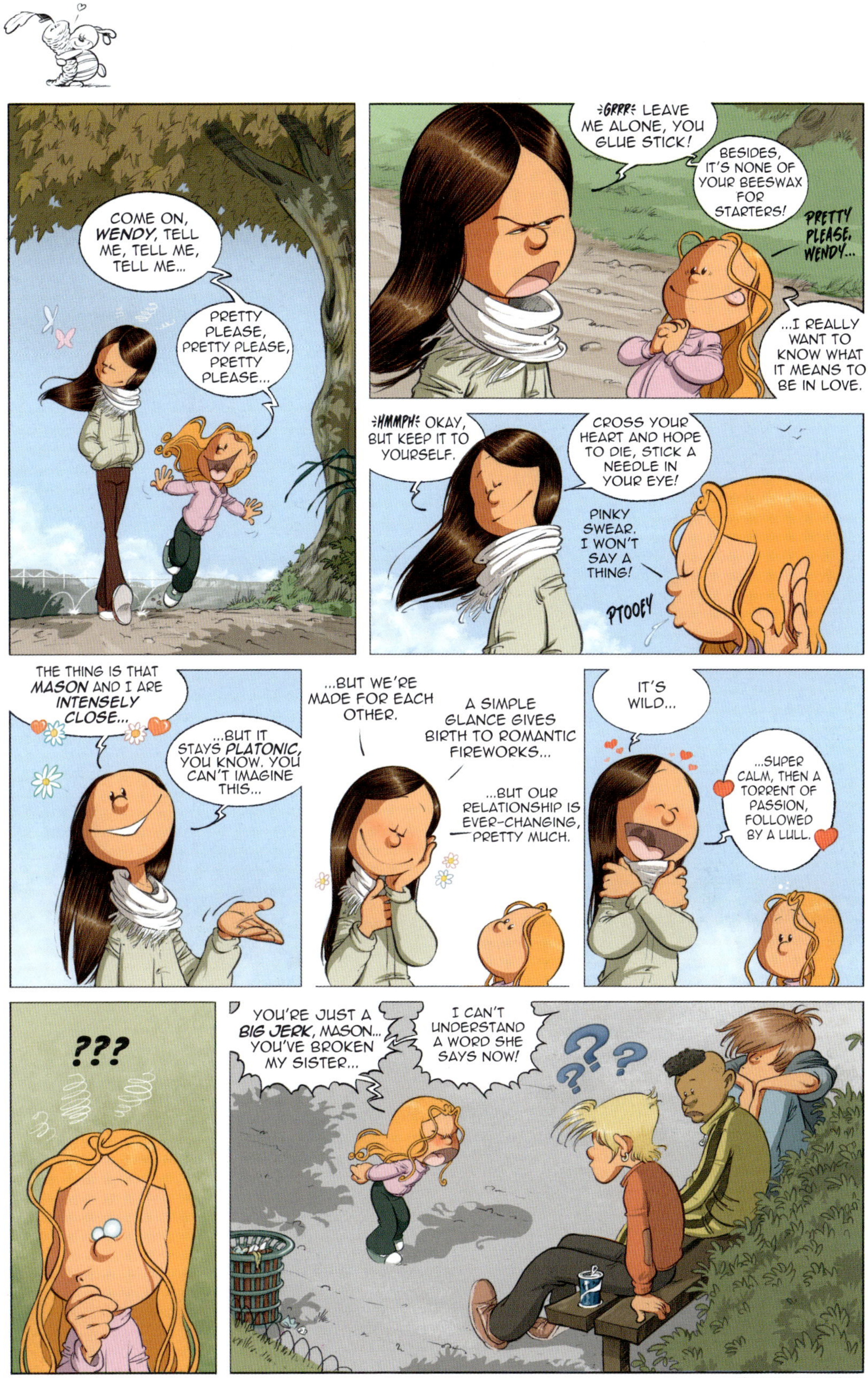

COME ON, WENDY, TELL ME, TELL ME, TELL ME...
PRETTY PLEASE, PRETTY PLEASE, PRETTY PLEASE...
GRRR LEAVE ME ALONE, YOU GLUE STICK!
BESIDES, IT'S NONE OF YOUR BEESWAX FOR STARTERS!
PRETTY PLEASE, WENDY...
...I REALLY WANT TO KNOW WHAT IT MEANS TO BE IN LOVE.
HMMPH OKAY, BUT KEEP IT TO YOURSELF.
CROSS YOUR HEART AND HOPE TO DIE, STICK A NEEDLE IN YOUR EYE!
PINKY SWEAR. I WON'T SAY A THING!
PTOOEY
THE THING IS THAT MASON AND I ARE INTENSELY CLOSE...
...BUT IT STAYS PLATONIC, YOU KNOW. YOU CAN'T IMAGINE THIS...
...BUT WE'RE MADE FOR EACH OTHER.
A SIMPLE GLANCE GIVES BIRTH TO ROMANTIC FIREWORKS...
...BUT OUR RELATIONSHIP IS EVER-CHANGING, PRETTY MUCH.
IT'S WILD...
...SUPER CALM, THEN A TORRENT OF PASSION, FOLLOWED BY A LULL.
???
YOU'RE JUST A BIG JERK, MASON... YOU'VE BROKEN MY SISTER...
I CAN'T UNDERSTAND A WORD SHE SAYS NOW!
CAZENOVE & WILLIAM

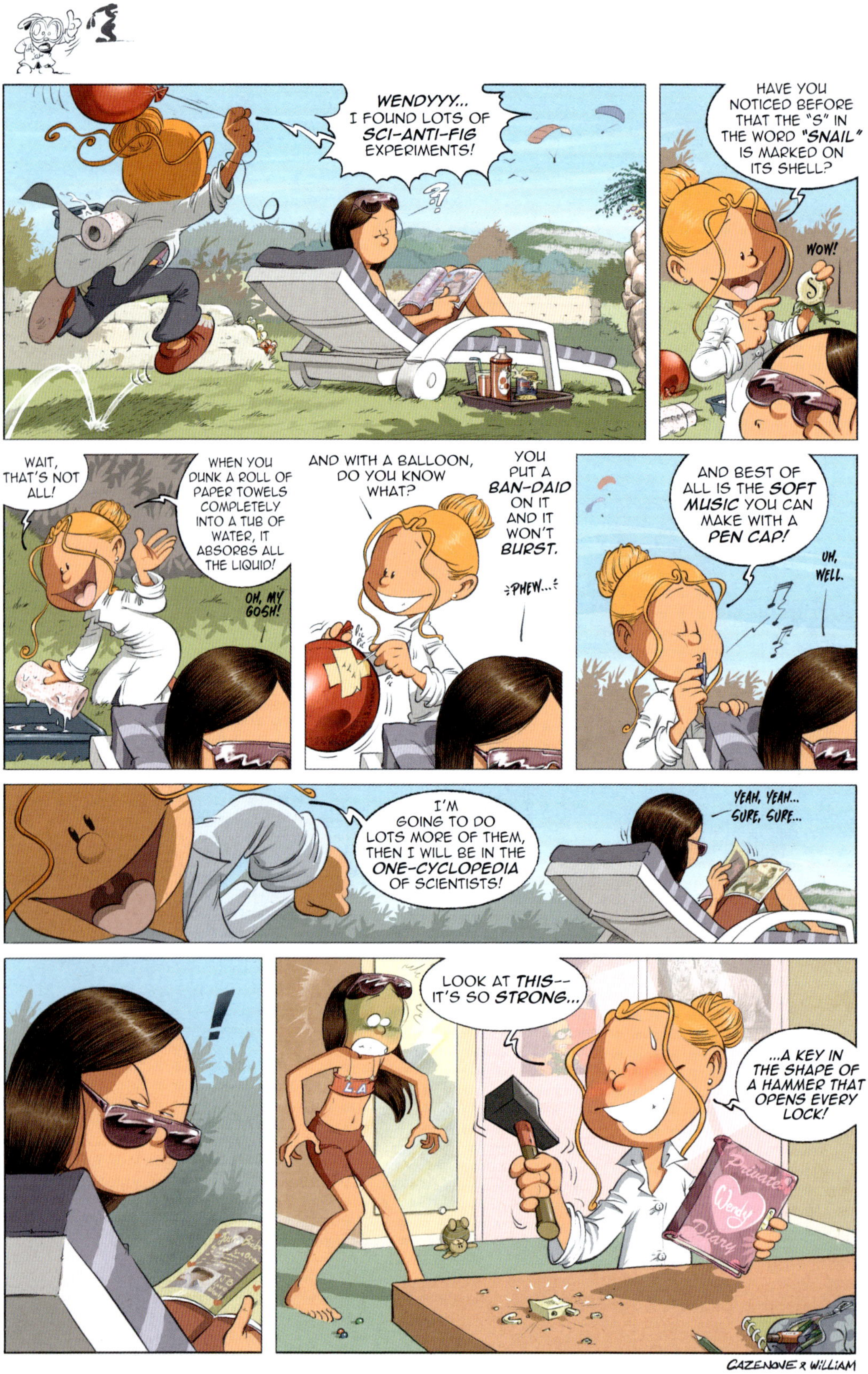
WENDYYY... I FOUND LOTS OF SCI-ANTI-FIG EXPERIMENTS!
?!
HAVE YOU NOTICED BEFORE THAT THE "S" IN THE WORD "SNAIL" IS MARKED ON ITS SHELL?
WOW!
WAIT, THAT'S NOT ALL!
WHEN YOU DUNK A ROLL OF PAPER TOWELS COMPLETELY INTO A TUB OF WATER, IT ABSORBS ALL THE LIQUID!
OH, MY GOSH!
AND WITH A BALLOON, DO YOU KNOW WHAT?
YOU PUT A BAN-DAID ON IT AND IT WON'T BURST.
PHEW...
AND BEST OF ALL IS THE SOFT MUSIC YOU CAN MAKE WITH A PEN CAP!
UH, WELL.
I'M GOING TO DO LOTS MORE OF THEM, THEN I WILL BE IN THE ONE-CYCLOPEDIA OF SCIENTISTS!
YEAH, YEAH... SURE, SURE...
!
LOOK AT THIS-- IT'S SO STRONG...
...A KEY IN THE SHAPE OF A HAMMER THAT OPENS EVERY LOCK!
Private Wendy Diary
CAZENOVE & WILLIAM

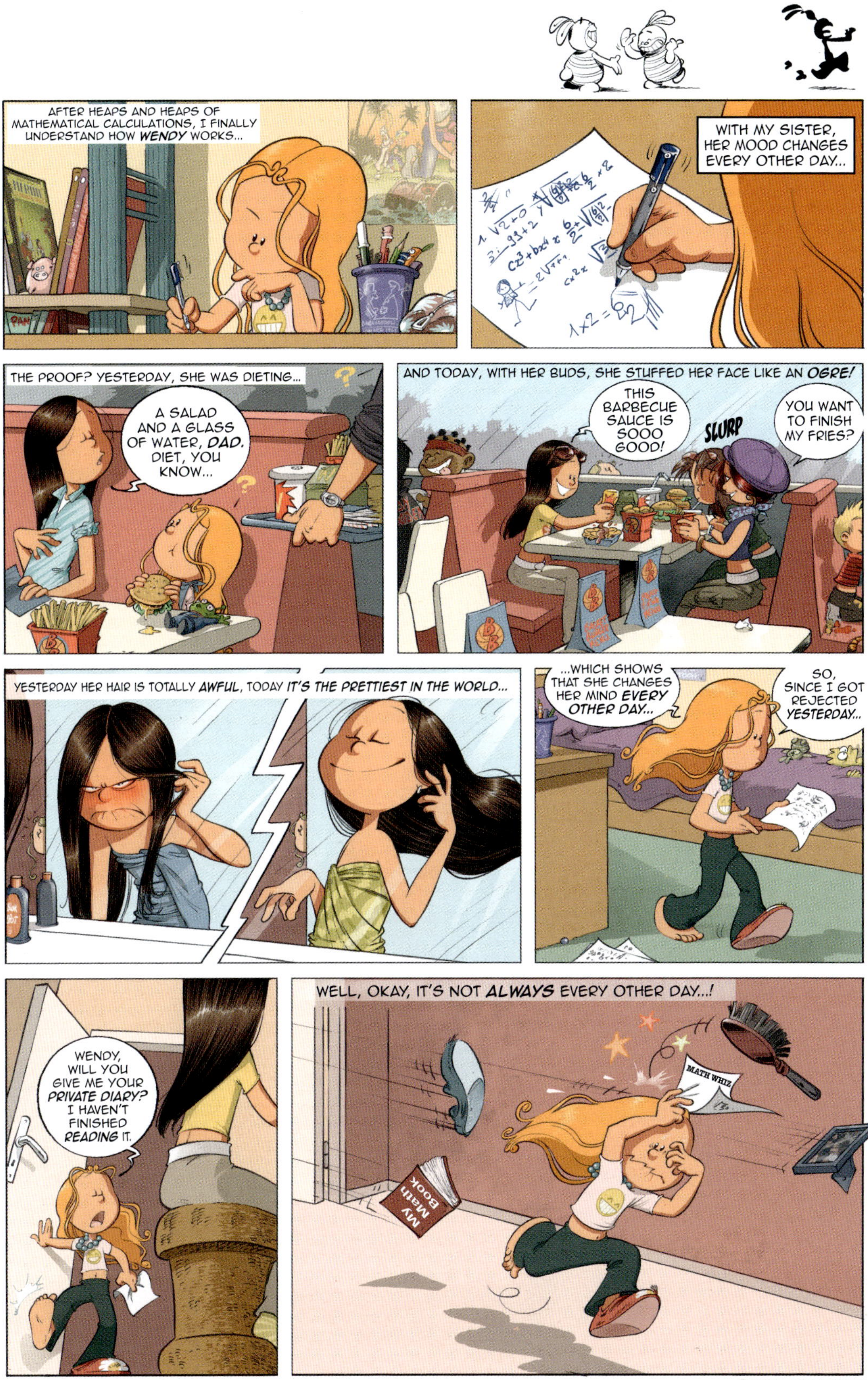

AFTER HEAPS AND HEAPS OF MATHEMATICAL CALCULATIONS, I FINALLY UNDERSTAND HOW WENDY WORKS...
WITH MY SISTER, HER MOOD CHANGES EVERY OTHER DAY...
THE PROOF? YESTERDAY, SHE WAS DIETING...
A SALAD AND A GLASS OF WATER, DAD. DIET, YOU KNOW...
AND TODAY, WITH HER BUDS, SHE STUFFED HER FACE LIKE AN OGRE!
THIS BARBECUE SAUCE IS SOOO GOOD!
SLURP
YOU WANT TO FINISH MY FRIES?
YESTERDAY HER HAIR IS TOTALLY AWFUL, TODAY IT'S THE PRETTIEST IN THE WORLD...
...WHICH SHOWS THAT SHE CHANGES HER MIND EVERY OTHER DAY...
SO, SINCE I GOT REJECTED YESTERDAY...
WENDY, WILL YOU GIVE ME YOUR PRIVATE DIARY? I HAVEN'T FINISHED READING IT.
WELL, OKAY, IT'S NOT ALWAYS EVERY OTHER DAY...!
MATH WHIZ
My Math Book
CAZENOVE & WILLIAM

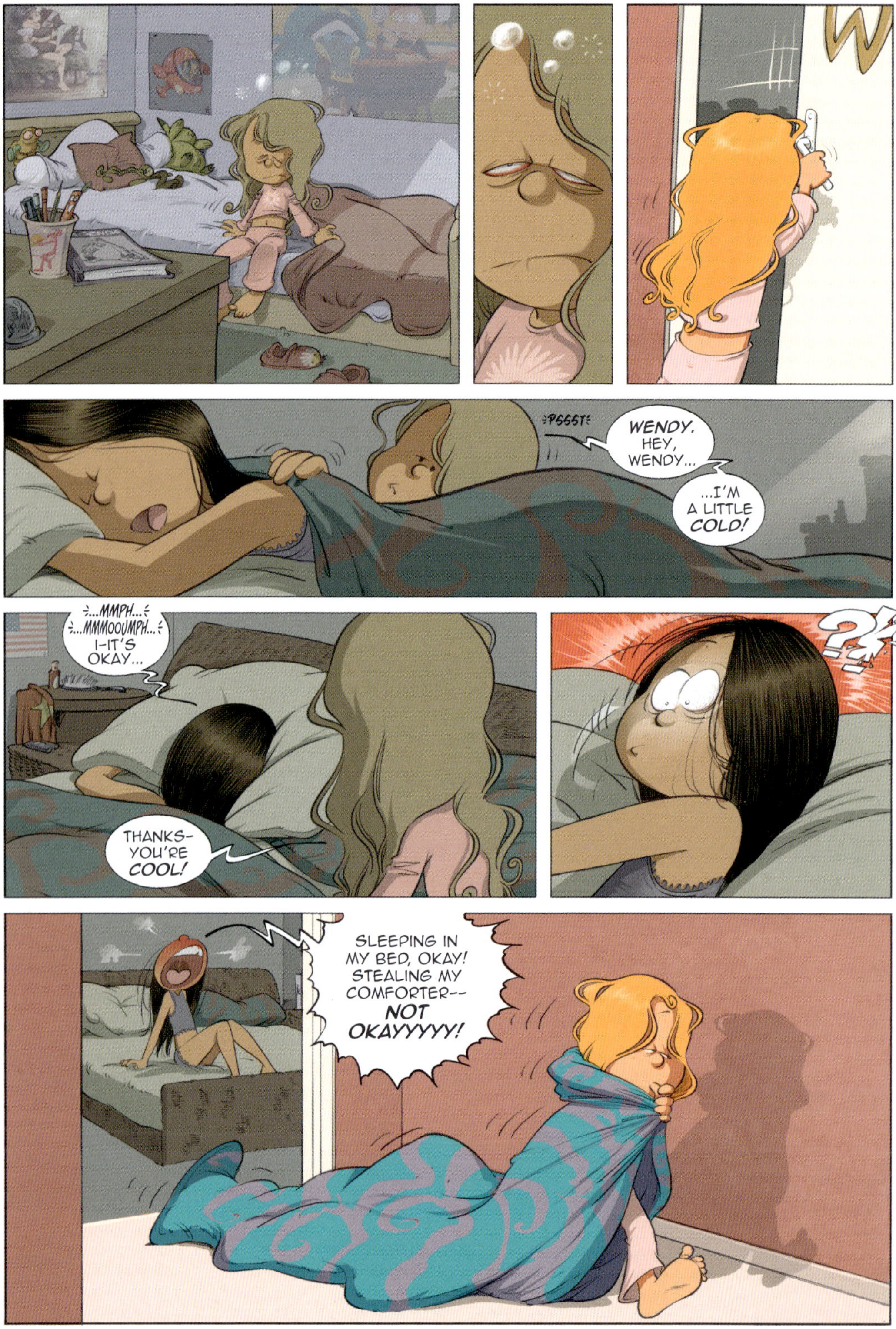
PSSST
WENDY. HEY, WENDY...
...I'M A LITTLE COLD!
...MMPH... ...MMMOOUMPH... I-IT'S OKAY...
THANKS- YOU'RE COOL!
?!
SLEEPING IN MY BED, OKAY! STEALING MY COMFORTER-- NOT OKAYYYYY!

CAZENOVE & WILLIAM

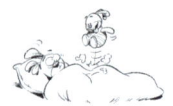

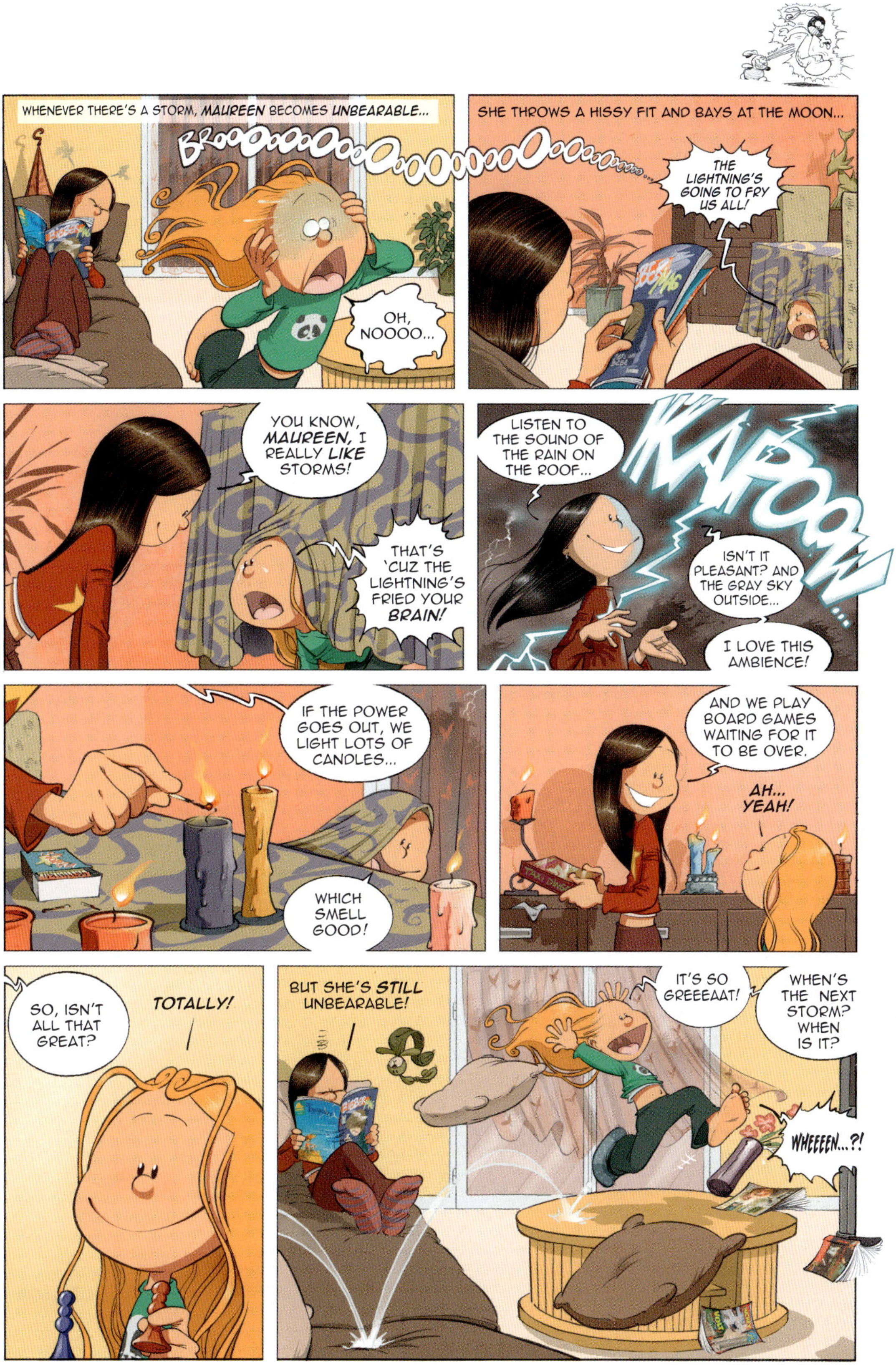
WHENEVER THERE'S A STORM, MAUREEN BECOMES UNBEARABLE...
BROOOOOOOOOOOOOOOOOOOOOOOOO...
OH, NOOOO...
SHE THROWS A HISSY FIT AND BAYS AT THE MOON...
THE LIGHTNING'S GOING TO FRY US ALL!
YOU KNOW, MAUREEN, I REALLY LIKE STORMS!
THAT'S 'CUZ THE LIGHTNING'S FRIED YOUR BRAIN!
LISTEN TO THE SOUND OF THE RAIN ON THE ROOF...
KAPOOW...
ISN'T IT PLEASANT? AND THE GRAY SKY OUTSIDE...
I LOVE THIS AMBIENCE!
IF THE POWER GOES OUT, WE LIGHT LOTS OF CANDLES...
WHICH SMELL GOOD!
AND WE PLAY BOARD GAMES WAITING FOR IT TO BE OVER.
AH... YEAH!
SO, ISN'T ALL THAT GREAT?
TOTALLY!
BUT SHE'S STILL UNBEARABLE!
IT'S SO GREEEAAT!
WHEN'S THE NEXT STORM? WHEN IS IT?
WHEEEEN...?!

CAZENOVE & WILLIAM

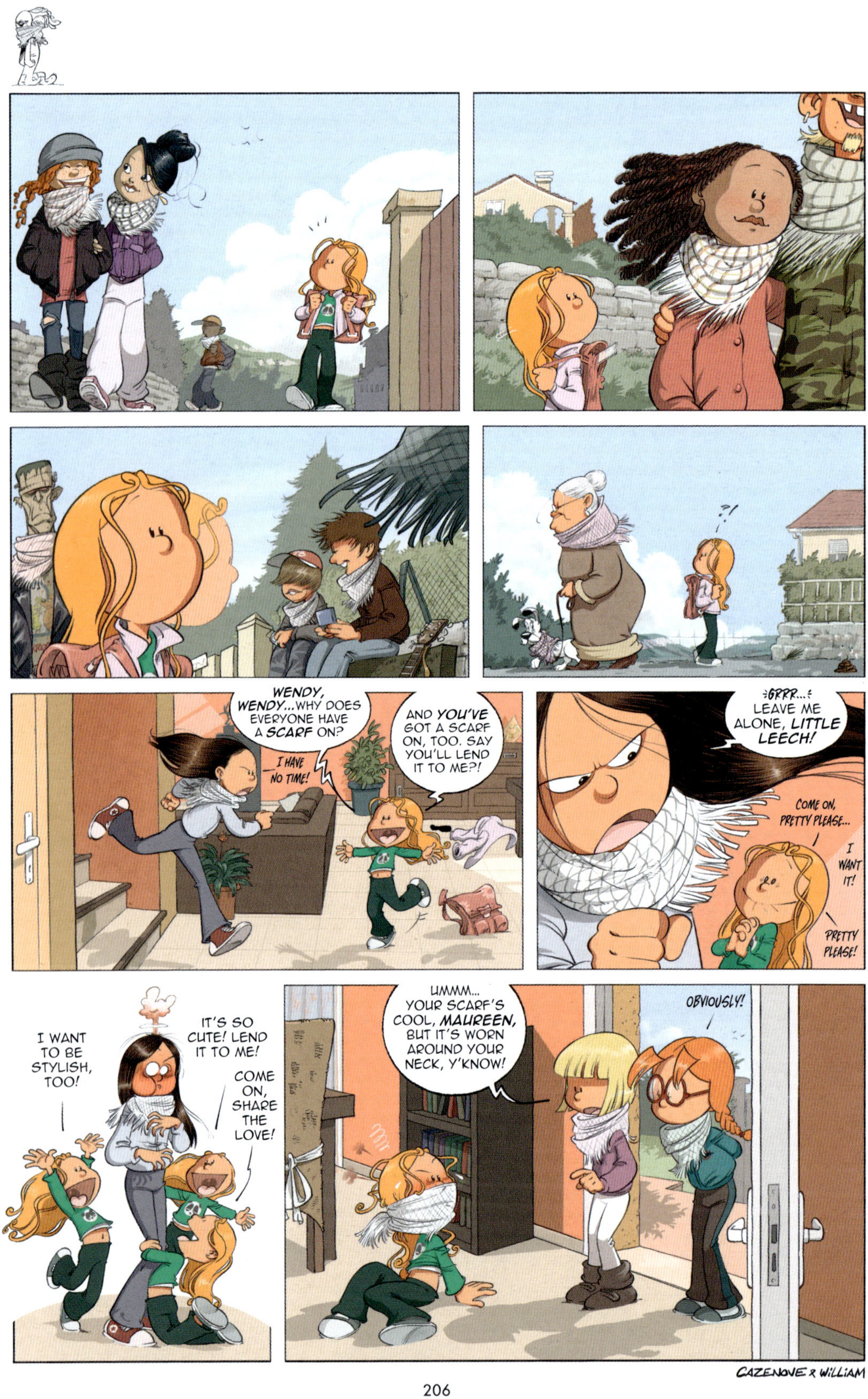
?!
WENDY, WENDY... WHY DOES EVERYONE HAVE A SCARF ON?
I HAVE NO TIME!
AND YOU'VE GOT A SCARF ON, TOO. SAY YOU'LL LEND IT TO ME?!
GRRR...
LEAVE ME ALONE, LITTLE LEECH!
COME ON, PRETTY PLEASE...
I WANT IT!
PRETTY PLEASE!
I WANT TO BE STYLISH, TOO!
IT'S SO CUTE! LEND IT TO ME!
COME ON, SHARE THE LOVE!
UMMM... YOUR SCARF'S COOL, MAUREEN, BUT IT'S WORN AROUND YOUR NECK, Y'KNOW!
OBVIOUSLY!
CAZENOVE & WILLIAM

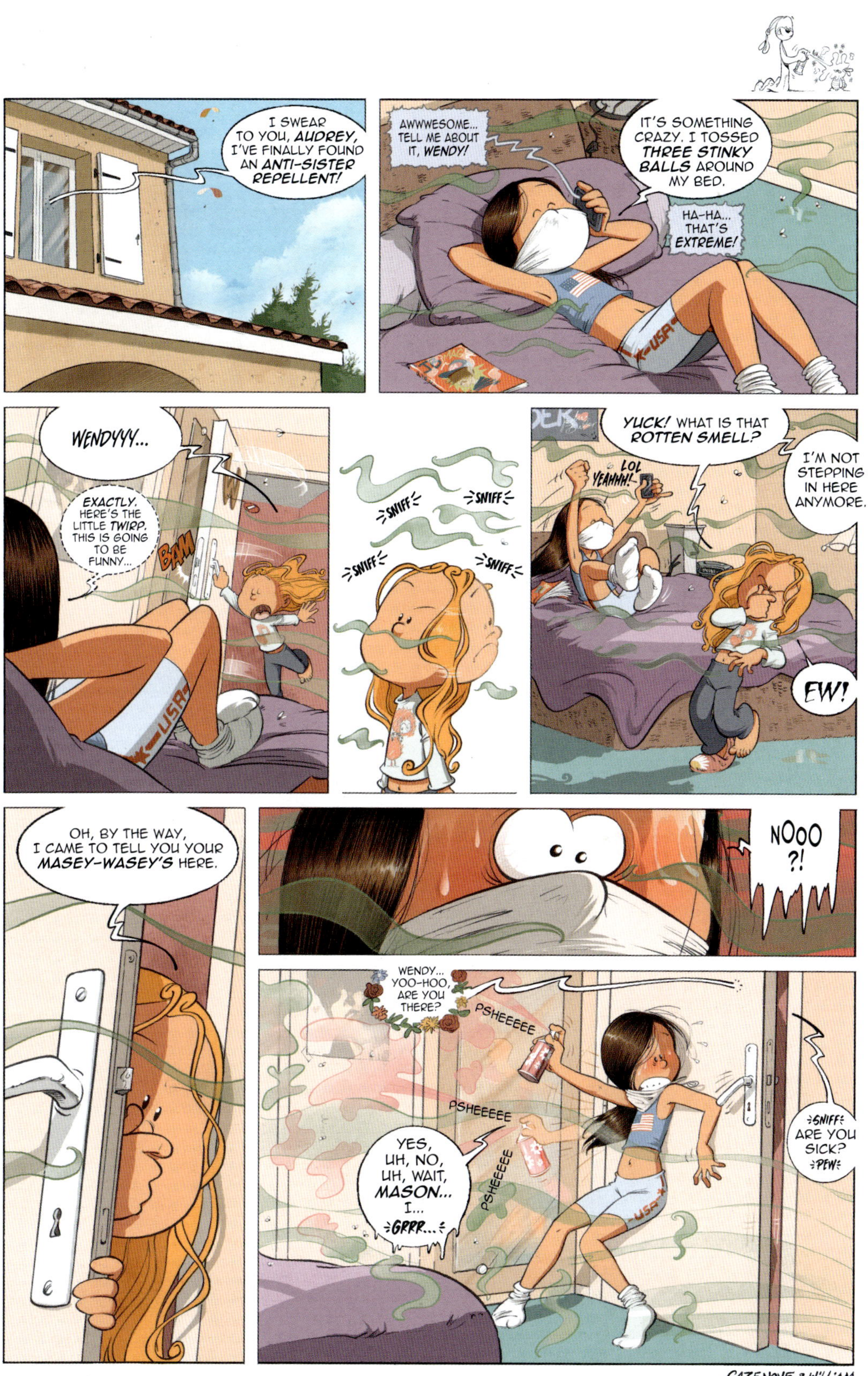
I SWEAR TO YOU, AUDREY, I'VE FINALLY FOUND AN ANTI-SISTER REPELLENT!
AWWWESOME... TELL ME ABOUT IT, WENDY!
IT'S SOMETHING CRAZY. I TOSSED THREE STINKY BALLS AROUND MY BED.
HA-HA... THAT'S EXTREME!
WENDYYY...
EXACTLY. HERE'S THE LITTLE TWIRP. THIS IS GOING TO BE FUNNY...
BAM
SNIFF
SNIFF
SNIFF
SNIFF
YUCK! WHAT IS THAT ROTTEN SMELL?
LOL YEAHHH!
I'M NOT STEPPING IN HERE ANYMORE.
EW!
OH, BY THE WAY, I CAME TO TELL YOU YOUR MASEY-WASEY'S HERE.
NOOO ?!
WENDY... YOO-HOO, ARE YOU THERE?
PSHEEEEE
PSHEEEEE
PSHEEEEE
YES, UH, NO, UH, WAIT, MASON... I... GRRR...
SNIFF ARE YOU SICK? PEW

CAZENOVE & WILLIAM

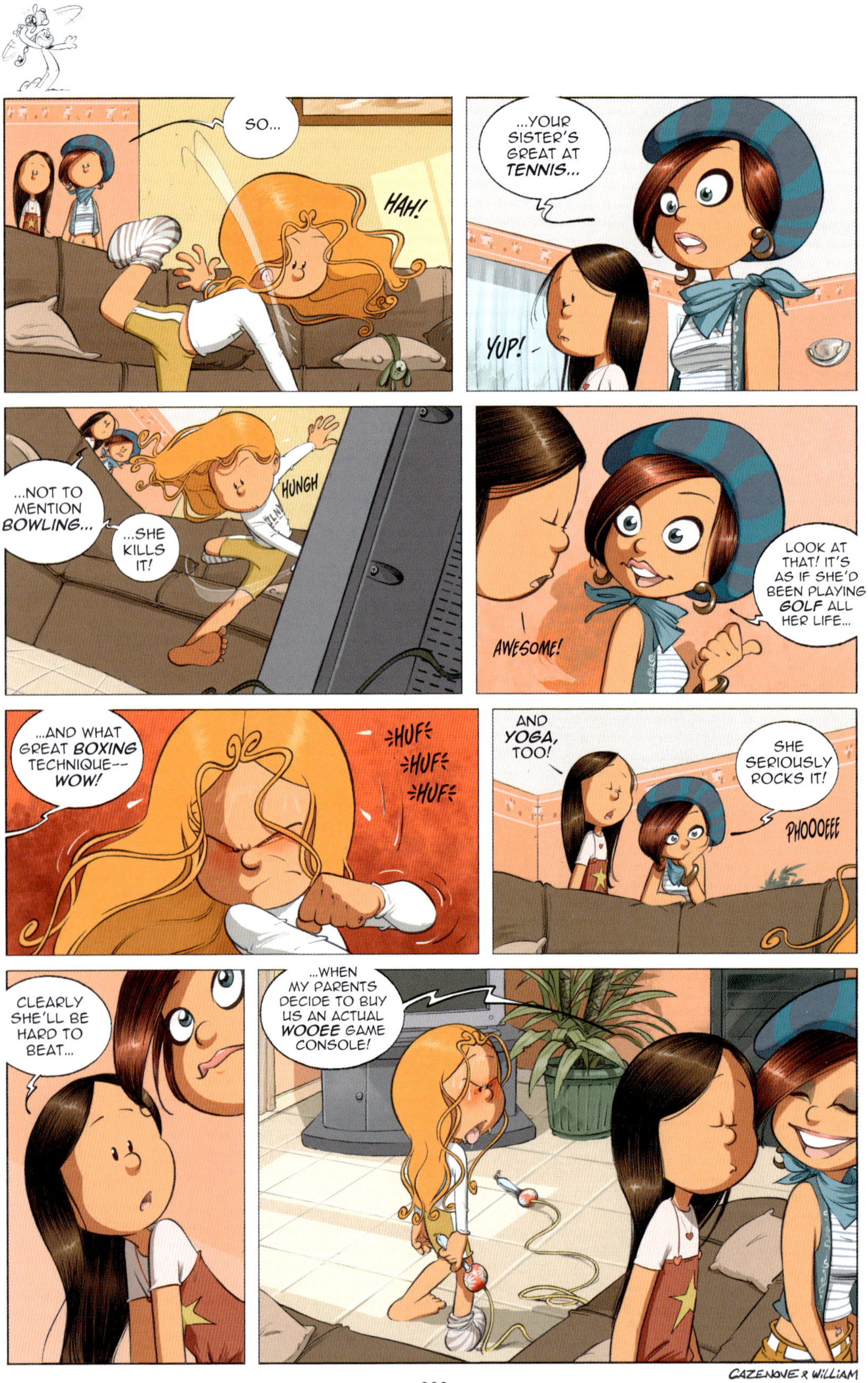
SO...
HAH!
...YOUR SISTER'S GREAT AT TENNIS...
YUP!
...NOT TO MENTION BOWLING...
...SHE KILLS IT!
HUNGH
AWESOME!
LOOK AT THAT! IT'S AS IF SHE'D BEEN PLAYING GOLF ALL HER LIFE...
...AND WHAT GREAT BOXING TECHNIQUE-- WOW!
HUF HUF HUF
AND YOGA, TOO!
SHE SERIOUSLY ROCKS IT!
PHOOOEEE
CLEARLY SHE'LL BE HARD TO BEAT...
...WHEN MY PARENTS DECIDE TO BUY US AN ACTUAL WOOEE GAME CONSOLE!
CAZENOVE & WILLIAM

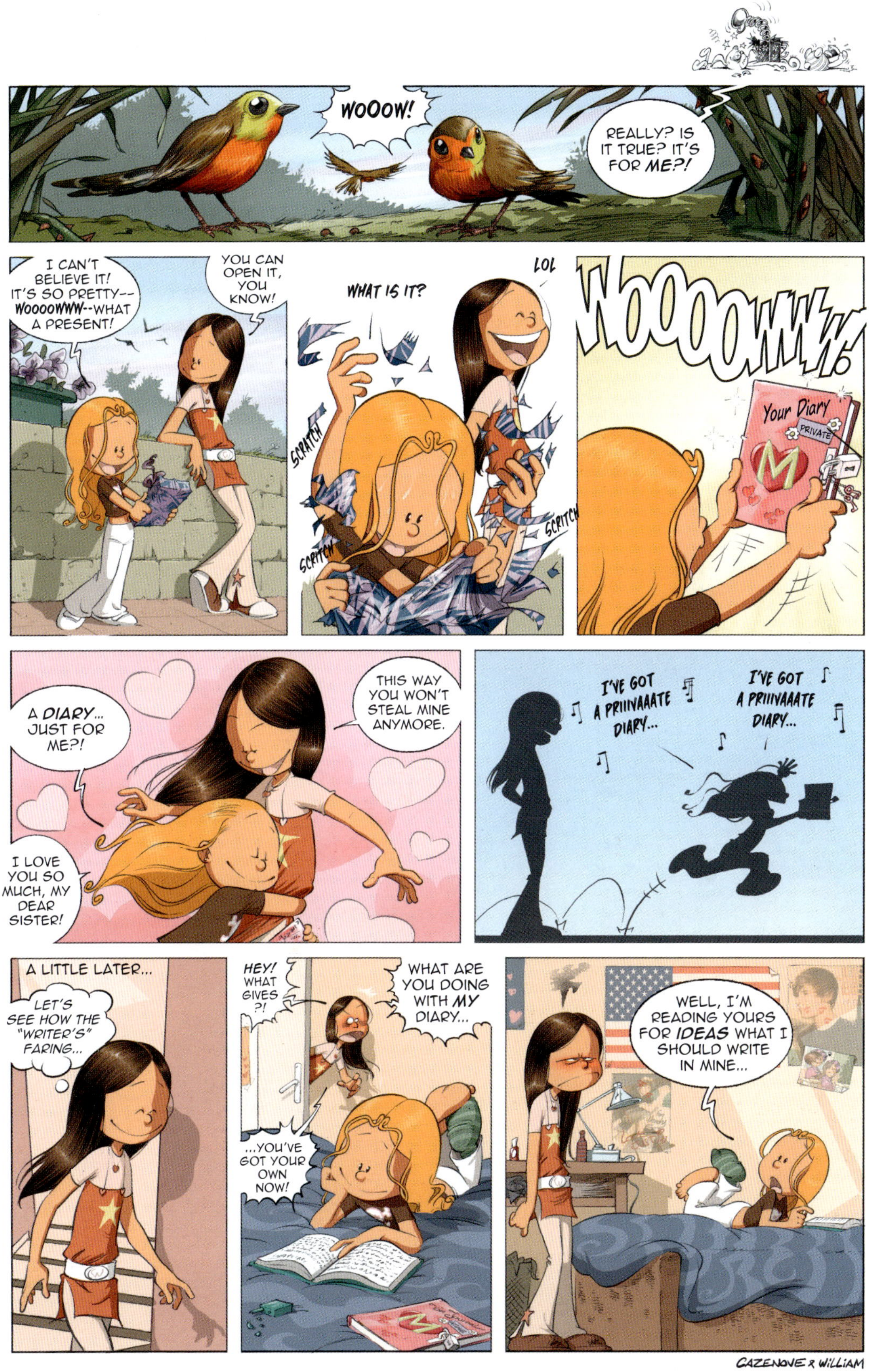
WOOOW!
REALLY? IS IT TRUE? IT'S FOR ME?!
I CAN'T BELIEVE IT! IT'S SO PRETTY-- WOOOOWWW--WHAT A PRESENT!
YOU CAN OPEN IT, YOU KNOW!
WHAT IS IT?
LOL
SCRATCH
SCRATCH
SCRATCH
WOOOOWWW!
Your Diary
PRIVATE
A DIARY... JUST FOR ME?!
THIS WAY YOU WON'T STEAL MINE ANYMORE.
I LOVE YOU SO MUCH, MY DEAR SISTER!
I'VE GOT A PRIIIVAAATE DIARY...
I'VE GOT A PRIIIVAAATE DIARY...
A LITTLE LATER...
LET'S SEE HOW THE "WRITER'S" FARING...
HEY! WHAT GIVES?!
WHAT ARE YOU DOING WITH MY DIARY...
...YOU'VE GOT YOUR OWN NOW!
WELL, I'M READING YOURS FOR IDEAS WHAT I SHOULD WRITE IN MINE...
CAZENOVE & WILLIAM

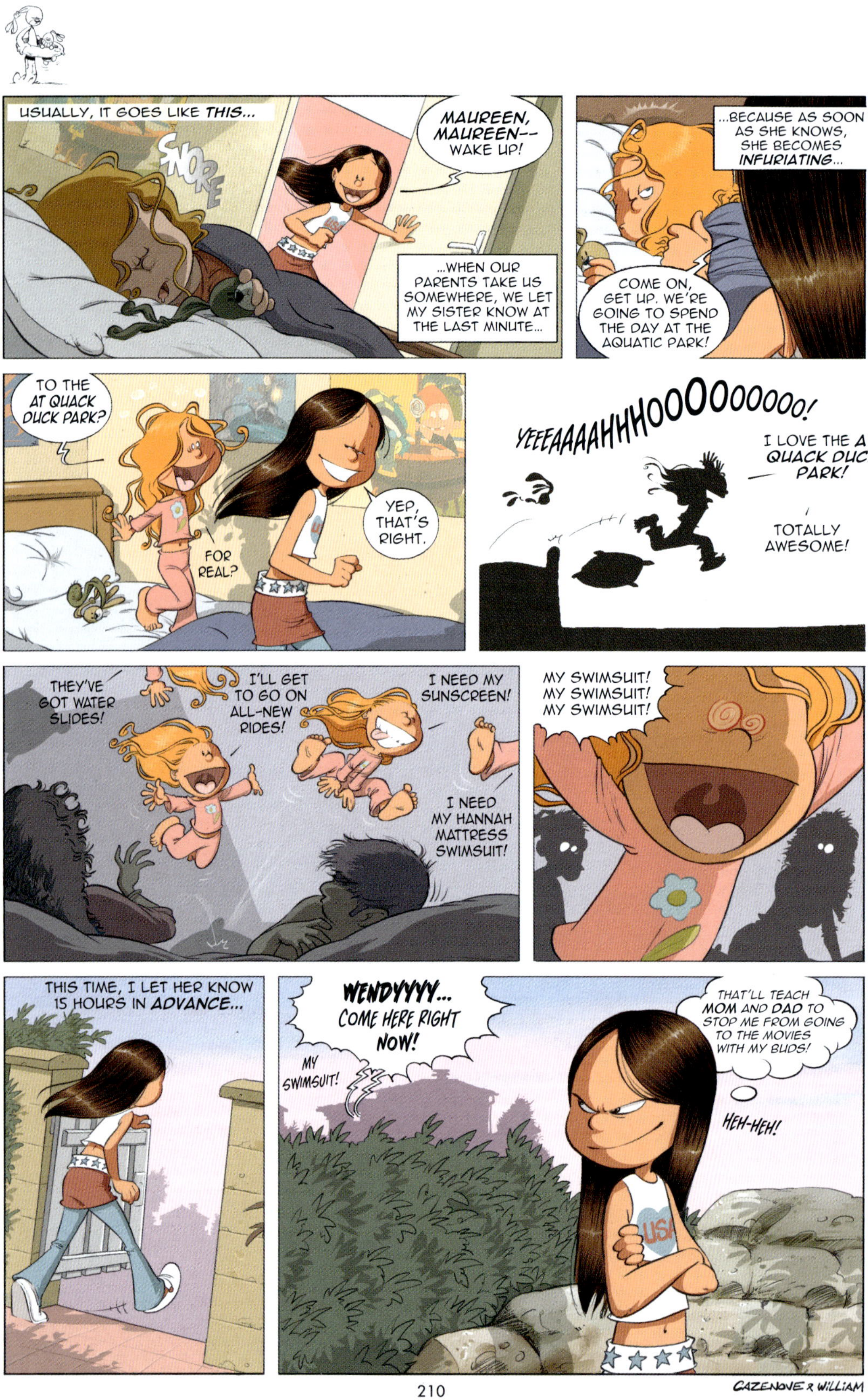
USUALLY, IT GOES LIKE THIS...
SNORE
MAUREEN, MAUREEN-- WAKE UP!
...WHEN OUR PARENTS TAKE US SOMEWHERE, WE LET MY SISTER KNOW AT THE LAST MINUTE...
...BECAUSE AS SOON AS SHE KNOWS, SHE BECOMES INFURIATING...
COME ON, GET UP. WE'RE GOING TO SPEND THE DAY AT THE AQUATIC PARK!
TO THE AT QUACK DUCK PARK?
FOR REAL?
YEP, THAT'S RIGHT.
YEEEAAAAHHHOOOOOOOOOO!
I LOVE THE AT QUACK DUCK PARK!
TOTALLY AWESOME!
THEY'VE GOT WATER SLIDES!
I'LL GET TO GO ON ALL-NEW RIDES!
I NEED MY SUNSCREEN!
I NEED MY HANNAH MATTRESS SWIMSUIT!
MY SWIMSUIT! MY SWIMSUIT! MY SWIMSUIT!
THIS TIME, I LET HER KNOW 15 HOURS IN ADVANCE...
WENDYYYY... COME HERE RIGHT NOW!
MY SWIMSUIT!
THAT'LL TEACH MOM AND DAD TO STOP ME FROM GOING TO THE MOVIES WITH MY BUDS!
HEH-HEH!
CAZENOVE & WILLIAM

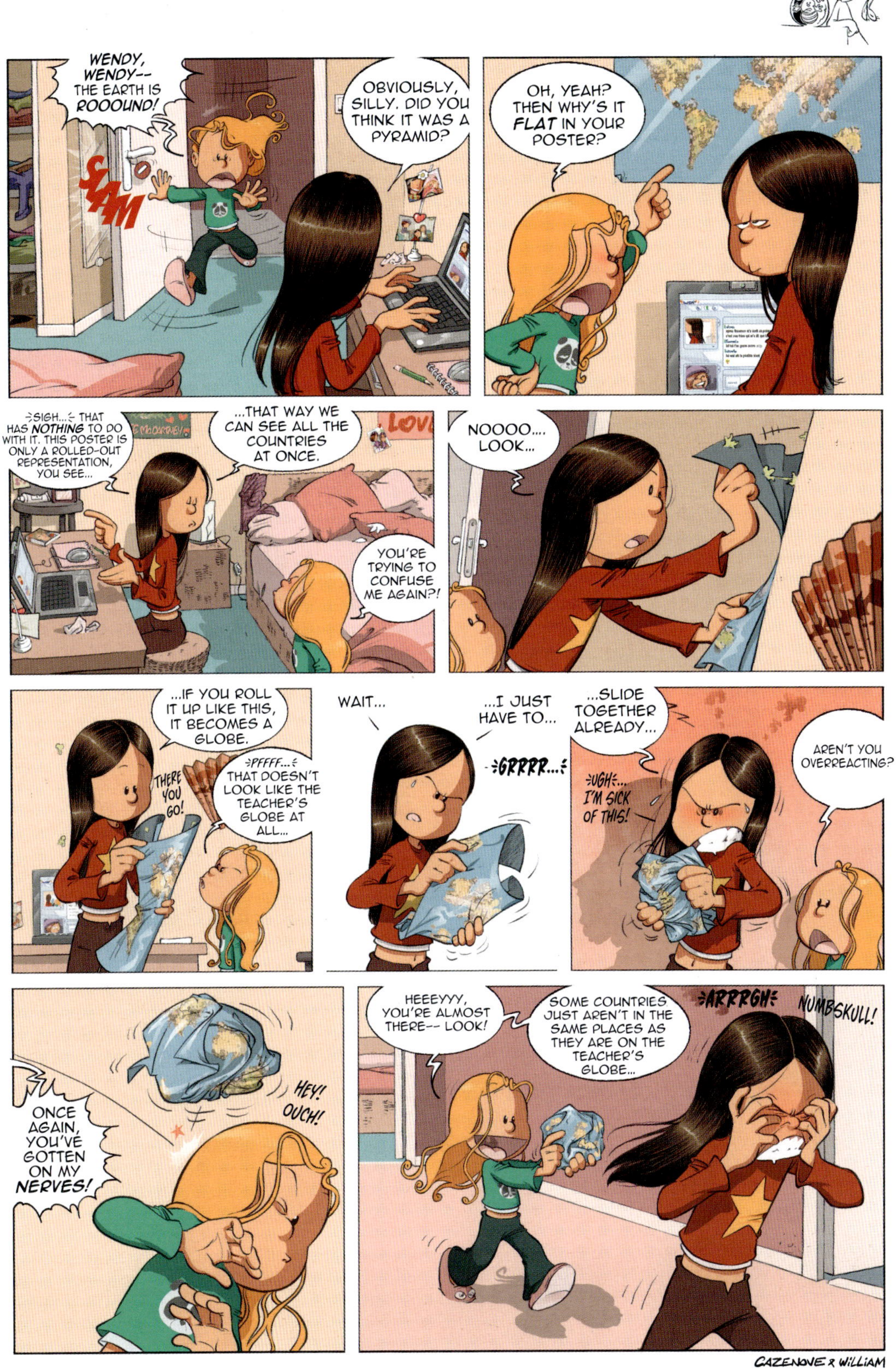
WENDY, WENDY-- THE EARTH IS ROOOUND!
SLAM
OBVIOUSLY, SILLY. DID YOU THINK IT WAS A PYRAMID?
OH, YEAH? THEN WHY'S IT FLAT IN YOUR POSTER?
SIGH... THAT HAS NOTHING TO DO WITH IT. THIS POSTER IS ONLY A ROLLED-OUT REPRESENTATION, YOU SEE...
...THAT WAY WE CAN SEE ALL THE COUNTRIES AT ONCE.
LOVE
YOU'RE TRYING TO CONFUSE ME AGAIN?!
NOOOO.... LOOK...
...IF YOU ROLL IT UP LIKE THIS, IT BECOMES A GLOBE.
THERE YOU GO!
PFFFF... THAT DOESN'T LOOK LIKE THE TEACHER'S GLOBE AT ALL...
WAIT...
...I JUST HAVE TO...
GRRRR...
...SLIDE TOGETHER ALREADY...
UGH... I'M SICK OF THIS!
AREN'T YOU OVERREACTING?
ONCE AGAIN, YOU'VE GOTTEN ON MY NERVES!
HEY! OUCH!
HEEEYYY, YOU'RE ALMOST THERE-- LOOK!
SOME COUNTRIES JUST AREN'T IN THE SAME PLACES AS THEY ARE ON THE TEACHER'S GLOBE...
ARRRGH
NUMBSKULL!
CAZENOVE & WILLIAM

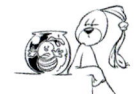

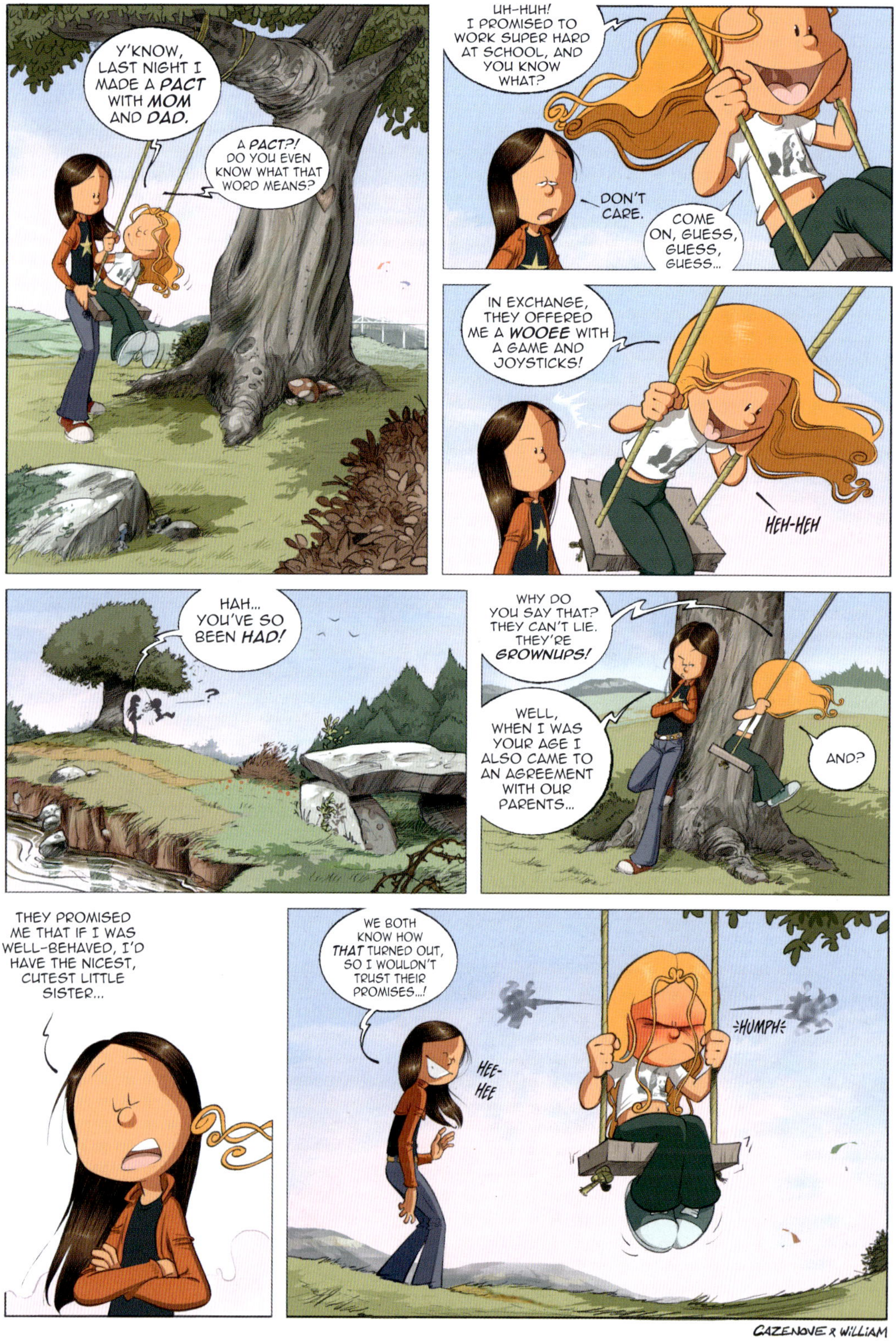
Y'KNOW, LAST NIGHT I MADE A PACT WITH MOM AND DAD.
A PACT?! DO YOU EVEN KNOW WHAT THAT WORD MEANS?
UH-HUH! I PROMISED TO WORK SUPER HARD AT SCHOOL, AND YOU KNOW WHAT?
DON'T CARE.
COME ON, GUESS, GUESS, GUESS...
IN EXCHANGE, THEY OFFERED ME A WOOEE WITH A GAME AND JOYSTICKS!
HEH-HEH
HAH... YOU'VE SO BEEN HAD!
?
WHY DO YOU SAY THAT? THEY CAN'T LIE. THEY'RE GROWNUPS!
WELL, WHEN I WAS YOUR AGE I ALSO CAME TO AN AGREEMENT WITH OUR PARENTS...
AND?
THEY PROMISED ME THAT IF I WAS WELL-BEHAVED, I'D HAVE THE NICEST, CUTEST LITTLE SISTER...
WE BOTH KNOW HOW THAT TURNED OUT, SO I WOULDN'T TRUST THEIR PROMISES...!
HEE-HEE
HUMPH
CAZENOVE & WILLIAM

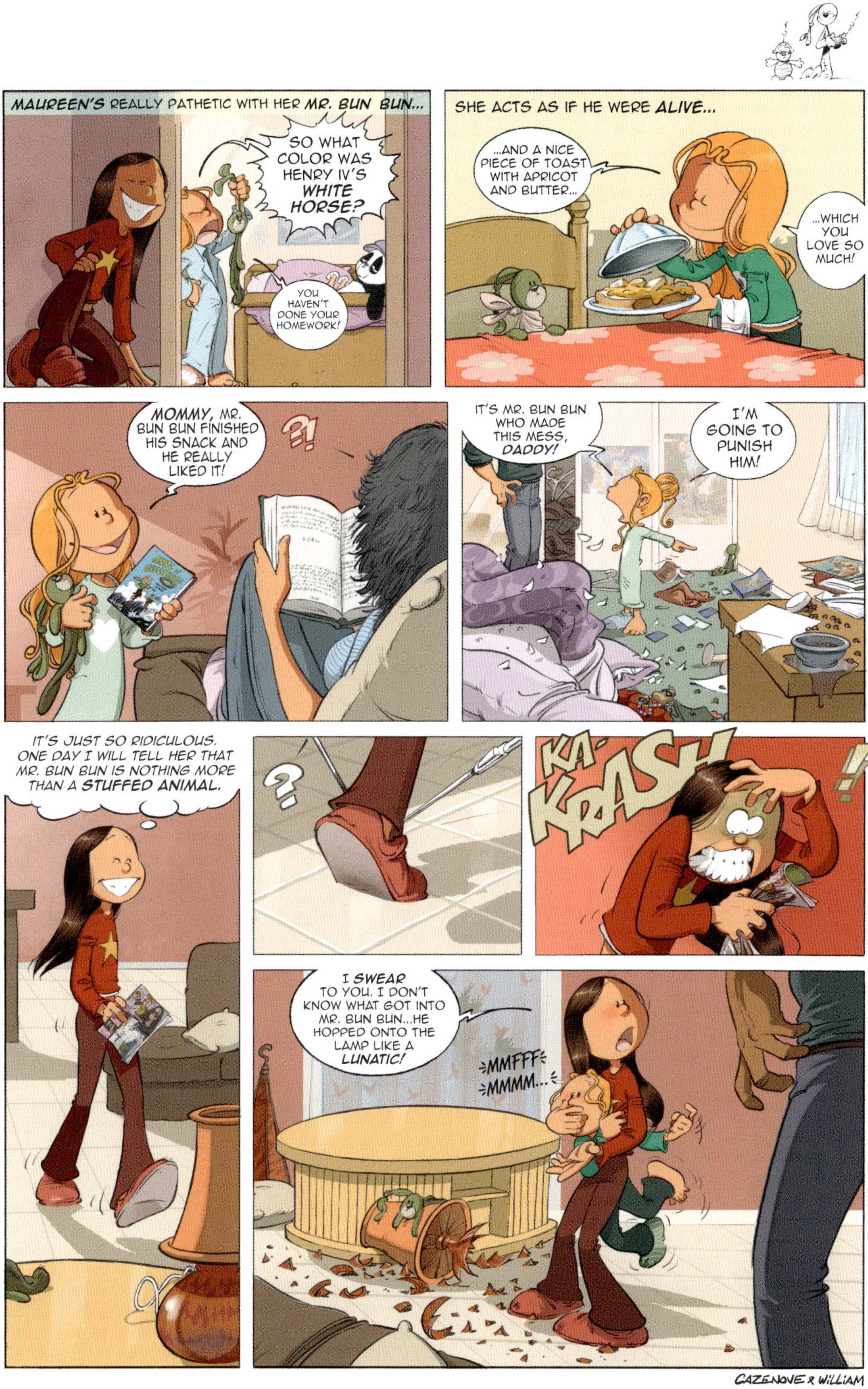
MAUREEN'S REALLY PATHETIC WITH HER MR. BUN BUN...
SO WHAT COLOR WAS HENRY IV'S WHITE HORSE?
YOU HAVEN'T DONE YOUR HOMEWORK!
SHE ACTS AS IF HE WERE ALIVE...
...AND A NICE PIECE OF TOAST WITH APRICOT AND BUTTER...
...WHICH YOU LOVE SO MUCH!
MOMMY, MR. BUN BUN FINISHED HIS SNACK AND HE REALLY LIKED IT!
?!
IT'S MR. BUN BUN WHO MADE THIS MESS, DADDY!
I'M GOING TO PUNISH HIM!
IT'S JUST SO RIDICULOUS. ONE DAY I WILL TELL HER THAT MR. BUN BUN IS NOTHING MORE THAN A STUFFED ANIMAL.
?
KA-KRASH
!
I SWEAR TO YOU. I DON'T KNOW WHAT GOT INTO MR. BUN BUN...HE HOPPED ONTO THE LAMP LIKE A LUNATIC!
MMFFF
MMMM...
CAZENOVE & WILLIAM

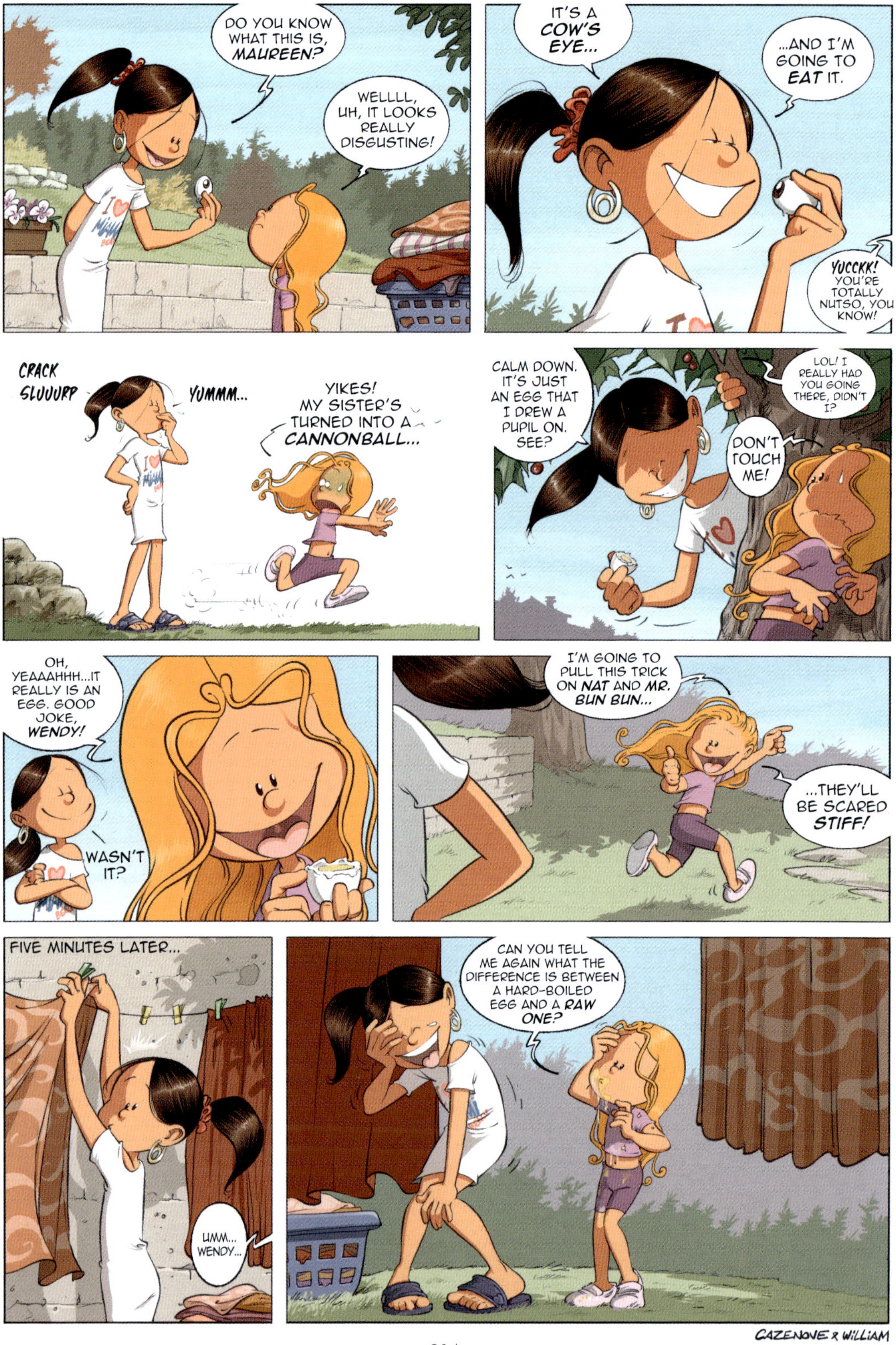
DO YOU KNOW WHAT THIS IS, MAUREEN?
WELLLL, UH, IT LOOKS REALLY DISGUSTING!
IT'S A COW'S EYE...
...AND I'M GOING TO EAT IT.
YUCCKK! YOU'RE TOTALLY NUTSO, YOU KNOW!
CRACK
SLUUURP
YUMMM...
YIKES! MY SISTER'S TURNED INTO A CANNONBALL...
CALM DOWN. IT'S JUST AN EGG THAT I DREW A PUPIL ON. SEE?
LOL! I REALLY HAD YOU GOING THERE, DIDN'T I?
DON'T TOUCH ME!
OH, YEAAAHHH...IT REALLY IS AN EGG. GOOD JOKE, WENDY!
WASN'T IT?
I'M GOING TO PULL THIS TRICK ON NAT AND MR. BUN BUN...
...THEY'LL BE SCARED STIFF!
FIVE MINUTES LATER...
UMM... WENDY...
CAN YOU TELL ME AGAIN WHAT THE DIFFERENCE IS BETWEEN A HARD-BOILED EGG AND A RAW ONE?

CAZENOVE & WILLIAM

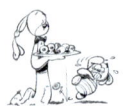

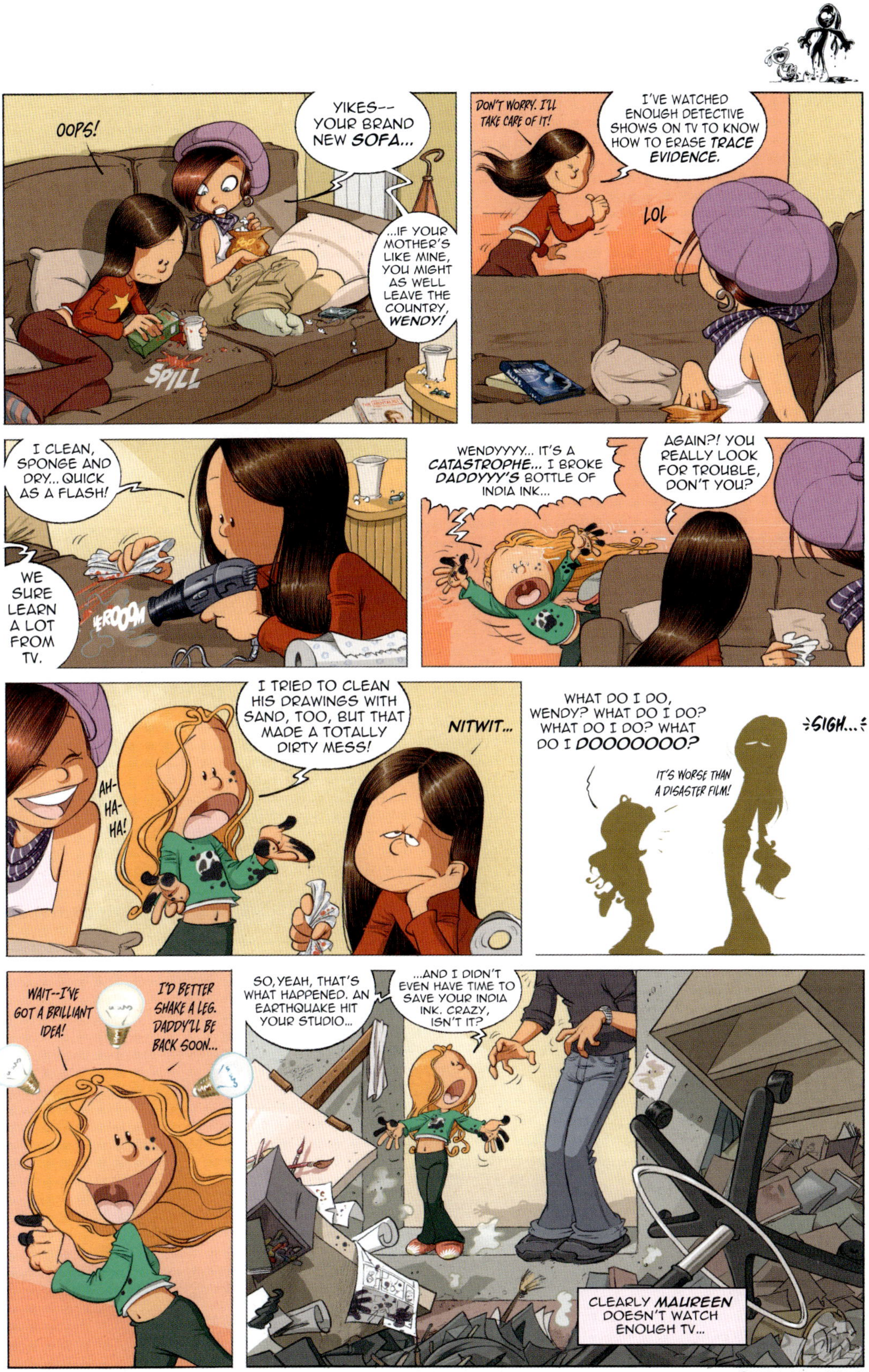
OOPS!
YIKES-- YOUR BRAND NEW **SOFA...**
...IF YOUR MOTHER'S LIKE MINE, YOU MIGHT AS WELL LEAVE THE COUNTRY, **WENDY!**
SPILL
DON'T WORRY. I'LL TAKE CARE OF IT!
I'VE WATCHED ENOUGH DETECTIVE SHOWS ON TV TO KNOW HOW TO ERASE **TRACE EVIDENCE.**
LOL
I CLEAN, SPONGE AND DRY... QUICK AS A FLASH!
WE SURE LEARN A LOT FROM TV.
VEROOOM
WENDYYYY... IT'S A **CATASTROPHE...** I BROKE **DADDYYY'S** BOTTLE OF INDIA INK...
AGAIN?! YOU REALLY LOOK FOR TROUBLE, DON'T YOU?
AH-HA-HA!
I TRIED TO CLEAN HIS DRAWINGS WITH SAND, TOO, BUT THAT MADE A TOTALLY DIRTY MESS!
NITWIT...
WHAT DO I DO, WENDY? WHAT DO I DO? WHAT DO I DO? WHAT DO I **DOOOOOOO?**
SIGH...
IT'S WORSE THAN A DISASTER FILM!
WAIT--I'VE GOT A BRILLIANT IDEA!
I'D BETTER SHAKE A LEG. DADDY'LL BE BACK SOON...
SO, YEAH, THAT'S WHAT HAPPENED. AN EARTHQUAKE HIT YOUR STUDIO...
...AND I DIDN'T EVEN HAVE TIME TO SAVE YOUR INDIA INK. CRAZY, ISN'T IT?
CLEARLY **MAUREEN** DOESN'T WATCH ENOUGH TV...

CAZENOVE & WILLIAM

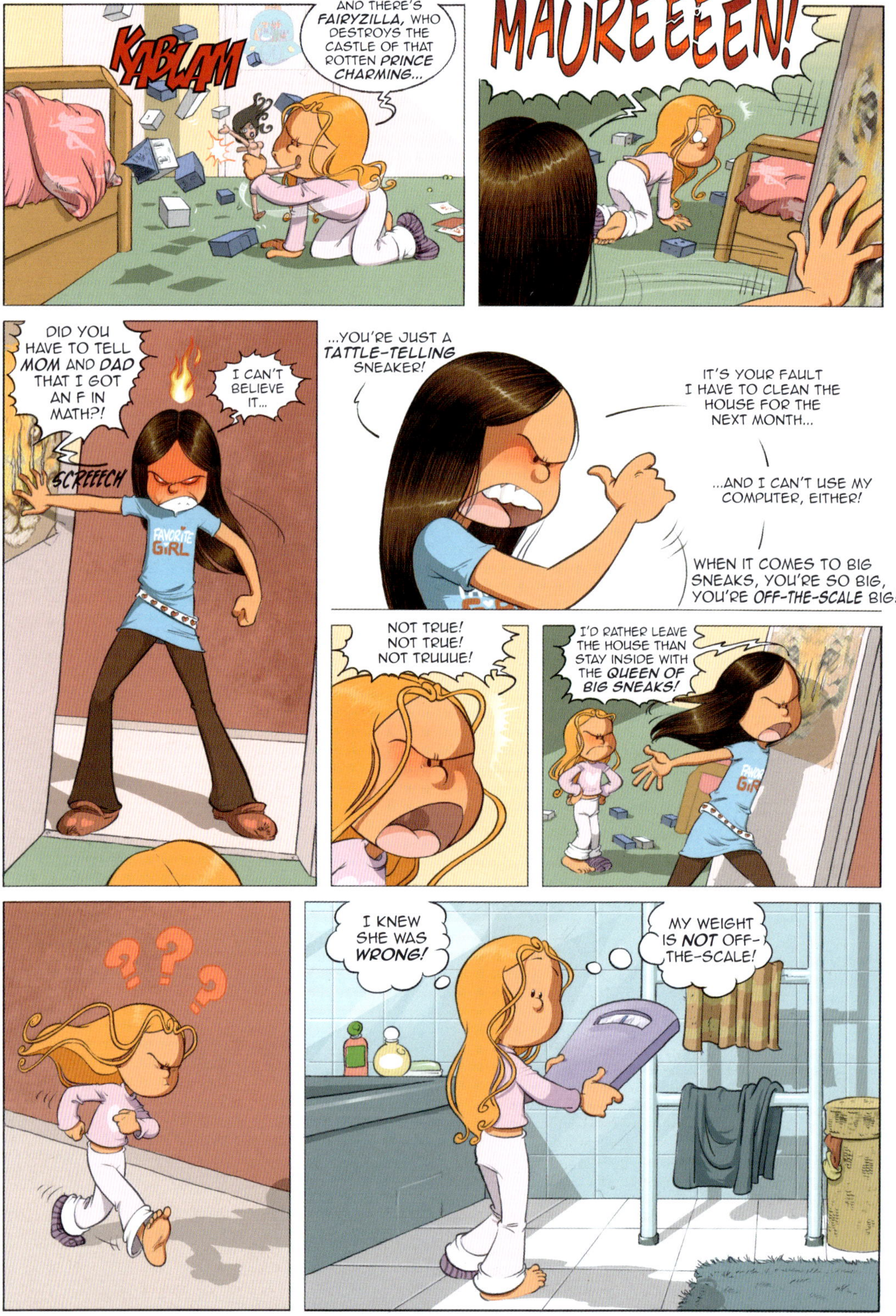
KABLAM
AND THERE'S FAIRYZILLA, WHO DESTROYS THE CASTLE OF THAT ROTTEN PRINCE CHARMING...
MAUREEEEN!
DID YOU HAVE TO TELL MOM AND DAD THAT I GOT AN F IN MATH?!
I CAN'T BELIEVE IT...
SCREEECH
FAVORITE GIRL
...YOU'RE JUST A TATTLE-TELLING SNEAKER!
IT'S YOUR FAULT I HAVE TO CLEAN THE HOUSE FOR THE NEXT MONTH...
...AND I CAN'T USE MY COMPUTER, EITHER!
WHEN IT COMES TO BIG SNEAKS, YOU'RE SO BIG, YOU'RE OFF-THE-SCALE BIG!
NOT TRUE! NOT TRUE! NOT TRUUUE!
I'D RATHER LEAVE THE HOUSE THAN STAY INSIDE WITH THE QUEEN OF BIG SNEAKS!
???
I KNEW SHE WAS WRONG!
MY WEIGHT IS NOT OFF-THE-SCALE!
CAZENOVE & WILLIAM

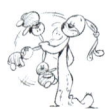

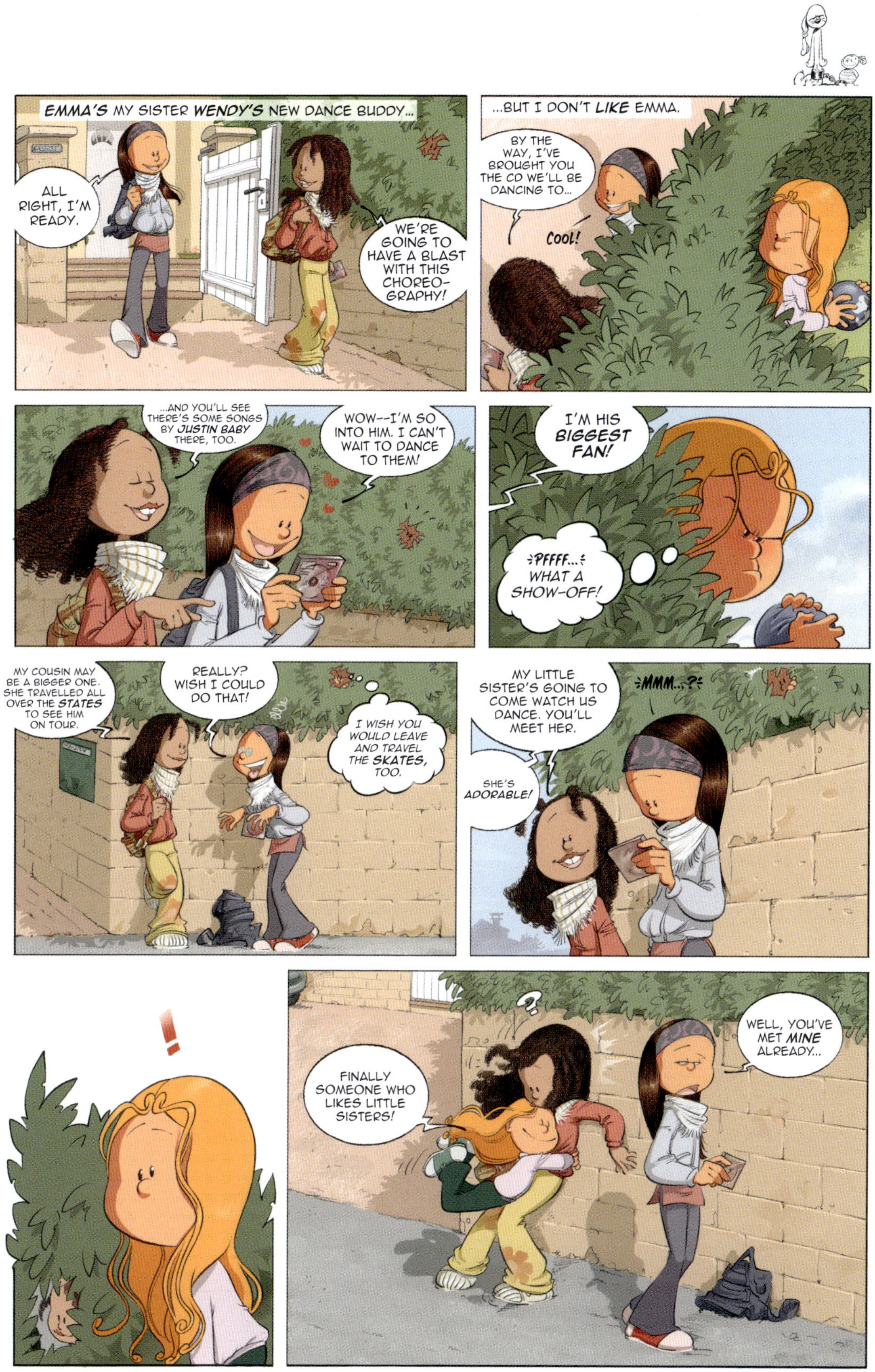
EMMA'S MY SISTER WENDY'S NEW DANCE BUDDY...
ALL RIGHT, I'M READY.
WE'RE GOING TO HAVE A BLAST WITH THIS CHOREO-GRAPHY!
...BUT I DON'T LIKE EMMA.
BY THE WAY, I'VE BROUGHT YOU THE CD WE'LL BE DANCING TO...
COOL!
...AND YOU'LL SEE THERE'S SOME SONGS BY JUSTIN BABY THERE, TOO.
WOW--I'M SO INTO HIM. I CAN'T WAIT TO DANCE TO THEM!
I'M HIS BIGGEST FAN!
PFFFF... WHAT A SHOW-OFF!
MY COUSIN MAY BE A BIGGER ONE. SHE TRAVELLED ALL OVER THE STATES TO SEE HIM ON TOUR.
REALLY? WISH I COULD DO THAT!
I WISH YOU WOULD LEAVE AND TRAVEL THE SKATES, TOO.
MY LITTLE SISTER'S GOING TO COME WATCH US DANCE. YOU'LL MEET HER.
MMM..?
SHE'S ADORABLE!
!
?
FINALLY SOMEONE WHO LIKES LITTLE SISTERS!
WELL, YOU'VE MET MINE ALREADY...
CAZENOVE & WILLIAM

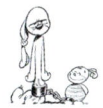

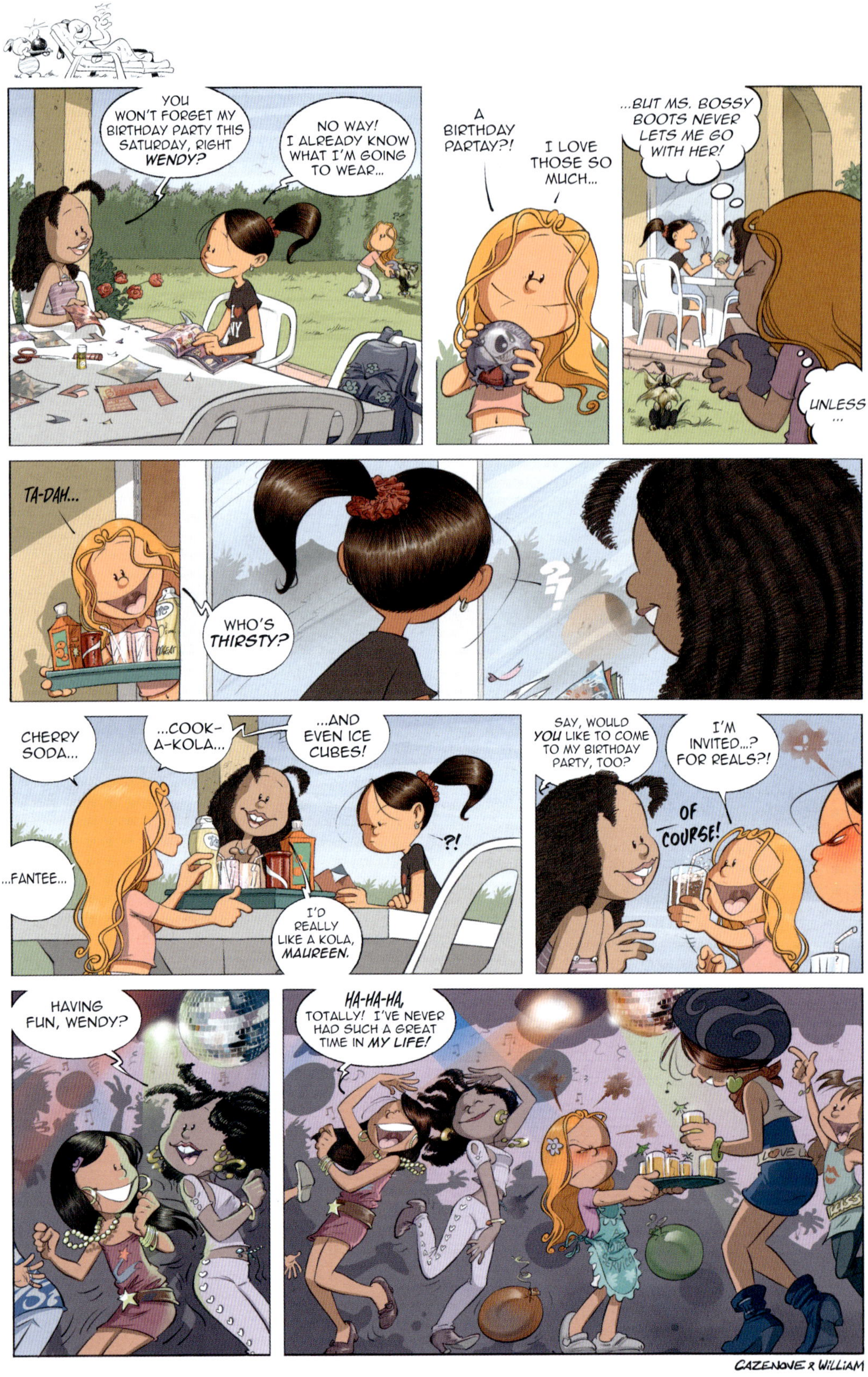
YOU WON'T FORGET MY BIRTHDAY PARTY THIS SATURDAY, RIGHT WENDY?
NO WAY! I ALREADY KNOW WHAT I'M GOING TO WEAR...
A BIRTHDAY PARTAY?!
I LOVE THOSE SO MUCH...
...BUT MS. BOSSY BOOTS NEVER LETS ME GO WITH HER!
UNLESS ...
TA-DAH...
WHO'S THIRSTY?
CHERRY SODA...
...COOK-A-KOLA...
...AND EVEN ICE CUBES!
...FANTEE...
I'D REALLY LIKE A KOLA, MAUREEN.
SAY, WOULD YOU LIKE TO COME TO MY BIRTHDAY PARTY, TOO?
I'M INVITED...? FOR REALS?!
OF COURSE!
HAVING FUN, WENDY?
HA-HA-HA, TOTALLY! I'VE NEVER HAD SUCH A GREAT TIME IN MY LIFE!
CAZENOVE & WILLIAM

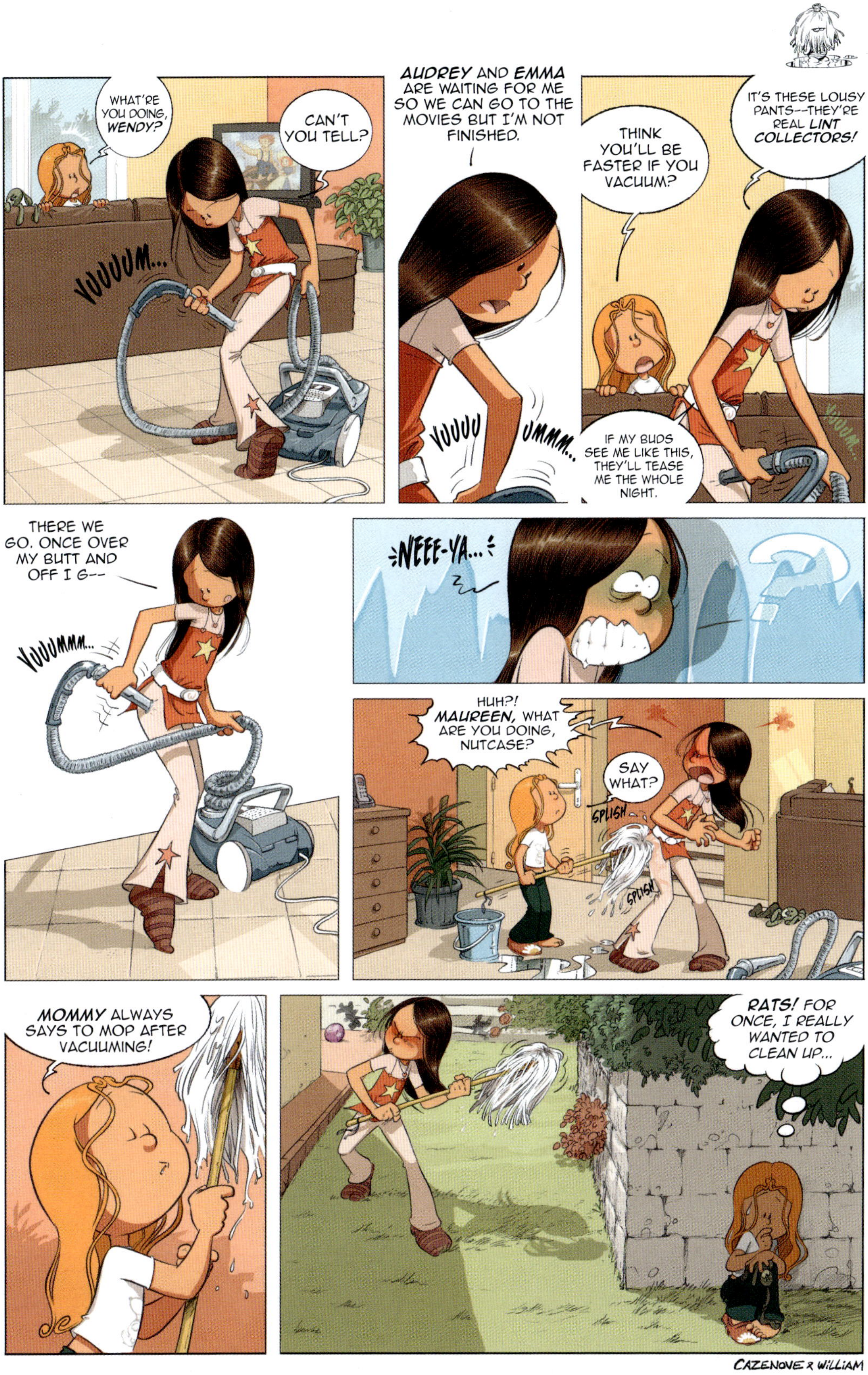
WHAT'RE YOU DOING, WENDY?
CAN'T YOU TELL?
VUUUUM...
AUDREY AND EMMA ARE WAITING FOR ME SO WE CAN GO TO THE MOVIES BUT I'M NOT FINISHED.
VUUUU UMMM...
THINK YOU'LL BE FASTER IF YOU VACUUM?
IT'S THESE LOUSY PANTS--THEY'RE REAL LINT COLLECTORS!
IF MY BUDS SEE ME LIKE THIS, THEY'LL TEASE ME THE WHOLE NIGHT.
VUUUM...
THERE WE GO. ONCE OVER MY BUTT AND OFF I G--
VUUUMMM...
NEEE-YA...
HUH?! MAUREEN, WHAT ARE YOU DOING, NUTCASE?
SAY WHAT?
SPLISH
SPLISH
MOMMY ALWAYS SAYS TO MOP AFTER VACUUMING!
RATS! FOR ONCE, I REALLY WANTED TO CLEAN UP...
CAZENOVE & WILLIAM

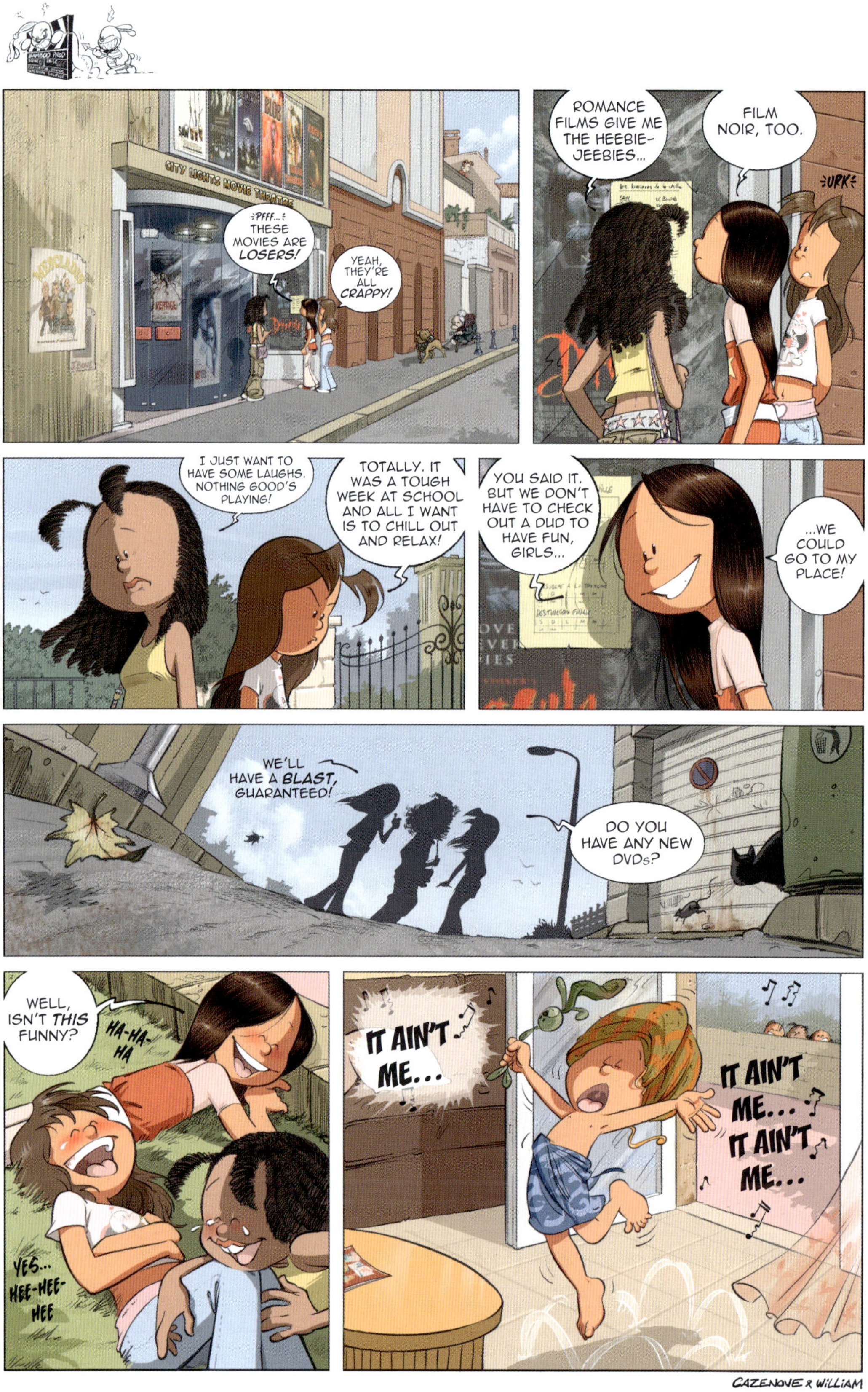
CITY LIGHTS MOVIE THEATRE
PFFF... THESE MOVIES ARE LOSERS!
YEAH, THEY'RE ALL CRAPPY!
ROMANCE FILMS GIVE ME THE HEEBIE-JEEBIES...
FILM NOIR, TOO.
URK
I JUST WANT TO HAVE SOME LAUGHS. NOTHING GOOD'S PLAYING!
TOTALLY. IT WAS A TOUGH WEEK AT SCHOOL AND ALL I WANT IS TO CHILL OUT AND RELAX!
YOU SAID IT. BUT WE DON'T HAVE TO CHECK OUT A DUD TO HAVE FUN, GIRLS...
...WE COULD GO TO MY PLACE!
WE'LL HAVE A BLAST, GUARANTEED!
DO YOU HAVE ANY NEW DVDs?
WELL, ISN'T THIS FUNNY?
HA-HA-HA
YES... HEE-HEE-HEE
IT AIN'T ME...
IT AIN'T ME... IT AIN'T ME...
CAZENOVE & WILLIAM

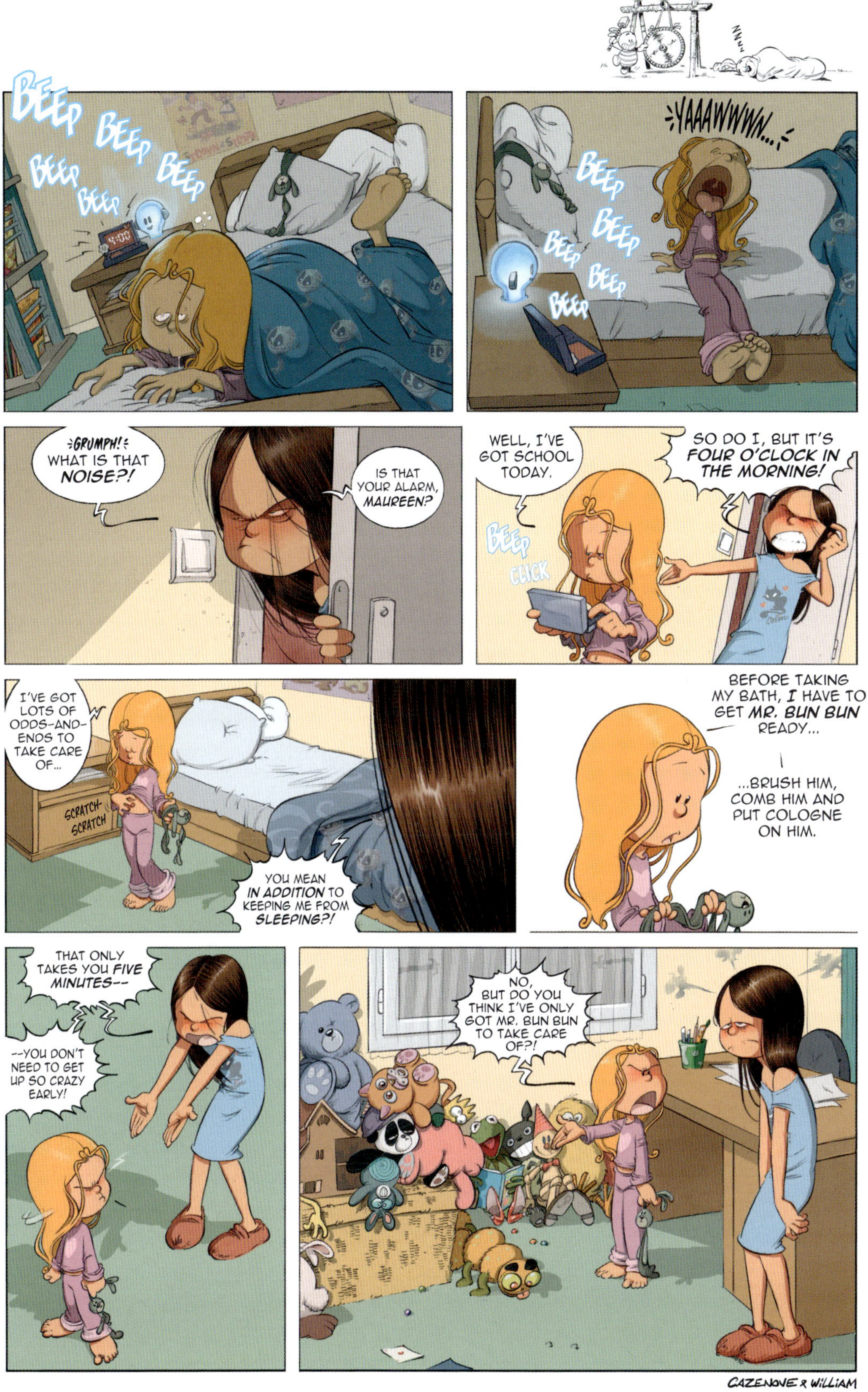
BEEP BEEP BEEP BEEP BEEP
YAAAWWWN...
BEEP BEEP BEEP BEEP BEEP
GRUMPH! WHAT IS THAT NOISE?!
IS THAT YOUR ALARM, MAUREEN?
WELL, I'VE GOT SCHOOL TODAY.
SO DO I, BUT IT'S FOUR O'CLOCK IN THE MORNING!
BEEP
CLICK
I'VE GOT LOTS OF ODDS-AND-ENDS TO TAKE CARE OF...
SCRATCH-SCRATCH
YOU MEAN IN ADDITION TO KEEPING ME FROM SLEEPING?!
BEFORE TAKING MY BATH, I HAVE TO GET MR. BUN BUN READY...
...BRUSH HIM, COMB HIM AND PUT COLOGNE ON HIM.
THAT ONLY TAKES YOU FIVE MINUTES--
--YOU DON'T NEED TO GET UP SO CRAZY EARLY!
NO, BUT DO YOU THINK I'VE ONLY GOT MR. BUN BUN TO TAKE CARE OF?!
CAZENOVE & WILLIAM

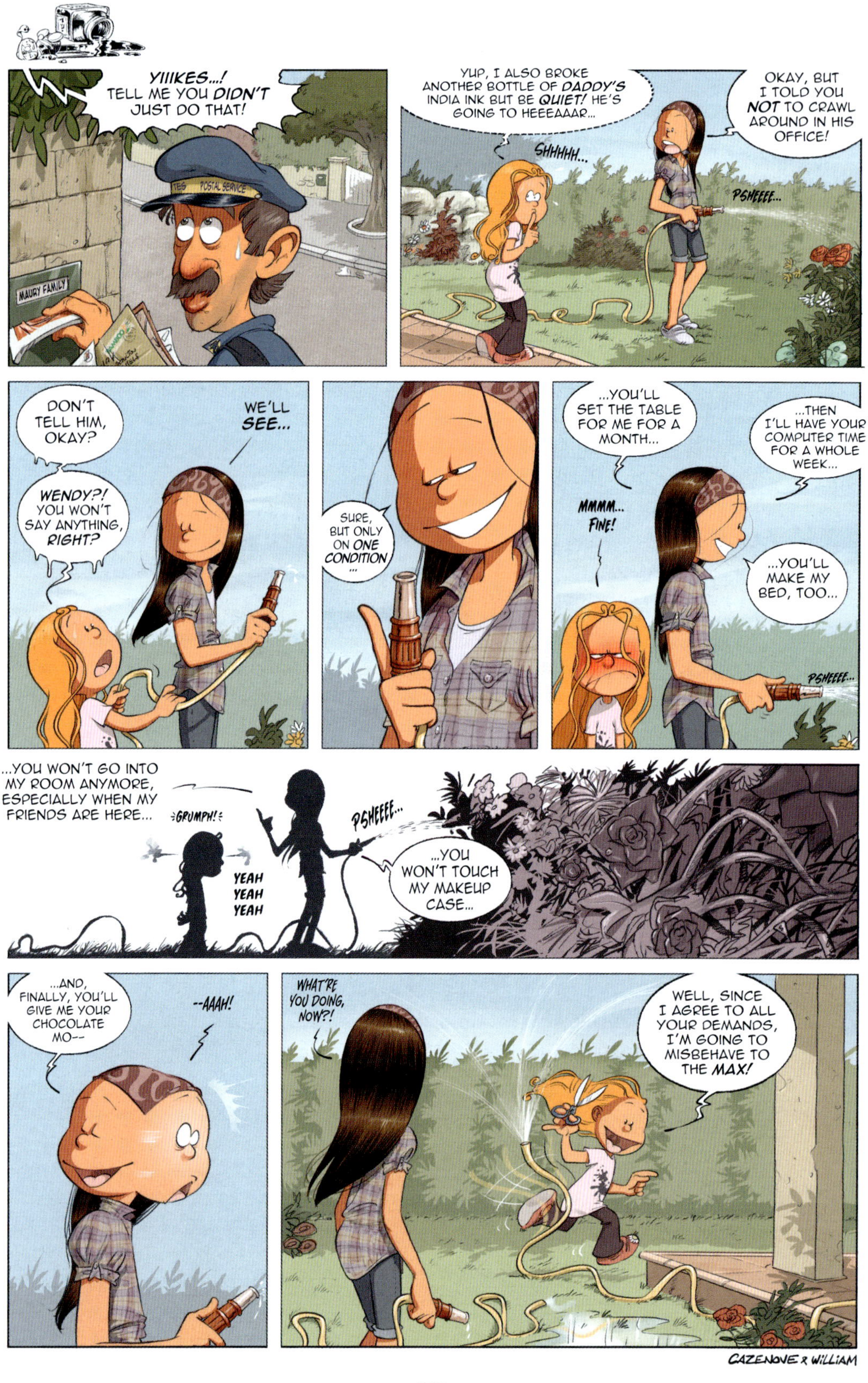
YIIKES...!
TELL ME YOU DIDN'T JUST DO THAT!
MAURY FAMILY
POSTAL SERVICE
YUP, I ALSO BROKE ANOTHER BOTTLE OF DADDY'S INDIA INK BUT BE QUIET! HE'S GOING TO HEEEAAAR...
SHHHHH...
OKAY, BUT I TOLD YOU NOT TO CRAWL AROUND IN HIS OFFICE!
PSHEEEE...
DON'T TELL HIM, OKAY?
WE'LL SEE...
WENDY?! YOU WON'T SAY ANYTHING, RIGHT?
SURE, BUT ONLY ON ONE CONDITION...
...YOU'LL SET THE TABLE FOR ME FOR A MONTH...
...THEN I'LL HAVE YOUR COMPUTER TIME FOR A WHOLE WEEK...
MMMM... FINE!
...YOU'LL MAKE MY BED, TOO...
PSHEEEE...
...YOU WON'T GO INTO MY ROOM ANYMORE, ESPECIALLY WHEN MY FRIENDS ARE HERE...
GRUMPH!
PSHEEEE...
YEAH YEAH YEAH
...YOU WON'T TOUCH MY MAKEUP CASE...
...AND, FINALLY, YOU'LL GIVE ME YOUR CHOCOLATE MO--
--AAAH!
WHAT'RE YOU DOING, NOW?!
WELL, SINCE I AGREE TO ALL YOUR DEMANDS, I'M GOING TO MISBEHAVE TO THE MAX!
CAZENOVE & WILLIAM

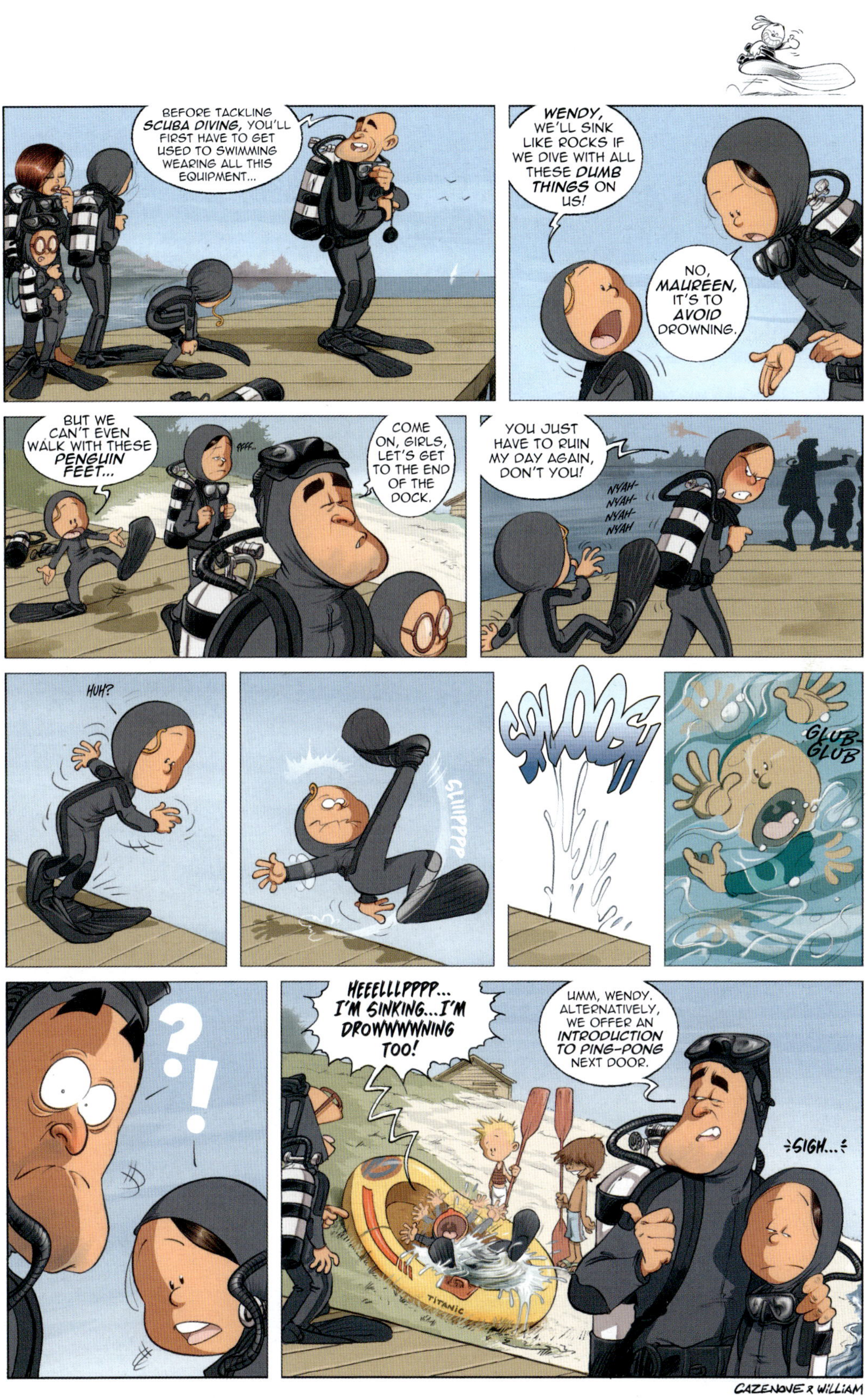

BEFORE TACKLING SCUBA DIVING, YOU'LL FIRST HAVE TO GET USED TO SWIMMING WEARING ALL THIS EQUIPMENT...
WENDY, WE'LL SINK LIKE ROCKS IF WE DIVE WITH ALL THESE DUMB THINGS ON US!
NO, MAUREEN, IT'S TO AVOID DROWNING.
BUT WE CAN'T EVEN WALK WITH THESE PENGUIN FEET...
PFFF...
COME ON, GIRLS, LET'S GET TO THE END OF THE DOCK.
YOU JUST HAVE TO RUIN MY DAY AGAIN, DON'T YOU!
NYAH-NYAH-NYAH-NYAH
HUH?
SLIIPPPP
SPLOOSH
GLUB-GLUB
?!
HEEELLLPPPP... I'M SINKING...I'M DROWWWWNING TOO!
UMM, WENDY. ALTERNATIVELY, WE OFFER AN INTRODUCTION TO PING-PONG NEXT DOOR.
SIGH...
TITANIC
CAZENOVE & WILLIAM

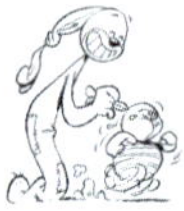

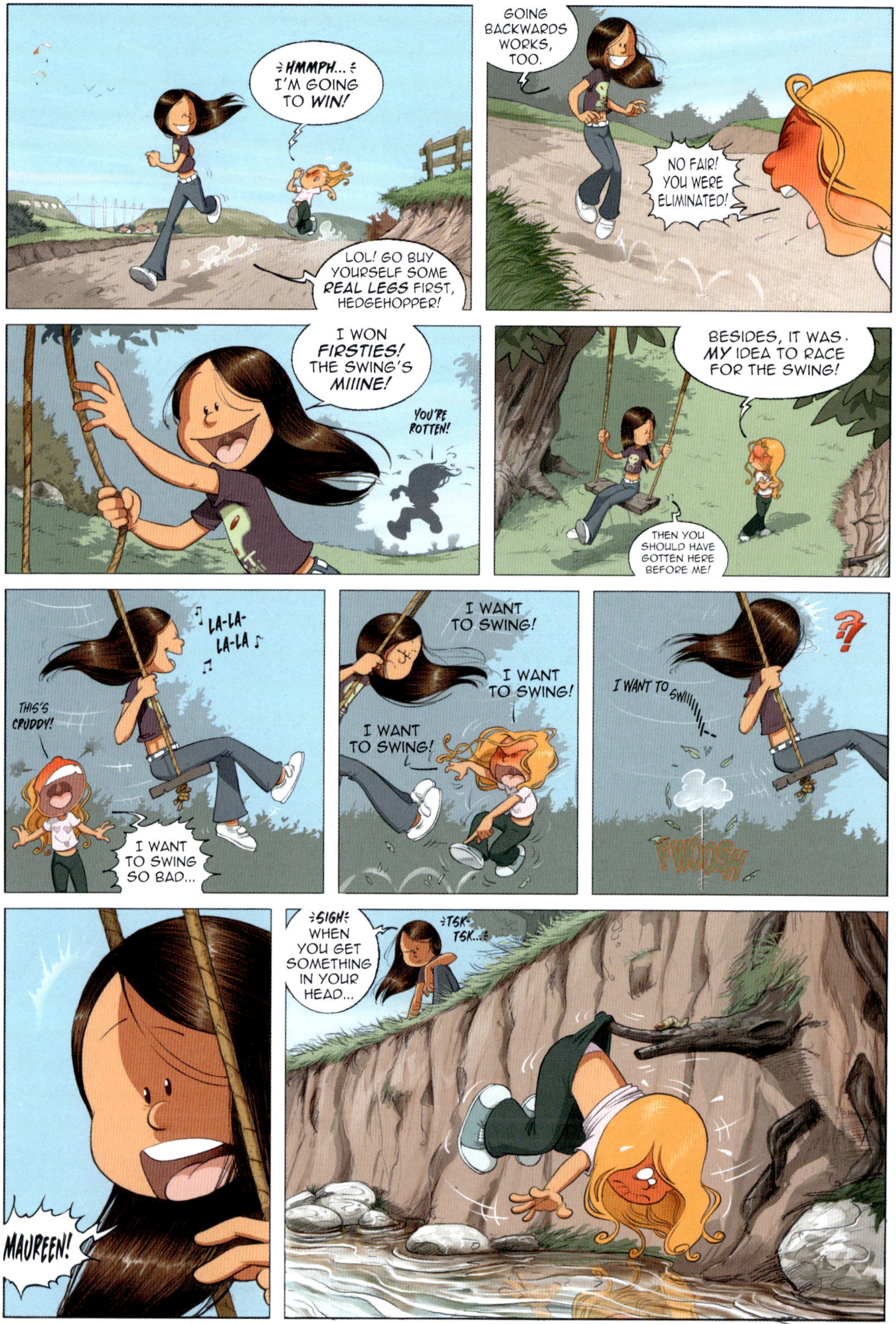
HMMPH... I'M GOING TO WIN!
LOL! GO BUY YOURSELF SOME REAL LEGS FIRST, HEDGEHOPPER!
GOING BACKWARDS WORKS, TOO.
NO FAIR! YOU WERE ELIMINATED!
I WON FIRSTIES! THE SWING'S MIIINE!
YOU'RE ROTTEN!
BESIDES, IT WAS MY IDEA TO RACE FOR THE SWING!
THEN YOU SHOULD HAVE GOTTEN HERE BEFORE ME!
LA-LA-LA-LA
THIS'S CRUDDY!
I WANT TO SWING SO BAD...
I WANT TO SWING!
I WANT TO SWING!
I WANT TO SWING!
I WANT TO SWIIIIIII--
?!
FWOOSH
MAUREEN!
SIGH WHEN YOU GET SOMETHING IN YOUR HEAD...
TSK TSK...

CAZENOVE & WILLIAM

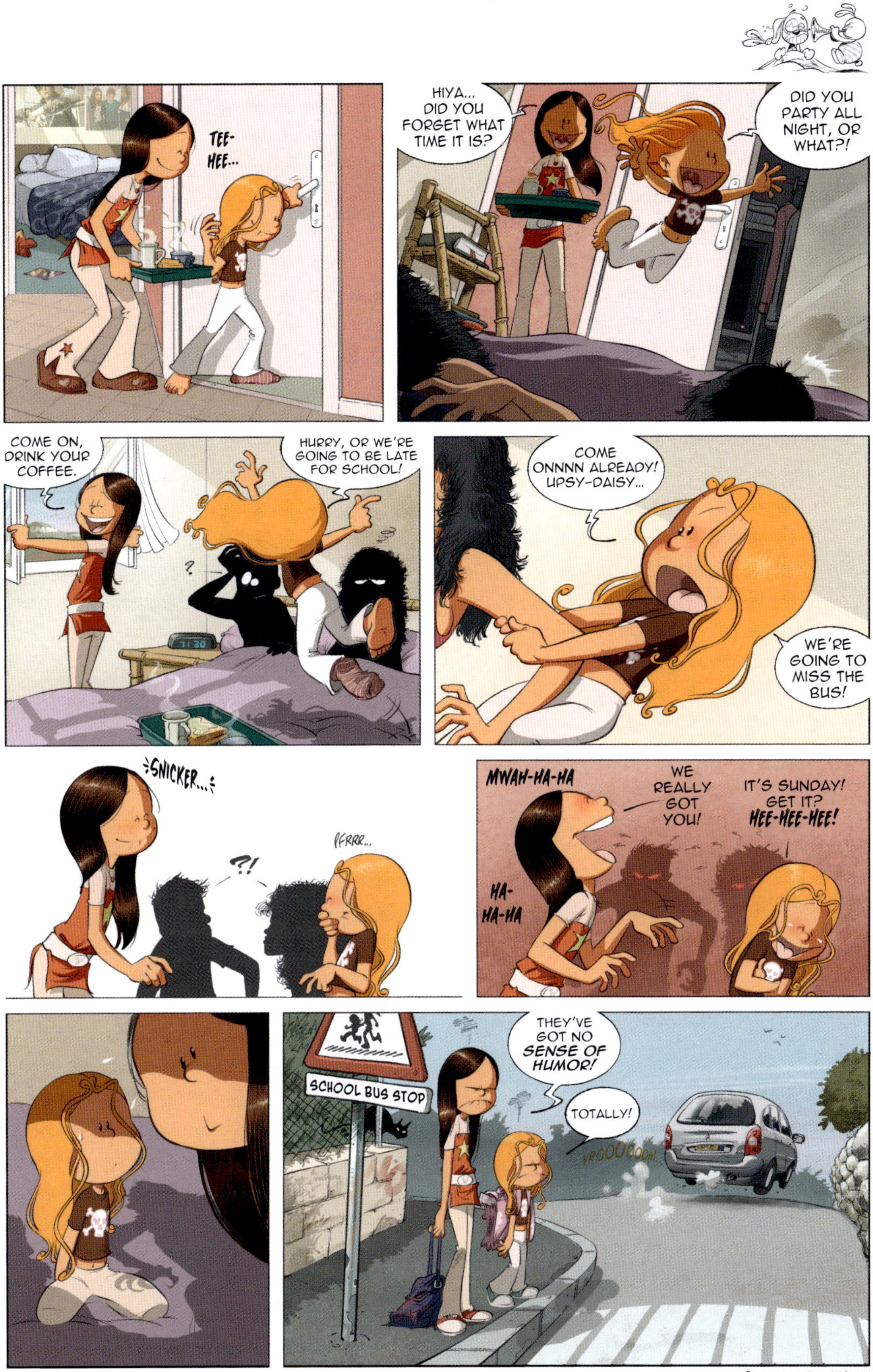
TEE-HEE...
HIYA... DID YOU FORGET WHAT TIME IT IS?
DID YOU PARTY ALL NIGHT, OR WHAT?!
COME ON, DRINK YOUR COFFEE.
HURRY, OR WE'RE GOING TO BE LATE FOR SCHOOL!
?
COME ONNNN ALREADY! UPSY-DAISY...
WE'RE GOING TO MISS THE BUS!
SNICKER...
?!
PFRRR...
MWAH-HA-HA
HA-HA-HA
WE REALLY GOT YOU!
IT'S SUNDAY! GET IT? HEE-HEE-HEE!
SCHOOL BUS STOP
THEY'VE GOT NO SENSE OF HUMOR!
TOTALLY!
VROOOOOOM...

CAZENOVE & WILLIAM

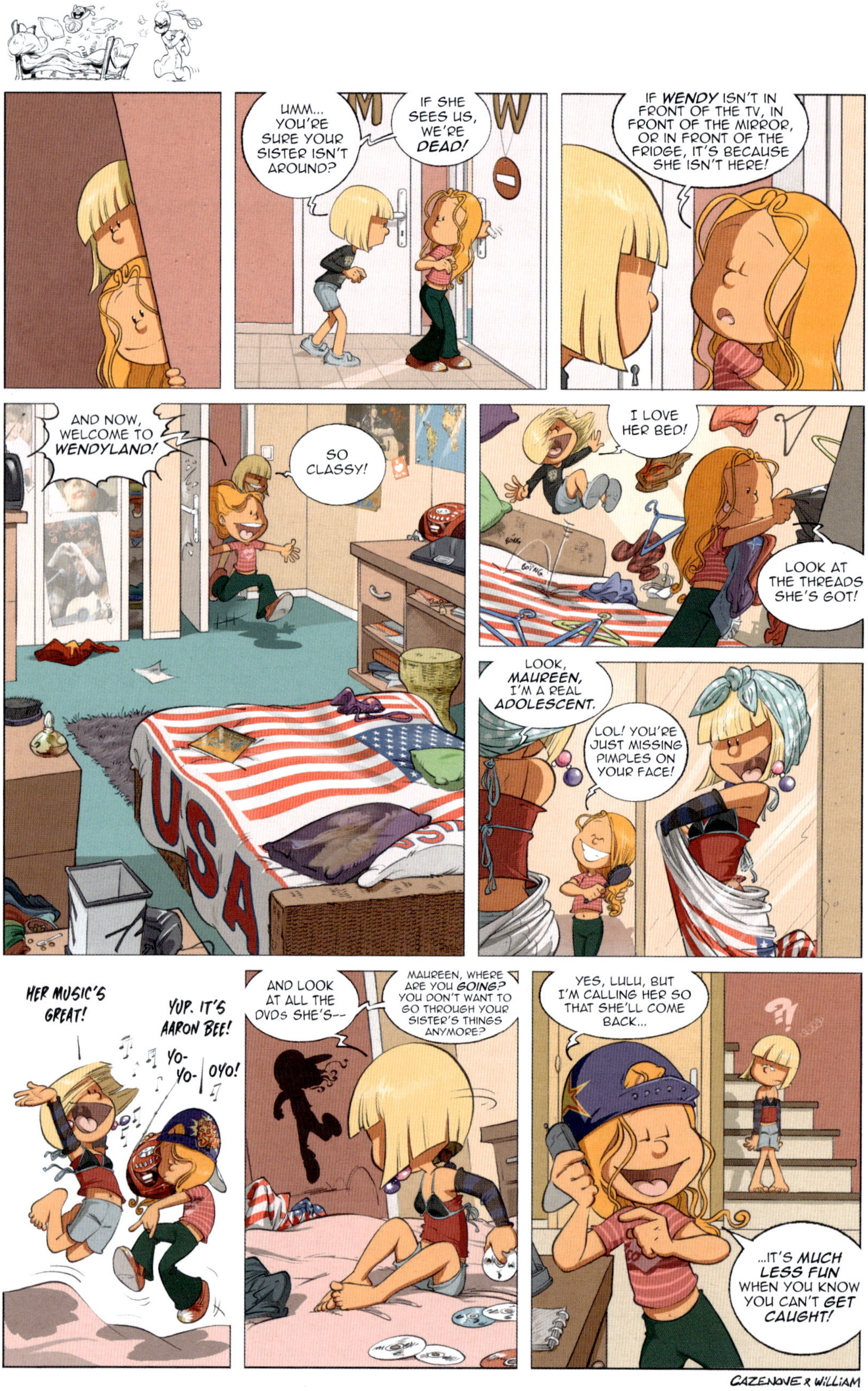
UMM... YOU'RE SURE YOUR SISTER ISN'T AROUND?
IF SHE SEES US, WE'RE DEAD!
IF WENDY ISN'T IN FRONT OF THE TV, IN FRONT OF THE MIRROR, OR IN FRONT OF THE FRIDGE, IT'S BECAUSE SHE ISN'T HERE!
AND NOW, WELCOME TO WENDYLAND!
SO CLASSY!
I LOVE HER BED!
BOING
BOING
LOOK AT THE THREADS SHE'S GOT!
LOOK, MAUREEN, I'M A REAL ADOLESCENT.
LOL! YOU'RE JUST MISSING PIMPLES ON YOUR FACE!
HER MUSIC'S GREAT!
YUP. IT'S AARON BEE!
YO-YO-OYO!
AND LOOK AT ALL THE DVDS SHE'S--
MAUREEN, WHERE ARE YOU GOING? YOU DON'T WANT TO GO THROUGH YOUR SISTER'S THINGS ANYMORE?
YES, LULU, BUT I'M CALLING HER SO THAT SHE'LL COME BACK...
...IT'S MUCH LESS FUN WHEN YOU KNOW YOU CAN'T GET CAUGHT!
CAZENOVE & WILLIAM

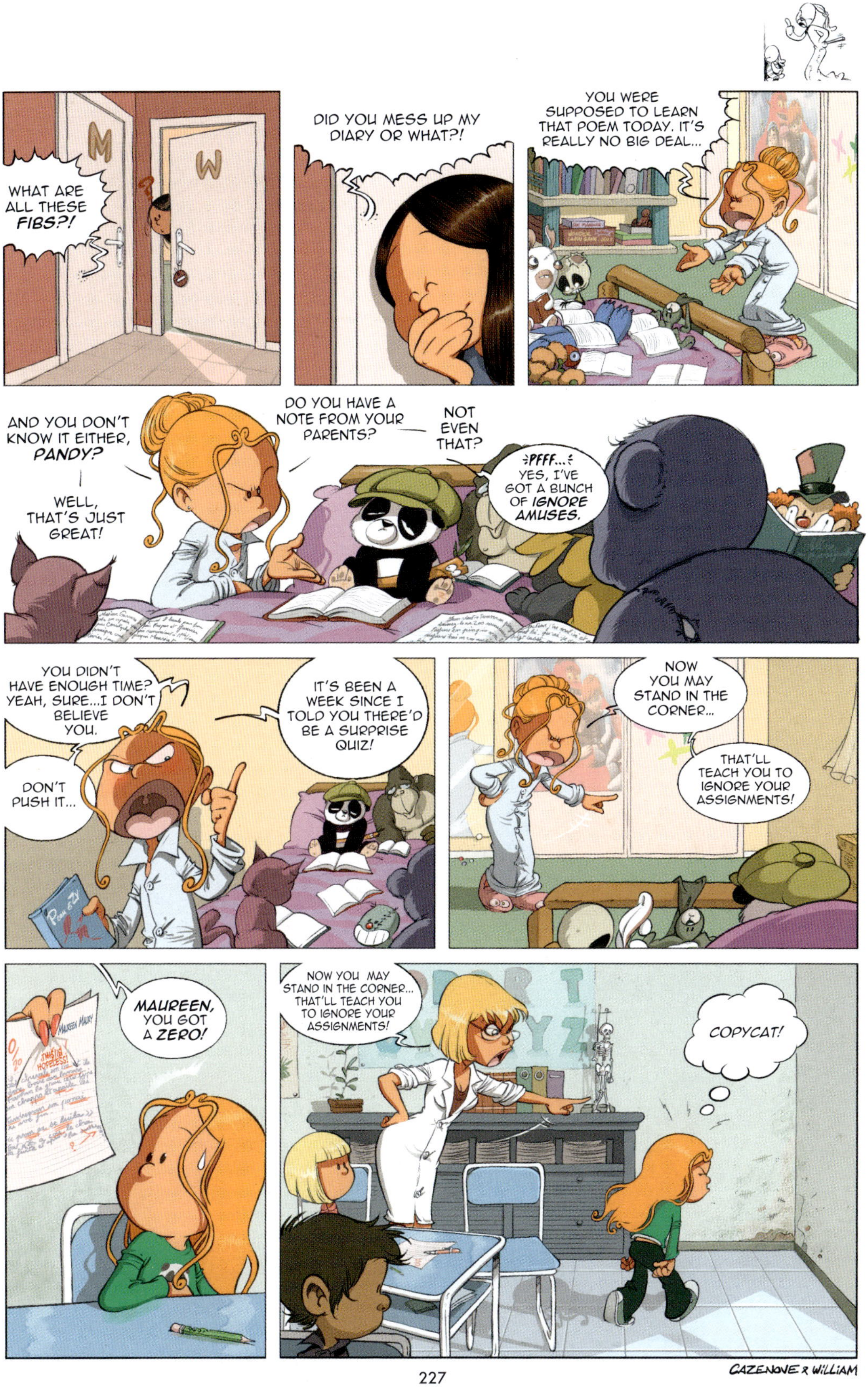
WHAT ARE ALL THESE FIBS?!
DID YOU MESS UP MY DIARY OR WHAT?!
YOU WERE SUPPOSED TO LEARN THAT POEM TODAY. IT'S REALLY NO BIG DEAL...
AND YOU DON'T KNOW IT EITHER, PANDY?
WELL, THAT'S JUST GREAT!
DO YOU HAVE A NOTE FROM YOUR PARENTS?
NOT EVEN THAT?
PFFF... YES, I'VE GOT A BUNCH OF IGNORE AMUSES.
YOU DIDN'T HAVE ENOUGH TIME? YEAH, SURE...I DON'T BELIEVE YOU.
DON'T PUSH IT...
IT'S BEEN A WEEK SINCE I TOLD YOU THERE'D BE A SURPRISE QUIZ!
NOW YOU MAY STAND IN THE CORNER...
THAT'LL TEACH YOU TO IGNORE YOUR ASSIGNMENTS!
MAUREEN, YOU GOT A ZERO!
NOW YOU MAY STAND IN THE CORNER... THAT'LL TEACH YOU TO IGNORE YOUR ASSIGNMENTS!
COPYCAT!
CAZENOVE & WILLIAM

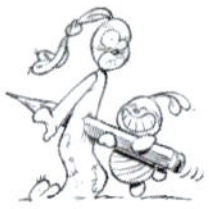

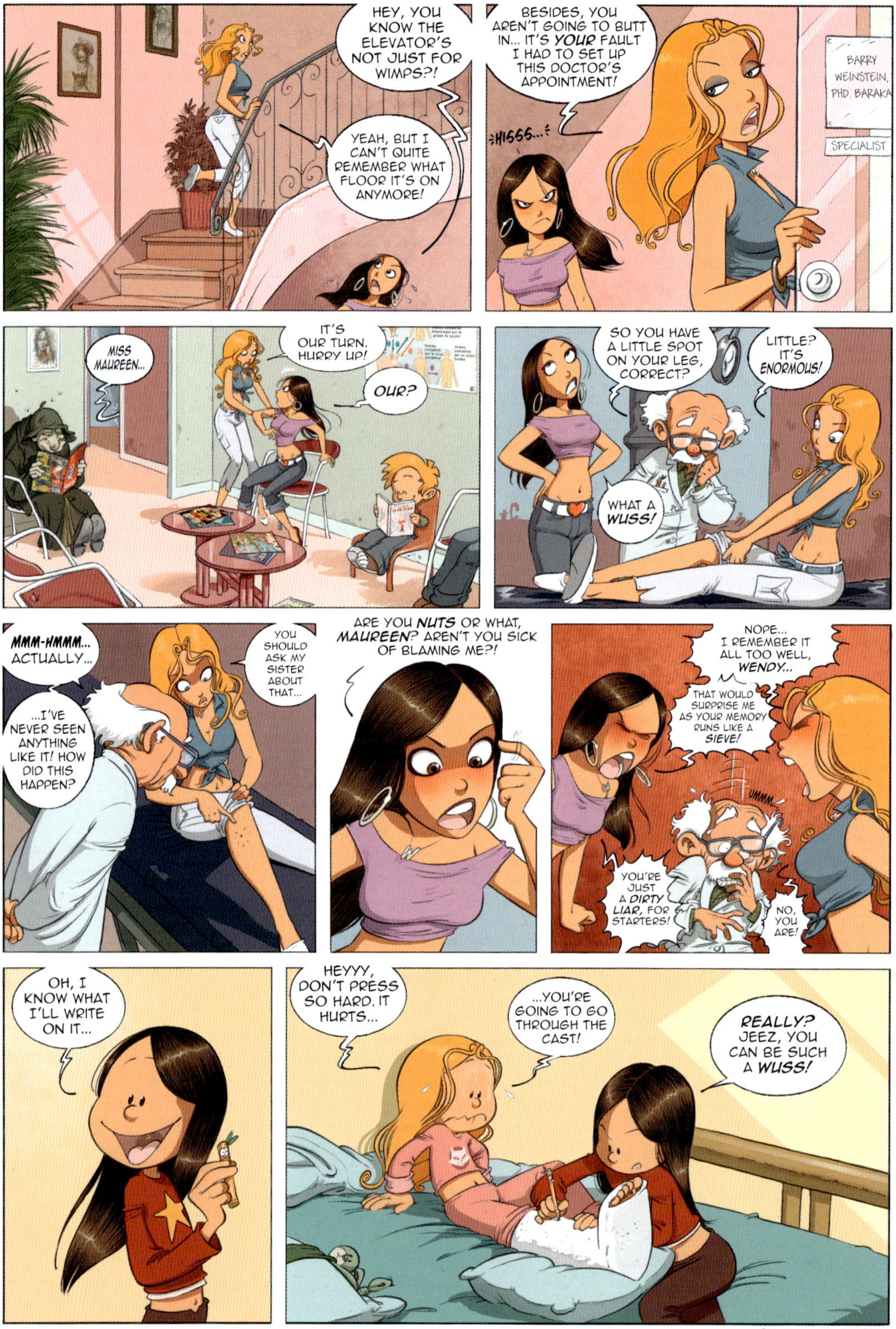
HEY, YOU KNOW THE ELEVATOR'S NOT JUST FOR WIMPS?!
YEAH, BUT I CAN'T QUITE REMEMBER WHAT FLOOR IT'S ON ANYMORE!
BESIDES, YOU AREN'T GOING TO BUTT IN... IT'S YOUR FAULT I HAD TO SET UP THIS DOCTOR'S APPOINTMENT!
HISSS...
BARRY WEINSTEIN, PHD. BARAKA
SPECIALIST
MISS MAUREEN...
IT'S OUR TURN. HURRY UP!
OUR?
SO YOU HAVE A LITTLE SPOT ON YOUR LEG, CORRECT?
LITTLE? IT'S ENORMOUS!
WHAT A WUSS!
MMM-HMMM... ACTUALLY...
...I'VE NEVER SEEN ANYTHING LIKE IT! HOW DID THIS HAPPEN?
YOU SHOULD ASK MY SISTER ABOUT THAT...
ARE YOU NUTS OR WHAT, MAUREEN? AREN'T YOU SICK OF BLAMING ME?!
NOPE... I REMEMBER IT ALL TOO WELL, WENDY...
THAT WOULD SURPRISE ME AS YOUR MEMORY RUNS LIKE A SIEVE!
UMMM...
YOU'RE JUST A DIRTY LIAR, FOR STARTERS!
NO, YOU ARE!
OH, I KNOW WHAT I'LL WRITE ON IT...
HEYYY, DON'T PRESS SO HARD. IT HURTS...
...YOU'RE GOING TO GO THROUGH THE CAST!
REALLY? JEEZ, YOU CAN BE SUCH A WUSS!

CAZENOVE & WILLIAM

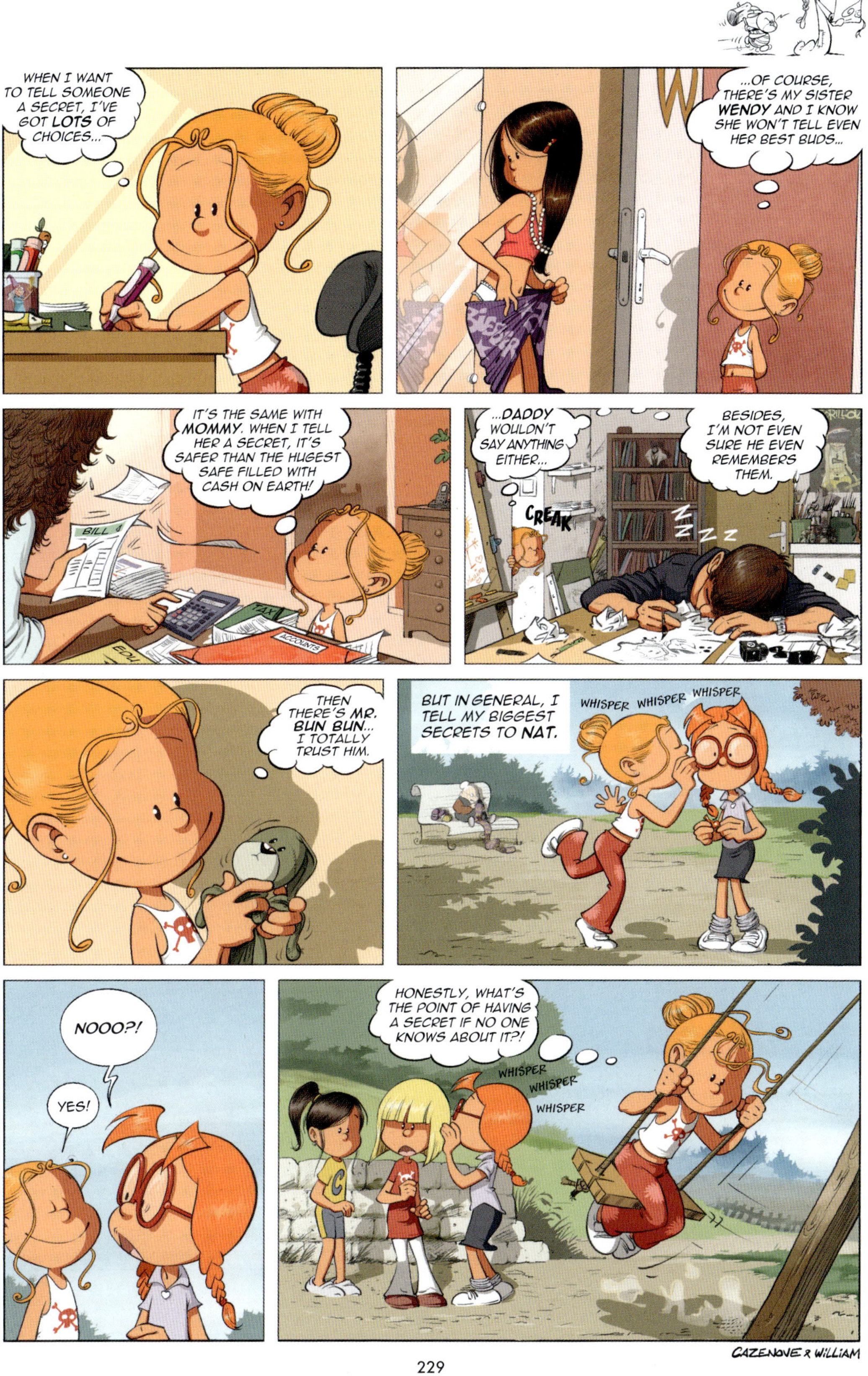
WHEN I WANT TO TELL SOMEONE A SECRET, I'VE GOT LOTS OF CHOICES...
...OF COURSE, THERE'S MY SISTER WENDY AND I KNOW SHE WON'T TELL EVEN HER BEST BUDS...
IT'S THE SAME WITH MOMMY. WHEN I TELL HER A SECRET, IT'S SAFER THAN THE HUGEST SAFE FILLED WITH CASH ON EARTH!
BILL
TAX
ACCOUNTS
...DADDY WOULDN'T SAY ANYTHING EITHER...
CREAK
BESIDES, I'M NOT EVEN SURE HE EVEN REMEMBERS THEM.
THEN THERE'S MR. BUN BUN... I TOTALLY TRUST HIM.
BUT IN GENERAL, I TELL MY BIGGEST SECRETS TO NAT.
WHISPER WHISPER WHISPER
NOOO?!
YES!
HONESTLY, WHAT'S THE POINT OF HAVING A SECRET IF NO ONE KNOWS ABOUT IT?!
WHISPER
WHISPER
WHISPER
CAZENOVE & WILLIAM

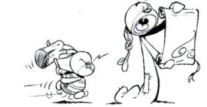

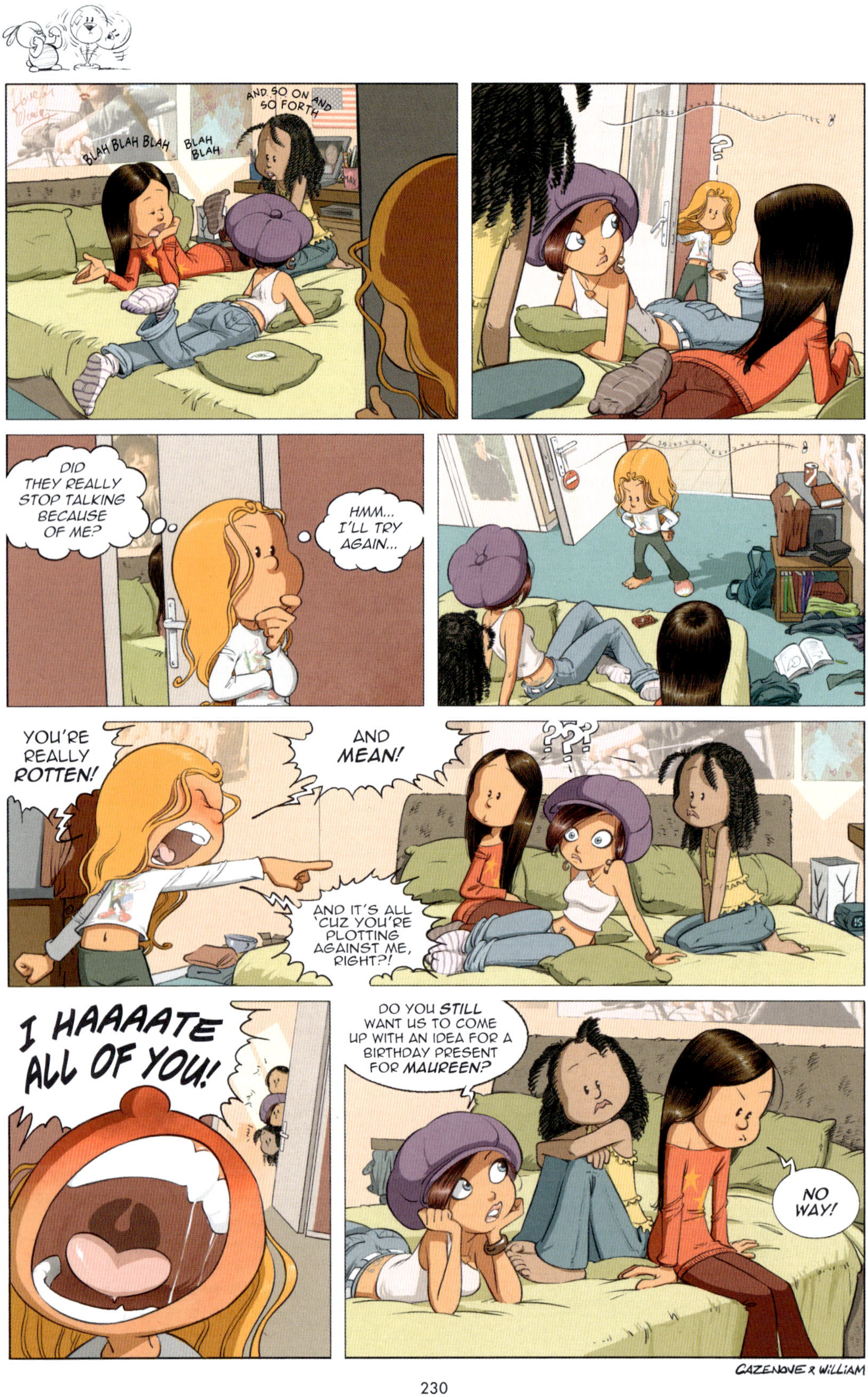
BLAH BLAH BLAH
BLAH BLAH
AND SO ON AND SO FORTH
?
DID THEY REALLY STOP TALKING BECAUSE OF ME?
HMM... I'LL TRY AGAIN...
YOU'RE REALLY ROTTEN!
AND MEAN!
AND IT'S ALL 'CUZ YOU'RE PLOTTING AGAINST ME, RIGHT?!
???
I HAAAATE ALL OF YOU!
DO YOU STILL WANT US TO COME UP WITH AN IDEA FOR A BIRTHDAY PRESENT FOR MAUREEN?
NO WAY!
CAZENOVE & WILLIAM

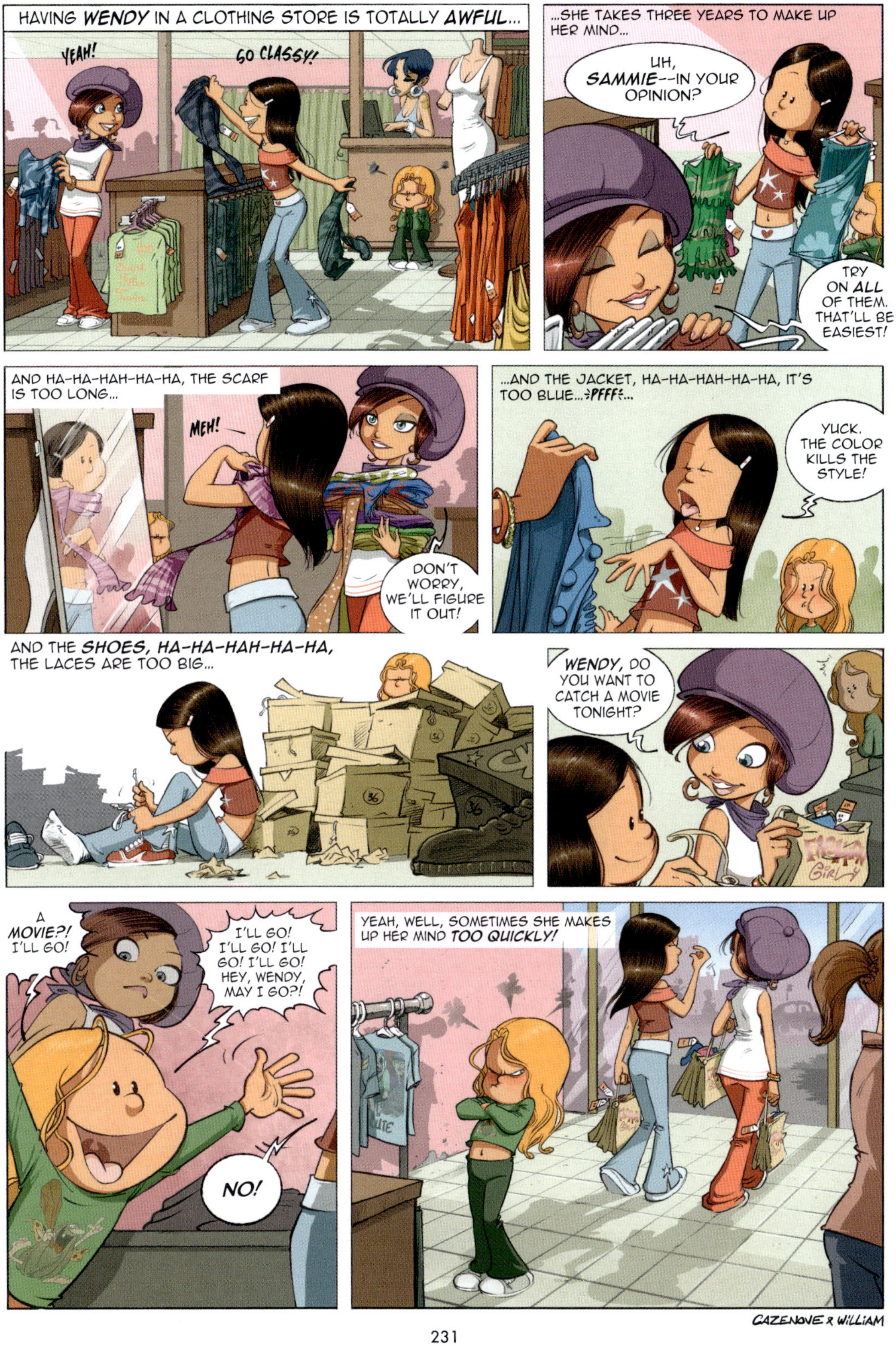

HAVING **WENDY** IN A CLOTHING STORE IS TOTALLY **AWFUL**...
YEAH!
SO CLASSY!
...SHE TAKES THREE YEARS TO MAKE UP HER MIND...
UH, **SAMMIE**--IN YOUR OPINION?
TRY ON **ALL** OF THEM. THAT'LL BE EASIEST!
AND HA-HA-HAH-HA-HA, THE SCARF IS TOO LONG...
MEH!
DON'T WORRY, WE'LL FIGURE IT OUT!
...AND THE JACKET, HA-HA-HAH-HA-HA, IT'S TOO BLUE...PFFF...
YUCK. THE COLOR KILLS THE STYLE!
AND THE **SHOES, HA-HA-HAH-HA-HA,** THE LACES ARE TOO BIG...
WENDY, DO YOU WANT TO CATCH A MOVIE TONIGHT?
A **MOVIE?!** I'LL GO!
I'LL GO! I'LL GO! I'LL GO! I'LL GO! HEY, WENDY, MAY I GO?!
NO!
YEAH, WELL, SOMETIMES SHE MAKES UP HER MIND **TOO QUICKLY!**
CAZENOVE & WILLIAM

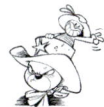

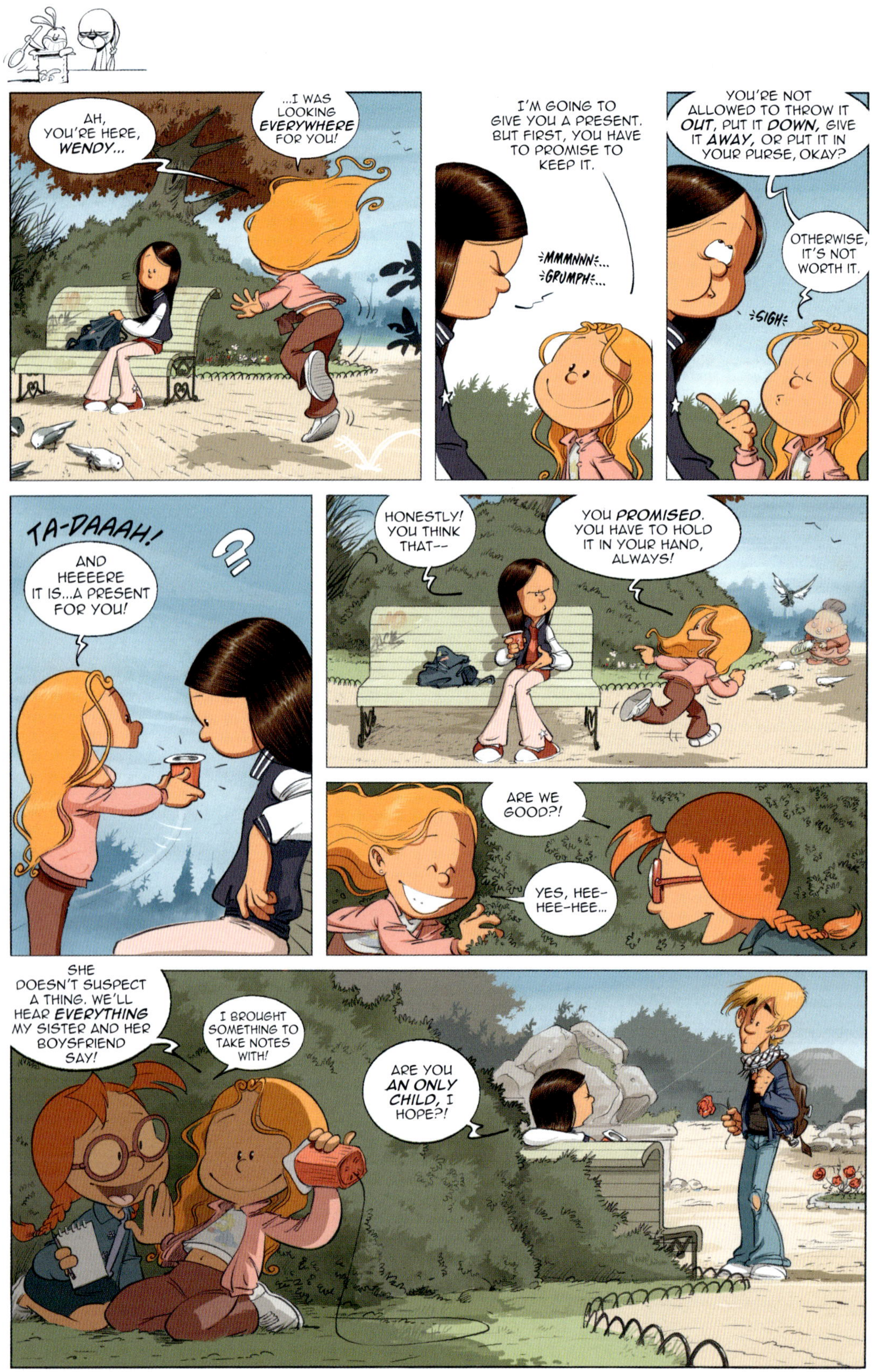
AH, YOU'RE HERE, WENDY...
...I WAS LOOKING EVERYWHERE FOR YOU!
I'M GOING TO GIVE YOU A PRESENT. BUT FIRST, YOU HAVE TO PROMISE TO KEEP IT.
MMMNNN...
GRUMPH...
YOU'RE NOT ALLOWED TO THROW IT OUT, PUT IT DOWN, GIVE IT AWAY, OR PUT IT IN YOUR PURSE, OKAY?
OTHERWISE, IT'S NOT WORTH IT.
SIGH
TA-DAAAH!
AND HEEEERE IT IS...A PRESENT FOR YOU!
?!
HONESTLY! YOU THINK THAT--
YOU PROMISED. YOU HAVE TO HOLD IT IN YOUR HAND, ALWAYS!
ARE WE GOOD?!
YES, HEE-HEE-HEE...
SHE DOESN'T SUSPECT A THING. WE'LL HEAR EVERYTHING MY SISTER AND HER BOYSFRIEND SAY!
I BROUGHT SOMETHING TO TAKE NOTES WITH!
ARE YOU AN ONLY CHILD, I HOPE?!

CAZENOVE & WILLIAM

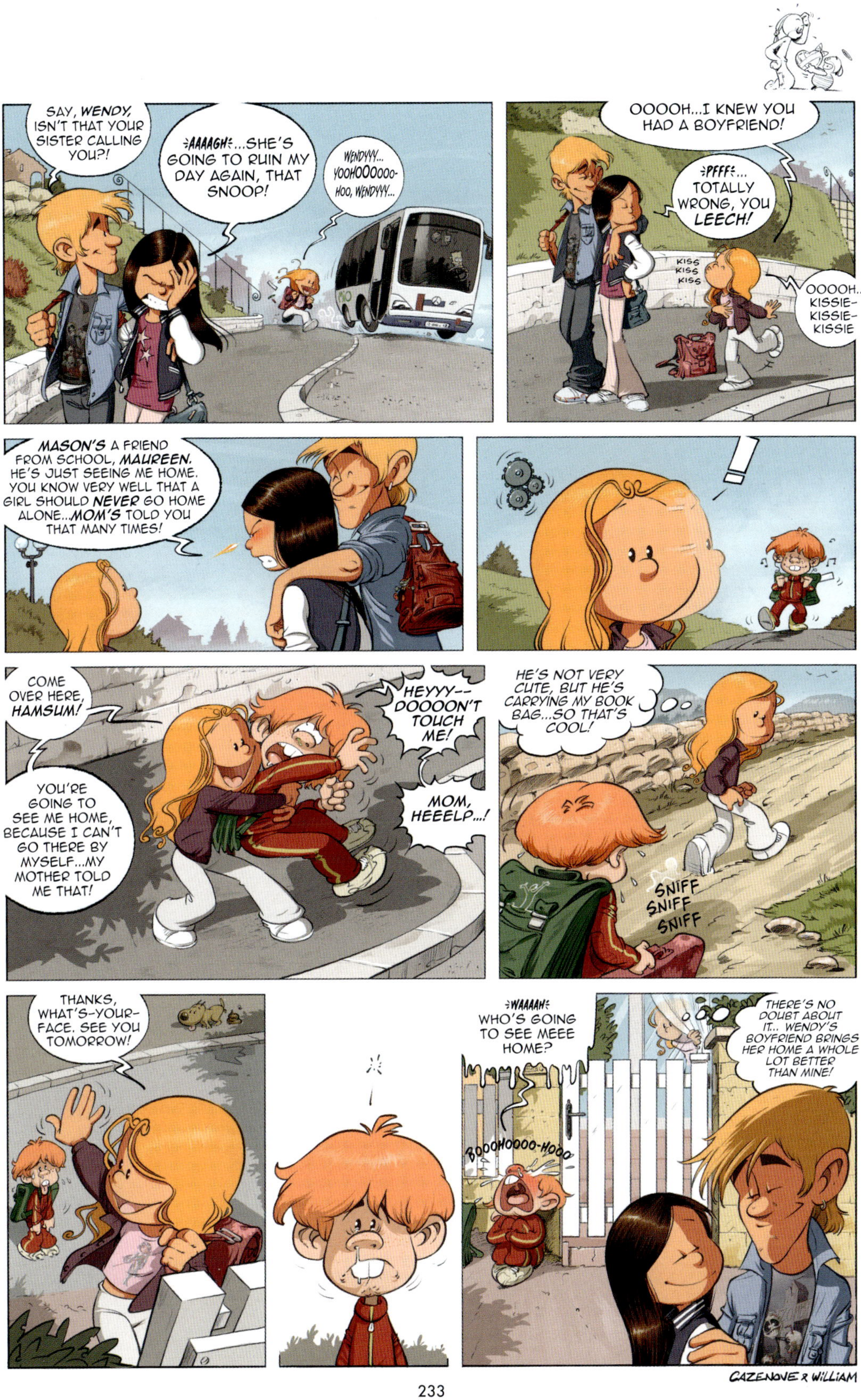
SAY, WENDY, ISN'T THAT YOUR SISTER CALLING YOU?!
AAAAGH...SHE'S GOING TO RUIN MY DAY AGAIN, THAT SNOOP!
WENDYYY... YOOHOOOOOO-HOO, WENDYYY...
OOOOH...I KNEW YOU HAD A BOYFRIEND!
PFFF... TOTALLY WRONG, YOU LEECH!
KISS KISS KISS
OOOOH... KISSIE-KISSIE-KISSIE
MASON'S A FRIEND FROM SCHOOL, MAUREEN. HE'S JUST SEEING ME HOME. YOU KNOW VERY WELL THAT A GIRL SHOULD NEVER GO HOME ALONE...MOM'S TOLD YOU THAT MANY TIMES!
COME OVER HERE, HAMSUM!
YOU'RE GOING TO SEE ME HOME, BECAUSE I CAN'T GO THERE BY MYSELF...MY MOTHER TOLD ME THAT!
HEYYY--DOOOON'T TOUCH ME!
MOM, HEEELP...!
HE'S NOT VERY CUTE, BUT HE'S CARRYING MY BOOK BAG...SO THAT'S COOL!
SNIFF SNIFF SNIFF
THANKS, WHAT'S-YOUR-FACE. SEE YOU TOMORROW!
WAAAAH WHO'S GOING TO SEE MEEE HOME?
BOOOHOOOO-HOOO
THERE'S NO DOUBT ABOUT IT... WENDY'S BOYFRIEND BRINGS HER HOME A WHOLE LOT BETTER THAN MINE!
CAZENOVE & WILLIAM

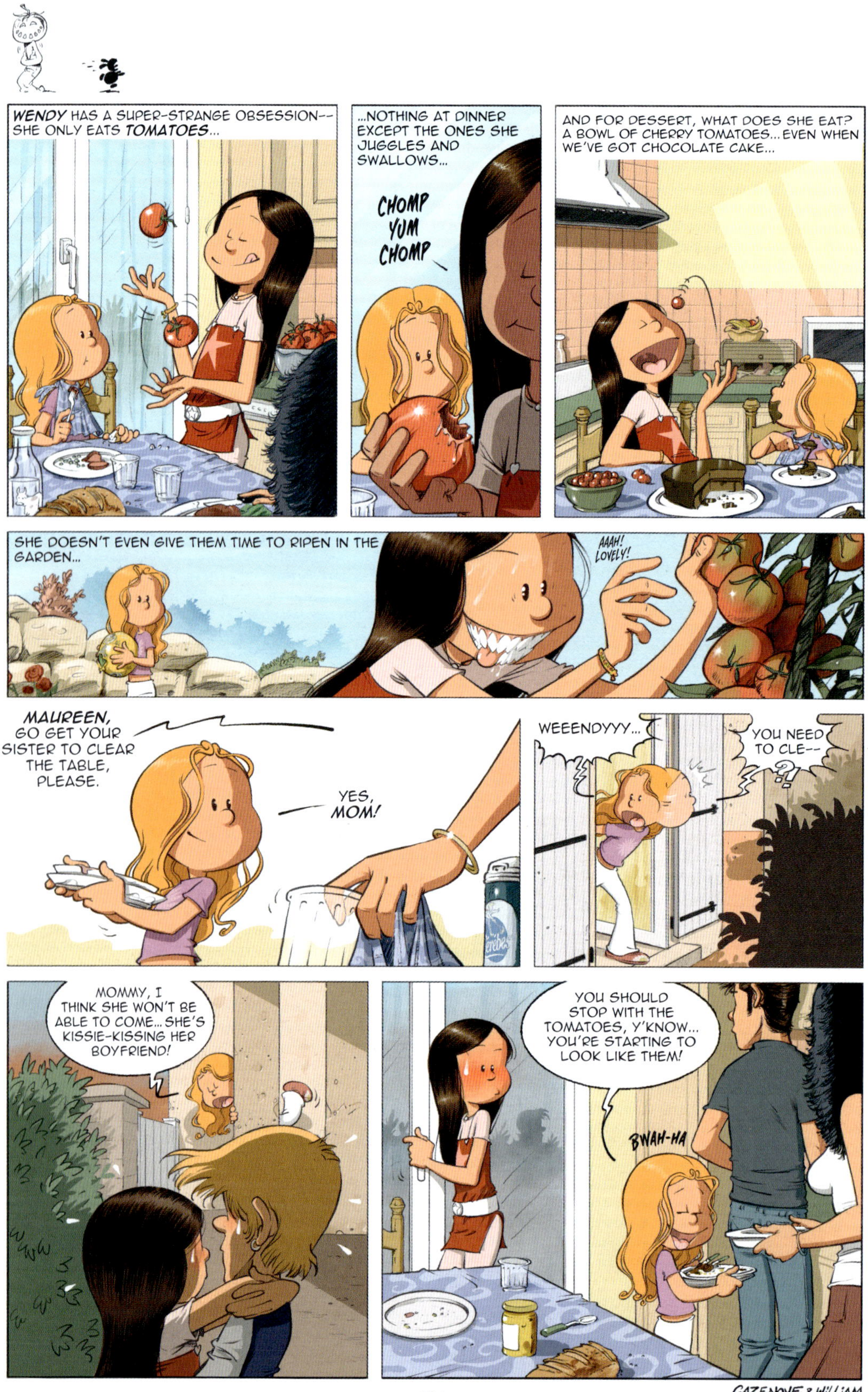
WENDY HAS A SUPER-STRANGE OBSESSION-- SHE ONLY EATS TOMATOES...
...NOTHING AT DINNER EXCEPT THE ONES SHE JUGGLES AND SWALLOWS...
CHOMP YUM CHOMP
AND FOR DESSERT, WHAT DOES SHE EAT? A BOWL OF CHERRY TOMATOES... EVEN WHEN WE'VE GOT CHOCOLATE CAKE...
SHE DOESN'T EVEN GIVE THEM TIME TO RIPEN IN THE GARDEN...
AAAH! LOVELY!
MAUREEN, GO GET YOUR SISTER TO CLEAR THE TABLE, PLEASE.
YES, MOM!
WEEENDYYY...
YOU NEED TO CLE--
?!
MOMMY, I THINK SHE WON'T BE ABLE TO COME... SHE'S KISSIE-KISSING HER BOYFRIEND!
YOU SHOULD STOP WITH THE TOMATOES, Y'KNOW... YOU'RE STARTING TO LOOK LIKE THEM!
BWAH-HA
CAZENOVE & WILLIAM

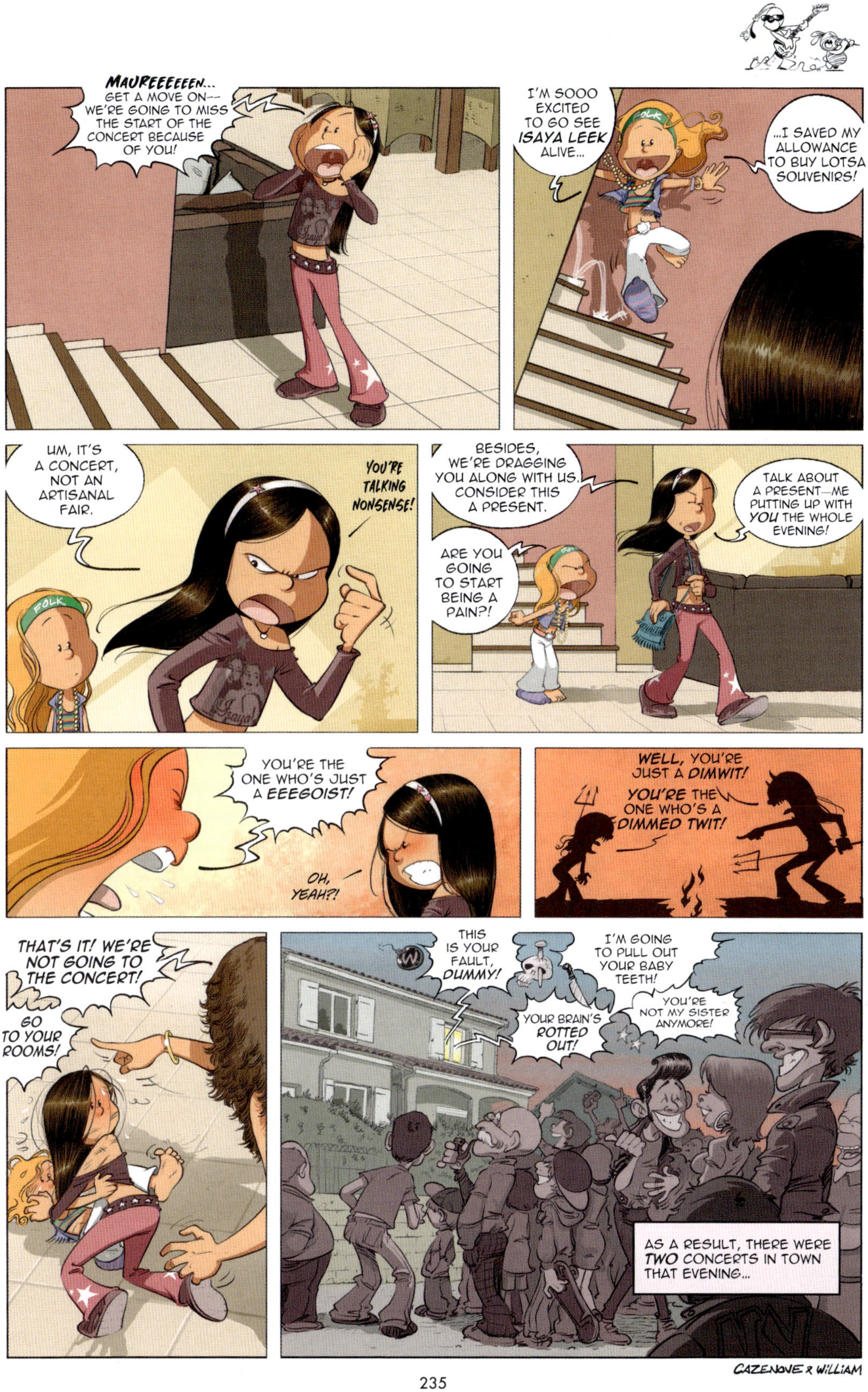
MAUREEEEEEN... GET A MOVE ON-- WE'RE GOING TO MISS THE START OF THE CONCERT BECAUSE OF YOU!
I'M SOOO EXCITED TO GO SEE ISAYA LEEK ALIVE...
...I SAVED MY ALLOWANCE TO BUY LOTSA SOUVENIRS!
UM, IT'S A CONCERT, NOT AN ARTISANAL FAIR.
YOU'RE TALKING NONSENSE!
BESIDES, WE'RE DRAGGING YOU ALONG WITH US. CONSIDER THIS A PRESENT.
TALK ABOUT A PRESENT—ME PUTTING UP WITH YOU THE WHOLE EVENING!
ARE YOU GOING TO START BEING A PAIN?!
YOU'RE THE ONE WHO'S JUST A EEEGOIST!
OH, YEAH?!
WELL, YOU'RE JUST A DIMWIT!
YOU'RE THE ONE WHO'S A DIMMED TWIT!
THAT'S IT! WE'RE NOT GOING TO THE CONCERT!
GO TO YOUR ROOMS!
THIS IS YOUR FAULT, DUMMY!
I'M GOING TO PULL OUT YOUR BABY TEETH!
YOUR BRAIN'S ROTTED OUT!
YOU'RE NOT MY SISTER ANYMORE!
AS A RESULT, THERE WERE TWO CONCERTS IN TOWN THAT EVENING...
CAZENOVE & WILLIAM

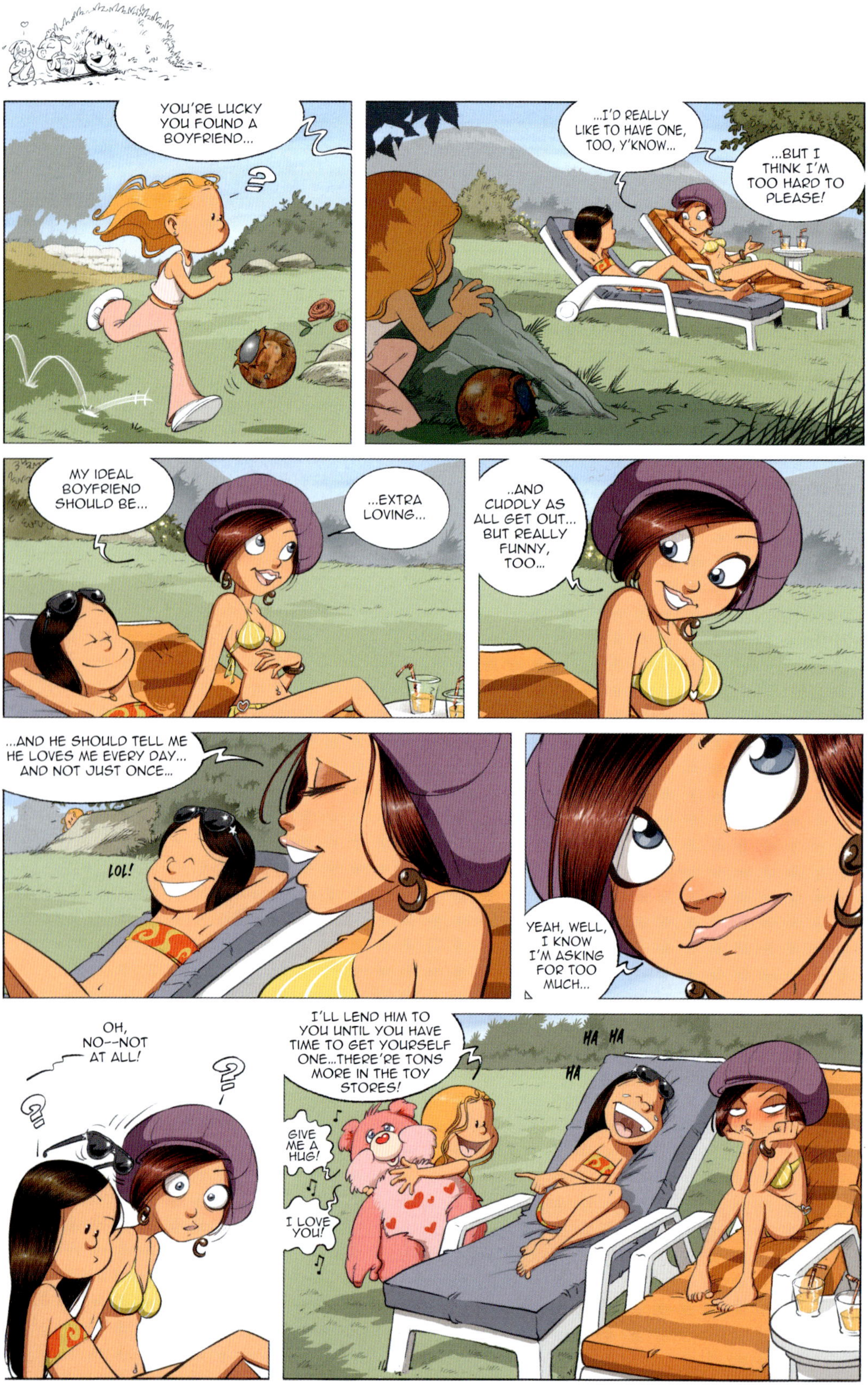
YOU'RE LUCKY YOU FOUND A BOYFRIEND...
...I'D REALLY LIKE TO HAVE ONE, TOO, Y'KNOW...
...BUT I THINK I'M TOO HARD TO PLEASE!
MY IDEAL BOYFRIEND SHOULD BE...
...EXTRA LOVING...
..AND CUDDLY AS ALL GET OUT... BUT REALLY FUNNY, TOO...
...AND HE SHOULD TELL ME HE LOVES ME EVERY DAY... AND NOT JUST ONCE...
LOL!
YEAH, WELL, I KNOW I'M ASKING FOR TOO MUCH...
OH, NO--NOT AT ALL!
I'LL LEND HIM TO YOU UNTIL YOU HAVE TIME TO GET YOURSELF ONE...THERE'RE TONS MORE IN THE TOY STORES!
HA HA HA
GIVE ME A HUG!
I LOVE YOU!

CAZENOVE & WILLIAM

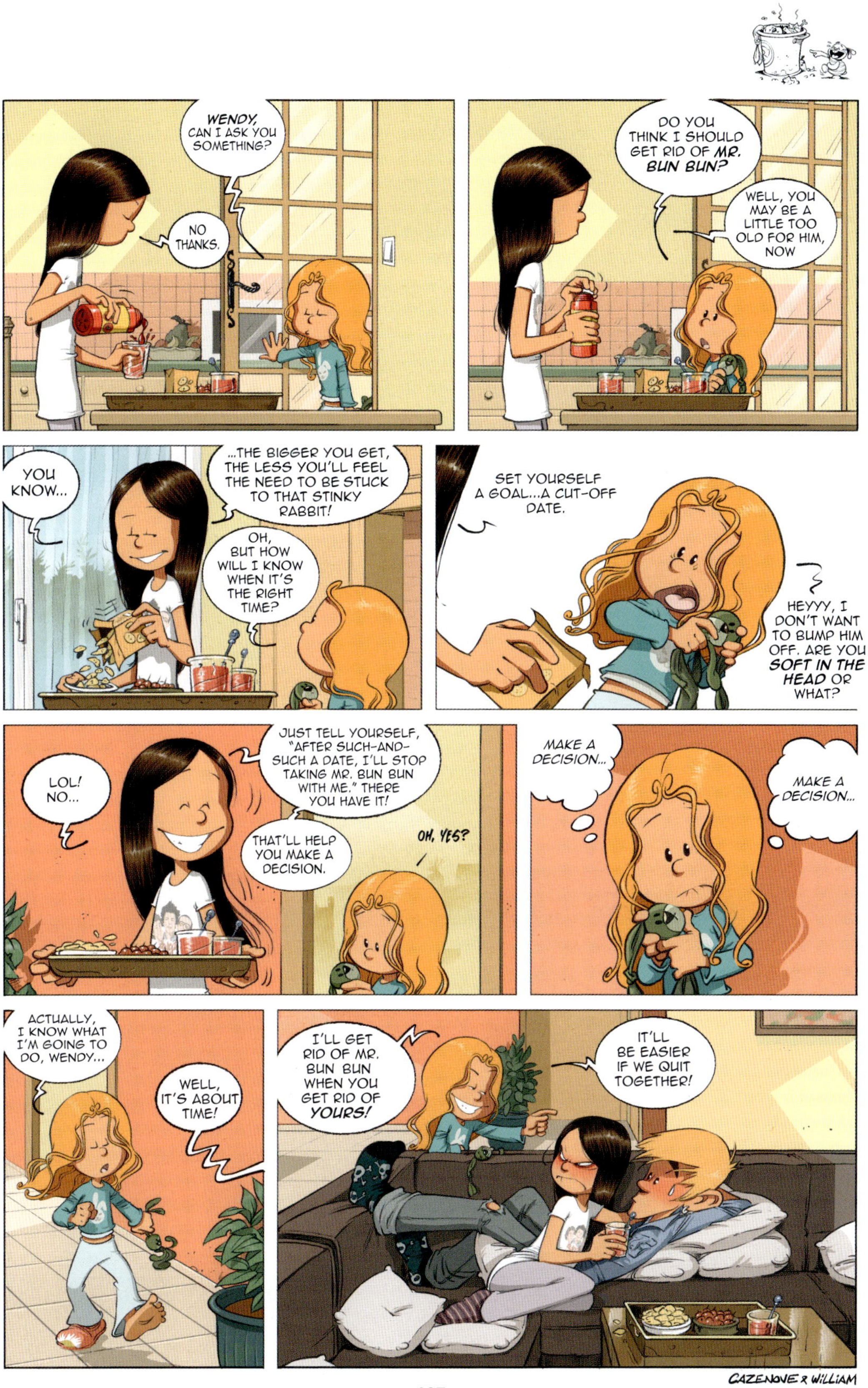
WENDY, CAN I ASK YOU SOMETHING?
NO THANKS.
DO YOU THINK I SHOULD GET RID OF MR. BUN BUN?
WELL, YOU MAY BE A LITTLE TOO OLD FOR HIM, NOW
YOU KNOW...
...THE BIGGER YOU GET, THE LESS YOU'LL FEEL THE NEED TO BE STUCK TO THAT STINKY RABBIT!
OH, BUT HOW WILL I KNOW WHEN IT'S THE RIGHT TIME?
SET YOURSELF A GOAL...A CUT-OFF DATE.
HEYYY, I DON'T WANT TO BUMP HIM OFF. ARE YOU SOFT IN THE HEAD OR WHAT?
LOL! NO...
JUST TELL YOURSELF, "AFTER SUCH-AND-SUCH A DATE, I'LL STOP TAKING MR. BUN BUN WITH ME." THERE YOU HAVE IT!
THAT'LL HELP YOU MAKE A DECISION.
OH, YES?
MAKE A DECISION...
MAKE A DECISION...
ACTUALLY, I KNOW WHAT I'M GOING TO DO, WENDY...
WELL, IT'S ABOUT TIME!
I'LL GET RID OF MR. BUN BUN WHEN YOU GET RID OF YOURS!
IT'LL BE EASIER IF WE QUIT TOGETHER!
CAZENOVE & WILLIAM

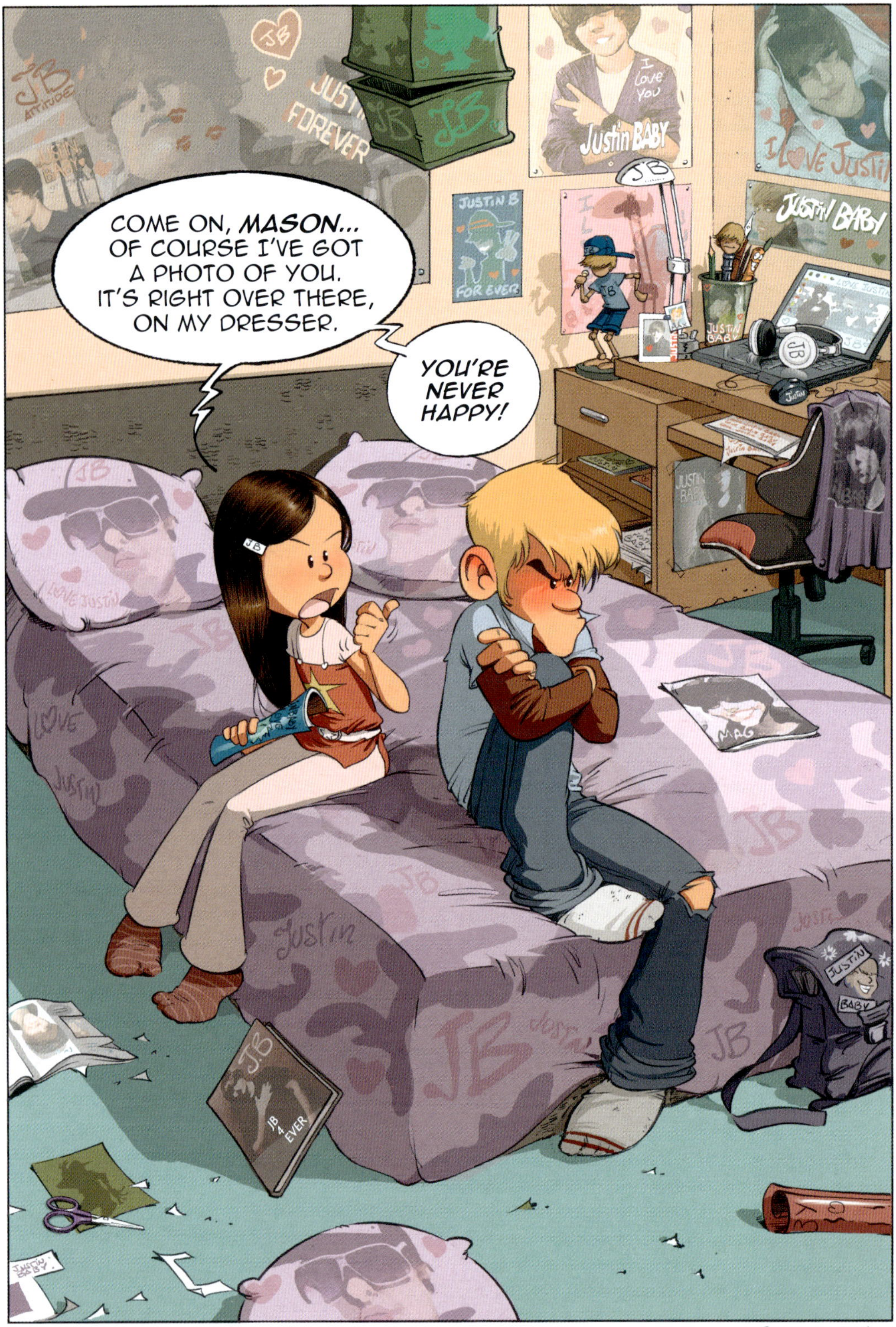
COME ON, MASON... OF COURSE I'VE GOT A PHOTO OF YOU. IT'S RIGHT OVER THERE, ON MY DRESSER.
YOU'RE NEVER HAPPY!

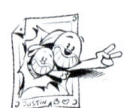

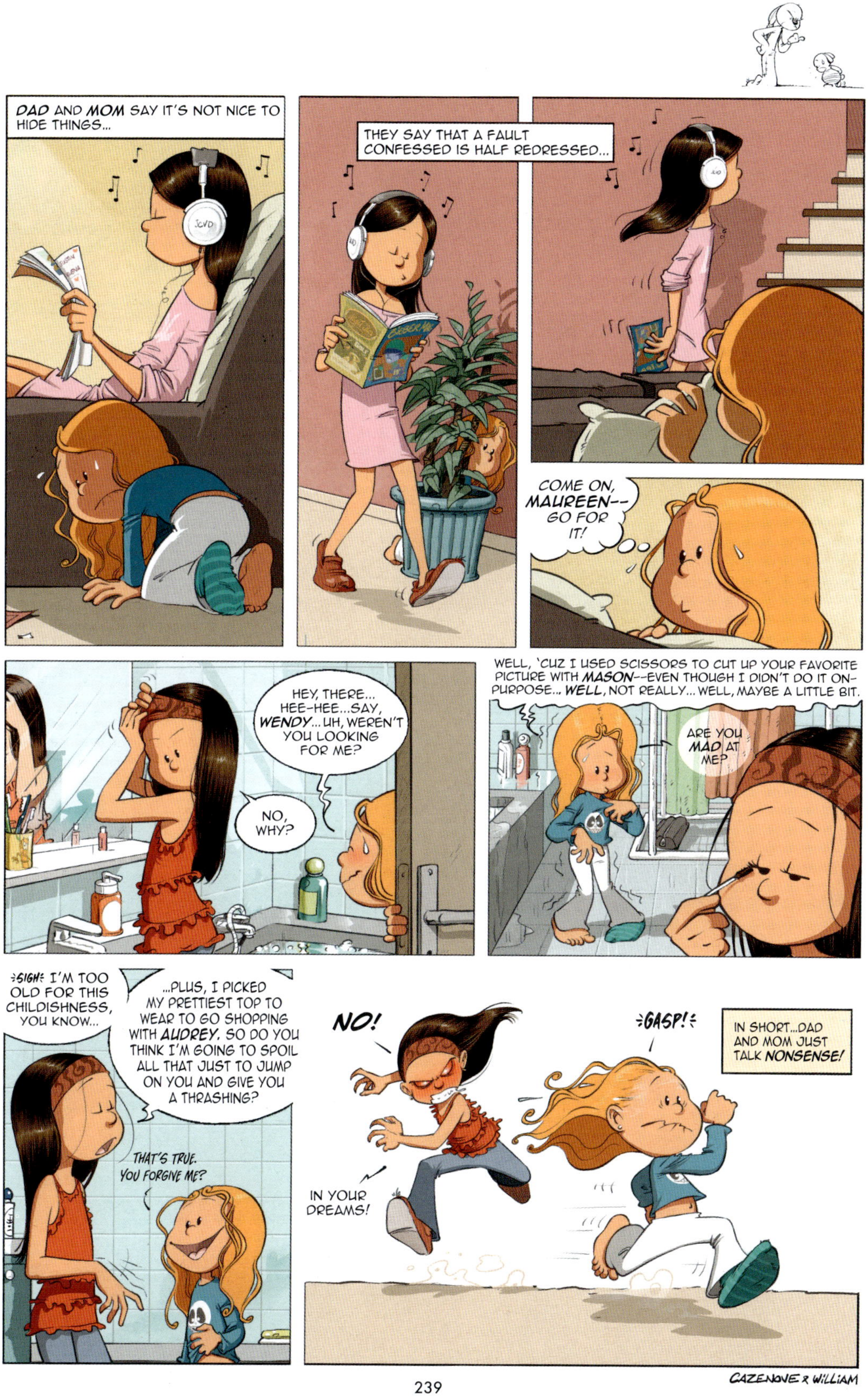

DAD AND MOM SAY IT'S NOT NICE TO HIDE THINGS...
THEY SAY THAT A FAULT CONFESSED IS HALF REDRESSED...
COME ON, MAUREEN-- GO FOR IT!
HEY, THERE... HEE-HEE...SAY, WENDY...UH, WEREN'T YOU LOOKING FOR ME?
NO, WHY?
WELL, 'CUZ I USED SCISSORS TO CUT UP YOUR FAVORITE PICTURE WITH MASON--EVEN THOUGH I DIDN'T DO IT ON-PURPOSE... WELL, NOT REALLY... WELL, MAYBE A LITTLE BIT.
ARE YOU MAD AT ME?
SIGH I'M TOO OLD FOR THIS CHILDISHNESS, YOU KNOW...
...PLUS, I PICKED MY PRETTIEST TOP TO WEAR TO GO SHOPPING WITH AUDREY. SO DO YOU THINK I'M GOING TO SPOIL ALL THAT JUST TO JUMP ON YOU AND GIVE YOU A THRASHING?
THAT'S TRUE. YOU FORGIVE ME?
NO!
IN YOUR DREAMS!
GASP!
IN SHORT...DAD AND MOM JUST TALK NONSENSE!
CAZENOVE & WILLIAM

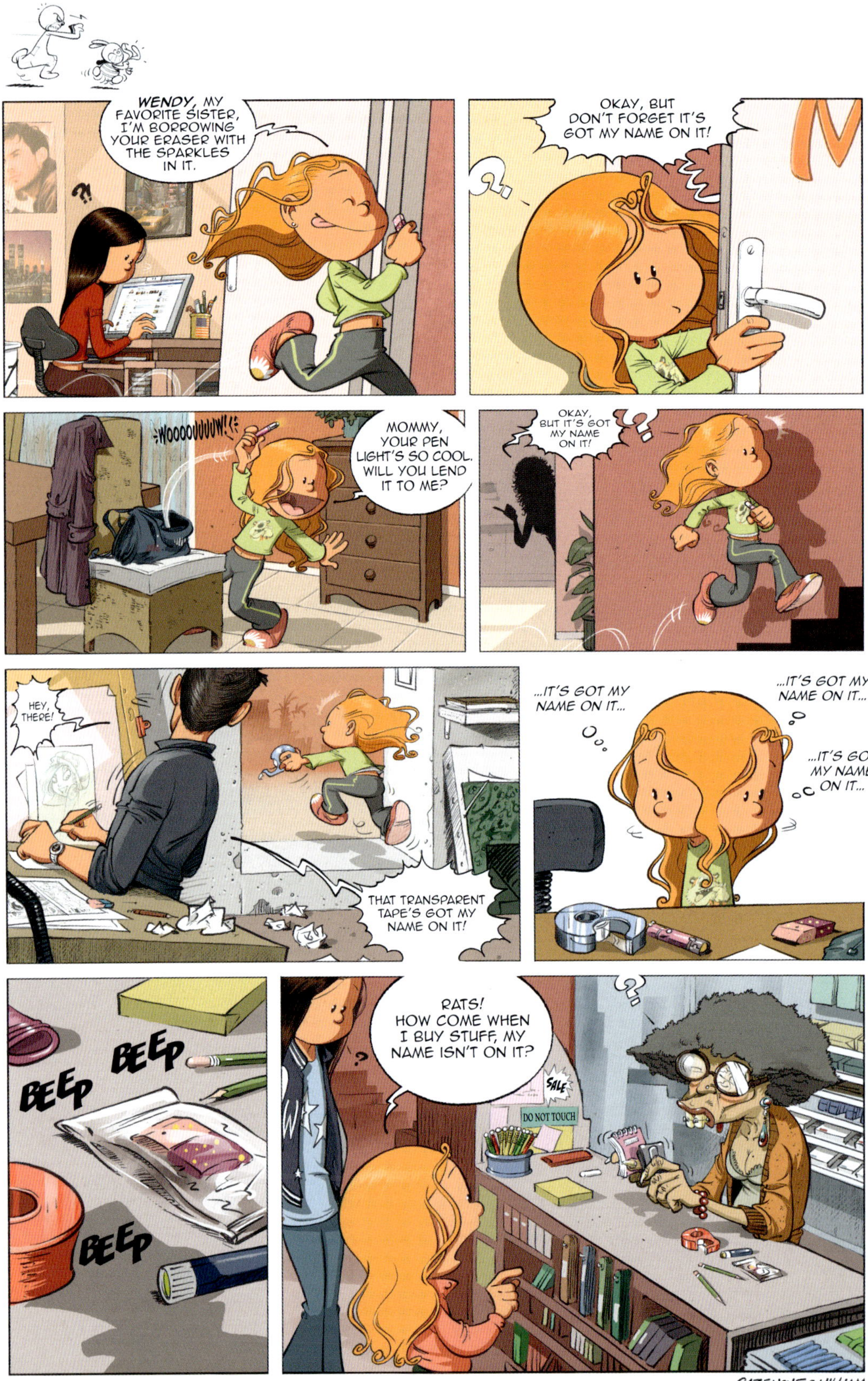
WENDY, MY FAVORITE SISTER, I'M BORROWING YOUR ERASER WITH THE SPARKLES IN IT.
OKAY, BUT DON'T FORGET IT'S GOT MY NAME ON IT!
-WOOOOUUUUW!-
MOMMY, YOUR PEN LIGHT'S SO COOL. WILL YOU LEND IT TO ME?
OKAY, BUT IT'S GOT MY NAME ON IT!
HEY, THERE!
THAT TRANSPARENT TAPE'S GOT MY NAME ON IT!
...IT'S GOT MY NAME ON IT...
...IT'S GOT MY NAME ON IT...
...IT'S GOT MY NAME ON IT...
BEEP
BEEP
BEEP
RATS! HOW COME WHEN I BUY STUFF, MY NAME ISN'T ON IT?
SALE
DO NOT TOUCH

CAZENOVE & WILLIAM

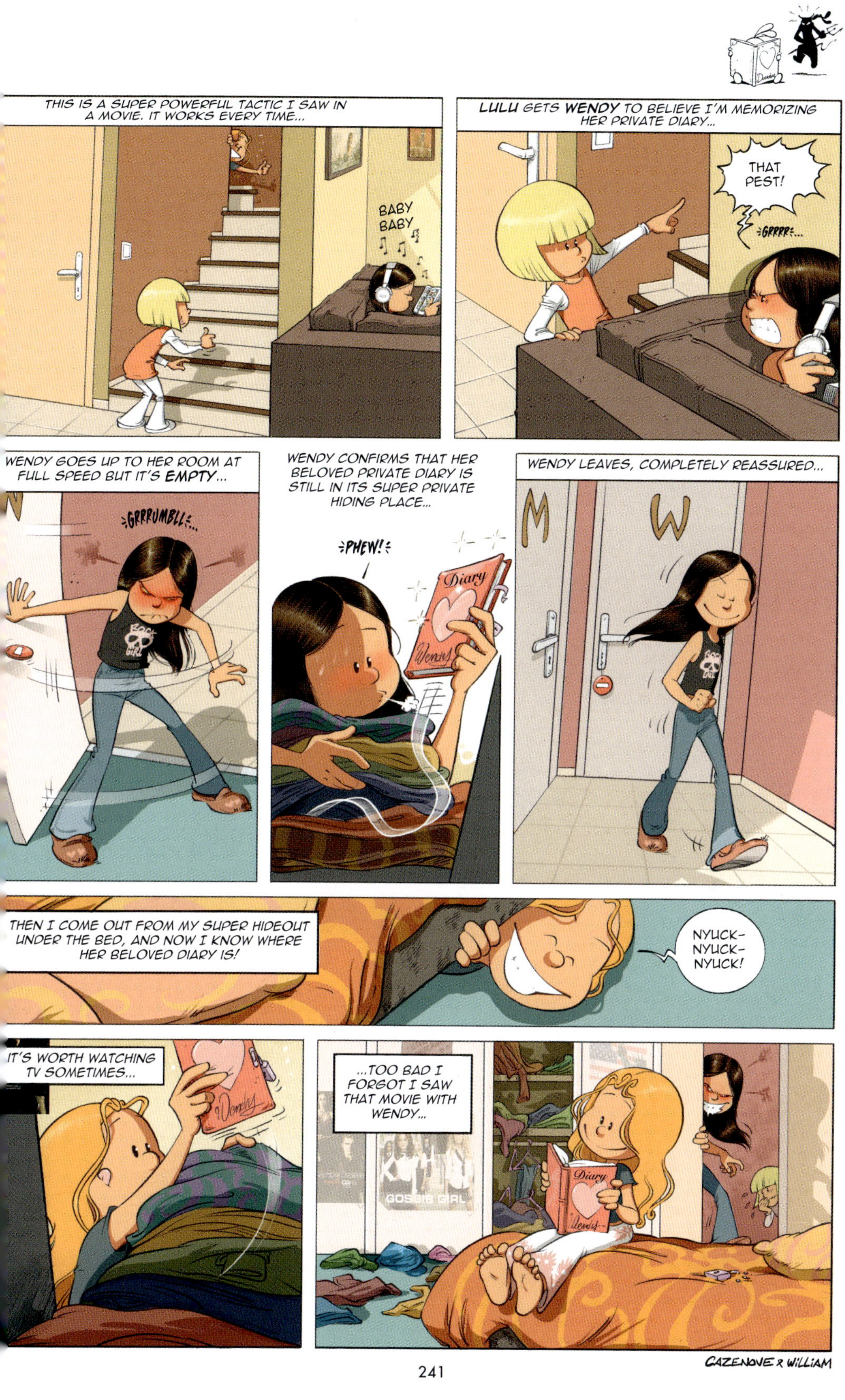
THIS IS A SUPER POWERFUL TACTIC I SAW IN A MOVIE. IT WORKS EVERY TIME...
BABY BABY
LULU GETS WENDY TO BELIEVE I'M MEMORIZING HER PRIVATE DIARY...
THAT PEST!
GRRRR...
WENDY GOES UP TO HER ROOM AT FULL SPEED BUT IT'S EMPTY...
GRRRUMBLL...
WENDY CONFIRMS THAT HER BELOVED PRIVATE DIARY IS STILL IN ITS SUPER PRIVATE HIDING PLACE...
PHEW!
Diary
Wendy
WENDY LEAVES, COMPLETELY REASSURED...
M
W
THEN I COME OUT FROM MY SUPER HIDEOUT UNDER THE BED, AND NOW I KNOW WHERE HER BELOVED DIARY IS!
NYUCK-NYUCK-NYUCK!
IT'S WORTH WATCHING TV SOMETIMES...
...TOO BAD I FORGOT I SAW THAT MOVIE WITH WENDY...
GOSSIP GIRL
Diary
CAZENOVE & WILLIAM

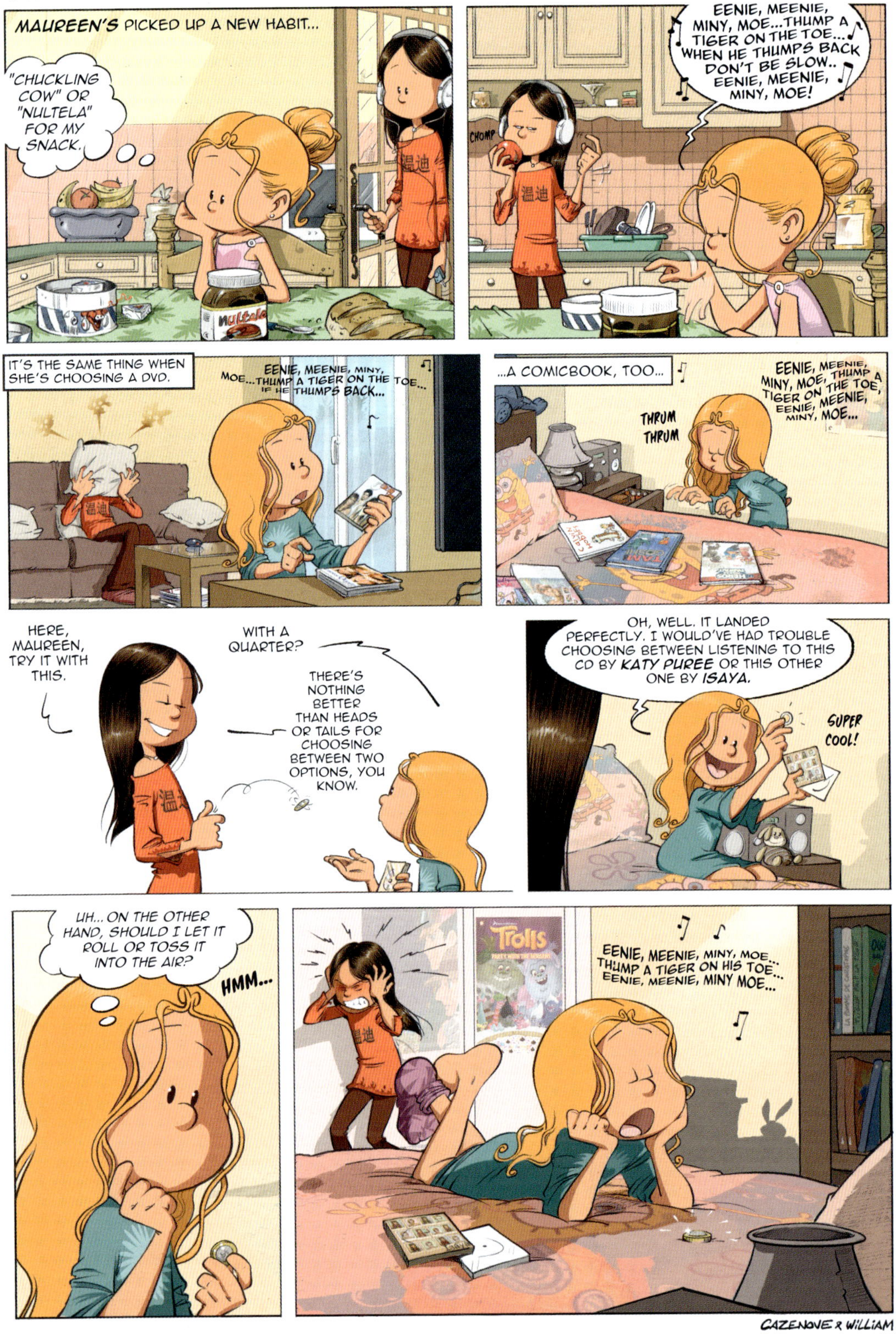
MAUREEN'S PICKED UP A NEW HABIT...
"CHUCKLING COW" OR "NULTELA" FOR MY SNACK.
EENIE, MEENIE, MINY, MOE...THUMP A TIGER ON THE TOE... WHEN HE THUMPS BACK DON'T BE SLOW.. EENIE, MEENIE, MINY, MOE!
CHOMP
IT'S THE SAME THING WHEN SHE'S CHOOSING A DVD.
EENIE, MEENIE, MINY, MOE...THUMP A TIGER ON THE TOE... IF HE THUMPS BACK...
...A COMICBOOK, TOO...
THRUM THRUM
EENIE, MEENIE, MINY, MOE, THUMP A TIGER ON THE TOE, EENIE, MEENIE, MINY, MOE...
HERE, MAUREEN, TRY IT WITH THIS.
WITH A QUARTER?
THERE'S NOTHING BETTER THAN HEADS OR TAILS FOR CHOOSING BETWEEN TWO OPTIONS, YOU KNOW.
OH, WELL. IT LANDED PERFECTLY. I WOULD'VE HAD TROUBLE CHOOSING BETWEEN LISTENING TO THIS CD BY KATY PUREE OR THIS OTHER ONE BY ISAYA.
SUPER COOL!
UH... ON THE OTHER HAND, SHOULD I LET IT ROLL OR TOSS IT INTO THE AIR?
HMM...
EENIE, MEENIE, MINY, MOE... THUMP A TIGER ON HIS TOE... EENIE, MEENIE, MINY MOE...

CAZENOVE & WILLIAM

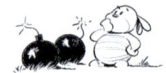

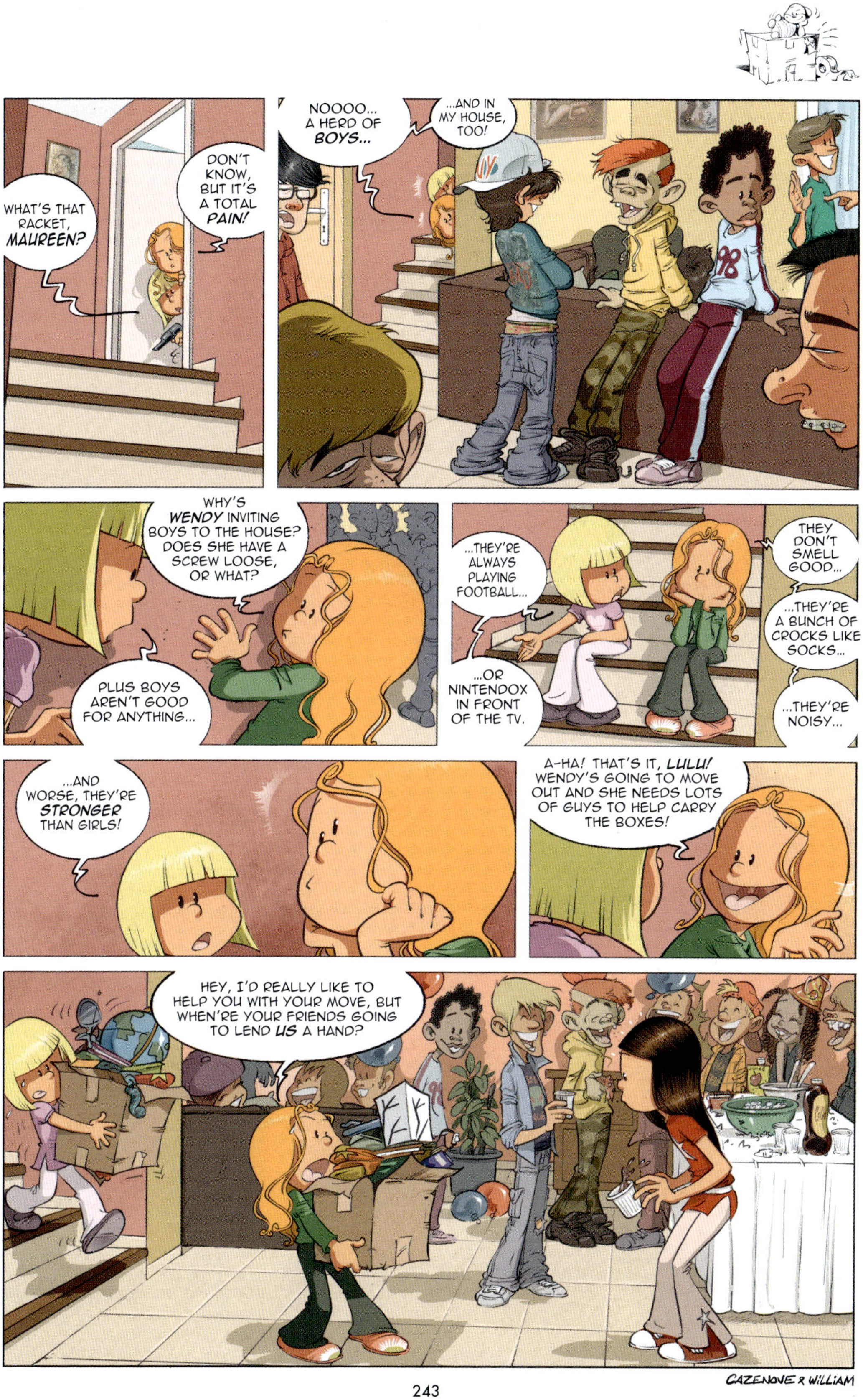

WHAT'S THAT RACKET, MAUREEN?
DON'T KNOW, BUT IT'S A TOTAL PAIN!
NOOOO... A HERD OF BOYS...
...AND IN MY HOUSE, TOO!
WHY'S WENDY INVITING BOYS TO THE HOUSE? DOES SHE HAVE A SCREW LOOSE, OR WHAT?
PLUS BOYS AREN'T GOOD FOR ANYTHING...
...THEY'RE ALWAYS PLAYING FOOTBALL...
...OR NINTENDOX IN FRONT OF THE TV.
THEY DON'T SMELL GOOD...
...THEY'RE A BUNCH OF CROCKS LIKE SOCKS...
...THEY'RE NOISY...
...AND WORSE, THEY'RE STRONGER THAN GIRLS!
A-HA! THAT'S IT, LULU! WENDY'S GOING TO MOVE OUT AND SHE NEEDS LOTS OF GUYS TO HELP CARRY THE BOXES!
HEY, I'D REALLY LIKE TO HELP YOU WITH YOUR MOVE, BUT WHEN'RE YOUR FRIENDS GOING TO LEND US A HAND?
CAZENOVE & WILLIAM

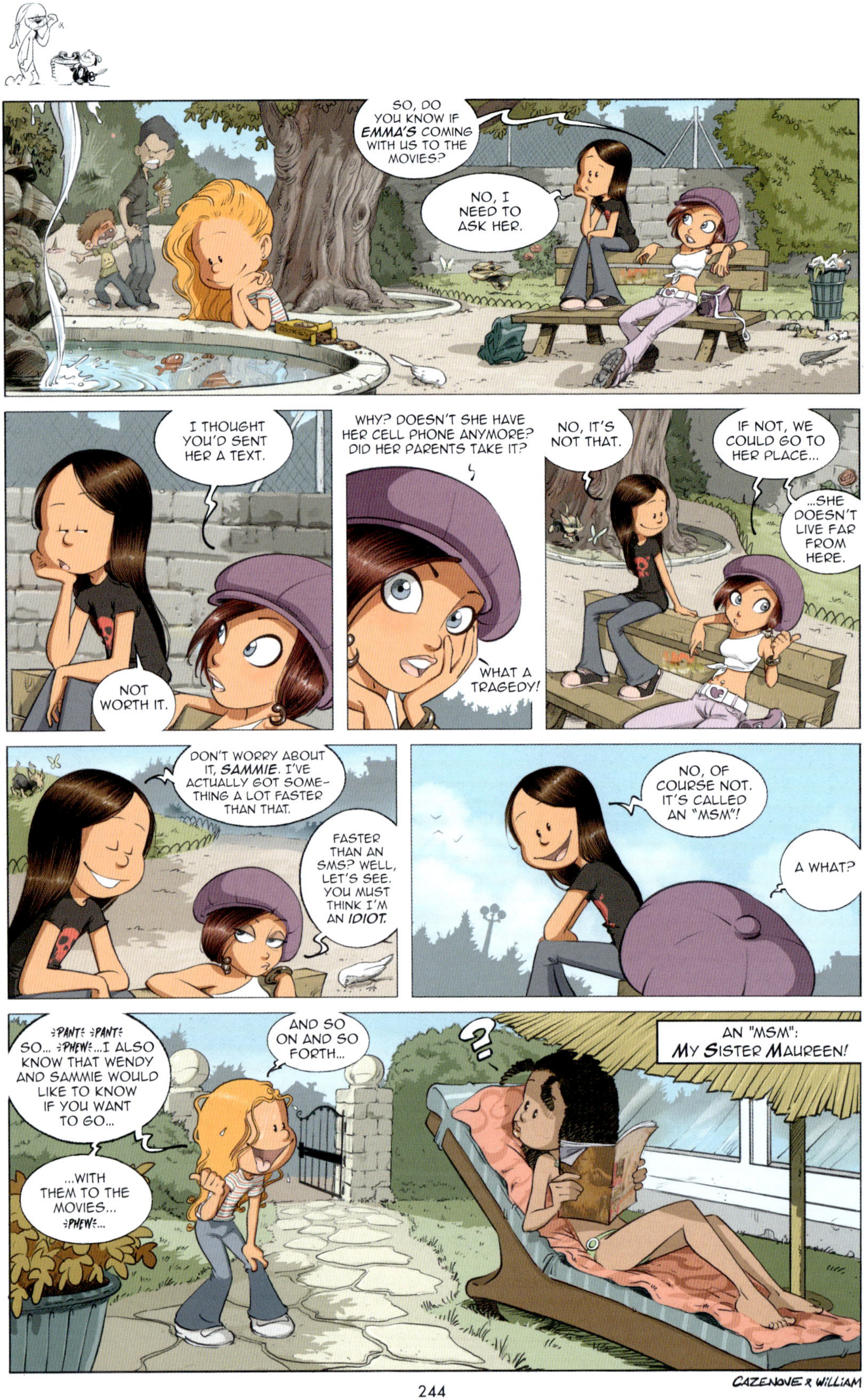
SO, DO YOU KNOW IF EMMA'S COMING WITH US TO THE MOVIES?
NO, I NEED TO ASK HER.
I THOUGHT YOU'D SENT HER A TEXT.
NOT WORTH IT.
WHY? DOESN'T SHE HAVE HER CELL PHONE ANYMORE? DID HER PARENTS TAKE IT?
WHAT A TRAGEDY!
NO, IT'S NOT THAT.
IF NOT, WE COULD GO TO HER PLACE...
...SHE DOESN'T LIVE FAR FROM HERE.
DON'T WORRY ABOUT IT, SAMMIE. I'VE ACTUALLY GOT SOME-THING A LOT FASTER THAN THAT.
FASTER THAN AN SMS? WELL, LET'S SEE. YOU MUST THINK I'M AN IDIOT.
NO, OF COURSE NOT. IT'S CALLED AN "MSM"!
A WHAT?
PANT PANT SO... PHEW ...I ALSO KNOW THAT WENDY AND SAMMIE WOULD LIKE TO KNOW IF YOU WANT TO GO...
AND SO ON AND SO FORTH...
...WITH THEM TO THE MOVIES... PHEW...
AN "MSM": MY SISTER MAUREEN!
CAZENOVE & WILLIAM

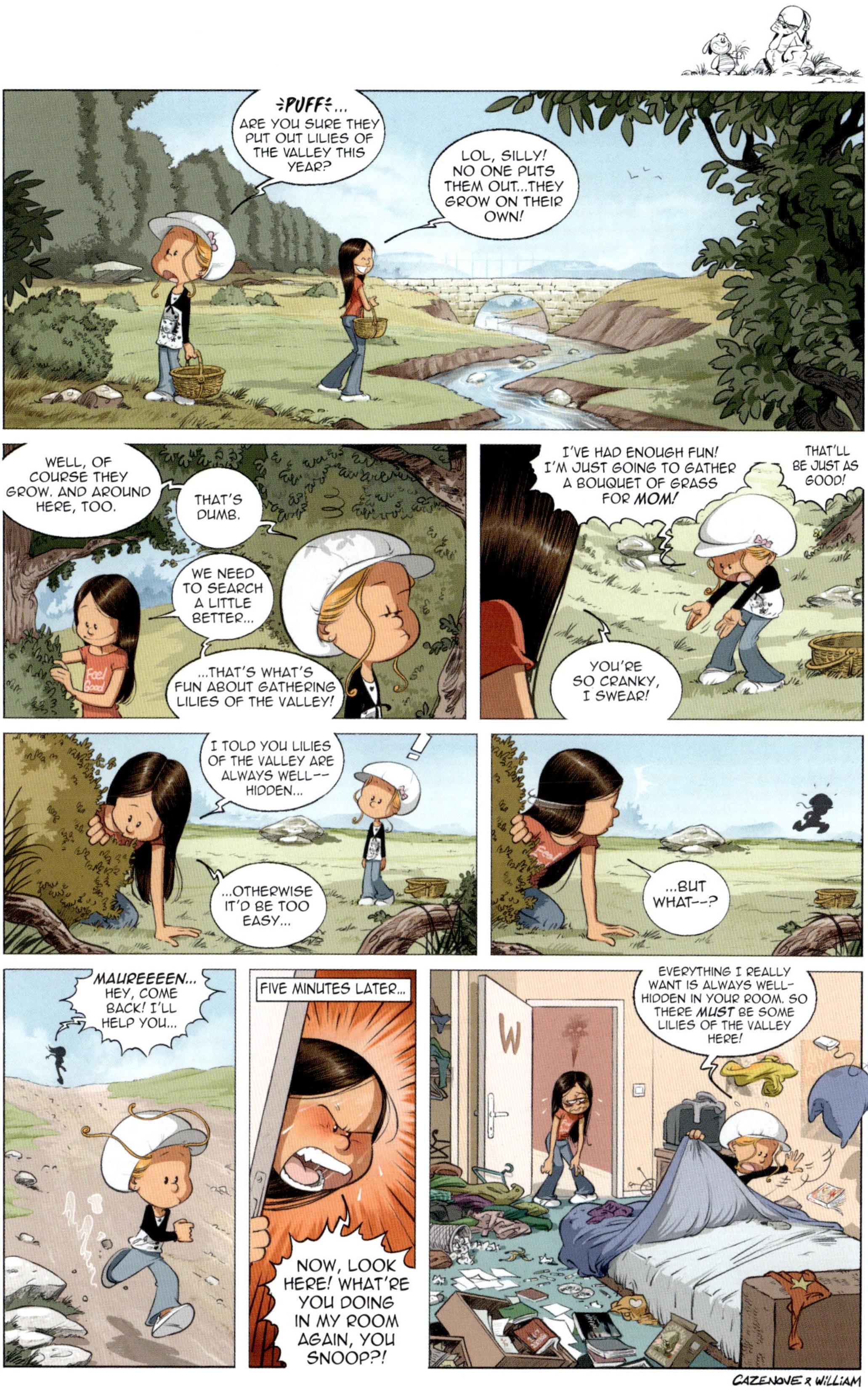

PUFF... ARE YOU SURE THEY PUT OUT LILIES OF THE VALLEY THIS YEAR?
LOL, SILLY! NO ONE PUTS THEM OUT...THEY GROW ON THEIR OWN!
WELL, OF COURSE THEY GROW. AND AROUND HERE, TOO.
THAT'S DUMB.
WE NEED TO SEARCH A LITTLE BETTER...
...THAT'S WHAT'S FUN ABOUT GATHERING LILIES OF THE VALLEY!
I'VE HAD ENOUGH FUN! I'M JUST GOING TO GATHER A BOUQUET OF GRASS FOR **MOM!**
THAT'LL BE JUST AS GOOD!
YOU'RE SO CRANKY, I SWEAR!
I TOLD YOU LILIES OF THE VALLEY ARE ALWAYS WELL--HIDDEN...
...OTHERWISE IT'D BE TOO EASY...
...BUT WHAT--?
MAUREEEEN... HEY, COME BACK! I'LL HELP YOU...
FIVE MINUTES LATER...
NOW, LOOK HERE! WHAT'RE YOU DOING IN MY ROOM AGAIN, YOU SNOOP?!
EVERYTHING I REALLY WANT IS ALWAYS WELL-HIDDEN IN YOUR ROOM. SO THERE **MUST** BE SOME LILIES OF THE VALLEY HERE!
CAZENOVE & WILLIAM

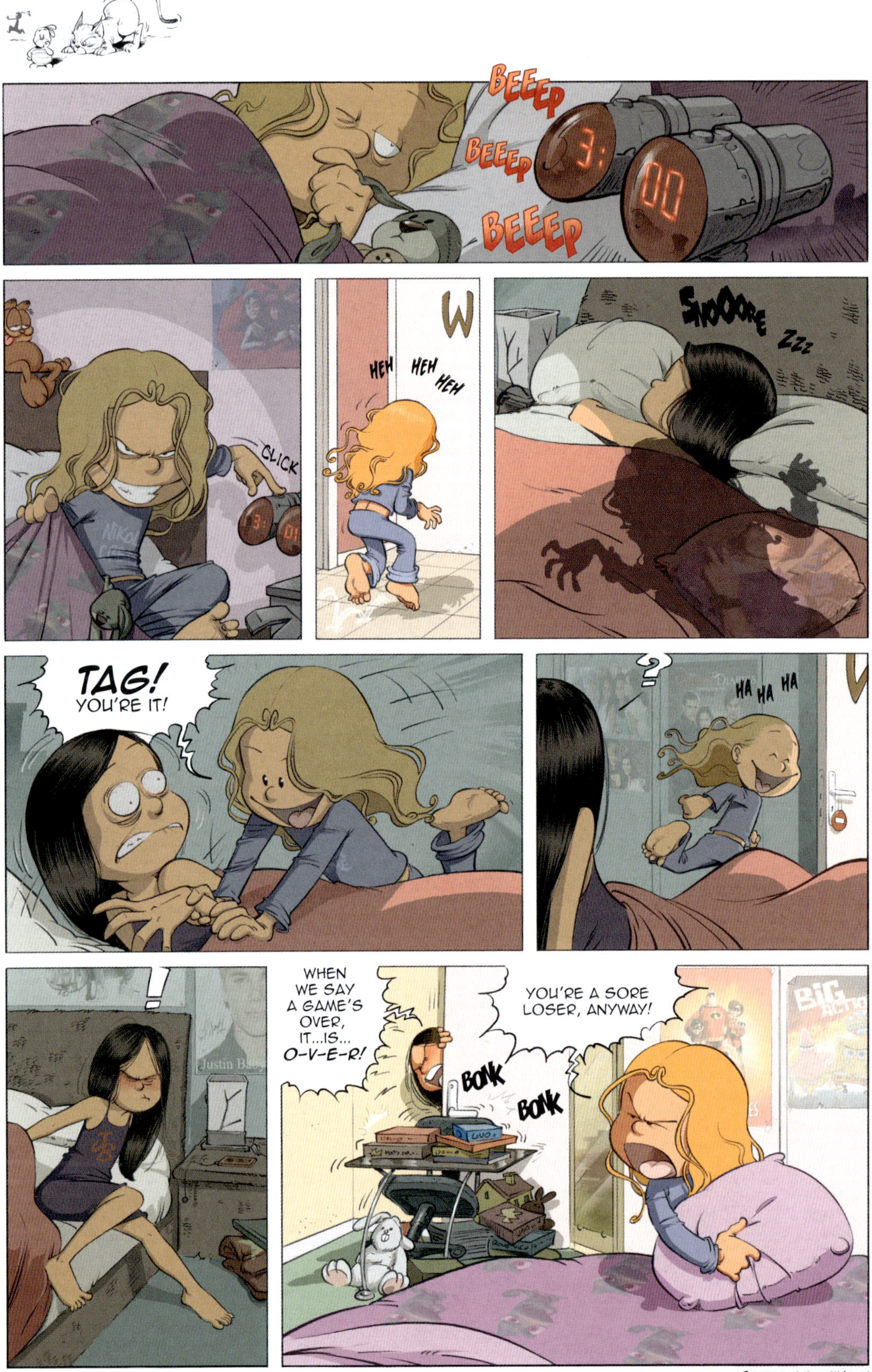

BEEEP
BEEEP
BEEEP
CLICK
W
HEH
HEH HEH
SNOOORE
ZZZ
TAG! YOU'RE IT!
?
HA HA HA
!
WHEN WE SAY A GAME'S OVER, IT...IS... O-V-E-R!
BONK
BONK
YOU'RE A SORE LOSER, ANYWAY!

CAZENOVE & WILLIAM

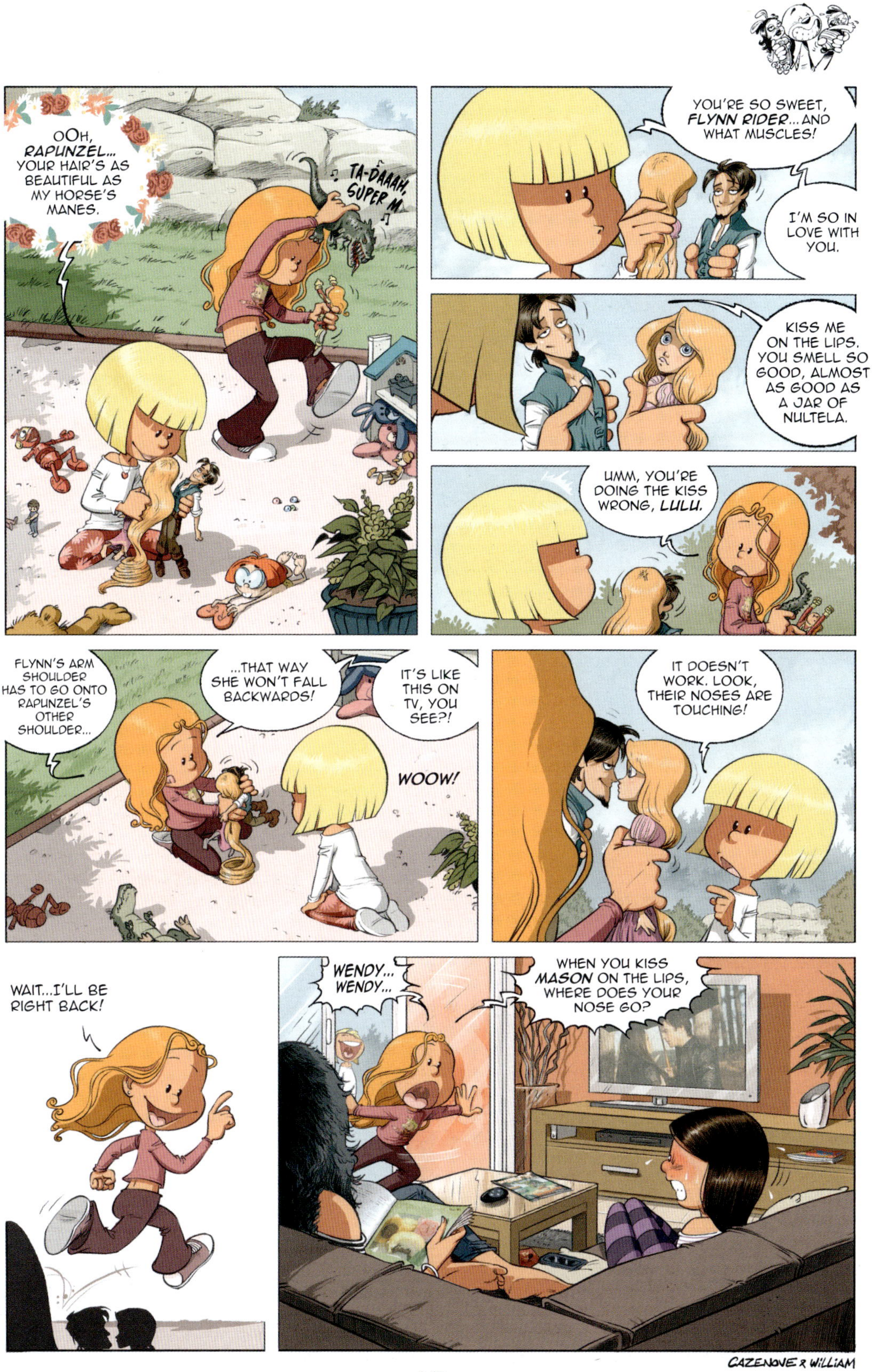
OOH, RAPUNZEL... YOUR HAIR'S AS BEAUTIFUL AS MY HORSE'S MANES.
TA-DAAAH, SUPER M
YOU'RE SO SWEET, FLYNN RIDER... AND WHAT MUSCLES!
I'M SO IN LOVE WITH YOU.
KISS ME ON THE LIPS. YOU SMELL SO GOOD, ALMOST AS GOOD AS A JAR OF NULTELA.
UMM, YOU'RE DOING THE KISS WRONG, LULU.
FLYNN'S ARM SHOULDER HAS TO GO ONTO RAPUNZEL'S OTHER SHOULDER...
...THAT WAY SHE WON'T FALL BACKWARDS!
IT'S LIKE THIS ON TV, YOU SEE?!
WOOW!
IT DOESN'T WORK. LOOK, THEIR NOSES ARE TOUCHING!
WAIT...I'LL BE RIGHT BACK!
WENDY... WENDY...
WHEN YOU KISS MASON ON THE LIPS, WHERE DOES YOUR NOSE GO?
CAZENOVE & WILLIAM

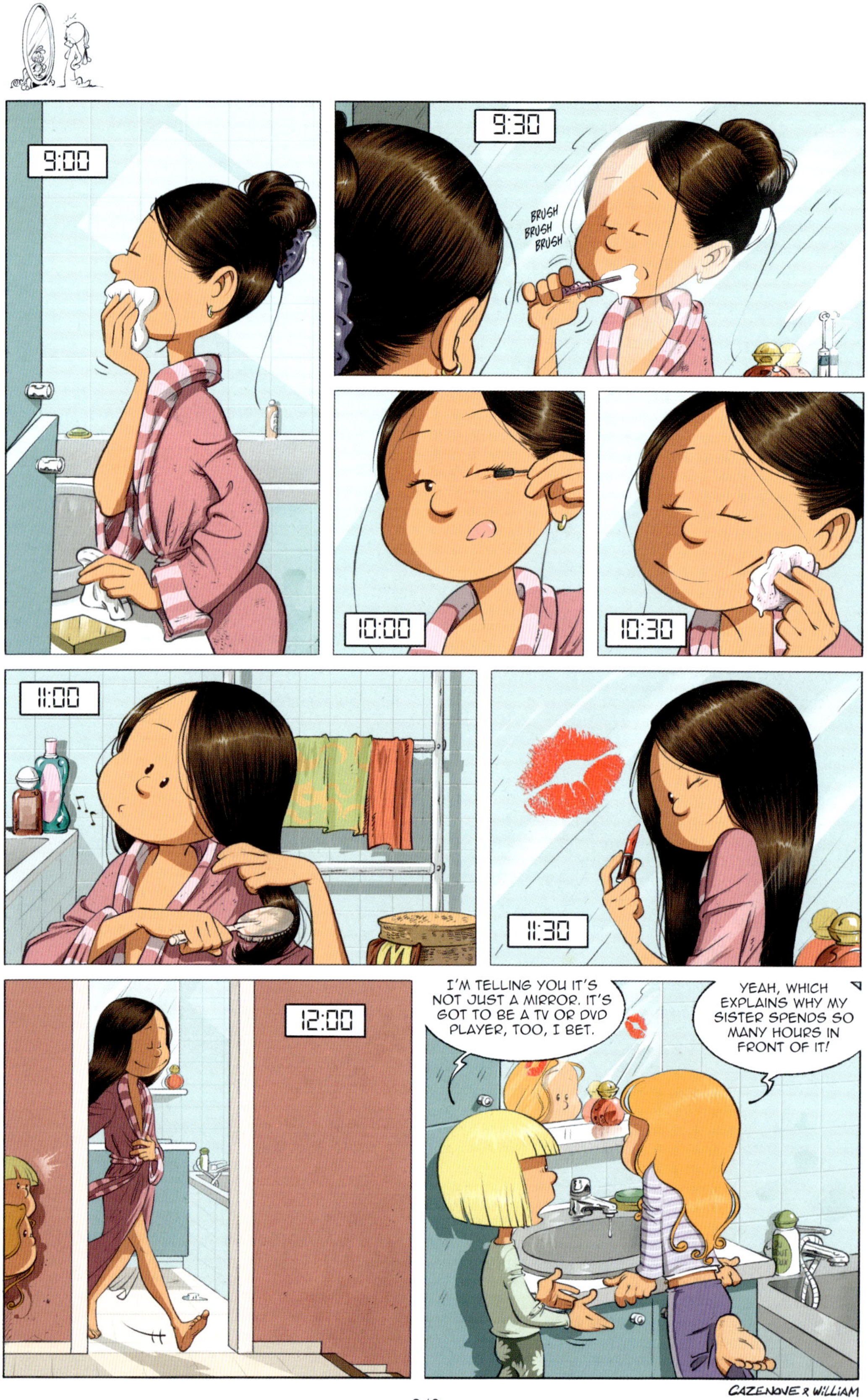
9:00
9:30
BRUSH
BRUSH
BRUSH
10:00
10:30
11:00
11:30
12:00
I'M TELLING YOU IT'S NOT JUST A MIRROR. IT'S GOT TO BE A TV OR DVD PLAYER, TOO, I BET.
YEAH, WHICH EXPLAINS WHY MY SISTER SPENDS SO MANY HOURS IN FRONT OF IT!
CAZENOVE & WILLIAM

WHEN I CAME HOME FROM SCHOOL THIS AFTERNOON, I HAD A STRANGE SURPRISE...

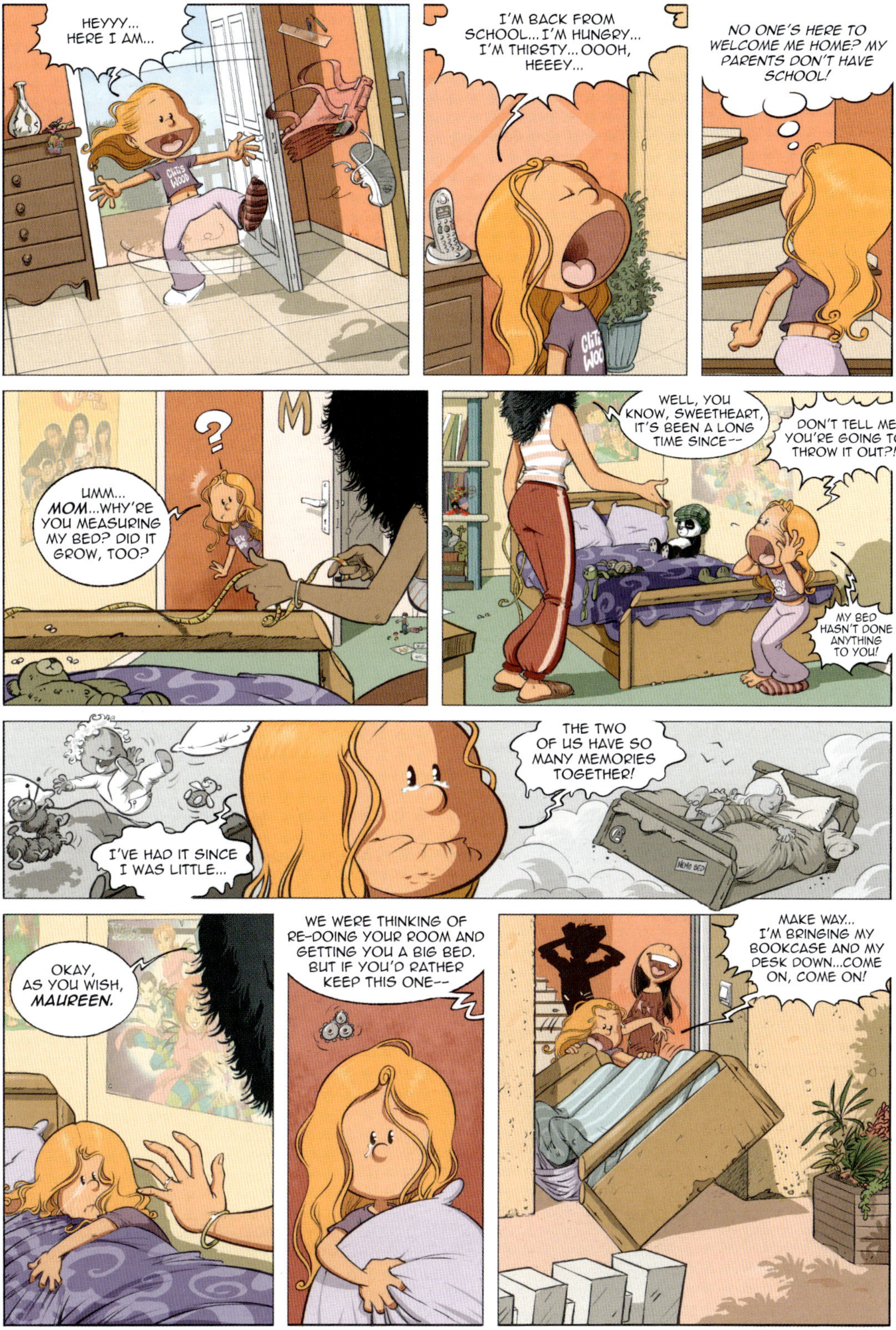
HEYYY... HERE I AM...
I'M BACK FROM SCHOOL... I'M HUNGRY... I'M THIRSTY... OOOH, HEEEY...
NO ONE'S HERE TO WELCOME ME HOME? MY PARENTS DON'T HAVE SCHOOL!
?
UMM... **MOM**...WHY'RE YOU MEASURING MY BED? DID IT GROW, TOO?
WELL, YOU KNOW, SWEETHEART, IT'S BEEN A LONG TIME SINCE--
DON'T TELL ME YOU'RE GOING TO THROW IT OUT?!
MY BED HASN'T DONE ANYTHING TO YOU!
I'VE HAD IT SINCE I WAS LITTLE...
THE TWO OF US HAVE SO MANY MEMORIES TOGETHER!
OKAY, AS YOU WISH, **MAUREEN.**
WE WERE THINKING OF RE-DOING YOUR ROOM AND GETTING YOU A BIG BED. BUT IF YOU'D RATHER KEEP THIS ONE--
MAKE WAY... I'M BRINGING MY BOOKCASE AND MY DESK DOWN...COME ON, COME ON!

CAZENOVE & WILLIAM

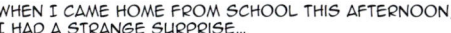

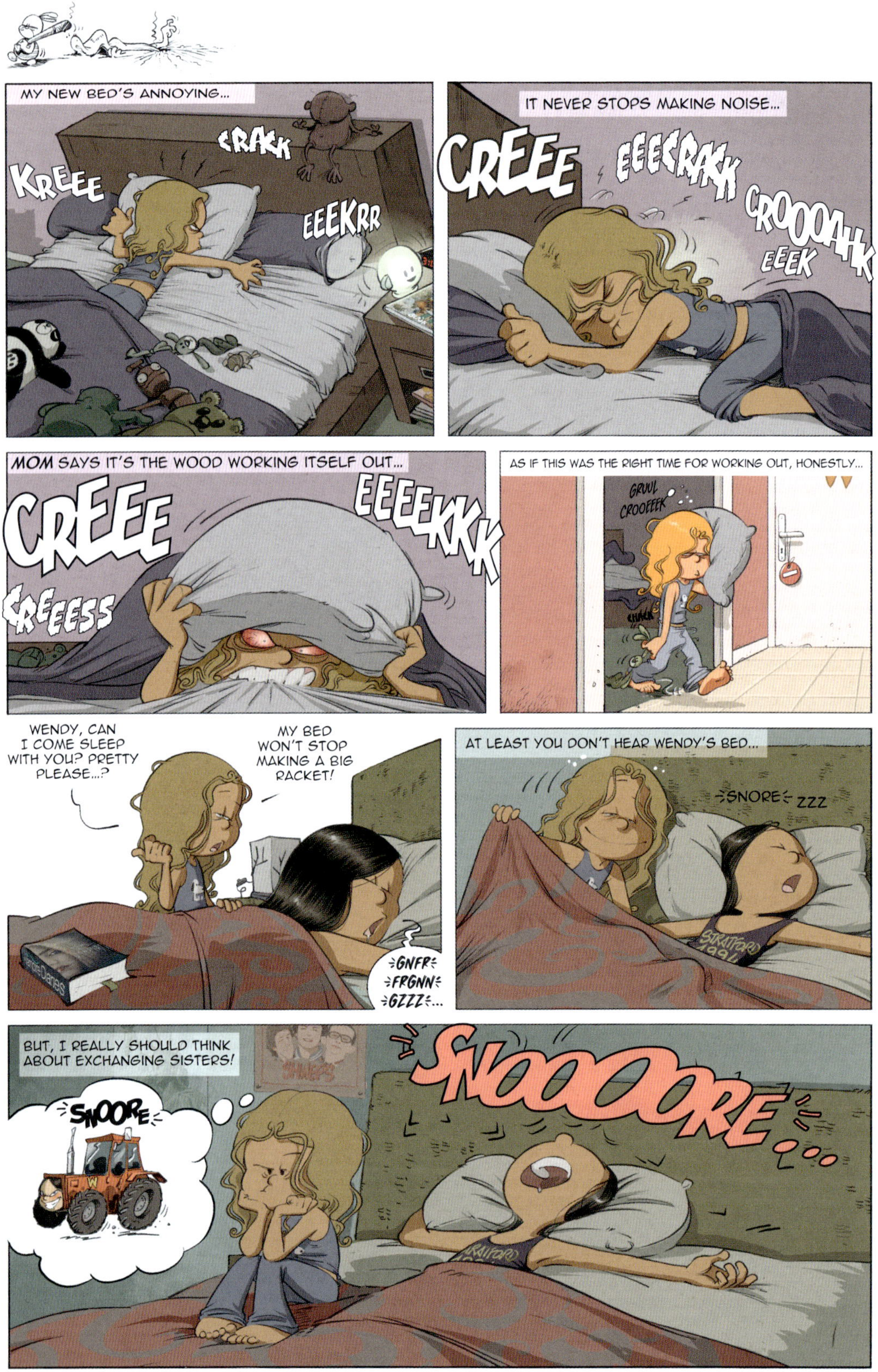

MY NEW BED'S ANNOYING...
KREEEE
CRACK
EEEKRR
IT NEVER STOPS MAKING NOISE...
CREEEE
EEECRACK
CROOOAHK
EEEK
MOM SAYS IT'S THE WOOD WORKING ITSELF OUT...
CREEEE
EEEEKKK
CREEESS
AS IF THIS WAS THE RIGHT TIME FOR WORKING OUT, HONESTLY...
GRUUL CROOEEEK
WENDY, CAN I COME SLEEP WITH YOU? PRETTY PLEASE...?
MY BED WON'T STOP MAKING A BIG RACKET!
GNFR FRGNN GZZZ...
AT LEAST YOU DON'T HEAR WENDY'S BED...
SNORE ZZZ
BUT, I REALLY SHOULD THINK ABOUT EXCHANGING SISTERS!
SNOORE
SNOOOORE...

CAZENOVE & WILLIAM

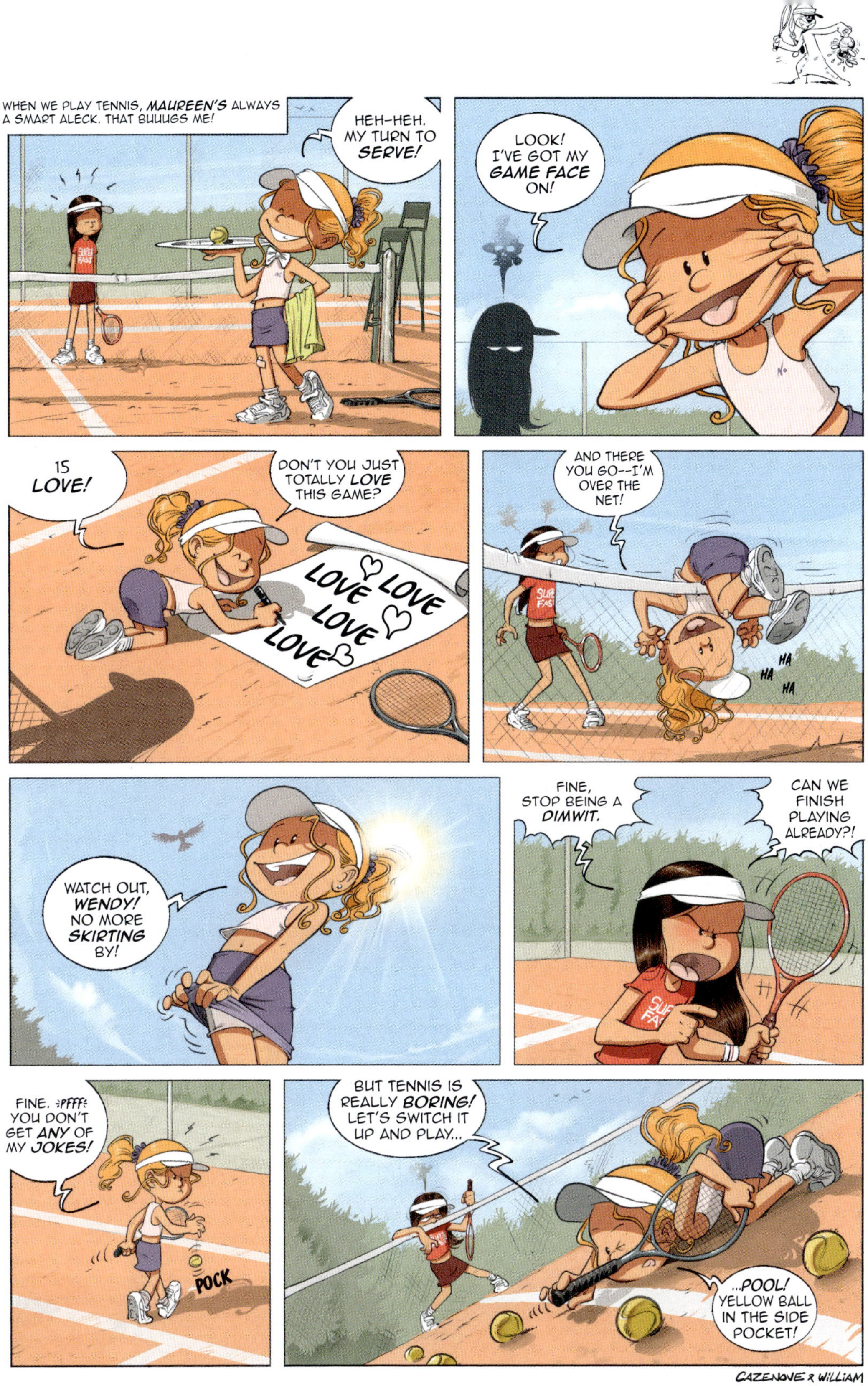
WHEN WE PLAY TENNIS, MAUREEN'S ALWAYS A SMART ALECK. THAT BUUUGS ME!
HEH-HEH. MY TURN TO SERVE!
LOOK! I'VE GOT MY GAME FACE ON!
15 LOVE!
DON'T YOU JUST TOTALLY LOVE THIS GAME?
LOVE LOVE LOVE LOVE LOVE
AND THERE YOU GO--I'M OVER THE NET!
HA HA HA
WATCH OUT, WENDY! NO MORE SKIRTING BY!
FINE, STOP BEING A DIMWIT.
CAN WE FINISH PLAYING ALREADY?!
FINE. PFFF YOU DON'T GET ANY OF MY JOKES!
POCK
BUT TENNIS IS REALLY BORING! LET'S SWITCH IT UP AND PLAY...
...POOL! YELLOW BALL IN THE SIDE POCKET!
CAZENOVE & WILLIAM

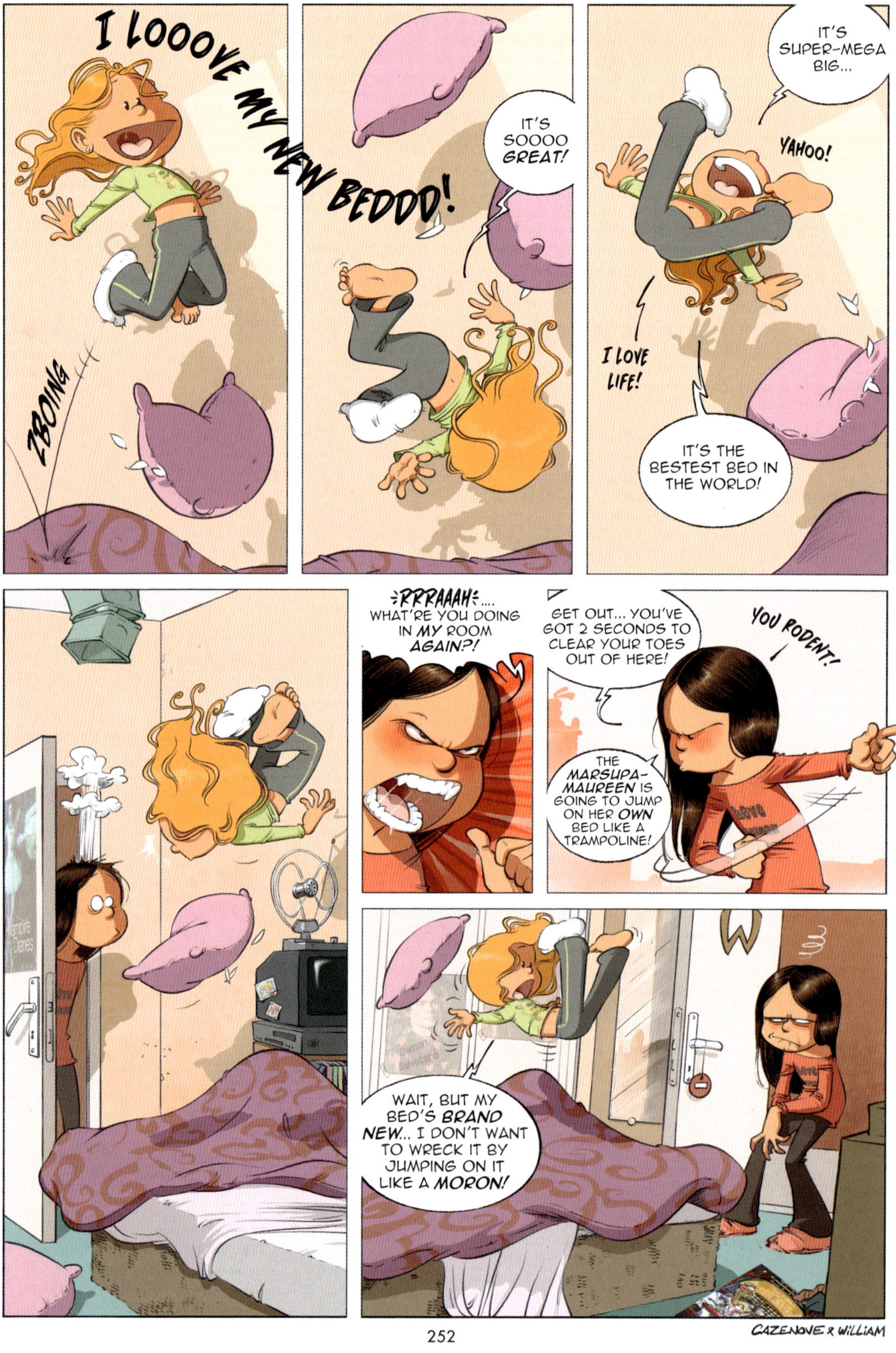
I LOOOVE MY NEW BEDDD!
ZBOING
IT'S SOOOO GREAT!
IT'S SUPER-MEGA BIG...
YAHOO!
I LOVE LIFE!
IT'S THE BESTEST BED IN THE WORLD!
RRRAAAH!.... WHAT'RE YOU DOING IN MY ROOM AGAIN?!
GET OUT... YOU'VE GOT 2 SECONDS TO CLEAR YOUR TOES OUT OF HERE!
YOU RODENT!
THE MARSUPA-MAUREEN IS GOING TO JUMP ON HER OWN BED LIKE A TRAMPOLINE!
WAIT, BUT MY BED'S BRAND NEW... I DON'T WANT TO WRECK IT BY JUMPING ON IT LIKE A MORON!

CAZENOVE & WILLIAM

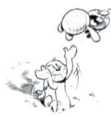

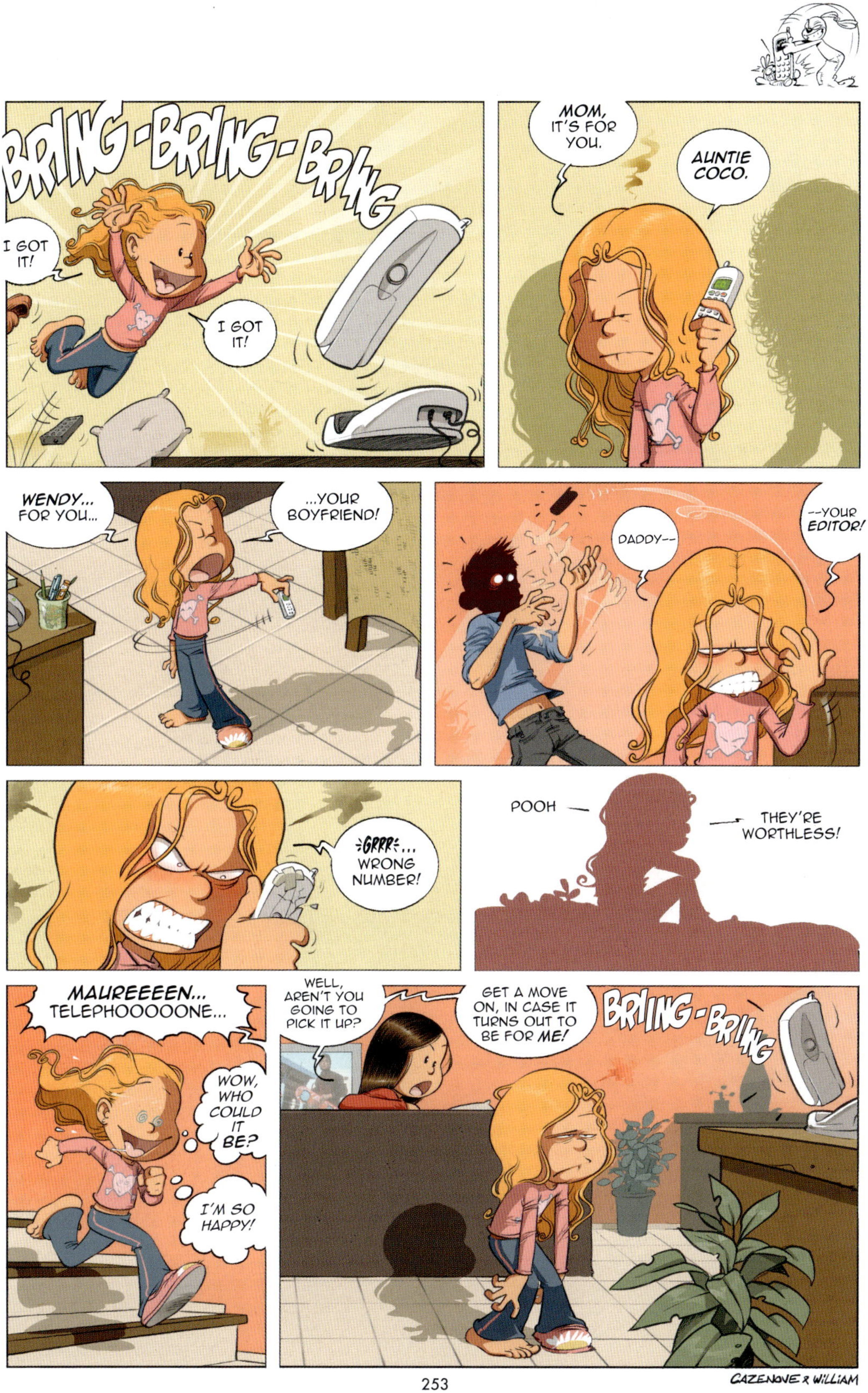
BRING-BRING-BRING
I GOT IT!
I GOT IT!
MOM, IT'S FOR YOU.
AUNTIE COCO.
WENDY... FOR YOU...
...YOUR BOYFRIEND!
DADDY--
--YOUR EDITOR!
GRRR... WRONG NUMBER!
POOH
THEY'RE WORTHLESS!
MAUREEEEN... TELEPHOOOOONE...
WOW, WHO COULD IT BE?
I'M SO HAPPY!
WELL, AREN'T YOU GOING TO PICK IT UP?
GET A MOVE ON, IN CASE IT TURNS OUT TO BE FOR ME!
BRIING-BRING
CAZENOVE & WILLIAM

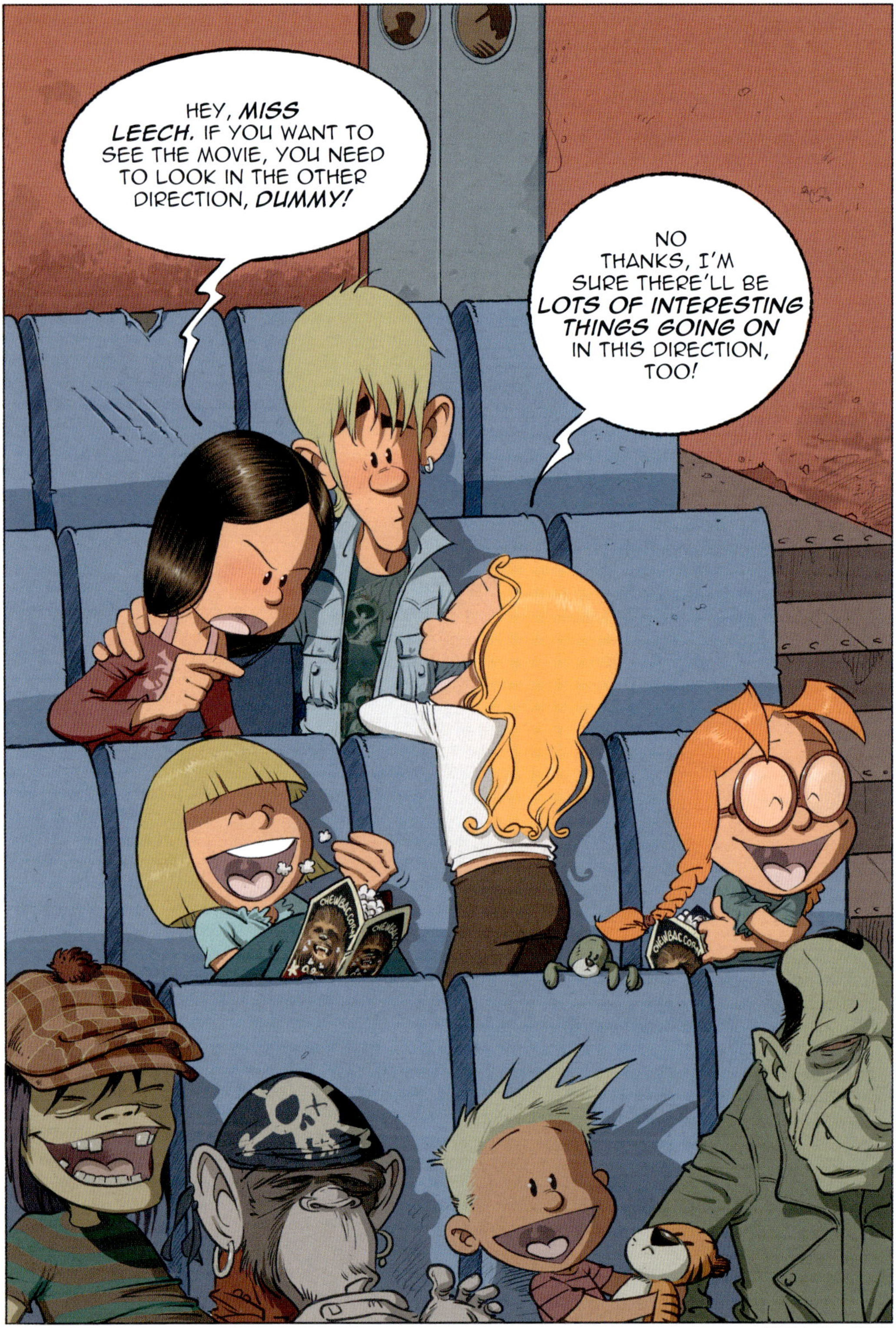
HEY, MISS LEECH. IF YOU WANT TO SEE THE MOVIE, YOU NEED TO LOOK IN THE OTHER DIRECTION, DUMMY!
NO THANKS, I'M SURE THERE'LL BE LOTS OF INTERESTING THINGS GOING ON IN THIS DIRECTION, TOO!
CAZENOVE & WILLIAM

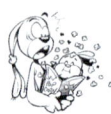

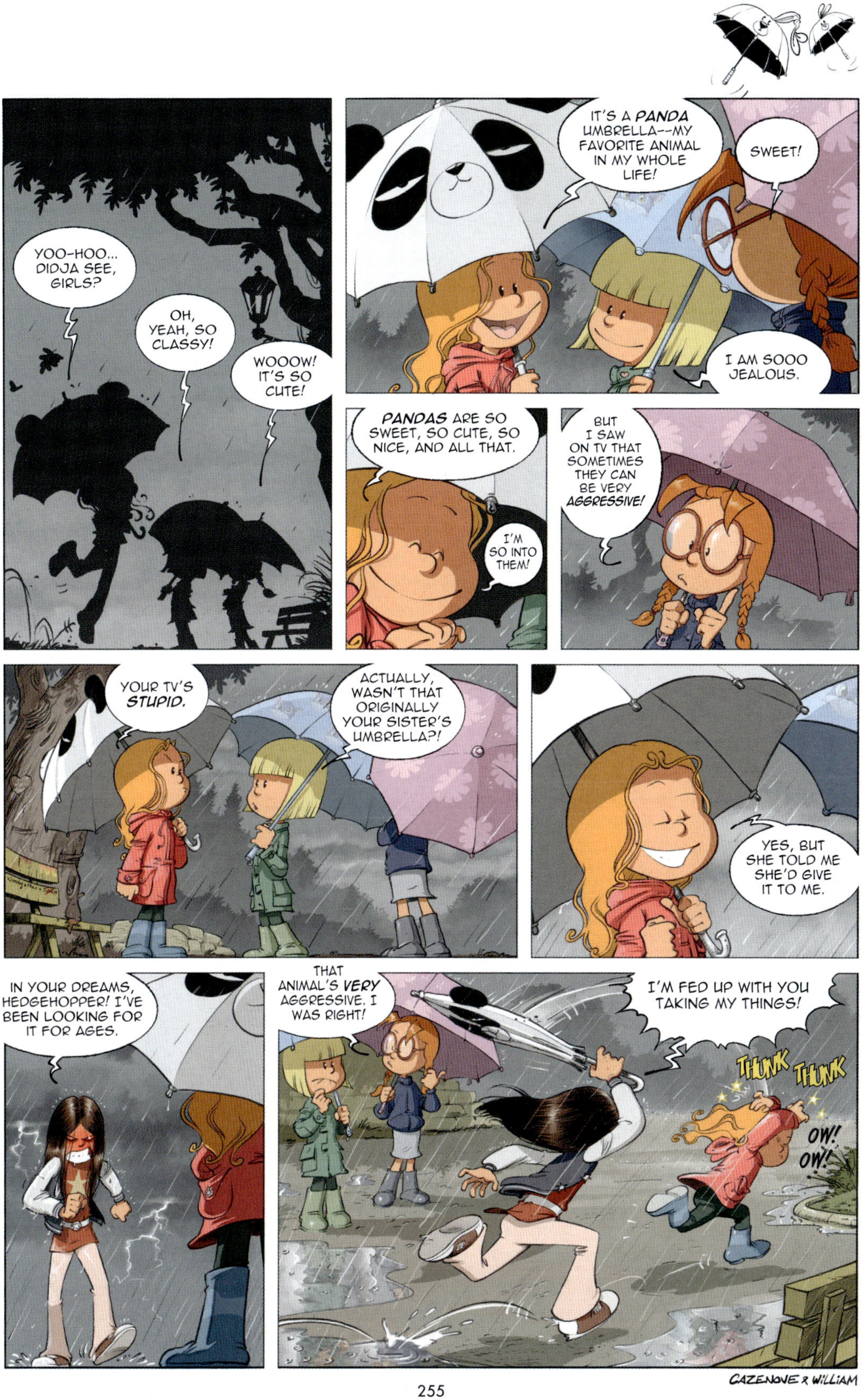
YOO-HOO... DIDJA SEE, GIRLS?
OH, YEAH, SO CLASSY!
WOOOW! IT'S SO CUTE!
IT'S A PANDA UMBRELLA--MY FAVORITE ANIMAL IN MY WHOLE LIFE!
SWEET!
I AM SOOO JEALOUS.
PANDAS ARE SO SWEET, SO CUTE, SO NICE, AND ALL THAT.
I'M SO INTO THEM!
BUT I SAW ON TV THAT SOMETIMES THEY CAN BE VERY AGGRESSIVE!
YOUR TV'S STUPID.
ACTUALLY, WASN'T THAT ORIGINALLY YOUR SISTER'S UMBRELLA?!
YES, BUT SHE TOLD ME SHE'D GIVE IT TO ME.
IN YOUR DREAMS, HEDGEHOPPER! I'VE BEEN LOOKING FOR IT FOR AGES.
THAT ANIMAL'S VERY AGGRESSIVE. I WAS RIGHT!
I'M FED UP WITH YOU TAKING MY THINGS!
THUNK THUNK
OW! OW!
CAZENOVE & WILLIAM

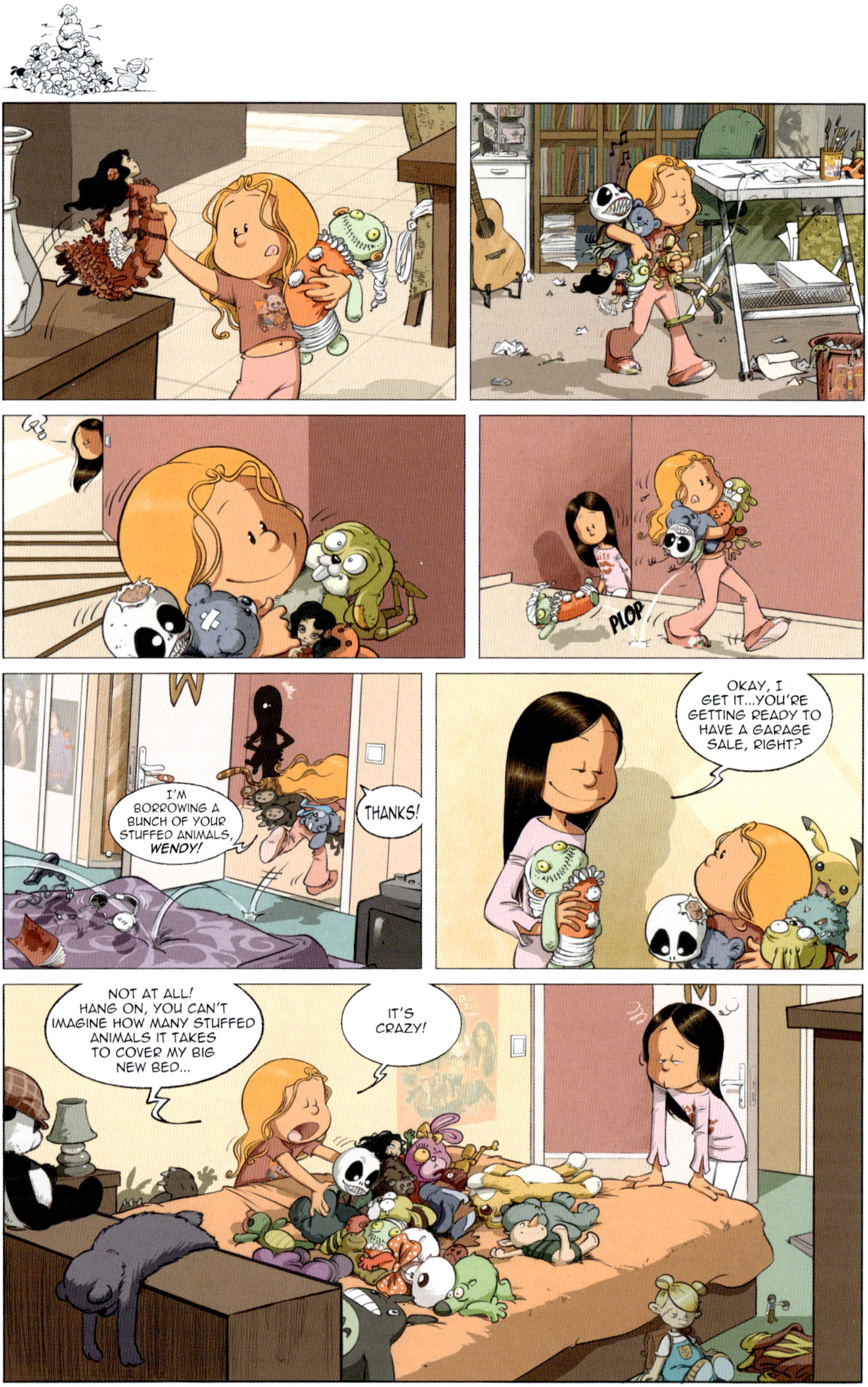
PLOP
I'M BORROWING A BUNCH OF YOUR STUFFED ANIMALS, WENDY!
THANKS!
OKAY, I GET IT...YOU'RE GETTING READY TO HAVE A GARAGE SALE, RIGHT?
NOT AT ALL! HANG ON, YOU CAN'T IMAGINE HOW MANY STUFFED ANIMALS IT TAKES TO COVER MY BIG NEW BED...
IT'S CRAZY!
CAZENOVE & WILLIAM

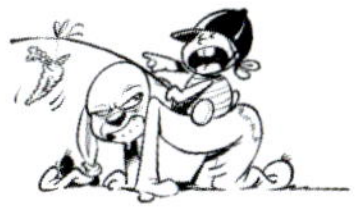

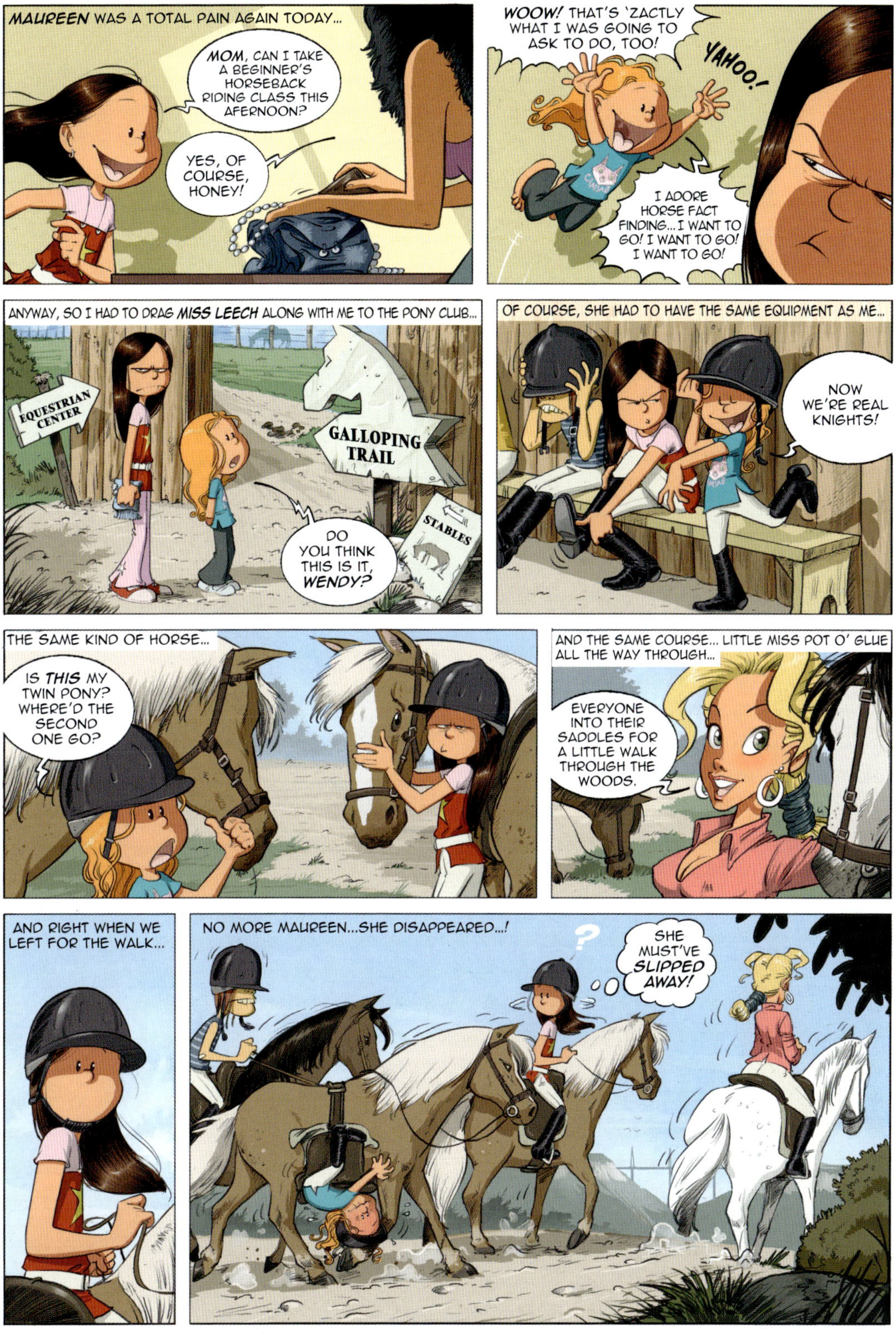
MAUREEN WAS A TOTAL PAIN AGAIN TODAY...
MOM, CAN I TAKE A BEGINNER'S HORSEBACK RIDING CLASS THIS AFERNOON?
YES, OF COURSE, HONEY!
WOOW! THAT'S 'ZACTLY WHAT I WAS GOING TO ASK TO DO, TOO!
YAHOO!
I ADORE HORSE FACT FINDING... I WANT TO GO! I WANT TO GO! I WANT TO GO!
ANYWAY, SO I HAD TO DRAG MISS LEECH ALONG WITH ME TO THE PONY CLUB...
EQUESTRIAN CENTER
GALLOPING TRAIL
STABLES
DO YOU THINK THIS IS IT, WENDY?
OF COURSE, SHE HAD TO HAVE THE SAME EQUIPMENT AS ME...
NOW WE'RE REAL KNIGHTS!
THE SAME KIND OF HORSE...
IS THIS MY TWIN PONY? WHERE'D THE SECOND ONE GO?
AND THE SAME COURSE... LITTLE MISS POT O' GLUE ALL THE WAY THROUGH...
EVERYONE INTO THEIR SADDLES FOR A LITTLE WALK THROUGH THE WOODS.
AND RIGHT WHEN WE LEFT FOR THE WALK...
NO MORE MAUREEN...SHE DISAPPEARED...!
?
SHE MUST'VE SLIPPED AWAY!
CAZENOVE & WILLIAM

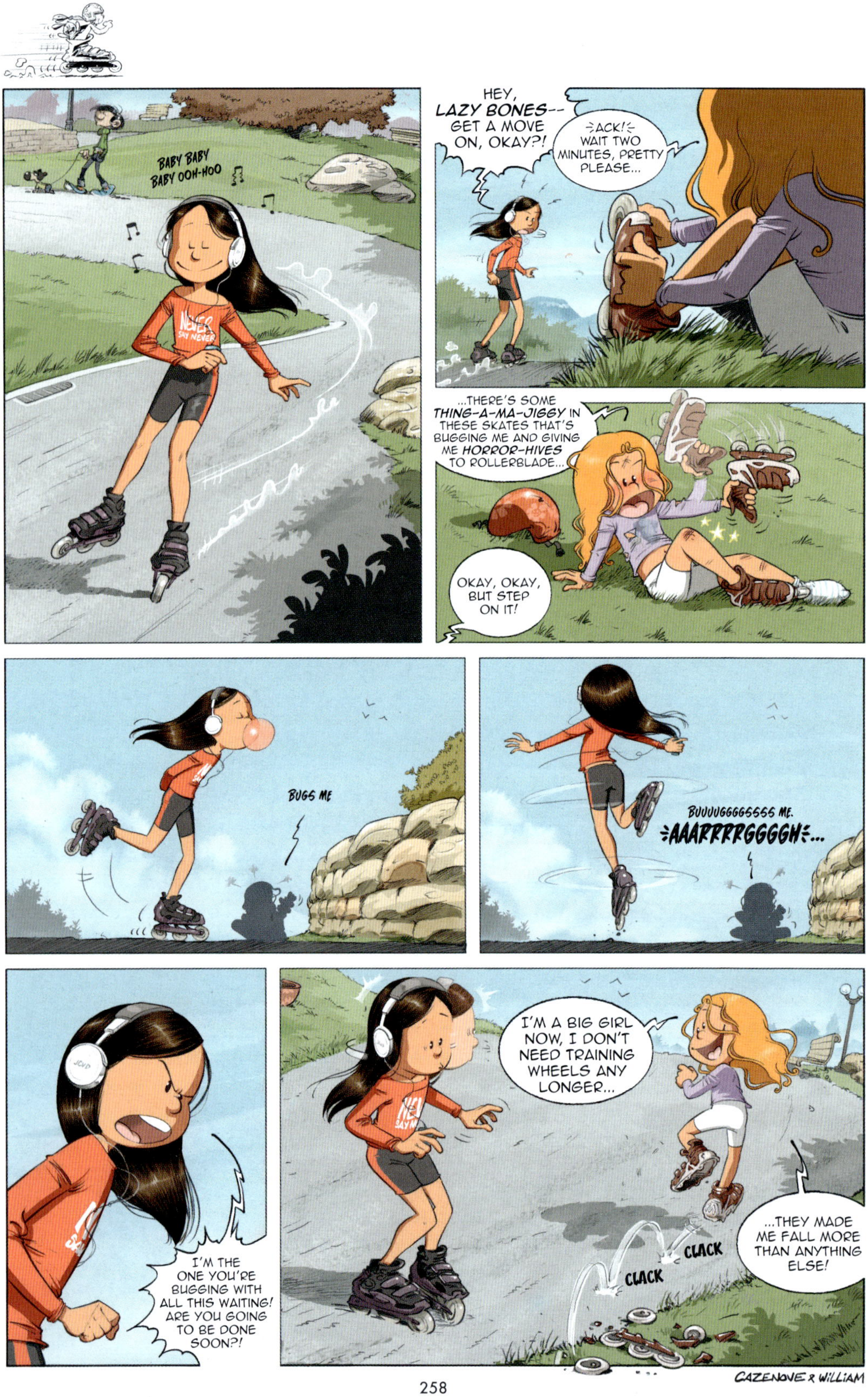
BABY BABY
BABY OOH-HOO
NEVER SAY NEVER
HEY, LAZY BONES-- GET A MOVE ON, OKAY?!
ACK! WAIT TWO MINUTES, PRETTY PLEASE...
...THERE'S SOME THING-A-MA-JIGGY IN THESE SKATES THAT'S BUGGING ME AND GIVING ME HORROR-HIVES TO ROLLERBLADE...
OKAY, OKAY, BUT STEP ON IT!
BUGS ME
BUUUUGGGGSSSS ME.
AAARRRRGGGGH...
I'M THE ONE YOU'RE BUGGING WITH ALL THIS WAITING! ARE YOU GOING TO BE DONE SOON?!
I'M A BIG GIRL NOW, I DON'T NEED TRAINING WHEELS ANY LONGER...
CLACK
CLACK
...THEY MADE ME FALL MORE THAN ANYTHING ELSE!
CAZENOVE & WILLIAM

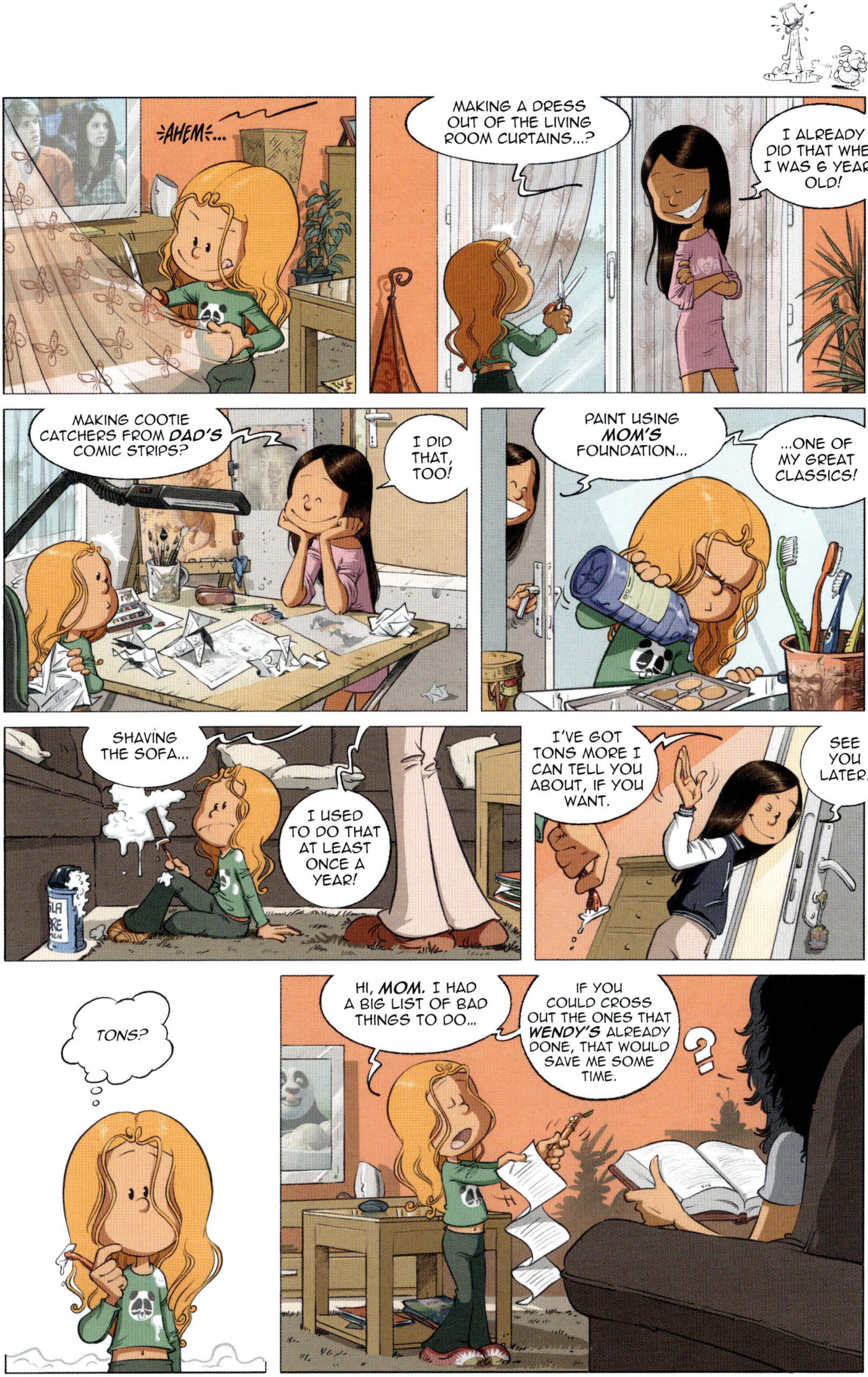
AHEM...
MAKING A DRESS OUT OF THE LIVING ROOM CURTAINS...?
I ALREADY DID THAT WHEN I WAS 6 YEARS OLD!
MAKING COOTIE CATCHERS FROM *DAD'S* COMIC STRIPS?
I DID THAT, TOO!
PAINT USING *MOM'S* FOUNDATION...
...ONE OF MY GREAT CLASSICS!
SHAVING THE SOFA...
I USED TO DO THAT AT LEAST ONCE A YEAR!
I'VE GOT TONS MORE I CAN TELL YOU ABOUT, IF YOU WANT.
SEE YOU LATER.
TONS?
HI, *MOM.* I HAD A BIG LIST OF BAD THINGS TO DO...
IF YOU COULD CROSS OUT THE ONES THAT *WENDY'S* ALREADY DONE, THAT WOULD SAVE ME SOME TIME.
?

CAZENOVE & WILLIAM

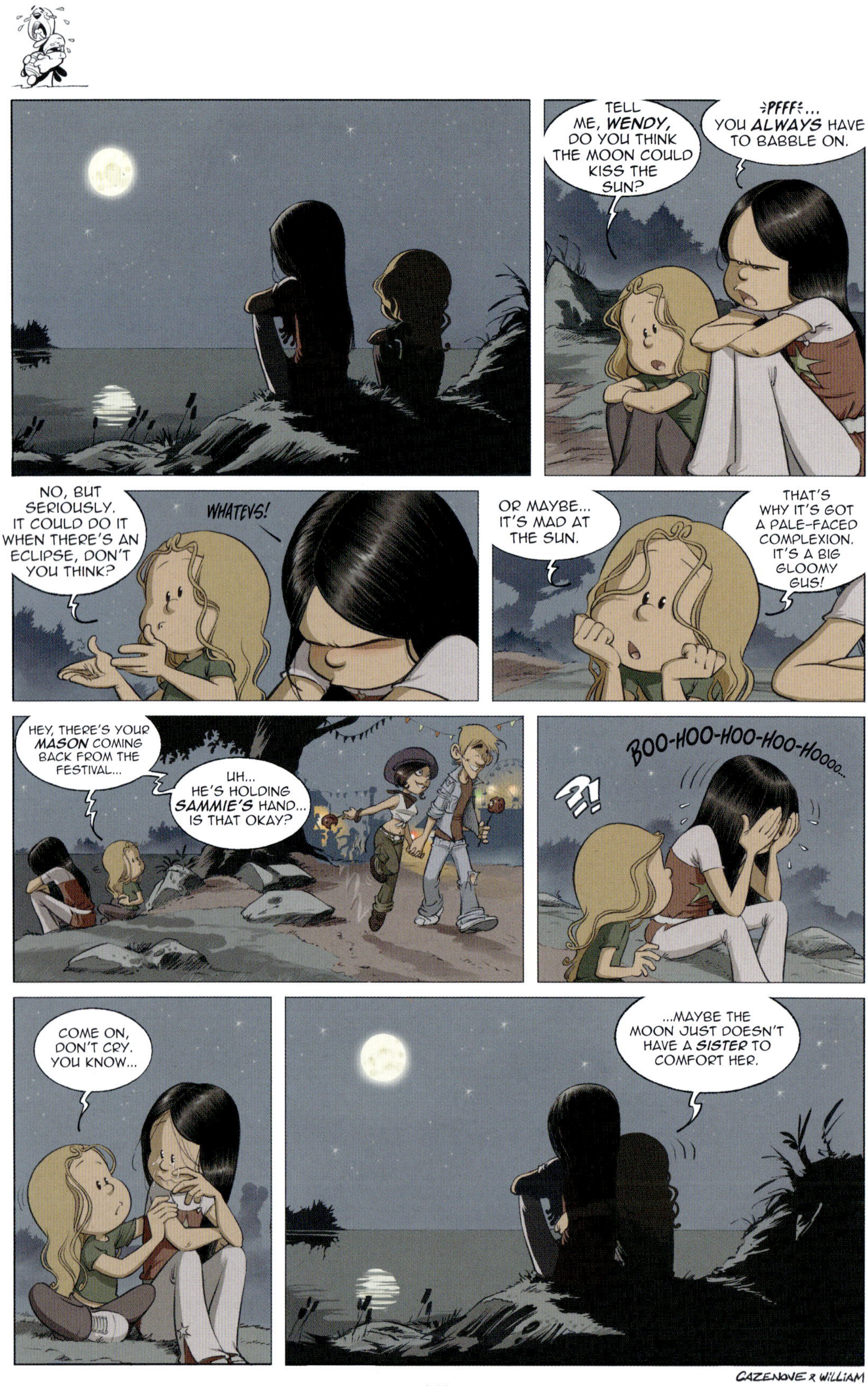
TELL ME, WENDY, DO YOU THINK THE MOON COULD KISS THE SUN?
PFFF... YOU ALWAYS HAVE TO BABBLE ON.
NO, BUT SERIOUSLY. IT COULD DO IT WHEN THERE'S AN ECLIPSE, DON'T YOU THINK?
WHATEVS!
OR MAYBE... IT'S MAD AT THE SUN.
THAT'S WHY IT'S GOT A PALE-FACED COMPLEXION. IT'S A BIG GLOOMY GUS!
HEY, THERE'S YOUR MASON COMING BACK FROM THE FESTIVAL...
UH... HE'S HOLDING SAMMIE'S HAND... IS THAT OKAY?
BOO-HOO-HOO-HOO-HOOOO...
?!
COME ON, DON'T CRY. YOU KNOW...
...MAYBE THE MOON JUST DOESN'T HAVE A SISTER TO COMFORT HER.
CAZENOVE & WILLIAM

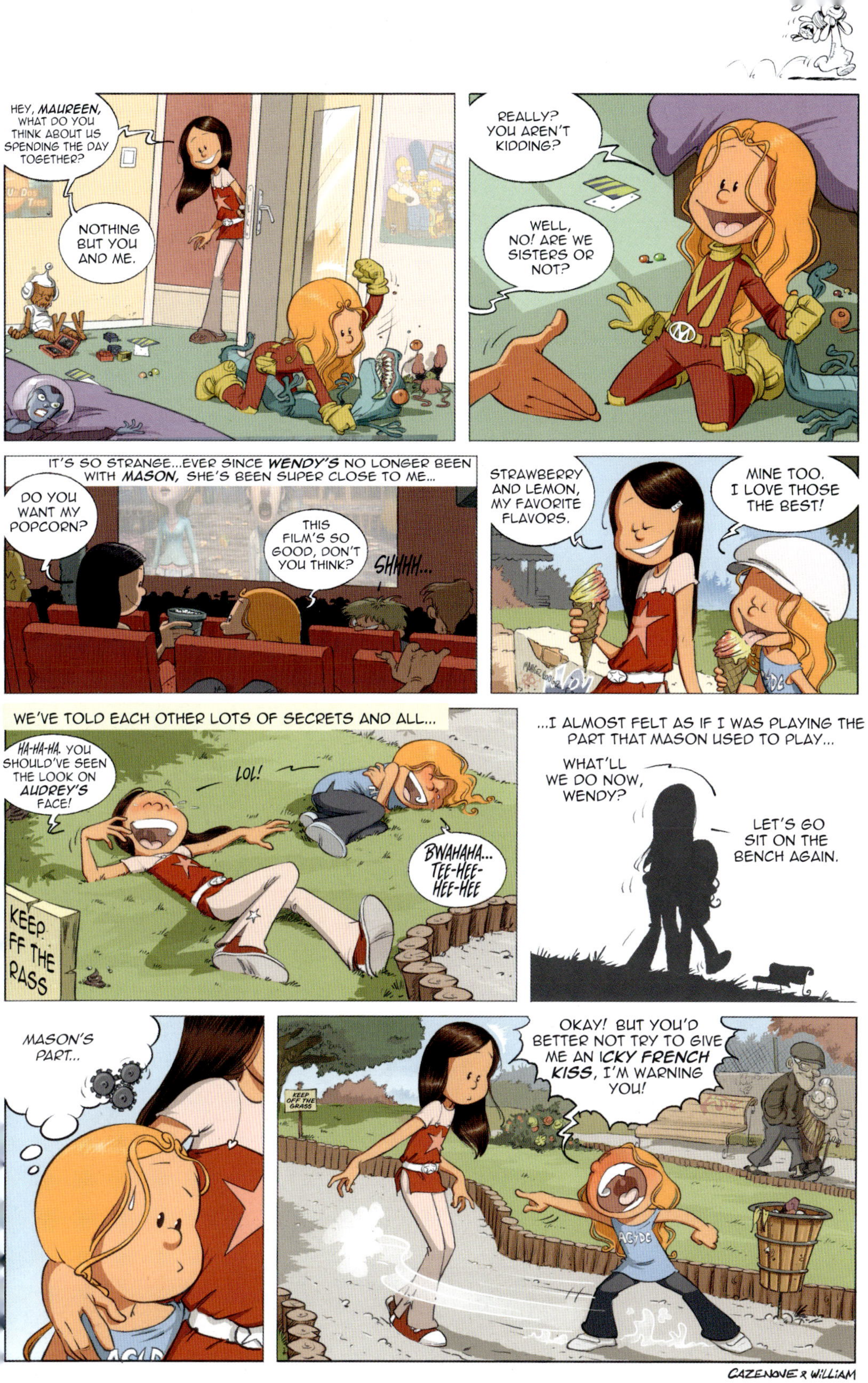
HEY, MAUREEN, WHAT DO YOU THINK ABOUT US SPENDING THE DAY TOGETHER?
NOTHING BUT YOU AND ME.
REALLY? YOU AREN'T KIDDING?
WELL, NO! ARE WE SISTERS OR NOT?
IT'S SO STRANGE...EVER SINCE WENDY'S NO LONGER BEEN WITH MASON, SHE'S BEEN SUPER CLOSE TO ME...
DO YOU WANT MY POPCORN?
THIS FILM'S SO GOOD, DON'T YOU THINK?
SHHHH...
STRAWBERRY AND LEMON, MY FAVORITE FLAVORS.
MINE TOO. I LOVE THOSE THE BEST!
WE'VE TOLD EACH OTHER LOTS OF SECRETS AND ALL...
HA-HA-HA. YOU SHOULD'VE SEEN THE LOOK ON AUDREY'S FACE!
LOL!
BWAHAHA... TEE-HEE-HEE-HEE
KEEP
FF THE
RASS
...I ALMOST FELT AS IF I WAS PLAYING THE PART THAT MASON USED TO PLAY...
WHAT'LL WE DO NOW, WENDY?
LET'S GO SIT ON THE BENCH AGAIN.
MASON'S PART...
KEEP OFF THE GRASS
OKAY! BUT YOU'D BETTER NOT TRY TO GIVE ME AN ICKY FRENCH KISS, I'M WARNING YOU!
AC/DC
CAZENOVE & WILLIAM

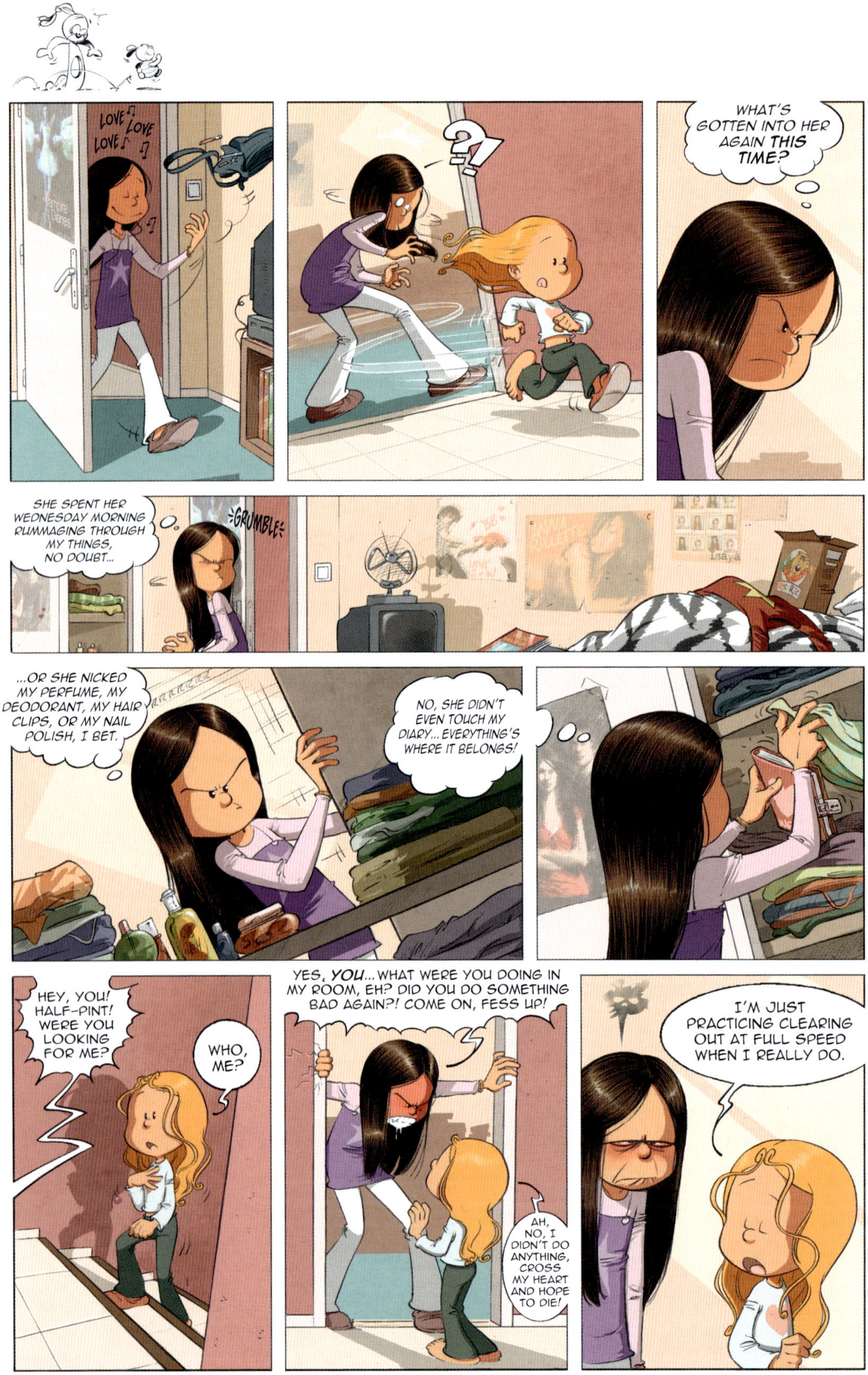

LOVE LOVE LOVE
?!
WHAT'S GOTTEN INTO HER AGAIN THIS TIME?
SHE SPENT HER WEDNESDAY MORNING RUMMAGING THROUGH MY THINGS, NO DOUBT...
GRUMBLE
...OR SHE NICKED MY PERFUME, MY DEODORANT, MY HAIR CLIPS, OR MY NAIL POLISH, I BET.
NO, SHE DIDN'T EVEN TOUCH MY DIARY... EVERYTHING'S WHERE IT BELONGS!
HEY, YOU! HALF-PINT! WERE YOU LOOKING FOR ME?
WHO, ME?
YES, YOU... WHAT WERE YOU DOING IN MY ROOM, EH? DID YOU DO SOMETHING BAD AGAIN?! COME ON, FESS UP!
AH, NO, I DIDN'T DO ANYTHING, CROSS MY HEART AND HOPE TO DIE!
I'M JUST PRACTICING CLEARING OUT AT FULL SPEED WHEN I REALLY DO.

CAZENOVE & WILLIAM

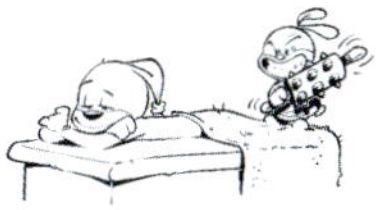

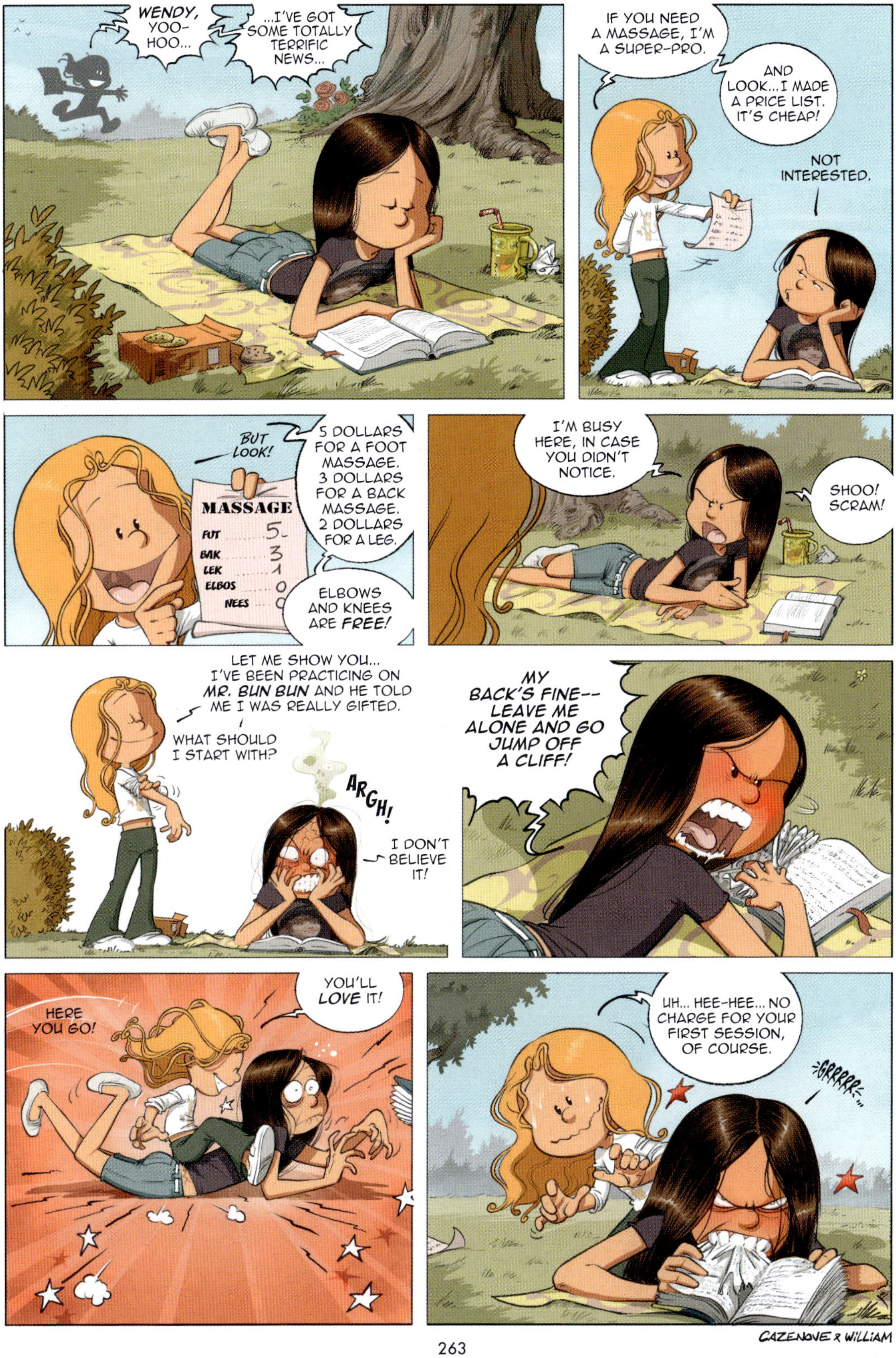

WENDY, YOO-HOO...
...I'VE GOT SOME TOTALLY TERRIFIC NEWS...
IF YOU NEED A MASSAGE, I'M A SUPER-PRO.
AND LOOK...I MADE A PRICE LIST. IT'S CHEAP!
NOT INTERESTED.
BUT LOOK!
MASSAGE
FUT 5
BAK 3
LEK 1
ELBOS 0
NEES 0
5 DOLLARS FOR A FOOT MASSAGE. 3 DOLLARS FOR A BACK MASSAGE. 2 DOLLARS FOR A LEG.
ELBOWS AND KNEES ARE FREE!
I'M BUSY HERE, IN CASE YOU DIDN'T NOTICE.
SHOO! SCRAM!
LET ME SHOW YOU... I'VE BEEN PRACTICING ON MR. BUN BUN AND HE TOLD ME I WAS REALLY GIFTED.
WHAT SHOULD I START WITH?
ARGH!
I DON'T BELIEVE IT!
MY BACK'S FINE-- LEAVE ME ALONE AND GO JUMP OFF A CLIFF!
HERE YOU GO!
YOU'LL LOVE IT!
UH... HEE-HEE... NO CHARGE FOR YOUR FIRST SESSION, OF COURSE.
GRRRRR
CAZENOVE & WILLIAM

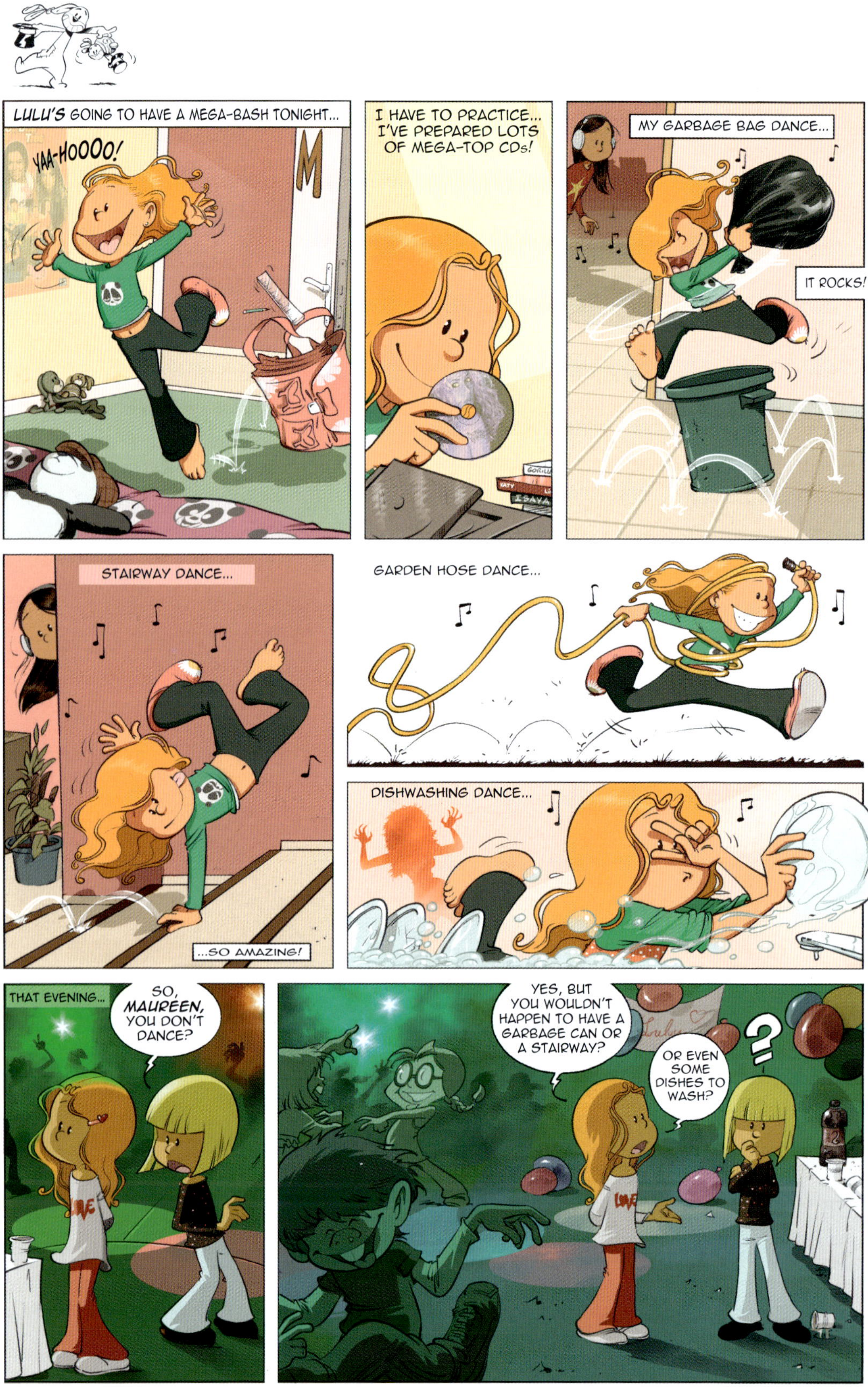
LULU'S GOING TO HAVE A MEGA-BASH TONIGHT...
YAA-HOOOO!
M
I HAVE TO PRACTICE... I'VE PREPARED LOTS OF MEGA-TOP CDs!
MY GARBAGE BAG DANCE...
IT ROCKS!
STAIRWAY DANCE...
...SO AMAZING!
GARDEN HOSE DANCE...
DISHWASHING DANCE...
THAT EVENING...
SO, MAUREEN, YOU DON'T DANCE?
LOVE
YES, BUT YOU WOULDN'T HAPPEN TO HAVE A GARBAGE CAN OR A STAIRWAY?
OR EVEN SOME DISHES TO WASH?
?
LOVE

CAZENOVE & WILLIAM

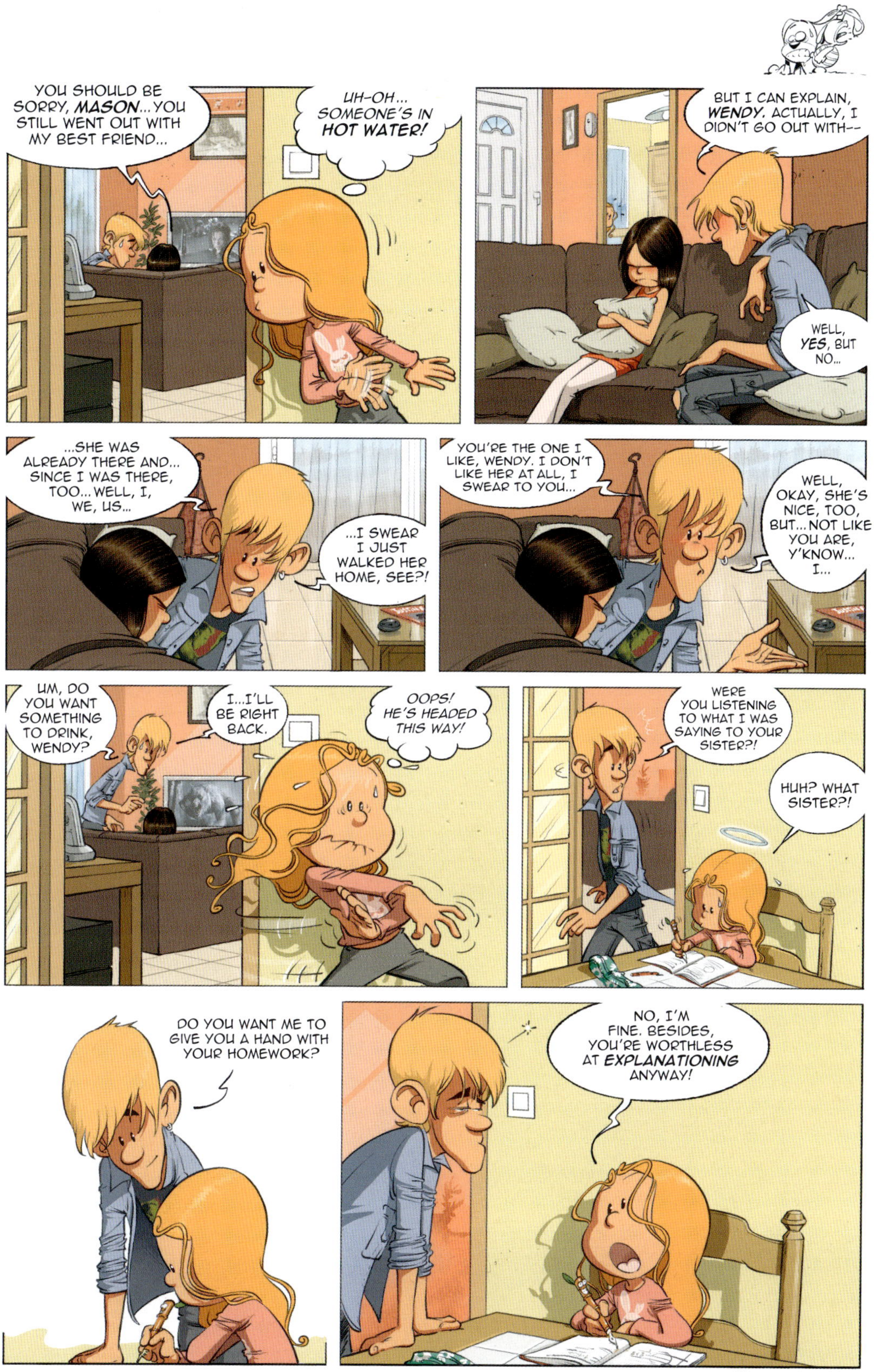
YOU SHOULD BE SORRY, MASON... YOU STILL WENT OUT WITH MY BEST FRIEND...
UH-OH... SOMEONE'S IN HOT WATER!
BUT I CAN EXPLAIN, WENDY. ACTUALLY, I DIDN'T GO OUT WITH--
WELL, YES, BUT NO...
...SHE WAS ALREADY THERE AND... SINCE I WAS THERE, TOO... WELL, I, WE, US...
...I SWEAR I JUST WALKED HER HOME, SEE?!
YOU'RE THE ONE I LIKE, WENDY. I DON'T LIKE HER AT ALL, I SWEAR TO YOU...
WELL, OKAY, SHE'S NICE, TOO, BUT... NOT LIKE YOU ARE, Y'KNOW... I...
UM, DO YOU WANT SOMETHING TO DRINK, WENDY?
I...I'LL BE RIGHT BACK.
OOPS! HE'S HEADED THIS WAY!
WERE YOU LISTENING TO WHAT I WAS SAYING TO YOUR SISTER?!
HUH? WHAT SISTER?!
DO YOU WANT ME TO GIVE YOU A HAND WITH YOUR HOMEWORK?
NO, I'M FINE. BESIDES, YOU'RE WORTHLESS AT EXPLANATIONING ANYWAY!

CAZENOVE & WILLIAM

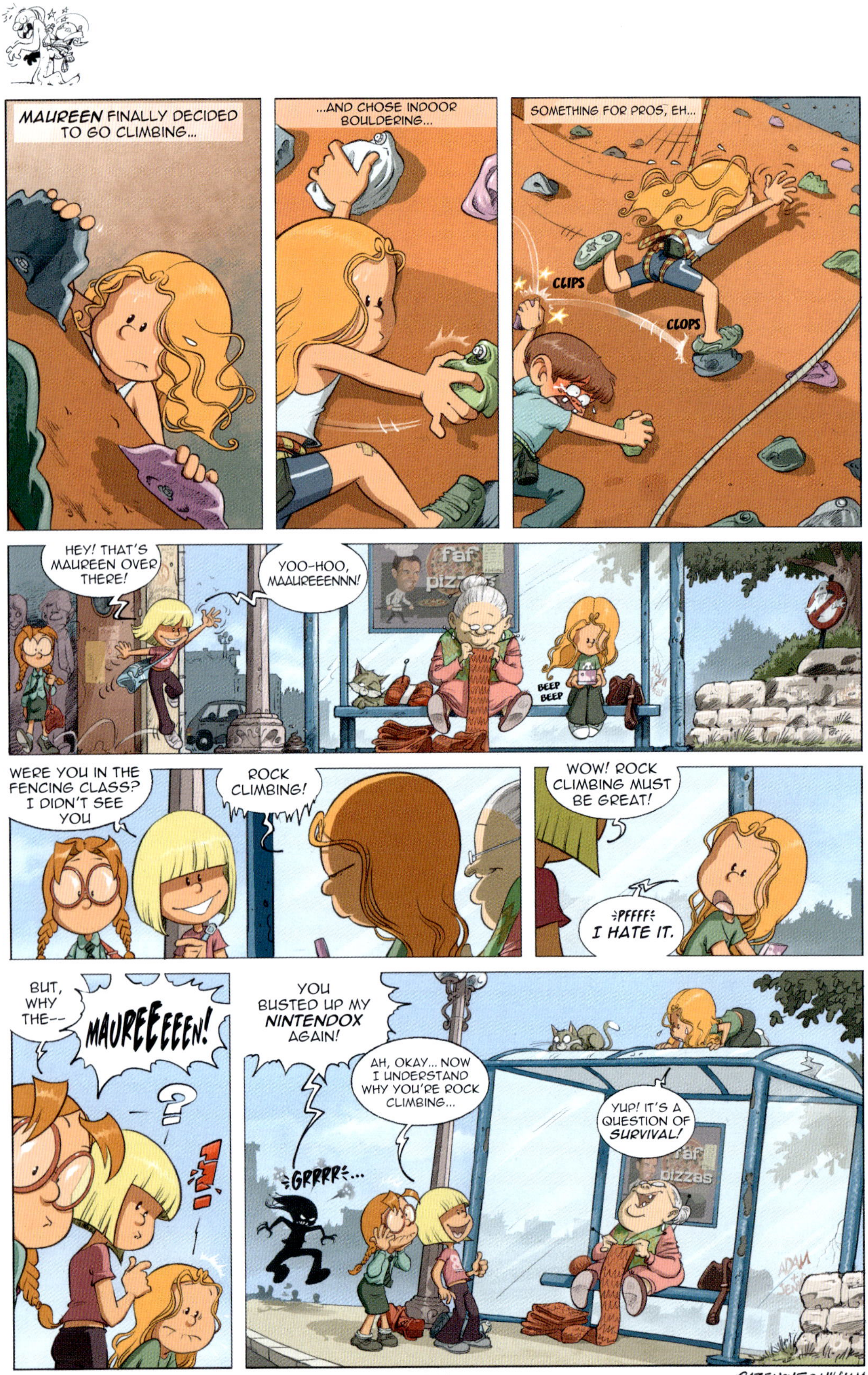

MAUREEN FINALLY DECIDED TO GO CLIMBING...
...AND CHOSE INDOOR BOULDERING...
SOMETHING FOR PROS, EH...
CLIPS
CLOPS
HEY! THAT'S MAUREEN OVER THERE!
YOO-HOO, MAAUREEENNN!
BEEP BEEP
WERE YOU IN THE FENCING CLASS? I DIDN'T SEE YOU
ROCK CLIMBING!
WOW! ROCK CLIMBING MUST BE GREAT!
PFFFF I HATE IT.
BUT, WHY THE--
MAUREEEEEEN!
?
!
YOU BUSTED UP MY NINTENDOX AGAIN!
AH, OKAY... NOW I UNDERSTAND WHY YOU'RE ROCK CLIMBING...
YUP! IT'S A QUESTION OF SURVIVAL!
GRRRR...
CAZENOVE & WILLIAM

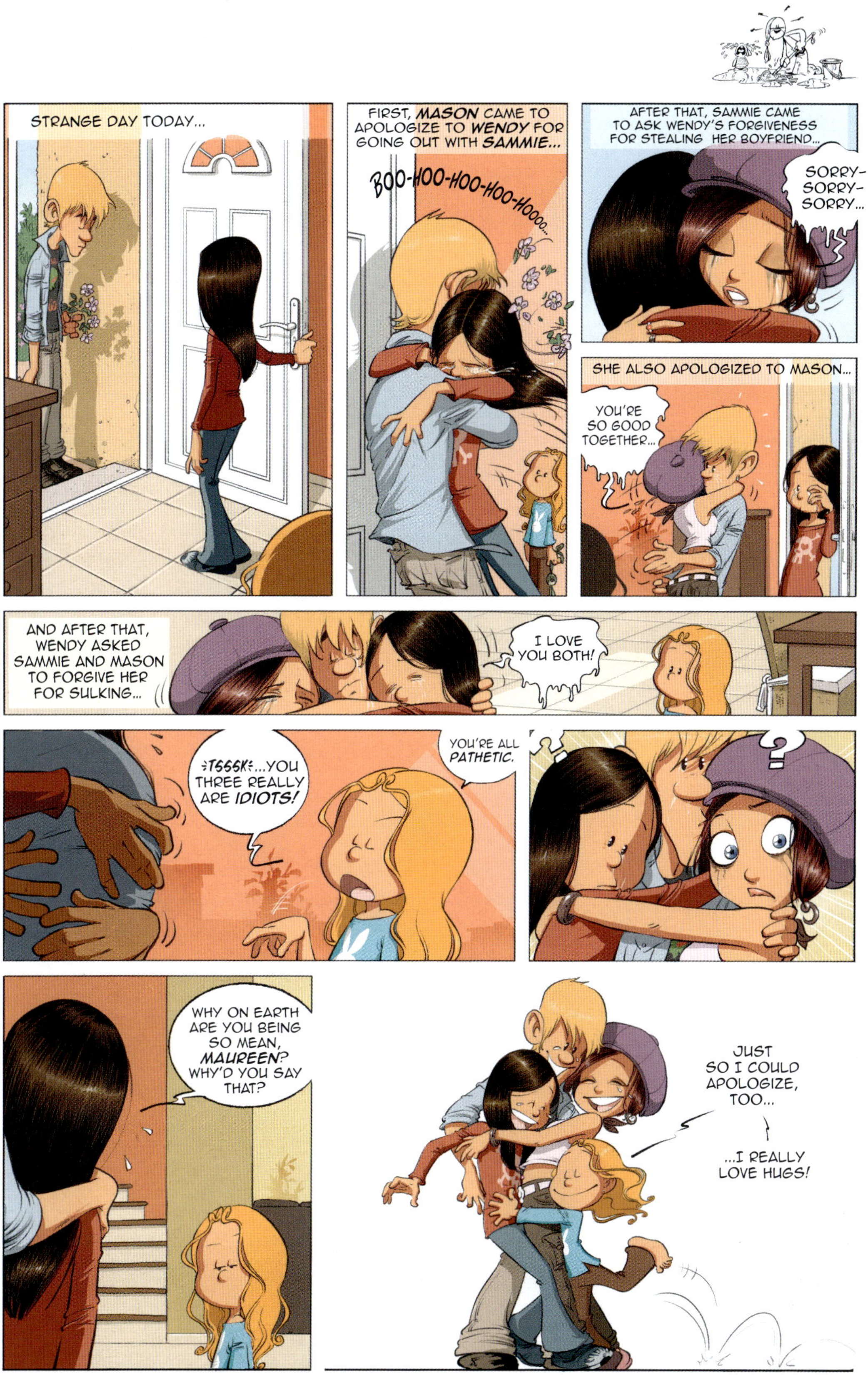
STRANGE DAY TODAY...
FIRST, MASON CAME TO APOLOGIZE TO WENDY FOR GOING OUT WITH SAMMIE...
BOO-HOO-HOO-HOO-HOOOO...
AFTER THAT, SAMMIE CAME TO ASK WENDY'S FORGIVENESS FOR STEALING HER BOYFRIEND...
SORRY-SORRY-SORRY...
SHE ALSO APOLOGIZED TO MASON...
YOU'RE SO GOOD TOGETHER...
AND AFTER THAT, WENDY ASKED SAMMIE AND MASON TO FORGIVE HER FOR SULKING...
I LOVE YOU BOTH!
TSSSK...YOU THREE REALLY ARE IDIOTS!
YOU'RE ALL PATHETIC.
?
WHY ON EARTH ARE YOU BEING SO MEAN, MAUREEN? WHY'D YOU SAY THAT?
JUST SO I COULD APOLOGIZE, TOO...
...I REALLY LOVE HUGS!

CAZENOVE & WILLIAM

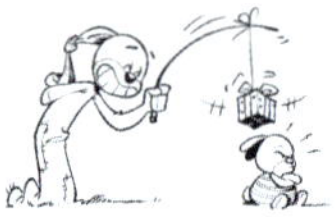

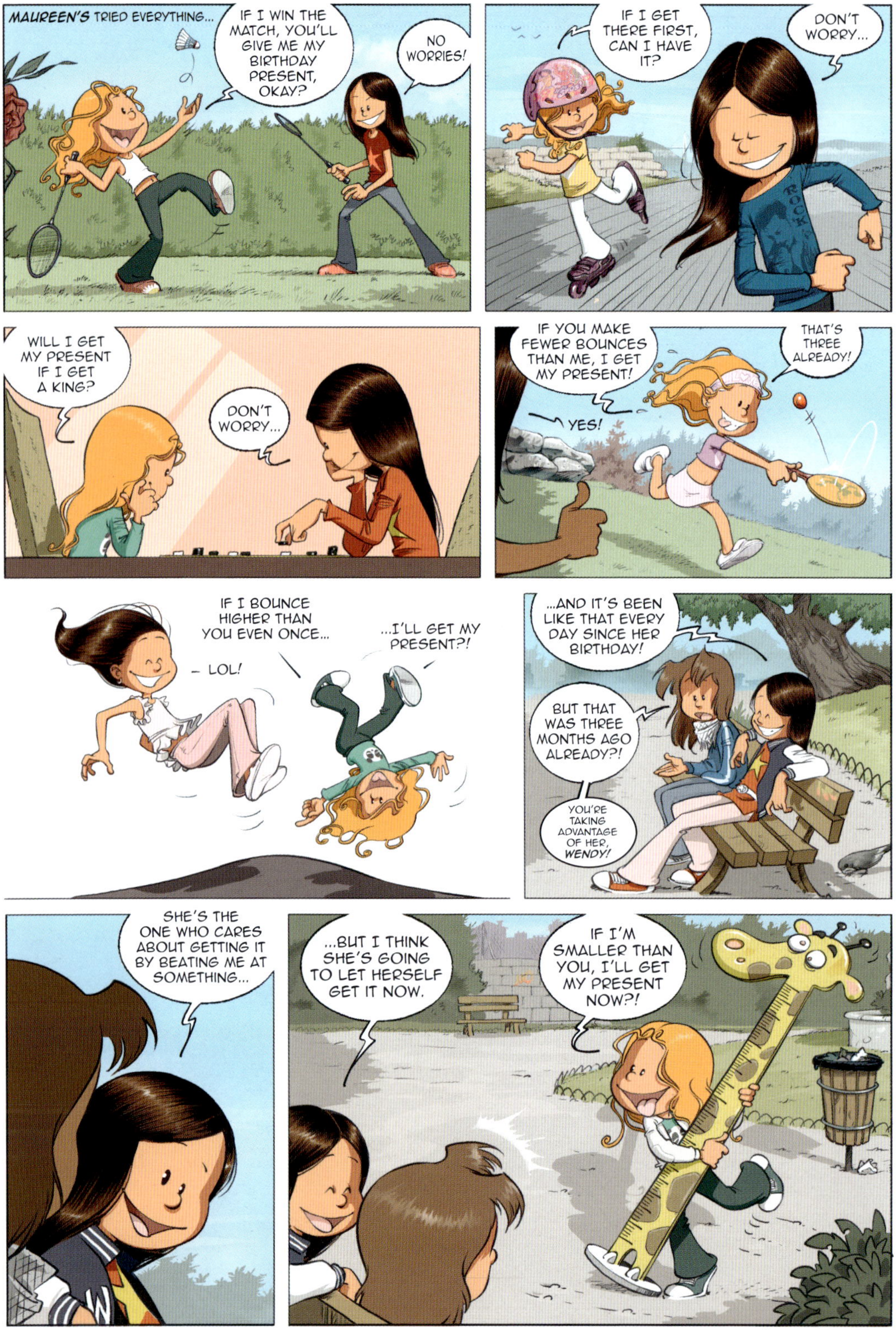
MAUREEN'S TRIED EVERYTHING...
IF I WIN THE MATCH, YOU'LL GIVE ME MY BIRTHDAY PRESENT, OKAY?
NO WORRIES!
IF I GET THERE FIRST, CAN I HAVE IT?
DON'T WORRY...
WILL I GET MY PRESENT IF I GET A KING?
DON'T WORRY...
IF YOU MAKE FEWER BOUNCES THAN ME, I GET MY PRESENT!
YES!
THAT'S THREE ALREADY!
IF I BOUNCE HIGHER THAN YOU EVEN ONCE...
...I'LL GET MY PRESENT?!
- LOL!
...AND IT'S BEEN LIKE THAT EVERY DAY SINCE HER BIRTHDAY!
BUT THAT WAS THREE MONTHS AGO ALREADY?!
YOU'RE TAKING ADVANTAGE OF HER, WENDY!
SHE'S THE ONE WHO CARES ABOUT GETTING IT BY BEATING ME AT SOMETHING...
...BUT I THINK SHE'S GOING TO LET HERSELF GET IT NOW.
IF I'M SMALLER THAN YOU, I'LL GET MY PRESENT NOW?!

CAZENOVE & WILLIAM

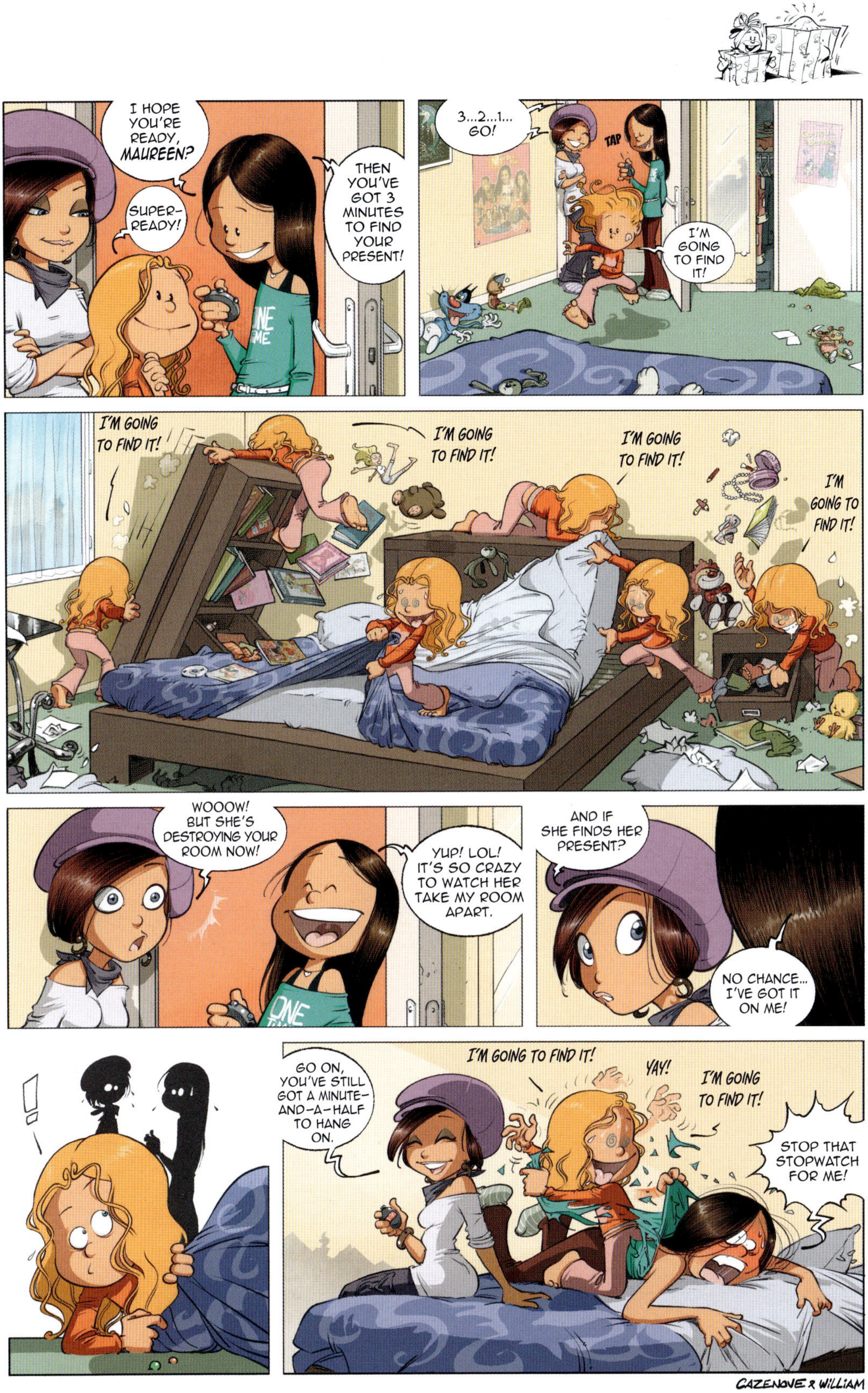
I HOPE YOU'RE READY, MAUREEN?
SUPER-READY!
THEN YOU'VE GOT 3 MINUTES TO FIND YOUR PRESENT!
3...2...1... GO!
TAP
I'M GOING TO FIND IT!
I'M GOING TO FIND IT!
I'M GOING TO FIND IT!
I'M GOING TO FIND IT!
I'M GOING TO FIND IT!
WOOOW! BUT SHE'S DESTROYING YOUR ROOM NOW!
YUP! LOL! IT'S SO CRAZY TO WATCH HER TAKE MY ROOM APART.
AND IF SHE FINDS HER PRESENT?
NO CHANCE... I'VE GOT IT ON ME!
!
GO ON, YOU'VE STILL GOT A MINUTE-AND-A-HALF TO HANG ON.
I'M GOING TO FIND IT!
YAY!
I'M GOING TO FIND IT!
STOP THAT STOPWATCH FOR ME!
CAZENOVE & WILLIAM

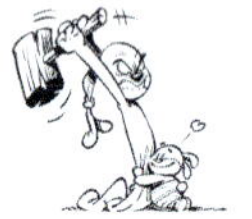

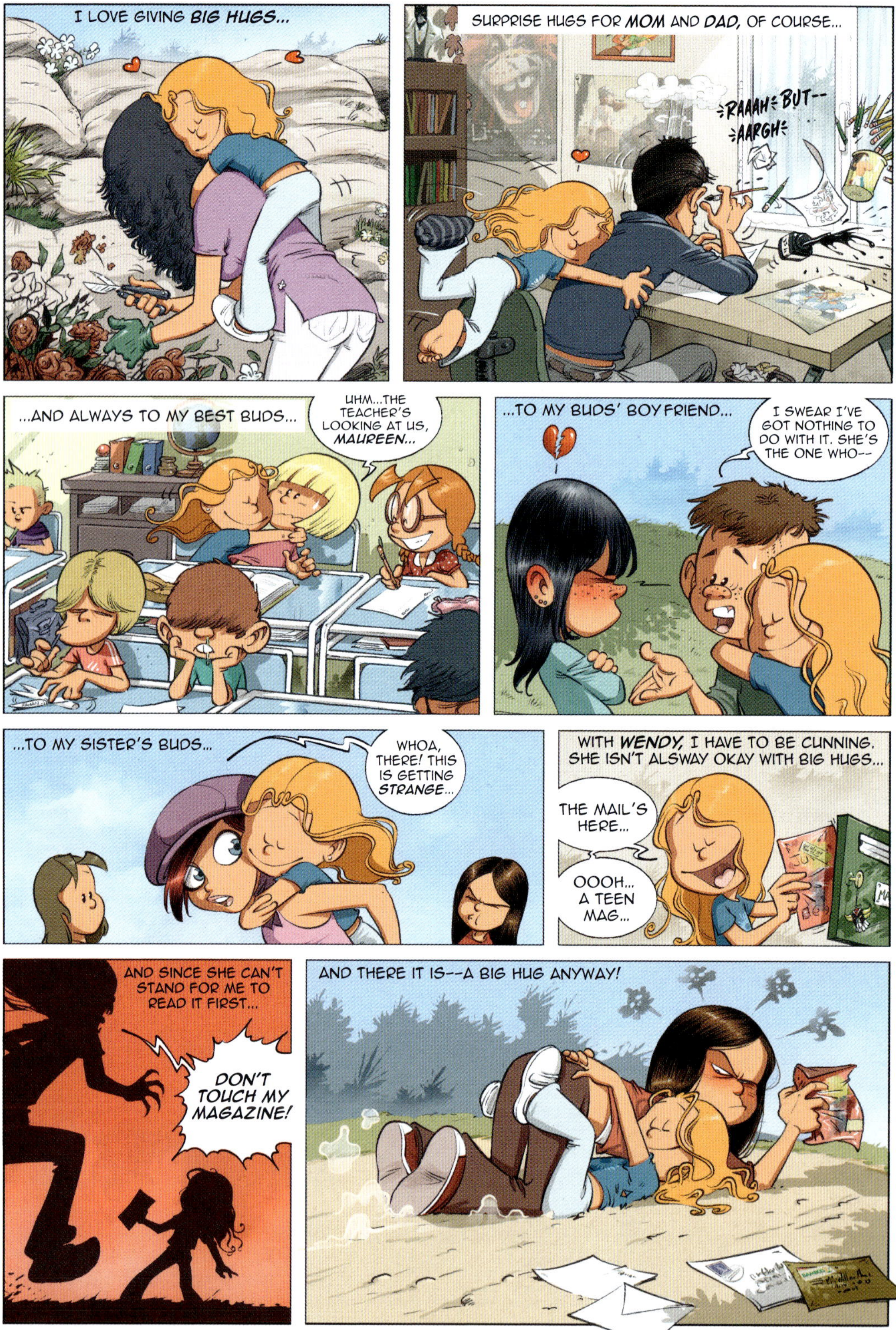

I LOVE GIVING BIG HUGS...
SURPRISE HUGS FOR MOM AND DAD, OF COURSE...
RAAAH BUT--
AARGH
...AND ALWAYS TO MY BEST BUDS...
UHM...THE TEACHER'S LOOKING AT US, MAUREEN...
...TO MY BUDS' BOYFRIEND...
I SWEAR I'VE GOT NOTHING TO DO WITH IT. SHE'S THE ONE WHO--
...TO MY SISTER'S BUDS...
WHOA, THERE! THIS IS GETTING STRANGE...
WITH WENDY, I HAVE TO BE CUNNING. SHE ISN'T ALSWAY OKAY WITH BIG HUGS...
THE MAIL'S HERE...
OOOH... A TEEN MAG...
AND SINCE SHE CAN'T STAND FOR ME TO READ IT FIRST...
DON'T TOUCH MY MAGAZINE!
AND THERE IT IS--A BIG HUG ANYWAY!

CAZENOVE & WILLIAM

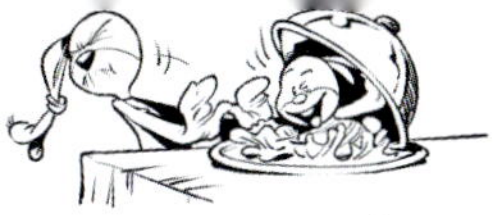

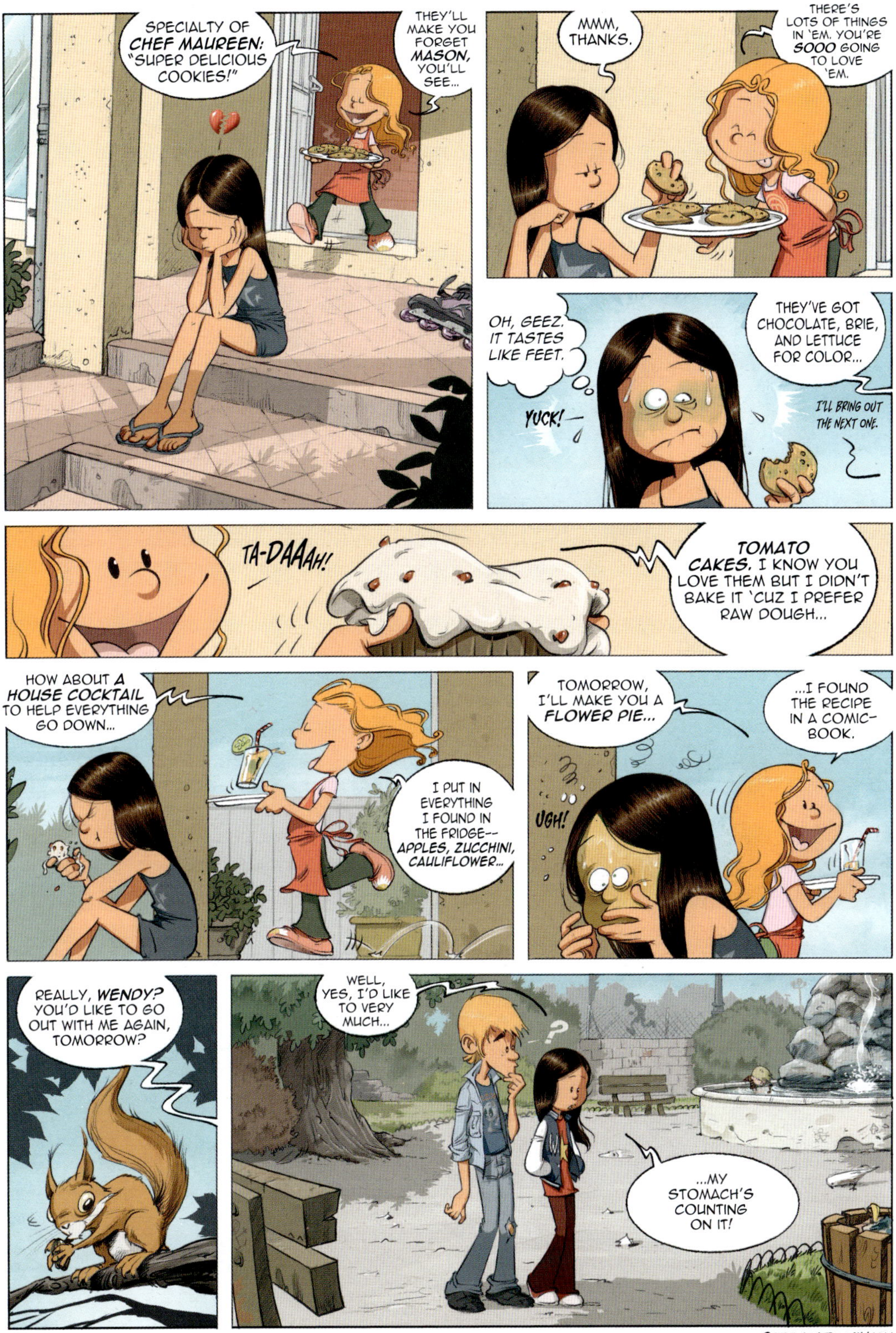

SPECIALTY OF CHEF MAUREEN: "SUPER DELICIOUS COOKIES!"
THEY'LL MAKE YOU FORGET MASON, YOU'LL SEE...
MMM, THANKS.
THERE'S LOTS OF THINGS IN 'EM. YOU'RE SOOO GOING TO LOVE 'EM.
OH, GEEZ. IT TASTES LIKE FEET.
THEY'VE GOT CHOCOLATE, BRIE, AND LETTUCE FOR COLOR...
YUCK!
I'LL BRING OUT THE NEXT ONE.
TA-DAAAH!
TOMATO CAKES. I KNOW YOU LOVE THEM BUT I DIDN'T BAKE IT 'CUZ I PREFER RAW DOUGH...
HOW ABOUT A HOUSE COCKTAIL TO HELP EVERYTHING GO DOWN...
I PUT IN EVERYTHING I FOUND IN THE FRIDGE-- APPLES, ZUCCHINI, CAULIFLOWER...
TOMORROW, I'LL MAKE YOU A FLOWER PIE...
...I FOUND THE RECIPE IN A COMIC-BOOK.
UGH!
REALLY, WENDY? YOU'D LIKE TO GO OUT WITH ME AGAIN, TOMORROW?
WELL, YES, I'D LIKE TO VERY MUCH...
?
...MY STOMACH'S COUNTING ON IT!

CAZENOVE & WILLIAM

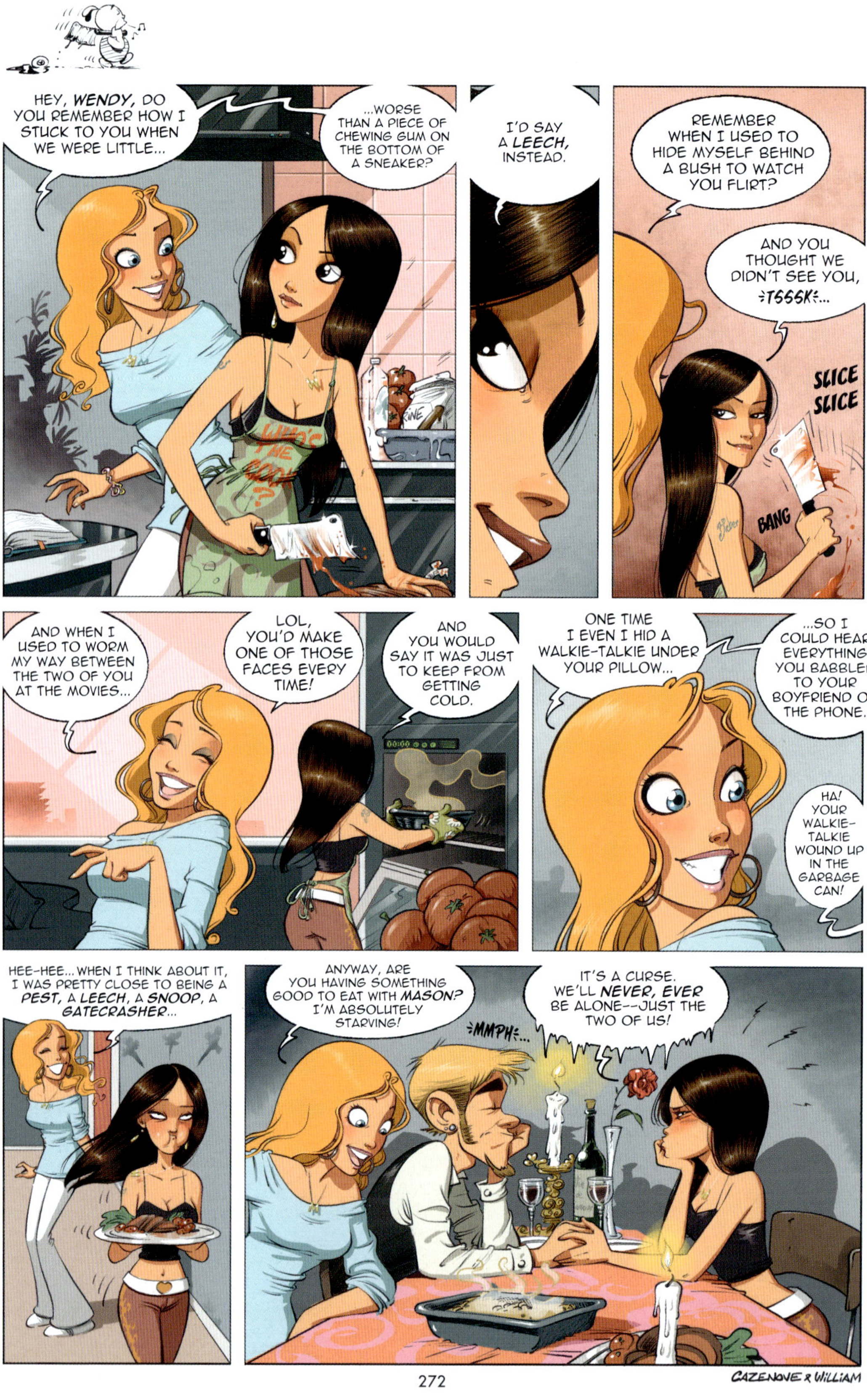
HEY, WENDY, DO YOU REMEMBER HOW I STUCK TO YOU WHEN WE WERE LITTLE...
...WORSE THAN A PIECE OF CHEWING GUM ON THE BOTTOM OF A SNEAKER?
I'D SAY A LEECH, INSTEAD.
REMEMBER WHEN I USED TO HIDE MYSELF BEHIND A BUSH TO WATCH YOU FLIRT?
AND YOU THOUGHT WE DIDN'T SEE YOU, TSSSK...
SLICE SLICE
BANG
AND WHEN I USED TO WORM MY WAY BETWEEN THE TWO OF YOU AT THE MOVIES...
LOL, YOU'D MAKE ONE OF THOSE FACES EVERY TIME!
AND YOU WOULD SAY IT WAS JUST TO KEEP FROM GETTING COLD.
ONE TIME I EVEN I HID A WALKIE-TALKIE UNDER YOUR PILLOW...
...SO I COULD HEAR EVERYTHING YOU BABBLED TO YOUR BOYFRIEND ON THE PHONE.
HA! YOUR WALKIE-TALKIE WOUND UP IN THE GARBAGE CAN!
HEE-HEE... WHEN I THINK ABOUT IT, I WAS PRETTY CLOSE TO BEING A PEST, A LEECH, A SNOOP, A GATECRASHER...
ANYWAY, ARE YOU HAVING SOMETHING GOOD TO EAT WITH MASON? I'M ABSOLUTELY STARVING!
MMPH...
IT'S A CURSE. WE'LL NEVER, EVER BE ALONE--JUST THE TWO OF US!
CAZENOVE & WILLIAM